REMNANT OF THE FALLEN

TIMOTHY HEATH

ISBN-13: 978-0-9897966-2-0
ISBN-10: 0989796620

For Xavier, Chance, and Serenity

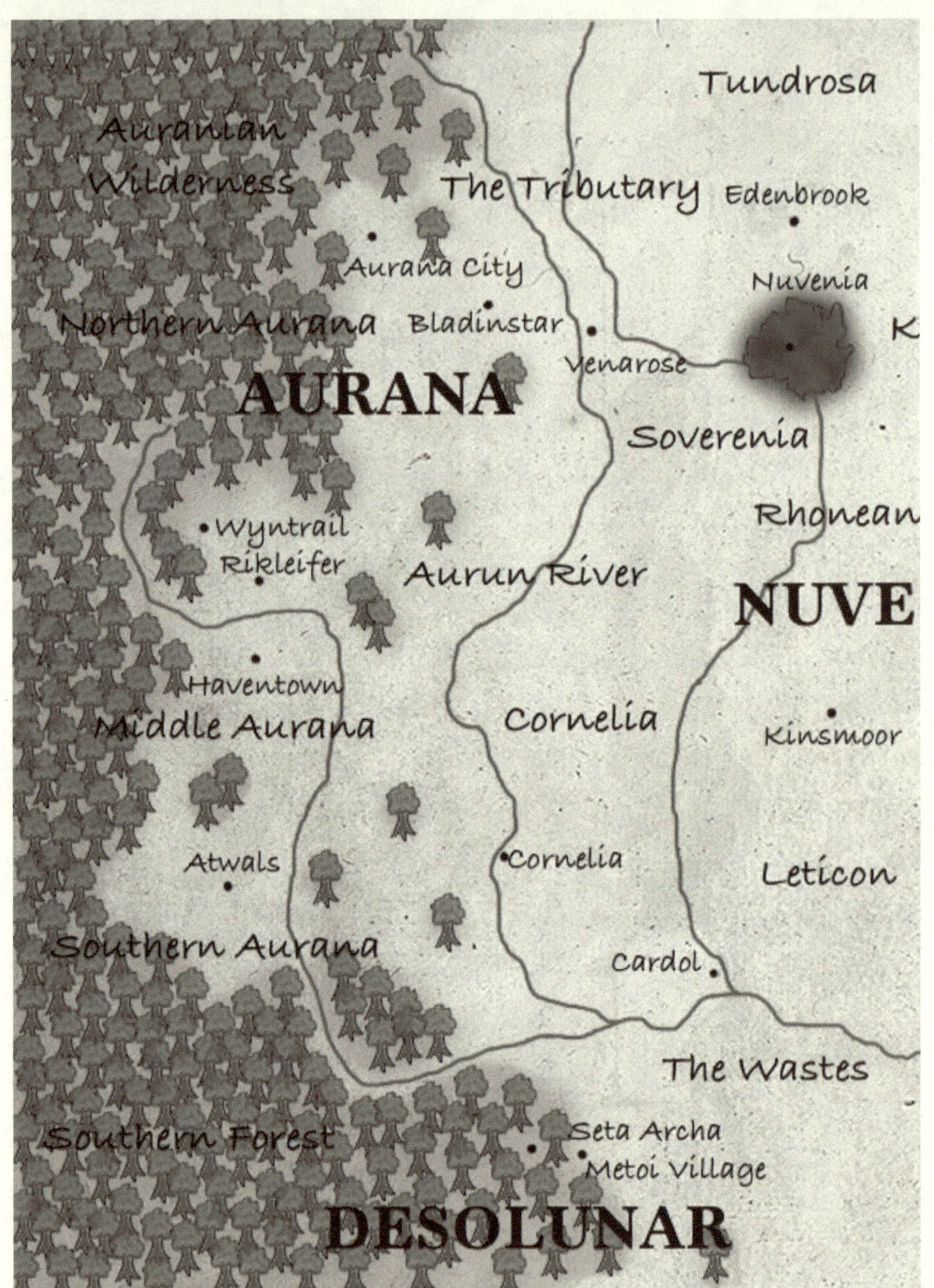
Tundrosa
Auranian Wilderness
The Tributary
Edenbrook
Aurana City
Nuvenia
Northern Aurana
Bladinstar
Venarose
AURANA
Soverenia
Rhonean
Wyntrail
Rikleifer
Aurun River
NUVE
Haventown
Middle Aurana
Cornelia
Kinsmoor
Atwals
Cornelia
Leticon
Southern Aurana
Cardol
The Wastes
Southern Forest
Seta Archa
Metoi Village
DESOLUNAR

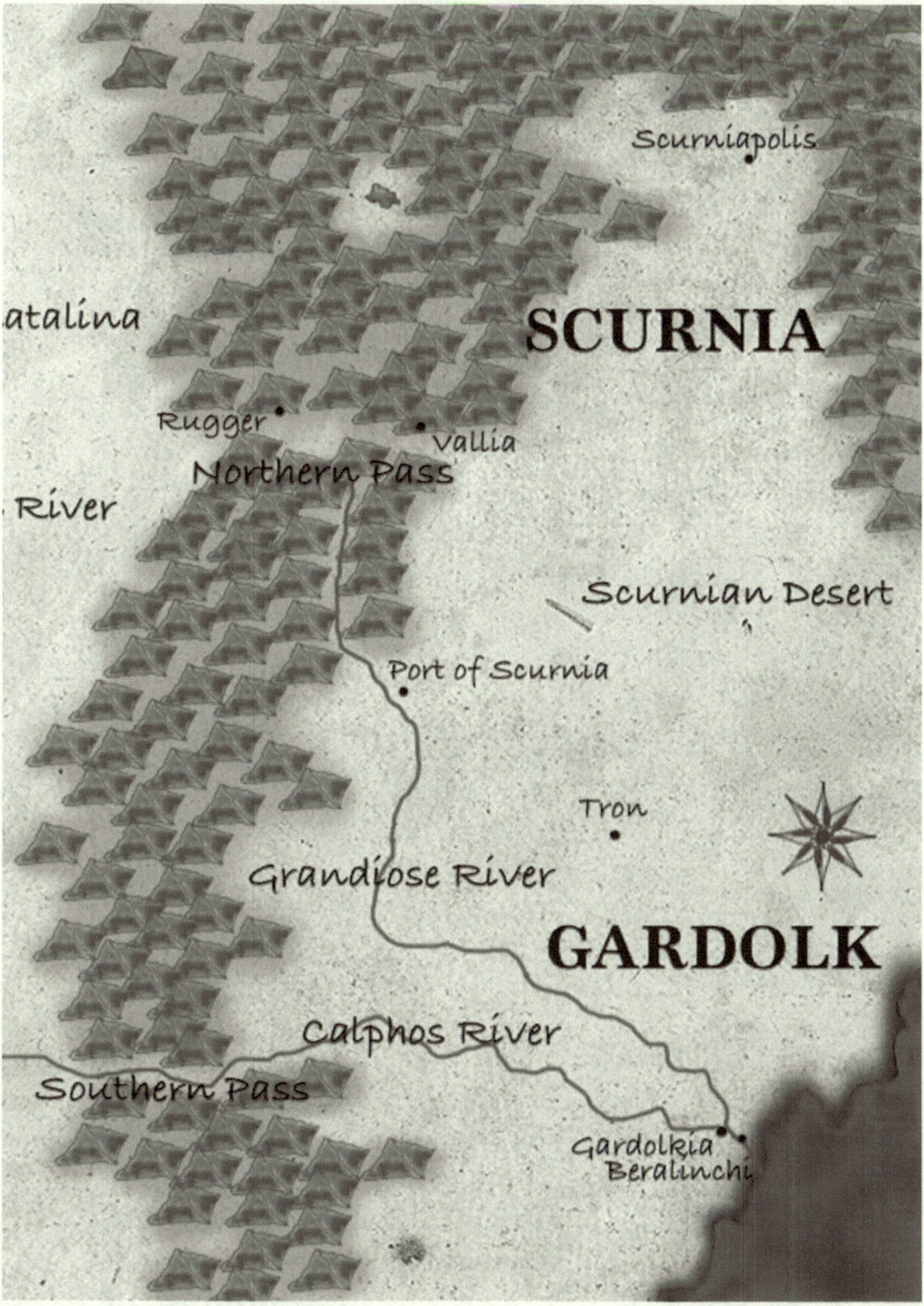

Scurniapolis
atalina
SCURNIA
Rugger
Vallia
Northern Pass
River
Scurnian Desert
Port of Scurnia
Tron
Grandiose River
GARDOLK
Calphos River
Southern Pass
Gardolkia
Beralinchi

Chapters

Prologue

An awkward crosswind blew across the wastelands of the Solunar Empire.

As the eldest tribal nation of the country, the Metoi tribe was very in tune with nature, despite the fact they lived in the Wastes. Led by the honorable Chief Aspectra, they were among the strongest of the many wasteland tribes of the Solunar Empire, and only bowed to its emperor. The Metoi were also the trusted information keepers of the empire, faithfully protecting records, folklore, and intricate knowledge from every corner of the young nation.

All around were only wastelands, the reason the lands were named the Wastes. People of the Wastes were very hardy people who had grown adapted to life in such a harsh environment. Almost all of them had adapted darker skin tones to resist the burning effects of the sun, many learned how to grow water-binding plants to collect the life-giving liquid from the atmosphere to later harvest and drink, and all intensely trained their men for warfare whether or not they intended to be warriors.

Standing about a fifteen-minute walk from the Metoi village, Chief Aspectra observed the territory around him as the dawn was breaking over the horizon. It was the nature of his people to be very observant of all that surrounded them, and to take these observations and analyze them very closely. Today, however, something seemed very different about the Wastes. Something that was not visible, but could only be felt. The unusual wind created a sense of disturbance within the chief, causing him to study his surroundings even more.

A couple of minutes later, the chief's wife came running to find him. She said very little upon arriving. She needed only look at her husband, however, to see that something was bothering him.

"A dark wind is blowing," stated Chief Aspectra, making his conclusion and vocalizing it so his wife could hear. "Something does not like the peace we have. Something wants to tear it all apart."

Next to him, his wife nodded.

In addition to his knowledge that he had built as a member of the Metoi, Chief Aspectra was also a very spiritual man. He was very in tune with nature, and so was his wife. Every sensation that felt wrong, every oddity present, he would question and attempt to determine if something more were present than what was observed. "We have only come to peace again recently," continued Chief Aspectra, as he put his hand around his wife's shoulder and started walking with her back toward the Metoi village. "Still, something tells me it will be short lived."

Aspectra's wife nodded. "I feel that sensation as well," she said. "All should be well, though, should it not?"

"One would think so," nodded Aspectra. "Emperor Arthur is trying to be a much better ruler than his father was. He has given each of us a voice in Seta Archa. There is peace, and there is prosperity, all in more areas of the world than there has been in years. And yet, a looming darkness hazes over my mind."

"How so?" asked his wife.

"I do not know," responded Aspectra. "However, something is not right nonetheless. It is as though I foresee that my death is imminent."

"Don't even say that," interrupted Aspectra's wife. "The Metoi need you, my husband. The last thing they need is you to be predicting your own downfall." It was very rare and culturally improper to the Metoi for a woman to speak so strongly like that.

Nonetheless, as a husband who respected the strong will of his wife, Aspectra turned around, placing his arm around his wife and turning to her as well. "Now, now," he began, "I did not mean to interject any fear into your heart. I still plan to be here for a long time." He said nothing of the improper nature of her comments.

"I do hope you mean that sincerely," responded Aspectra's wife.

Chief Aspectra nodded. "Of course I do," he responded as he wrapped his other arm around her shoulder, let go of the first arm, and turned back toward the village.

There was a horrifying sight. Aspectra's eyes widened instantly.

Almost as if his premonitions of a black wind were true.

A cloud of smoke and a wave of black were approaching the Metoi Village. A look of horror came across Aspectra's face. Immediately, he bolted for the village, his wife following him as quickly as she could.

Quickly they ran toward the village, running as fast as possible. It would not be long until they were there, but every second counted. The minutes seemed like hours, as their fears escalated.

As they arrived into town after running for at least ten minutes, Aspectra and his wife saw what was the black flash they had seen: hundreds of troops dressed in the old black uniforms of Desolunar. Instantly, Aspectra became very suspicious as he entered his village, as he knew that the new uniforms of the Solunar Empire contained orange trim and looked distinctively different from the old Desolunar uniforms. It meant that, for all Aspectra knew, there were two possibilities: this was a unit of troops that had not had one soldier obtain a new uniform as of yet, or this was a rogue unit not under the control of the Solunar Empire.

All around Metoi Village, these troops were standing in formation and had weapons drawn. This made Aspectra feel threatened as he walked into his village. Why would an armed band of troops, belonging to his nation of the Solunar Empire or not, be here? What was their purpose? The answer was straight ahead as Aspectra looked forward and saw one man on horseback in the entire crowd. He was standing amongst the troops in the center of the village, and was almost silent, yet he was signaling orders to his troops. Aspectra took a very good look at the man and recognized him instantly.

It was General Sayo, one of the most loyal generals to the former state of Desolunar.

Aspectra certainly had no fear now. By all means, he knew that Sayo knew he was in the wrong for bringing his troops through the Metoi village, and Aspectra was ready to throw the book at him. Fearlessly, Aspectra approached General Sayo while his wife stood back. He walked past all of the troops surrounding him as though he were ignoring their presence altogether. When he was within a few steps of Sayo, Aspectra began, "General Sayo, what are you doing here? Why have you brought your men here?"

Sayo remained silent.

"You are in direct violation of Solunar Empire statutes which dictate that troops are to stay away from all villages of The Wastes without prior authorization, and I have given none for you," added Aspectra. "I will have you know that this will go into my monthly report to the emperor, and that you and your men will be disciplined for this action. Now, as ruler of the Metoi, I order you, pull your men out of my village."

Still, Sayo remained like a rock: emotionless and unwavering.

"Well, are you going to do nothing but stand there?" continued Aspectra as he raised his voice.

Sayo turned his head to the right, and then to the left. Then, he raised his hand, and said, "Light it."

For a split second, Aspectra was puzzled.

Then, he saw what was happening.

The troops of Sayo's unit were beginning to firebomb the buildings of the Metoi. Innocent tribal villagers were rushing out of their homes, and chaos was setting in inside the village. The sky reflected a red dawn as the fires grew higher. Within a matter of seconds, his village was in flames. Aspectra looked around and all he saw was fire. His village, that which he swore to protect, was burning to the ground. A great feeling of sadness swept through his heart.

Then, as he stood there and watched his village burn, in shock from what he was seeing, Sayo drew his sword and pointed it directly at Aspectra. Death stared him in the eyes.

The old Desolunar did not take prisoners. Sayo was a general who never took prisoners himself. Chief Aspectra knew that Sayo would make sure he was dead. Several of the men around Aspectra also drew their weapons and pointed them at him. And Aspectra knew what was coming.

"How dare you!" he exclaimed hysterically, making sure what would be his last words were heard. "How dare you walk into this land of the Metoi and annihilate our people? How dare you turn your back on your own nation? You may kill me today, General Sayo, but I promise you, one day you will regret it! You will regret it!"

Aaaaaargh!

Everyone stabbed Aspectra simultaneously, executing him on the spot. As they withdrew their weapons, his body collapsed to the ground.

From a short distance away, his wife shrieked.

That drew Sayo's attention. He walked his horse over to her and pointed to her with his finger.

Instantly, that drew a shot of fear into her veins. She was watching as her village was burning and her husband was murdered. And now she was staring into the icy cold glare of the hell-bent general who was the cause of it all.

General Sayo then changed the direction of his finger, pointing it west toward the city of Seta Archa. He spoke no words, but the message was clear. Aspectra's wife took heed of it and fled to the west alone, watching her burning village crumble as she left. She had no time to care for her fellow Metoi, knowing she would be killed if she stayed.

The message was to run. Run to Seta Archa and tell the emperor. Tell him of the plight of the Metoi, and of who did it. It was a signature, a strong message to the new Solunar Empire, that not all wanted it to exist.

Chapter 1

A Renewed World

Somewhere in between the extremes of phantasmal space lie the realms of existence, where the seven magical energies collide and form what might be known as a world. To the mortal, it is simply "the world", but to the immortal, it is referred to as "the mortal realm".

On one of these planes of existence is this realm. It is home to the mortal beings, most being of a civilized nature. Mortals are known to be able to manipulate some amount of magic with enough study, but oftentimes steel is their strongest weapon. The mortal realm is a place where light and darkness are in balance, and elemental magic is the dominant controller of the realm. Many had turned to worshipping the "nameless ones", the terms they had for the images in their head of immortals. Ultimately, however, what they really saw was their own creation and not a reality.

Though the political landscape had changed much over the course of history, through eras of nomads, of tribes and feudalistic small kingdoms, five large kingdoms remained to this day. These superstates were Aurana to the northwest, Nuve in the north-central, Scurnia in the northeast, Gardolk in the southeast, and the Solunar Empire in the deep south. The Solunar Empire was the most recent to arrive.

Three months have passed since a great war, known unofficially to the mortal as the Desolunar War, was ended. Thanks to a sixteen-year-old boy by the name of Kevin Trent Stryker, the kingdoms of Aurana, Nuve, and Scurnia were unified and brought together to end the conquests of the Desolunar dictator and cultist, Demonicus. With guidance from Professor James Magnon, he had helped to overthrow the king of his homeland of Aurana and install the king's son as the new ruler, reinvigorating the nation. He then proceeded to Nuve and boldly used his new position as the Vanguard of Aurana to help broker a temporary armistice to unify Nuve. After assisting in the strategies used and participating in the Battle of Middle Aurana, fought in his hometown of Rikleifer, he joined the Battle of Seta Archa. There, under a blackened sky as Demonicus sought to cover the world in darkness, he ran into the heart of the city, helping to depose Demonicus as top commander General Sayo was forced to retreat.

To the immortal, the more key point of these events would never be known to the mortal. Kevin was the son of the legendary Vincent Stryker and co-incidentally able to bear the Sword of Purity, a blade powered by the sacrifice of a god. With Professor Magnon's daughter Caitlin by his side, Kevin revealed the innocence of the god Tyrinion, whose Professor James Magnon persona was a disguise, and pursued the immortal Setadev, the true perpetuator of the conquest of the realms. By using Setadev's own greed against him, Kevin and Caitlin destroyed the immortal conqueror and his entire realm.

Formerly, the land of Desolunar sat where the conquest had come to an abrupt conclusion, in particular focused at the city of Seta Archa, the capital of Desolunar. Left in its place were people in panic, needing someone to trust and someone to lead them, to provide for them and give them protection and peace. Desolunar, however, was no more, and despite the fact that it provided little for its people, it provided more than anarchy ever could.

In the place of the disposed dictator Demonicus, his seventeen-year-old son and Kevin's best friend Arthur Falchor rose to power on the basis of being the "heir of Desolunar". He inherited land of what was left after all of the claimed lands that had previously belonged to the countries of Aurana and Nuve were returned to their respective nations. Forming a new imperial government alongside a council representing all corners of his new empire, Arthur Falchor became known as Emperor Arthur of the Solunar Empire, and began to lay down the groundwork for what would become a new nation in a renewed world.

Arthur placed a great deal of his trust in his new prime minister, the eighteen-year-old Rachel Reinhart. Very quickly, she was becoming Arthur's most trusted advisor as well as the executor of his orders. Out in the field, however, Arthur's will was imposed by his two new Vanguards, Rouge and Resa Kirkwood, a pair of young women who knew the empire better than most and stood behind Arthur all of the way.

Together, Arthur, Rachel, Rouge, Resa, the tribal chiefs of the Wastes in the eastern side of the empire, and a few elected officials from Seta Archa made up the new Imperial Council of the Solunar Empire. With the voices of many in the ear of Arthur, the future of the Solunar Empire appeared to be very promising. At this point in time, however, winter had set in and the cold weather was proving very difficult for the young nation. Since a great deal of Seta Archa had been damaged three months before and rebuilding was still in the process, many of the people of the Solunar Empire were struggling to survive, their stockpiled food resources depleted by the recent war. Though the recent seventeenth birthday of their emperor had been a reason to celebrate as of late, the city of Seta Archa was suffering.

On one of these such days in the midwinter, Arthur Falchor stood in the throne room of Seta Archa's capital building, the very same one where three months ago he and Kevin Trent Stryker had disposed of the dictator Demonicus. Since Arthur had thrown Demonicus out through the window in their encounter, the glass had been repaired in the triangular pyramid, and through it Arthur saw his new surrounding domain.

A knock came from the floor, from the trap door that was the entrance to the throne room. "Enter," called Arthur.

At this call, the door popped open and up the last couple of stairs walked Rachel Reinhart, the prime minister of the Solunar Empire. During the time of the battles to stop the conquest, she was a traveling partner with Arthur for a great deal of the time and a friend to everyone involved. At the age of eighteen, she was older than Arthur, but still she respected him for all that he had done.

Dressed in a regally-decorated black and orange dress, the colors of the Solunar Empire, Rachel was the second most powerful woman in the world, second only to Queen Mildred of Gardolk. Still, it was never about the power to Rachel, nor the fact that she held a great amount of power for a woman. It was all about helping Arthur and being a positive change for the world.

"Arthur," she began, as she closed the trap door behind her, "we anticipate the arrival of Chief Aspectra of the Metoi tribe anytime now. His scheduled regular visit is fast approaching."

"Very well," nodded Arthur. "I will be ready for his visit, then." Arthur's response seemed quite distant.

Picking up on this, Rachel asked, "What's wrong, Arthur? You don't quite seem like yourself. It's been several days now I've noticed you're behaving unusually."

Arthur shrugged. "I haven't been myself for a while, Rachel. Not since the war ended, at least." He sighed.

In that moment, Rachel saw that Arthur was bearing a heavy burden, and what she was seeing was his struggle to carry it. "I know what you mean," she said. "So much has changed since then. We're now the rulers of a whole other land that was never our home to begin with."

"I don't just mean that," interrupted Arthur. He let out a sigh as he looked out the window again. "As much as Kevin loved the questing, and I hated it and only kept up with him out of respect for trying to rescue me, I kind of miss those days of being out there and traveling the world. Now I'm here as the emperor of a land that I helped try to destroy, because I descend from someone to whom I wish I wasn't related."

A smirk came to Rachel's face. "But it's not the same land," she said. "You're the emperor because you stepped up to do the right thing for people who really needed it. You gave back the lands taken from Aurana and Nuve in the war. You've rebranded the country and given people a reason to live in peace, even if times are tough now. You've recalled all of the military units of the former Desolunar…"

"And still several units remain out there," interrupted Arthur again.

"Why is that stressing you out?" responded Rachel. "They'll be back. They're your people now, and they know that."

Arthur took a breath. "They're my people, Rachel, but at the same time they're not. Why would they have any reason to trust me? Why would they want to come back to an entirely different land from what Desolunar was?"

Rachel rolled her eyes. "And I thought I was supposed to be the skeptic here," she commented, knowing that Arthur and the rest of her friends had constantly joked about her realistic and skeptical attitudes on life. "Look, Arthur, everything's going to be okay. The soldiers will come back because they're your people, you're their lord, and because they have their families here. You have to trust that everything will be as it should, and if it doesn't, figure it out from there."

Arthur looked like that had slightly changed his feelings. He glanced quickly at Rachel before turning back to the window. "I'm glad I asked you to help me run this country," he said. "I appreciate how you can be the voice of reason in a difficult time."

Aside, Rachel smiled briefly, but looked back at Arthur in concern. She owned Arthur her life, too, since he had saved her from imprisonment and possible execution once. Being here to help him was the least she could do to repay him.

At that instant, the trap door flew open. "My lord! Arthur!" exclaimed a young lady's voice as it drew nearer. A figure emerged from the trap door opening, revealing itself to be the nineteen-year-old co-Vanguard of the Solunar Empire, Resa Kirkwood. As one of the Vanguards, she was dressed in a new Solunar Empire uniform, with a very unique twist: instead of being all black with orange trim, a diagonal line divided her uniform from her left shoulder to her right side, and below it the uniform was orange with black trim instead. Her older half-sister Rouge wore a similar uniform, and both wore the traditional red and black triangle vanguard patches as their rank on the sleeves. The bottom of Resa's outfit was a short skirt, as magic capabilities were enhanced by wearing flowing garments and having open skin. By contrast, her sister Rouge wore shorts and a skintight top as part of her uniform to allow her to be agile, as was common for practitioners of her Toronaga martial arts.

Upon seeing Arthur staring out the window, Resa stopped and said, "Oh dear, I apologize if I am interrupting anything."

Arthur turned around and said, "No, not at all." He then started stepping toward Resa, with Rachel walking next to him. "I must say, though, it's a little unusual you didn't knock first or anything before walking in."

Resa offered a curtsey. "I'm sorry, but it is urgent and I thought

I should get to you as soon as possible."

"Urgent?" asked Arthur. "What's the news, Resa?"

"I'm not quite sure," answered Resa, "but the wife of Chief Aspectra of the Metoi is here to see you, alone."

Arthur raised an eyebrow. That was highly unusual, indeed. "Marilynn is here?" he asked. "Without her husband?"

Silently, Resa nodded. "Completely by herself," she said. "Marilynn was very out of breath, like she ran the whole way here by herself. I asked her why she needed to see you right away, but she said she wouldn't say unless it were to you directly."

"I see," acknowledged Arthur, worried. He knew Aspectra, and he knew Marilynn quite well by now; not only was Aspectra a member of the Imperial Council, but Marilynn often accompanied him and showed herself to be the brains behind her husband. "And where is she at right now?"

"With my sister Rouge," said Resa. "They're at the bottom of the stairs right now, waiting for you."

Quickly, Arthur took a glance over at Rachel, then back to Resa. "Very well, then," he said. "Send her in."

"Right away, my lord," bowed Resa as she turned around to walk down the stairs. She closed the trap door behind her.

As soon as she left, Arthur said, "I swear I'm never going to get used to that. Resa's supposed to be a friend, not simply a minion."

Rachel rolled her eyes. "Oh, come now, Arthur," she began, "you know full and well that Resa's not your minion and she doesn't think of herself that way. And neither does her sister Rouge, and neither do I."

Arthur merely shrugged, just trying to keep the thought out of his mind. Then, he changed the subject. "Now, for what reason could Marilynn be here on her own?" he asked. "It makes little sense. The Metoi normally don't allow women to travel on their own, much less the chief's wife. And even if she were, it is almost time for Aspectra himself to be arriving anyway."

At that second, the trap door swung open again. "I guess you're about to have your answer," said Rachel.

The first ones through the trap door were Rouge and Resa

Kirkwood, the two Vanguards of the Solunar Empire. Upon entering, they gave way for Marilynn, the wife of Chief Aspectra of the Metoi. Rouge then closed the trap door as Marilynn made it to the top.

Marilynn was a middle-aged woman, dressed in ragged cloth to cover herself. Her long black hair was the longest of any of the Metoi, which was her right as the wife of the chief. Tattooed on her skin were many small symbols, including the symbol of the Metoi – a tribal design of a spiral with five points projecting from it like a star – and several heart shapes and others as symbols of love and devotion to her husband. "My emperor," began Marilynn as she bowed, "it is an honor to have you listen to what I have to say today."

"Of course," said Arthur. "I am always honored to hear what you have to say, Marilynn. However, I sense that today's matter is not good, is it?"

Marilynn shook her head. "No, it is not," she said, as tears started to well up in her eyes. She looked so exhausted and sad that Arthur could tell this was not something good at all.

Seeing this, Arthur walked over to his desk, picked up the chair from it, and sat it behind Marilynn. "Please have a seat," he said, as he gestured to Marilynn. "You look wiped out, like you need a rest."

Before taking the seat, however, Marilynn bowed. "My emperor, you are all too kind," she said as she sat down.

"It's nothing, really," responded Arthur, as he walked back over to where Rachel was standing. "Now, what is it that you have to share? And where is Chief Aspectra?"

"That's what's wrong," said Marilynn, as more tears started pooling up in her eyes. She started to cry. "He's dead."

Immediately, Arthur's eyes widened. "Tell me what happened," commanded Arthur, now incredibly concerned. "What brought upon Aspectra's death?"

Marilynn was having a hard time trying to put together the words, but still she was trying to place all of her effort into it as she sobbed. "I was with my husband before it happened… we were watching the Metoi village from a distance when suddenly we saw this black wave approaching." She paused, trying to suppress her tears. "We ran back to the city to find out what was going on, and what we saw was shocking. They were… soldiers, but not Solunar soldiers. They were Desolunar soldiers wearing the old black uniforms, and they were being led by General Sayo."

General Sayo. Desolunar's former top general. Arthur and Rachel glanced at each other briefly.

"My husband ran to confront Sayo fearlessly, but as he did, the soldiers started to firebomb the village. Then, Sayo and his men killed my husband… then they left with the village burning…" Marilynn was crying so hard now that she could not make the words come out. "Some of us escaped… but Sayo pointed me here… as he destroyed everything… and killed many…"

Rachel stepped forward and placed her hand on Marilynn's shoulder, trying to be reassuring. "Take it easy, now," she said. "We all feel for your loss, and we'll take care of you and the Metoi."

"Before we do anything, though, answer me this," added on Arthur. "Where are the Metoi now? Is the village still standing?"

Marilynn shook her head, still trying to dry as many of her tears as possible. "I don't think so," she said. "Without the village and without Chief Aspectra, the Metoi are weak. I would think the Metoi have gone to a sacred place on our lands, to search for resources until they can rebuild our home."

Arthur nodded. "That's the important part, at least. We'll do our part, then, and I promise you that you can count on us." Then, Arthur turned to Resa. "Take care of Marilynn, would you, Resa? See to it that she is tended to and taken care of here in the capital building."

"As you wish," said Resa. She then knelt over to help Marilynn out of the chair, moved the chair aside, and then led Marilynn to the stairs. Marilynn offered a curtsey as she stood up in gratitude to the emperor, before following Resa down the stairs.

Almost as immediately as the trap door closed, Arthur put his hand over his eyes and shook his head. "Just great," he said.

"I feel so sad for the Metoi," added Rachel, somberly.

"You know, with the Metoi out of the way, the balance in the Wastes has been destabilized," commented Rouge. "With Chief Aspectra out of the way and the Metoi tribe severely weakened, it is likely that someone will make a move out there and start a chain reaction that will bring the entire area of the Wastes into chaos."

"How so?" asked Arthur, a little confused. "Wouldn't the Toronaga come to the aid of the Metoi? They're allies."

"Probably," answered Rouge, who was half-Toronaga but was not raised in the Wastes. She was relying on her knowledge of the area from having visited the Toronaga several times previously. "At the same time, I guarantee you someone would make their move and attempt to increase their power by capturing the Metoi. One group jumps in, whether or not the Toronaga are present, and they all jump in and try to capture the Metoi lands. It's a very fragile balance."

Arthur sighed. "Well, damn," he said. "So now we have two problems: stabilizing the Wastes until the Metoi can control their own area again, and bringing General Sayo to justice for this attack."

"If I may make a suggestion," said Rachel, "I think I might have an answer to the first problem, if we can move fast enough to keep it from destabilizing at all."

"And that would be?" asked Arthur.

"Something simple and forceful," Rachel responded. "Why not just impose martial law on the Metoi lands? I know you really don't want to use our troops that much, but in this case it might be the best way. Send some of our troops to the Metoi lands and have them secure the area and protect it from attack. Let the military govern the lands until the Metoi have rebuilt, and put someone in charge that you know you can trust."

Considering this for a second, Arthur responded, "I really don't want to have to do something like that, but it does sound like the only real option for the moment." Then, Arthur glanced over at Rouge. "I trust that you and your sister are capable of handling such an event, Rouge. I know I can trust the two of you to maintain control of the Metoi lands until they are ready, if I supply you with enough troops."

"We can certainly do that," nodded Rouge, herself not a military leader but someone who carried influence in the empire. "And what of General Sayo? What can we do about him?"

"Probably nothing," said Rachel, shaking her head. "Marilynn said Sayo and his men appeared quickly and left with the village still burning. Clearly they weren't looking for anything or trying to take a piece of land themselves. That makes them unlikely to return."

Rouge nodded. "I see," she said, taking out one of her knives and starting to flip it around in her hand. "The question is, then, what will you do about him?"

"That would depend on Sayo's motives," responded Arthur. "As Rachel said, Sayo wasn't looking for anything, whether it be wealth, land, or anything of that sort. It's obvious now that he's not in favor of the Solunar Empire as much as he was for Desolunar several months ago. Hmmm…" Arthur pondered, deep in though, "an act of terrorism, perhaps? Trying to send a message to us here in Seta Archa?"

"It would be a pretty strong message, Arthur," said Rachel. "If you remember Vincent Stryker's report after the battle a few months ago, he mentioned that General Sayo was a traitor to Aurana. Treason must not be past his thinking, but even so, why flaunt it so boldly?"

Arthur nodded. "I see your point. Even if he simply wanted to take a shot at us, what could Sayo have wanted with the Metoi?"

"There may be one question even better," added Rouge. "Why did Sayo let Marilynn live?"

Arthur and Rachel stopped in their tracks as they hit the next floor. What Rouge had said had struck them hard. "She would have had to have escaped the city, wouldn't she?" asked Rachel.

"No," answered Rouge. "One thing I know about General Sayo from my days in the state of Desolunar is that Sayo prefers to, and knows how to, control every aspect whenever possible. He burned the village to destroy it for whatever reason that we don't know yet, but if any Metoi escaped at all, which is what Marilynn implied, it is because he let them escape." She paused. "He knew about the Metoi and who they are. He knew who Marilynn was—her tattoos make that very evident—and I guarantee you he saw Marilynn if she and Aspectra were both in the village when it was burning, as Marilynn said she was."

Rachel shook her head. "Then why would he let Marilynn live? Why let her get to Seta Archa and tell us about what happened?"

"Because he wanted us to know what happened," realized Arthur.

Bewildered, Rachel took a second to gather herself. "Somebody doesn't want the Solunar Empire to exist, and that's the message he chose to send." She paused. "What do we even know about General Sayo, anyway?" asked Rachel, as her head raised. "What could drive someone to do something like that?" She looked to Rouge.

"I'm afraid I can't help much," said Rouge. "Resa and I were specialists with the Desolunar government when we were here, not part of the army. All I know about Sayo comes from what Demonicus had said. Sayo was his top general, and someone he trusted, but that's about it."

Rolling his eyes, Arthur answered, "Little to go off of, and much destruction as a result. This day just keeps getting better and better."

At that moment, although she was hesitant to do anything, a very slight smile cracked from Rachel's face. That statement was the kind of sarcasm that Arthur used to have all of the time. It was his primary tool for humor, and he used it all of the time. Despite the seriousness of his current role, maybe the same old Arthur was still in there. "So now we have to figure out a solution," she then commented. "Chances are that General Sayo is not anywhere within the Seta Archa vicinity. It would make little sense for him to let Marilynn be a messenger if he were headed this way."

"I agree," nodded Rouge.

Arthur shook his head. "I don't know what to do about it," he said. "If Sayo is that dangerous, we can't send troops out to him and expect to win. The army is still so worn down and needs to be rebuilt. Yet things will only get worse the more we wait, of course, so we can't wait to get it completely combat-ready again."

"I know," considered Rachel. "And I bet Sayo doesn't negotiate, either, or he would've sent a ransom note or something." She paused as she gathered her thoughts. "What we need is someone who can go out there and track down and either capture or kill General Sayo. Take out the headpiece and the rest crumbles around it."

Considering the suggestion for a moment, Arthur said, "That's a solid idea, and I see the logic in it. But even if it were to work, who could we send? Who would be willing to go and capture General Sayo? I don't know if we have anyone."

"We could do it if we didn't have to secure the Metoi," acknowledged Rouge, referring to herself and her sister, "but ideally, you're going to want someone who knows about Sayo's motivations. Someone who can get inside his head, you know? And you're going to want someone who can hide amongst his men too. As women, although my sister and I are excellent masters of disguise, we would stick out like sore thumbs out there in the Wastes."

Arthur thought hard about this. Then, the perfect idea hit him. "Don't worry, I think I know someone," chuckled Arthur as he rolled his eyes. "Rachel, can you take a letter for me?"

Walking over to the emperor's desk, Rachel pulled out a piece of paper and a dry feather pen. She then pulled out a sealed container of ink. "I do," she said, as Rouge brought the chair back to the desk for her to sit down.

"Awesome," said Arthur. "Prepare to take a message for me."

Rachel nodded, dipping her pen in the ink and preparing to write on the paper.

"This is going to be a letter," continued Arthur. "Address it from Arthur Falchor of the Solunar Empire, Capital Building Main Office, Seta Archa, Solunar Empire."

"Gotcha," nodded Rachel, as she jotted it down, not thinking to question why he was not using his official title in the address. "And who should I address it to?"

Arthur took a quick breath. "Kevin Trent Stryker and Caitlin Amelia Magnon, Rikleifer, Aurana."

Rachel's eyes widened. There was a moment of pause. Then, Rachel became excited. "Kevin and Caitlin are coming?" she asked, growing more and more eager. "Really?"

"Mhmm," nodded Arthur. "They're perfect, Rachel. And they're our friends, so you know they'll gladly accept the job. I hate to ask such a favor of them, but he'll do it if we ask them nicely."

Instead of getting upset about putting a friend on such an assignment, though, Rachel jumped up and down. "Awesome, Arthur!" she said, really excited. "It seems like it's been so long since we've seen Kevin and Caitlin. Maybe we can bring them by here first?"

"Brilliant idea," acknowledged Rouge. "Though if I'm not mistaken, I believe Caitlin's sixteenth birthday is coming up."

"Oh, right," nodded Arthur. "Still, we should see if she can come down as well. I know she will have to register soon, but maybe we can work around that." He paused for a second. "Now, shall we get down to business on this message? This is serious business, and though it involves our friends, we can't let that get in the way of the facts before us."

Rachel and Rouge nodded in the affirmative. It was going to be very exciting if Kevin and Caitlin would be willing to come back to Seta Archa to help out, but there was still important work to be done, something neither of them could forget. They could not lose sight that this invitation was for an important reason that had to take priority.

Chapter 2

Living Life

It was a cold winter's evening in the City of Dreams itself—Rikleifer, Aurana. Despite how cold it was outside, now was a time for enjoyment within the massive Rikleifer Stadium. A tradition of the world, especially in Aurana, dangerball games were often played in the evenings by the light of torches all around a stadium. As cold as it was, no one minded because of how fun the experience was. After all, tonight was a home game for the local top-league team, the Rikleifer Rangers. They were playing their rivals, the Aurana City Force.

Sitting around the middle levels of the stadium, somewhere on the home side of the field, were Kevin Trent Stryker and Caitlin Magnon. Together they were sharing a blanket out in the cold stadium, enjoying the game that was just starting. It was hard for Kevin not to get noticed nowadays, but he was still trying not to be. In the last three months, his status as Vanguard of Aurana had drawn him some unwanted attention, usually positive but still unwanted because Kevin wanted no part of celebrity. Still, his apparel made it difficult for him to hide; Kevin wore his Auranian military jacket wherever he went, but unlike most men of the military, he kept it open, exposing his red shirt he wore underneath. This, to him, was part his personality and part because he was not a military person.

Kevin looked over to see Caitlin shivering a bit. She was wearing her solid white dress with the red trim, and though it covered her full body from her neck to her feet, she was still shivering. "Are you sure you don't want my jacket?" asked Kevin. "It's not much, but it ought to keep you a little warmer, at least."

Caitlin shook her head. "No thanks, Kevin," she said. "You'll be even colder than me if you do that." Because of the crowd around, Caitlin did not want to light a fire to warm up.

A snicker came to Kevin's face. "Don't worry about it," he

chuckled. Then, he pointed down toward a set of men in the stands closer to the field. None of them were wearing shirts. "See those guys?" he said. "I used to be one of them."

"You *what?*" asked Caitlin, stunned.

Kevin laughed. "You heard me," he said. "Last year, I joined them down there without wearing a shirt for a game or two. It was my attempt to try and socialize a little bit."

By now, Caitlin was glaring at Kevin. Quickly, Kevin recognized this as the "you're an idiot" look. Still, Kevin found it funny because it was a pretty typical reaction to not wearing a shirt out in the cold of the winter.

That Caitlin had reacted like that at all, Kevin realized, would have been surprising a few months ago. It had been several months before, while on a journey to help a god get home and unify the lands against Desolunar to rescue Arthur, that Kevin had met Caitlin. The daughter of a professor of magic, she was a dedicated spellcaster who had devoted her life and all of her studies to the arcane arts. In maintaining this dedication, she kept her emotions tightly guarded at the time, including behind a magical barrier. Even so, she and Kevin found common ground between each other to connect and form a friendship. Quickly, she became an instrumental piece to his quest, and it was not long until he started falling for the emotionless girl. Then, one night, Kevin told Caitlin he loved her, which broke the magical barrier protecting Caitlin from her emotions. Caitlin decided shortly after that not to have the barrier restored, instead wanting to explore the feelings of happiness she now had traveling with Kevin.

It naturally came out later that Caitlin's father was actually a god himself, and that she was an angel as a result. She had access to a unique form of divine power, but it only manifested whenever she felt a strong connection to Kevin or needed to rescue him. It was discovered as part of their falling in love. Since the end of the war, Kevin had been trying to show Caitlin all that she had been missing from life, to allow her to explore her new feelings, and the dangerball game was one such event.

"I swear, there's just some things I'm never going to get," said Caitlin, as she shook her head. "Why would a bunch of guys do that?

It just seems so illogical to me."

"Not at all," laughed Kevin. "It's just one of the things men do for team spirit, and being up there without their shirts on shows they're dedicated to their team. Sometimes they'll even use some dye on their bare chests in the team's colors to show their support too."

Caitlin shook her head. "I still don't understand," she said. Then, she curled closer to Kevin.

Kevin ruffled the blanket around a little bit to make sure Caitlin was covered well with it. Kevin could not help but smile a little bit as he looked down at Caitlin curling up next to him. Their relationship had become very affectionate, especially in the last three months now that they had more time to spend with each other without other focuses. It was not uncommon for them to snuggle together if they had the opportunity.

As she rested her head on Kevin's shoulder, Caitlin asked, "So, I know we played dangerball before with our friends, but can you explain to me how the game works?"

Kevin set to explaining the rules of the game.

Despite listening intently, Caitlin shrugged. "I guess I didn't really get what I wanted out of that," she said. "I still don't understand why they play it when it's this cold outside. It's not like it helps your athletic performance or makes it comfortable."

"Ah, it's just tradition," laughed Kevin. "Besides, what else are we supposed to do in the winter around here?"

"Beats me," shrugged Caitlin. "I'm trying to figure out what there is to do other than study and practice magic."

Ever optimistic, Kevin did not let this comment get him down. "There's plenty," he said. "Hey, take a look, the game's about to start."

The loud sound of a whistle signaled the start of the game. As the game began, Kevin and Caitlin watched as the Rikleifer Rangers played intensely. The game proved to be aggressive and violent, but also a dominant performance by the Rangers. As the game went on, it was clear there was no real contest. Rikleifer won the game handily, in an affair that lasted a couple of hours.

With the game over, the stadium crowds began to disperse, and the people of Rikleifer started heading to their homes. Kevin and

Caitlin left together holding hands, with Caitlin wearing the blanket they had brought draped around her shoulders in an attempt to keep warm. "So, what did you think of the game?" asked Kevin, with one arm up in the air celebrating with some of the dispersing crowd casually.

"Oh, it was all right, I guess," said Caitlin, still too cold to give any kind of energetic response, positive or negative. "Good to see Rikleifer won tonight, at least."

"It's always a good thing," joked Kevin. "I love to go to these games every now and then, at least. There isn't another one until next week, though."

Caitlin pulled the blanket tighter around herself. "That's fine by me," she said. "Why can't they play these games in the summer? It's cold out here."

"They *do* play it in the summer," laughed Kevin. "And they play it in the winter, too. Come to think of it, I don't really know if there's a time people stop playing dangerball completely, since it's kind of the popular sport around here. The professional teams take a couple of breaks in the hottest weeks of the summer and the coldest parts of the winter, but there's not a season where they completely stop."

"I still don't know how much of this I can take," said Caitlin. "I'm sorry, Kevin, but I just don't think I like being out a cold night like this."

Inside, Kevin knew Caitlin had a valid point, and he accepted that. The nighttime winter dangerball experience was not for everyone, after all. And Kevin did remember his first time going to a game during the winter at night, and he remembered complaining to his mother about the experience as well. "That's okay," he finally said. "I won't make you do it again. Still, don't you think the experience was worth it?"

Caitlin was trying to think about what to say. Reluctantly, she said, "I guess."

Kevin rolled his eyes. Sometimes it was clear that Caitlin was still the same person she had always been, even if she had a few more emotions than before.

Then, the snow began to fall in large flakes, as the last of the day gave way to night. Kevin saw Caitlin start to stare at the snowflakes, as if she were seeing them in a different way for the first time in her life. She seemed fascinated by what she saw.

"Are you enjoying the snow?" Kevin asked.

"It's beautiful," said Caitlin, as her eyes lit up.

Seeing an opportunity, Kevin said, "Not as beautiful as you."

That made Caitlin blush. "Oh stop it," she giggled, "you're embarrassing me!"

Embarrassment. Now that was a new one. Kevin had seen Caitlin be embarrassed a couple of times before, but it was still something rare. Hearing that Caitlin was embarrassed actually brought him up a couple of levels in how he felt about taking Caitlin on this trip. It was not actually that she was embarrassed that made him feel that way; it was that she had felt a strong emotion she was relatively unfamiliar with. That it was related to a comment about her appearance, which she did not value to the extend she did her intelligence or her magic strength, was also surprising.

Still, they were teenagers, after all. The thoughts of his relatively new intimacy with Caitlin had made Kevin think a great deal. She smiled so bright at times like this, it made him happy to finally see the special side of Caitlin that he had been looking for since they had first met. He was absolutely in love with this young woman.

Yet, at the same time, there was another thought within Kevin as well. He was, after all, only sixteen, albeit just a couple of months from his seventeenth birthday. He and Caitlin both had a lot of life to live. As young as they were, were they rushing into things too fast? Granted, neither one really had relationship experience before to help guide them through this. Kevin had only had crushes before Caitlin, including on Rachel Reinhart about a year and a half before, and Caitlin had cared not for human connection prior to meeting Kevin. The thought had also run across Kevin's head that perhaps he had other people to meet in his life, that maybe there was more out there than just Caitlin. Sure, Caitlin made him a very happy person, but could it be possible that they were not united in their futures?

At least for now, none of that mattered. Kevin was happy where he was, and he and Caitlin would tackle those hurdles as they came up.

For now, though Caitlin was staying with him for long periods of time, there was still a little bit of distance between them that kept things from getting too complex, and for now it made the situation very stable and kept their relationship very close.

As they walked back to Kevin's house together, hand in hand, it felt as though these happy times might last forever. Peace was present in Rikleifer, and all throughout Aurana. Things were quiet and tame around the city, and there was little for anyone to worry about.

That evening, Kevin and Caitlin spent the night together at Kevin's house, as they did every night. It was a quiet and peaceful, although it was pretty cold. The winter snow that fell was fairly light and none of it was sticking to the ground.

As Kevin prepared dinner, Caitlin sat on Kevin's bed and pulled out a book. It was a diary that she had been keeping since returning with Kevin to Rikleifer three months before. Her every thought and feeling that she could remember, she was now keeping recorded in this little book. To her, it was a nice way of seeing how far she had come since she had been an individual lacking in emotional feelings. While Kevin was working on dinner, Caitlin knew he would be busy for a while, so she pulled out a feather quill and a container of ink, and started writing another entry into her diary:

Two nights before the half moon of the second month of winter, also known as identifying date 2048157, at Kevin's house, Rikleifer, Aurana.

I went to a game of dangerball tonight with Kevin. It was so cold that I think I nearly froze solid. Fortunately, Kevin was there with me and he did what he could to keep me warm. Sharing a blanket with him, strangely enough, had a very neat feeling to it. There's some sensation of closeness that comes with it that I never would have expected to experience from such a simple thing. That being said, I'm not sure I want to go out while it's so cold unless it's necessary. I used to keep myself inside as much as possible when the cold became unbearable, but the idea of going out into it for recreation still strikes me as being a little odd.

Every time I've gone out into the cold for recreation so far, though, I've had a lot of fun with Kevin. He's still very much the same as he was before the winter: kind, mature, but also fun-loving and in many ways happier than he had been before. Although I'm sure I know the answer, I still wonder for certain if, just as how being with him makes me happier, that my presence by his side and being in his life makes him happier too. I guess maybe that's just the way love works; it takes two people thinking the same things and feeling the same feelings, even if they can't know for sure what the other is thinking or feeling. Sure, I could go in and read Kevin's mind with my magic, but to do so would be very rude and I wouldn't have any of it, especially since he can't read mine. Maybe that's just the way things are meant to be, and I'm all right with that.

I don't think I would have been all right with that a few months ago, though...

Caitlin had to stop at this point. She had certainly put an interesting thought into her head. Before she gained emotion, she did read Kevin's mind once without asking him. In many ways, the old Caitlin would have done anything to maintain control of a situation. Now, she was more willing to go where the situation would take her. Though she didn't know for sure, maybe that was something that human emotion added into her personality, and she was glad to accept that. It felt more human, at least.

With those thoughts past her, and with others in mind, Caitlin went back to writing. She left some space between before she kept writing:

The truth is, though, that I think this inability to know for sure is causing doubt in my heart again. I thought I was over this a long time ago, after realizing that I was scared that I couldn't be a traditional girlfriend or wife for Kevin. I guess, though, that it's not that easy to get rid of doubt while truly feeling emotions, especially now that I'm not suppressing them. It's hard to be trusting and not to be skeptical sometimes.

It's not that I distrust Kevin, or anything like that, but the logical side of me wonders sometimes if Kevin fell in love with me just because I was the only girl who didn't see anything wrong with him when I met him, or if it was just because we were traveling together, or something like that. It's made me wonder, too, if I fell in love with him just because he was the only one to see something more in me than anyone else ever had. On that part, though, I'm convinced that whether or not that was the way it happened to start, I love him now and wouldn't ever want to let him go. What makes it different the other way, though, is the possibility that Kevin might find someone that he may decide he likes more and start pursuing her. If that happened, I would be very heartbroken and alone. I just don't know. I don't want such bad thoughts to keep pressing on my mind, but they do. What will I do if Kevin ever finds out I'm thinking such a thing? That in itself might drive him away...

Caitlin stopped. She forgot how she was intending to finish this entry. Briefly she looked around for a moment, as if trying to find what she had been thinking. Already feeling a sort of way, worried about herself, she flipped through the diary to the end cover, where she had a few papers with poems sandwiched between the cover and the papers of the book. Perhaps a poem could help her remember.

These were poems that she had copied down from a book of poetry inside Rikleifer's library, a small single chamber inside its castle. Sometimes for enjoyment, she and Kevin would travel there together and read books together, since they had a shared love of fantasy adventure stories. Caitlin would also read poetry at times, and when she really liked one she read, happy or sad, she would write it down to save in the back of her journal.

She opened one and read it.

Shattered glass rains from the sky.
Shattered glass, it rains so dry.
It's cold and hard, an icy cry
From the heart that only wants to die.

Shattered pieces, all that remain
Of a romantic woman who felt the pain
From a man whose love was only a game;

It was life's most tragic shame.

Her heart of glass was smashed to bits;
It was so fragile it felt all of the hits.
Love, that passion, everyone of its
Powerful memories would cause crying fits.

As pieces fell, she fell asleep,
So depressed from her on-stricken grief.
"She'll never wake." 'Tis the common belief,
As shattered glass rains, falling in her sleep.

Quickly, Caitlin folded up the paper, enclosed it in her diary, and shut the cover. She had just thrown her mind into a dark place. After she put her diary away, she put her face in her hands, wondering whether or not these thoughts could really be scaring her so badly. Why did she have to have such dark thoughts, and why did they have to keep haunting her? Was it caution, or was it paranoia? Could she not get rid of her fears?

"Dinnertime, Caitlin!" came a call from Kevin from the small kitchen outside of the bedroom. Immediately, a smile came to Caitlin's face. Something about remembering he was there brought a smile to her face. She picked herself up and walked out into the kitchen, ready for a nice warm meal and to be with Kevin again.

As she sat down at the table, Kevin also took a seat and asked, "Writing in your diary again?"

Caitlin nodded. "Of course. It seems to be the best way for me to process these emotions I'm feeling."

Kevin smiled. "Other than talking about them?"

"Maybe," laughed Caitlin.

For the rest of the night, they spent their time together simply enjoying each other's company before heading to bed. The night was peaceful, and there would be much opportunity to rest for whatever might be in store the next day. It was a quiet night, as the snow continued to fall, leaving the ground caked in a layer of white powder.

Chapter 3

An Authentic Message

Early in the morning, just a few hours later while both Kevin and Caitlin were still sleeping, there was a loud knocking at the door. The sun had just poked its head over the horizon, and the nighttime was just wearing off. The knocking woke Caitlin up, though not very well. Knowing that someone should get the door, she pushed herself out of bed and threw on her dress. Then, she walked to the door and opened it slowly.

At the door stood a man dressed in a black uniform with orange trim. "Pardon me for waking you up so early," he began, "but would you happen to be Caitlin Amelia Magnon?"

Caitlin rubbed her eyes. "I would be," she said.

"Excellent. So I am at the right place," responded the man. "Is Kevin Trent Stryker here with you as well?"

"He's asleep in the other room," said Caitlin. "In fact, so was I until you knocked on the door."

The uniformed man bowed. "I apologize for waking you both up," he said, "but I was instructed to get here as soon as possible, and I did not want to wait. May I come in and speak with you both? It is urgent."

Rubbing her eyes a little bit, Caitlin had to gather herself. She knew Kevin would not like being woken up early, but if this man at the door claimed it was urgent, she knew Kevin should probably be up to hear about it, whether he liked it or not. Of course, Caitlin had her own curiosity now as well. What was going on that brought this man here? Why did he want Kevin and her to meet with him? The only way to find out was to wake Kevin up and let him know about it so they could start the discussion.

Before she walked in to wake Kevin up, Caitlin asked the stranger to wait in the kitchen area. Then, she headed over to Kevin's bed, knelt over him, gently put her hand on the side of his face, and said delicately, "Kevin, you have to get up now."

Kevin's sleepy eyes barely cracked open to see Caitlin above him. He then took a quick look outside the window in his room. His eyes then shut again as he said, in a low and tired voice, "Can't you let me sleep in today, Caitlin? There's nothing really important that we have to be up this early for."

"Much as I'd like to let you, something important has come up," Caitlin responded. "There's someone here to see us, and he says it's urgent."

Underneath his eyelids, Kevin was rolling his eyes. Business before pleasure, after all. Then, he opened them again and said, "All right. Can you grab my Vanguard jacket, Caitlin? I'd like to have it this morning if we're meeting with someone."

"Sure thing," said Caitlin, as she turned around to grab Kevin's jacket off of a chair in his room. She then left while Kevin dressed himself. Out of precaution, Kevin secured the Sword of Purity to his side, unsure of what would come of this meeting. A "locked sword", it was keyed to him and created by the sacrifice of a god. Kevin had used it as part of his journey to end the conquest of the realms several months before, but for the past three months he had no need to use it.

Walking out, still a little groggy, Kevin and Caitlin took seats at the table in the kitchen area. They invited the stranger to do the same, which he did. The first thing Kevin noticed was the stranger's uniform, and it interested him a bit. A black military uniform with orange trim, was not something he was familiar with.

"I am sure you are curious why I'm here," began the stranger, as he took his seat. He then reached into his jacket and continued, "I have a very important message for you, and I was told to deliver it as soon as possible." The stranger pulled a sealed envelope from his jacket.

Kevin nodded. "Interesting," he said, as he reached across the table to take the letter. "And where would this message be from? Where are you from?"

"I am a soldier of the Solunar Empire," answered the stranger. "A courier, to be specific. This message comes straight from my lord himself, Emperor Arthur."

That made Kevin and Caitlin look at each other. They both knew exactly who he was talking about: their good friend Arthur Falchor. Arthur and Kevin had grown up as best friends in Rikleifer, and it was Arthur's kidnapping by his father that motivated Kevin's actions several months ago.

"Please read it right away," continued the courier. "My lord wishes that you read it as soon as possible. I flew here by gryphon as quickly as possible to deliver this message."

Kevin and Caitlin simultaneously nodded. If it was a letter from Arthur that was delivered by gryphon, then it had to be important. Carefully, Kevin opened the envelope and unfolded the letter, holding it in such a way that Caitlin could read it as well. They both leaned toward each other to read it silently.

Arthur Falchor, Emperor of the Solunar Empire
Capital Building Main Office, Seta Archa, Solunar Empire

TO: Kevin Trent Stryker
Rikleifer, Aurana
URGENT

Dear Kevin and Caitlin,

It feels as though we have not talked in a long time. I apologize for this, knowing that much of it is my fault for not keeping in touch, but affairs have been arising very quickly here in the new Solunar Empire, and unfortunately much of this has kept us from finding the time to contact the two of you.

Unfortunately, however, one of these affairs has gone out of control in recent days, and I am forced to ask you both for a favor. During the past few weeks, we have been calling back all of the old Desolunar troops, giving them new Solunar Empire uniforms, and letting them rest with their families. However, one of Desolunar's most talented generals, known as General Sayo, has been rampaging against the new empire. He has already destroyed one town, and I fear that he may have enough force to throw off the whole empire.

My people have suffered for a long amount of time, and they need not suffer any longer. For this reason, I beg of you, will you lend us some aid? The courier I have sent will provide a ride to Seta Archa, and we will have time to meet up beforehand. If you choose to accept, I will brief you further of the situation upon your arrival.

Sincerely, and always your friend,
Arthur Falchor

As they both finished the letter, Kevin and Caitlin looked at each other again in surprise. What were they to do? There were a lot of questions to be answered about this letter. Above all, there were more concerns for Arthur and all of the friends Kevin and Caitlin had left behind in the Solunar Empire: Rachel, Rouge, and Resa.

Kevin quickly skimmed the letter a second time. As he did, he started to realize that Arthur's voice in the letter sounded as though it were one of desperation. Though it was stated in a fairly formal way, it was still a last-ditch effort that would never have been sent unless Arthur had no other alternative.

Kevin turned and looked at Caitlin. "Is Arthur in trouble?" he whispered.

Caitlin took another glance over the letter. "It certainly looks that way," she said. "I have to wonder what this worry is with one of the old Desolunar generals. Kind of seems like a political issue, but if it were, Arthur wouldn't be asking us for help."

Kevin nodded. Something was not right with this. Very familiar with Arthur's handwriting, Kevin could tell that the letter was not written by Arthur himself. The handwriting was far too neat for that. Still, however, there was something about the handwriting that seemed very familiar, almost as though even though it did not belong to Arthur, it belonged to someone that Kevin knew. That was good enough for Kevin. "I'm pretty sure it's authentic, Caitlin," he whispered. "I think we have to go, as soon as possible."

"Agreed," Caitlin whispered back, trusting in Kevin's words. "We have to find out what Arthur needs, at least."

So it was settled, then. Kevin turned toward the messenger and said, "Thank you for delivering this. We appreciate it."

The messenger nodded. "It is only my duty to my emperor," he said. "Now, the emperor also offers his courtesy by allowing you to ride with me by gryphon back to Seta Archa. Will you accept this?"

"Of course," acknowledged Kevin. "The quicker we can get there, the better. However, we will likely have some errands to run before we go, so can we save that ride until tomorrow morning?"

At first, there was an awkward look on the face of the messenger. Kevin and Caitlin were slightly confused by this, as well as worried that they may have upset this man. But in a second, his face changed to an awkward chuckle. "I never thought you would say that," he said. "I've been trying to get here as quickly as possible, and it's left me short on sleep and my gryphon exhausted. We could use a little time to recuperate."

"Certainly," nodded Kevin. "You're welcome to stay here, if you'd like."

The Solunar Empire soldier bowed. "I'm honored," he said, some of the exhaustion leaking through his voice.

Kevin shook his head. "Of nothing," he responded. "Please, let me show you to a bed."

As he finished these words, Kevin prepared himself for something he knew he would not like. He showed the soldier into his mother's room, which he allowed Caitlin to use when she stayed with him. The soldier thanked Kevin for the room and, with his gryphon already secured outside, almost immediately took to rest. Just outside of the room, Kevin asked Caitlin to come with him as he leaned out the door.

Outside, it was still quite cold. None of the snow from the previous night had stuck to the ground, leaving only dead grass and a cold ground behind. Winter in Aurana typically looked like this, since Aurana was mostly meadow and forest outside of its cities and towns. "I guess I'm sharing a room with you tonight," Caitlin stated, somewhat reluctantly. "Are you sure it was a good idea to leave him in your house by himself? You did just meet him a few minutes ago, you know."

Kevin nodded. "I know, but take a look at the guy," he said. "He's worn down, and there's nothing in there that would be of value anyway even if he were looking to loot my house. Besides, if we're going to the Solunar Empire tomorrow, we need him and his gryphon to get there, and it would help if they were well rested."

Caitlin just shook her head. "I suppose you're right," she said. "He definitely has to be carrying an authentic message from Arthur. Was it Arthur's handwriting, Kevin?"

"No," responded Kevin. "Arthur doesn't write that neatly." Then, finally realizing whose handwriting it was, Kevin snapped his fingers. "But I'm willing to bet you it was Rachel's. She's always had very nice handwriting, since back when we were in school together at the Rikleifer Academy."

"Ah, so that's whose it was," said Caitlin. "Come to think of it, I do remember hearing that Arthur made Rachel his prime minister when he took the reins down there. It's going to be really nice to see both of them again, my half-brother and my best friend..." Caitlin stopped at this point and turned her head to Kevin. "That is, other than you, of course, Kevin," she added, a little nervous that she may have implied something.

"If you say I'm your best friend," Kevin smiled back. He then reached down to hold Caitlin's hand, which she more than willingly accepted. "It sounds like we do have some serious business down there with whatever's going on."

"I won't forget that," nodded Caitlin, with a little wink. "Hopefully the serious stuff won't take too long, though, so we can spend more time with Arthur and Rachel, and Rouge and Resa too. Plus, I've got to make sure I'm back here in Aurana in time for registration."

"Right," acknowledged Kevin. He knew full and well what Caitlin was talking about.

At any Auranian citizen's sixteenth birthday, it was their responsibility to register with a government office because sixteen was the legal age of adulthood. Registration was fairly simple: just a checkup on the person's legal records of their birth and life, logging a legal name to be carried into adulthood for certain, and approval of adulthood. It had to be done exactly on the person's sixteenth birthday, or else the Auranian government would usually add some kind of penalty, including extra work to be done for registration. Kevin had gone through registration himself just a few months before, and he knew it was not very painful, just a slight roadblock for a day. Being out of the country at the time, however, would be a bad idea.

Caitlin was fifteen at the moment, but she was fast approaching her sixteenth birthday, when she would legally become an adult. She could not wait, because that would also mean she could register as a wizardess, the highest ranking of spellcaster, with the Aurana Department of Magic Affairs, giving her the legal right to practice magic as a career across the world. Very few wizards were registered with any of the governments of the world, and most who trained in the arts never achieved the top-level qualifications to be able to practice it legally.

Together, Kevin and Caitlin continued to walk deeper into Rikleifer, holding each other's hand as they did so. For now, though it was cold outside, nothing could be warmer than the thoughts of being with their best friends soon enough.

"I forgot to ask, where are we going?" asked Caitlin, as they walked along.

Kevin chuckled. "Oh yeah, I did forget to say something," he said. "If we're going to the Solunar Empire, then there's someone we should say goodbye to, first."

Chapter 4

The Retired Warrior

Kevin's father, a man by the name of Vincent Stryker, was a retired general of the nation of Scurnia, far to the east of Aurana. That was, however, until the most recent war with Desolunar had brought him out of retirement. Originally, Vincent Stryker had been born in Aurana, in the city of Rikleifer. At the age of two, his family moved to Scurnia, where he grew up. Very quickly, the young Vincent Stryker became very active with the Scurnian army, joining it as soon as he was eligible at the age of sixteen, and by the age of thirty, he was already an influential general in the Scurnian military, smack dab in the middle of the time of the Alliance-Daritel War, when the Daritel tribe of the Wastes took over Seta Archa and began to terrorize everything in their path, invading north and conquering large swaths of land at a frightening pace.

Scurnia was very fortunate that Vincent Stryker arose at the time that he did. It was his genius that had allowed him to plan a bold and daring surgical strike directly on the city of Seta Archa behind enemy lines, ending the war that had been ravaging a good portion of the world. His force of Scurnians, coupled with an Auranian unit, managed to pierce into the heart of the walled city of Seta Archa and decimate the Daritel. Of course, there was more to the story than just what was being seen by most. Vincent Stryker also carried with him a second duty as the "pure one", a man chosen by the gods themselves to be their champion. Given a weapon blessed by the sacrifice of king of gods Vinz Larinion, the Sword of Purity, he was also tasked with a request from the gods to bring down the puppeteer behind the Daritel, a fallen god.

In that task, Vincent failed.

As much effort as Vincent had placed into defeating the puppeteer, he ultimately found his efforts futile and his strength depleted. His Sword of Purity, despite being a powerful weapon containing divine power, was unable to break his opponent. Realizing this, Vincent made a difficult decision. He cut a deal with the puppeteer for his life and laid down his sword, entrusting it to his friend, War Commander Milton "Ironman" Eukert of Aurana. After the end of the war, Vincent fled to Aurana, abandoning his commission with the Scurnian army. Then, he returned to the city of his birth: Rikleifer. While there, he met a woman by the name of Lavinia Trent, whom he began courting. They were never truly married, but they remained together for four years, by the end of which they had a son.

That son was Kevin Trent Stryker. Vincent and Lavinia had registered him together and planned to get married to bind their lives together, but the dark voice of the puppeteer returned. There was a great amount of danger in staying with Lavinia and Kevin, Vincent realized, so with Lavinia's blessing, Vincent left Aurana, never to return. He trusted Lavinia to hide the identity of Kevin's father and fled to Scurnia, settling in the city of Tron on the border of Scurnia and Gardolk. There, he served solely an advisory role on a come-and-go basis with the Scurnian military, who refused to forsake their great general despite his leaving four years before.

Still, Vincent Stryker was finding himself very disillusioned with life where he was. It had felt as though because of his decision and what had happened four years before, his life was virtually over. Looking to escape from the sickness of society, he planned an escape to a region in western Scurnia where he could be away from society forever. He fled to a cave along the treacherous Cliffs of Vallia, where he could live in peace without any disruption from society ever again. Over that course of time, his body had become old and started to have problems. Sixteen years had passed in Scurnia, and Vincent Stryker quickly accelerated to the age of fifty. That was when Kevin Trent Stryker had finally found his father after so long of not knowing. Kevin was already taking up his attempt to stop the puppeteer and his even stronger dominion of Desolunar.

Now, Vincent was retired from battle. His poor health was growing even poorer because he had continued to push himself, and he was simply finding it harder and harder to keep going. Knowing this, the Duke of Rikleifer, Edmund Cleary, offered to the man that he and his nephew King Andrew II had considered "one of Aurana's greatest treasures" to be cared for in the Castle of Rikleifer by the duke himself. Vincent accepted because it would place him in Rikleifer, close to his son. He and Kevin were finally able to develop a true father-son relationship for the first time thanks to that.

It was him that Kevin and Caitlin were coming to see on this day. Kevin wanted to make sure he said goodbye to his father before leaving for Seta Archa.

The Castle of Rikleifer's outer walls were almost always left with open doors to allow everyone into its courtyard. It was, for all intents and purposes, just a business building on the inside with an array of government offices and small businesses that sold to the people who came here to do bureaucracy. Only in times of war were the gates locked and the castle turned into a military installation. Kevin deeply recalled being involved in the last time that happened, at the Battle of Middle Aurana.

Passing through the external gates of the castle and directly into the castle's core, Kevin and Caitlin proceeded to the middle of the castle to the duke's office. As the city's ruler, the duke was a responsible leader who had helped to preserve Rikleifer as the "city of dreams" it had claimed to be. He took no credit for this, but many praised his leadership nonetheless. Despite taking no credit, the duke did take a great deal of pride in his city, proud of the accomplishments of his people. The duke was, however, a regal man who was accompanied by the same traditional thoughts of the ruling class as many of his ancestors.

After being cleared by security to enter the innermost part of the castle and leaving his sword with them, Kevin and Caitlin proceeded down the hallways of the government sector in the middle of the castle to the duke's office. They stopped right in front of the door, and as Kevin knocked on the door, Caitlin said, "I wonder what kind of condition your father is in. It's been a couple of weeks since we saw him last."

"He's probably the same he's always been," answered Kevin, "but the duke did say that he wanted to make sure my father's health was closely monitored, so I guess we'll have to see."

Caitlin nodded. "Guess so," she said. "He's a survivor, at least."

"Mhmm," acknowledged Kevin. Then, he paused for a minute, listening for anything behind the door. "It sounds like the duke is in there," he said, as he knocked a little harder on the door.

As Kevin pulled his hand back from the last knock, the door swung open and behind it was a tall man dressed in a regal green uniform with blue and red accents to a cape across his shoulders. "I heard you the first time," he said, as he ran his free hand across his head to press his flat black hair. "Kevin Trent Stryker, I am certainly honored that you have come to visit today."

Pretty quickly, Kevin and Caitlin fell to their knees, being that they were in the presence of the duke; Edmund Cleary, Duke of Rikleifer. "It is an honor to see you, my lord," Kevin said as he knelt down with his left hand over his right fist."

Unlike his nephew King Andrew II, who disliked these traditional signs of respect, the duke reveled in them. "Rise," he commanded. Then, he proceeded to speak normally. "Kevin and Caitlin, I am glad to see that both of you have come back again. Here to visit Vincent again, I presume?"

"Yes sir," responded Caitlin. "We're leaving soon on a trip, and we wanted to say goodbye to him before we left."

"Ah, but of course," nodded the duke, in full understanding. "In that case, would you both be willing to come inside for just a moment?"

Kevin and Caitlin glanced at each other for just a second, and both of them nodded. "We'd be delighted to," answered Kevin, as he and Caitlin proceeded into the office. Behind them, the duke closed the door, before heading to his seat behind the desk. Kevin and Caitlin took seats in the two chairs in front of it.

As the duke sat down, he adjusted himself several times in his seat before finally getting comfortable. "All is well with your father for now, but in his own perception, he is better than he is. Do you understand what I am saying?"

Shaking his head, Kevin responded, "Not really."

"I get it," interrupted Caitlin, looking over to Kevin. "Your dad's recovering, but he's not content with sitting here all of the time."

The duke nodded. "Precisely, Caitlin," he responded. "It concerns me that Vincent Stryker has this spirit that does not let him simply sit around. While it has proven itself very admirable over the years as Vincent has led thousands of troops and accomplished more than anyone could ever dream to do, it makes it difficult for him to get the proper rest he needs to treat his aging body. I can only hope he has not further injured his back recently from all that he has been doing."

Kevin rolled his eyes a little bit. He could recall only a few months before seeing his father for the first time, looking like a withered old man in a cave, older than his age actually was. After that, however, when Vincent had donned his old red Scurnian war uniform and had picked up a sword, he seemed to keep the chronic problems he had been having from getting the best of him, all the way through the Battle of Seta Archa. Though Kevin had not returned to Aurana with his father at the same time, he did recall his father's story of the return trip. According to Vincent, his back had begun to tense up again as he returned, and he was fortunate to have the duke's offer to be taken care of to make sure he would be able to live without handicap. Clearly, his body had taken a great deal of abuse over the years and needed to be treated better.

"That's my dad for you," Kevin finally responded, with a serious tone. "So, is that why you wanted to pull us aside for a moment?"

"Precisely," acknowledged the duke. "I was hoping I could get your cooperation and have you ask your father to ease up. We have him on several physical and dietary regiments to try and keep him healthy, which he continues to resist while working more with his swordplay and walking around here in boredom." He paused for a moment. "Your father is one of Aurana's most valued treasures, even if his life is far more significant in Scurnia. What he has done for Aurana, like what you have done, is most certainly worthy of recognition, which is why I have taken it upon myself to protect and rehabilitate him. However, I cannot do everything."

Silently, Kevin nodded. "I understand," he said. "And I am grateful to you for your kindness to my father."

"You are welcome," responded the duke, with a nod. "For his sake, though, will you help to make sure he keeps to his programs, at least until he is healthy enough to live without difficulty on his own?"

There was a momentary pause. "The best I can do is ask him," Kevin finally answered. "No more, and no less. I can't make him do anything, even if I wanted him to, but I can see if he will."

Caitlin laughed a little bit as she looked at the duke. "That's his father for you," she chuckled.

For just a second, the duke's response was a serious, silent glare. Then, suddenly catching Kevin and Caitlin by surprise, he started laughing very hard. "Oh, how right you are!" he laughed. "Ah, it is difficult to be serious about Vincent Stryker sometimes. Though he has been difficult, my staff always enjoys him. I only ask for your help in keeping him down for a while because I am concerned for him, even if I do enjoy his presence and his antics."

Despite the smiles on the faces of Caitlin and the duke, Kevin still had a serious look on his face. As much as the duke was finally starting to come around and laugh, he did take his father's well being very seriously. Now that he understood the duke's concerns, he did understand the worry.

The duke noticed Kevin's reaction, and decided to continue delicately because of this. "I do apologize if I worried you, Kevin."

Kevin gently shook his head as he tried to keep smiling. He would be all right as long as he managed to see his father today nonetheless and saw him in good condition.

"Now, then," continued the duke, "I must ask, Kevin, because I find it curious. It has not been long since you and Caitlin came to visit Vincent. Why are you back so soon already? Miss your father that much?"

Seeing Kevin was still trying to shake off fears for his father, Caitlin responded, "Not exactly. Something has unfortunately come up in Solunar, and the Vanguard and I must leave to address it."

The duke rolled his eyes. "I am not surprised," he responded. "Solunar was left in such a mess after the Battle of Seta Archa. Is your friend Arthur managing well down there?"

There was a second's pause. Then, Kevin and Caitlin each

shook their heads awkwardly. "We really don't know," answered Kevin. "That's what we're going to find out. We received a hand-delivered letter today via gryphon transport from Seta Archa that there is a situation going on down there, and Arthur has asked for our help."

"Very well," nodded the duke. "Solunar is out of your jurisdiction, but if Arthur has invited you, then I see no reason for you to be forced to stay in Aurana. After all, right now it is a peaceful time and there is likely little need for you here at this moment. You have said it yourself to me before, Kevin: one must not forget about their friends and those who they have sworn to protect."

Kevin nodded. "Thank you, my lord," he said. "We'll be heading out tomorrow morning, in order to get there as soon as possible."

"That sounds best," nodded the duke. "Keep in mind as well, of course, that we here in Aurana do support the stability of the new Solunar Empire, provided Arthur keeps to his promises. When you are down there, you represent Aurana as well. As such, I would like to keep a report of the situation, if you would allow me to do so. It would definitely help your record as the Vanguard of Aurana if we kept records of your official activities."

"Meaning you're making this an official activity?" asked Caitlin.

The duke nodded. "Absolutely," he said. "In other words, should something come up in Aurana, Kevin will not be required to report in and acquire an assignment if necessary, because he is already assigned."

"Wow…" said Kevin, very surprised. "You'd really do that for us? On so personal a task?"

Again, the duke nodded. "Of course," he responded. "You are the Vanguard, after all. Your rank may be ceremonial and your position very high, but you are still a part of the Auranian military, after all. Furthermore… for all that you did for your country in the Battles of Middle Aurana and Seta Archa, you deserve as much respect and generosity as we can give you."

Shaking his head, Kevin responded, "I'm not sure I really deserve all of that."

Silently, the duke nodded, taking a slight pause as well. "Regardless," he began, "that is my gift to you. Go and do what you need to do without worrying about us. Besides, I do not think there would be anything more to please King Andrew II more than a little diplomacy with the new, smaller nation of the Solunar Empire."

King Andrew II was one of Kevin's good friends, after Kevin helped him to ascend the throne. Though their friendship had been forced together somewhat by Caitlin's father, Professor Magnon, Andrew and Kevin had begun to be very good friends over the course of their meeting, with Andrew even calling Kevin one of his most valuable retainers. Andrew had given Kevin the title of Vanguard of Aurana, the first one named in fifty years, after Kevin had helped Andrew ascend to the throne and displace his misguided father. It was more than a sign of respect for Andrew to give Kevin the title; it was a sign of friendship.

"Now, you two had better get to visiting with your father, Kevin," continued the duke. "He's on the roof of the northwest tower of the castle, right now, by himself. Part of his rehabilitation has been practicing artistic swordplay using specific movements, to keep himself sharp without straining himself."

"Gotcha," winked Kevin as he and Caitlin stood up. They showed the duke a respectful bow. "And thank you for everything."

"Of nothing," said the duke in a nice tone. "Now get going, I'm sure your father would love to see you."

Acknowledging this, Kevin opened the door, and he and Caitlin left through it. They left the duke sitting at his desk by himself.

With the door closed, Kevin started looking around. He looked down one hallway, then down the other. Then, down one, and down the other again. "What's up?" asked Caitlin, noticing this.

"Uhm…" Kevin chuckled awkwardly, "I forgot which way the northwest tower is."

Caitlin started laughing. "You want to try *northwest*?"

Looking down at Caitlin, Kevin rolled his eyes as he laughed. "I'd expect something like that out of Arthur, not you," he laughed. "Which way is northwest?"

"It's to your left," she continued to laugh. "Now come on, let's go see your father before the duke questions why we're here."

The walk to the northwest tower was very much like the walk through the castle. Simple stone walls sat on all sides, as various offices and areas linked up to these small hallways. At the end of the hallway was the stairway up the northwest tower. There was little to it, being that there were no rooms in the tower. The stairway only served for access to the turret at the top, where arrows could be rained down from a higher point than the wall surrounding the castle. Needless to say, during times of peace it made for a quiet spot within the Castle of Rikleifer.

As Kevin and Caitlin reached the top, they opened the trap door, allowing a beam of sunlight down into the dark stairwell. Kevin was the first to step up, as he noticed his father, Vincent Stryker, leaning against a battlement as he stared out toward the west. From the turret atop the northwest tower, the cold winter morning was evident all around. A coating of snow and frozen ground dotted the landscape all over, and people below were walking around wearing thick jackets or wrapped in blankets. The chill in the air was not terribly bad this morning, but it was enough to be noticeable.

Quickly, Kevin turned to Caitlin and put his finger to his lips, asking her to be very quiet. He wanted to surprise his father with being there. But, as Caitlin closed the trap door behind her, she accidentally dropped it and let it slam back to the floor.

Almost instantly, Vincent drew his katana and had it at Kevin's neck.

Kevin raised his hands in surrender. "Hey, easy, dad. No need to be so paranoid all the time."

It took Vincent a second to lower his sword, the *Lavinia*, named for Kevin's mother. "I'm so sorry, Kevin," he said, without even saying hello. "It's so instantaneous anymore." Carefully, Vincent then sheathed his sword and walked back to the battlement to stare off again.

Slowly, Kevin and Caitlin walked over to Vincent and leaned on the battlements themselves, each on one side of Vincent. "It's all right, dad," began Kevin. "We really didn't mean to startle you like that. I was kind of hoping we could surprise you in being here, and it just didn't work out so well, did it?"

Awkwardly, Vincent chuckled a little bit. "I guess not," he said, as he put his arm around Kevin's shoulders. "It really is pleasant to see you here, though, my son." He then turned his head toward Caitlin. "And my future daughter-in-law, too."

Almost instantly, Kevin took a couple of steps back from his father in surprise that he had made such a comment. "Hey, whoa, dad!" he exclaimed. "We're not anywhere near even thinking about that point just yet."

Caitlin was a little nerved by that. "Yeah, that'd be a little weird, wouldn't it? We've only known each other a few months."

"Probably so," nodded Vincent Stryker. "It was only a joke, anyway. Still, it's good to see you kids again."

"Good to see you too, dad," nodded Kevin. "So, what's with the quick draw? Something on your mind?"

"Nothing more than usual," responded Vincent as he shook his head. "I never let you see that before, Kevin, but the truth is, living in a cave like I did for years and years made me very paranoid. Even Sammy had to be careful when coming to see me sometimes, to be sure I would not snap and attack him. Anyone approaching was like a threat to me, in my head."

Kevin shook his head, worried about his father. Caitlin answered, in her usual logically thinking self, "Being in an environment like that makes you a bit of a recluse, and with seclusion and isolation comes paranoia and instinct."

Vincent chuckled a little bit as he looked over at Caitlin in response. "You're your father's daughter, that's for sure. That's the same kind of response he would have."

"I guess so," laughed Caitlin. "That's always him, with the logical answer and little thought to the sympathetic."

"Ah, don't worry about the sympathetic," chuckled Vincent again. "I know from you that you do mean it."

"Indeed. With that kind of reaction, though," continued Caitlin, "it's no wonder the duke is worried about you."

Vincent rolled his eyes. "And it figures he'd send you two up here to tell me. Just like him, can't do it himself."

Kevin put his hands up. "Actually, that's not why we're here to see you today, dad, but the duke did ask us to mention it while we were here. He sounded pretty worried about you; he said you haven't wanted to take it easy while you've been here and he's afraid that that's not good for your body."

"Bah," exclaimed Vincent. "No one ever tells me to sit still. That's why I still carry this thing," he said, as he flashed his sword quickly, and snapped it back into its scabbard. "Swordplay is an art form, after all, and if nothing else during this time of peace, practicing with it up here helps me to stay flexible without worrying about injury."

"It's not about the swordplay," frowned Kevin, "although I might have something to say about nearly striking me with it. Have you even tried to rest your back while you've been here?"

There was a moment's pause as Vincent thought. Then, he shook his head. "Not exactly," he said, "but listen to me. Kevin, when you brought me back into action, the problems with my back pushed themselves aside so I could fight with you. It was only on my way back to Aurana, accepting the duke's gracious offer, that it tensed back up and became sore like it had been before. Perhaps, then, it is staying active that will do me best, as long as I watch my back and take care not to injure it further."

"It could be," answered Kevin with a weak response. He really did not want to get in between the duke and his father, and start a bunch of drama that was pointless. "Although," he began, with a new thought, "perhaps if you manage to get your back better, you might be able to go back to Scurnia to visit with Sammy again. It has been a while since we all have seen him."

"That would be pleasant," acknowledged Vincent. "Blasted old centaur-man has such a self-conscience about his horse legs that it keeps him from being involved with society. Someday, Kevin, I hope that maybe someone will do for him what you have done for me."

"Someday, someone," said Kevin, as he crossed his fingers.

Vincent Stryker merely nodded again and changed the subject. "So, then, if my health is not why you are here, what does brings the two of you here today? You two just came to see me a couple of days ago. Is something wrong?"

Kevin shook his head. "I don't really know," he said, "but

we're going to be leaving for Seta Archa tomorrow morning. Arthur sent us a letter about some kind of emergency he's having down there, and he wants our help with it."

Sighing, Vincent responded, "That's why you're here. You had to let me know you're leaving town."

"We thought it was the best thing to do," added Caitlin.

"And it likely is," nodded Vincent Stryker. "What's the emergency?"

Kevin took a breath. "It sounds like someone is causing havoc in the Solunar Empire. A rogue general named General Sayo attacked one of its towns."

Immediately, Vincent's eyes widened. "You must be extremely careful!" he exclaimed. "That man is dangerous!"

"You know him?" inquired Caitlin.

"Know him? He was one of my very best friends for years!" exclaimed Vincent. "We served together in the Alliance-Daritel War, and he was a top commander in Aurana." He balled one hand into a fist, before letting it go, pausing for a moment while Kevin and Caitlin observed his frustrations. "Martin Sayo was a commander in the Aurana Protection Forces during the Alliance-Daritel War. We served together in a coalition force along with Eukert and Bryant, whom you fought alongside at the Battle of Middle Aurana. He became a traitor to his country, and a traitor to our friendship, after Atwals fell to Desolunar during the Desolunar War. As I understand it, he's also the one who attacked Eukert and his men when you found him and saved his life."

Kevin clenched his fists, remembering that battlefield vividly. It was a memory he would never forget. "That son of a…"

Interrupting, Caitlin grabbed him by the arm, trying to settle him down. She then looked at Vincent. "So he became a Desolunar general after that, I would presume."

"He did," acknowledged Vincent. "Eukert, Bryant, and I actually fought him at the Battle of Seta Archa three months ago. He escaped. Clearly, we were in the wrong to let him live."

Taking a breath, Kevin tried to respond calmly. "Clearly not," he said.

"We should have known," Vincent nodded. "General Sayo is extremely clever, ruthless, and well planned. He barely speaks, but when he does, it's because his words need to make an impact. If you are going after him, you need to be extremely careful, because there will not be a contingency he has not planned for."

Shaking his head, Kevin said, "I hope that's not the ask Arthur has for me," he said. "I'm not sure I'd know how to hunt someone down."

Caitlin chimed in. "Rouge and Resa would know. We'll just have to find out what they have in store for us."

"Indeed; I am sure that Arthur, being your best friend, would be mindful of your safety." He paused for a second. "You just have to do what you have to do sometimes. And he needs you because you always defend those you have an obligation to protect."

With a smile, Kevin nodded. "You said that before, back when you had to justify to Professor Magnon about why we needed to go into the Battle of Middle Aurana."

"That's true," acknowledged Vincent. "Kevin, my son, I am glad to see that you have not forgotten my words. It disappoints me that for so many years, I could not do that for you."

A nerve was touched there. Kevin had never been raised by his father, and had only met him a few months before. For so long before that, however, Kevin had only wondered what it would be like to have a father, and had desired one for such a long time. And now that he had his father, there was almost a slight awkwardness to the whole thing. There was a long pause as Kevin thought about this.

Then, Vincent Stryker continued, "You two have my blessing to do whatever you need to do, but I advise you to be mindful of the danger General Sayo presents. I'm sure I'll be looking forward to your return every day."

Nerved as Kevin was, he managed to nod his head and say, "Thank you, dad. We'll come back and see you again as soon as we return to Aurana. Who knows, maybe we'll be back within a week."

"Really depends on whatever he needs down there, though," added Caitlin. "We'll just have to see. I hope it doesn't take too long, because I have to get registered pretty soon."

Kevin nodded. "We'll make sure you get taken care of," he said as he wrapped an arm around Caitlin. "After all that we've all been through together already, how bad could it be?"

"That may be true," acknowledged Vincent, "but keep in mind, Kevin, you should never take any situation lightly. It's never smart to forget that you should never lower your defenses." He paused and looked at Caitlin, before looking back at Kevin. "And put your trust in her. I have yet to see her steer you wrong."

Silently, Kevin nodded. He was not the naïve kid anymore that he had been a few months before. From all that he had gone through, he had rapidly developed into a battle-hardened warrior. Plus, he was absolutely right about Caitlin. He looked at Caitlin for a moment.

Caitlin nodded as well, knowing Vincent Stryker was right. She would make sure Kevin was not led astray. And she too had that sense of obligation, to make sure her friends Arthur and Rachel had every opportunity to succeed and for their people to be safe. Not only was it personal, but to her this was what being a wizard was all about.

Looking back at his father, Kevin had a more confident look. "I won't forget," he said, with a very serious tone. "I'll still be on my guard at all times."

"I hope you will remember that," replied Vincent.

Again, Kevin nodded. He was ready for this one.

And so, with a hug and a close moment, Vincent and Kevin wished each other the best as they prepared to part ways. Caitlin also hugged Vincent in a sign of him accepting her as a part of the family, as well. It would be a while before they would be able to see each other again. Kevin and Caitlin had to be off quickly, though. They wanted to leave Rikleifer tomorrow morning, in order to reach Arthur as quickly as possible.

In order to be ready for anything possible, they had to stock up on supplies, before taking the arranged gryphon flight to Seta Archa. As Kevin thought about getting his supplies for the trip, he recalled the familiarity of everything involved with that. It meant strapping the Sword of Purity back onto his belt and keeping it nice and tight. It meant getting to travel around with Caitlin again, bringing around old memories of the conquest of the realms, and his journey to stop it.

Sure, it may not be a fallen god he was chasing now, or a dictator with dark ambitions, but whatever the task would be would be important nonetheless. He was not a hero, so he had told himself, but he was the one willing to do it. So too was Caitlin, whom Kevin felt was more of a hero than he ever could be.

The day passed quickly, and all the while, Vincent Stryker kept practicing his artistic swordplay into the twilight, his son having long since left by now. At the edge of the sunset, however, Vincent decided to sheathe his sword and head back into the castle. As he put it away, though, Vincent felt an odd crosswind. He stopped for a moment and mumbled to himself, "An odd wind?" Then the wind blew stronger, for just a moment, and then faded off completely. It had hit for just one second, before disappearing. As it did, Vincent's eyes widened. He said it to himself, in realization as he stared at the sunset.

"Something's not right."

Chapter 5

Pursuit of the Remnant

It was becoming painfully clear to Arthur, the more he watched over his city of Seta Archa, that his people were suffering. Though he was doing all he could for them, they continued to struggle with a great many issues. Every day, Arthur hated his role as emperor a little bit more. Simply put, this was not the life that he had wanted to lead. He could hardly see how anyone could enjoy this job unless they were looking merely to usurp the power involved in it and not actually care for their people. As his people struggled to survive and he was looking to put the broken Solunar Empire together as something new, the fact that General Sayo was out there terrorizing his people was more than a thorn in the emperor's side. It was, as Arthur had seen it due to the fragile state of the empire, a knife blade pointed at his country's heart.

Now what was there to do? Arthur's mind was starting to break down every day. His worries were slowly starting to catch up with him, tearing him apart and making him feel weaker and weaker. He found himself doing more and more of what his father had done before: sitting in his throne room atop the capital building, and staring out the glass sides of the triangular pyramid structure at the surrounding city of Seta Archa.

In worriment over what was going on with Arthur, Rachel Reinhart spent much more of her time watching him and making sure he did not collapse. Secretly, silently, she held herself together as she did everything she could to care for him in these stressful moments, taking responsibilities for resolving issues with the empire when Arthur was too stressed to make the right decision, as well as trying to help keep Arthur's head in the game. There just seemed to be so little about this whole mess that she could help to resolve outside of standing in for him in the bureaucracy of running the empire. All Rachel could do was watch Arthur change in front of her eyes, become more depressed, and talk to him and try to slow down how quickly this came about. She watched on as Arthur was undergoing a drastic metamorphosis of character. His normally sarcastic, yet joking sense of humor, was vanishing. It was being replaced by serious concern and contemplation over reality. His normally carefree lifestyle was being crushed by a weight of heavy responsibility.

And Arthur knew it, too. It did bother him that he knew he was not able to be himself in front of his friends anymore, yet he had to continue thinking about his people first. That was the way it had to be if he was to take care of them. If only it did not need to be so taxing on his mind.

Rachel had always considered herself to be a realist, but never to the level she was seeing in Arthur. In fact, though she had a great amount of responsibility herself as the prime minister of the Solunar Empire, she began to wonder if maybe she was starting to become more idealistic, more of a dreamer. She could not really be sure herself, but something was definitely changing within her as well. The more Rachel stood and watched Arthur degrade, the more she began to feel desperate to get him some relief. The only question was, how do you relieve the tension of someone in his position?

Breaking the silence in the room was a loud thud below the trap door. "Enter," called Arthur, without turning. Rachel merely stood in her place, still looking downtrodden by Arthur's depression.

In response, the door flew open, and a Solunar Empire soldier walked up through the floor and closed the door behind him. Then, he walked right over to Arthur's desk and left an envelope there. "Message for you, sir," he said, as he nodded and walked back to the trap door.

As soon as he had left, Rachel took a couple of steps closer to Arthur and asked, "Why didn't you acknowledge him? That's not like you at all."

Arthur shook his head, still depressed. "I don't feel like me at all, Rachel," he said. "I feel like my father." He took a breath, after a long pause. "I sit here and watch upon Seta Archa, and I see its people struggle to stay fed, to survive the winter. I can only stand back as some try to tear them all to shreds. Yet despite the power I hold as emperor of the Solunar Empire, there is so little I can do for them sometimes. How can anyone do this?"

Rachel merely sighed. That encapsulated everything she feared he was feeling. There was nothing she could really say to try and encourage him, nothing that would lift his spirits. Put simply, there was a great deal to be depressed about.

Not hearing any response from Rachel, Arthur went about opening the letter on his desk. He tore open the envelopes and carefully unfolded the paper within, noting that the note was written in red ink. That color of ink was traditionally used for death sentences.

Carefully, Arthur read the message over. It had no addressee or other information, no signature, only a message.

You who have called for the fall of mighty Desolunar will soon see how its vengeance will strike back on you. The "Solunar Empire", as you call it, is unfit to be in existence. Its people are weak, its resources are depleted, and its armies rally around those with real power.

The remnant of the fallen still exists, and I assure you, it is very much alive. It is coming, and soon a new wind will sweep over Solunar, as the empire is replaced by the essence of strength.

Beware, "Emperor Arthur". Your time is coming...

Arthur merely shook his head as he put the letter down, not even bothering to finish reading the note. It was not something unexpected to receive, but it was something quite dark to read nonetheless. "So they finally have a name at last," he said as he shook his head.

There was a confused look on Rachel's face. "What do you mean?" she asked. "What's inside that letter?"

"Not a whole lot," shrugged Arthur. "It merely seems like 'the remnant of the fallen' has decided to spit in our faces, that's all."

Rachel rolled her eyes. "That's what they're calling themselves now? That's got to be the dumbest name I've ever heard."

Shaking his head, Arthur reluctantly agreed with Rachel. It seemed to be more of just a term in the letter than the name they were officially using, but that was irrelevant. "Regardless," he said firmly, "they're still a dangerous group. I'm not going to take this lightly."

Rachel put her face in the palm of her hand. There was little she could do. She started to stare out of another of the triangular pyramid's three windows that comprised its sides on the top level where the throne room was. It was staunchly similar to the way Arthur had done it for days and days before. Just outside of that window, a gryphon was landing carefully right beside the pyramid. It was a little bit of an odd sight to see, since there were other, more open areas to land a gryphon, even in the tightly packed city of Seta Archa. Nonetheless, Rachel had seen it happen before in her short time as prime minister, so the sight itself was not too unusual.

Curious as to who was landing, however, Rachel watched closely as the gryphon descended in front of her. Plain as day at the gryphon's front was a Solunar Empire soldier, not an uncommon sight at all. Behind him were two people: a boy in a green uniform with a red and black triangle patch on the side, and a girl in a white dress with red trim accents.

Kevin and Caitlin.

Instantly upon recognizing them, Rachel's face lit up. "Arthur! Arthur!" she exclaimed, "they're here! They're here!"

"They're here?" asked Arthur, slightly confused. "Who's here?"

"Who else would be here?" Rachel asked back. "Who did you summon for that we'd be so excited to see?"

Excitement came to Arthur's eyes upon realization. He almost sprinted out of his chair toward the trap door. Rachel was really surprised, but pleasantly so, as she followed him down the stairs.

At the next floor down, Arthur did not bother to think about the lift to the bottom in the torch-lit hallway. Instead, he ran for the next set of stairs and continued going down the large triangular pyramid-shaped capital building. Down four floors he continued, until he hit the very bottom. There, he bolted straight for the east exit, the side where the gryphon was landing. Rachel was struggling to keep up, as she found that running down the stairs in a dress that fell to her ankles was more difficult than she imagined.

Outside, the gryphon finally touched the ground as Kevin Trent Stryker and Caitlin Magnon flipped off of the gryphon's back. So too did the soldier who had went to get them from Aurana. While Kevin adjusted the position of his sword and Caitlin straightened her dress, the soldier approached the emerging Arthur, saluted, and said, "My lord, I have brought your guests here as you requested."

Quickly, Arthur gave a salute to the soldier. "Thank you," he said, bowing to show his respect. "You are dismissed for a while. Take it easy, and go relax with your family."

That surprised the soldier, himself a former Desolunar soldier. Arthur's benevolence was indeed great. At this, he saluted back to Arthur and started walking his gryphon down the street to a nearby military stable.

Immediately afterward, Arthur turned to look at Kevin and Caitlin. "Well, well, well, long time no see, stranger," he said directly to Kevin.

Kevin laughed. "It's good to see you too, Arthur," he said as he and Arthur grabbed each other's hand and pulled close for just a second.

As Kevin and Arthur let go, Caitlin came up to Arthur and gave him a hug. "It's good to see you again, brother," she said.

A smile came to Arthur's face. "Good to see you again too, sister," he said. It had only been found out about three months ago that Arthur and Caitlin were actually half-siblings, related by the same mother, Christine Falchor. Arthur, about a year and a couple of months older than Caitlin, was fathered by former Desolunar dictator Demonicus; whereas Caitlin's father was Professor James Magnon.

Pretty quickly after Arthur and Caitlin let go of one another, Rachel walked over and gave Caitlin a big hug as well. "Caitlin! I've missed you so much!" she exclaimed.

Caitlin returned the hug as well, a little surprised at Rachel's reaction. "I missed you too, Rachel," she said. "I'm glad to see you again."

"And to you too," responded Rachel as she let go. Then, she turned to Kevin and hugged him. "And don't think I forgot about you too," she continued.

"Of course not," answered Kevin back, chuckling a little bit. As he and Rachel let go, Kevin turned to Arthur and asked, "How have you been, Arthur?"

Arthur shook his head as he started heading into the pyramid, causing Kevin, Rachel, and Caitlin to follow him. "It hasn't been good," he said. "I'm going to be honest with you, Kevin. The new Solunar Empire has not been off to a good start so far."

"Oh?" asked Kevin. "I'm really sorry to hear that, Arthur. Then again, I bet you inherited quite a bit of a mess here."

"Sure did," nodded Arthur, somberly. "Man, I miss Rikleifer so much. Never thought I'd say I missed anything about being in Aurana, since it was such a boring place to live, but I'd rather be there and not have to deal with all of this."

Caitlin shook her head. "So why did you decide to take the mantle of command here when Larion offered it to you?"

All Arthur could do was shrug his shoulders, as the group turned up the stairs. "I guess I thought it was the right thing to do. For everyone here in Seta Archa left without a home, for the tribes in The Wastes to stay together… it was what was right for them. They trusted me already, and I was their source of hope."

"That's what being the heir of Desolunar does for you," remarked Kevin.

Arthur glared over at Kevin for that one. Kevin knew that that was something Arthur did not want to think about: the position of respect he had from people who had never known him before simply because he was the son of Demonicus, the dictator of Desolunar. Arthur was still very bothered by the fact that Demonicus was his father, and he hated to be reminded of that, but he knew Kevin meant no harm. "I suppose," he finally answered. "Really, though, Kevin, at the time this all came up, we all thought you were dead. It was right after that massive explosion, before Larion told us that he and the gods had intervened and saved your life. I thought about what you'd tell me to do, and I thought you'd tell me to do what was right."

Kevin gave a slight nod. "You did do the right thing, Arthur. Because of that, Caitlin and I are going to help you as much as we can, okay?"

"Mhmm," acknowledged Arthur. That was all he needed to reply with.

Quietly, Caitlin leaned over toward Rachel. "What's going on?"

she asked. "What's with Arthur? He doesn't seem like himself."

"He hasn't been himself in such a long time," responded Rachel as she shook her head. "Arthur's just not the same person he used to be anymore. He's become so much more concerned about every little detail and hasn't been able to enjoy himself in so long. Even I feel like I'm letting him down from all of this."

"It's not your fault, though," whispered Caitlin. "You're his prime minister, not his…"

"No, Caitlin," interrupted Rachel, still keeping her voice down so Kevin and Arthur would not hear. "This isn't about my job. As a friend, I feel like I'm letting him down. Regardless of how much I seemed to dislike Arthur on our quest three months ago, I owe him my life. I don't know if I've ever told him how much of a friend I see him as now."

All Caitlin could do at this point was nod. They would have to talk about it later.

At this point, the group came to the trap door. Arthur opened it, inviting everyone into his throne room. It was all too familiar a sight for Kevin, the place where he and Arthur had come into confrontation with Demonicus three months before. For Arthur, though, it was the place where he ran his country, despite its history. "Nice to see the glass got fixed in here," joked Kevin, recalling that day three months before. "In all seriousness, though, I like what you've done with the place. You really can see all of Seta Archa from here."

"And more," added Arthur, as he strolled to his desk. He took a seat, and then invited his hand out to Kevin and Caitlin to sit in chairs in front of it. Respectively, they took two of the three seats in front of Arthur's desk, and Rachel took the third.

Arthur put his hands together as he set them on his desk. "There is something much, much darker out there, however, Kevin. Beyond what you can see from the top of this building, something tragic has happened, and it could be coming to destroy all of Solunar."

"What is it?" asked Kevin.

Slowly, Arthur lowered his head. The stress was getting to him.

Seeing this, Rachel turned to Kevin and Arthur, and began to explain. "A few days ago, there was an attack on the Metoi tribe of the

Wastes. The entire village was destroyed, burned to the ground, and the chief was killed." She paused for a second. "The Metoi are a very special tribe to us, guys. Not only are they a protected tribe of Solunar and the keepers of information for us, but Arthur and I were helped by them during our escape from Seta Archa a few months ago. Chief Aspectra of the Metoi was one of our greatest aids. The attacker sent Marilynn, Chief Aspectra's wife, to Seta Archa to tell us what happened. His goal seems to have been to send a message to us by destroying our closest allies within our country, and we're worried that eventually he'll come to Seta Archa and try to overthrow what we're building here and bring back Desolunar."

Caitlin put her face in the palm of her hands. "I should have guessed," she said. "It only makes sense that when you start a new government, there will be some uprising against it. After all, Demonicus led here for quite a while. Surely there were some who supported his ideals."

Rachel nodded. "Indeed," she said. "It was General Sayo, who was Demonicus' left hand man, if Pseudo was his right." She was referencing a visual clone of Kevin who had attacked him previously, and it took a combined effort of Kevin and Caitlin to kill him.

"Sayo is a major threat," acknowledged Arthur, as he raised his head. "Marilynn also confirmed that he had troops with him. That puts him in a position to make a power play whenever he wants. And with the country as fragile as it is, I can't have him going around trying to destabilize it, or else there might be a civil war." He paused. "The more I learn about this city, and these lands, it seems like they've been in chaos for a long time. The people who live here deserve peace."

Kevin looked at Caitlin, then looks back and nodded. He too had desired peace for Aurana, and now he had it. Now Arthur was fighting for peace for the people he was asked to lead. "What do you need us to do?"

"I need you to go into the Wastes and hunt down General Sayo," Arthur said. "I need him taken into custody and brought here, or killed."

Immediately, Kevin put the palm of his hand over his eyes, as he leaned on the desk.

"I don't think that's something we're able to handle," Caitlin answered. "We're not assassins. That sounds like a better job for Rouge and Resa, if I'm being honest."

"Except we can't do that," chimed in Rachel. "We thought of that already, but right now the balance of power in the Wastes is heavily destabilized with the plight of the Metoi. We have to put someone in charge out there to hold the Metoi lands safe until they can hold their own, and quite frankly, with what's going on with General Sayo we believe that Rouge and Resa are the only ones we can trust to make that happen. We don't have enough trust in any of our generals right now to do the right thing and not jump to Sayo's cause."

Caitlin cringed. "So the only other people you could call, were us."

Arthur nodded. "Precisely," he said. "I'm sorry I had to ask you to come down here and straighten out my mess, but there's just not a lot of options out there. It's difficult to trust my forces when so many were loyal to Demonicus before, and it's evident that they aren't all high on what we're trying to do. You're kind of my last option."

Kevin was now starting to see what kind of stress Arthur had been going through since taking the reins in Solunar. With drastic problems to fix and very few tools to do it with, Arthur was struggling at the command of Solunar. Kevin figured that it would be likely for even the most experienced rulers to have trouble in this kind of situation, but for Arthur, an inexperienced leader, it must have been a nightmare.

"Hey, it's all right," interrupted Kevin. "That's what we're here for, Arthur. In fact, the Duke of Rikleifer made this an official mission for me, so Caitlin and I won't have to worry about business in Aurana."

"Well, that's a good thing," answered Rachel. "Least you guys won't be worrying about what's going on back there."

"That means that all there is is what's ahead," acknowledged Kevin. "Do you have a plan for getting it done?"

Arthur and Rachel looked at each other for a second. Then, Arthur set his head down again, as Rachel continued, "Not really. We were hoping that you might be able to work something out. The only real thing we have is that we need you to go out there and track down

Sayo."

Caitlin rolled her eyes. She was not one to enjoy wild goose chases.

"Don't be dour about it," said Rachel, catching that reaction. "We'll put all the intel together that we can before you go, and give you everything we can to help you succeed."

Kevin nodded over to Caitlin. "She will," he said.

More and more, Rachel was really showing herself to be a leader. To both Kevin and Caitlin, this was becoming more and more evident the more they spoke with her. It had really impressed both of them significantly, as neither one of them had been sure before how Rachel would manage as the prime minister of the Solunar Empire. It appeared from her current personality, though, that she was ready for it.

"I know," nodded Caitlin. "It's up to all of us to make this work."

Rachel smiled a bit. "For sure, Caitlin. Maybe this is really our time to shine."

Instantly, Kevin raised an eyebrow. "Rachel, is it just me, or are you actually becoming more of an idealist and losing that realistic skepticism?" he asked.

"Oh, maybe a little bit," answered Rachel, as she glanced back over at Arthur.

At the same time, Kevin and Caitlin stared at Rachel, before staring at each other. Using her abilities in mind magic, Caitlin projected into Kevin's head an odd telepathic communication:

Something seems really off about her, too. How is she the optimistic one here?

Maybe it's her self-defense mechanism. She does seem like she's had some positivity come into her life, at least.

I wonder what that could be...

"What in the world are you two doing?" interrupted Rachel. "Why are you guys just staring at each other like that? It doesn't even look romantic or anything, just kind of weird."

"Uh, nothing," responded Caitlin quickly, not wanting to let Rachel know what was going on or that she and Kevin had a way to talk behind her back while being in front of her. "It's nothing, really."

Kevin nodded. "What she said," he said.

"Oh, I see how it is," Rachel chuckled. "Collective denial, huh?"

"If that's the way you see it," joked Kevin, "then, yes."

"Can we please get down to business here?" interrupted Arthur, who had been silent for a while.

Everyone stopped. There was definitely something wrong with Arthur, and everyone could tell. He was not himself at all, and the more Kevin and Caitlin saw it, the more they began to realize it. Arthur was not even close to being the real Arthur Falchor anymore. Emperor Arthur had taken over; a depressed man who let the worries of his country get to him. Kevin, Caitlin, and Rachel all knew that they had to lift Arthur's spirits. They had to save their best friend.

At this point, there was a heavy knocking on the trap door. Arthur stood up, in what appeared to be a bit of paranoia, and mumbled, "Oh, for crying out loud... Enter!" Before the door could open, though, Rachel stood up and brought Arthur back down to his seat, trying to get him to calm down.

The trap door swung open and from the stairs came two girls slightly older than Kevin and company, dressed in uniforms of orange and black with red and black triangle patches on the sides. Everyone instantly recognized them, even though Kevin and Caitlin had never seen them dressed as such, as Rouge and Resa Kirkwood. Kevin and Caitlin instantly stood up when they saw the Kirkwood sisters, knowing what would come next out of one of them.

They were right. The second she saw Kevin and Caitlin, Resa started dashing toward them. "Kevin! Caitlin! I've missed you both so much!" she exclaimed as she nearly tackled them. Resa extended one arm around Kevin and the other around Caitlin to hug them both.

Both Kevin and Caitlin started laughing a little bit. "It's good to see you too, Resa," commented Kevin.

Behind Resa, Rouge was laughing as well as she slowly walked toward Kevin and Caitlin. She knew her younger sister well enough to know that was going to happen. With a smile on her face, Rouge walked up to Kevin and Caitlin as Resa let go of her hug and said, "It's a pleasure to see you guys again."

"It's great to see you too, Rouge," said Caitlin, smiling.

Of all the friendship ties between these six friends, the ones between Kevin and Caitlin, and Rouge and Resa, had to be the oddest. It was only a few months ago that Rouge and Resa, then serving as unwilling assassination specialists of Desolunar, tried to kill Kevin and Caitlin. Fortunately, Kevin and Caitlin managed to thwart this assassination attempt and make friends with the two sisters by offering them an option that would keep them from any further harm.

Resa was almost childlike in some ways, yet possessing the mature qualities of kindness and friendliness in others. Rouge, by contrast, was cold and calculating, but also caring.

"Rouge, do you want to give a status report to Arthur?" said Rachel, from her seat. "It may actually brighten him up."

"Oh yes!" said Rouge. "I almost forgot!" Then, Rouge took a couple of steps closer to Arthur's desk. "The unit you asked me to gather is on its way to Metoi Village. They should have the area secured before any tribe out there can jump on an assault on the Metoi, and we'll be out there before too long to lead them."

Arthur only managed a slight nod. "Good," he said. "But what if Sayo strikes again? He could remove our defense, and we would lose many people."

"That's the one thing," said Rouge. "There's no way to be sure Sayo won't take it back, as we don't know how many men they have, but we don't have many right now."

"We don't even know what he's up to," added Resa. "Would he even do that?"

Arthur slammed his fist to his desk in realization. "Damn," he said. He was clearly frustrated.

Caitlin shook her head. "Don't fret too much, Arthur," he said. "Maybe someone in the empire knows. Time to gather intelligence, perhaps? Does anyone know Sayo?"

"There is someone in this building who knows him," added Rachel.

There was a pause in the air. Everyone looked over at Rachel.

Again, Arthur shook his head. "I was hoping we wouldn't have to resort to talking to him, but I guess we have no choice, do we?"

"I really don't think so, Arthur," responded Kevin, knowing of whom Arthur was speaking.

Letting out a sigh, Arthur answered as he stood up, "Very well. The sooner we get this over with, the better. Kevin, if you would please come with me. Rachel, if you and the rest of the girls wouldn't mind, I'd appreciate it if you would check on Marilynn really quick, and then meet us at the stairs to the basement."

Rachel answered, "All right. I'll make sure there's not a crowd where you're headed." She knew Arthur would rather not share this with anyone, and was only doing so with Kevin because he had an innate trust for the Vanguard of Aurana.

Arthur had to pay a visit to someone, and he had to do it regardless of the distaste he had for it. He brought Kevin with him as he prepared to head to the dungeon in his capital building. The walk down there took several minutes.

Chapter 6

Negation of Glory

The former leader of Desolunar and Arthur's father, Demonicus, remained locked up in the seldom visited dungeon of the capital building in Seta Archa. Strangely enough, this was done at Demonicus's request after the battle of Seta Archa three months before. Demonicus had said that he wanted a second chance to be a father after what had happened to him, but that at the same time, he knew that he deserved a long prison sentence and was lucky to have his life.

Arthur had gone to visit his father a couple of times before, but always visited him alone. Demonicus was still a source of shame for Arthur, and he still was not comfortable knowing who his father was and what atrocities he had committed. Nonetheless, Arthur had some desire to know his real father, since he had never truly known his real mother and was raised by someone who told him she was his mother. Raised in Rikleifer, Aurana, Arthur was raised by Rita Falchor, an alcoholic and abusive woman by nature. As it would turn out, however, Rita was only his aunt, and his mother had died about a year after he had been born. Arthur had still not been back to see his aunt since taking the role of emperor of the Solunar Empire, nor did he care, knowing how she had treated him.

Part of finding out who Arthur's real mother was also led him to find his half-sister, Caitlin Amelia Magnon. It became a little bit of a twisted irony that he and Kevin had ran into Caitlin on their quest months before, much less that Kevin and Caitlin would become so close as they were, without any of them knowing about Arthur and Caitlin's shared mother.

As Arthur descended the stairs into the dungeon of his capital building, he could only hear his footsteps and those of Kevin behind him as they walked across the hard stone floors. Then, quietly he walked down the hallway toward the narrow door with a small window covered by bars. Behind that door sat Demonicus, the disposed ruler of the former state of Desolunar. He spent his day doing as he had always done: sitting in that tiny prison cell, thinking. In his dark red robes that he traditionally wore, he moved not, but upon hearing footsteps, he said, "Hello, Arthur."

"Hello, Demonicus," answered back Arthur in a cold, undaunted voice. Arthur had no respect for his father, and thus no emotion to show him. It had not been so long ago that Demonicus was Arthur's sworn enemy.

Demonicus stood up and nodded as he approached the window. "And hello to you too, pure one," he said, addressing Kevin with an unwavering tone. "Been a long time, has it not?"

Kevin responded crossly, "I would prefer 'Kevin', if you don't mind," he said.

"As you wish," nodded Demonicus, as he paced around a little bit in his cell. "What brings the two of you down here today?"

Desiring not to spend longer with Demonicus than he had to, Arthur said directly, "I have a favor to ask of you. I need some information."

"Oh? Is that so?" asked Demonicus, with more curiosity. "And what exactly would that be?"

Arthur paused for just a moment. "What can you tell me about General Sayo?"

Demonicus walked to the door again. "So, he has not returned with the troops after all," he snickered. "I knew that would happen. He was at my beck and call, my most trusted general, and even I feared him."

Standing at that window, Kevin stood stunned. Demonicus was a source of fear to many; his assumed name came from being known as "the conqueror's chosen demon". How could he fear one of his own trusted tools of his influence?

"Spare none of the details," interrupted Arthur. "Tell me as much as you know about him, from start to finish. I want to know absolutely everything."

"I understand," nodded Demonicus. "General Martin Sayo was in charge of my army directly. What I know of his early history is little, other than that he was associated with the famous Vincent Stryker, the general that brought down the Daritel before my nation was even created. What I do know begins with the Desolunar invasion of the city of Atwals, about fifteen years ago. In that invasion, then-Commander Sayo of Aurana stood against me, but our men overwhelmed his. Atwals was burned to the ground, on my orders, and Sayo was captured." He paused briefly. "Nonetheless, despite my policy not to take prisoners, I saw potential in Sayo and knew he had the capability to be an outstanding general for Desolunar if only I could convince him somehow. When I discovered of his foolish pride for his home, I had found my key: convincing him that Desolunar was his new homeland and Atwals was now in Desolunar."

"A classic case of the abducted joining the abductor," said Arthur. "Continue."

Demonicus nodded. "Sayo quickly rose back through the ranks to become my most trusted man, my left arm. Pseudo, my gift from my master, was my right. Though Pseudo was the one designed for my rule, it was Sayo who became the one I could trust when I myself had concerns."

"I'm a little confused here," interrupted Kevin. "If that was the case, then why did you fear him, as you say you did?"

"Why would I not fear him?" asked Demonicus, turning the tables. "As I just told you, he was my most trusted general. Not only did he know all of my secrets, but he also knew more about how Desolunar functioned than anyone else, and knew every weak point in this country. That made him a dangerous man, even if he worked for me."

"I see, by putting him in a position of power it makes him capable to reverse the tides on you," answered Kevin, understanding the rationale. "He could do damage to you that no outsider could ever do."

"Exactly," affirmed Demonicus. "And given that I convinced Sayo to turn his back on his home country, what was to prevent him from doing it again in the future? Dangerous people are not born; they are made. By doing as I did, I made Sayo the most dangerous man in Desolunar."

It took everything Arthur had to keep from rolling his eyes at his father. He knew, quite well, that Demonicus had committed a great number of atrocities in the former state. To presume that anyone but him could be the most dangerous man would be to overlook the disposed dictator's tyranny. Still, Arthur did not seek to interrupt, knowing that he needed as much as he could get about General Sayo.

"May I ask," began Demonicus, "what brings you to me about the general?"

Shaking his head, Arthur said, "Nothing that you should be concerned of."

A deep glare came to the eyes of Demonicus. "So my assumption was right after all. He has not returned yet, has he? Instead, he continues to resist, to attack and fight on, not with the support of the new empire."

"Such is the case," Arthur finally nodded. Afraid of being struck in his capital city, he then asked, "Would Sayo, by any chance, be aiming to come after you and try to break you loose?"

Demonicus shook his head. "Fat chance," he said. "Though I had great trust in General Sayo, he knew as well that if I did not take prisoners, and he did not take them, then there was no purpose for rescuing prisoners. I would not be surprised if what you are seeing stems from one of two things: either he has found a new lord to serve, or he has chosen to break away for whatever reason." He paused for a second. "Still, you should heed one warning, my son, and heed it well. General Martin Sayo is a dangerous man, and pursuing him is likely to result in grave consequences unless strategically planned. The man is a genius of military strategy and a master of preparation and stealth."

"I will," nodded Arthur. He then started stepping away from the door and toward the exit. Kevin turned and stared at him for just a moment, surprised that he was just walking away like that.

Inside his cell, Demonicus put his face in the palm of his hand. Then he said, "Hold on, son."

Son. The one word Arthur never wanted to hear from Demonicus. Yet Arthur hesitated to take another step.

"Is that all you came for?" asked Demonicus. "You are only here to take your information and leave?"

Arthur paused for a second. He knew what Demonicus was

getting at, but still he did not want to think about it. "That is all it will be for now," he said, without turning. "If you're looking for forgiveness or acceptance as my father, you're not going to get that for now." Then, Arthur walked off and back up the stairs from the dungeon.

Demonicus merely sighed and sat back down in his cell.

Kevin, though, did not move. He let Arthur walk off, realizing that Arthur's frustration with merely seeing his father was getting in the way. If Kevin were to go after General Sayo, however, he needed to know more. Noticing this, Demonicus perked up and asked, still unwavering, "What more do you want to know, pure one?"

"Some parts of this whole thing don't make sense," Kevin responded, getting down to business. "I need your help to understand why General Sayo is doing what he is doing."

Shaking his head, Demonicus sat back down in the cell. "Very well, then," he said. "Clarify to me what Sayo has done. Tell me what my son would not."

Knowing that he was about to feel bad about talking behind Arthur's back about his affairs, Kevin continued, sure that he needed more from Demonicus. "Sayo attacked the village of one of the Wastes tribes, the Metoi. They burned the village and sent the chief's wife to Seta Archa to send the message of it happening."

"A very clear-cut message indeed," considered Demonicus. "Hmmm… I would suppose that Sayo had no business out there?"

"Nothing that Arthur or I know of," said Kevin.

Demonicus crossed his arms. He was thinking deeply. "The Metoi tribe was always my tribe of information keepers, but then burning the village would be counterintuitive to collecting that info. Sending the chief's wife back as a message is a pretty strong tactic, and one with a lot of guts, too. That would be just asking for attention."

"Sayo certainly has our attention now," added Kevin.

"And that is what he wants, I assure you," responded Demonicus. "I would beware, pure one. This whole instance sounds like General Martin Sayo has set up a trap for Arthur. That is the only reason I can think he would send such a message: to intentionally antagonize Arthur and draw him out of Seta Archa. If it would not work the first time, surely at some point Arthur would see enough suffering in the Wastes to go there himself, even if it was with a force, and then Sayo would arm his trap and snap it on him."

A lot of thoughts went through Kevin's head as Demonicus said that. If this whole situation was really an elaborate trap, that meant he would have to be careful going out there, as well. Sayo would probably be ready for Arthur to approach on a direct route with forces, at some point in time. Sneaking in with a little bit of stealth to remove General Sayo would likely remove the trap and let Arthur get control of the force Sayo controlled, and thus seemed like the most prudent idea. The sooner it could be done, the less damage that could be done by Sayo.

Then, Demonicus straightened up and walked toward the window bars again. "Please, pure one, or Kevin if you prefer, if you do only one thing, please do this. Do not allow my son to fall into the trap. Regardless of what my past actions have shown, I do care about my son and I want him and his new nation to succeed where I have failed."

There was a momentary pause.

As he looked away, Kevin shook his head.

"It is true," continued Demonicus, trying to explain himself. "I let him go from here, with the Sword of Corruption, after I captured him while I was ruling Desolunar. I never did want to bring him to harm."

Clenching his fist, Kevin turned around. "Never wanted to bring him to harm? You possessed him with tracer magic to attack me! Every attack you executed, you also attacked him!" He stepped in closer. "You have shown me nothing to prove that."

There was a sigh from Demonicus. He dropped his head. "I know I have not," he said. "Still, my request stands. Please, keep my son out of any trap that has been set for him. Only you can protect him."

Kevin was not one to listen to anything Demonicus requested, mostly because of the torment and attempts on his life that Demonicus had tried on Kevin before. However, this was a request that Kevin could definitely honor. He let down his attitude, put his fist to his chest, and said, "I will do that." Then, he turned his back, as if to leave, but stopped before he could. He continued, "Don't get me wrong,

Demonicus. I am not above forgiving you for what you did, someday, perhaps. Now, however, is not the time." Kevin then paused for another second. "No one who shows legitimate remorse should be forever shunned."

Demonicus merely nodded, although Kevin did not watch him do it. He continued on, "Beware of one more thing, pure one. If you are to be the one going after General Sayo, he is likely to have many troops and many Enlighteners from the Shadows with him. He will be very difficult to get to."

That made Kevin turn around. He had had a couple of run-ins with the Enlighteners from the Shadows before, including Demonicus himself, who Kevin knew was one of them. Their saying, *Wondamer Notuerew,* translated meaning "Negation of Glory", had been stuck in Kevin's head for quite some time. With an icy glare, Kevin stared through the bars and directly into the eyes of Demonicus. He asked, with a cold tone, "What can you tell me about the Enlighteners from the Shadows?"

Slowly, Demonicus sat back down in his cell. He was taking his time, being very quiet until he reached the floor.

Kevin wondered why he was taking his time.

As Demonicus finally made it to the floor, he began, "There is so much of this you do not know, pure one. In this case, what you do not know may eventually bring about your downfall and that of everyone else who stands against the Enlighteners."

"Then educate me on them," said Kevin firmly. "Unless, of course, you have some stake in the Enlighteners that you are not sharing, in which case I will let Arthur know you are not truly devoted to changing your life like you promised him. I know you were an Enlightener yourself."

There was not a pointy response from Demonicus. "Very well," was what he simply said. "If that is what you wish, then I will tell you about the Enlighteners."

Nodding, Kevin prepared to listen very closely to this explanation.

"The Enlighteners from the Shadows are a very old group," began Demonicus. "I, of course, was a member, but it is likely that they have forsaken me by now due to my failure here at Seta Archa and my imprisonment. You may be familiar with another one of the administrators of the organization, if you acquired the Stripe of Fire from him."

That rang a bell in Kevin's head. A very loud one, at that. Kevin could remember pursuing the Seven Stripes of the Elements as part of his search for how to take Kron home. One stripe he acquired was the Stripe of Fire, which Arthur and Rachel fought for at the Ancient City against an Enlightener who was destroying the ruins. " I had assumed he worked for you," added Kevin, with this in mind.

"No," answered Demonicus. "The Enlighteners are a fragmented group, with no complete central core running it. I was an administrator for my group, merely a local leader, and he was one of many other administrators in the world. I only know of him from the stories I had heard through Enlightener channels on someone who had the Stripe of Fire, and knew he would bring it to me when the time was right."

"That brings about another question," interrupted Kevin. "How did the Enlighteners know about the stripes?"

"How else do you think?" Demonicus barked back, pointedly. "The Enlighteners have been around a very long time, and they have one person the group was formed to serve, operating in secrecy to destroy knowledge."

The sudden realization just hit Kevin there. "Setadev," he said.

"Precisely," responded Demonicus. "My master created the Enlighteners from the Shadows for the purpose of destroying information that would potentially lead to his downfall or the prevention of his goals. For that, he bribed the original Enlighteners with power when he founded his city here in Seta Archa. From then on, however, future generations of Enlighteners have done so out of tradition and belief, yet they all served his purpose. Although such an audacious move would likely serve as a trap for Arthur, it also serves the motivation of the Enlighteners, as well."

A trap? Kevin realized it was all too perfect. With a poor military force, all it would take to capture him would be to get him outside the walls of Seta Archa. A dark fear was brewing in Kevin's mind, as he listened in surprise at what he was hearing. Perhaps there was not solely a few remaining elements of Desolunar floating around to cause havoc, but remaining elements of Setadev as well. Several words that Setadev had said in his defeat rang out in Kevin's mind again, repeating themselves as Kevin wondered about the Enlighteners from the Shadows:

You cannot defeat me, for I am nothing.

Was this what Setadev had meant by saying such words?

"I was an Enlightener, that is true," continued Demonicus. "So are hundreds of others that still live on today. And the truth be told, Setadev's influence spreads to all of them. Each Enlightener shares that influence, that power. Being an Enlightener was not solely about devotion, though. It was about gaining power."

"Power?" asked Kevin. "You've said that quite a bit. What power?"

Demonicus paused for a moment. "Divine power," he said.

Kevin gasped a little bit.

"Setadev blessed all of his Enlighteners with a slight bit of divine power over the course of all of his existence," continued Demonicus. "Of course, it would not be enough, even combined, to overthrow him. It did, however, give incentive to become an Enlightener and help accomplish his mission. Strength in battle and disappearance upon defeat to spare your life… that is the power Setadev gave to all of his Enlighteners."

"So that's how you survived that fall!" exclaimed Kevin, realizing the missing piece to how Demonicus had been alive after being thrown out of the top of the capital building. Kevin was starting to realize that both Demonicus and the other Enlightener he had seen before had used the same effect on him.

"Yes, indeed," answered Demonicus. "Let me warn you, though, that General Sayo is likely to have many of the Enlighteners with him. He is not one himself, but he has likely allied with those sympathetic to the old Desolunar, which would certainly include the Enlighteners. I would not be surprised if they sought him out and perhaps encouraged him to begin this little crusade."

It was a warning not to be ignored, and Kevin realized this.

“Thank you,” he said to Demonicus. "I appreciate what you have shared with me. Someday, I may be willing to forgive you for what you have done.”

The changed man of Demonicus nodded. “Of course,” he said, as he sat back down in his cell. There was little he had actually wanted to say to Kevin of a personal nature, given that he and Kevin had been sworn enemies for so long. Despite saying that he could possibly forgive Demonicus someday, Kevin also had little more he wanted to say.

Suddenly, there was a scream from down the hallway. Instantly, Kevin’s ears perked up.

“Kevin! What are you still doing down there?” It was Arthur’s voice.

Kevin gave a quick nod of acknowledgment and quickly rushed back to the stairs, running up them as fast as he could. He was not sure he wanted to give a real goodbye to Demonicus, anyway. After all, despite what he said, Kevin was not yet to the point of forgiving Demonicus for his crimes. At the top of the stairs, Arthur, Rachel, Caitlin, Rouge, and Resa were waiting for Kevin. It had only taken him a few seconds to get there.

“What in the world were you doing down there for so long?” asked Arthur. “I was wondering where you were.”

Kevin looked very distant. Somehow the words of Demonicus had phased him to a great extent. Seeing this immediately, Caitlin took to Kevin’s side and asked him, “What’s going on, Kevin?”

Shaking his head, Kevin sighed. “I really don’t know entirely,” he said, “but Demonicus gave me some information on the Enlighteners from the Shadows.” He took a breath. “They’re a group of Setadev’s, although I don’t think anyone here is surprised to hear that. What I didn’t expect, though, is that Demonicus warned me they could have the influence of General Sayo.”

“What would they want with him?” asked Arthur. “Their leader has fallen and their deity has met his demise. Surely there’s not much for them to do, is there?”

Caitlin turned to Rouge and Resa. “Do you two know anything about them?”

"Not really," responded Rouge. "Demonicus had several of them around him quite a bit, all wearing these dark red hooded robes like what he used to wear all of the time, but that's about it."

All Kevin could do was ponder. There was not a whole lot to go off of here. Even with Demonicus's help, there was not a whole lot known about the Enlighteners from the Shadows.

"I think the best Demonicus could come up with is that it matches their ideology," Kevin tried to reason. "They like destroying knowledge, and being an Enlightener grants them power."

Pondering the implication, Caitlin asked to the group, "Does General Sayo project power?"

Rachel nodded. "From everything we've heard about him, he does. The man says little and lets his actions speak for themselves."

"It wouldn't be too hard to be attracted to that, if power is what you crave," reasoned Rouge.

Resa, though, shrugged. "Kinda doesn't sound like that's all, though. Is that really enough?"

Arthur looked at Kevin. "Was there anything else?"

"One thing," acknowledged Kevin. "Demonicus thinks this might be a trap for you."

With that, Rachel and Arthur looked at each other. "That would explain the letter," Rachel said. "It makes more sense than a random attack and an attempt at intimidation."

"Well, that's a relief," interjected Arthur as he rolled his eyes. "At least we know now that the whole purpose of this kerfuffle is to try to kill me."

"Hey! Would you lighten up?" Kevin responded snappily. "Jeez, Arthur, I don't ever think I've seen you so depressed. I'm going to go out there and bring Sayo back so you can take his head yourself if you want. How long are you going to be so pessimistic about stuff?"

Arthur shook his head. "Look, Kevin, it's not like I don't trust you," he said, in a depressed tone. "If I didn't, I wouldn't have asked for your help in the first place. But after Sayo, what's next? Who's to say someone else won't show up and try to do the same thing?"

Immediately, Rachel walked up behind Arthur and put her arm around his shoulders. "You will," she said. "You'll be able to be both a strong ruler and a happy one. The people of Solunar love you, Arthur, and once we get through this winter and this uprising together, I think you'll be able to be a lot happier. And you know I'll share the burden of leading this country with you. You won't be alone all of the time."

That was a move that had pleasantly surprised Arthur. He had always called Rachel a cynic, but here she was showing optimism. Arthur could tell she was trying to lift him up, and it did make him feel slightly better to know that. In response, Arthur gave only a meek answer after a minute of pause. "All right," he finally said.

"So what's the plan here, guys?" asked Resa. "How are we going to do this?"

"Like this," answered Rachel, as she let go of Arthur. Now was the time to show a downtrodden Arthur how she could help share his leadership burden in her role as prime minister. "Rouge and Resa, you two will go to the Metoi lands to help keep them secure. Stay at the village and help rebuild it, if you can. We'll send orders by gryphon to have the nearest unit go to the village, but for the purpose of evaluating if there is any other damage between here and the Metoi lands, you guys will go on foot."

"Yes, ma'am" acknowledged Rouge and Resa simultaneously. Resa, in particular, seemed excited by the orders.

Caitlin looked at Kevin. "We'll need a few days before we can set off after Sayo," she answered. "I don't want to make this wait, but I have to complete my adult registration in Aurana in a couple of days. If I don't, I could actually get into a lot of trouble between the legal stuff and losing out on my wizard license." She anticipated that Kevin would follow her lead.

Surprisingly, however, Kevin shook his head. "Actually, I think I'll go along with Rouge and Resa. From there, I'll figure out where to go next in tracking down General Sayo."

"What?" asked Caitlin in surprise, interjecting. "Why in the world would you do that, Kevin? I thought we established already that we work as a team."

Everyone stared at Kevin for a second. "I'm afraid we may lose Sayo's trail if we don't," answered Kevin. "Rouge and Resa can walk me out to the Metoi, and maybe they can sort out which way Sayo went, so the trail will be more fresh. I can wait up for you then so we can grab him together." He took a breath. "After everything that's happened already, what's the worst that could happen this time? The Sword of Purity will give me all the advantage I need to take down Sayo. It's never let me down."

Rouge and Resa looked at each other for a moment. They appeared to be considering whether or not Kevin was right about that. Despite being trained assassins, they looked uncertain if it was a good idea or not.

It felt far too dangerous for Caitlin to think it was safe. But, she loved Kevin and wanted him to do what he felt needed done, and she did not feel like Kevin was trying to exclude her. "I can't stop you, I suppose," she said. "All I ask is that you stay safe. Don't think this will be easy just because you're going up against a military general and not a god."

"Hey, now, I didn't say that," interrupted Kevin. "I don't think it'll be easy, Caitlin. I just know what must be done, and I'll trust in my sword and my experiences out there, and I'll find Sayo so you can catch up with me and we can finish the job together. I promise I won't chase him without you."

Caitlin reached out and grabbed Kevin's hand. Though she was worried for Kevin, she did have all of the faith in the world in him. "I trust you," she said, as she leaned in and kissed him on the cheek. "You can do it, locate Sayo, and then we'll be back together again to take care of business."

At this, Rachel, Rouge, and Resa all smiled. How could they not love the spirit of Caitlin? Even now she exuded an inner strength that could only be admired. Kevin reached an arm around Caitlin, hugging her.

"So we have a plan, then," Arthur finally said after a moment's pause. "Are you going to be leaving first thing in the morning?"

"I think that would be best," answered Kevin. "The sooner this is over, the sooner you can get your country back."

Rouge and Resa also nodded in agreement.

"Very well," said Arthur, with a slight change in his mood.

"Then perhaps we could have some fun tonight, with the six of us back together for the first time in a long time," added Rachel, as her eyes lit up. "We can have supplies gathered and get some time to relax, too."

Arthur shook his head. "I don't know," he said. "I would feel bad about relaxing while our people struggle."

In response, Kevin put his arm around Arthur. "Can't work forever, Arthur. You've got to take some downtime every now and then."

"Say what?" snapped Arthur, in a slightly humorous tone. Even Kevin had to be glad to hear a stunned reaction; however; at least it snapped Arthur out of his cycle for a minute and back to his normal, sarcastic self. "Excuse me, Mr. World Hero, but who said you could take a day off?"

"Oh, come now, Arthur," interrupted Caitlin, taking the response from Kevin. "Even Kevin and I took a little downtime when we were traveling together. Yeah, we kept moving continuously, but when we had to stop, we took advantage of the time to relax and grow closer. I don't know if we could have kept going without it."

Kevin nodded, ignoring the "world hero" bit he despised hearing. "She's right, you know," he said. "Arthur, we've done this when we were all together, so we don't lose our sanity. We're friends. We can't forget why we are."

Everyone else agreed, and nodded as well.

There was a long pause, before Arthur said, "Then let's do that."

Finally. There was something to be happy about, at last. Arthur was finally going to take a little time to relax.

For the next few hours, Kevin and company took the time to relax and enjoy all of the time they had. In particular, Kevin and Caitlin spent almost all of their time holding hands while they all had fun, using their chance to stay as close to one another before having to part the next day. The six friends spent most of their time catching up with one another. Truly, they had missed each other during the three months they had been apart. With the hope that things would improve even greater in the next few days, all of them tried to forget all of their worries, if only for a few hours.

When the night fell, Kevin and Caitlin spent the night together, their last before being separated. Little did they know, however, that their separation would be much longer than either of them would have ever imagined.

Chapter 7

The Wasteland Expedition

The next morning, Kevin left early with Rouge and Resa. Caitlin, Arthur, and Rachel all said their tearful goodbyes in the morning, knowing that it would be a while before they would be reunited again. There was business to be done today, however, and for now, that had to take precedent.

As Kevin had found out early on the trip, the dense forests around Seta Archa were more navigable than he imagined, despite having no visible roads. The pathway to the east and into the Wastes, for example, was marked with periodic signs nailed to trees letting travelers know they were heading in that direction. It was a poor system, but Seta Archa was meant to be a difficult city to find.

Within a couple of hours of walking, the forests started to disappear and the ground appeared more barren. A slow transition occurred over the next few moments of walking as the forest faded into the Wastes, a region of the Solunar Empire with little water and little life.

The tribal people who resided here were among the last in the world, as none of the kingdoms really wanted to invade and dominate it. Wars between the tribes were not uncommon, although many of the tribes were docile and only a few were provocative. The region had ultimately decided to attach itself to the former kingdom of Desolunar to help keep its own peace after the Daritel uprising that led to the Alliance-Daritel War twenty years ago. Though they did so without representation, in looking to keep them with the new Solunar Empire Arthur had invited all of them to take part in his new Imperial Council, an offer most of the tribes accepted.

As the walk went on, Kevin was starting to feel a little sweaty. Although it was still the winter and much of Desolunar was covered in snow, there was little snow to be seen in the Wastes. A few patches sat around every now and then, but the Wastes had increased temperatures on average compared to other regions. Rouge and Resa were next to him, each a little sweaty themselves. The walk was wearing everyone down a little bit, especially as going into the Wastes meant less life-sustaining land. The trip had taken some time to reach Metoi Village, but there was not much longer left to go.

To Kevin, it had only felt like yesterday since the first time he had met Rouge and Resa Kirkwood, the two vanguards of the Solunar Empire. In all actuality, it had been about three months. At that time, Rouge and Resa were two assassins working on the basis of a death threat for Desolunar, and had been assigned to kill Kevin. Their attempt had failed, however, on the basis of Kevin's cunning and awareness, as well as Caitlin's resistance to magic attacks. After that, Kevin saw the good in the two sisters and understood why they did what they did, and sure enough, they became friends very quickly after that. It took a little bit longer to make Arthur and Rachel friendly to them, however, since hearing the story left them paranoid as to whether or not Rouge and Resa were really that good inside.

As they continued into the wastes, Kevin asked, "You know something? Back when we were in Seta Archa, I think I forgot to ask how you two have been."

"Oh, Kevin, getting forgetful, aren't we?" joked Resa, laughing a little bit. "We're your friends too; you're not getting off that easily."

"I wouldn't quite put it that way," interrupted Rouge. "But to tell the truth, we've been fine, Kevin. You're a Vanguard yourself; you know how that life goes by now."

Kevin shrugged. "Not really," he said. "I don't really have an active role in Aurana like you guys have here. There's no real need for one. I'm sure Arthur's got you guys busy everywhere, though."

"Kind of," answered Rouge. "Maybe, Kevin, we need to let you know how things have really been here in the Solunar Empire since you left after the battle. I don't think Arthur or Rachel told you how things have really been."

Merely nodding, Kevin was intent on listening.

Rouge looked over at her sister. "Tell him what it's been like, Resa."

Quickly, Resa took a breath. Then, she shook her head. "I'm not really sure if this will help, but this is how it's been, Kevin. After the battle, and after you left, there was a lot of chaos still around Seta Archa. There was kind of a huge aftermath of resistance and confusion, until Arthur really stepped up. He explained in a couple of speeches that while Demonicus had been forced to step down, he would rise and bring prosperity to the new Solunar Empire he was forming. This involved several changes: a move to his new imperial government and the formation of an imperial council, the return of lands wrongly taken from Aurana and Nuve, the freedom for all Solunar citizens to move as they pleased, the rights of women to be treated as citizens just as men were, and the recall of the old Desolunar troops, with an eventual goal toward demilitarizing and letting those who wanted some rest to get it."

Kevin nodded. All of that made sense so far.

"Things didn't really go to prosperity right away, though. With so much of Seta Archa destroyed in the aftermath and a great deal of struggle with famine and deficiencies during the winter, the Solunar Empire was struggling right away. Arthur really didn't like his job, and as things got worse, he got worse. He's been retreating back because of the way things have been, and it's made him reclusive."

Suddenly, Kevin became worried. How bad were things going for his best friend, Arthur Falchor? He listened on as Resa continued.

"Really, it's been Rachel guiding things along and keeping them moving without Arthur really present mentally all of the time. She seems to have a knack for this sort of thing, but it hurts her a lot to see Arthur's mental state decline." She paused for a second." You know, maybe it's just me, but I think Rachel really has a thing for Arthur that she won't tell anyone about."

Kevin's eyes widened. "Really, now?" he asked. "Now that would be pretty interesting, but I wouldn't believe it for a second."

"Well, I can't really be sure," responded Resa, "but Rouge and I have kind of seen that every now and then. She spends a lot of time with him in his throne room, although that's to be expected since she's the prime minister. There's more to it, though. I think I can sort of sense it when I see her interact with him."

Now, Kevin was really surprised. He could recall all of Rachel's cynicism, her attitude, and her seeming dislike of Arthur during their travels together months ago. He had known Rachel for a couple of years now overall, and knew that Arthur was not really the type of person that she would go after.

"So what about yourself?" asked Rouge to Kevin, breaking a second of silence.

"Huh?" asked Kevin.

Rouge let out a quick sigh. "Well, Kevin, you just had us explain how we have been and how Solunar has been. How have you been, back in Aurana?"

"Yeah, got something you want to share, Kevin?" added Resa. "We shared with you, so now you share with us."

Kevin chuckled a little bit. "All right, all right," he laughed. "I'll tell you a little bit, then. After the battle, Caitlin and I returned together to Seta Archa, after that whole thing where the gods spared my life. You two remember that, right?"

"It was a little bizarre, but I do remember," answered Rouge. "First time Resa and I met the gods from the Realm of the Angels, if that's right. I don't really know; you tried to explain it to me quite a few times how this whole thing worked out and what the gods really are, who we met and how you're tied into them."

"Even though they're not really, just kind of think of them as the nameless ones we all learned in religion," said Kevin, "but that they have names and they asked me to stop their counterpart and former member Tyrinion, who it turned out was actually innocent; and the first god ever, Setadev, was the real evil one. I don't really think I can make it simpler than that."

"Works for me," interjected Resa.

Rouge shrugged. "I guess," she said.

Kevin shook his head. He knew it was not an easy concept to understand. "Anyway," he continued, "as you remember, the gods brought Caitlin up to the Realm of the Angels after the battle to come and meet me, like I asked for. Then, we came back together, and said our goodbyes and such after we found out Arthur, Rachel, and you two were staying in Desolunar, or what is now Solunar. We went back to Rikleifer, and Caitlin now lives with me in my house. I've been collecting my vanguard salary and saving it for a rainy day, and I've tried really hard in the last three months to show her the truth about real life and all of its beauty, its positives, everything good about it."

"A little worried she might someday revert back to her emotionless state you've told us about before, huh?" asked Rouge.

"No, nothing like that," answered Kevin. "It's just that I think she needs to see the best parts of the world and make up for all that she's missed, that's all." He reached for his canteen he was carrying to take a drink.

A deceptive look came to Resa's eye. "Speaking of the best parts of the world, have you two gotten so close yet as to connect up parts of your skin other than your lips?"

Almost as instantly as Resa said that, Kevin's face turned red as he spit out the water he had been drinking, in surprise. "What?" he exclaimed. "Resa, was that supposed to be an implication of…"

Resa just gave a funny look with a smile at Kevin.

Kevin put the palm of his hand over his face. He was trying to hide a laugh, actually finding the comment quite humorous. Still, Rouge and Resa caught a snicker escape from the young male. "Look, you two, no… just, no."

In response to Kevin's embarrassment about the whole situation, Resa started giggling. Rouge, just a little more serious than Resa, said to Kevin, "It's nothing to be embarrassed about. You're a teenage boy, Kevin. Surely the thought of it has crossed your mind more than once."

"I'd still rather not talk about it," responded Kevin, sounding a little frustrated.

Rouge chuckled a little bit. "Now, now, we're all young adults here," she said. "I'm twenty-one, and I'll tell you right now, Kevin, that when I was just a couple of years younger, I already had quite the reputation for… well… such acts."

Rolling his eyes, Kevin laughed and said, "That's really more than I needed to know."

Laughing a little bit more, Rouge answered. "Then this is even more. Resa over there has a bigger reputation than I do."

Kevin's eyes actually widened at that one, as his head turned toward the younger sister. Resa always seemed like the more innocent of the two. Resa started laughing hysterically when Kevin looked over at her.

"I really don't see why I need to know this," mentioned Kevin, looking really embarrassed.

"That's because I haven't gotten to the point yet," answered Rouge. "The point is, Kevin, that it's perfectly normal for you to be thinking about it, even if you won't say anything. In fact, I'll even bet that she's thought about it more than once too."

Speechless at that thought, Kevin had to take a second to compose himself. "That doesn't mean I want to be a father just yet," Kevin frowned. "It doesn't seem like it would be right for quite a while."

"Why not?" asked Resa. "You *are* going to marry her, aren't you?"

Kevin just looked away at that comment.

Immediately, Rouge reached over and hit her sister in the shoulder. "Resa, don't jump to conclusions. Look at Kevin for a second. What you said just bothered him."

The second she saw Kevin's reaction, though, Resa realized that she had gone a little far with that one. She did not need Rouge's comment to put that one together. "Oh my gosh, I'm sorry, Kevin. You want to talk about it?"

Lifting his head, Kevin began, in a depressed tone, "There's not really a whole lot to say. I really like Caitlin, there's nothing wrong about that. We moved really quick to get to where we are, though, and honestly it's just not a thought I've kept in my mind a lot. I don't even know if I'll even be with Caitlin forever."

"Really? You don't think so?" asked Rouge.

"I didn't say that," answered Kevin. "Look, I'm not saying I don't like Caitlin or anything like that." A tear came to one of Kevin's eyes. "The luckiest thing to ever happen to me was that I met Caitlin by chance. I never thought I could find someone so special, yet so knowledgeable and strong. In fact, I was a little skeptical for a while, before I met her, that I would find any girl at all who would want to be with me. But this all happened so quickly, within weeks of meeting. What's to say I won't someday move on past Caitlin, or that she would want to move past me? I just don't know for sure if I'm ready to say I'll be with Caitlin for the rest of my life."

"How could you?" interrupted Resa, as if she were stunned. "How could you even say that?"

"Easy, Resa," interrupted Rouge, as she put her hands up to stop her sister. "Kevin's got a valid point, more valid than you might think right now. Let me put it into perspective, though. How many boyfriends have you and I had, between the two of us, that we thought we'd be with forever and then turned out not to be?"

Resa thought about it a second. "I suppose you're right," she said, "But still, Rouge, it is Kevin and Caitlin we're talking about, here. They're so special, it's almost like they were made for each other, in an odd sort of way."

Rouge shrugged. "Well, Resa, maybe we shouldn't expect so much. I mean, it's only been a few months they've known each other. And they are quite a bit younger than us, Resa."

Again, Kevin rolled his eyes. "Thanks for the support, ladies," he said sarcastically.

"Only trying to help," laughed Resa.

Kevin and Rouge had no response. They had stopped.

"Hey guys," began Resa, "what's…" She then stopped herself, as she saw what they were looking at.

Metoi Village was utterly demolished. Only a few burned-up remains stood around. The entire village had been decimated.

"Oh, dear gods," said Rouge, finally breaking a long bit of silence. "Sayo really pulled no punches with this place. He wasted the entire village." She waved Kevin and Resa on, knowing they had to walk into the town itself to survey the damage.

All around, splintered fragments of wood and clay were everywhere. Any building that was still standing appeared to be too unsafe to enter, for fear of collapse. To see such destruction in such personal sight startled Kevin so badly as he looked that he had to make sure his heart was still beating at some points. Gray ashes were scattered everywhere, appearing very distinct against the dark red clay ground. Some of them were still quite warm, a distinct feeling considering it was currently the wintertime. It was all over the village, becoming the symbol of what the village was now. It was only ash.

Kevin slowly shook his head, extremely distraught at what he had seen. This was above and beyond a normal war action. This was a war crime. "I don't think I've ever seen the destruction of so many innocent lives," he said. "Who could be so cruel?" Though Kevin had an answer for who that person was, he had no idea what that person was like. There was still very little that Kevin knew about General Sayo, after all.

Rouge took another look around. "I don't see any troop encampments," she observed. "We sent men this way. Where are they? They should be here by now."

"Perhaps with the Metoi themselves, if they've made it this far," answered Resa after a moment of thought. "Marilynn did say the Metoi likely retreated to a sacred place on their lands. And we did tell them to protect the Metoi first and foremost."

"That is true," nodded Rouge. She looked around again. As she did, however, a strong wind buffeted her as well as Kevin and Resa. The force was strong enough that each of them lifted their arms in a protective stance; it was that bad. It took Kevin and company a second to regain their balances.

The breeze died down quickly, and soon enough no trace of it was visible across any part of the surrounding wastelands. "That was weird," commented Resa.

"In more ways than one," said Rouge, as she shook her head. "Winds normally go from west to east. This one went east to west. That was an odd crosswind."

Kevin just shook his head. "Let's hope that's all it was," he said, as he started to approach the destroyed Metoi Village. "This village doesn't need anything more."

Quickly, Rouge and Resa followed suit. "Here's a thought," commented Rouge, as they continued to the burned village. "If Sayo let Marilynn live to send us a message, then why would he leave other

Metoi alive as well? That's what Marilynn told us happened, but Sayo must have easily had control over the entire village to cause such destruction. He could have, without a second thought, destroyed the entire Metoi tribe without breaking a sweat."

"Maybe they just got away or weren't in the village, or something," responded Resa.

"No," answered Rouge, shaking her head. "That's not what happened, Resa."

"But Rouge," whined Resa, unintentionally showing her immaturity, "how can you be so sure of that? I don't get it. How come you think that Sayo might just have missed a few people?"

Again, Rouge shook her head. "Because it's not like him, Resa."

"I still don't get it," said Resa. "How can it be 'like someone' not to miss a few people in a whole village?"

This time, Kevin took the answer. "Because, Resa, General Sayo is not like most other men," he said. "My father suggested it before Caitlin and I left Rikleifer, and my visit with Demonicus confirmed it to me. Sayo could have locked down the village effortlessly and kept anyone from escaping. If he had them all captive, then he must have let some of them go if they have survived. However, he still killed their chief and some of the Metoi, anyway."

"So why?" asked Resa.

"Your guess is as good as mine," answered Rouge. "Kevin, do you have an idea?"

Kevin responded skeptically, "Only one, something my father told me once last month. When all else makes no sense whatsoever tactically, default to human compassion."

By this point, the group had reached the middle of the burned village. Resa walked away, noticing something. "I wouldn't call this kindness, Kevin," interjected Rouge.

"Neither would I," answered Kevin, as he shook his head. "I was looking for a word, and obviously found the wrong one. But maybe he let up, somehow. It factors into how we understand the general."

Rouge shot a glance at Kevin. "Are you suggesting these

people don't deserve to be avenged because someone was kind enough not to kill all of them?"

"Oh, no, not at all," answered Kevin. "I totally understand. But the one thing I learned about it was that there's more important things to fight for than vengeance. Like protecting the innocent, and those you love. There are the remaining people of the Metoi, as well as the innocent, well-meaning people of Solunar to protect and defend. It's all about the way you see things, you know?"

Rouge rolled her eyes. "However you see it, I guess. I only wish I were going with you so I could kill Sayo myself."

"That is, if you could beat me to it," commented Kevin.

Instantly, Rouge looked over at Kevin oddly, almost infuriated by an insult to her ego. Rouge was, after all, a former assassin and an expert stealth fighter. She started flipping up one of the knives she kept in a holster on her belt. "Don't forget who's the faster fighter here, Kevin. I've knocked you out before, remember?"

"Yeah, back when you and your sister tried to kill me," scoffed Kevin. "Didn't you lose that little confrontation, anyway? I think I recall having my sword at your neck at some point in there."

"Be glad we're friends now," Rouge scoffed, as she put her knife away, "because if not, I would prove you wrong once and for all."

Smiling at Rouge, Kevin said, "And that's just one of the many reasons I'm glad to have you as my friend. But seriously, if we ever fought again…"

Kevin let off of his response. A horrifying sight of the damage of Metoi Village sank in on the perceptions of the two. They walked by a Metoi house where it was evident the family had not escaped. They saw several skeletons amidst the ruins of the house. Ash coated the ground all around. Everything was demolished, burned to the ground. It was a total loss.

Kevin was seeing nightmares. Several months ago when he found the Sword of Purity that was strapped to his belt, he saw a battlefield littered with dead soldiers. They, at least, knew they had to be prepared for the possibility of their deaths. This family would not have.

"This can't be," he said. "No one is this heartless."

"I don't have a word for this," Rouge said, stunned. "Even assassins have a code. We kill but we don't let them suffer." She paused. "I'm afraid they likely did."

"What harm could the Metoi have brought to Sayo that caused him to do this?" Kevin exclaimed. He was visibly upset.

In response, Rouge shook her head. "Maybe nothing. Maybe everything," she said. "Somehow or another, we'll know soon enough, though. Soon enough, if you or Caitlin don't kill him, Kevin, I'd like to wrap my fingers around Sayo's neck, and get some vengeance for the Metoi."

"No," interrupted Kevin firmly. "Not for revenge. That is the wrong reason to fight. But it will be me who kills Sayo."

Suddenly, Rouge glared at Kevin. "And why not me?" she asked.

"Hey guys!" interrupted a shout from Resa a good distance away. "I think I found something!"

Immediately, Kevin and Rouge started running toward her. No time to continue this conversation now. As Kevin and Rouge approached, they saw Resa kneeling on the ground, pointing toward what appeared to be a large amount of footprints heading south. Some were printed in the ash, others in the deep red clay. The prints were much more organized than what was in the rest of the city, where chaos appeared to have taken place. "These are all newer boot prints," she said. "You can tell by the shapes in the prints. All of our newer Solunar Empire shoes have these kinds of stitching lines, but the older Desolunar ones don't have them."

Kevin started to understand what Resa was saying. "So the men you guys sent over here were here and headed south?"

"Sure enough," nodded Resa. "As I remember right, Sayo never came back to Seta Archa, so his men wouldn't have these shoes. There's also several tracks of bare feet in the dirt here, too. Those probably belong to the Metoi. That would mean, presuming I've got this all right, that the Metoi fled southward and our men either followed them or accompanied them."

Taking a deep breath, Kevin responded. "That's a relief."

"Indeed," added Rouge. "Nice job, Resa. You know a lot more

about bootprints than I do, that's for sure. Anything from any older-issue boots here? Something that would link us to the direction of Sayo's men?"

Resa shook her head. "Not that I've seen just yet," she said. "But I'd say that's a good thing, so far. Means that Sayo didn't follow the Metoi, if it turns out there aren't any prints from his men heading south."

A sigh of relief came from Rouge. "We lucked out, then. Still, we'll have to go there, Resa. I'm sure the Metoi still need our help."

"Right," nodded Resa. "Looking around, though, these prints were hard enough to find in the ash. How easy could it be to find another set?"

Kevin, Rouge, and Resa looked around. The wind was sweeping across the land, brushing ash over the shoe prints. Disappointed, Kevin sighed. This was going to be a lot more difficult than he had hoped.

An idea then came to him. The Sword of Purity had served many times to guide him before when he was lost. And perhaps, it would be able to guide him again. Though it had done its job and fulfilled its mission to end the conquest of the realms, Kevin was hopeful that the sword would still be helpful in guiding him.

After he had let Rouge and Resa know what he was thinking, Kevin carefully pulled out his sword and raised it in front of him. He gently whispered, "Someone has to put an end to General Sayo. You are the only one that can help me. Where do I need to go?"

A minute went by, and nothing happened. Then, a flash.

Instantly, Kevin blacked out, falling backward into the ash.

Be warned, pure one, echoed a voice in Kevin's head, as he lay knocked out, *if you truly seek General Sayo, you will find yourself betraying everyone you know. Be warned... your sword will guide you, but advises you against pursuing Sayo alone.*

Then, another voice started up, this one a little different. *Seek Sayo. Only you can restore the peace to Solunar. This is your fate.*

"Hey, are you all right?" echoed the voice of Rouge.

Kevin cracked his eyes open. Sure enough, Rouge and Resa were both bending over him, making sure he was all right. "I think so," responded Kevin, as he stood up and brushed himself off.

"Are you sure?" asked Resa. "I mean, it's not normal for people to just pass out like that."

As Kevin brushed himself off, he nodded. "I'll be fine," he said. "I'm still not completely sure what that was, but I can keep going." He lifted the Sword of Purity. "You ladies catch up with the Metoi. I'm going after General Sayo myself."

Rouge shook her head. "You don't have to do this," he said. "You told Caitlin you would wait for her. Sayo won't be so far away that you can't catch up after Caitlin gets here."

Kevin flipped his sword up. "No," he stated firmly. "I've seen enough. How many more families need to suffer like the one that burned to death in their house? I can't allow this to happen to anyone else. The sooner this ends, the better."

Again, Rouge shook her head. "Persistent, as always," she said. "It's both your most rewarding characteristic as well as your biggest weakness."

"Kevin's persistence is part of what made us friends with him, Rouge," added Resa.

At this, Rouge tilted up an eyebrow. "I suppose you have a point, Resa," she acknowledged. "Just understand that we won't protect you if Caitlin comes to find you and gets angry that you went without her." She paused for a second. "Even so, Kevin, we're still missing a direction in which to follow Sayo. We still don't know where he is."

"Maybe not," acknowledged Kevin, "yet there is a way to find out if I can get an answer." He then eased his grip on the Sword of Purity, allowing it to sit loosely in his hand. Then, the sword started lifting itself up, just as Kevin hoped it would. Several times before, the Sword of Purity had dragged Kevin to somewhere he needed to be, and he hoped it would do so again. As the Sword of Purity lifted up again, Kevin felt it pull him to the east. He firmed up his grip again, to make sure that he did not lose the sword by its own forces. By the time the sword reached its highest point, parallel to the ground, the tip was glowing, pointing definitively to the east.

"Interesting, indeed," contemplated Kevin, as he stared at his sword. “I would say we have a direction, now. The Sword of Purity never lies.”

Seeing this, Rouge looked to the east. “Why would Sayo go deeper into the Wastes? If he has troops with them, he would constantly need to rest and refresh them, since they are in an environment like this. Heading further in would pose a risk to the health of his men without resting them first in a more bearable environment, and he knows that.”

“Maybe there’s an oasis out there somewhere?” asked Resa.

Kevin added, “The tribes out there have to be getting water somewhere. If Sayo knows their source, he could be tapping into it.”

“But ‘tapping into it’ isn’t really the term,” commented Rouge. “Logistically, it would be more like draining it, and every source he and his men visited. The tribes of the Wastes are relatively small for a reason. Resources, even around the source points of what sustains the life of the natives, are very tight here. Part of why the Wastes are so hard to cross is due to the resource problem. Add to it that the Wastes tribes are very aggressive, and sending troops here is essentially writing a death sentence for the men that come here.”

As Rouge finished explaining, Kevin leaned in to Resa and whispered, “Your sister’s well versed in military tactics, I see.”

“She’s not just a skilled assassin; she’s a military genius,” Resa whispered back. “She reads military books when she’s bored.”

Rouge shook her head, catching only bits of what Kevin and Resa were talking about. She then enunciated, “Furthermore, it’s not like General Sayo at all to make such a move, where he’s putting his men at pointless risk. If he actually is out east, there must be something that makes him want to stay out there, more than simply any plan to destroy everyone out here. He knows to take better care of his men, and would not let any emotion control him to the point of sacrificing his men. Only strategy would make him do that.”

“Regardless of the reason,” Kevin responded, “I still have to track him down. We can worry about the reason later.”

For a minute, Rouge paused. Then, she said, “Have you been listening to anything I’ve been saying, at all? I’m not just reciprocating observations, Kevin. Something is suspicious about this whole thing. I really think you should be very careful if you're planning to go out there."

Kevin nodded. "I bet that's the trap for Arthur that Sayo suggested." He paused, as he stretched. "But this can't wait. Even without Caitlin, I'm ready," he said.

"Oh, fine," shrugged Rouge, giving up. "Just be careful out there. We'll tell Caitlin where you went if we see her, so she can catch up to you and curse at you any way she sees fit."

In contrast to her sister, Resa walked up and gave Kevin a hug. "We'll head south and assist the Metoi. See you soon, okay?"

A smile came to Kevin's face. "Will do," he said.

And with this, Kevin wished Rouge and Resa his best goodbyes as he headed on to the east, alone. If General Sayo were to be defeated, his fall would have to be as quick as possible. Memories of the battlefield several months ago, and the village burned to ash today, ran through Kevin's mind. Both were caused by General Sayo. For the benefit of all of Solunar, from the Wastes tribes to the people of Seta Archa to Kevin's best friend Arthur Falchor, this was something Kevin had to do immediately.

Still, the message of the Sword of Purity was solidly in Kevin's mind. Why were there two voices, anyway? And even weirder, why were they telling Kevin opposite things? Was one voice not really the sword talking? Why did Kevin black out when he asked the Sword of Purity where to go? Maybe there was something wrong, but regardless, Kevin was not going to be bothered by this. Not while there were people suffering, and friends who needed his help. Even Rouge's suspicions added on top of it all could not stop him now.

Several hours later, Kevin was starting to get very sweaty. He had been traveling nonstop for a while, and in the wastelands, such a trip was starting to get rough. Thoughts of returning home to Rikleifer were dwelling in his mind, keeping him sane across the long trip. He missed Caitlin, and thought again about whether or not he should have waited for her as he said he would do. Still, he felt strongly he was doing the right thing.

As the sun reached the edge of the horizon, Kevin caught a glimpse of a light reflection in the difference. Being alert, Kevin carefully approached, using the terrain to his advantage. There were a few embankments up ahead, which let him approach out of the vision of anyone watching from the other side.

Kevin stopped at the embankment. Then, he looked over it, and saw what he was looking for. The other side of the embankment was a steep drop, perhaps about half the height of the capital building in Seta Archa. Below it, there were tents everywhere, from the edge to a great distance further east. This had to be General Sayo's unit, and they were fully equipped with long-range travel gear, it appeared. It was indeed a large unit, and well equipped too, but something struck Kevin as a miss here. Though this unit was obviously able to use the temporary base they had as a launch point for many attacks in the Wastes, they did not have many resources to draw off of in the surrounding area, not even an oasis as he and Resa had suggested earlier. Kevin was sure someone as strategically gifted as General Sayo would know that.

Knowing he would be easily identified if anyone caught a glimpse of his Auranian uniform, Kevin removed his jacket and tied it around his waist for now. Of the tents he saw from the embankment, Kevin saw one that had a symbol painted on it. It was a white letter "D", which made it stand out amidst all of the black fabric tents. Kevin figured this letter stood for Desolunar, but he could not be sure. It also appeared to be a larger tent than the rest out there. It had to be the command tent, Kevin thought to himself.

Quickly, the sun was starting to sink below the horizon. If Kevin were going to move, he would have to move now. Waiting for nightfall and the cover of darkness would make it much more difficult for Kevin to check the tents, especially since the tents were made of black fabric. Carefully, Kevin crouched down and wedged his sword in the steep side of the embankment. Then, as he had done once before, Kevin dropped himself over the edge, using the Sword of Purity lit up to precisely the right amount of energy to let him fall without free-falling, at a controlled slow speed.

Kevin reached the bottom of the embankment with a soft impact, and immediately he sheathed his sword and crouched down. He took a couple of moments to work out an approach. He saw the command tent just a few tents away, toward the middle of the unit. It looked like they had place the command tent nearer to the embankment to take advantage of the relative protection it would offer, as the embankment was a little too steep to climb down safely.

With care, Kevin advanced, being careful not to be noticed. He stuck as close to the tents as he could, knowing the black fabric would make him harder to see through the tent walls. As Kevin stopped right at the command tent, he breathed a sigh of relief. He had not been caught. Being cautious had let him to his destination safely. Knowing what should come next, Kevin carefully lifted up the edge of the large tent, and rolled underneath it.

Kevin felt himself hit something solid as he rolled into the tent. It was a solid row of wooden boxes, likely full of supplies. He saw enough to see he was behind the boxes safely before rolling himself back to being face down, in order to remain out of sight as he listened carefully.

He heard the tent flap on the other side raise.

After he heard it close again, another voice, just on the other side of the boxes, said, "General Sayo, how did your inspection of the men go?"

"Well," responded another voice. "The men are perfect to my standard. I am not sure, however, that they may be to yours." Kevin figured from the response that the man answering the first man was General Sayo, having just entered the tent. Perfect timing, Kevin thought to himself.

"Now, Sayo, I know you demand perfection," began the other voice, "but I demand absolute perfection. Why, then, do you think that we began this little operation? It is ultimately the goal of perfection, nothing more. And perfection, the kind I desire, can only be achieved in one way."

"Yes, master, I understand," bowed Sayo.

Master?! Kevin could not believe what he had just heard Sayo say. Did Sayo just call someone else master?

That changed the entire dynamic of what Kevin had to do. Killing Sayo would likely not accomplish the goal of stopping this force, now. He was not the headpiece of this operation after all. But that brought upon an even bigger question. Who was the headpiece now?

"Very well," answered the other man. "For now, though, it will have to do. Please seal the tent flap, Sayo, for there is much to do."

There was a pause in the air as Sayo tied the tent flap tight with some string.

"What do you have in mind, master?" asked Sayo, after finishing the ties.

Quietly, the other man, without looking, stepped back closer to the crates. "Let's start with this, shall we?" he said. Then he reached down, grabbed Kevin by the neck, and lifted him into the air.

Discovered! But how?

Kevin struggled to try and break the man's grip. "Let go of me!" he exclaimed.

The man stared into Kevin's eyes. "You were not so wise to come here, Kevin Trent Stryker. Did you really think you could evade me forever?"

The face was all too frightening. And all too familiar.

"Pseudo!"

The grip of Kevin's deformed fake tightened. His voice deepened, "And now you see how the game is played."

Kevin's eyes widened even more with an even darker realization. "Setadev," he said.

And as he said that, General Sayo hit Kevin in the back of the head with the crossguard of his sword, knocking out the young Vanguard of Aurana.

Chapter 8

The Teacher

Magic, although a much rarer art than it had been in millennia before, was still being taught in a few places. One of these rare schools of magic was the excellent Bladinstar School, in the middle of downtown Bladinstar, Aurana, about a day's walk east and slightly south of Aurana City, and a good distance northeast of Rikleifer. It was headed by Headmistress Sarah Haughton, a longtime expert in magic and bureaucracy.

Sarah Haughton held a wizard license, but never truly felt like she had the right to call herself a wizardess. She attributed this failure to her inability to generate the levels of magic energy necessary to achieve such a level. However, Sarah set herself apart in the magic world by becoming intimately involved with government and politics. She had been an administrator of magic affairs in cities all across Aurana at various points in her career, and had been an advisor to King Arnold VIII. Upon request, she was also made an advisor to the current king of Aurana, King Andrew II, although she stayed in Bladinstar to to continue operating the school. Existing in a city of tourism thanks to its location close to the border with Nuve and its facilities that made it convenient and desirable as a stopover, the school was a common tourist attraction as well, being that it was one of a handful still in existence.

Sarah's most tenured professor at the school, and also close personal friend, was Professor James Magnon, who had been teaching since before she was a student at the same school herself. Tenured for many years and a department head, Professor Magnon was almost ageless. Of course, there was more behind that story than Headmistress Sarah Haughton, or anyone, more or less, really knew. In all actuality, Professor James Magnon was not a magic man of agelessness or anything like that. He was a god.

James Magnon's real name, at least the one he had five thousand years ago, was Tyrin Amtensen. As a god, he took the shortened name of Tyrinion and became well known and respected as the god of darkness. A little over five thousand years ago, Tyrin Amtensen, a revered wizard who was a little reclusive, started listening to the teachings of a zealot. This traveling zealot claimed to have found a power greater than all of them, known as divine power. Interested, Tyrin joined this zealot, who was rounding up only the very strongest people he could find that believed in what he had discovered.

That zealot's name was Setaeus Demota. The author of a book called *Immortality is a Truth*, which outlined his teachings and discoveries, Setaeus had more dreams and aspirations than anyone could have fathomed. To conquer the world would seem to be such a silly idea that only children would have, yet Setaeus secretly harbored these dreams. After leading his nineteen followers to the Realm of the Angels and making them gods, as well as himself, Setaeus took the name of Setadev, asking his followers to take shorter, one word names as well. The only one who did not was Setadev's personal assistant and second-in-command, Vinz Larin. He instead changed his last name to *larinion*, changing its meaning in the *rengan* language to "light and father to all".

When Tyrin Amtensen, now known as Tyrinion, learned of Setadev's true ambitions of conquest, he reported them to Vinz Larinion and made sure he spread the news to the other followers, as well. The time had come to force Setadev out, and for good. Setadev was furious, but the gods' attempt to strip Setadev of his immortality had failed. Seeing that he was best to bide his time, however, Setadev feigned being depowered and returned to the mortal realm. He made some foundings for a few years, such as the city of Seta Archa in the Solunar Empire, before disappearing and staying off the radar for thousands of years.

For about four thousand and eight hundred years afterward, the Realm of the Angels prospered in a way Setadev never could have imagined. From above, albeit with a minimum amount of interference to let the mortal realm live by itself, the gods protected their mortal brethren. Life continued greatly, until Setadev set his long-brewing plan into motion. Knowing that Tyrinion was the current carrier of the Stripe of Life, that which could create immortality, and also knowing that it was Tyrinion who had exposed his real intentions, Setadev took control of Tyrinion with a piece of tracer magic he had placed millennia before in the god of darkness. With the control, Setadev forced Tyrinion to attack his home in the Realm of the Angels, using every ounce of power he had. When Tyrinion snapped out of it and realized what was happening, he was horrified and immediately fled to the mortal realm, fearing repercussion for the crime he did not commit with his own mind.

This made Tyrinion the ideal candidate to be blamed for the uprising of a tribal nation twenty years ago, falsely believed to be the force behind the kingdom of Desolunar, and the one who placed a curse over the Realm of the Angels to keep any gods from escaping. All of these were incorrect, however. Tyrinion had never committed either of these things. It would take Kevin Trent Stryker to prove all of that wrong.

Nowadays, Tyrinion was still teaching in Bladinstar. It was his passion, as he had come to discover. Despite still being displaced from his home, although by choice this time, Professor Magnon found peace in being an instructor and being in the mortal realm where he could be closer to his daughter. He was the teacher. He was the professor. He was the man at peace, after so long at war.

In the late evening, the professor did as he liked to do sometimes. He stood on the roof of the Bladinstar School, watching the sun set in the distance. Lately, however, something had been bothering him. He could not place his finger on exactly what it was, but he felt some very bad premonitions. For the last couple of days, he spent several hours on the roof, standing as still as a statue but meditating and allowing the wind to blow through the slicked-back points of his faded blonde hair. Something about the wind in particular seemed to be a source of his anxiety. On this night, Sarah Haughton had been looking for the professor. As Sarah came up through the entrance to the roof, she said, upon seeing the professor, "James, have you been up here all this time? I have been looking for you for a while now."

Without turning, the professor nodded.

Sarah then sighed. "You know, I am not so sure I know what has been wrong with you lately," she said. "You have been awfully studious of the winds lately. Quite a bit, I have seen you up here listening, observing, and considering."

Professor Magnon shook his head. "It is nothing," he said. "Merely some signs in the recent winds have made me very curious, is all."

With that, Sarah walked up to the professor. "When you say it that way, I know it is not just another one of your curiosities, James," she commented. "I know you well enough to know that. Tell me, what sensation have you felt?"

There was a slight pause. Then, the professor finally turned his head to the headmistress. "It is the oddest of crosswinds, Sarah," he said. "One that blows in the opposite direction that winds normally do."

"Interesting," considered Sarah. "Is it linked to some kind of prophecy, perhaps?"

This time, the professor shrugged. He knew prophecy as just words of a writer with no credibility trying to forecast the future. "You know I place no stock in the words of 'prophets'. One who claims to be a profit is no more or less correct than someone who takes a wild guess."

At this, Sarah became quite cross. She folded her arms and said, "You do not have to lie to me, Professor Magnon. I know you well enough to know that although you believe that, you've seen enough documented instances of prophecy that you can't completely ignore the possibilities."

A smirk came to the professor's face as he lowered his head again. "Well, believe as you will," he said. "Belief is, after all, sometimes what keeps people moving more than other forms of motivation."

The headmistress rolled her eyes. "A point of fact, for sure," she said. "Still, I only wish you would tell me the truth. After so long, I had thought that you trusted me, Professor Magnon. It only appears now, though, that I was wrong."

"It is nothing like that," interrupted the professor. "Sarah, I am glad you have been more than just my student for so long, but I need you to understand that sometimes spreading unconfirmed information is more dangerous than not spreading it, even if it might be crucial to know. Belief in the false is more dangerous than not knowing at all." The professor had recalled teaching this lesson quite a few times. Mostly, however, he had used it for his own benefit, and he would admit to it if someone asked him. However, there was validity in what he taught, from some perspectives. The last thing needed to solve any problem was hysteria, after all. And furthermore, information in the wrong hands could lead to devastation.

"I understand," acknowledged Sarah calmly. "I am not here to pry at you, Professor Magnon. What is yours to keep secret is yours to know, alone."

"Indeed," nodded the professor. He then closed his eyes and stood cross-armed, feeling the wind blowing his robes around.

Sarah then shrugged. "It is also what keeps you alone."

That made the professor raise an eyebrow. What was the headmistress getting at?

"It is who you are, much as you are my mentor," said the headmistress. "I mean no disrespect, of course, but you are always so busy with your work or your studying, and keeping what you learn on the cutting edge all to yourself, that you have few friends and collaborators."

Professor Magnon was surprised. Sarah had analyzed him so well, and he knew it. He was proud, now more so than ever, that Sarah had learned well from being his student for years. "You are still as sharp as the most dangerous swords," he said back to Sarah. "I will not deny that I am a recluse." He turned to her. "Clearly, I have taught you well."

"I always do say that I learned from the best, James. Yet sometimes I wonder what lessons I'm missing in your secrets. You are so private that I'm not even sure that I know when you're at the school half of the time, unless you make your presence known."

"I guess," responded the professor, cracking the slightest bit of a smile. He would often simply arrive and begin his work, without making himself known…

Professor Magnon's jaw dropped. He had a frightening thought. He only needed to feel the crosswind one more time to confirm it. Sure enough, the odd wind began again in a few seconds, and the professor felt it. He stood silent, trying to study it.

Feeling the wind as well, Sarah brushed the side of her short gray hair with her hand. "That is odd," she said. "But how could it…"

Suddenly, the wind picked up.

Professor Magnon and Headmistress Sarah Haughton had to brace themselves as the wind buffeted them. It was a very strong wind that nearly blew them off their feet. An even stranger sensation kicked up in the wind as well. Then, as suddenly as it had arisen, the wind disappeared. As Sarah lowered her arms, she cursed under her breath. Then, she said, "What in the world was that? A strange crosswind?"

There was no response from the professor. Sarah looked over to see the professor's eyes open wide, and locked in that position.

"No," he said, as the wind died down, "it cannot be! It cannot be!"

"Professor, what's going…"

Quickly as he could, the professor bolted for the stairway into the building. He ran, as fast as he could, for his office. Sarah tried to follow him as fast as she could, but could not run quite as fast as the professor. Reaching his office, the professor reached up for the top shelf of his bookcase and ripped down a large, old book. He slammed the book to his desk and instantly started flipping through the pages, at a frantic pace.

The second Sarah reached the professor's office, she asked, "What's going on, Professor Magnon?"

"There is no way this can be!" exclaimed the professor again, turning back to his bookshelf and reaching for a few more books, as rapidly as he could. "Something is very wrong," he continued as he opened these books and thumbed through them, as well. "But what went wrong? How can this be?"

Closing the door to the professor's office behind her, Sarah walked up to the professor's desk and slammed her hands down on the edge, grabbing the professor's attention. "Tell me what that wind was, James. Clearly, you know exactly what is throwing you into a panic right now."

There was no more good that hiding would do. Not from someone as smart as Sarah Haughton, that was for sure. She did deserve to know the truth. Still, the professor did not stray away for even a second as he continued to move through the books on his desk. "That wind was a sensation of a presence over five thousand years old, Sarah. A zealot known as Setaeus Demota used to send such winds to places using divine power as a way of telling of his forthcoming arrival. He tended to use it as a taunt."

"Professor Magnon, divine power is only a theory," dismissed Sarah. "And how would you know about this zealot?"

"Because," began the professor, slamming one book shut and opening another one, "I have experienced it myself, and I have listened to his teachings, in person."

"Listened to his teachings? But how? Unless…"

"I am a god, Sarah," remarked the professor, finally. "I am an immortal, one of those who dare to call themselves gods."

Sarah's eyes widened. "Oh, James, you don't need to flatter yourself. You can't possibly be…"

"I am absolutely serious," interrupted the professor, as he slammed another book shut and turned to grab more. "Sarah, when have you known me to play a prank on you?"

There was a slight pause as Sarah tried to process all of this. "So then… you mean it? You're actually a god?"

The professor slammed another book shut. "In a manner of speaking," he said. "I have been alive for over five thousand years on the basis of divine power, since my inception as a god. I was born a mortal, but made an immortal."

Sarah's hand finally dropped from her mouth. "Oh my gosh," she said in amazement. "Somehow, I think I've believed it all along in my heart, but never could believe it in my head. How you've barely aged since you taught me as a young student, and how you could be so much smarter than everyone who I've ever seen perform magic before…" Then, Sarah shrugged her head, as if to snap out of her mind getting stuck on the fact. "Then why tell me the truth, professor?"

Finally, Professor Magnon slammed his books and looked

straight at Sarah. He then shook his head. "Perhaps for no reason," he said. "Perhaps because you were smart as a girl when you were my student and you are still a very intelligent woman today who can use the knowledge. Perhaps because you have been the closest thing I have to a friend. The exact reason, I am not sure if even I know."

Awestruck, Sarah Haughton had no response.

The professor continued to flip through his books. "What did we miss?" he kept asking aloud to himself. The book open in front of him was a prophecy book, and while the professor was not a believer in prophecy, he was desperate for any answer at this point. One of them that he was looking for was one that the gods kept close about this situation. Then, the professor began reciting that prophecy, "A hero will arise and end the conqueror's rampage..."

"But his wrath will only be delayed," interrupted Sarah Haughton. Professor Magnon's head turned up to face her, in surprise, as she continued, "The conqueror's evil shall seep through the realms and his influence will spread. He will cause great pain and suffering, unless the purest of heroes can stop him. The reign of evil can be defeated, but victory will be difficult. The first one will fail no matter what, but the second might succeed, should he be able to stand out against the evil flow and survive. The odds are against the light, and darkness will expand. Beware, all who know this prophecy, for the conquest of the realms has already begun."

"Sarah," began the professor, surprised, "how do you…"

"You left it open on my desk one day," interrupted Sarah, "in one of your prophecy books. Is it true, professor? Or, should I say, your holiness?" She was still so awestricken by this concept of Professor Magnon, her trusted teacher for years and fellow co-worker, as well as the one she might call her best friend of her later years, being an immortal.

Professor Magnon nodded. "There are similarities to reality, but it is more likely to be coincidence." The professor took a quick breath. "You do not need to call me 'your holiness', though. It feels very out of place."

"Well, I can't exactly call you 'professor' anymore, can I?" asked Sarah. "James Magnon probably is not your real name, either.

What is your name, anyway?"

Again, the professor stopped. Lies would not help him anymore. "My name… my real name… is Tyrin Amtensen," answered the professor, "also known among the immortals as the god Tyrinion."

To the professor's surprise, a smile actually came to Sarah's face. "So, no such thing as nameless ones, as in what religion teaches us?"

"All depends on how you see it," answered the professor. "Maybe we are the nameless ones, or maybe we are not. Regardless of how you see it, James Magnon is as real of my name as Tyrin Amtensen is. It has been my name, the only one I have used, for a century and a half."

"Then you have really lived more than a hundred and fifty years, have you not?" asked Sarah.

"I already told you that I have lived for five thousand," responded the professor. "One hundred and fifty-one years is solely how long I have been bound to this realm and lived as James Magnon, wizard and professor of magic."

For another second, Sarah paused and shook her head. "But then why… there is so much I just cannot understand…"

"Save it for later," interrupted the professor. "This is not the time to discuss this," he continued as he flipped open another book.

Sarah stopped. This was time to be serious. Something had the professor panicking. Anything about him being a god would have to wait.

As the professor continued to flip through another prophecy book, a paper fell out. Since the professor was not stopping, Sarah picked up the paper and read it. It was a poem:

Take thy sword and raise it high,
For tonight you will spread your wings and fly.
A journey starts to stop the bad
Who walks around in darkness clad.
The hidden angel will be your guide
And you will find others in your stride.
Along the way you will find tools,

But remember there are certain rules
Such as how you must protect
Energies so they will not defect,
For should he claim any one part,
The end of the world will break everyone's heart.
Seven powers, yes they are
Of stronger powers than the stars
That watch from above, overhead
As you lay down in your bed.
The powers of light, and earth and sky
And fire and ice and darkness and life;
Collect all seven, and there will be
Your weapon of choice in the fight to see.
The amazon shall hold the first,
But her fate shall not be the worst.
The phoenix guides you to another
And the centaur protects the power's brother.
An evil beast of existence
Holds another as he will prance
While he slowly begins his kill
Unless a secret is revealed.
One is kept by a man of magic;
Another by a god so tragic,
Made so by a vicious lie.
Several times it has made him cry.
The last is held by the darkened heir
Whose evil is seen everywhere.
This power, though, is not the end;
There are two more things to get to defend
The world from complete collapse.
The Key of Hearts, which might lapse
Out of your memory, but remember it so
Because it is needed to reverse evil's flow.
But when all is said and done,
You must merge two into one;
And should you survive all blasphemy,

You have a small chance at victory.

As Sarah Haughton glanced over the poem, she said, "Why do you have one of the *Letters to the Adventurer* poems in your book?"

"Sarah, what are you talking about?" asked the professor, confused.

"I'm talking about the poem that fell out of your book," answered the headmistress. "I've studied literature before. I doubt this came from a prophecy book."

"It was something my daughter found and gave to me," the professor answered. "You know it?"

"I do," she said. "It's by a known 'prophet', written as part of a series."

Still confused, the professor shook his head. As the pieces came together, he realized something. This could be a prophecy that was formatted in the style of a modern language poem, and Sarah implied it was one of a set. Maybe there was more to this poem, and it was the key for which he was looking. Suddenly understanding this, he questioned, "Are you saying this was published in a book of poetry?"

"That's exactly what I'm saying," responded the headmistress. "This is the first poem from a series called the *Letters to the Adventurer*. They were written in the early part of the language transition period when the dominant language became our modern one over *rengan*, by Clavius Lekion Stryker Dominous, some three hundred years ago."

Clavius Lekion Stryker Dominous. Maybe a distant relative of Vincent and Kevin Trent Stryker. Suddenly the fear was that, if it could be a prophetic poem, it was very likely to be relevant. As the professor thought about it, he responded. "Sarah, do you have a book with these poems in it?"

With confidence, Sarah nodded. "I believe I have at least a partial record. It is in my office." She turned for the door. "I'll be right back, with it."

Quickly, Sarah started sprinting out the door, headed for her office. As she did, an interesting thought came to the professor's head. He stared down at this poem, knowing now it was one of a series. Was there more to fulfill?

There were far too many unknowns in dealing with this, and this reason was one for why the professor disliked prophecy. Too many unknowns, too much speculation, and too many questions arising from trying to answer others. The professor's analytical and questioning mind was working in overdrive, yet there were only more questions arising. Even the professor had to admit, he was purely speculating by this point.

He needed more help, from people who would understand what he was talking about. Though Sarah Haughton knew a great deal and now held Professor Magnon's secret of being a god, she would likely not be able to consult with the professor on a level that would be necessary for the situation. She held no knowledge, nor gravitation of the importance of what Kevin, the professor's daughter, and the rest of their friends had accomplished three months ago in defeating Setadev. Sarah could only be so much help. Explanation could only go so far in showing Sarah what was happening.

The gods, however, would understand.

For a second, the professor was afraid of that thought. He had not been home to the Realm of the Angels in a long, long time. Granted, he had been welcomed back home whenever he wanted to return, so it would not be as though the professor were an unwelcome visitor. Still, the place held a stigma to the professor. Maybe it was time for him to overcome his fears again.

Chapter 9

Careful Considerations

The light of a single candle was the only glow in a pitch-black tent.

Nightfall had set in, and Kevin Trent Stryker was still knocked out, tied to a heavy box, also with his hands bound. As the dusk subsided into the pitch-black clouded winter night, he was still unconscious. The only two people in the tent, otherwise, were General Sayo and Setadev, in the guise of Pseudo.

Slowly, Kevin did start to gain consciousness. His head still hurt terribly from being hit so hard, and his eyes were starting to come into focus. "Is he awake yet, General Sayo?" asked Setadev, as Kevin started to wake.

Sayo stepped close to Kevin, and observed him for a second. "He is starting to move a little bit, master. He should be awake shortly."

"Excellent," remarked Setadev. He walked up to Kevin, gave him a hard smack across the face, and said, "Wake up!"

The smack was very painful, but it did give Kevin a little bit more consciousness. As his eyes opened wider, Kevin expressed a great look of surprise as he stared into the eyes of Pseudo, his distorted duplicate.

Formerly, Kevin had believed that Pseudo was a general of former Desolunar dictator Demonicus, a creation of Setadev's that was designed to take his appearance and shape. He had previously appeared exactly like Kevin himself, but had his own distinct personality. Pseudo was wearing a very tattered uniform from the old Desolunar forces. In Kevin's encounter with Pseudo, Kevin had, with Caitlin's help, stabbed Pseudo through his chest and kicked him off the side of the Cliffs of Vallia in western Scurnia. The wounds and impact should have been enough to be more than fatal.

"Stunned to see me, are you?" echoed the voice of Setadev from Pseudo's mouth. "Somehow I am not surprised that your feeble, little mortal mind has such emotion."

Quickly, Kevin tried to gather his words. He was not going to let Setadev intimidate him again, if he could afford it. "My mind may be mortal, but it has bested you before," he said.

"Bested me?" questioned Setadev. "Oh, pure one, how many times have I said it before, and how many times must I say it again? You cannot defeat me, for I am nothing. The fact that I am here should prove to you that you have bested no one. You failed, Kevin Trent Stryker. You failed to extinguish me, and because of that, I am still here. You may have won the battle, but you failed to end the war."

Kevin looked slightly confused, and very fearful. "I don't even know who you are," he said. "Are you Pseudo, or are you Setadev?"

Setadev started laughing, in his dark, evil laugh. "I am both," he said. "All of Pseudo is Setadev, but not all of Setadev is Pseudo. Do you understand, or should I explain? Nay, I do not think your mortal mind has such comprehension, so I should explain." He stepped back and turned his head. "Pseudo was my creation, Kevin Trent Stryker. Knowing that you were the 'pure one' spoken of in prophecies, I designed every aspect of this form after you. Designing him gave me one additional option, too: the ability to make him immortal. I made Pseudo immortal by placing a piece of myself within him." He turned. "When you stabbed him through his chest and threw him off the ledge, he was only being kept alive by this piece of myself, although he could not move, and his body was lifeless in all other aspects. And when you brought me to my physical demise by giving me all Seven Stripes of the Elements at once, the piece activated, and I was reborn in the body of my creation, at the bottom of the cliffs. And now that you know, how many more pieces do you think I have scattered? Now, pure one, you will be unable to ever bring an end to me."

Kevin scoffed. This was definitely Setadev, given the excessive monologuing. Kevin was frustrated, seeing as how he had completely missed destroying Pseudo entirely and allowing Setadev to live in this way. Obviously the term "immortal" held some weight: stabbing Pseudo through did not kill him, although fully disintegrating Setadev did. Still, despite his frustration, Kevin wanted to maintain a strong persona, with no fear. Setadev would prey on his fear if he held any. "Or so you say," he said. He then glared over at General Sayo. "And what are you supposed to be? Demonicus falls, and suddenly you become Setadev's lapdog? Have you no honor, Sayo?"

Sayo said nothing.

"He knows whose side will play most favorable," remarked Setadev, "and that is why he and his men are with me."

Sighing, Kevin shook his head. "Pathetic," he said, directly to Sayo. "You're no better than the master you worship."

With this, Setadev walked up to Kevin and smacked him across the face again. "Throw another insult, and the next time, I will start taking away your limbs."

"Why don't you just take my head?" demanded Kevin. "You've got me right where you want me, clearly. You said you swore revenge upon me." He was speaking out of anger, not even thinking. The fact that Kevin had people to protect meant nothing for the moment.

Setadev rolled his eyes. "All in due time, my impatient friend," he smiled as he stared into Kevin's angry face. "I am not surprised you think I would simply take your head and be done with it, because you do not know how the game is played."

Kevin became even more cross. "Then enlighten me, if you will. How do you play this little game you play?"

"In a darker way than you can ever imagine," laughed Setadev. "You see, as I will not be allowing you to escape my clutches alive, you might as well know a few details about my plans, so that they may eat at you for every minute that you breathe, until I finally allow you to die. This entire force I have assembled is here to help me accomplish my goal. As you can see," Setadev continued as he took a step back, "I am in a weakened state without my original body. That is true, but you have not destroyed all of my power. I know of a way to regain it, and I will allow you to witness as I become myself once more."

"And just how do you plan to recover all of this power?" asked Kevin.

Setadev glared directly into Kevin's eyes. "That, you will never know, Kevin. I would not tell you any detail that might directly impact the results of this little journey. However, you will be coming with us, as I wish for you to witness my return to power, and the full extent of my revenge, before you die."

"Fine, then," answered Kevin. "Then why attack the Metoi? Why set up this encampment in the middle of nowhere?"

"Why, have you not guessed?" inquired Setadev, with a very pointy tone of voice. "What interest would I have in pathetic tribes that live in a wasteland? Furthermore, what interest would I really have in the Solunar Empire? You can ignore the fact that it was once Desolunar; you remember how I abandoned Demonicus to bring you to me, some three months ago."

"Then it is a trap," nodded Kevin. "Why would you want to trap Arthur, though? He's not the one who destroyed you."

There was a slight pause. Then, Setadev started laughing hysterically. "You still do not get it, do you?" he asked, still laughing. "Who said anything about Arthur Falchor? This trap was for *you*, pure one."

Kevin's eyes widened. His mouth dropped.

"Yes, and now you see how the game is played," continued Setadev, more serious. "I knew that when faced with the potential destruction of his own country, Emperor Arthur would call only someone he could trust to help. And, as he knew you were the only one he could trust that could do the job, I knew I could isolate you by this method, and take you captive."

Still, Kevin was in disbelief. How could he have been so foolish? Who else would Arthur have asked to come to the Wastes when his military was still in disarray and he needed someone that he could trust? Rouge was right for sure; Kevin should have taken a minute to consider all of the oddities that presented themselves while investigating. And he should have waited for Caitlin.

Setadev let this soak into Kevin's mind. Then, he continued, "You are mine, Kevin Trent Stryker. Perhaps you should have heeded the warning of your sword before you came to find me."

"You knew!" exclaimed Kevin, shocked. "How did you know the Sword of Purity tried to warn me not to come here?"

"Isn't it obvious?" returned Setadev, not leaving any blank time after Kevin asked his question. "Or did you simply not recognize the second voice, the one that told you to pursue General Sayo?"

In response, Kevin glared into Setadev's eyes. He had a feeling he knew the answer to this one.

"That is correct, Kevin," said Setadev. "Your thoughts have the right answer. That voice was mine, pure one. Now, do you know how my voice made it into your Sword of Purity?"

Kevin was speechless.

"Your silence does not surprise me," Setadev continued, "yet in this case it is appropriate. This one, you will not know the answer. However, as you can tell, my power far surpasses anything you can fathom, even beyond that of your sword." Then, Setadev leaned in and put his face right in front of Kevin's, to leave a stinging comment. "Proof, as you can see, that you cannot be the hero the gods wanted you to be!"

Whack!

Setadev's hand came to his face, in surprise. He wiped it off, quickly.

Kevin had spit in his face.

"My sword is not what makes me, you overconfident schmuck!" a furious Kevin responded. Very much, he was ignoring the consequences of his actions in order to stand strong to Setadev. "I'm no hero, Setadev. I made myself what I am, and my sword is only one tool I use. I didn't need it to beat you the first time, and if you take it away from me, I won't need it to beat you again."

Again, Setadev smacked Kevin hard across the face. Somehow, Kevin figured that was coming. "Oh, pure one, you should consider yourself lucky that I do not want to kill you just yet. Otherwise, I would make sure you died a very painful death for disrespecting me in such a way. Still, I have other plans for you, so I suppose that I can be patient for a more thorough revenge."

Kevin flared hard, full of rage. "You won't get away with this, Setadev. The gods will be on to you sooner than you know it. When that happens…"

"They will do as they have always done," interrupted Setadev. "Not one of them has ever had the power to bring me down, not even

Vinz Larinion himself. No, they fear me far too much to launch an assault on me, even if they found me in this weakened state. And even if they were, Ralios Larion is an ineffective leader who will never be able to motivate his fellow immortals to true action."

Kevin was furious and frustrated, but there was little he could do. Taking a deep breath, and trying not to get too antagonized, he changed the subject. "Stop talking in circles and get to the point. So what are you going to do with me?" he asked.

Setadev stopped pacing. Then, he chuckled. "Looking forward to your stay, huh?" he asked, getting in Kevin's face again. "Very well, then, allow me to tell you this much. You may have guessed that I bound your hands to keep you from calling your sword to you, but that does not matter anyway as I have your sword in the protection of General Sayo."

"I figured that much," answered Kevin, frustrated. "That still doesn't explain your intent."

"Because you will find out my plans for you soon enough," continued Setadev, "except for one thing. I swore revenge on you for what you did to me, and I will have it. And just as I also promised you, I will get my revenge on the angel as well."

Instantly, Kevin's pupils shrank. "No!" he exclaimed. "You dare lay one finger on Caitlin, and I promise you I'll have your head!"

"And just how will you do that, pure one?" Setadev answered, this time starting to pick up his own emotion as he glared right at Kevin, sticking his face up to Kevin's.

Kevin could only glare back.

"You see, pure one," continued Setadev, "I am well aware of your relationship with Tyrinion's daughter. I know she is more than simply your companion. And before I end your life, I believe I am going to toy with hers, and cut it short before you."

"No! You had better not touch her, you son of a…"

"Do not finish that sentence," interrupted Setadev, stopping Kevin from finishing what he was exclaiming. "I grow tired of talking to you, pure one. Instead, I would much prefer to shut you up." Setadev then turned to General Sayo. "Hand me my purple powder dart."

Sayo did what he was instructed without words, giving a dart tipped with purple powder to his master. It was a drug Kevin was familiar with, having been struck with a dart coated with purple powder before. As Setadev prepared to bring the dart to Kevin's neck, Kevin exclaimed, "You had better make sure that dart knocks me out good, because when I wake up, I'll be coming after you."

"Oh, pure one, your continued fight amuses me," responded Setadev, as he stabbed the dart into Kevin's neck to knock him out, "but it will all be futile."

Then, Setadev removed the dart.

Quickly, Kevin was starting to fade. Within a few seconds, he had lost consciousness. Setadev waved his hand in front of Kevin's face just to be sure that he was unconscious before turning to General Sayo.

"Pity, indeed," Setadev said to General Sayo, as he cleaned the tip of the dart with a handkerchief from his jacket pocket. "The gods find one mortal to challenge my rule, and even he is terribly feeble. How humorous, indeed. Perhaps if they had chosen you, Sayo, they may have had more success."

Sayo said nothing.

Amused, Setadev continued, "Oh, does that thought bother you, General? Might you be the slightest bit jealous?"

This time, Sayo shook his head and then spoke. "Not at all," he said.

For a second, Setadev paused. "Ah," he began, "as expected, you speak only to those you respect. As you were disciplined for my son, you have been disciplined for me as well. Still, the question stands, despite your apparent discipline, General Sayo. Might you be the slightest bit jealous?"

"My answer stands," responded Sayo firmly, maintaining his discipline. "Not at all."

Continuing to press on his top general, Setadev then asked, in a prying tone, "Or does it bother you that this boy is the son of your former friend, Vincent Stryker? Do you possibly have some past allegiances in your heart somewhere, Sayo? Ones that I should be aware of?"

"Not at all," again answered Sayo's voice.

Setadev glared at Sayo for a moment, as if studying him. Then, he relented. "Very well," he said, as he stepped around the general. "Make sure to tie up our guest, and set him in a box with only a few holes for air."

"Is such precaution truly necessary?" asked Sayo. "It seems cruel."

"If it is cruel, so what?" Setadev pointed out, getting angry in his tone of voice. "Such precaution is necessary to prevent him from knowing our location once we begin the move to the new base of operations. We must begin the procedures as soon as possible."

General Sayo nodded. "As you wish, sir. I now request the full procedure that you wish for me to carry out."

"Must you always be down to business and never savor the moment?"

Sayo said nothing.

Setadev looked at Sayo. After a moment, he relented. "Very well, General," he said. "We will begin the move to the fortress as soon as possible, from where we can contact our peers and organize the retrieval. Your orders are to begin moving the troops as soon as I leave. I have some business to begin in order to set our plans in motion, but I will meet you and the troops there, to begin the second phase."

"Of course," acknowledged Setadev. "Your orders will be carried out. And what of the boy?"

A dark chuckle came to Setadev's lips. "Within the fortress is a series of holding cells. Each is too small to be considered a dungeon, but the entire area is very dark and creates the effects of one. Put him in one of them, and have him force-fed aphrodisiacs."

Sayo raised an eyebrow. "*Aphrodisiacs?*" he asked, absolutely surprised. "Why in the world would you want to give the prisoner those?"

"Oh, I have my reasons, Sayo," continued Setadev. "You can acquire them, of course, right?"

Reluctantly, Sayo nodded. "I can," he bowed. "I have an apothecary present within my troops, as an assistant to our medical personnel. Certainly he will know how to make any chemical you wish."

"Excellent. Then 'blue soup' will be the desired choice," acknowledged Setadev. "Yet, still you are curious, I can sense. Sayo, do you really wish to know why I will force a drug down this boy's throat that will make him unable to resist the temptations of a female?"

General Sayo kept himself as reserved as possible. "I must admit, I do find it a bit curious," he said.

"My specific plans, General, I will not share with you."

Sayo shrugged, in frustration. "It seems as though there is little that you wish to tell me," he said, "and I am beginning to find it difficult to listen to you, Setaeus Demota. What you keep secret will only serve to…"

"To keep everything as it should be," interrupted Setadev. "Let the mortal be mortal, and the immortal be immortal. Do not challenge me, General."

"Yet all of this focus on the boy, does it not bother you that it may interfere with the mission?" asked General Sayo. "You are putting more effort into capturing this boy and torturing him than you are on your own revival and conquest."

"Oh, Sayo, my dear top general," began Setadev, as he put his hand on Sayo's shoulder and shook his head, "what am I going to do with you? I am surprised that for someone as brilliant as you are, you do not see how the game is played."

Frustrated, Sayo brushed off Setadev's hand and continued, "I am not talking about that, my lord. It only seems that your focus is a little…"

"Sayo, do you want to be the most powerful mortal man on the face of the world?" interrupted Setadev, as he started leaning on Sayo's shoulder. He then stuck one hand out and began gesturing as he started to to explain, "This whole world can be yours as long as you obey me and give me your full and unwavering devotion. I can make you the most powerful person in the world. That is, next to me, of course. All you have to do is shut up and follow me. You have your orders, so can you do this for me?"

Sayo glared for a moment. "Yes, sir," he said reluctantly.

"Good," acknowledged Setadev. "You will have about an hour

or so to lock the boy in the box before the powder wears off. I will be leaving in a minute to handle my business, and prevent a certain thorn from stabbing us in the side. In the meantime, I want you to have the men ready to leave in two days, and prepare to move out."

"As you wish," acknowledged Sayo, with no emotion.

Chapter 10

Inner Thoughts

"State your name and business."

Caitlin was back in the castle in Rikleifer. She had to rush back to Aurana in order to be registered on her sixteenth birthday, as anticipated. Arthur arranged for a gryphon flight so that she could make it back on time. Aurana's laws on registration were very strict, likely for bureaucratic reasons and the tediousness of pulling records.

"My name is Caitlin Amelia Magnon," she said to the operator behind the window in the castle's records office. "I'm here to complete my mandatory adult registration.

The young male operator nodded. "Very well," he said. "Is today your sixteenth birthday?"

"It is," answered Caitlin.

Much as she should have been excited for this day, Caitlin could not be. In her heart, though she was very excited to be turning sixteen and legally considered an adult, she was sad for the fact that Kevin could not be with her today. She had really wanted him to be there with her for such a momentous occasion, not to mention the day that celebrated her life.

"All right," said the operator. "Please have a seat on the bench in the corner. A legal representative of Aurana will be out in a moment with your file, so we can complete the registration process."

Nodding, Caitlin walked over to the bench and sat down. Finally, she would legally be an adult, just like all of her friends. She could go anywhere freely without having to ask her father's permission —although she did that already, anyway, knowing her father trusted her and would not mind. She could do anything within the laws of adults without worrying about the laws on children. She could finally get her wizard license to practice as a professional.

Gently, Caitlin ran her fingers through her long, straight red hair.

It seemed to be a little longer by now than she remembered it being. She wondered if maybe her magic works had been the cause. In her short course of time with Arthur and Rachel, Caitlin was willing to give some demonstrations of her power, just for fun, and it had left her pretty exhausted. Yet just like muscles and how working them makes them tougher, using a lot of magic and draining oneself led to more energy building back up than had been there before. It was complex to explain to anyone, but such energy, as Caitlin had explained to Arthur and Rachel after showing off some of her spells, sometimes would exude itself in the body, such as through more rapid hair growth or nail growth.

As she ran her hand through her hair again, Caitlin twirled it a little bit, thinking about twisting it into a shape. She knew that Kevin liked it when she kept her hair down, calling it an example of her free spirit, but with him not here at the moment, she considered putting it into a tail of some type, just to see what it looked like. Tying it into two tails on either side of her head with ribbon was a thought she was toying with in her mind.

Then, Caitlin straightened her dress out a little bit. She thought about it a little bit, as well. Caitlin had had that dress for a few months now, having traded for it because she thought Kevin would like it. Of course, she really liked it too, or else she would not have traded for it. The color white was often one of the wizardess, the highest rank in magic for a female. And to Caitlin, the red trim all over gave her dress a lot of personality, regardless of the fact that it was floor length with long sleeves, and essentially covered her from her neck to her toes.

Caitlin had always been very comfortable in dresses, both before and after she regained her emotions. They had a great deal of use in magic as a comfortable, flowing garment for females, since open skin led to greater energy conduction and thus more magic potential. The airy design of a skirt bottom on a dress allowed Caitlin's legs to be exposed under her dress, and was open enough for great magic conduction. Given that it was winter, however, Caitlin was wearing a pair of white leggings under her skirt to help keep her warmer. For the moment, keeping warm in the winter was more important than conducting magic.

Still, magic was not the only reason Caitlin liked wearing dresses. She typically just enjoyed the feel of them when moving around. She usually kept to the completely covering ones, but she usually did not like having lots of fluff or excess fabric to get in the way. The top piece on her current dress that reached over her shoulders and draped down her sides, also white with red trim, was the one exception in that she liked the way it looked and it did not interfere much with her movement.

Suddenly, the door beside the operator opened. An older gentleman appeared, and said, "Miss Magnon, if you would please follow me, we will continue with the registration process."

Caitlin stood up, nodded, and followed the older gentleman past the windows and into an office. She took a seat at the little table, and the older gentleman in nice clothes took a seat next to Caitlin. He laid out several folders and said, "These are your records. We just need to verify them and grant you your adulthood certification, okay?"

"Okay," nodded Caitlin.

"All right, then," began the gentleman. He rustled through one of the folders, and took out a sheet of paper. He also grabbed out a feather pen and dipped it in a container of ink. Then, he turned to Caitlin and asked, "Would you like to keep your legal name as Caitlin Amelia Magnon?"

Normally a pretty quick question to answer, Caitlin had to think hard about this one. There was a pretty big complication in the way. Though Caitlin had always known herself to have the last name Magnon, she had only recently come out to find out about her father's real name and identity, and Caitlin wondered if it might make more sense to change her last name to Amtensen, which is what it should logically be. That was, after all, her father's real last name, even if no mortal knew his true identity. Still, that was also a reason not to take that last name. It might be a risk to her father and to her to do that, not to mention the fact that no one would recognize why she would take that last name and that she would have a hard time justifying the reason for the change to the official she was talking to.

So, she finally answered, "No. Caitlin Amelia Magnon is who I am."

"All right," acknowledged the gentleman. "I will note your name and date of birth in the records, then." He then shuffled through his papers on Caitlin. Noticing an oddity in one of them, he said, "Hmmm… well, this is strange, Caitlin. Your official records are here, and were filed within two weeks of your birth date, as required by Auranian law, but you do not have any parents listed."

"Yeah, uhmm…" interrupted Caitlin, thinking hard on what to say, but only coming up with a slanted version of the truth, "my mother died in childbirth, and it had distraught my father so much that I guess he didn't file all the paperwork."

The gentleman considered this for a moment. "Okay, I suppose I can see that. Still, Caitlin, it's abnormal not to have at least one parent listed for the records. The registering parent is supposed to list himself or herself, and both can list only if both are present, per Auranian law. It's your right, if you wish, to request an inquiry and have your father questioned, if he is still alive, to correct the mistake."

"No, it's all right," responded Caitlin quickly, wanting to keep her father out of the way of the government of Aurana. The less questions were asked about him, the better he could maintain his identity. "It's not a big deal to me anyway."

"Okay," nodded the gentleman, writing something down on the record. "Educational experience to be listed?"

Caitlin answered, "Home taught. My father taught me everything I know."

"All right," said the gentleman. "Any certifications?"

"Yes," answered Caitlin. "Aurana Department of Magic Affairs, Sorceress-class. I will be pursuing my wizard certification after we are done here."

The gentleman's eyes widened for a second, then reduced as he wrote this down on the record. "Wow," he said. "We do not have many people who have any magic certification listed at all, much less at your level. You must be quite talented."

"So I hear," laughed Caitlin.

After another second of writing, the gentleman continued, "Do you have a trade or other source of income?"

Shaking her head, Caitlin answered, "Not at the moment. I

guess you could say I'm a student of magic, but that's about it. No income from that, though I may earn some when my wizard license is attained."

"Okay," acknowledged the gentleman, as he wrote more down. "That being said, are your basic necessities being supplied by criminal activity, or by friends and family?"

"Friends and family," nodded Caitlin. "I stay with a friend of mine at times, and when I stay by myself, I know how to live off the land."

The gentleman nodded as well, as he added to his paperwork. "All right, there is only one more question. Have you had a child, or are carrying one at the moment, that you know of?"

Caitlin shook her head with certainty. "No," she said. She kept this response short and simple.

Yet, for just a second, the question made Caitlin think. If Caitlin considered the fact that had she been asked less than a year ago if she would ever carry a child, she would have said no. The whole activity of raising a child would interfere too much with her works as a magic caster. After she became close to Kevin, however, the thought of being a mother was starting to crawl around in Caitlin's mind. It was little more than something to ponder at this point rather than a serious thought, but whether or not she could ever bear children was still a question. Being that Caitlin was half-immortal thanks to her father being a god, something that had never been accomplished before, Caitlin was not sure just how her body would function in such a situation, and if it would work like a normal, mortal female, or not. After all, immortals were capable of having children with immortals too, yet Caitlin was the first ever child of a mortal and immortal pairing.

At that same time, while contemplating these ideas, Caitlin was stricken with a sense of hesitation about her relationship with Kevin, and even considered the possibility that it may not happen between them. Something had not seemed right in the past three months. Though Kevin and Caitlin spent almost all of their time together, and did pretty well for the most part during that time, their relationship had not advanced further than what it was. Caitlin became nervous, very rapidly, that this stalling out might be from Kevin reconsidering their relationship. There were other possibilities to consider, though, and Caitlin recognized that. She knew that she was still getting used to having so many emotions that she may not have realized how fast she wanted to keep going, or that Kevin may have wanted to take it slower. Still, the fear spread through Caitlin like a wildfire, despite her best efforts to quell it. Could she keep this emotion under control, too?

"All right, then," said the gentleman, as he marked down a few final comments. "I will make sure to have this filed properly, and approve your adult certification." He then rose and offered to shake Caitlin's hand. "Congratulations, Miss Magnon."

Caitlin stood up and shook the man's hand. "Thank you," she said.

The gentleman nodded. "You are welcome," he acknowledged, as he walked Caitlin to the door. "If you have any questions, feel free to come back to the records office, and we will try to answer them for you. Have a nice day, Miss Magnon."

"You too," nodded Caitlin, as she turned for the door.

It was still a cold day outside in Rikleifer, so as Caitlin left the records room and headed through the castle for the exit, she pulled the arm sleeves on her dress tight to make sure they covered her arms and kept tight to her skin. She also checked the white winter leggings she was wearing underneath her skirt, to make sure she had them pulled tight as well. On a cold day like this, it was important to stay warm.

Within a couple of minutes, Caitlin was outside the castle again. She decided not to visit Kevin's father while there, mostly because he was pretty busy with his rehabilitation. Recalling the last time that she and Kevin had interrupted him and knowing of his growing paranoia, she thought it might be best to let him continue uninterrupted as much as possible until he could see his son again and know that his son's trip had been a success.

Just north of the castle in a separate building was a small office of the Aurana Department of Magic Affairs. Here, Caitlin entered to attain her wizard license. Her brief examination included a skills test as well as an ethics test, demonstrating that she was skilled enough at magic not to hurt someone accidentally, able to perform magic at the highest levels it was known to be capable, and that she knew when and when not to use certain kinds of magic. Caitlin passed with ease within a couple of hours, and was granted a license which would be filed with the government of Aurana. She now had the legal right to practice magic as a career and sell her services as a wizard, if she chose to do so.

With that, Caitlin left and headed for Kevin's house, where she was staying while in Rikleifer. She had allocated the whole day to get these processes done, and now in the early afternoon she had already completed them. Tomorrow morning, the gryphon flight would return to take her back to Seta Archa.

During her walk, Caitlin thought about Kevin. Something about being with Kevin just made Caitlin ever so happy. Even when they might disagree every now and then, or not see eye to eye on a particular topic, she always found her way back to him. On everything, they worked together when they had the opportunity, although Kevin did tend to be a little protective of Caitlin and wanted to ensure her safety when doing something hazardous.

As Caitlin walked back to the west, toward Kevin's house, one of these memories came to mind. She came to find herself daydreaming about her life, only wondering how the future could get even better than the present.

"Hey Caitlin, where are you?"

Caitlin walked out of Kevin's bedroom to find Kevin in the kitchen, standing on the first rung of a ladder leaning against the wall. "I'm over here, Kevin," she said. "Just doing a little reading. What's up?"

"I'd say I am right now, given where I am," laughed Kevin, poking fun at the fact that he was standing on the ladder. "Can you do me a favor and hold this ladder steady for me? There's a hole in the roof up here, and I'm going to place a small piece of thatching up here to fill it before it rains and starts leaking in here."

With a smile, Caitlin nodded. "Sure thing," she said. "How long has that hole been up there, anyway?"

"Beats me," answered Kevin, as Caitlin grabbed the sides of the ladder, allowing him to climb higher with less risk of falling. He took his patch piece of thatching and slipped it into the hole. As he began to adhere the patch into the roof with a handful of adhesive from a jar, he continued, "I just noticed daylight coming into it a few minutes ago. With all of this freezing rain we've been getting lately, I'd rather not take a chance on the cold coming in and forming ice everywhere."

"Or getting us sick," added Caitlin.

Kevin nodded. "That's true," he said. "I have a feeling I'll have to replace the roof next summer, when it's warmer. I don't think it's been replaced in a while, and it will likely keep springing leaks until it is replaced."

"Time to get some new thatching, then," mentioned Caitlin. "Don't worry, Kevin," she said. "When next summer comes, I'll be looking forward to thatching the whole roof with you."

"No," stated Kevin firmly, in response. "I'd really rather that you not, Caitlin. I'll do it myself."

Almost stunned, Caitlin let go of the ladder as she put her hands to her hips. "And why is that?"

As Kevin finished off the last little bit of sealing around the patch, he answered, "Thatching a roof is dangerous business. I've never done it myself, but I know it is. I really don't want to see you get hurt doing it, by falling off the roof, or through it, or anything like that."

Caitlin just rolled her eyes. "Together we survived an onslaught from a banished god, two major battles, and some dark cloud called the Existence, and you're concerned about me thatching a roof with you?"

Kevin started stepping down from the ladder, not realizing that Caitlin had let go of the siderails. "Look, Caitlin, it's not that…"

Suddenly, Kevin came crashing to the ground.

"Kevin!" shrieked Caitlin, as she rushed to his side to help him, "are you all right?"

Without Caitlin holding the siderails of the ladder, the flimsy stick ladder slid backward across the floor when Kevin attempted to step down. This caused the whole ladder to fall to the ground, taking Kevin with it, straight to the floor. Instantly, Kevin's hands went to his head, as though he had hit it pretty hard. Fortunately, he had hit it against the rungs of the ladder as he fell, and had not cut his head open. Still, Caitlin was in panic mode until she helped Kevin to sit up and saw he was still conscious and had only bruised his forehead.

"Oh my gosh, Kevin, I am so sorry," apologized Caitlin as she put one hand to her mouth. She was kneeling down next to Kevin, who was sitting on the fallen ladder. "I really didn't mean to let go of the ladder; I didn't want to hurt you."

Kevin was still clutching his head, in pain from bumping it. He was pretty sore in a couple of other spots on his body, too, from where the ladder broke his fall. "It's okay, Caitlin," he said. "I just bumped my head, that's all. At least the patch is in place so I won't have to climb the ladder again."

Seeing that Kevin was going to be okay, Caitlin stood back up and offered her hand to Kevin. "Here, let me help you up," she said. "I'll take you back to your room."

Slowly, Kevin did reach for Caitlin's hand, and took it. "Thanks," he said, as he lifted himself mostly by his own power. As he stood up, Kevin's other hand was still on his head. By now, there was a fairly visible dark bruise on his forehead from where his head hit the rung of the ladder.

At least there was not terribly much to do today. Caitlin knew Kevin could afford to take a little rest. After all, Caitlin figured that the two of them spending a little bit of time together might be the best thing for him to forget his injuries.

As they walked into the bedroom, Caitlin took a quick glance out the window. It was a cold winter day outside, but Kevin's house was still reasonably warm thanks to the small iron stove in the kitchen. It might stay warmer now since Kevin put the patch in the roof. There was snow falling outside, coating the ground in white and shining the sky in reflecting sparkles of white. For once in what seemed like most of the winter so far, there was snow instead of freezing rain.

Carefully, Caitlin helped Kevin to sit down on the bed, and he then turned himself to lay down, with a hand still clinched on his forehead over the bruise. Then, Caitlin sat herself down and twisted herself sideways, so she could lie on her side and look directly at Kevin. She stroked Kevin's forehead gently, as a bit of healing magic glowed from her hand to treat the bruise, and said, "I'm really sorry, Kevin. I hope you're okay."

"It's fine," shrugged Kevin, as he let go of the bruise. "Are you all right, Caitlin? I wasn't sure if the ladder kicked out and hit you in the leg or not."

Caitlin reached down and grabbed her right leg for a second. She had not been injured by the ladder, having stepped back far enough to be out of its reach when she put her hands to her hips before. Still, what Kevin had said had brought back the memory of having her right leg broken against a brick wall a few months before, during the Battle of Middle Aurana. "No, I wasn't hit at all," said Caitlin.

Kevin breathed a small sigh of relief. "At least you're all right," he said. He had a little smile on his face with that realization. Even though he was the injured one, he cared more about if she was hurt or not.

For a second, Caitlin smiled. Then, recalling the discussion they were having before Kevin slid to the ground, she began, "Really, Kevin, now I'm worried about you replacing the thatching on that roof by yourself. You worry about me too much; sometimes, you need to worry about yourself, and let me help you when I can."

Still, Caitlin was not quite sure if she had sold Kevin on that fact or not. Certainly she admired his chivalrous nature and desire to protect her, but at the same time, she wanted to be able to do anything with him that she wanted. They had already survived more danger than most couples would ever see in their lifetimes. Perhaps there would be a way she could convince him of that, at some point. That little incident with the ladder had happened over a month ago. Yet despite that, the memory seemed so fresh in Caitlin's head.

Despite it all, nothing was going to pull her from Kevin's side. She was so devoted to him. Several times before, Caitlin had debated with herself as to whether or not it was true affection she was feeling or just a side effect from Kevin being the one to open her heart when he told her that he loved her the first time. That had been a factor in her being hesitant before, but in the past couple of months, Caitlin had no hesitation at all. She was certain, and she was sure.

About changing Kevin's mind about dangerous situations, however, Caitlin was starting to consider consulting Rachel Reinhart about it. As Rachel was very feminist-minded and likely would be seen as a great symbol for the advancement of women in society thanks to her position as Prime Minister of the Solunar Empire, she might have some ideas. Also, as a good friend to both Kevin and Caitlin, she might also be able to sit down with Kevin and talk to him personally.

While she thought about this, Caitlin had arrived at Kevin's house. She walked in and put her new papers down on the table, proof of her registration as an adult and her new wizard license. A little chilled from walking so much in the winter, she went to the corner stove and lit a fire with her magic. Then, she warmed her hands for a few minutes by the heat of the stove.

A few minutes later, she walked to the bedroom that used to be Kevin's mother's room. It was here that she slept when she stayed with Kevin. They'd had to share a bed before, but it was more comfortable for both of them, and more modest, that they slept in separate rooms. Neither bed was large enough to sleep more than one person comfortably, anyway. Under the bed, Caitlin kept her diary. She always left it here, even when she was away, and when she returned she would write in it.

Today, she had so many thoughts that she just had to write them down:

Several days since last entry:

Registration is done. I finally have my wizard license. It feels like I have everything I've worked for. I won't stop training in magic and I'll always want to be even better than I was before, but I think my wizard license was the last major milestone I know of. I'll need to make more if I want to keep growing.

I really miss Kevin. It's been a few days now that we've been separated, longer than we have since we first met. I don't know if it's a sign of weakness, but it's an odd feeling not having him around. I guess that when I worried about if I was growing distant from Kevin, that maybe I was wrong after all. Time apart from him has made me only want to be closer to him again.

Maybe it's nothing to afraid of. Maybe I'm not weak, and it's just normal for a teenage girl like myself to want to be with my boyfriend. It seems like it's normal for Kevin to want to be with me...

mostly. I'll admit that sometimes I don't know what's normal and what isn't. I just love him. It feels so hard to explain sometimes, but there's such a powerful special feeling every time we're together that makes me so happy. And he seems so happy too.

I long to feel that feeling again soon...

Satisfied, Caitlin put her diary down. She headed to the front of the house and decided to step outside for a couple of minutes. All of the snow that had previously fallen was accumulated all around the road, although the road itself was clear. However, it was currently snowing at the moment, leading Caitlin to believe that the snow would be replaced soon enough on the roads. Fallen, tan blades of grass were all across the fringes of the road where it was visible, and frost was developing in patches all over. For the moment, there was little to no wind. All around, the houses were covered with frost and snow. Caitlin stopped and admired what she saw, finding beauty in everything.

On the window ledge in front of Kevin's room, a couple of birds were searching for food. Amazing it was that they were able to survive in this cold weather, although it did appear that it was not easy for them to do so. Their nest was built into a tree, sheltering them from the cold wind when it blew. Then, one of the birds flapped down to Caitlin and landed on her shoulder. Caitlin turned her head to look at the bird and smiled. She noticed that the little bird appeared to be shivering.

"I don't have any extra food, but I'll help you, little birdie," smiled Caitlin, as she put the little bird on her right index finger and moved it in front of her. Then, with her left hand, she snapped her fingers, creating a tiny magic spark of flame. Carefully, she held the bird close to the flame coming from her fingers, while being very careful not to torch the bird.

The bird sat on Caitlin's finger for just a minute, warming up before taking off again for the ledge. The sight was majestic for the short moment that it had lasted. The little bird must have a lot of work to do, Caitlin reasoned to herself, as she watched it go back to searching for food. She wondered if maybe it had a family to support, or if it was supporting itself. Since the other little bird had flown away already, it was hard to tell whether or not that bird may have been a part of the family of this particular one.

Shortly afterward, the two birds appeared again on the ledge, and Caitlin caught a glimpse of her new friends chirping together. They looked to be communicating to one another. Again, Caitlin watched the birds, admiring the beauty of their work.

Suddenly, however, the birds took off. For a moment, Caitlin wondered why. It had appeared as though they had been spooked.

The wind started picking up. Nothing unusual.

Then, it became a crosswind, and started blowing in the opposite direction. It started changing directions afterward, shooting in all sorts of directions.

That's unusual, Caitlin thought to herself.

And then, the winds picked up, nearly knocking Caitlin off of her feet.

She raised her arms and braced herself as the wind buffeted her. "Something's not right," she said to herself, as the wind pushed hard against her. It continued to intensify and intensify harder and harder.

Then, nothing. The winds stopped. The snow falling seemed to freeze in place. It was as if time itself had suddenly stopped moving forward. This had happened to her once before, Caitlin realized. Was a god appearing?

Then, the light of a teleportation gate opened in front of Caitlin.

Chapter 11

Shattered Glass

As the gate formed, Caitlin's eyes widened. The winds intensified, even though everything still appeared frozen in time. Caitlin had to keep her arm up to prevent the wind from buffeting her.

Slowly, the winds started to die down as Caitlin lowered her arms and watched someone walk out from the gate. For a second, it almost looked like Kevin. "Kevin, is that you?" she asked.

Then, as he stepped out in full, it was apparent that it was not Kevin. The deep scars across his body and face told her who it was she was really looking at.

It was Pseudo.

The gate closed behind him as Pseudo appeared. The clearly distinctive voice of Setadev then said, "How predictable to find you at the pure one's house. I thought you would be here." He paused for a second. "Surprised to see me, angel? I am surprised the winds of my presence did not alert you to me."

"You!" exclaimed Caitlin, as she dropped her arms, and then raised her right one in a position to shoot magic, if necessary. She realized it was Setadev whom she saw, and immediately recognized that she was in danger. "How are you even alive?"

"That is none of your concern," responded Setadev, "because you will never understand how the game is played."

That phrase was a telltale sign of who Caitlin was actually looking at, and the lack of glowing eyes meant that he was not being possessed by tracer magic. Somehow, Pseudo actually was Setadev and not just a puppet. Caitlin stared directly into Setadev's cold eyes. "What do you want?" she asked. "If you're here for the pure one, then I hate to disappoint you, but he's not here."

"Heh," chuckled Setadev as he approached Caitlin, "interesting indeed, angel. You are as defiant as your father. Besides, I know the pure one is not here. I am not here for him."

"My name's Caitlin, not 'angel', if you don't mind," said Caitlin. "And if you know that Kevin is not here, then you can just turn around and walk away. I have no interest in talking to you about anything."

Setadev shook his head. "You wish, angel," he said. "I am not here to simply walk away. I will destroy you first."

The audacity of that comment angered Caitlin. "I'm afraid I can't allow that," she responded with discipline, as she charged a ball of fire. She was intent on defending herself from Setadev, still a little lost as to why he was here, now.

Silently, Setadev nodded. "Very well, then. As you wish." Suddenly, Setadev leapt out and attempted to strike Caitlin with his forearm.

Caitlin ducked out of the way at the last second and launched her fireball, only to watch it dissipate against him. No luck, Caitlin thought to herself. Quickly looking for a counterattack, Caitlin unleashed a beam of darkness, one of her stronger attacks. Setadev was ready, however, and blocked the attack with one hand held out. The blast kept going and going for a moment, until Caitlin realized it was futile to continue, letting up the beam. As the beam dissipated, Setadev said, "A fan of darkness magic, are we? How completely unfitting for a figure of purity."

Frustrated, Caitlin lit up a beam of light in her hand, using her manipulation skills to shape it into a lightning whip. It was one of her most advanced techniques. "My father is the god of darkness, if you haven't forgotten. But, if you feel that I must show some light, Setaeus Demota, then why don't you let me purify your soul?"

"Then purify me, if you can!" demanded Setadev.

Without a second of thought, Caitlin rushed at Setadev and unleashed the full power of her lightning whip.

Setadev used only his arm to block every shot.

As fast as she could, Caitlin moved from one shot to another, moving with lightning speed. Every strike was full of power. Every lash was full of fury. Rarely did Caitlin ever want to use such deadly force, and her true power as a wizardess was revealed as she unleashed these powerful whips of lightning.

She stopped for a moment and let the whips disappear. Setadev was still standing, completely unfazed by the attack. He started chuckling, before he began to laugh hysterically. "You cannot defeat me, for I am nothing. You cannot purify what is already pure. I am more pure than you are, than your friend the 'pure one' is, than any of the gods are."

"I don't believe that, even for a second," denounced Caitlin.

"Oh, but you should," nodded Setadev, stepping closer to Caitlin as he continued to talk. "After all, good and evil, purity and corruption, are only the concepts of those who claim to have them or accuse others of being them. To say that something is pure and good, or that something is corrupt and evil, is only to claim your own opinion. Those inspired by one or the other have named their creations for their beliefs." Setadev then started stepping closer to Caitlin again. "Still, I would not expect you to understand that, for you are immature and young. Perhaps an admirable quality for your image of innocence, yes, but for as intelligent as you believe yourself to be, you seem to miss so many of the basics."

"Perspective is one thing, Setadev, but morals are what show whether or not you are pure or corrupt," responded Caitlin defiantly. "Even you can't change that, and your morals are definitely corrupt."

For a second, Setadev paused. Then, he set his hand on Caitlin's shoulder, getting a shocked reaction out of her. "In this reality, perhaps. I do realize that, angel. However, soon, the reality will change, and I will be the controller of this reality. And he or she who controls reality controls morality and all of its aspects." Then, Setadev leaned in. "Can you not see it, angel? A unified world, under one ruler who keeps the peace. There would be no more war, no more destruction, none of that. Tell me, angel, is my vision so different from yours?"

Caitlin turned and glared at Setadev for a second, and then backed away several steps from him. "It is, because you have oversimplified things, Setadev. One man should not ever rule the entire populace."

"Ah, a quote from your father?" asked Setadev. "One that has become a solid piece of deity philosophy, for sure. Perhaps, however,

Kevin has not been so indoctrinated with your philosophy and will agree with me."

"You will not touch him," again Caitlin boldly stated, raising her hands in a defensive stance again. "If you want to get to him, you will have to go through me first."

To Caitlin's surprise, Setadev began laughing hysterically. "My dear girl," he began, "how little do you understand? I already told you I know he is not here. If I were coming for Kevin, I would not show up here. I have come for *you*."

Caitlin was confused. "Why?" she asked.

Setadev chuckled. "Because I already have the pure one."

Instantly, Caitlin's eyes widened, and her hands came to her heart. Were her worst fears really coming true? All she could think about was Kevin. She had been bluffing to Setadev about having to go through her to get to Kevin, knowing Kevin was in Solunar to track General Sayo. Had Setadev been two steps ahead of her? But worse yet, was Kevin in danger? Defiantly, Caitlin responded, "You won't be harming Kevin. I will make sure of that."

Setadev nodded. "If you say so, angel, but allow me to ask you a question. How can you stake such a claim when the pure one is in my control? How do you not know that I have harmed him already?"

"I may not know for sure, but I don't need to know until you're gone," answered Caitlin, as she appeared to charge more energy, "How do I know that you really have him, and you aren't bluffing?"

Suddenly, Setadev only smiled. "I set the trap that lured him out and caught him. After all, why else would someone walk out into the Wastes alone?"

Caitlin gasped. That was where Kevin was.

"Why else would someone stir havoc in the Wastes?" continued Setadev, seeking to explain, as well as rub salt into the wounds he was tearing open. "I could not care less about Desolunar, or the newly formed Solunar Empire. I could not care less about Aurana, Nuve, Scurnia, or Gardolk. The only cares I have are two things: revenge on the pure one and you, and conquest of the realms to fulfill my destiny to control reality."

"You'll never control reality," responded Caitlin.

“That may be what you say,” answered Setadev, “but regardless of what you believe for the moment, my entire operation out in the Wastes was designed to lure Kevin out.” He paused briefly. “General Sayo? He is my pawn. And just as he and I predicted, attacking out in the Wastes made Arthur Falchor, Emperor of the Solunar Empire, call for the pure one to help him. And just as I predicted, the pure one went out there alone. The setup was perfect, and the trap snapped.”

Caitlin shook her head in denial. “He wouldn’t go out there alone, not without me. You’re lying."

“Funny you would think that, because he did. You clearly do not know him as well as you think you do.” said Setadev. "The pure one is mine, angel. And if you will not crumble and submit to me so easily, maybe he will.”

That was the last straw.

“No!” screamed Caitlin. She blasted at Setadev with a strong beam of darkness magic.

Setadev had only a second to roll out of the way, but he did so with ease.

Seeing that she missed, she stopped. Caitlin turned o face her challenger. “Kevin would never succumb to you, not ever! Even if you have him as your prisoner, I promise you he is fighting you every step of the way!”

“He will soon enough,” scoffed Setadev. “If you so much as doubt that, then you are an overconfident fool. Perhaps a problem you have underlying, angel? You think you are strong, yet you have developed so much reliance on that boy that it borders on codependence, perhaps? You think he can do no wrongs?”

Caitlin said nothing, but tightened her fists.

Seeing this, Setadev glared into her eyes as he stepped forward. “Yes, angel, I do know of your fears. I can see right through you, and I can pierce into your aura and read all of its intricacies, far beyond anything that anyone else could ever know, even yourself. I can see all that you are, and everything that you can never be.”

Suddenly, Caitlin’s fists were shaking. Setadev was getting on her nerves, and was starting to get to her.

“I know you are upset,” nodded Setadev, cooling his voice as he approached Caitlin, "but I see no reason as to why you should be upset with me. All I have done is tell you the truth, and nothing more than that. If what you see is different from what I see, then it is time to forget what you know and move on. The future is arriving, and the end of the times of war is near. Soon, there will be peace and utopia, and there is nothing you can do to stop it."

Caitlin's eyes were stone cold. They were engaged in a steely glare at Setadev.

"Oh, does that bother you?" Setadev continued as he leaned in, getting right in Caitlin's face. "Are you worried? I can assure you that you have no need to worry, for everything will be all right, whether or not you are still alive by tomorrow. The world will keep moving, I can assure you of that. The future under me will be a good one."

Without warning, Caitlin smashed Setadev in the face with a burst of fire from her fist. It knocked back and blinded Setadev enough for Caitlin to hit Setadev with a beam of darkness magic. This time there was no dodging. Caitlin hit Setadev square in the chest, knocking him back and against the ground.

Setadev slid a long way backwards. Still, as Setadev was an immortal, even if in the form of Pseudo, Caitlin was sure that such a blow in no way was going to be fatal. Certain of this, Caitlin walked over to where Setadev had stopped, seeing that his eyes were wide open as he sat up from the ground. "The future is only good *for you* if I let you have your future, Setadev. No one else is better being under your thumb."

"And yet you failed to provide your alternative," breathed Setadev, trying to brush himself off as he stood up. Clearly, he was in pain; a first for Caitlin to have ever accomplished. There were even more scars across Setadev, and his golden robes were dirtied. "You have done nothing for 'everyone', despite all your best efforts. All you have done is tried to protect the pure one as an excuse to stay close to him."

"You can stop insinuating things, Setadev," Caitlin said firmly.

There was a moment's pause. Then, an awkward chuckle came from Setadev. "Are you actually listening to yourself?" he laughed, as he straightened himself up. "Look at yourself, angel. You are the daughter of Tyrinion. You have the blood of both mortal and immortal running through your veins. As I understand it, you used to have the peerless devotion to magic that would have made you great. And furthermore, you are an angel with power never seen before, by the mortal and the immortal." He paused for a second. "Now look at yourself. You have grown soft with emotion, just as you once feared you would. You are no longer the powerful being you were before; instead, you have been made weak by your peerless devotion and allowance of emotion to control your actions. Fear, passion, and uneasiness, all of these control you now. All of these make you irrational. You had so much potential, and the pure one forced you to throw it all away."

Caitlin stood with a defiant posture. "That's a lie!" she exclaimed. "Kevin never forced me to do anything. And I'm stronger because of him. What makes you human is what makes you stronger."

"Not true," smirked Setadev, without allowing even a second's pause. "What makes you stronger is the power you wield, and the ambition you have. Anything else is merely a distraction. Only the strongest are truly strong."

In response, Caitlin rolled her eyes. "Like you, right?" she asked in a frustrated tone. She should have figured that any verbal defense she had against Setadev's comments would never be taken by the fallen deity who had lived and plotted revenge for over five thousand years.

A glare showed again in Setadev's eyes. "Precisely," he said.

"Really, now?" asked Caitlin, charging up energy. "Then why don't we test that theory?"

Setadev chuckled. "Feisty, aren't we?" he asked. Then, he raised his arms. "Since words will not sway you, it is time for my action to do the talking."

It was time for the showdown. The duel.

Angel versus fallen deity. Surely one for the ages.

As was tradition in duel or showdown formats for fighting, whether by the sword, the arrow, magic, or by all three, Caitlin took up a battle stance. Hers favored a quick unleashing of magic, with one arm extended to shoot magic and another back for defense. Setadev took one as well, favoring another leaping forearm smash with both of his fists up and his right arm extended further than his left. They stood about ten steps from one another.

Whoever flinched first would signal the other to attack. The showdown would begin when one of them flinched.

For a moment, both of them stood as still as rocks.

There was no movement.

The silence seemed to continue forever. Suddenly, Setadev flinched. He moved so much it seemed deliberate.

Caitlin seized the opportunity, launching another beam of darkness. Hers would be the first shot. After a few seconds, she let down the beam, in order to observe the damage caused.

Setadev was still standing. He had deflected the whole beam.

Knowing what had happened, Caitlin knew she had no time to waste. She immediately started rushing toward Setadev, her arms charging light magic. Delivering her shot at point blank range would give him no chance to block it. As soon as she made it, however, Setadev ducked out of the way, and Caitlin had to stop herself as soon as she could.

That was Setadev's opportunity. He leapt and pummeled Caitlin with his forearm.

It was no ordinary smack. Setadev was charged with divine power, even if he was not in his most powerful form anymore. Caitlin was decked hard sideways, and she sailed right across the road into the side of Kevin's house. A visible dent in the wall, caused by the impact, was where Caitlin had finally stopped sliding.

For a moment, Caitlin was not moving as she stopped sliding. For another moment, there was silence. Setadev took up another battle stance, staring directly at Caitlin.

Within the next moment, Caitlin was moving around. Her fist tightened, as she slowly started to pull herself up the side of the house to a slumped position She was very scuffed up and appeared to be in pain. But she was alive at least, and not dead.

"So I was right," acknowledged Setadev aloud, as he watched Caitlin stand up. "You are immortal, after all. An interesting result, indeed. I had wondered which property, immortal or mortal, an angel would carry."

Caitlin was slumped against the wall, still on the ground. She was breathing hard, feeling completely decimated. A cut was on her forehead, bleeding moderately. Caitlin reached up and felt the cut, staining her hand with blood. She then took a look at the blood on her hand.

It was pink, a lighter hue than blood should be.

White was the color of the element of life. Although Caitlin did not know it, bleeding white was also a signature of immortals, as life ran more prominently in their veins than fire, the element that led to mortals bleeding red. She was bleeding a mix of the two colors. Likewise, it was also the first time she had been cut open in a very long time, the first that she had not healed one before it could bleed. As she stared at the blood on her hand, even though a million questions came to her mind, only one thing came out of her mouth as she looked back at Setadev. "That hurt," she said.

"I am sure it did," nodded Setadev. "Yet, believe me when I say that I will put you through much more pain than that." He started walking toward Caitlin again, this time brimming with confidence in his walk. "This day, however, is almost over."

Caitlin took a few deep breaths, still trying to catch it again. She was still trying to put everything together on what had just happened. "You deliberately flinched," she said.

"That is correct," acknowledged Setadev. "A completely legitimate move in showdown, although a dirty one at that. I knew what your first attack would be if I gave you the opportunity, and I read you correctly."

Infuriated, Caitlin tried to stand up. "Then what are you waiting for?" she demanded. "I'm still up for a second round!"

"Oh, my dear angel," responded Setadev, as he put his hand on Caitlin's shoulder and kept her down, "why continue? There is no need for a second round. You have already heard me say that I have the pure one already. Why would I need to get past you? You are my objective."

Still defiant, Caitlin answered, "Even if that is the case, I still will put an end to you."

And again, Setadev chuckled. "Your continued resistance amuses me, angel," he began, "yet I forgive you for it for now, because you do not see how the game is played. Your struggle to protect the pure one is admirable indeed, angel, and even I must admit that as foolish as such signs of devotion to a figure of futility are, devotion is a quality worth of recognition nonetheless."

Caitlin said nothing. She was too worn down to keep arguing.

"Yet your devotion is very poorly placed," continued Setadev. He was lightening his dark voice, in an odd and unusual way, although his tone still possessed some of its normal characteristics. "As a matter of fact, to tell you the truth, I feel sorry for you. Tell me, angel, is your relationship with the pure one solely based on the fact that he made you a more emotional person?"

Exhausted, Caitlin breathed heavily. "Of course not," was all she could say, all that she had breath to say.

"Oh really, now?" asked Setadev, still maintaining that somewhat lighter tone that he was using. Something seemed sinister about it, like it was not right. "I don't buy that for a moment. I believe that you need him more than he needs you, because he changed you in such a way that you are now codependent."

Caitlin was breathing heavily. She tried to resist, to stand against Setadev's pressure, but she had no energy to do so.

In a creepy manner, Setadev took his free hand and stroked Caitlin's hair. "Oh, but I suppose that is the innocence and purity that angels are said to have, is it not?"

Disgusted by Setadev's behavior, Caitlin did the only thing she could. She spit at Setadev in the face.

Taking his hand off of Caitlin's shoulder, Setadev wiped the spit from his face. "Persistent, aren't we?" he said. "Just like how you persist in putting up with that boy who is the 'pure one'. But let me tell you something." Setadev leaned in.

Caitlin's eyes widened as she felt helpless.

Setadev placed his free hand on the other side of Caitlin's head, and had both palms flat against her temples. His hands began to glow, as he spoke.

"He doesn't care about you. You mean nothing to him."

All of it hit like a thunderbolt all at once

"No!" Caitlin screamed as pulled herself to her knees, as Setadev stepped back. Instantly, tears were in her eyes. She cried for almost a minute. Everything had crushed her. Her teary eyes looked up at Setadev and exclaimed, "You're lying! You have to be!"

Setadev waved a finger across both of his eyes. "Look into them, and tell me I am lying."

Caitlin looked into Setadev's eyes. They were cold and steely. No flinching.

Immediately, Caitlin fell back to the ground, leaning all the way down. She became incredibly erratic. "No!" she exclaimed. "Why? Why? Why? Why? Why?" Her arms were pounding the ground, and her face was almost to it.

Another drop of blood fell from the cut on her head. Caitlin was still crying on the ground. In that moment, she felt her life, as she knew it, was destroyed. So much sadness was present.

Across from her, Setadev was still chuckling with an evil tone. He set his hand on the back of her shoulder again, although he did not lean down. "Such a tragedy indeed, but one that I find so interesting. It reminds me of an old poem once, a personal favorite of mine over the years." He paused for another second. "Now, how did it go again? Ah yes, now I remember. Shattered glass rains from the sky. Shattered glass, it rains so dry. It's cold and hard, an icy cry…" Setadev paused for a moment before continuing, as he looked directly down at Caitlin, "from the heart that only wants to die."

The words echoed in Caitlin's head. They were words she had kept in the back of her diary. Even while she was crying, those words haunted her.

Setadev chuckled again. "Well, now, I can see you might need some alone time," he began, sarcastically. "Therefore, I shall take my leave, so that you may have your time alone. I will come back for you when I feel like it."

There was a pause from Setadev. Caitlin was still crying.

"I will, however, give you one warning for now," he continued. "Do not, under any circumstance, come after the pure one. You will only find pain and destruction down that path. I do not wish to see the world's only angel destroyed when I forge my world, but if you try to resist me again, I will see it through." Then, Setadev wound another teleportation gate. "Until later, angel. When the world is mine, I will come back for you."

As Caitlin continued to cry, she lifted her head to look upon Setadev. He was walking through the teleportation gate.

And as quickly as it opened, it slammed shut again.

Silence filled the air.

The tears were still in Caitlin's eyes, as her head slunk down to the ground again. She could not resume her angel form. The doubt was now firmly planted in her mind. Whether or not it was the truth had little impact for now.

While she was still pounding the ground, so upset with herself, Kevin, and Setadev, Caitlin's necklace popped out of the neck space of her dress. She had kept it tucked in at all times, knowing what it had meant to her. Now that it had fallen out, however, she took the opportunity to reach for it and pull it off of her neck. She examined it carefully, remembering what it meant.

The actual string was simply that—a long yet normal piece of twine. Hanging from it was the real treasure. It was a little pink key, not of gold, or of silver. It was just a little piece. The bottom had a key stem, with the projections like any other key, but the head was molded into the shape of a heart. The whole key was shaped like a long, winding piece of the same thickness, save for the projections, which made a heart shape of the empty space in the head of the key, as well.

Caitlin had spotted this key in a jewelry store window in Aurana City, and Kevin promised to get it for her, in what was the greatest emotional gesture she had ever received before. Months later, Kevin had given her this key. This was a perfect symbol of their relationship together. Caitlin cried a little harder as she looked at this key. Regardless of the fact that she was holding this particular key, she was not sure if it meant anything anymore.

Another sad thought came to Caitlin's mind. Several months ago, she had promised and swore to Kevin, up and down, that she had alleviated any doubts about him in her heart. Now, she felt like she had lied to him. It was there again, worse than it had ever been before.

Breaking her promise to her beloved was not a good feeling.

The snow was starting to fall harder all around, and the road was starting to get snowed up again in a light coat. Knowing she had to get up and moving again before she was covered in snow, Caitlin managed to stand up and tried to dry her eyes. They would only get so dry, however.

Again, Caitlin stared at her necklace, wondering how much Kevin really did love her. She did know, however, that it was not going to be best for her to do nothing about it.

She needed help.

She needed someone who she could talk to. Her father could be someone, but who knew where he could be at this moment? Arthur and Rachel could be another, if they were not in Seta Archa, almost two weeks away on foot. And who knew where Kevin was, to talk with him directly? Setadev could have been lying about keeping Kevin captive, after all. If he was serious, then something even worse was happening.

Something had to change. Caitlin had to figure out what to do next, no matter what kind of frantic and depressing thoughts were going through her mind. Yet, despite this, Caitlin felt helpless. It was as if, in one fell swoop, all the excitement that had started this day off had been taken away, and in the same motion, her life was now wrecked.

Her father had to know Setadev was back. That had to be the first thing to do, to notify him. But where would he be? Magic could only carry her so far.

Teary-eyed as she could be, Caitlin pulled herself int Kevin's house, wondering if it was really her home anymore.

Chapter 12

Urgent Business

Tyrinion was in a panic. If Setadev was really still alive, then he was a greater danger than anyone could have ever imagined. The long-held belief that the gods had had about Kevin Trent Stryker was wrong. He and his Sword of Purity could not defeat the powerful founder of those who dare to call themselves gods.

No. That was too grim of a thought for him to have right now.

Regardless, he had to speak with the gods on this issue. That meant returning home—to the Realm of the Angels, where he had not been in over a century and a half. There was a lot of past animosity keeping him from returning home. With a leave of absence in hand, signed by Sarah Haughton herself, Professor Magnon waited for the late night to arrive, when the sky was dark and all of the torches around Bladinstar had been extinguished. Then, he rushed to the roof of the Bladinstar School. It had been a long time since he had done this. Using the abilities of his divine power, Tyrinion lifted himself into the air, and began to ascend higher and higher. As he reached into the sky, he passed clouds very quickly. Below him was the city of Bladinstar, sitting calmly against the dark background of the world.

This was a good feeling. Knowing that flight was impossible by mortals, Tyrinion had intentionally not used this particular power of his since he went into hiding. To use it again felt so energizing, so refreshing. He truly felt like a god again.

As Tyrinion went higher and higher, the night started to fade into daylight. It was not time for sunrise, though. Quite simply, Tyrinion was crossing over the line between the mortal realm and the Realm of the Angels. Remembering at what point he was, Tyrinion closed his eyes as he continued higher.

When he stopped, he opened them, to see a familiar yet heavenly sight. Golden clouds formed the ground below, but the sky itself was crystal clear. Only one building stood, and it was a large, seemingly infinitely high tower. This building was Angel Tower, shaped like a tall cylinder and constructed in white stone.

There was nobody around when Tyrinion looked around. That was a fairly typical appearance when the gods were busy with a project. Everyone would be inside the tower, probably working on one thing or another. As Tyrinion approached the stairs that led into Angel Tower, he saw one god standing on the top of the staircase. He appeared to be in contemplation about something, as he was staring off into the golden-cloud landscape. Instantly, Tyrinion recognized him.

It was Kronius, a messenger god. Not too long ago, Kronius had been trapped in the mortal realm and, going by his mortal name of Kron Kalavere, asked Kevin to help him get home. Instead of being able to help Kevin with that, however, he ended up helping Tyrinion for quite a while, upon request. During the whole trip, however, Kronius believed that he was talking to Professor James Magnon and thought that Tyrinion was the conqueror that needed to be stopped. All of the gods had, at the time, believed that the latter was true, until Kevin finally identified the professor as Tyrinion, and Tyrinion identified the conqueror as Setadev, all of which turned out to be true.

Kronius had lived only a few centuries so far. Because of this, and because of his induction into the gods after being chosen, he was in the lowest of the three *de facto* classes of gods: the original gods who traveled with Setaeus Demota to the Realm of the Angels, the immortal children of those gods, and those inducted since the originals into the gods. His third-class status also gave him only a low position, as a messenger god. Despite this, Kronius was looking to better himself ever since the Battle of Seta Archa, taking regular private lessons in magic and philosophy with Tyrinion. He hoped to grow his position by growing himself, and he found the lessons he had learned from Tyrinion to challenge the paradigms he had long believed.

As Kronius stood contemplating, he happened to glance down, and saw Tyrinion walking up the stairs. It was a surprising sight. "Oh my," he said, as he noticed. Instinctively, he asked as he recognized the professor's form, "Professor Magnon, have you finally returned home?"

"I have," nodded Tyrinion, "though I hesitate to call it home."

His red outer and black inner robes stood in stark contrast to those of Kronius, which were white with blue and green streaks. "It is an honor to see you again too, Kronius. Please forgive my unannounced intrusion."

"I would not consider it an intrusion," Kronius answered. "After all, you have welcomed me into your house in Wyntrail every week for lessons for the past three months. The least I can do is ensure your return to the Realm of the Angels is not treated as an intrusion, even if I know as much as not to roll out a red carpet for you."

Professor Magnon nodded. "It is appreciated. Certainly, you have grown much wiser in the past year."

Past year. Tyrinion was emphasizing not how long ago he and Kronius had last seen each other, but Kronius's total growth since starting to work with Tyrinion several months before. Kronius gave a slight bow, very appreciative of Tyrinion. "I would certainly hope so," he said. "I do believe, after all, that I have an excellent teacher who opened my mind to a great number of possibilities."

Tyrinion had little to say. He was not one to take praise very much, and only believed that he was doing his job when he was teaching. That was where his addiction to teaching others came from, the knowledge that others were learning because of him.

"What brings you back to the Realm of the Angels?" Kronius continued, in curiosity. "Have you finally decided to come back on a permanent basis?"

Shaking his head, Tyrinion answered, "No, Kronius. I have far more urgent business here, and I must speak with Ralios Larion immediately. Something has arisen that should not be."

Not one to take any warning from Tyrinion lightly anymore, Kronius immediately nodded. "Larion is in his office," he said. "If you would like, I can take you to him."

Again, Tyrinion shook his head. "No need to worry about that, Kronius. I am sure I remember my way there." He then turned, twisted a teleportation gate, and started walking through it.

As he walked through it, Kronius exclaimed, "Tyrinion, I am pretty sure that Larion would not want you to enter that way unannounced; that, he might consider an intrusion…"

The gate disappeared and Tyrinion was gone. Kronius rolled his eyes, knowing the professor tended to march to the beat of his own drum, and turned away to contemplate further.

Upstairs several stories, Larion was sitting at the desk in his elegantly decorated office. It was coated in gold all over, and even the desk was gold. The only thing not colored gold in the office was Larion himself, and his royal red robes that he wore. A large picture of Vinz Larinion hung at the other end of the room, as a salute to the man he once called his lord. Having existed for approximately three thousand years, Ralios Larion was the child of two lesser-known gods. He served as a god to royalty in his years of service, under the archetype of light. However, when Vinz Larinion decided to sacrifice himself to create the Sword of Purity, he chose Ralios, the very same god of royalty, to lead, sending shockwaves among the community of gods who expected Vinz Larinion to pick one of the original gods to be the king. In commemoration of Vinz Larinion, Ralios took the name of Larion, a name meaning "light of great power". This was meant to be a spin on Vinz Larinion's adopted twist on his last name, which translated to "light and father of great power". More often than not, Larion became his most common name in reference.

While busy writing some documentation for the official histories, the opening of a teleportation gate in his room completely startled Larion, who jumped back from his desk for a second. He stood up, preparing for his unwelcome visitor. Much to his surprised, out walked Tyrinion from the gate. Quickly, Tyrinion turned around and closed the gate.

"Do you not know how to knock?" joked Larion.

"Perhaps," answered Tyrinion. "Hello, Ralios Larion. It has been a while, has it not?"

"It has, Tyrinion," said Larion, as he approached Tyrinion and extended his hand. "A couple of months or so since we last spoke about affairs. Welcome back to the Realm of the Angels."

Tyrinion did shake Larion's hand. "Thank you," he acknowledged, "but I have no plans to stay."

Larion nodded. "I did not reason you would, Tyrinion. Still, as I have told you before, this is your home, and you are welcome here whenever you please. While you are here, though, is a change in wardrobe not in order?"

Reluctantly, Tyrinion acknowledged the request, not finding it necessary but not wishing to argue. "As you wish, my lord," he said, as he rolled his eyes. He then waved a hand over his robes, and the red outer robes he wore turned purple, with a black centerpiece on his front, in the shape of a square turned so the corners were pointing straight up, down, left, and right. The black inner robes were still black. Then, Tyrinion reached back and pulled a hair tie from the back of his robes, grabbed the numerous points of his slicked-back blond hair, lengthened them in the process, and bundled them in the tie, forming a small tail. His face also looked slightly younger as the effects of his divine power changed that. Though he still appeared to be in the typical middle ages of a mortal man, he looked about a decade younger than his previous appearance had. This was the Tyrinion everyone could recognize. This was the original appearance of the former god of darkness.

"Excellent," acknowledged Larion. "Now that is the Tyrinion I remember from my younger days here. Now, you are no longer simply Professor James Magnon."

"I suppose," answered Tyrinion reluctantly. He was used to his assumed name now and he felt as though it was his own. "My lord, for your own elder appearance, I had hoped you might treat things in a more mature manner than this."

Larion frowned for a second. Though his appearance was more elder than Tyrinion's, he was two thousand years younger. "Remember, Tyrinion, one must not forget about the simple pleasantries of life and the impacts they truly do have. Here you should be as you are, not behind your disguise."

"If you say so," answered Tyrinion skeptically.

Larion nodded. "I do say so," he said. "Now, let us get down to business. What brings you back to the Realm of the Angels today?"

Knowing that Larion was right about the business, whether or not he agreed about Larion's perspectives on life's pleasantries, Tyrinion took a deep breath. "Something awful," he began. "Lord Ralios Larion, there is a dark sensation blowing around the mortal realm."

"Blowing around?" questioned Larion.

Tyrinion nodded. "Literally. I have been studying the winds for some time, and I have noticed several odd peculiarities that are unnatural. All of these changes have come since Setadev fell three months ago. At first, they only seemed like odd winds blowing around periodically, and they would occasionally gain strength. And then, earlier tonight, the winds finally materialized into crosswinds, blowing contrary to their normal directions."

"Setadev's signal of his arrival," acknowledged Larion.

Surprised, Tyrinion responded, "You know of the signal?"

"I do," acknowledged Larion. "I have read Setaeus Demota's *Immortality is a Truth*, and I know of the messages he used to send. He would send the winds with his divine power to inform that he was planning to arrive somewhere. A wind blowing in the opposite direction was an old sign from the lore that change was coming, and Setadev modeled his signal after that."

Immediately respectful, Tyrinion bowed. "You are much more learned than I would have ever imagined, Ralios Larion. I can now see why Vinz Larinion chose you, and not an older god, to rule. You have the intangibles to become a greater god."

"Now, now," began Larion, raising his hands to the level of his eyes, "let us not get to that topic as of now. We can discuss that story on another day, Tyrinion."

"Agreed," nodded Tyrinion. "You can likely tell where I am going with my point. I fear that Setadev has returned again."

For a moment, Larion glared. His mind started racing with a new fear. Setadev. The one long mistaken for Tyrinion. The criminal who had tried to conquer all of the realms. A very bad thought came to Larion's mind. "One of the stories told to me from Kronius upon his return was that Vincent Stryker, the original pure one, struck a deal with Setadev for his own life, and we thought you… I mean Setadev, had been defeated then. Do you think Kevin did the same?"

Tyrinion ignored the comment about him, knowing that years of believing one thing when something else was true was going to be hard to shake for any of the gods. "Absolutely not," he finally answered, in complete confidence. "My daughter went with him into the realm below. She told me everything, in the complete truth. And, bear in mind, that Kevin did collect all of the Seven Stripes, and used them in defeating Setadev."

Larion nodded. "True," he said. "I do not mean to doubt Kevin at all by asking that question. Let us assume, then, that Kevin did defeat Setadev as your daughter described, by giving Setadev all seven of the stripes all at once, causing his body and the entire realm below to disintegrate. Is it possible that he would have planned for this, and had a backup plan in case something like this were to happen?"

"Heh, *a* backup plan?" scoffed Tyrinion. "My lord, if I know Setadev, he has likely had *many* backup plans since the day he began his conquest. The man is dangerous, Larion. He is aggressive, coldhearted, conceited, and vindictive, yet he is also devious, genius, and highly intelligent. Keep in mind, we still refer to his writings for a great many things."

"As I am aware," acknowledged Larion. Then, he straightened up and approached a little closer to the fallen god of darkness. "Tyrinion, you may know Setadev better than anyone. You are the one who pointed him out, five thousand years ago, as a danger to us all. I ask that you tell me, as no book can, what you know of Setaeus Demota. We must know if something is in that history that may help us assess the threat."

Quickly, Tyrinion sighed. "I dislike recalling this history, but I will for you," he said. "When I first met Setaeus Demota, I was not Tyrinion at all, of course. I was Tyrin Amtensen, master wizard. He was Setaeus Demota, zealot of the secret to immortality. As we know now, Setaeus Demota found the Stripe of Life, one of the Seven Stripes of the Elements, and used it to make himself immortal. Divine power came as a side effect to it, and the power he wielded in divinity made him incredibly strong. He gathered only the strongest he could, and that is why only a total of twenty became immortals.

"He then guided us to the pathway that led to the Realm of the Angels, blessed us with the same divine power that he had found the secret to—which we now know of as the Stripe of Life, one of the Seven Stripes of the Elements that is now missing—and began to form the power structure that we now know as the gods. However, as time went by, it seemed as though something was very odd about his behavior. To call it reprehensible would be an understatement. To call it maniacal would be to underestimate his genius and arrogance."

"I see," acknowledged Larion, gesturing to Tyrinion to continue.

Doing as he was instructed, Tyrinion continued. "Setadev often told us that we did not see, as he put it, 'how the game is played.' After he had brought us here, he would try to convince us that all of us were shortsighted and that because he was not, he should become the leader, a 'king' of gods. Though we still use the title today to maintain order, the way Setadev ruled was tyrannical. Had we not stopped him, he would likely be the ruler of the realms like he is trying to accomplish now." Tyrinion paused for a second. "We had no choice but to stop him, and I urged Vinz Larinion to strip Setadev of his immortality, which we then carried out. Yet perhaps we really were shortsighted, because we failed to do this and also failed to recognize that we were unsuccessful. I would guess that Setadev probably recognized at some point that we had failed, yet went into hiding after a short return to the mortal realm. It would seem to be reasonable that he did so in order to wait until we all had forgotten about him, so that he could then execute his plans for revenge and none of us could see him until it was too late."

Larion nodded. "It is fortunate that the pure ones came around when they did, then."

"Very," acknowledged Tyrinion. "I would have fought Setadev to the end, if need be, but I doubt I have the power to come close to him. There is something to be said about the pure ones, Vincent and Kevin Trent Stryker. They are not immortal, yet possess more resolve that most of us here."

Larion nodded. "Quite," he said. He then shifted back to business. "If he has returned, then we must find a way to silence Setadev for good. If he has truly survived such a blow that the pure one dealt to him, though, then it is likely that Setadev is currently in a weakened state. Perhaps the best mentality here is to strike when the iron is hot."

"My thoughts exactly," nodded Tyrinion. "On that note, Larion, I have a question for you. Have you heard of the *Letters to the Adventurer*?"

Shaking his head, Larion answered, "Not that I am aware of."

"You should be," snapped Tyrinion. "For all the cataloguing of prophecies that happen here, it is a set of prophetic poems."

Suddenly, Larion's eyes grew wider. "It is part of a series?" he asked.

"Indeed," nodded Tyrinion. "My daughter actually showed it to me, as she and Kevin found it with one of the stripes. Recently, I showed it to the headmistress of the school where I teach. She recognized it as one of a series of poems called the *Letters to the Adventurer*, written a few hundred years ago by a little-known poet named Clavius Lekion Stryker Dominous. Related to Kevin, perhaps?"

"Maybe," answered Larion. "Did you find any more poems?"

Tyrinion sighed. "Sarah went and found a poetry book, but it only had two poems in it by Clavius. Like I said, Clavius is not a well-known poet of history. Both poems were *Letters*, numbered one and two, although Sarah informed me that she knows more exist."

Larion shook his head. "I thought you did not believe in prophecy?"

"I do not," asked Tyrinion. "But I know you, and many of the gods, do. Perhaps you would be interested in this." He passed Larion a slip of paper.

As Larion unfolded it, it became clear that he was reading the second prophetic poem, the second of the series of *Letters to the Adventurer*:

The world moves in mysterious ways,
And the sky goes through cycles on all days.
Much is the same about the bad
Who walks around in darkness clad.
He uses the shadow to hide, protect,
And create masks to make others defect.
Beware the lure of protecting your friends,
Or else a curse he will hold over your heads.
He's gunning for you, but you he won't kill;
He prefers to snare and force into you a pill.
He'll change you, break you, destroy all you are,

Demolish your reputation near and far;
Then he'll take away the one you love,
Break hearts like dropping a glass dove.
And when you have nothing left, and he drains your regret,
You will become his most powerful asset.
A source of power has emerged, a powerful gate
From the seven powers' disintegrated fate.
Another dimension is open somewhere
And if he crosses the rift, all will despair.
Ancient weapons are all abound;
He knows them all, and will search 'til they're found.
Those who watch from above, overhead,
Will not be able to rest in their beds
Once the truths of all are revealed
And the Great Conqueror returns completely healed.
Begin will the greatest trial, as winter falls;
The two of you must prove that love conquers all.
Betrayal, pain, deception, sadness,
Endure them all and the Key will glow with happiness.
Only by love's triumph over adversity, over hate
Can access be granted to the transformation gate.
And if you two can finally become one,
The Great Conqueror will have no choice but away to run.

Larion set down the paper. "This one seems dark," he said. "Upon a general reading, the poem reads like a warning. Though its meanings are cryptic, I fear that there may be great danger on the horizon."

"I concur," added Tyrinion. "Especially now more than ever, I fear for my daughter's safety. If you presume that this prophetic poem is addressed to Kevin, I fear that something bad is going to happen to him."

"Then we must warn them," nodded Larion. "We owe that much to the pure one and your daughter, at least. They fought for us when no one else could, and they are still our best hope at defeating Setadev. Until he is defeated, the peace in the mortal realm will not last, and we will be forced to remain vigilant here in the Realm of the Angels. The conqueror must fall, for the good of us all."

Tyrinion paced around the room a little bit. "We need a plan of action, Larion."

Knowing what decision must be made, Larion stated firmly, "We must assemble the gods again. Let us collect a few ideas and decide on the most prudent decision as a group, so we may have the best one."

Crossing his arms, Tyrinion responded, "Contrary to what you believe, I do not think that democracy or consensus can help us here. However, it may be good to have a brainstorming session, if you believe that might work."

"It might," acknowledged Larion. "Let us convene the security council. That group would be the best ones to discuss the matter."

Although he was used to working on solutions by himself, Tyrinion could see Larion's rationale in this argument and thought that it could be reasonable. "Very well," he said. "About how long do you think it will take?"

For a brief second, Larion considered the mathematics. "If I signal everyone, it should take about an hour or two. We will likely hold the meeting in the meeting room. There are some gods in the mortal realm right now, so they will take the longest to arrive.

"All right," nodded Tyrinion. "Then, while we are waiting on them, I shall go and have a word with Vincent Stryker. Perhaps he knows something about Clavius that we do not know."

An odd look came to Larion's face. "Tyrinion, if you are so concerned about your daughter and the pure one, why not head to them first? I understand your business-first mantra that you live by, but in this instance I would think that it would be much more appropriate if you went to them first to be assured of their safety."

"I will be doing that when I arrive," he said. "My daughter and the pure one live in Rikleifer, Aurana, where Vincent Stryker also currently resides. As I deal with things in Rikleifer, I can verify their safety."

Larion nodded. "Okay," he said, "but I have a better idea. Bring them with you. All three of them: Kevin, Caitlin, and Vincent.

They have all been here before, and it would give us a chance to show them the poem. Furthermore, if Setadev is still out there, then they should know of his presence."

"Very well," acknowledged Tyrinion. "I agree with that suggestion. They all can be of help." Then, without skipping a beat, Tyrinion turned for the door, but instead of heading for it, spawned another teleportation gate. "I will be back in about an hour or two, in time for the meeting. Until then, farewell."

"Hey! Tyrinion, wait for a..."

Too late. Tyrinion had already walked through the gate and closed it.

Typical, Larion thought to himself as he shook his head. That was just like Tyrinion: always about the business first. It was enough that he had forgotten about all of the pleasantries of life.

Or perhaps not. He did seem to have a close watch on his most valuable pleasantry of all. Caitlin was always on his mind, and he did desire to protect her no matter what penalty would come first.

Either way, Tyrinion was always going to be welcome in the Realm of the Angels. Larion knew that given the opportunity, Tyrinion could be a dangerous individual just like Setadev, but the former was so much more reserved than the latter. Quite simply, Tyrinion just did not have the dark ambitions in him to do it. He was much more concerned with keeping things in good shape than trying to contort the world to his own visions.

Larion had to get started, and he knew it. Quickly, he activated the recall beacon using his divine power, and then walked out of his office. He had a meeting to plan, and a room to help set up.

Chapter 13

A Darker Truth

On top of the castle in Rikleifer, Vincent Stryker was once again practicing his swordplay. He was on the turret of the northwest tower, swinging his sword in all directions. He did it with such smoothness and grace that one might not be able to distinguish his swordplay from a ballet.

Vincent Stryker was still trying to rehabilitate his back. Over the years, he had damaged his spine, made worse by the fact that he spent over a decade living in a cave without any medical care. In a sense, he had fallen from grace. No longer was he in the shape of the legend that he supposedly was. Had it not been for the fact that he had come out of retirement and returned to society to help his son Kevin, he would have truly been seen as such.

The day was cold and snowy. Under his old tattered Scurnian war uniform, he was wearing thick padded clothing. Though usually used in defense to help protect against sword slashes, Vincent was using them to stay warm in the cold winter weather. He had them tight around his limbs and wore gloves and heavy boots, in order to keep himself well insulated.

Around and around Vincent flipped his sword. He was spinning it in circles in front of him. Every move was elegant, yet quick. Thrust behind. Spiral around to a forward strike. Upward throw, and grab to pound to the ground.

A vortex sound came from behind Vincent. One that he heard.

Kneel to the ground, and flip around to thrust upward in the opposite direction, toward the vortex sound.

Right into the face of Tyrinion, who had his hands raised.

"Easy, Vince," said Tyrinion, in a slightly frightened tone. "You don't need to be quite so paranoid."

Realizing who he was looking at, Vincent Stryker sheathed his sword again, and stood up. "Tyrinion. I am sorry to point my sword at you, but what brings you here today?"

Tyrinion thought little of the sword being pointed at him, although he did find this reaction out of Vincent Stryker to be odd. "Unfortunately, a lot does, old friend. I hate to trouble you while you are recovering, but I must speak with you right away."

Vincent finished sheathing his sword, and spat at the ground. "Recovery? Is that what we're calling it now?"

For a moment, Tyrinion was confused. "Well… yes, that is what you have been here for, is it not? That is why I came here to find you, because my daughter had told me the Duke of Rikleifer had taken you in."

Now, Vincent rolled his eyes. "Then this is some brilliant idea of recovery, huh? If the reason I am here is simple recovery, then you or your daughter could have healed my back with your magic some time ago. No, Tyrinion, I am not here for recovery. I am here because the Duke of Rikleifer does not want me to disappear again."

"Pardon me for asking, but I fail to understand why you accepted his offer, then," asked Tyrinion. "You seem to be so upset about this, yet it was your decision to come here and live under the care of the Duke."

Raising a hand up a little bit, Vincent answered back, "That was only so I could live closer to my son. Still, the Duke's strict regiment is not what I signed up for, and furthermore if I were to leave the castle, I would have to go far away or the Duke would try and bring me back in."

Seeing that Vincent was irate, Tyrinion asked, "You have never been bothered by seeing me before, and yet I sense your rehabilitation here is not the true source of your anger. Why are you so upset to see me?"

There was only silence for a second.

Then, Vincent stared directly into Tyrinion's eyes. "Why didn't you come to see me, Tyrinion? I have spent three months in this asylum. We lived together through a great number of things, and survived because of each other. Our children even love each other. If I am really the 'old friend' that you called me earlier, then you would have come to see me here. Heck, I don't even know if I should call you Professor Magnon or Tyrinion"

Looking into Vincent's eyes, Tyrinion could see that this was only part of the frustration of the tired warrior. Still, he could tell it did nag on Vincent Stryker quite a bit. Years before, Tyrinion, in the guise of Professor James Magnon, had helped Vincent Stryker a lot through his trials in the aftermath of the savage war. Then, he was inextricably tied back into Vincent's life as the old general's son dared to challenge Setadev, the conqueror. As Vincent had struggled through so much mental strain, especially after his failure at the very end of the savage war, it had been Tyrinion who had helped him survive through it all.

Still, business before pleasure, after all.

"I do apologize," Tyrinion decided to answer. "You can call me James, if you like. I think that would be fitting of old friends."

Silently, Vincent nodded, as he looked out upon Rikleifer.

Tyrinion continued, "I have been busy, very much so, recently. In fact, it is because of this business that I have come to see you today. I need your help."

"Setadev survived, didn't he, James?" asked Vincent.

Tyrinion was absolutely stunned. "How did you figure that out? I fear such is the case."

"Then you have undoubtedly felt it too," Vincent Stryker answered. "The dark crosswind, the one that is always present when he is about to arrive. I have felt it before when I was preparing to confront him the first time. I felt it a couple of weeks ago, but I could not understand what it was, other than that it gave me a premonition of dread. Today, I remembered where I had felt it before."

"Indeed, I have sensed the same," acknowledged Tyrinion. "I have also taken the matter to Ralios Larion, king of gods, and he agrees with me. We will be meeting in an hour or so to discuss matters."

Vincent nodded. "I am glad someone else has picked up on this, then. What help do you need from me?"

Tyrinion paused for a second. "Does the name 'Clavius Lekion Stryker Dominous' sound familiar somewhere in your family tree?"

"Not as far as I am aware of," answered Vincent. "Then again, my knowledge of my family tree is actually very slender. I did not grow up with a father, so any knowledge of that might have died with him."

That was not the response Tyrinion was hoping for. "Then this may be a more difficult connection to establish," he said. "Vincent, it is important for me to let you know this. Although you know I am a skeptic when it comes to matters of prophecy, I believe that I may have stumbled on a series of poems that could be a prophecy related to Kevin. The coincidences between the writing and actual events so far are too great to ignore. The series was written by someone named Clavius Lekion Stryker Dominous a few hundred years ago."

"So that is why you asked that question," realized Vincent. "If that is the case, then have you discovered the whole series?"

Tyrinion shook his head. "No," he said, "but I did find a second poem. The gods will be discussing it in the meeting. I am planning on taking you with me, if you would be willing to return to the Realm of the Angels."

"Me?" asked Vincent.

"Yes," nodded Tyrinion. "And your son and my daughter, too. If Setadev is back, then it impacts all of us as much as it does the gods. If there is another prophetic poem, then Kevin needs to hear it, too."

Vincent Stryker sighed. "Then you are going to have a problem. My son and your daughter left town a couple of weeks ago. They said they were headed to Seta Archa, because Arthur Falchor sent them a letter asking for help."

Now, Tyrinion was stunned. Though he knew his daughter Caitlin was very independent and would do as she wished, he thought for certain that Caitlin would have told him if she and Kevin were going anywhere for an extended period of time. Then, a thought came to him, the realization of what day it was. Today was Caitlin's sixteenth birthday, and that meant that she would be here in town to register for adulthood. Tyrinion did not think his daughter would want to deal with the late registration penalties, if given the choice. If she was here, then it would be likely, more or less, that Kevin was in town as well.

Realizing this, Tyrinion told Vincent about this. "We may want to check by Kevin's house, then," he said after explaining the situation about his daughter's birthday. "You know how Kevin and Caitlin are.

They are inseparable. If they came back for Caitlin's birthday and registration, then they might be here in town."

"I wonder why they would not have visited me, then," added Vincent. "My son usually does whenever he is in the castle."

Tyrinion looked up at the sky for a second. Though it was very cloudy and snow was falling, he could tell it was still the early evening. "Perhaps they have not come to register Caitlin yet," he answered. "There is still some time left before the offices inside close for the day."

Vincent thought about it for a second. "Then let's go to find out if they are here, shall we?" He straightened the cuff on his jacket. "I am pretty sick of this place, anyway."

Nodding, Tyrinion headed for the trap door and pulled it up. "It is a nice day for a walk, is it not?"

For a moment, Vincent looked up, then looked down at the ground outside of the castle. Then, he looked directly at Tyrinion. "Your sense of humor is terrible, James," he said.

Tyrinion only smiled and nodded. Knowing he was in the presence of Vincent Stryker, and now knowing Vincent had some attachment issues to him, he recognized that in this case, it was important to keep a lighter spirit for Vincent. Though Tyrinion was very business motivated, he did know there were times to have emotion, both for business and for himself.

Together, Tyrinion and Vincent walked through the castle, and were out of the gates within a few minutes. They then headed across the west road, toward Kevin's house. As Rikleifer was designed in concentric circles with several roads crossing the diameter, and the castle was in the exact center of the city, the west road was connected directly to the castle. It was still a cold and snowy day outside, and the ground was frozen all around. A coat of snow was everywhere. The walk would take a short while, as Kevin's home was closer to the edge of Rikleifer than it was to the center.

To Vincent, though, things were a little too familiar. He began, with a slight sense of awkwardness, "Tyrinion, I should let you know that I have not been to Kevin's home since I have been here. In fact, I have not been to the home at all since I was living with Lavinia, more than a decade and a half ago."

“Afraid you might trigger some reminiscent memories?” Tyrinion asked.

Vincent gave a slight nod. “Maybe,” he said. He pulled out his katana as the two of them continued walking. “Lavinia Trent meant a lot to me, old friend. It was more than just a time frame that resulted in my son. After I put down the Sword of Purity, I didn’t carry a weapon during the whole time from then until I left Rikleifer. When I had one made for me,” he said as he pulled up his sword to show Tyrinion, “it seemed only natural that I had to name the sword for her.”

“I bet she was special,” acknowledged Tyrinion. “I know the feeling myself. The way you talk about Lavinia Trent reminds me a lot of Christine Falchor, Caitlin’s mother. That same special feeling can last, even after short relationships.”

“Mhmm,” said Vincent. “When I felt the dark crosswinds, earlier, it took me a while to connect them to where I had felt them before. It was the same wind that was present in Rikleifer shortly before I left. I felt them… felt his presence again. He knew where I was, and he knew that he had no reason to keep me alive. That’s why I left… I loved Lavinia, and I wanted so badly for us to raise our new son together, but if Setadev knew where I was,.I was afraid he would come after Lavinia and Kevin too. So I had to flee, run back to my homeland of Scurnia.”

“I see now how you recognized it,” Tyrinion said. “A darker truth than I had believed at first, yet at least it allowed you to identify the odd winds.” He paused for a second. “Speaking of Lavinia, out of curiosity, allow me to ask you how you met Lavinia Trent. Since you were from Scurnia, even if you were born in Rikleifer, Aurana, how did you end up here after the savage war?”

Awkwardly, Vincent chuckled, as he prepared to recall his past. “Well, I guess you could say that I was pretty tired of war after the end twenty years ago. I was very depressed after my failure to defeat Setadev, even though the battle in Seta Archa was a complete success, so I decided to leave the army and follow my newfound friends Eukert, Bryant, and Sayo home to Aurana. It seemed like a good idea to get away from everything for a while, and maybe give myself an opportunity to clear my mind of everything that had happened. After all, since I was born in Rikleifer but had no memories of the city, it seemed like a fun little trip to take to return to where I came from."

"You are fortunate the Scurnian army did not charge you with desertion," stated Tyrinion.

"Oh please, James, I may have resigned my commission to them anyway, but I could have deserted and they would have chosen to do nothing to me. The public relations disaster in Scurnia would be tremendous, after that battle and everyone knew what I did to win it."

Tyrinion nodded. "Fair enough. Go on."

Vincent continued, "On our way to report back to Aurana City, we stopped over in Rikleifer. That's where I met Lavinia, in the offices in the castle. We had stopped by there to check in, as the nearest military office was there with Atwals being destroyed, and it was there that I saw her. She was working as a scribe in there, copying down records. She was so friendly… and that was the best thing I remembered about her when we first met. So, I left my sword with Commander Eukert and started living my new life with Lavinia. We lived together for quite a while, and we did all right. I took on some handyman work to make a living in Rikleifer, and that let us live well. We were planning on getting married at some point, but when I found out that Lavinia was pregnant, we had to readjust our plans a little bit so we could be sure we had enough money to raise Kevin. So, we decided to put it off." He paused for a second. "Later that year, around this time of year, actually, Rita Falchor moved down the street from us. She was one of Lavinia's childhood friends, and so was Rita's sister, Christine. I only wish we had seen Christine more often before she passed away."

Tyrinion nodded. "By that time, Christine was already in my care. Had the two of you met with Christine more often, it is likely that we would have met earlier than we actually did. We did not meet for another couple of years, by the time you were in Scurnia, as I recall."

"You recall correctly," answered Vincent. "Still, it baffles me that when Rita moved in, she called Arthur 'her child', and furthermore that neither Rita nor Christine never told us that Rita's son was actually Christine's. We know now, of course, that Arthur was really Christine's son, yet Rita was always persistent that Arthur was her son."

Contemplatively, Tyrinion thought for a second. "I can think of two reasons for the first part, and perhaps one for the second. Rita, as you know from all that you know about her, was an alcoholic, and she may have forgotten the truth. After all, if Arthur is to be believed, she still is one. Or, perhaps, Rita believed she had adopted Arthur into her family, and in that way he was her son. Christine knew that Rita had possession of Arthur, even though Demonicus himself failed to make that connection when he gave Arthur away to be raised outside of Desolunar. She told me she was planning to retrieve him someday when she thought Demonicus would not be following her anymore, but we never reached that point before Christine died."

Vincent nodded silently, himself quite familiar with that story by now. "A terrible tragedy," he acknowledged. There was a slight pause Vincent gave before he started again. "Anyway, to continue the story, Lavinia gave birth three or four months later, and Kevin was born in the springtime. We registered him together, and signed the certificates, and all of that. When the winds came to haunt me, though, I told Lavinia that I had to leave, and she understood. I also made it clear to her that I wanted Kevin to think that his father had died before he was born, so that way he would not grow up with the shame of having been abandoned by his father. I guess someone told him about me, though." After that, he glared at Tyrinion.

Tyrinion rolled his eyes. "Kevin needed to know," he said. "We needed it as leverage in overthrowing King Arnold IX. Everyone knows the story of the Sword of Purity and that no one other than you can hold it. Showing he could showed a lineage that one might consider noble." He was ignoring the fact that Arnold IX did not consider it as such, but the end results were secured anyway.

"I know," acknowledged Vincent. "It was the way it had to be. You are a good friend, James. I believe that everything worked out the way it should."

Giving no verbal response, Tyrinion nodded.

Kevin's house was at the corner in front of them. Tyrinion and Vincent walked up the road to it, noticing the puffs of smoke coming out the top of the house. The stove in Kevin's small kitchen was burning, providing heat for the house. It was a sign that someone was there.

Tyrinion walked up to the door, and attempted to turn the handle. The door was locked. "They locked the door," he said to Vincent, as both of them stood in front of the door. "Maybe they are out and about somewhere."

"Could be," said Vincent. "Left the stove on to keep the place warm?"

"Probably," answered Tyrinion. "Would you want to come home to a cold house when it's this cold out here?"

Vincent chuckled. "No, I don't think so at all," he said.

Suddenly, the piercing sound of crying ripped through the air.

Tyrinion and Vincent looked at each other. "Did that just come from inside the house?" asked Vincent.

Nodding, Tyrinion said, "I will get the door." Then, before Vincent could even react, he opened a teleportation gate and went through, appearing on the other side of the door. Then, he opened the door from the inside. He moved so quickly and so seamlessly that there was no delay or wait at all.

"Don't you know there's such a thing as knocking on a door?" asked Vincent, reluctantly shaking his head after the door had been opened. "Besides, Kevin gave me a spare key to this house."

Hushing Vincent, Tyrinion responded quietly, "The crying is coming from the far bedroom. Let us find out what is going on before we worry about the door."

Quietly, Vincent acknowledged as he shut the door behind him. He then followed Tyrinion to the far bedroom, taking caution not to make too much noise just yet. In the bedroom, though, was a surprising sight.

Lying on Kevin's mother's bed, curled up to herself, was Caitlin. She was crying while clutching the blankets of the bed tightly. Her face was in the pillow. Never before had Tyrinion seen his daughter so upset. This was a new, and scary, experience.

Seeking not to startle his daughter with his surprise presence, Tyrinion let out a mental signal that he knew Caitlin would receive. The message was, *turn around, I am here for you.*

A couple of seconds later, Caitlin rolled over and lifted her head from the pillow to see her father. Her eyes were puffy and soggy, showing that she had been crying for quite some time. Though her father looked significantly different than he had ever appeared to her before, she still recognized him as her father. She reached her free arm up, as if asking her father to hug her.

In response, Tyrinion leaned down and hugged his daughter. He stayed held to her as she clutched tighter. "I am here for you, Caitlin. I will always be here for you, my daughter."

Caitlin kept crying, but it did make her feel better to have her father with her. "Thank you, father," she said, as another tear rolled down her face. She swung her body around, so she could stand up. As soon as she did get up, though, she went right back to hugging her father.

Knowing that Tyrinion and Caitlin needed a father and daughter moment, Vincent Stryker turned and headed out of the bedroom. With the room to themselves, Tyrinion loosened his hug, and looked at his daughter, straight into her teary eyes. "Why are you so sad?" he asked, with an honest and sincere tone.

The tears were still rolling from Caitlin's eyes. She struggled to make any words come out. All that emerged from her crying were fragmented syllables from each time she tried to start a sentence.

"It is okay, Caitlin," said Tyrinion compassionately, as he angled his forearms higher to place his hands on the side of his daughter's head while she continued to hug him and cry. "You do not have to say a word. Just please, let me in so I can see for myself and help you."

Caitlin said nothing. She continued to cry, but let her father place his hands on her head. She knew he was asking to read her mind, and it was only ethically acceptable to do so with permission. She felt it would be easier this moment than talking.

Unleashing the intricate webs of light and darkness magic that allowed for mind reading, Tyrinion closed his eyes and started to view the inner thoughts of his daughter. As long as Caitlin did not resist, he would be able to read everything. It was a technique that he had used many times before.

Inside Caitlin's mind was a gigantic sense of loss and sadness. Tyrinion had never seen this in his daughter at this level before.

Everything was playing out in her head for the professor, allowing him to catch glimpses of what had been happening.

He saw Kevin venturing out on his own from Seta Archa, leaving Caitlin behind. He saw her return to Rikleifer on her own, knowing that her registration had to happen. He saw someone appear and attack her. He heard that person say that he had Kevin as his prisoner. He heard that person tell her something to tear her apart. Instantly, he looked around elsewhere, and found all of the damage that had been done.

Horrified, Tyrinion stopped using magic and opened his eyes. "Who did this to you?" he asked. He was afraid he knew the answer to that question.

Instead of answering, Caitlin turned over and cried even harder.

"Shh, shh," the professor attempted to quiet his daughter. "It will all be all right." Tyrinion attempted to reassure his daughter, as he tried to focus himself back into taking care of her first. "Did Setadev put his hands to the sides of your head?"

Caitlin said nothing. Her crying was loud.

Tyrinion connected the dots, based on the images he had seen in Caitlin's head. Not only was Setadev back, it seemed, but he was also going after those who had brought him down. Tyrinion was not sure, however, if Setadev was doing so simply for revenge, or if he had considered Caitlin a danger to him.

Taking a peek out the door to the room, Tyrinion took a quick consideration of all the time that he had spent in the mortal realm since leaving the Realm of the Angels. Then, he turned back to his daughter. "Caitlin," he began, taking a brief pause as he sympathized with her, "I promise you we will fix this. Setadev hit you with a mental shatter spell. I can fix this, but I need you to let me work on this. It could take me hours to repair the damage he's done."

In her crying fit, Caitlin gently nodded as she lay on the bed.

With this response, Tyrinion called to Vincent Stryker. When Vincent arrived back at the door, Tyrinion met him there, refusing to let him see Caitlin.

"Is she going to be all right?" asked Vincent Stryker, as he looked down at Caitlin.

"Physically, yes, although she's visibly injured," answered Tyrinion. "Mentally, I am not so sure. That said, it would seem from this whole incident that your son may have been captured by Setadev, if you trust Setadev's own words."

Though Vincent was nervous of anything happening to his son, he knew as well as Tyrinion did to be very wary of anything Setadev said. "What happened?" he asked, unsure of what was going on.

"It would seem that Setadev attacked my daughter," answered Tyrinion again. "For that alone, I swear I will destroy him. He did something so inhumane to her…" Tyrinion caught himself in his anger, and calmed down. "In any case, our worst fears are true. Setadev is indeed back again."

Again, Vincent frowned. "Then what made Caitlin so upset?" he asked, confused. "I still am not quite sure that I understand."

"He told her that he captured your son, and that your son does not care for her," answered Tyrinion. "But before we jump to conclusions, I believe that was accompanied by a shatter spell. It is a kind of magic that destroys the psyche and can make one unable to control themselves mentally or emotionally. This is an ancient magic, one so old that I have not see it used for thousands of years." He paused for a moment. "Setadev knows what kind of power my daughter has because of her connection to your son. I believe he tried to break it."

Vincent Stryker was awestruck. "We had better find Kevin as quickly as we can."

Agreeing with Vincent, Tyrinion turned to his daughter. "We do," he said, "but we have things to do first. I need to repair Caitlin's psyche; it could take me hours to do so. Then, we need to tell the gods that Setadev is back."

Nodding, Vincent acknowledged.

"Do you know where your son went?" Tyrinion then asked. "How would Setadev have isolated him from Caitlin?

"Kevin and Caitlin received a request for help from Arthur Falchor of the Solunar Empire," explained Vincent. "It sounds like they were having trouble with attacks from an Auranian traitor turned Desolunar general named Sayo."

Instantly, Tyrinion glared back at Vincent. "Friend of yours?" he asked. "I can only presume so based on the way you described him."

"Used to be," answered Vincent. "Also one of Desolunar's top generals in the last war. He had a showdown with myself and our old war buddies at the Battle of Seta Archa, which we won, but we couldn't kill him. And Kevin would have…" The realization that Tyrinion was touching on with the pointed question just hit Vincent, "known that."

Tyrinion nodded. "Perfect bait," he said. "I have a bad feeling about this. I think someone may have set up Kevin to be snared. Whether or not Setadev has him, Kevin is in danger."

Chapter 14

The Silent General

From the shadows, they carry light.

Out of the darkness, they gleam. Yet, they remain in the shadows.

In *rengan,* their saying was *Wondamer Notuerew.* Translated, it meant "negation of glory".

This was the saying of the Enlighteners from the Shadows, an ancient group with almost five thousand years of history. Established by Setaeus Demota as a means of maintaining a foothold in the mortal realm before going into hiding in the realm below, the group spent much of its time destroying ancient relics and knowledge in order to prevent their master from having any ancient weaponry or knowledge used against him. Of course, none of them knew this real purpose, and believed only that by eliminating the past could they continue to move on into the future.

Within Setadev's current entourage of troops and assembled factions were many such Enlighteners. They were easily identifiable by their dark red robes, each with a hood that was usually worn in such a way as to obscure the eyes, and a gold chain with a tag containing the initials "WN" on their necks, standing for *Wondamer Notuerew*.

Little was really known about them to most in the mortal realm, and that included the old troops of Desolunar that served Setadev. General Sayo himself had no idea who the Enlighteners were or what they were capable of, but he was determined to find out.

Currently, the entire wasteland camp was being packed up for the move to the fortress. The pure one had been secured, just as Setadev had wanted. It was time for the next steps to take effect.

Martin Sayo continued to ask himself what those next steps were. Much as Sayo spoke little except to those he served under, he did have a great deal that he considered. Once considered to be one of

Aurana's great military geniuses, as opposed to his former friend War Commander "Ironman" Eukert's powerful charisma, Sayo had risen to the rank of commander very quickly in Aurana. Upon the end of the savage war, however, Sayo spent much time contemplating his future, and after talking it over with his friends, he decided to take the same route as fellow friends Vincent Stryker and John Bryant, and retire from the military. They had all had enough war for a while. Only Eukert stayed with the army.

Sayo retired to his hometown of Atwals, where a few years later, the city was attacked and burned to the ground. The once valiant commander was then captured, but offered an interesting deal by a younger Demonicus, who allowed him to serve in the Desolunar army. Sayo accepted, in order to protect his own life and those of his family. Over time, Sayo's brilliance quickly shined bright, and Demonicus promoted him as far as to make the general his left hand man. Only Pseudo stood higher, as Demonicus's right. After years of serving, Sayo had become completely loyal to Desolunar, and was not afraid in the least of attacking his old homeland, even units led by his old friend, Eukert.

After a showdown defeat at the Battle of Seta Archa a few months ago, Sayo retreated into the Wastes with his men, and headed north to the Calphos River to find suitable ground that could support his men. He realized as he left that Seta Archa was lost, and decided not to return. On the banks of the Calphos, however, Sayo ran into Pseudo again, who disclosed everything about his true identity: Pseudo was a fragment of the once great fallen god, Setadev.

A fearsome sight on the battlefield, Sayo had served without question under the man he now calls his master. However, as time had gone by, more and more questions without answers were arising.

As Sayo collapsed the command tent while his men were working on packing up their supplies, an Enlightener approached Sayo. He was dressed as any Enlightener was, in the typical red hooded robe. Sayo only glanced at the Enlightener, to acknowledge his presence, before turning back to his work.

"I understand that you wish to know more of the Enlightener ways," said the Enlightener, in a fairly deep voice. "Our leader has told us so. He has mentioned how you have expressed your curiosity."

Sayo said nothing.

The Enlightener, however, had an understanding of General Sayo. He knew not to be offended by Sayo's lack of remarks. "Your silence speaks to me," he continued. "Our leader is very much like our inspirational founder. He sees more than man could possibly ever see. He has seen from you a similar greatness."

Again, Sayo said nothing, and made no reaction.

"Do you have a desire, my general?" asked the Enlightener. "A dream, perhaps? You will find that much is possible when you become one of the Enlighteners from the Shadows, and swear the oath. There is a great imbuement of power that comes from the brotherhood that can make you powerful."

In response, Sayo turned his head for a second, then turned it back to continue his work.

"Ah, so does power drive you, General?" asked the Enlightener upon seeing this reaction to his last comment. "I can see it within you, brother. You are already a powerful individual. If you will learn with us, we can help you to harness that power and become truly great."

Sayo continued to work.

It was then that Setadev, having returned from where he had gone before, stepped up behind the Enlightener, causing him to pause. Sayo, however, did not budge.

"Why, Master, I did not expect you to return so soon," the Enlightener said while completely stunned. He had been caught off guard.

"Spare me of it," responded Setadev. "You know of my power. I am the reincarnation of Setaeus Demota himself, and as such, I have all of his powers. Could you not assume that I would know of ways to travel quickly and finish my businesses in all due speed?"

"Yes… I mean no… I mean…" stuttered the Enlightener, trying to find the correct answer to this question, "I mean of course I knew you could. Your presence at this moment, however, has surprised me."

Setadev put his hand in his face, almost in shame. "Whatever," he said. "As I know you intend your loyalty and belief, I will not do anything to you for now. Are you bothering General Sayo?"

"Of course not, sir," answered the Enlightener, putting a little more confidence into his voice. "I was only doing as your intentions were, sharing the glory of the Enlighteners from the Shadows with our mighty General Sayo. After all, how can he truly share the enlightenment we all find in you without understanding the Enlightener philosophies?"

Setadev glanced over at General Sayo, who turned around to face him. Sayo only stared as a response. Using this, Setadev turned back toward the Enlightener. "Leave him be for now," he instructed. "General Sayo speaks only to those he respects. If he does not answer you, then he does not respect you. Should he decide to become an Enlightener, he will do so on his own. It matters little to me whether or not he adopts the principles."

The Enlightener nodded awkwardly. "Yes, sir," he said, as he turned and walked away. There was nothing else to discuss.

As the Enlightener walked away, Setadev then approached General Sayo, who was still packing down his command tent. When Setadev was only a slight distance from Sayo, the general turned to face his master. "You may rest easy," began Setadev. "My Enlighteners do tend to be a little forceful with their wishes. Still, their order is a powerful pillar of support for our troops."

Sayo began walking with his master around the command tent. "I do not see how," he said. "They seem to be a distraction."

"Ah, I am sure that they do for now," answered Setadev. "To you, I would presume that they seem like religious fanatics. And that is because they are. They worship the ground on which I stand. Yet this fanaticism is useful in quite a few aspects. Because of the beliefs I have instilled in them, they have found a great deal of ancient technology and knowledge. Most of this has been destroyed so it cannot be used against me."

"Part of the scheme," nodded General Sayo.

In response, Setadev shook his head. "No," he said. "Not a part of the scheme at all. Part of the backup plan, general. Bear in mind that you are the only one here who knows my true identity and story, and even the Enlighteners do not realize that I am their true founder."

"Indeed," nodded General Sayo, knowing the truth of Setadev.

"I presume your trip was a success?"

Setadev nodded. "It was," he answered. "The angel should not be a threat to us for quite some time. I do fear her power, Sayo, and it is only her that I fear."

Sayo raised an eyebrow, but said nothing.

"I have theorized, through research with divine power and its effects, that the angelic form of divine power might possibly be incompatible with immortal divine power," continued Setadev. "If such is the case, then her power could be devastating to us."

For a second, Sayo looked away. "I do not understand," he said.

"Of course you do not," interrupted Setadev, "because when it comes to the immortal and divine-related affairs, you do not see how the game is played. However, it is only fair, as you would not understand even if I told you everything. Such information for someone in your position would only be trivial and pointless."

General Sayo shrugged, as he continued with his work. "Why tell me, then?"

Setadev glared into Sayo's eyes for a moment. "You are a part of this backup plan, too," he began. "Therefore, you will someday figure out from what I have told you, everything that you will ever need to know. The information may be trivial, but it has already sparked your curiosity. I can tell. Explore that curiosity, Sayo, and maybe you may someday see how the game is played. Yet you should be humble as you do, because you must remember that had I not been defeated by that measly boy that we have locked in the box, gagged, and tied up, we would not be executing this plan right now."

There was a slight pause. "And you would have never had any use for me," Sayo finally answered.

"Not at all," said Setadev, without a second of pause. "I will not lie to you, Sayo. I can see that you have some understanding when it comes to that matter, but do you really know how the game is played?"

Sayo said nothing. He turned his head away.

"This is your army," continued Setadev, noting Sayo's response. "You took the opportunity to aid me, and because of that, I will reward you and your men when we are done. Already, you have done well by setting the trap for the boy. Yet we are not done, Sayo. We must continue with the next phase of the plan."

"To the fortress," acknowledged Sayo. "From there, I have no idea what your plans contain, except that your objective is in the caverns."

Setadev nodded. "That is correct," he said. "You remember your orders."

"Then I still don't understand why the Enlighteners are here," Sayo mentioned.

Rolling his eyes in frustration, Setadev answered, "Allow me to enlighten you, then, and show you how the game is played. How would I have a fortress already if I did not have a group that has taken care of it for me during the many years I have been gone?"

Now, Sayo had the answer. "It is their fortress," he realized.

"Correct, in a sense," said Setadev. "The fortress is the construct of the largest and most powerful of my Enlightener groups. You see, my Enlighteners from the Shadows encompass more membership than what you see here. All around the world, numerous factions of Enlighteners exist. Each group is powerful, each is led by a veteran administrator, and each falls under the umbrella of the fortress. No orders are given, of course, but communication happens from group to group through this fortress as a relay point. And this fortress is well hidden in plain sight by its remote location."

"Which way will we be marching the troops, then?" asked Sayo, implying that he wanted to know where this fortress was.

Raising his right arm and turning, Setadev pointed in a direction.

Upon seeing the way Setadev was pointing, Sayo said, "You must be joking."

"It is no joke," answered Setadev. "It is a more remote region that you could possibly imagine. From there, the caverns are only a few days away."

"Very well, sir," acknowledged Sayo. "The gear should all be packed away within the next couple of hours. I suggest we march our men to the Calphos River for supplies before we continue on to the fortress."

Setadev nodded. "We shall do that," he said. "And on that note, let me give you this, as a symbol of my appreciation." He unbuckled his sword belt, which had a short sword and scabbard attached to it.

Without question, Sayo attached the short sword and scabbard to his own sword belt, on his left side behind his normal sword. There were now two swords on his belt. As Sayo was aware that he had very little skill with a two-sword combat style, he preferred to have both swords on the same side of his waist so that he could draw either one with his right hand–his sword hand–if need be.

"The short sword you have now is made of antite," continued Setadev. "This makes it more fragile than steel, but completely resistant to magic. If you strike someone with it and open a flesh wound, it will block their ability to use all magic for quite some time. It will also absorb any magic attacks fired at it, if you can block them with it. I have no need for this sword, so you may have it in case of emergency. But understand that this sword was extremely difficult and expensive to create, so you had better take care of it or I will ensure your end is not pretty."

Sayo said nothing.

After a moment's pause, Setadev began again, "I sense that you have another question, Sayo. You wonder why I would take everyone to this fortress instead of directly to the caverns, if we are stopping for supplies at the river."

Sayo said nothing.

"My Enlighteners who have located this ancient weapon are still trying to establish a secure and private route through which we can discretely transport so many troops," began Setadev. "In the meantime, it would make the most sense to regroup in a safe place."

"Not to mention your plans for the boy," added Sayo.

"Ah, the most satisfying part of all," commented Setadev. "I do have quite the plan for him. General Sayo, now that we are in a more familiar understanding with one another, and I sense that you wish to know more about what is in store, would you like to know what I have planned?"

There was a slight pause. "I would be lying if I did not admit I am the slightest bit curious," said the general. "Your request for aphrodisiacs stunned me."

Rolling his eyes, Setadev picked up, "Yet they are so useful for this plan." He paused for a second. "As you can see, my current body is, in many respects, very much identical to that of the pure one. It is damaged, however, by the scar the false emperor gave me across the eye, and the amount of energy it took to restore this body after being impaled by the pure one and kicked off a cliff."

"I understand this body is an artificial creation," nodded Sayo.

"Indeed," nodded Setadev, "and one that could not be killed completely without disintegrating the body." He paused for a second. "I plan to use a similar technique of creation in order to break the bonds associated with the pure one and his angel. Under the heavy influence of such aphrodisiacs, not only will the pure one lose control of his inhibitions, but also he will lose his grip on reality, on what is real or not, and who is who. I will use that effect to disillusion the pure one and place him with a false companion. As time passes, he will forget all about his old life until he is nothing but an empty shell, and every amount of devotion he once had to love, friendship, family, duty, and everything else, is gone. Perhaps all that will be left will be thoughts of his false companion, but for certain once all of that is gone, he will submit to me. Then, and only then, will I have what I desire."

Though he said nothing, Sayo was awestruck. It was true that Sayo was a traitor to his homeland of Aurana and now consequently to the Solunar Empire and was likely not one to speak on matters of honor, but he found what Setadev was speaking of doing was completely dishonorable. For the longest time, Sayo had considered himself to be a man of honor. He believed very much in the same code as did his old friends, in the warrior's way. Such a path included honor and dignity, even if war was often dirty and damaged the innocent. In that case, Sayo considered that to be an unfortunate consequence of war.

This, however, was torture. Plain and simple.

Still, Sayo remained the silent general. He said nothing.

Seeing this, Setadev resumed, "I will let you let that soak in for a little while. Do as you wish in the time being, but be prepared to move out soon. And tend to the box and make sure the pure one has enough food, water, and air to last the entire trip, will you? None of my efforts will be worth it unless he survives the trip to the fortress."

With that, Setadev stuck something in Sayo's hand and walked away. As Setadev walked off, Sayo opened his hand to see that what was there was a small golden necklace with a tag marked with the initials "WN".

Wondamer. Glory. *Notuerew*. Negation.

Negation of glory. The creed of the Enlighteners from the Shadows. Some things were clear to General Sayo now. There was no chance, none at all, that he would join the Enlighteners. Something was so wrong with their mental state that Sayo considered such a move would make him stupider.

Come to think of it, Sayo thought to himself, what was he doing anyway? He and his men had followed Setadev because Setadev, in the form of Pseudo, was the second-in-command of Desolunar, before the fall of Demonicus and loss at the Battle of Seta Archa. Everything there had simply seemed to fall apart, and what was a perfect defense had been bested, oddly enough.

Only Sayo knew of Setadev's true motive and identity. Everyone else believed he was Pseudo, leading the mighty army of Desolunar to take their homeland back. None of them knew that Arthur Falchor, Demonicus's son and the fabled heir of Desolunar, was the one running the new Solunar Empire. Had they knew, it was likely they would all be resting back in Seta Archa, participating in Arthur's demilitarization and rebuilding processes. Yet not even General Sayo knew that. What had set Sayo and his men apart from the rest of the old Desolunar troops was that Sayo's unit had actually retreated during the battle, in part due to Sayo's loss during a showdown with his old friends Vincent Stryker, "Ironman" Eukert, and John Bryant; and in part due to the fact that he saw the city was lost and that his unit was likely fighting for nothing as enemy troops stormed into the city.

There was so little hope left, it seemed. Sayo took a brief glimpse out amongst his packed-down camp to see many of his men still hard at work, and he began to worry for them. Though he was a silent general, he was not one without emotion. He did care for his men and believed that just as they fought to protect their homeland and beliefs, he fought to protect them.

Still, there was a faint dream for General Sayo. He had

wondered what it would be like to be back in the days of the savage war again, fighting alongside his three best friends. Those days seemed so long ago by now. Where was the hope that he needed? Sayo was not sure if he or his men could ever have the lives they wanted with Setadev. Was it not the dream of every man and woman to live the best life possible?

Sayo's eyes drifted to the box where Kevin Trent Stryker was being kept prisoner. Perhaps, Sayo thought to himself, the hope for the future he was looking for was locked in that box. Regardless of how little Sayo knew of Kevin, he knew that Kevin had defeated Setadev before, even though Kevin was mortal whereas Setadev was not. Even if Kevin had stood against Desolunar before, was it possible that he knew something that General Sayo did not?

The silent general now had a conundrum on his hands. Looking over at Setadev, there was little that he could do for now. Now, Sayo had much to think about. But perhaps, when the time was right, he would make his move.

Until that time, Sayo began packing up his command tent again. There was still much work to be done. For now, Sayo would have to remain diligent, and not let Setadev know his mind was full of thoughts of desertion.

Chapter 15

Violations

It had been a rough night for Caitlin. Her mind in tatters from the shatter spell, she found herself utterly unable to control her emotions. Her father stayed by her bedside all night as she screamed, working tirelessly to repair as much of the damage to her mind as he could.

In the middle of the night, Caitlin finally fell asleep as her father continued to work. Professor Magnon had actually hoped this might happen, as it would allow Caitlin to get some rest while he worked. So much damage had been done by this ancient spell, and only he had the magical talent to fix it.

Regardless, Caitlin would never be the same again. Even if the professor was able to fully fix her mind with no remnants of the damage—which he was not capable, although he could get close—the amount of trauma that she had suffered would leave scars on her mind forever. It was such a powerful suggestion, as Caitlin was being rendered mentally shattered, that Kevin did not care about her. Had she any level of her mind, she would have thrown such a comment away as Setadev trying to throw shade on everything. With her mind broken and unable to protect itself from such an attack, she experienced the most powerful feeling of loss that she had ever felt.

As he finished his repairs, Professor Magnon breathed a sigh of relief. He knew he had done the best that he could. He also knew, now more than ever, that he wanted to get his hands around Setadev's neck. It was one thing for him to have personal issues with Setadev. It was another altogether for Setadev to attack his daughter and do this to her.

Late in the middle of the night, the professor, having just finished, walked out to the kitchen. He was exhausted from the tedious effort. Vincent Stryker had since retired to the castle for the night, to sleep in his quarters. The professor, alone in the dark, sat down in a chair at the kitchen table, hoping to catch his breath. He ended up passing out at the table, overexerted from the strain so much effort for an extended amount of time had taken him.

In the morning, Caitlin woke up late, much later than she normally did. As she looked around and started to pull herself up, she felt very sore. What had happened to her had broken her body as well as her mind. Even though she had been healed, the aches and pain would not be gone for quite some time.

Neither would the mental scars.

She felt utterly ridiculous, losing herself like that yesterday, and she had a sensation of feeling violated. Her father could hopefully explain it. Yet the thoughts and the fears still remain. Did Kevin really not care about her? It preyed on every hesitation and worry she had. And if Kevin really went off on his own, when he told Caitlin he would wait for her, and was captured, that only seemed to back up these fears.

Surely whatever had happened, Caitlin knew her father could explain. Figuring everything out with her feelings, however, Caitlin felt there was one person with whom she could speak. That person was Rachel Reinhart, who Caitlin considered her best friend after they fought together and spent plenty of time talking with each other several months ago. It was unusual to Caitlin to feel like there was someone better to speak with than her father, but she felt that Rachel could relate with her when she just needed to talk about everything.

After she had the chance to speak with both, she had made up her mind that she had to go after Kevin, with or without help. If he was in trouble, and she had no reason to believe that Setadev was fabricating that story, then she was going to rescue him.

Having taken some time to touch herself up with some healing magic and make sure she was ready to travel, Caitlin took a quick look in the small silver mirror in Kevin's mother's old room. She still looked a little roughed up, a sign of the beating she had taken yesterday. This was not something her magic could heal; she could heal any cuts or injuries, but superficial damage would need to heal on its own. She did take a few extra moments to brush her hair, feeling she needed to be somewhat presentable when she faced her father, to show him that she had not given up.

With that and feeling she was as ready as she ever would be, Caitlin left the room. She was surprised to find her father slumped over in a chair in the dining area, which was something she had never seen. He had clearly exerted a lot of effort.

Gently, Caitlin tapped on her father's shoulder, as she sat down at the other chair at the small table.

Professor Magnon was roused. He was pleasantly surprised to see his daughter, as presentable as she could make herself. "Good morning," he said to her. "Are you okay?"

"I think I'm as okay as I'm going to be," answered Caitlin. "I hope you are. I'm not used to seeing you in this condition."

Tired, the professor smiled. "I am fine. You need not worry about me." He paused for a second, feeling that he had to address the elephant in the room. "I am presuming, given your ordeal, that you want answers?"

"Of course," acknowledged Caitlin, seeing that her father was getting to the point and leaving the formalities, a trait that was not uncommon with him. "You know I was attacked. Last night was the worst night of my life, and this morning I still don't feel quite right. I remember feeling like I couldn't get myself together yesterday. What happened to me?"

The professor lowered his head. "Something very evil, and very unethical," he answered somberly. "You, of course, remember how wrong it is to read someone's mind without their permission. It is even more wrong, the ultimate of mind magic crimes, to destroy someone's mind."

"Is that what happened to me?" Caitlin felt even more violated.

Silently, the professor nodded. "Yes," he said. "It is not a kind of magic that has been taught for thousands of years, but Setadev clearly demonstrated he knows it and has no fears of using it. It's called a 'shatter' spell—light and darkness magic used within the mind to tear apart the psyche and destroy one's ability to think or react. Sometimes it can also be placed with a suggestion, to make one believe something and be unable to rationally deflect it."

It occurred to Caitlin that, remembering what Setadev said to her in that moment, that he placed a suggestion that Kevin did not care about her. Recognizing that fact was not enough to dissuade her fully, but it let Caitlin recognize that Setadev was trying to sever the connection between her and Kevin. She was now more resolved than ever that she had to find him, and rescue him from Setadev's clutch.

A little weary, the professor then stood up. "I am planning to get Vincent Stryker, and we will head for the Realm of the Angels. I have already warned the gods that Setadev is back, based on the presence of the crosswinds he is fond of using to announce his coming. We are going to meet soon. I think it would be best if you came along."

Shaking her head, Caitlin said, "With all due respect, father, no. I understand what has happened to me now, but I can't let Setadev run off with Kevin. As much as he said things to hurt me and attacked my mind to try and force the fears upon me, I don't think Setadev was lying when he said he had Kevin captive."

Logical as ever, the professor nodded, understanding his daughter's position. "I think you are correct," he acknowledged. "It is not like him to fabricate his stories as he likes to boast about his accomplishments." He paused for a second. "How will you find him? We do not even know where he is being held. You could spend months searching the mortal realm and never find him. Slow down and think for a minute."

"No," answered Caitlin. "I know where I am going. I am headed for Seta Archa, and I will follow his footsteps. By following the same path he did, I can follow the trail straight to him."

"Then at least let me come with you," interjected Tyrinion. "Let me speak with the gods, and then when I return I can escort you to Seta Archa personally and we can follow Kevin's trail."

Caitlin shook her head, confident in what she knew. "I can't let you do that, father." Her tone was still very isolated and lacking in emotion. "Some things, you have to figure out yourself."

Immediately, Tyrinion turned his head to Kronius and glared for a second. Kronius had a stunned look, as though he was not expecting such a response.

"This is what I have to do," continued Caitlin. "This is my journey, father. And I have to do it myself. I have to go back to Seta Archa, I have to follow him, and I have to find him."

Tyrinion reached out and grabbed his daughter's shoulder, stopping her. "Caitlin, I know you love him, but you have to stop and think for a second. This is not smart. You are putting yourself in a high level of danger if you should encounter Setadev by yourself again."

Caitlin's attention was caught by these comments. As she looked into her father's eyes, she could see the legitimate concern he had. He was not simply lecturing; he was deftly afraid and completely worried for his daughter. By contrast, Tyrinion could see that there was determination in his daughter's eyes. Her eyes were fixed, focused, determined. Nothing was going to deter her.

"I will be strong, father," Caitlin responded. She then stood. "And I'll have my friends from the Solunar Empire with me, if it comforts you." She took a breath. "I've been taken by surprise once. I won't let that happen again," she continued.

Tyrinion sighed. "Are you sure that this is what you want to do?" he asked. "It is no bother to me to go with you."

Caitlin shook her head. "No, father," she said. "I have to do this, and I have to do it alone. I will not let Setadev get the best of me." She paused for a second. "Maybe it's a bit selfish, but I won't have any answers for myself if I don't do this."

Suddenly, Caitlin's behavior made a bit more sense. "You have something more you are looking for, do you not?" asked the professor. "You are not usually the type to let your pride precede the stronger option."

"I do," Caitlin finally admitted, but without backing down. "I cannot hide anything from you, father. I have to save the one I love… and I have to find out if our love is real or not. I have to know why I let the doubt get to me, and if I am missing something inside or if I am truly seeing something in Kevin that I was never meant to see."

"Meaning you are not sure whether or not to trust him," realized the professor. "Setadev's words have rung truer with you than it should.

In response, Caitlin only looked down. This was hurting her more that she realized. What Setadev had said to her, even knowing it was done in a way to impact her harder, had really struck her nerves harder than she had realized before. She knew that Setadev had to be lying about Kevin, and that Kevin would never do something to break her heart. Yet Caitlin was much more afraid than that; if not of Kevin possibly not caring for her, then of herself not being able to believe in their love deep in her heart. The hollowness in her heart would not fill itself in simply because of what she was told by others.

In that moment, the professor realized she needed to do this for herself. As he nodded to his daughter, he hugged her close. "It is all right, Caitlin," he said. "Please take care of yourself while you do this. Every day, I am so proud to have you as my daughter."

The cracks of a smile started to show in Caitlin's face as she hugged her father. "I love you, father," she said. "Thank you for understanding."

And with that, the professor let go of his daughter. Those were words that, months ago, he never expected to hear from his daughter. She was a different person now, and that was in part thanks to Kevin Trent Stryker and in part thanks to her desire to explore the new feelings she was having. Even though the professor knew his recommendations were being ignored, he knew it was not for lack of care from his daughter.

Alone for the time, Caitlin felt as though she still had so much to process. She pulled out her diary and set it on the table, knowing that she would be leaving it behind soon. She needed not to be carrying excessive things while she was traveling, so the diary stayed in Kevin's house. She took out a pen and began to write out her feelings, not even bothering to take the time to check the identifying date:

A few days since the last entry:

I don't know if I really know who I am anymore. Having my mind destroyed, even though I now have it back thanks to my father, has shattered me to the core. I remember everything that happened. I remember how I reacted, and how overcome I was. I have never felt so much upsetting emotion in my life. Even as I'm coming to embrace feeling emotion and leaving my discipline behind, I still think of myself as a mostly professional person except when I'm alone with Kevin. It's hard to believe I could fall apart like that and not be able to pull myself out of it.

Is this what having feelings is supposed to be like, when you have absolutely no restraint? Do we all really use some level of emotional restraint even when we don't think we are? And how many people say what they feel and how many lie and try to hide it?

I know who said it, but it reinforces all of the doubts I've had. When you cry about something for hours, no matter how much sense it makes, it seems like it has a lasting effect regardless. At least I feel it has for me. Maybe it's because I felt something so strong for so long.

Maybe it's because I still feel a bit of it now...

I feel lost and conflicted. I feel like my mind has been violated.

And yet at the same time... I'm really worried about him. I can't believe anything Setadev says, but I know if he says he's captured Kevin, then he has. I haven't forgotten that he could be suffering right now, and if he isn't, then I'm sure Setadev will make him very soon.

Why would Kevin run off without me? He promised he wouldn't. If he had just listened to me, this never would've happened. I'm so angry at him... and yet, I love him and need to be with him again. No matter how mad at him I am, or worried I am for our future, I don't think I could be mad when I'm with him. I would just be happy. That must be what love is.

Is it? Or is it codependency, like Setadev tried to say? I hope not. I do love Kevin but I know I can't only be capable because I'm with him. I have to be strong on my own.

There's a lot I need to know, but for now I know this: I will do whatever I need to do to save him. I need to do this logically, but... all I want to do right now is run to him. I want to bring him home, back to me and back to our friends. I miss him so much...

Gryphon flight will be here soon. I need to be ready to go. No time to waste.

Caitlin put the diary away. She knew she would not return to it for quite some time. Despite the fact that she felt she wrote something not as coherent as her usual diary entries, she saw how it was a reflection of her current mental state. It was still relieving to get some of that feeling out onto paper.

She missed Kevin. She worried for him. At the same time, she still felt a little broken. No amount of magic would fix that.

Within a short amount of time, the gryphon flight from the Solunar Empire had returned to pick up Caitlin. She made her way out of Kevin's house to catch it; simultaneously, the professor left at the same time to meet up with Vincent Stryker. As she prepared to board, she gave her father a big hug and thanked him again for everything. She promised to him that she would stay safe, and with that she boarded the gryphon to head back to Seta Archa. The gryphon took off at the command of the soldier flying it, and as it left Caitlin saw her father turn to head toward the castle.

As they ascended, Caitlin turned to face forward. Her mind was racing with everything that had happened and everything that needed to happen. Such violations from Setadev could not go unpunished. Shattering her mind was one thing. Kidnapping Kevin, the boy she loved and who had changed her so much, was another.

She had to talk to her friends in the Solunar Empire to find out where Kevin had gone and how he had gone off alone, if Setadev was right. She needed to talk to Rachel, to process her feelings and get some advice. And she needed the support of those who had stood by her through difficult times. Yes, her father was one of those people, but as Caitlin reasoned, being a teenager meant that she really wanted her peers.

And in the end, Caitlin reckoned, she might learn a little bit more about herself in the process. That is, she might realize that lesson once she had smashed in Setadev's face.

Chapter 16

Council of the Gods

Professor Magnon was once again Tyrinion as he arrived in the Realm of the Angels, as he changed his appearance to suit the wishes of Ralios Larion. Tyrinion had brought Vincent Stryker with him, who had been here before. It was a familiar sight to both, except for one thing. Above, the sky was completely overcast, in stark contrast to its normal cloudless appearance.

"The warning clouds are out," commented Tyrinion. The meeting room should be ready for this security council meeting."

"We had better get moving," added Vincent Stryker, staring in a bit of awe. Although he had been here before, he had never seen the warning clouds.

The stairs to Angel Tower were in front of the trio, and at the top of them were Kronius, the messenger; and Chatka, the deity of peace and war. They were checking the gods who were arriving from elsewhere in the realm, or from visits to the mortal realm. It took the trio less than a moment to reach them.

Upon seeing Tyrinion, Chatka was pleasantly surprised. "Tyrinion," he began as he reached out to shake the former god of darkness's hand. "So, the redeemed one has finally returned after all."

"If you want to call me that," answered Tyrinion reluctantly. "Have you any idea what the emergency council is about?"

"No," Chatka frankly said. "Do you?"

"Yes," nodded Tyrinion. "I brought it to Larion's attention. I fear that Setadev is back, and he has now proven it by attacking my daughter."

Chatka nodded. "Then we had better start the meeting at once," he said. "Come, one and all, and let us head to the assembly." At this, Chatka waved and started down the hallway into the tower.

Together the group walked into the tall, stone structure of Angel

Tower. After a couple of turns down hallways, they had reached the eponymous meeting room, of which there was only one to which the gods referred. Inside, the meeting room in Angel Tower seemed to go on into infinity. White space expanded to no limit, and it appeared that the room extended in all directions, even beyond the door. A person could literally be unable to walk to the end of the room. Fortunately, no one was ever lost, for if someone went far enough in one direction, they would end up back where they started. All of that design was simply for effect.

A rectangular table and chairs were set up, and all of the chairs were filled by gods. Tyrinion, Chatka, and Vincent took positions near Ralios Larion, king of gods, at the head of the table. Also seated at the table were a few other deities, members of the gods' security council: Jarnis the god of plants, Datyrios the current god of darkness, and Necnea the goddess of time. Larion gave a quick nod of acknowledgment to the professor and to Vincent Stryker, and they nodded back. They remained standing, expecting to speak, as they looked at the gods seated at the table. All fell silent as Larion began to speak.

"Fellow deities of the Realm of the Angels, those who dare to call themselves gods," began Larion, with a formal introduction, "I am glad everyone could be here for the convening of this security council. The past few hours have revealed some disturbing truths. I understand that many of you do not know why we are here, but the emergency we have may be far greater than what we have experienced before. Please welcome back Tyrinion, as he elaborates further on the situation."

As Tyrinion stepped up to the edge of the table, there was an air of awkwardness in the room. The gods were still trying to clarify their mental images of Tyrinion, knowing now that Tyrinion was not the conqueror who had made them live in fear for the past twenty years. Those that had not been personally involved with the incidences surrounding the conquest were those who were still realizing all that had happened. Tyrinion knew the best approach to keep respect was to keep his comments as formal as possible.

"Gods and goddesses of the security council," began Tyrinion, a very adept speaker and lecturer, "in the past few weeks, crosswinds have been flying around the mortal realm. These winds seem to hit for only a few seconds before fading. Now, as those of you who are older recall, such a sign is that of the forthcoming arrival of Setadev, the former king of gods whom we cast out a long time ago." He paused for a second. "These winds, however, are not the only evidence we have found. His presence has been seen, and he has made it known. It seems evident now that Setadev has returned."

There was a collective gasp across the room. Larion was forced to call for order, to allow Tyrinion to continue.

"At first, the signals in the winds seemed only to be hypothetical. However, we know now, from only the last day, that this information is not hypothetical. We have a confirmed sighting of Setadev. Perhaps even worse," continued Tyrinion, taking a slight pause because he was finding difficulty in saying what he was about to say, "is the possibility that the pure one himself may have already been captured by Setadev."

Suddenly, Jarnis, the pale green robe-clad deity of plants, interjected from near the head of the table. "How can this be so?" he asked. "What happened to him?"

Tyrinion shook his head in response. "I do not know," he said, "but he returned in the form of Pseudo, a created person in the shape of the pure one that is distinguishable by the damage he has sustained to one of his eyes. Supposedly, he also has a partner." He turned and nodded at Vincent Stryker.

Knowing this was his turn, Vincent Stryker picked up the speech. "Allegedly, he may be working with someone from the old Desolunar forces named General Martin Sayo, who escaped the Battle of Seta Archa with a small unit. Martin Sayo is a dangerous military general, not the least of which because he has been willing to change his loyalties before. He's generally a tricky military planner, and one who leads with stoicism, needing few words to express his commands. If he is loyal to Setadev, he adds a level of danger in engaging Setadev in a military battle to get to him." He looked back at the professor.

"We bring this up to express the trap that was set," continued Tyrinion. "According to my daughter, she and Kevin went to Seta Archa on request from Arthur Falchor, whom you will recall we installed as the new leader in the region. He has since established the Solunar Empire as Desolunar's replacement. Arthur had been having trouble with Sayo, who had been attacking his people. He asked the pure one and my daughter for help with this matter." He paused. "My daughter had to return to Aurana for a required government procedure, and while they were separated, Setadev attacked my daughter and claimed that he had taken the pure one. I have no reason to believe he would lie about that."

There was a collective gasp from the gods at the table.

"It seems clear what we must do," added Larion, as he stepped forward to take the table head again. "If we can find the pure one, we can find Setadev as well. Then, we will have the opportunity to rid our realms of this menace ourselves…"

"And how do you intend to do that?" interjected Datyrios, the current god of darkness, from the middle of the table.

Larion fell silent.

Datyrios, a younger-appearanced god dressed in black robes with purple trim, then rose from his seat. "Has it not crossed your mind that even the pure one never defeated Setadev? Surely Setadev is a menace that must be dealt with, of course, but to say we will simply 'rid our realms' of him is a serious oversimplification of the problem."

Though Datyrios was a younger god known for his contrarian viewpoints that normally stood against anything the majority of gods believed, most recognized that in this case, he had a valid point. How was Setadev to be defeated if he had not been defeated when the pure one had an opportunity, and was believed to have done so?

"An excellent point," acknowledged Larion, who, despite his own personal distaste for Datyrios, had to agree with him. "To answer this question, we must know how Setadev survived. The accounts given to us by the pure one indicate Setadev's death was caused by a cataclysm of energy that arose from being given all Seven Stripes of the Elements at once, generating a reaction that tore apart his existence and disintegrated both himself and the entirety of the realm below. Is there any possible way he could have survived that?"

There appeared to be a general state of confusion amongst the gods as they contemplated the answer to that question. Several of them were discussing the possibilities with each other. None of them had the answer.

A grim truth seemed to come out of this statement at the same time, however. "It would seem that disintegration is the way to kill an immortal," commented Tyrinion, without fear of this fact. "The lore theorizes on it in some of our most ancient texts. It was what claimed the life of Vinz Larinion, as we all witnessed in his sacrifice to create the Sword of Purity. It did kill Setadev, and we know that. So, if we know that Setadev was disintegrated, and thus died in the only way immortals can die, then how could he have survived? Surely being fully disintegrated into one's core elements is not something from which one can recover."

Silence filled the air. No one had any idea.

Vincent Stryker, though, had one. Taking a breath, he began, "I saw Kevin kill Pseudo several months ago when Kevin ran him through with the Sword of Purity, and then kicked him off of a cliff. It seems apparent now that he is not dead."

Tyrinion realized what had happened now, and his eyes widened in surprise as he connected the dots. "And if Setadev did not have the Stripe of Life to bestow immortality on someone, there is only one other possibility of which I can conceive that he created another immortal."

That answer had more implied to it than its simple words. And the gods knew it.

"My gods," answered Jarnis, the god of plants, stunned as he stood up from his seat. "Setadev has learned how to fragment himself."

There was a collective gasp across the table, followed by chatter. Larion had to call for order again. "Now, let us not suddenly become afraid of the possibility of this being true," he began, maintaining a confident tone in order to reassure his gods. "Let us look on the positive side of this. If he is indeed back, then it is likely he is in a severely weakened state." He continued to address the council.

As Larion continued to talk, Vincent whispered in Tyrinion's ear. "Why is there all this fear of Setadev fragmenting himself? I'm not sure I fully understand."

Nervous about how to answer, Tyrinion looked away for a

second. "It is because if Setadev can fragment himself once, he can do it multiple times. It has been a fear of the gods for quite some time that someone could split himself or herself apart like that. The reason for that is that just as we believed we could imbue immortality and create gods, we believed we could take it away, too. In this way, we had a check on an immortal who would go astray; though we had failed on Setadev, I think we all still believed we can take away immortality if we learned how to use the Stripe of Life. If someone can fragment parts off, however, then one would have to de-power or somehow kill all of the parts to eliminate the immortality. It creates an escape route, and allows one to impose their will almost continuously by doing so, because it would be nearly impossible to track down all of one's fragments."

Vincent just sat in amazement for a second. He did not realize just how dangerous this made Setadev. He started listening again to what Larion was saying. Larion was monologuing, "If we can find Setadev and strike while the iron is hot, we may be able to catch him early enough. We know of one fragment, and if more emerge, we will deal with them as they come. This shall be our goal now, to find Setadev and bring him to justice, no matter what he has up his sleeve."

Tyrinion leaned forward. "We need a plan now to track him down. To do so, we need to find out where Setadev is heading. I anticipate he will likely be looking for something that he can use to strengthen himself to his old strength, if he has truly fragmented himself. Setadev does not like to feel weak."

No one had an answer.

Larion then took the head again. "One thing has been clear is that Setadev is, admittedly, smarter than all of us combined at the moment. Everything that has happened from the moment he was cast away five thousand years ago until now has all been carefully and meticulously planned out. Not only that, but it appears from the look of things now that his plan has several failsafes built into it as well. He must have had a way to acquire such knowledge without any of us picking up on it."

Necnea looked at Larion. "Five thousand years is a long time to plan," she said. "And a long time to acquire knowledge."

Tyrinion then added, “He also has the assistance of a cult that worships him, called the Enlighteners from the Shadows. They believe in the conqueror, and that he is it.”

“Are you suggesting he’s taking advantage of a group that believes in a mythology far older than him?” questioned Jarnis. He was referencing an old set of beliefs known as the trinity, of the existence of a conqueror, a destroyer, and a guardian.

“I am,” nodded Tyrinion. “I do not know if he actually founded them or if he simply took the place of their deity, but they are a group that still has a great deal of magic talent. Demonicus was one.” He paused for a scone. “This is no ordinary organization of humans. They are extremely fanatical and devout, and dedicated to destroying knowledge that could interfere with their conqueror’s mission. They accomplish this through their magic.”

“This may be the greatest danger,” chimed in Datyrios. “A shame that our species is easily manipulated.” He sighed. “Yet we are no closer to knowing Setadev’s target, which is what we must know if we are to stop him."

This was a very valid concern, Larion thought to himself. “Then this is what we will do,” he began to announce, raising his voice slightly. “We must go through our archives again, and any bit of knowledge we have. We have to know what Setadev is going after. If we can find that, we can intercept him before he gets to it.” Then, he paused before continuing, “Are there any questions or objections?”

The highly esteemed goddess of time, Necnea, dressed in elegant lavender robes, rose from her seat near the head of the table. One of the original gods to arrive in the Realm of the Angels, Necnea had been married to the long-time king of gods Vinz Larinion, before his self-sacrifice to create the Sword of Purity. Even after his fall, however, she still held a great deal of respect amongst her fellow immortals because of her intelligence, unique workings with time flow, and power. “There is a fact of truth we are missing here,” she began, in a firm tone. “That fact is that the sooner we can catch Setadev and ensure the safety of the new pure one, the better. Our strategy, as it stands so far, does not play to that strength. I do, however, like the idea that constant research provides us with the best option of finding the solution."

"Then do you have an idea as to how we might resolve this?" asked Larion.

Necnea nodded. "I do," she said. "We have, counting Tyrinion who is present here today, eighty-five of the most brilliant minds our universe has ever seen. While we have archives that will take a great period of time with which to deal, surely we can allow a couple of gods to enter the mortal realm, incognito, and attempt to find leads amongst the mortals that will lead us to him. Essentially, we can form a tracking team that can try to locate Setadev and what is his objective. By combining the bookwork with the fieldwork, we may be able to work together faster to find him, and the pure one."

There was a pause as Necnea took her seat again, as was customary for gods as they finished what they had to say at a meeting. "Now that is a plan I like," said Larion. "I would completely agree with Necnea's points in every sense. Are there any objections to this plan?"

No one raised a hand or stood. Not even Datyrios. Larion glanced over at him to see him actually nodding in agreement.

"Then we have our plan," continued Larion, noting the response from the table. He then turned to Necnea. "As this idea was yours, Necnea, and you seem to have a clear idea as to what kind of things we need to look forward to, would you like to head up the field team?"

Necnea was surprised by this move, but she did legitimately want to help. She had her personal reasons for wanting to be in the field; mostly, she secretly wanted to get her hands around Setadev's neck for everything that he had done, including being the driving factor behind her husband sacrificing himself. She silently nodded, and then said, "I would be honored."

"Very well," acknowledged Larion. "I would reason that a team of three gods would be the most appropriate size for this field team. This way, we have enough if splitting off is necessary to follow multiple leads, and in case any one of the team comes into danger, that person has two gods to protect him or her. As I declare this will be such, I need two more volunteers for the field team."

There was silence across the table. Being on the field team

could be quite dangerous if Setadev was on the loose, and everyone at the table recognized that. Fearlessly, however, Tyrinion stood. “I will join the team,” he said. “I will return to the mortal realm and continue my work to end Setadev regardless, so perhaps it would be best if I worked as part of a team this time.”

There was two now. Would one more step up to the challenge?

After another minute of silence, one did.

Kronius stepped up from near the table head and raised his hand. “I will go,” he said confidently. “I have traveled with the pure one before, and I owe him many favors. If finding Setadev will lead to him, then I wish to go and repay my debt to him.”

Larion looked over at Kronius and nodded at him, knowing how much Kronius had shown as of late. Though he was of the lowest class of gods, brought in from the mortal only a few hundred years ago, he had shown a great deal of courage in the past year, more than any god had shown lately. Ending only three months before, one of Setadev’s longest strategies against the gods was a seal he placed on the Realm of the Angels, preventing any god from leaving the realm. Kronius was accidentally trapped on the mortal side of the barrier, and had wandered for twenty years to find a way home. He found Kevin Trent Stryker, and further helped the cause in the mortal realm further by supporting Professor James Magnon, who he later came to find out was the falsely accused god Tyrinion. Thanks to their efforts, Kevin was able to find and destroy the seal, freeing the gods once again.

“I shall go as well,” interjected Vincent Stryker. “If doing so will lead me to my son, then it is something I must do."

“Then our team is assembled,” acknowledged Larion, as he nodded to Vincent Stryker. He then turned back toward the full table. “The rest of the gods will begin our research immediately. Our situation appears cryptic, but the overall message is clear. We are not out of danger yet. If we wish to end this threat to the realms once and for all, the key piece in unraveling the secrets behind Setadev’s location and activities. We need only find out where the key goes in order to find what knowledge it unlocks.” He paused for a second. “With that, we are dismissed.”

At this call of dismissal, Jarnis and Datyrios rose and departed with Larion, following him to assist in gathering the gods to begin their mission. They left Necnea, Kronius, Tyrinion, and Vincent Stryker in the room.

"Next question," stated Vincent Stryker. "Where do we start?"

Kron looked at Vincent. "I think we should start by finding out what the Enlighteners from the Shadows are doing. If Tyrinion is right, they will be doing something to support Setadev at this time, and they will not be able to be quite as subtle as him."

Necnea nodded. This made sense.

"Come to think of it, I might know someone we can ask," answered Tyrinion. "Let us start by heading to Bladinstar, in the province of Northern Aurana. My office is there, along with someone who might know of a few Enlighteners."

"Might as well be as good as any place to start," nodded Kronius.

Also acknowledging this, Necnea added, "Then it is agreed."

"Right," said Tyrinion, as he ran his fingers through his hair. Necnea and Kronius both observed as it shortened, past where Tyrinion tied it off. The tie fell to the ground, no longer holding anything. Still, Tyrinion's hair remained slicked back, which he then scattered into various points by rubbing his hand across the back. He then waved a hand over his robes. They changed color from purple to red, and the centerpiece across his chest disappeared. His face also took a slightly older appearance.

Now, he was Professor James Magnon once again.

"I had been growing tired of that," he informed Necnea and Kronius. "This is my identity, and I am most comfortable with it." The professor straightened his robes for just a second. "We should not have too much trouble with our appearances, as we would likely appear to be members of the magic community. You might want to make sure, however, to use your mortal names, in case we are being watched by Setadev or his Enlighteners. We will not fool Setadev, but his Enlighteners are not likely to be as educated as he is."

Necnea nodded. "Are you to remain 'Professor James Magnon', then? You will not use your true name?"

"Yes," answered Tyrinion. "As I said, this is my identity."

Chapter 17

Tremors of Vengeance

Around the city of Seta Archa, the earth was often at peace. The shelter of the surrounding coniferous forest protected the massive city from running out of supplies, providing groundwater from wells that supplied the city despite its location away from any river. It was a slightly different sight from anywhere else in the world, because only the southern forest was mostly coniferous, and nowhere else was there a city that survived quite like Seta Archa did.

Arthur Falchor and Rachel Reinhart were the rulers of this city, albeit somewhat unwilling rulers. Neither of them had even seen the city until a few months ago. Still, this was their empire.

It was a dismal day outside. The weather had warmed up a little bit, but this ended up leading to worse conditions, as snow turned to rain, which then froze as it hit the ground and made slick patches of ice everywhere. Altogether, it was a nasty day for the city. Likewise, it was a day that would disturb its emperor, as well. Quietly, Arthur stood watching out the windows of his throne room at the top of the pyramid, only wondering what was to come. From a short distance away, his prime minister and friend Rachel Reinhart stood watching him, only wondering whether or not she would be able to keep him from losing himself in his stress.

The serious affairs of being the emperor had changed Arthur dramatically. He was no longer the fun-loving, sarcastic, and egotistical seventeen-year-old that he once was. Instead, now he was serious, isolationist, and very much alone. And Rachel hated it. It simply was not the real Arthur. Rachel stood next to Rouge and Resa Kirkwood, wondering when he would snap out of it.

"So, it is done," said Arthur, as he refused to turn away from the window.

"Uhm…" began Resa, having a little trouble with answering a

distant Arthur, "yes, it is done. The Metoi have named a new leader and will rebuild their village very soon. A representative of the Toronaga came to visit us to volunteer their services, as well. They are strong enough together that the Metoi should not be threatened in the Wastes, and neither should the regional stability. Our men have already returned to Seta Archa."

Arthur silently nodded. That was some good news, at least. If only his misery could come to an end. This city was a curse to him now. It held him down, kept him from being free. He had more responsibility now than any other man in history, he felt. That responsibility was something that he knew he had to do, and desired to maintain because he did care about the people in his new empire, but he hated the procedures and stress of it all.

He simply stared out the north window of his capital building again, looking upon his city. It seemed so cold now, given that it was the deep winter. Much of Solunar was still coated in a layer of snow, although snow was quite sparse in the Wastes due to the more arid climate that made up the region. On top of every building in Seta Archa, however, was a thick layer of snow. Snow covered the ground, the walls of the city, and even the trees beyond the city. Across the wall and along every road in the city, torches burned to light the way in the winter night. The light from these torches reflected off of the snow, lighting up the entire city in a unique sort of way and reflecting a dim red color into the overcast night sky. Arthur looked out to the wall, where armed guards once patrolled the city walls from atop them. Now, the walls and battlements were barren except for the torches.

Arthur's eyes drifted to the entrance of the main thoroughfare, now abandoned. Thoughts of running through that entrance before ran through his mind, as he had done so during the Battle of Seta Archa. It now sat empty all of the time, as travel over the wall via gryphon airlift or ladders were the more preferred methods of entering or leaving Seta Archa.

Suddenly, speaking of a gryphon airlift, he saw one coming in from far away. He could make out little from the distance, but Arthur thought to himself that it would be awfully peculiar for someone to enter the city that way via an airlift.

Rachel still stood nearby, confused by Arthur's unmoving, fixed stance. "Arthur, are you…"

"I see someone coming in via a gryphon flight, and I think I know who it is," he interrupted. "Rouge, grab your binoculars."

Almost immediately, Rachel stepped over to the window, as Arthur pointed out to her the flight. "It's a little hard to see, but that's the person, right there," he said.

"What's the word?" asked Rouge, passing the binoculars to Arthur. "What do you think?"

"I think it's my sister," Arthur answered, as he confirmed by looking through the binoculars. "It's Caitlin." He tossed the binoculars back to Rouge, who caught them.

Stunned, Rachel asked, "Alone?"

Arthur nodded. "Other than our soldier who flew her in, yes."

Instinctively, something about watching the flight made Rachel feel uneasy, as if she could tell that something was wrong. Suddenly, she took off and bolted for the stairs.

"Rachel?" asked Resa, as Rachel took off. She was too late, though. Rachel was already making her way down the first flight of stairs to the ground level.

Quickly, Arthur looked over to Rouge and Resa, and signaled for all of them to head down the stairs and follow her.

Hurriedly, Arthur, Rouge, and Resa ran down the stairs. Rachel, though, was way ahead of them. "What in the world is going on?" asked Rouge, as she continued to run down the stairs with Arthur and Resa. They made it down the first flight and around to the next.

"I don't know," answered Arthur. "Rachel must be worried sick about her."

Resa took a quick breath as she continued slightly behind Arthur and Rouge. "We're all close, but Rachel and Caitlin, I'm sure, are closer than most of us are individually to each other. Maybe she just wants to see Caitlin that badly."

"Or maybe she's afraid something's wrong," added Rouge.

Arthur could not discount that possibility. Something had to give here, and he needed to know what was happening. He would be very happy to see his sister again, but if it were under grave circumstances, the mood would very much be toned down.

Finally, Arthur, Rouge, and Resa made it to the bottom of the stairs. They ran toward the exit to the triangular pyramid-shaped capital building, to see Rachel almost there already. She ran headlong into Caitlin, and after each of them stopped to see who they had found, they immediately hugged each other. Arthur and the Kirkwood sisters caught up to them in a few seconds.

Instantly, a tear came to Rachel's eye. "Caitlin, I missed you so much, my best friend," she said.

"And I missed you too, Rachel," answered Caitlin.

Carefully, as Rachel and Caitlin let go of one another, Arthur hugged his sister as well. After a second, however, Arthur noticed a tear on her cheek, which he wiped off as he let her go. Rachel had been absolutely right. "What's wrong?" he asked.

"Something's gone terribly wrong," Caitlin answered, trying to keep herself together without getting too emotional again. "Kevin's been captured!"

Immediately, Arthur's eyes widened. Everyone else appeared stunned.

"How?" Arthur immediately asked. "Who has him, Caitlin? Is it General Sayo?"

Caitlin stopped to take a breath and catch herself again. "No," she said, "or possibly, but it can't be entirely him if that's the case." She then paused again. "Setadev is back."

Arthur raised his hand and waved everyone in to pay close attention to him for a second. "We had better head back for the throne room right away," he said. "We must discuss this as soon as possible."

There was a unanimous nod among everyone present.

Together, Arthur, Caitlin, Rachel, Rouge, and Resa walked together back up the stairs to the throne room. Any good spirit left was gone. Everything was very serious now, yet Arthur and Rachel had to continue to ask themselves, what was going on? Rouge and Resa were also deeply concerned as well.

The walk seemed to take forever, but within a few minutes, everyone was in the throne room, where the three glass windows formed the tip of the pyramid, above the large wood and stone base painted in black. Although the top of the pyramid was sealed and normally quite warm, today it felt as though the cold outside was permeating into the throne room.

As soon as Resa slammed the trap door as she was the last to enter the throne room, Arthur immediately said, "Tell us everything, Caitlin. What's going on?"

"Hey, easy, Arthur!" demanded Rachel as soon as Arthur finished, appearing to be bothered by Arthur's promptness. "She's our friend and your sister; you don't need to be so forceful."

"It's all right, Rachel," interrupted Caitlin with a gentle tone, lifting her hand to gesture for Rachel to ease up. "Arthur is right to be concerned. Everything is most urgent for us to discuss."

Casually, Arthur made his way over to his desk and took a seat. He invited everyone else to share the couch and chairs he had next to his desk. Rachel and Caitlin took chairs; Rouge and Resa shared the couch. Regardless of what anyone thought about Arthur's urgency, he did have care for his friends, and had sat everyone down mostly to make Caitlin comfortable. He could tell whatever had happened had clearly hurt his sister, but he needed to know what happened so he could do something about it.

Caitlin began, taking a breath of air, "I need your help to find Kevin. Here is what has happened," she paused as she interlocked her fingers and tried to recount her story without getting upset. "You guys already know that I went back to Rikleifer by gryphon a few days ago to get ready for registration. While I was there, I ran into Pseudo. He was still alive."

"That doesn't make any sense," said Arthur. "We killed him, didn't we? Kevin ran his sword straight through him and kicked him off of a cliff."

"We did," nodded Caitlin, "and at the same time, we never could have killed him."

"How do you figure that?" asked Rouge.

Caitlin shook her head. "Pseudo is Setadev," she said. "Or at least, he is a part of Setadev. The form was Pseudo, but the voice and the power was clearly Setadev. If Pseudo is really a piece of Setadev, that means that Kevin couldn't have killed Pseudo by stabbing him through and sending him off a ledge, because he's immortal and can't be killed like that. He does, however, have Setadev's consciousness and memories, and a lot of his power."

There was a collective gasp.

"I am lucky to be alive," Caitlin continued, "but that's only because Setadev doesn't want me dead. He did, however, attack me and tried to permanently destroy my mind. I'm grateful my father found me and repaired the damage that was done." She paused for a second. "Now, I have to follow where Setadev has gone, to save Kevin."

Rachel looked confused for a second. "Caitlin, how do you know that he has Kevin captured?"

Caitlin let out a deep breath. "Because Setadev told me. At the same time, he didn't just tell me. He knew, to the letter, about the situation in the Wastes that Kevin went out to resolve. He told me he had set up everything that had happened out there."

Something snapped in Arthur. He immediately rose from his chair. "Is Sayo working for him?" Everyone looked at Arthur for a second. He had something he was getting at.

"Yes," nodded Caitlin. "Setadev implied that."

"Damn!" exclaimed Arthur, as he slammed his fist on his desk. "So we were set up, then." He then shot a glance to Rouge. "Where did Kevin branch off from you and your sister?"

"At the village," answered Rouge. "We walked by the destruction in the village and Kevin saw a house that was burned down, and you could see the dead bodies. That really galvanized him, that he said he needed to put an end to this now. He followed the direction his sword told him to go."

A bit surprised, Caitlin thought about that. Kevin went off on his own to do good, but ultimately was being ruled by his passions. He would have been better to wait, regardless of the opportunity he felt he had. She understood why he did what he did, but she was frustrated that he chose to act rashly.

In disbelief, Arthur shook his head. "Amazing," he said, sarcastically. "If that was the setup to lure Kevin into the trap, then it can only be Setadev. Kevin believes he can trust that sword, I know."

"That's so elaborate, though," commented Rachel, stunned. "If Setadev is back, we know he would have reason to go after all of us for revenge, but a reason so simple doesn't sound like him."

"He must be after the whole empire," suggested Arthur. "We displaced his kin and his foundations, and he has taken Kevin as the first in getting back at all of us."

Again, Caitlin shook her head. "No, Arthur," she answered. "Not us. Only Kevin. Setadev made it very clear he didn't care about any country, or about you or your people. He wants revenge on Kevin, and on me. Anything or anyone else he uses, is merely so he can use them for his benefit, including using you to lure Kevin out into the middle of nowhere, where the trap was set."

"So we were used," scoffed Rouge, as she scuffed her shoe agains the floor. "All because we are friends with Kevin. Are you sure it is Kevin and you that he wants?"

Nodding, Caitlin responded, "He attacked me to make that very clear."

"He *what*?" interrupted Rachel, surprised.

Caitlin looked down for a minute. "He tried to kill me," she admitted, going back to something she did not want to talk about very much. "He said he didn't want to destroy the world's first and only angel, but the way he attacked said otherwise." Tears came to Caitlin's eyes. "After he did, he told me some words. Some very, very dark words, that still resonate." Her tears started to flow even more as she recounted the words, the same as was in her poem in the back of her diary, "Shattered glass rains from the sky. Shattered glass, it rains so dry. It's cold and hard, an icy cry…"

"From the heart that only wants to die," answered Rachel, wrapping an arm around Caitlin. "I've read that poem. Caitlin, I'm so sorry."

Resa picked herself up off of the couch and kneeled down at Caitlin's side. She was trying to be encouraging.

Rouge stood up and started flipping one of her daggers around. "So, it looks like we have a rescue operation to conduct," she said, maintaining her cool. "Resa, you and I owe our lives to Kevin. Perhaps it is time we return the favor."

"No," interrupted Caitlin. "I have to do this one myself."

Rachel rolled her eyes. "Caitlin, you sound like Kevin when you say that," she said. "He's our friend too, you know. You don't have to try to rescue him by yourself. We can get the army ready, and we'll go in and save him. You've been through enough; let us take care of things from here on..."

"You don't understand," interrupted Caitlin. "Rachel, I know we're the best of friends, and I know that you, my half-brother, and Rouge and Resa would do anything for me. Following Kevin, though, is something I have to do myself. I wish I could explain, but I can't, and I'm sorry."

A little frustrated, Rachel shook her head. Never before had Caitlin been so stubborn about going it alone. "Please don't make the same mistake Kevin made," she said. "Have you learned nothing from his loss?"

"I do know," said Caitlin. "But now, I don't have a choice. You need to keep your empire stable in case Pseudo decides to let Sayo run wild on the empire. Plus, I can move quicker on my own."

Reluctantly, Rachel looked at Arthur. "I guess it's your decision, my emperor," she said. "What will you allow?"

Everyone looked at Arthur. He had his answer already in mind, as he sat back in his chair, much more relaxed than he had just been. "If Caitlin wants to go by herself, we have no right to force her to take our army with her. I realize that Kevin is my best friend, but I can trust Caitlin to do this herself. However, I insist that if you are going to follow in Kevin's footsteps, that you should spend the night here to rest up and get a good meal while you are here. The Wastes tend to be very unforgiving."

Rachel just looked at Arthur, stunned.

Caitlin stood up and bowed. "Thank you, Arthur," she said. "Thank you so much."

Arthur nodded. "It is nothing," he said. "Now, Rouge and Resa, would you two be willing to take Caitlin down to the kitchen? Have the chef make a filling meal tonight, and make sure it is full of nourishing foods. We can speak more on the issues later."

"As you wish," nodded Rouge. She and Resa both stood up and

took Caitlin with them. Rouge then opened the trap door, and grabbed the inner part of the handle to close it as soon as she was through the exit.

Resa and Caitlin walked down the stairs first, as Resa asked Caitlin, "So what would you like to have for dinner tonight?" Clearly, they were ready to have a relaxing, casual discussion and not have any worries for a while. Before anymore could be heard, Rouge descended the first couple of stairs as well and shut the door.

Instantly, Rachel turned to Arthur, furious. "What the hell?" she asked in a very rude tone. "What is wrong with you? You know that letting Caitlin go out there on her own is basically letting her kill herself!"

"Relax," answered Arthur calmly, not rising from his seat. "Caitlin is very intelligent. She should not have a problem out in the Wastes. We will make sure she has adequate supplies with her to make it all the way across, if need be. And under current imperial law, none of the tribes will attack a lone traveler. I'm not so sure the Aequina will listen to that, but even so, she should be safe from them."

"It's not the Wastes I'm concerned about, Arthur," continued Rachel, still very upset. "Did you not hear her say that Setadev is back? He could easily kill any one of us if he wanted. He already tried to kill her once, and you know he will threaten her again. Everyone in all of the realms is in danger if Setadev is running around again."

"Oh, I heard," answered Arthur, still keeping calm in his chair. "That does make me worry, but there's little I can do to control my half-sister if she wants to save Kevin on her own." He paused for a moment. "But I agree we can't let her kill herself."

"And how do you plan to do that?" asked Rachel.

Arthur hesitated. "Honestly, I was going to ask you that question," he said.

Rachel sighed. It would not be long until it was late. "I don't know," she said reluctantly. "Maybe we can give it the night and see if we have any ideas tomorrow."

Silently, Arthur nodded. So little seemed like it could be done in such a hopeless situation. His best friend captured by a traitor to the Solunar Empire and his fallen deity boss, Arthur was doing his best to stay strong. Even so, he felt the tremors of vengeance being sent by Setadev and General Sayo. And all of that was for simply choosing to exist, to try and create a better world for a city that had been beleaguered by war for decades, of which Arthur had no prior connection, and being friends with someone who later found out he could carry a glowing sword.

In his mind, he was panicking, but he had to try not to show that to anyone, least of all Rachel.

Chapter 18

Best Done Alone

For the rest of the evening, Arthur made sure to treat Caitlin like an honored guest. He treated her and their friends to a good meal, nothing befitting of an emperor since Arthur did not want to eat better than his people, but enough of a hearty meal for Caitlin to have the energy to go in the morning. The two, along with Rachel, Rouge, and Resa, ate together before adjourning to quarters for the night. Caitlin was given a nice room in the pyramid, elegantly decorated but lacking any windows. She had a couple of candles to keep the room lit.

A little later that night, darkness had fully set in and everyone went to bed. Before the sun could rise, however, Caitlin was awake. She was restless, thinking about what needed to be done today. She missed Kevin dearly and she had to find and save him, no matter what it took. Knowing she had to say goodbye to her friends before she left, however, Caitlin decided to leave her room and take a walk around.

Arthur had instructed his palace guards to let Caitlin go wherever she pleased and not to ask questions or obstruct her. He wanted her to feel welcome here in his capital. This gave her the freedom to go wherever she wanted. She thought about going outside, but since it was cold and snowy, Caitlin wanted to try and enjoy as much of the warmth of being in this building as she could before she left for the day. Therefore, she decided to climb up to Arthur's throne room, atop the pyramid, to look out upon the city of Seta Archa.

As she looked out upon the city, Caitlin saw everything that her half-brother did on a regular basis. The stars were out above, mapping out the sky. Below, a few torches were burning around the city, but dark silhouettes inside the walls etched out the outlines of homes and buildings. Looking out and thinking about everything this city had gone through in the past twenty years or more, Caitlin realized this was perhaps it at its most peaceful in that time.

It was warm in the throne room, even behind such large panels of glass. Caitlin was still a little sore from being beaten a couple of days ago, so the warmth helped her feel a little more comfortable. Though she did not fear it, she was not looking forward to being out in the cold, where the soreness would feel worse. Unfortunately, there was not time to wait for her wounds to fully heal. Every day that passed would make it more difficult for her to find Kevin, and increased the danger to his life.

"I've seen this look before," echoed a voice across the room. "Your brother does this a lot."

Caitlin looked over to see Rachel in the throne room, walking toward her. She had never heard the prime minister enter. "You're up quite early," she said.

"As are you," Rachel pointed out, as she briefly adjusted her black and orange dress. "For me, it's part of the job. I have to be awake before my empire is." She looked at Caitlin. "I get the feeling that this morning, it's the same for you."

Sighing, Caitlin shrugged. "I suppose so," she said to Rachel. "I couldn't sleep very well. I haven't for a few days."

Gently, Rachel sat down on the couch nearest to Caitlin, and invited her to sit down. "I'm sorry," she said. "I'm guessing a few reasons?"

Reluctantly, Caitlin sat down next to Rachel. She had wanted to talk with her friend, but she still felt a bit ambushed given the situation, as though this were not fully on her own terms. As she sat down, she simply shook her head.

"I get the feeling you really want to talk to me," Rachel then said.

"Rachel, I've missed talking with you. I think, other than Kevin, you're probably my best friend," said Caitlin. "Secretly, I've hated that you live so far away from me, and that if you hadn't taken Arthur's offer to be his prime minister, you'd be living in Rikleifer with Kevin and I."

Smiling a bit, Rachel answered, "You never even knew me when I was in Rikleifer." She sighed, looking a bit more down. "But I get it. We could've had lots of hangouts together, maybe we'd visit the castle library together or shoot some targets in a shooting gallery, or go explore the shops together."

Caitlin looked at Rachel oddly. "Explore… the shops together?"

"I'm only kidding," Rachel laughed. "It's something a lot of ordinary teenage girls do together. It's not really my thing, and I guess it's not really yours, either."

At this, Caitlin shrugged. "Maybe if I were bored," she said. She paused. "I feel like we had barely become friends by the time we were separated. Now, I could really use one, but I don't know if I've invested enough in you to use your help."

"When you say that, you sound like what Arthur used to call 'the old Caitlin'," joked Rachel. "I agree, we'll have to hang out more when this is all said and done. Hopefully after this winter we shouldn't be so busy all of the time."

Silently, Caitlin nodded. That sounded like a good idea, but her mind was anywhere except on fun.

Noticing Caitlin's mind being elsewhere, Rachel then asked, "That gets me thinking, since we're talking about hanging out more often, why do you want to go after Kevin alone?"

Taking a deep breath, Caitlin answered, "It's just something I have to do."

"You sound like Kevin when you say that," Rachel responded. "Maybe you two are cut from the same cloth a little more that I realized."

"It's not that," Caitlin responded. "I had my mind shattered, Rachel. My whole psyche destroyed." She started to sound distraught, reminded of a very bad memory. "And in that moment, all I could do was cry and scream while the last words Setadev told me resonated in my mind: that Kevin doesn't care about me."

"Oh, Caitlin," a surprised Rachel said as she tried to comfort Caitlin, "you know that isn't true…"

"Is it?" asked Caitlin. "Are you sure about that?"

Rachel stammered, caught off guard by the reaction. "I mean… I'm pretty sure of it. You're clearly not, though, are you?"

Caitlin leaned forward and put her face in her hands. "I thought

I was. But now… I can't forget it."

Looking at Caitlin deeply, Rachel asked, "You believe Setadev?"

"No, of course not," Caitlin said. "I have no reason to believe he's lying about capturing Kevin, but…" She paused.

"Do you worry he's right about Kevin not caring?"

"I don't know," Caitlin broke down, a tear falling from her eye. "I don't have any reason to believe him, but… if you knew how sad I was, and the trauma I endured feeling that…" She looked up at Rachel. "It sounds ridiculous, I'm sure, but with a shattered mind the slightest doubt and fear turned into the most powerful emotions I've ever felt in my life. And that emotion I felt… was tragedy."

Silently, Rachel took a breath for a moment. She knew in this moment she had to be there for her friend. "It doesn't sound ridiculous to me," she said. She then connected the dots. "Is this why you want to go off alone? You need to find out for sure?"

"Is it so ridiculous an idea?" asked Caitlin.

"For you to want to find out, no. For you to want to go alone and do it, yes." Rachel was trying not to be frustrated as she explained. "Kevin was captured because he defied your advice and your request, and he went off alone. If you do as he did, you'll be subjecting yourself to the same fate."

Caitlin shrugged. "I won't let Setadev capture me."

"I'm sure Kevin said the same thing. And now you want us to sit on the sidelines while you go and make the same mistake?"

"You have an empire to run, Rachel. I can't take you away from that."

"Forget the empire for a moment, Caitlin. I could let Arthur stay here and run it; it's his job as the emperor, anyway. You could use my bow. Or I could even bring some military as long as we stay in the empire."

"Rachel, I appreciate it. I really do," Caitlin said as she put her hands in front of her. "But this is best done alone. If the trap is sprung, and Setadev thinks he's taken me out of action, he won't be expecting me." She paused. "Because Sayo is with him, he could be expecting you, or anyone else from the Solunar Empire. That could put the whole empire in danger."

"That doesn't make me feel better about sending you off alone!" answered Rachel, frustrated. She shut down for a moment, not really sure what else she could say to Caitlin. Her friend still had a broken mind of sorts, causing Rachel to worry that Caitlin was doing this too impulsively and recklessly.

Then, Caitlin put her hand on Rachel's shoulder. "Hey, I've got this," she said quietly but with a bit of confidence. "I'll be all right, and one way or another, I'll bring Kevin back."

Reluctantly, Rachel looked up and nodded her head. "I can't stop you," she said, nervously, "so I guess I have no choice but to trust you." She paused for a second. "I hope you haven't lost faith in him. He's a little weird at times and a bit awkward, but I have every reason to believe he loves you."

Quietly, Caitlin nodded. "I know," she said, consciously knowing that but subconsciously wracked with chaos. "He has some explaining to do in why he decided to go without me," she said, as she sounded a bit more determined. "I can't even imagine that I know exactly where he went."

"Beats me," shrugged Rachel. "Sayo could be anywhere out there." Then she thought of something. "But I know who might know. If you head out to the Metoi village, where Kevin was, you should seek out Marilynn, Lady of the Metoi. Her husband was the chief, Aspectra, who was killed by Sayo and his men. She is also a Metoi leader herself, and someone whom we respect greatly, although she doesn't always have the highest opinions of us." Rachel paused. "If anyone knows where Kevin might have gone out in the Wastes, it would be her. Although she has evacuated the Metoi from the village, she is likely still there, either picking up the pieces or safeguarding any books or records that haven't been damaged in the attack."

Caitlin nodded. "Thanks, Rachel," she said. "I'll make sure I seek out Marilynn. Any way I would recognize her?"

"She's a middle aged Metoi woman, and she usually wears traditional garb," Rachel answered. "She also has a huge tattoo on her shoulder of a spiral inscribed in a star, which is the Metoi symbol."

A spiral inside a star. "I'll remember that," Caitlin said.

"You're a great friend. Even when you don't agree with me, you're willing to help me."

"Just remember you owe me one," smiled Rachel. "You know, when we're not out saving people for a change. Maybe I'll need some magic help, or to talk about books, or to help pick out a wedding dress."

At that last bit, Caitlin laughed a little bit. "I'm sure that'll be a while," she said. "I don't imagine you get the chance to do much dating when you're the prime minister of an empire."

"No, but I have my pursuits," said Rachel. "And I'll leave it at that."

"Oh really?" asked an interested Caitlin. "Now who would that be?"

"I'm not going to say."

"Come on, tell me." Caitlin was getting a bit excited.

That made Rachel happy to see, but she would still protect her secrets. "Not going to happen," she said. She started to look a bit embarrassed, like she really did not want to say.

Not quite knowing her limit, Caitlin continued to ask, "Why are you so embarrassed? Is it a man you're not supposed to have? Or is it another woman, maybe?"

Rachel's face turned very red. "It's not another woman," she shrugged off the question. "And I told you, I'm not saying anything. I don't care if you try to read my mind or not, you're not getting it. Not now, at least."

It was at this moment that Caitlin realized she was overstepping. Her understanding and ability to control the excitement of her emotions only went so far while she learned how to harness them properly. "I'm sorry, Rachel," she said. "I really don't like that I get a little childish when I get upset or excited."

Confused, Rachel asked, "Childish? Who told you that? Was it Kevin?"

Caitlin shrugged. "Kevin has never said 'childish', but he's said I light up like a child sometimes." She paused. "Setadev called me childish, and…" she blew out a long exhale, "he was right. In that moment when he got under my skin, I overreacted like a child. I can't ever recall losing my discipline like that before I started embracing emotions."

"That can happen, but it doesn't make you 'childish'," Rachel commented. "Everyone processes things differently. If that's the way you react in the heat of the moment, what of it?"

Sighing, Caitlin nodded. She then said, "By the way, I wouldn't read your mind. It's highly unethical to do so. Your secrets can be your secrets."

Quietly, Rachel thought for a moment. Then, she looked around, before leaning in to Caitlin. She made her decision. "Can you keep a secret?" she whispered. "I've never told anyone this."

"I'm sure I can," acknowledged Caitlin.

Rachel whispered in her ear.

Immediately, Caitlin became excited. "You're kidding!"

"I wish I were," Rachel said, almost smiling because she lifted a small weight off her chest.

"Does he know?"

"No. You're the first I've told."

"I get it now," Caitlin said. "Your secret is safe with me. I really hope you can make it work out."

Rachel smiled. "Now that's the Caitlin who's my friend," she said.

At that moment, the trap door opened, and up walked Arthur into the room. He was actively yawning and his clothes were crooked on his body, as though he were too sleepy to dress himself. The sun itself had not yet risen, so this was not wholly unreasonable. "What's all this?" he asked tiredly. "Why are you ladies up so early?"

The two ladies giggled at him.

Before long, Rouge and Resa were up as well, and everyone was enjoying breakfast and conversing in the throne room. It would not be long, however, before Caitlin said that she had to go. She had direction in mind and knew what she had to do.

And although Rachel had her doubts, she trusted Caitlin to keep herself safe. Caitlin had a good point about what would happen if the empire were involved. Even so, the fact that Kevin had been captured doing the same thing made her worry for her friend.

As Caitlin left, Arthur and company said their goodbyes to her at the base of the pyramid. Arthur offered her a horse if she wanted to try and catch up, but Caitlin declined, knowing that she was not trained at horseback riding and that horses would be unlikely to find enough to eat or drink in the Wastes. Everyone wished Caitlin well and that they would all be together again soon. Then, as she set off, Arthur and Rachel headed up to the throne room to watch Caitlin depart while Rouge and Resa went to meet with the city's defenders on its wall.

Rachel said, "You know, I feel a bit better today about Caitlin going off on her own. I still don't feel great about it, though. She's just so stubborn sometimes."

"I know," nodded Arthur. "I feel the same way. And that is why we are going to get the army ready to follow our own pathway."

That answer came out of nowhere. "Huh?" asked Rachel, confused.

"Rachel, we can let Caitlin follow her own path," continued Arthur, this time assuming a more upright position in his chair. "At the same time, we can't let her do this herself, and we can't let Kevin come to any more danger. I want to rescue him too, you know." He paused for a second, as Rachel listened, intrigued. "We have somewhere we can go, with the army. Sayo has one, but so do we. If we spend a couple of days regrouping them here, we can head out together and launch a rescue of our own. If we are good enough, and we will be, then we will save Kevin and keep Caitlin from ever coming into any harm."

"Wow," said Rachel, cooling down. She took a seat in one of the chairs. "I guess I owe you a little more credit, then. You must've slept on it to show me today that you really do know what you're doing."

"Well, what did you expect?" asked Arthur, starting to regain that classic sarcastic tone that he had had before he became emperor of the Solunar Empire. "I'm not that kind of idiot, remember?"

Even Rachel had to lighten up, with some sense of excitement over Arthur sounding more like his old self. "Or maybe you are," she joked, as she crossed her legs.

Arthur rolled his eyes. "Yeah, yeah, yeah," he said. "Look, this is serious business, though. Caitlin may beat us to him, in which case things probably will be as they would otherwise. If nothing else, though, we will have reinforcements ready to help her if that's the case. We will have to play this right."

"Indeed," nodded Rachel. "You do know that Caitlin would likely be very upset with us if we beat her to it and she found out we didn't really let her rescue Kevin by herself, right?"

"I do," acknowledged Arthur, "but I would rather keep her safe than keep her from getting upset. Plus, this has been our issue since Sayo first attacked the Metoi. The Solunar Empire needs this action as much as Kevin needs it. If nothing else, we are resolving this issue for our own people, not to mention saving our best friend's life and hopefully putting a permanent end to Setadev this time."

Rachel let out a deep sigh. "That last part will be awfully hard, Arthur, especially without Kevin. Even if we rescue him, we have no Seven Stripes of the Elements left to help him like we did last time. We'll have the gods, I'm sure, but we may still not have enough to beat him for good."

"That's the risk we'll have to take," nodded Arthur.

A thought came to Rachel's mind. "Does that mean we're leading this unit by ourselves?"

Arthur started smiling. "It does," he said. "The two of us, along with Rouge and Resa. We'll leave the council here to govern in our absence, and we'll take off to save Kevin, as well."

"Really?" asked Rachel, excited. She was glad to get the taste of adventure again, to leave the sedentary life of governing the empire. She was also glad to get to travel with Arthur again, but in a strange sense like she had never felt before.

"Really," answered Arthur confidently. He could tell now, as his emotions of frustration and depression started to clear up by the thoughts of going to adventure again, that Rachel was acting funny. She was no longer a cynic or a realist; somehow she had gained a sense of idealism that mixed with her realist concerns. There was something funny about the way she was acting, as though she was acting weird.

Arthur could not place his finger on it, though. He knew it was not dangerous, so he had little to be worried about.

"Awesome!" Rachel nearly jumped for joy. "I guess I had better dig out my longbow and quiver again. You had better get your Sword of Corruption. Don't you love it, Arthur? It'll be just like old times again!"

Arthur nodded in acknowledgment. Then, he clenched his fist. Though this excitement about getting to travel again and start questing had snapped Arthur out of his somber attitude, a deep sadness was in his heart for his best friend, Kevin. Nothing could overcome that.

Kevin and Arthur had been friends for as long as they had lived. It was an irony, in some senses, that Arthur's mother and aunt were close friends with Vincent Stryker and Lavinia Trent, Kevin's parents, when Demonicus sent Arthur's aunt Rita off with Arthur to live outside of Desolunar. She chose Rikleifer, just down the street from Kevin's family, and as a result the two boys grew up together. Even without their parents, they had become the best of friends.

They had shared their dreams together, their ambitions and desires. And, when Arthur was discovered with Kevin by Kronius, Arthur became a crucial part of Kevin's quest. Now, with his best friend missing, Arthur knew that he had to save his best friend. Having seen him only a couple of weeks before made it that much more cement.

Tempted to make sure the real reasons for the trip were secure with Rachel as well, Arthur looked to see Rachel very deep in thought, and sad. Clearly, as the excitement of leaving Seta Archa had waned off, the emotion of Kevin being missing had hit her hard as well. Everything in her focused mind was shifting over to the goal of saving Kevin and making sure Caitlin would be safe.

Then, she realized something. "How will we know where to go?" she asked. "You said we have somewhere we can go with the army. Where is that?"

Arthur only leaned back in his chair for a moment. "Someone is hiding something from us. He did not tell us something. Wherever that something is, will tell us where to go next."

Chapter 19

Another Consultation

Darkness…

Everywhere he looked, there was only darkness.

He was kneeling on the ground, in the darkness. "Father, why?" he asked.

There was no response.

"I did all that you asked me to. I imposed your will. I searched for the seven powers that you told me to. Why did you forsake me? Why?"

Audibly, there was no sound. Only silent breathing echoed in his head.

"I know it was you. I know you are why my plans did not succeed. My plans, though, were all in the name of your glory. They were for your greatness. Why did you have to destroy them? Why did you use me?"

You do not see how the game is played!

Instantly, Demonicus snapped out of his sleep, in complete surprise. It had all been a dream, yet one that had seemed so real. As he tried to regain himself, he thought only of the days of watching his kingdom from the top of his triangular pyramid, and of who was watching out through there now.

His mind was only at an awkward peace during those days. Demonicus had been a much more fragile individual than he had led himself on to be at that time, relying heavily on the voice of his father as his guidance. Though he was a man with the blood of many on his hands, never did he really enjoy taking blood. It was all about absolute victory, and as such, taking no prisoners and obliterating everything in his path was his strategy, the one that was his philosophy in war.

Outside, it was still nighttime, although Demonicus could not tell that from his cell. Arthur kept him locked up as punishment for all that he had done, which he had felt that he deserved. Every day, Demonicus was paying for the blood stains on his hands.

The sound of footsteps came from down the hall. Two sets, Demonicus realized. Quite unusual, indeed. The only one who ever visited was Arthur, and he always visited alone—save for the time he brought the pure one with him.

This time, though, Arthur was accompanied by Rachel.

Immediately, Demonicus stepped to the door. "You have returned," he said. "What brings you here today, my son?"

Again, the last two words struck Arthur hard to hear, but he did not let them bother him too much. "Business, Demonicus," he said. "You didn't tell me something before, and I'm here to find out what that is."

Demonicus flicked his eyebrows. "Really, now? If you do not know what it is that I did not tell you, then why do you believe that I did not tell you something?"

"Because you lied," glared Arthur. "Or at least, you omitted certain truths to the stories of your regime."

"And what makes you believe that?" asked Demonicus.

With no fear, Arthur looked straight through the bars in the window of the door, into the eyes of Demonicus. "Your father," he said, referring to Setadev and the term Demonicus sometimes used to refer to him.

There was a moment's pause. Then, Demonicus turned around and walked toward the back wall of his cell. "The voices," he began, with a long pause following, "the voices… he has returned after all. But how?"

"Why don't you tell me?" interrupted Arthur.

Suddenly, Rachel tugged at Arthur's sleeve. "Take it easy, Arthur," she said. "In this case, I don't think he knows. Perhaps it is possible that Demonicus didn't know anything about it until you mentioned it to him just now."

"No," interrupted Demonicus, as he turned around again. "You are wrong, minister. I have just heard his voice again, just before you arrived."

"Then you're receiving messages from him," stated Arthur.

"In a manner of speaking," nodded Demonicus. "However, they are not so much what you might consider 'messages'. My father has long since forsaken me."

Rachel took a step toward the door. "Why would he forsake you?" she asked, in a more pointed tone.

Demonicus shook his head, and then spat at the ground. "You are quite naïve for a young ruler, minister. You would not realize, therefore, that my father abandoned me at the Battle of Seta Archa a few months before. To him, I am merely a pawn, and when he had no more use for me, he allowed me to fail."

"I realize that," acknowledged Rachel, "because I was there. My question, however, is still valid. We know he is still alive, Demonicus. Why did he forsake you?"

There was a slight pause. Then, a grumble from Demonicus. "He never cared," the middle-aged Demonicus finally said aloud. He took down his hood, revealing his shock of faded blonde hair and blue eyes, not surprisingly similar to the look of his son, Arthur. The look sent a jolt up Arthur's spine. He certainly could see the resemblance he shared to his father now, and why he looked so different from his half-sister, Caitlin. "He set me up to fail, I am sure," Demonicus continued. "Even now, in my dreams he haunts me. When I beg him for the answer, he tells me only that I do not see how the game is played."

Arthur and Rachel looked at each other for a second. Then, Arthur addressed his father. "We think he's running loose in Solunar somewhere. It looks as though he made a copy of himself in the form of Pseudo."

Demonicus let out a sigh, in interruption. "I thought he had been killed," said the former leader of Desolunar. "My men reported to me that the pure one stabbed him through with his sword and kicked him off of a ledge."

In response, Arthur glared through the window in the door. "You know better," he said.

Looking confused, Demonicus asked, "What do you mean?"

"Don't lie to me, father!" exclaimed Arthur, getting frustrated. "You had to have known all along that Pseudo was a creation of your father. You had to have known that he must have been forged of his divine power."

"Of course," nodded Demonicus, interrupting his son. "I knew that my father created Pseudo. How else would someone who looked exactly like the pure one serve alongside me and be my second-in-command?"

"That's not what I meant, and you know it," stated Arthur, getting even harsher with his tone.

Letting out a sigh, Demonicus said, "I don't know what you want. What are you trying to say?"

Arthur was getting angry, and it seemed like his blood was going to boil as he clenched his fists tight. But Rachel, seeing this, put her hand on Arthur's arm. "Ease up, Arthur," she said calmly. "We didn't know until just now. Maybe he doesn't know as much as we think he does, either."

So much, Arthur wanted to be angry with his father. Yet Rachel was right; if Arthur himself had not known, then the knowledge may have eluded Demonicus as well. He then looked at his father, with a more stern yet less frustrated appearance. "Pseudo is not just your father's creation, Demonicus. He is your father, or at least a fragment of him."

Demonicus's eyes widened. He turned and marched around in his cell. "The voices," he mumbled to himself, but loud enough that Arthur and Rachel could hear. "The messages, the continued torment… it all makes sense now why it has continued. He just will not leave me alone."

Rachel and Arthur looked at each other, puzzled. They were trying to make sense of what Demonicus was saying, but it was difficult because of his mumbling. Then, Demonicus cleared his voice and spoke up. "What you are saying, then, is that my father is still alive because he divided himself up prior to his death."

"That is exactly what we are saying," responded Rachel. "Setadev lived because Kevin never actually killed Pseudo, as we understand it. Our source tells us that although Kevin ripped through Pseudo and caused injuries that would have killed any mortal, Pseudo was not killed because he was immortal."

There was a long pause. Then, a dark chuckle from Demonicus.

"What do you find so funny?" interrupted Arthur.

Demonicus had to stop chuckling to respond. "My son, do you not believe that you are overthinking the matter? The simpler explanation would be that the pure one never destroyed my father, as you believe he did. After all, my father is immortal too. How could he kill one and not the other, if both were immortal?"

Logical question. But Rachel had an answer. "Don't deny it," she said. "Kevin wasn't alone; he had Caitlin with him. You can't tell me they both are hiding such a hideous lie."

"Perhaps," Demonicus said as he stepped back to the window. "I am not one to speculate, however. Regardless of the reason he is still alive, the situation is now worse."

That made Arthur freeze up. "Worse?" he asked. "How is it worse? Tell me!"

Rachel could tell Arthur was getting feisty. He felt as though Demonicus was hiding something, and she could agree with that sentiment.

As he normally did when pressured by his son, however, Demonicus stepped back and sat back down in his cell. He took a second to pause, before continuing. "My son, I am glad that you do not know my father the way that I know him. I am glad that you have never known him as I have."

Again, Arthur rolled his eyes. "I'm still a little touchy about the 'son' aspect, if you don't mind."

"I understand that," answered Demonicus, "but your harboring of me was well meant for that purpose."

It was. Arthur could not deny that. It was the whole reason Arthur had let Demonicus live after the Battle of Seta Archa, much less keep him where he was.

As Arthur thought on this aspect briefly, Demonicus continued, "If there is one thing my father has that distinguishes him from any other man, it is a temper and a desire for revenge. He does not tolerate failure very well at all. I am sure that he does recognize by now that the failure was his, and all involved in his downfall will be the most susceptible to his anger. My guess would be that this anger would start with the pure one for being the one to destroy him."

Arthur and Rachel looked away for a second. They were very painfully aware of what Caitlin had told them.

Noticing this, Demonicus asked, "It has begun already, has it not?"

Neither Arthur nor Rachel gave a response.

Demonicus bowed his head. "I understand," he said. "Captured or killed?"

After a moment's pause, Rachel answered, "Captured, but we fear that he may have something sadistic planned for Kevin."

"I see," nodded Demonicus. "Whether or not you believe me, minister, the pure one does have my respect." He then turned to Arthur. "My son, I want you to know that as well. When you came down to see me before, the pure one stayed to ask more questions of me. He also told me that he was not beyond forgiving me someday, and for that I will always respect him whether or not he does. Anyone who would even consider that is someone to which I owe a great deal of gratitude."

Again, Arthur looked away. Rachel realized that being in Demonicus's presence was bringing him down, and to think anyone would forgive his father hit him on the head with the real issue at hand: whether or not he would be willing to forgive Demonicus.

"Then will you help us?" she began to Demonicus. "Surely you do know something about this whole situation that will be helpful to us. Where he might be going, what he might be doing… anything of that sort."

"Of that, I know little," answered Demonicus, "but I can hypothesize."

"Then do it," ordered Rachel. "What can you tell us?"

With this, Demonicus took a breath, walked around his cell for a minute, and sat back down. Clearly, he was nervous. At first, Rachel thought it was because he really did not want to say anything about it, that it was not in his true interest. Then it hit her. Setadev was not only speaking to Demonicus, but was able to issue repercussion to him as well. Demonicus mumbled about "the voices" before, almost as if he feared them. He was working up the courage to defy the repercussions and speak about the matter to his son.

Pausing for another minute, Demonicus took a deep breath. "As I warned the pure one before he left on his expedition, General Sayo is very likely to have many Enlighteners from the Shadows with him. I am sure that the pure one told you before he left what I told him; that the Enlighteners are a group of my father's design, and of his teachings and will."

"I recall," answered Rachel. "Go on."

Demonicus took another breath. "The Enlighteners have been playing against the pure one all along. Without a doubt, my father is relying on them as a support network. He did much the same when Desolunar existed, to increase his vision and the number of minds working for his goals. Now, I am sure with Desolunar gone, he has made the Enlighteners his primary network to support him." He paused for a second. "If Sayo is with them as well, as I believe he would be, then chances are Sayo is only a satellite of this network. My father would not entrust his mortal realm network to a force as small as his is in comparison to the power of a whole country or the worldwide spread of an ancient group he founded."

"Do the Enlighteners have a headquarters he might go to?" asked Arthur, interrupting.

There was another short pause. "Sort of," answered Demonicus.

"Sort of?" asked Arthur.

Demonicus nodded. "It could be called one, but it is not exactly one. The Enlighteners operate as a fragmented group without direction in each individual circuit of the group, aside from the voice of the father. There is, however, a relay point they use for communication with one another. This is how I gained my knowledge of other Enlighteners around the world: through messengers via the relay point."

"What kind of relay point?" asked Arthur. "Is it a building or something? An underground structure, or somewhere else hidden?"

"No," answered Demonicus. "It is in plain sight."

Arthur and Rachel stood cold for a second. Something about that answer made it seem as though the Enlighteners had more gall than they had previously suggested.

"The relay point is known amongst the Enlighteners as the Fortress of Da Leval," continued Demonicus. "It is built out of white stone, and in my opinion is a magnificent structure. Quite lovely in the summer time, although the landscape it sits on is not well complemented in the winter by any structure…"

"Get to the point," interrupted Arthur, noting Demonicus's rambling.

Immediately, Demonicus corrected himself, knowing the importance of this business. "All around the world, only the Enlighteners from the Shadows know of where this structure is located. Any intruders into the region, as few as they are, are usually taken captive and executed, in order to protect this secret fortress."

"And where is it?" asked Rachel.

Demonicus said the location.

Rachel just shook her head in response. "No wonder it can be hidden in plain sight," she said. "Really, though? Why would anyone build a fortress there?"

"We all know of the rumors," added Arthur. "They must have some guts to build there."

"They do," nodded Demonicus. "That fortress is several thousand years old, but even before then, the events that gave such a land its reputation were already taking place. Needless to say, it is the best protection system available to such a place. Even if they cannot truly rise up, the dead guard the fortress better than any living soul could."

"So it seems," nodded Rachel.

Arthur turned to Rachel. "I guess we know now where we have to take the army," he said. "Whether or not Setadev is there, toppling that fortress will be very important to removing the Enlighteners from Solunar for good, and crippling Setadev's network."

"I would be careful of doing that, if I were you," interrupted Demonicus, with caution in his voice. "Though it may be your only course of action, the ghosts of war are not very forgiving, you know."

Nodding, Arthur turned to Rachel again, but this time he whispered in her ear, "We should discuss this further without Demonicus. Regardless of the rumors, there's more at stake here."

Rachel silently nodded.

With this acknowledgment, Arthur no longer desired to see his father. However, this time he was not simply willing to walk away. He gave a bow, and said, "Thank you. That will be all for today." Then, he turned down the hall and walked off.

As she watched him walk away, Rachel just shook her head. Then, she started to follow him.

"Wait, please."

The voice came from back down the hall again.

Though he did not turn around, Arthur did stop where he was. He waited for Demonicus to continue.

"If you do find the pure one, tell him that I am sorry," continued Demonicus. "I am sorry to him for everything I have done against him."

"Why don't you tell him in person?" Arthur shouted back, without turning. "He will be back here soon enough, and you can say it to his face then." And with that, Arthur stormed off. Rachel followed close behind.

It was a short walk out of the dungeon area, and Arthur slammed the access door behind him. He wanted no more of his father for today.

When they were out of the dungeon with the door shut, Rachel asked Arthur, "So, shall we begin the regrouping phase? It will take a while until our men are ready to march."

Arthur raised a hand. "Hold on that for a second," he said. "Rachel, we need to think this through before we do anything."

"And how do you figure that?" asked Rachel. "I thought you said we would be doing anything necessary to rescue Kevin."

For a quick second, Arthur chuckled. It was just then that he realized Rachel was a little more of an idealist and less of a cynical realist than she had been before. Perhaps if he had had the vigor for life before, like the energy he had now, he would have noticed that. Still, there were serious issues to discuss. Arthur had to maintain his mindset while he discussed them with Rachel. "We will be," he continued, with a confident air. "However, we do need to be sure of our approach. I have no worries in dealing with the rumors around where we are headed, but I do have an issue with taking our armies outside of Solunar without permission. Not only is that trespassing and an act of war, but given the invasions from this area of land in the last twenty years from both the Daritel and Desolunar, such a move might incite mass hysteria again and lead to the destruction of the peace we have made in the Solunar Empire."

"Oh..." said Rachel, as she realized his point, "I almost forgot about that. You're right; how do we move the army outside of the country without inciting fear? Once we touch the soil of another land with our army, that is an act of war."

Arthur rolled his eyes. "Obviously we will be minimizing our time with that by marching our men through our own territory as far as possible before taking them out. So, we will want to have plenty of maps ready and we will want to carefully plot out our route. I trust that you can delegate that task, Rachel?"

"I can," nodded Rachel. "What about walking into foreign territory with the army, though?"

Letting out a sigh, Arthur said, "I guess we'll just have to risk it," he said. "We have to do it, for Kevin, and for the future of the Solunar Empire. We don't have a future until Setadev is no longer a threat, and that includes the empire, not just us."

Rachel had no qualms about it, knowing that she wanted to save Kevin. "Right," she nodded, in full agreement. "This is too important for us to ignore." She paused for a moment. "Maybe the rumors will actually help us in this case. There won't be a lot of people anywhere near where we're headed."

Brilliant. Lucky break, if there ever was one. "Hey, that just might work," said Arthur, as his tone lightened up. "It's worth a shot, at least. Let's just hope it goes well."

"Indeed," nodded Rachel.

There was a very long moment of silence. Arthur leaned back against the wall to which he was nearest. Neither one said a word for a moment. "Rachel, where have I been?" interrupted Arthur, breaking the silence.

"Huh?" asked Rachel, confused.

"Where have I been?" asked Arthur again. "It is a simple question, Rachel; I would hope that you would be able to answer it."

Rachel was confused. "I guess I don't understand you, Arthur."

"I'm sure you do," answered Arthur. "You have watched me

look over this city in a gloomy daze for the last couple of months now. You know more about me than most do; maybe only Kevin knows more. I don't know where I have been, but I haven't been here in the past three months."

Aha! Rachel realized what Arthur was talking about now.

Arthur continued, clutching his fist together. "It's just a shame," he paused, "that it took finding out that my best friend has been captured, to bring me back to sanity."

Nodding, Rachel added, "Imagine what it did to Caitlin, on top of everything else that happened to her."

"I can only imagine," said Arthur. With that, thoughts of his half-sister ran through his mind, as he leaned back against the wall and closed his eyes. Though Arthur and Caitlin were still working on becoming close siblings, having only recently discovered their biological relationship, they were already good friends. As Kevin had become very close with Caitlin, Arthur had to become friends with her as well in order to keep up with his best friend.

The combined pain of losing his best friend and seeing his half-sister hurt so badly by it had brought Arthur back into the real world. Though he was sarcastic and excited again, inside he hid his overwhelming sadness and determination for what he had to do now.

Seeing him so contemplative, Rachel walked over to Arthur and hugged him tightly, almost without thinking about it. "We'll save him soon enough," she said. "In the meantime, we have to be strong for both of them."

She was right. Arthur knew it. He had to be strong. Then, he realized something. Something that was out of place. Since when was Rachel hugging him? She had never been like that before.

His eyes instantly popped open. "Rachel, what are you doing?" he blurted out, surprised.

Instantly, Rachel, let go. She was stunned. "I'm sorry, I…" She backed off, almost horrified. "I'll be back." With that, she bolted off.

Clearly she was making an excuse, but to Arthur, one thought kept running through his head as he watched her run away.

What was that all about?

Chapter 20
Stratagems

"I'm sorry, Professor Magnon, but how do you know this source of your information, again?" asked Vincent Stryker.

In the city of Bladinstar, in Aurana, Professor James Magnon was grouped with Necana Larin, Kron Kalavere, and Vincent Stryker, the former two being the gods Necnea and Kronius. They stood together on this cold winter evening in front of the Bladinstar School of Wizardry and Sorcery, which had a simple design in the shape of a brick. Fires burned around the city even as the night was starting to set in, keeping its denizens warm in the cold, windy weather. An adamant Vincent Stryker, being the only one who was not a god in this traveling party, was a little impatient but felt he was in the right, given his worry for his son, Kevin. Professor Magnon could not agree more, himself being a parent and knowing what came from the necessity to protect one's children.

"She is the headmistress of this school," answered Professor Magnon, as he invited everyone into the building. They followed him as the professor elaborated. "Sarah Haughton was one of my students, and though she is not the strongest of magic casters, she is very well educated. She is also very tied in with diplomacy and international affairs."

"If she is so well educated, does she know of your identity?" asked Kronius.

The professor nodded. "She does," he answered. "I told her only yesterday."

Necnea shook her head. "You do know that Larion would be quite upset with you for sharing our existence with a mortal, correct?"

"I do know, but in this case I believe it will be helpful," answered the professor. "If Sarah can give us the information we need, without restriction, then we will be better off in the end. Also, I feel as though she deserved to know," he continued as he looked away for a second and his tone softened. "I have worked with Sarah Haughton for the better part of a half century. She was my student for years before becoming the master of this school."

"And a friend," added Vincent, causing the three gods around him to turn and look at him. "The way you say that indicates you do have some sense of care for her."

Tyrinion nodded. "You speak the truth, Vincent Stryker. You and your son seem to share the same sense of logic."

As the group continued down the hallway into the school, the barren solid stone of the school stood in contrast to the grandeur of Angel Tower in the Realm of the Angels. There was nothing special to be found in the structure of the school, and it made those present wonder why Tyrinion had wanted to teach at this school for years and years. Of course, to the professor, it was all about the students and his passions.

Within a few minutes, the group had arrived at Professor Magnon's office. It was by far the largest office in the school, containing two windows, a large bookcase, a desk with podium, and also a raised circle for demonstration and work with magic casting. There was, after all, no teacher greater than Professor James Magnon.

Professor Magnon held the door open and let everyone else in. "Wait for a moment here," he said. "I will go and get the headmistress." He then left, leaving Necnea, Kronius, and Vincent Stryker inside.

As soon as the door was closed, Kronius started looking around in awe. The professor's office appealed to him greatly, having never seen his workspace. "This is amazing," he said.

"Really?" commented Necnea, as she looked as well. "This is certainly not a grandiose sight to me. Simply an office with a casting platform, that is all."

"Ah, but Necnea, you have to look beneath what you see," remarked Kronius. "Tyrinion… er, the professor, has undoubtedly constructed most of what this school is today, and this is his office. I bet that almost half of those books on his bookcase, he has written himself."

Vincent looked up at the size of the bookcase. "Knowing him, I bet he has written much more than this."

Necnea rolled her eyes. "Nice," she said with sarcasm, almost unimpressed. She was not scornful of the professor, but only that it was relatively small by comparison, herself being used to much larger facilities. "Still, we have a much more impressive library in the Realm of the Angels. If we needed any information at all, we could always reference the information there."

Hearing this, Kronius turned, looked at Necnea, and shook his head. "No," he said. "That is not true at all. You will not find a great deal of this in the Realm of the Angels. What the professor has learned, he has written down, and much of it is unknown to us."

"Oh, really?" asked Necnea, skeptically.

"Yes, really," nodded Kronius.

"Prove it."

"Fine, I will. Do you know anything about removing anti-magic afflictions, Necnea?"

Necnea shook her head. "Not as far as I am aware of. If you are referring to antite--antimage metal—there is no way to remove the affliction, except to wait out the effects."

"And that is where you are wrong," stated Kronius. He started looking through the bookshelf, and a minute later found what he was looking for. It was a copy of *The Rise of Dictators, The Fall of Kings* by James Magnon, a book that the professor had recommended to Kronius as part of his continuing studies. Kronius continued, "I have read parts of this book. He just finished writing it last month, based on his studies of magic, and has not brought a copy to the Realm of the Angels. Now," he paused, "tell me if you have ever found anything like this."

He flipped to Section 6, Chapter 29: Removal of Anti-Magic Afflictions:

While they are rare, anti-magic afflictions can be nasty to a spellcaster. Usually anti-magic afflictions are temporary and do not require anything but time to wear off. These lengths of time can be reasonably long, sometimes lasting years. Most, however, are minor.

No permanent occurrence of an anti-magic affliction has ever been documented, though a couple of undocumented cases have occurred, suggesting that a weapon capable of the permanent removal of magic from a person could be possible.

Most anti-magic afflictions are caused by the mineral antenz and its processed form, antite—better known as antimage metal. While its potency depends on the content of antenz fused into the iron used to make antite—which compromises the strength of the iron—generally antimagic afflictions do not last any great length. This is, however, what caused the death of many spellcasters during the Mage Genocide; when users of magic were temporarily disabled, they could not defend themselves from weapons any further. In some cases, magic has been used to strengthen the antimagic effect, creating a paradox in logic; however, it has been shown that as more magic is absorbed into antite, the anti-magic effects are actually strengthened.

In order to more quickly remove one of these afflictions, one must first have slight magic control back to them. While it varies among people and the power of the anti-magic affliction, a usual measure of the point for this cure to work is the ability to spontaneously light a spark of flame equal to the power of a small burning flame. Once that is achieved, create a magic spark, similar to an orb or ball, but very small, as larger forms of magic are likely unachievable until the very end of the natural healing process. This spark should have a half-light and half-darkness composition.

Once this spark is created, turn it within yourself, and use the magic of internal sight to follow the magic spark as you guide it. Search for areas that appear to be normal in the dark field you see but without color, and touch it with both sides of the spark. Once every area is taken care of, remove the spark and dissipate it. Magic control should be fully restored by this point.

What I have come to learn from the effects of antite is that it works by absorbing magic into itself. As more is absorbed, the vacuum intensifies, and elemental magic is even more easily dissipated by the miracle metal. However, as is usually the case, dissipation of any form of anti-magic has been shown by me to be negated by the dimeric use of the primary elements, light and darkness. Their opposing effects offset the disturbances that cause loss of magic function, and as long as it is used with extreme care and very precise control, can be used in restoring those whose magic has been drained by antite.

As Necnea read through this passage, Kronius noted, "Much of the chapter after you get past the actual treatment is about antite and how it can do what it does." He paused for a moment. "My understanding is a couple of months ago, the professor found out his daughter had been hit by an antite arrow in the Battle of Middle Aurana," he said, referencing the large battle in Rikleifer that Kevin, Caitlin, Rachel, and Vincent Stryker had participated."

Next to Kronius, Vincent Stryker nodded in acknowledgment. "She asked Kevin not to tell her father at the time. She must've finally broken down and done so."

Kronius picked up from there. "Professor Magnon told me that led him to commit a lot of time to researching how to reverse antite, and he found a method, even though it takes a lot of skill to pull off. Supposedly the only people who know about this method are him and his daughter, since he taught it to her once he discovered it."

"Are you certain about that?" asked Necnea.

"Absolutely," nodded Kronius. "Do not misinterpret me, Necnea. I am not saying that Tyrinion is all knowing or anything of that sort, but he has learned things we do not know or have recorded. He has had experiences that none of us have ever had, and he has invested his time and efforts into learning things we have never been able to discover without him."

"It comes with the solitude," echoed a voice from the doorway.

Kronius, Necnea, and Vincent turned to see Professor Magnon standing in the doorway with a woman slightly older in appearance next to him.

Noticing this, Professor Magnon stepped fully into his office, and the woman followed him. "When one has a great deal of excess time, it is often beneficial to spend that time learning new things and teaching oneself to become stronger. And likewise, if we are to believe that knowledge is power, then it was and still is equally important to document the new things learned and the strengths gained so that the power is not lost, although some knowledge is best left undistributed until the proper time."

Vincent Stryker offered a bow. Kronius and Necnea nodded as well.

Professor Magnon acknowledged them. He then continued, as he stepped aside to indicate his companion, "Allow me to introduce to you Headmistress Sarah Haughton of the Bladinstar School." Then, the professor turned to Sarah and indicated to Kronius, Necnea, and Vincent. "Let me introduce to you Kron Kalavere, a faithful messenger. Next to him, Necana Larin, mystic of time. And next to her, Vincent Stryker, who bears the title 'Vincent the Pure One'."

Sarah bowed. "I am honored," she said. "Can I presume that all of you are gods, as well?"

Before anyone else could answer, Professor Magnon did. "Two of them are. Necana Larin is the goddess of time, Necnea; and Kron Kalavere is the messenger god Kronius. Vincent Stryker, however, is mortal. I am surprised you did not recognize his name."

The realization hit Sarah then. Vincent Stryker's name, of course, was fairly well known worldwide for those who had been old enough to remember the Alliance-Daritel War vividly. "Of course," she said. "My apologies."

"It is nothing," nodded Vincent. "Consider it my honor to make your acquaintance, Mrs. Haughton."

"Please, call me Sarah," responded the headmistress. "I have never been married, so 'Mrs. Haughton' would be quite inappropriate anyway."

Vincent nodded.

Professor Magnon then continued, "Vincent is also the father of the boy who is dating my daughter."

Rolling his eyes, Vincent sighed. He wished Professor Magnon had not put things quite that way. Such facts as the last one he stated were irrelevant for the moment.

"That same boy is now in trouble, Sarah," continued the professor. "As I mentioned to you before, the signatures of Setadev are floating around again. It seems evident now that he is still alive, and we now have reason to believe that he has captured the boy, as well.

Therefore, we need to find Vincent's son, as quickly as possible."

"I see," nodded Sarah. "Do you believe he might be the one to whom that poem from the *Letters to the Adventurer* by Clavius Lekion Stryker Dominous was addressed?"

The professor responded in the affirmative.

Necnea was stunned. "You know of the prophecy?"

"Prophecy?" responded Sarah, confused. She looked to the professor. "I thought you did not believe in prophecy?"

At this point, the professor looked up and addressed Sarah. "I do not, but we must treat it as one," he said. "At this time, we have little to lose by not doing so, and we have few other leads at this moment."

Reluctantly, Sarah nodded. "It is from a series of poems called the *Letters to the Adventurer*. They were written a few hundred years ago by a poet named Clavius Lekion Stryker Dominous, who served as an advisor to a king in the last days of the Third Era. Supposedly he was believed by some to be a bizarre character, especially since he claimed to be able to see the future, and that is why he was hired to be an advisor to a king."

Thinking hard, Necnea thought this story sounded familiar. "I think I remember reading of this in the histories," she said. "His supposed foresight was a scam, unable to provide his ruler with the information he needed to prevent an invasion, and their fortress was ransacked with the king's surrender and Clavius's execution so his foresight, if it were real, could not be used agains them." She paused. "The invading kingdom, as I recall, did not last long beyond that as it was defeated and conquered by feudal Aurana, in the formation of the superstate kingdoms at the start of the Fourth Era."

"You must know your history well," commented Sarah. "I don't know all of it, but you sound quite grounded and confident in it."

Necnea nodded.

Sarah then turned to Professor Magnon. "James, unfortunately I checked my books, and I don't have more than the first and second poems in the series. I fear that any further may have been lost to history, but there was enough information in the records to imply there were originally more than two."

Professor Magnon sighed. "We will have to make do," he said. "Is the one I showed you one of the two?"

"Yes, it is the first," acknowledged Sarah. "And I have found the second. And I have analyzed it." Sarah took a piece of paper out of her pocket. It was folded up and took several unfolding steps to fully unravel. She laid it flat on the professor's desk, revealing it to be the second poem from the *Letters*. The poem was printed in black, and in several places Sarah had added notes, written in blue, in the margins.

The world moves in mysterious ways,
And the sky goes through cycles on all days.
Much is the same about the bad
Who walks around in darkness clad.
He uses the shadow to hide, protect,
And create masks to make others defect.
Beware the lure of protecting your friends,
Or else a curse he will hold over your heads.
He's gunning for you, but you he won't kill;
He prefers to snare and force into you a pill;
He'll change you, break you, destroy all you are,
Demolish your reputation near and far;
Then he'll take away the one you love,
Break hearts like dropping a glass dove.
And when you have nothing left, and he drains your regret,
You will become his most powerful asset.
A source of power has emerged, a powerful gate
From the seven powers' disintegrated fate.
Another dimension is open somewhere
And if he crosses the rift, all will despair.
Ancient weapons are all abound;
He knows them all, and will search 'til they're found.
Those who watch from above, overhead,
Will not be able to rest in their beds
Once the truths of all are revealed
And the Great Conqueror returns completely healed.
Begin will the greatest trial, as winter falls;

The two of you must prove that love conquers all.
Betrayal, pain, deception, sadness,
Endure them all and the Key will glow with happiness.
Only by love's triumph over adversity, over hate
Can access be granted to the fusion gate.
And if you two can finally become one,
The Great Conqueror will have no choice but away to run.

She sat down in the chair at the desk, as the others circled the professor's desk, standing. "Literature just happens to be one of my many interests," Sarah added. "This one referred to the one 'who walks around in darkness clad', might this be the person you refer to as Setadev?"

"I've never been sure of that," nodded the professor. "If this were a prophecy, it would depend on interpretation. I was for many years the god of darkness, after all." He looked away for a moment.

So did Kronius, who felt ashamed with the same thought as the professor.

Sarah was confused by this. "Why the reaction?" she asked. "Professor, I do not understand your shame by that. Just because Setadev has returned and the first one played out already, as you said before, does not mean you have failed…"

"It is not that," interrupted Kronius, seeing the professor did not want to speak. "For the longest time, the gods—myself included—presumed that Setadev had been dead for millennia and that the one who the first poem was written about was Tyrinion."

Tyrinion. Sarah realized that Kronius was referring to the professor, remembering vaguely that that name was his deity name. Knowing the professor as well as she did, Sarah dropped the subject. "The first few lines seem to indicate that he might be able to disappear and reappear with some crafty tricks, and can play people off against one another. He would seem to be strategically very gifted." She paused for a moment. "The next couple of lines, however, definitely serve as a warning. 'Beware the lure of protecting your friends, or else a curse he will hold over your heads.'"

Professor Magnon nodded. "My daughter told me that Kevin,

the young man we have been mentioning, left for the Wastes region of the Solunar Empire. His best friend is the new emperor of the region, and it sounded as though the new country was being endangered by a rogue general. Kevin left to help with that, and we believe it was there that he was captured."

Sarah sighed. "The coincidences seem quite strong," she said. "At the very least, if this is a prophecy and can be presumed to be true, we can be assured that for now his life is safe, and that he is in no danger. However, looking at the next few lines tells me that it is likely he is going to be psychologically stressed in some fashion." She started pointing to the next lines in the poem. "Though the lines are a little cryptic, what is implied is that the individual listed in the poem as the Great Conqueror, which I can only presume is this Setadev that you have told me of, has an agenda to break Kevin's spirit, defame him, and tear apart any relationship he might have."

"No wonder he attacked your daughter, Tyrinion," noted Necnea.

Tyrinion shook his head. He still refused to believe it as a prophecy, but even he was starting to see the parallels with reality. He then stared at Sarah.

Taking the hint from the professor's reaction, Sarah continued, "I am intrigued with how the poem declares that the addressed one will become the Great Conqueror's most powerful asset. That part, I cannot help you with. The next part, however, begins to speak in ways that are more coherent with the imagination that the real world, even for the gods, I am sure. It speaks of an opening to another dimension that is a 'source of power', and connects it to at least one ancient weapon of some type."

"Might it mean the opening to the Realm of the Angels?" suggested Vincent Stryker.

Necnea shook her head. "I doubt that would be so," she said. "While I would not be surprised if the realms were interpreted as other 'dimensions', Setadev knows where that opening is already and could have taken it at any time. Therefore, I am doubtful that that is what is meant by 'another dimension'."

As Necnea and Vincent discussed this, Kronius looked at

Tyrinion to see him very contemplative in his thought processes. He knew something.

"Is something on your mind?" asked Kronius.

Tyrinion said nothing, but stepped over to his bookshelf, and passed another book to Kronius. "Only slightly," he said. "Flip to chapter 96 and start reading."

Kronius nodded.

He looked at the book cover. It was titled *Stratagems: The World As We Know It and How to Use it Adequately* by Professor James Magnon. Another one of the professor's books, this one from a couple of years ago based on the date in the cover.

Immediately upon recognizing this, Kronius set the book down on the desk and flipped through it, making his way through it quickly. He stopped when he hit the 96th chapter, and began to read.

Chapter 96: Different Dimension Possibilities

This book, as those who eventually read through the whole of it will recognize, has been devoted to the research of various stratagems of general use by using the world around us; whether for war, peace, or any reason, as many possibilities and logical solutions have been examined and evaluated. One would not truly understand the whole of stratagems, however, if one did not examine the possibilities that lie all around us. Although it may seem fictional, evidence suggests that there may be the possibility of different dimensions aside from realms. The utilization of such theory could eventually prove to be dangerous knowledge, but for now, it is only theory. By phantasmal space theory, all of the realms lie in planes on a column. The evidence for this theory is supported by the translocations of the realms and the spaces in between them, lending to this argument. However, what if our series of realms is but one column in a network?

Though we understand little about the people who existed here tens of thousands of years before us, their lore that they left behind may serve as indicators of potential discoveries we have yet to make. The issue then becomes a hypothetical that leads us to ask if our column is the only column in existence. It is a possibility we cannot deny, if we expect to be rational, and it is my belief that such is the case, that there are other dimensions, more so than just realms. As more becomes clear with phantasmal space theory and its implications, we must also evaluate a new theory, which I have termed dimensional space theory. We may not be able to see them, but what is there to say there is not some alternate reality out there?

Unfortunately, the truth is that there is little to say of dimensional space theory so far. In order to understand it, we must someday find the courage to discover a pathway to one and explore it. If it proves to be false, then the theory can be rejected, but not until that moment. For the moment, what can be said about dimensional space theory and the possibility of other columns can only be extrapolated from lore. No piece of lore makes direct reference to different dimensions, and that is true. However, dimensional space theory could serve as an explanation for several events discovered in the old texts.

For example, let us take a case of matter rearrangement. There is an old story, several thousand years old, of a female jeweler who wanted to make the most beautiful gemstone in the world for a princess to wear in her tiara on her wedding day. To accomplish this, the jeweler supposedly took one of every kind of beautiful blue and white gemstone she could find, and combined them all into one very large light blue gemstone, the theme color of the princess's kingdom. Then, the jeweler cut it and formed the largest and most beautiful gemstone imaginable, and the princess's wedding became very successful. Now, we know already that combining gemstones is an impossibility with physical means, or even magical ones. This problem could be solved, however, by the possibility of different dimensions. As moving to another column could be conceived as a different reality, it would be completely plausible that energy and matter can change abruptly at a dimensional shift, and even an incomplete passage could have the ability to change reality at its fringe. This goes in line with studies on teleportation gates and their unstable fringes; at the edge of the gates, a little bit of matter distortion occurs where the rifts begin to dissipate. Now, take that studied fact and apply it to a dimensional gate, where if it were to exist the energy would have to be much higher to fully penetrate through the fabric of reality. The distortion of the incompletely open areas, or perhaps an incomplete access point in itself, would have the potential to reorganize matter and energy into one form.

Of course, at this point, everything that can be said about dimensional space theory is only hypothesis. Someday, more work will have to be done that stretches the limits of what is possible, to determine if the theoreticals and hypotheticals that suggest the existence of alternate dimensions and the effects of dimensional shifts are actually true. The possibilities are nearly endless.

Kronius stopped at this point. Much of the rest of the chapter seemed to continue to speculate on whether other events in lore could be tied to "dimensional space theory", as he called it, and suggested but also questioned the possibility.

Speculation from the professor. That was a rarity, indeed. Still, the theory made some sense, at least. Who was to say that there was no such thing as another dimension? Of course, one could not equally say that there was such a thing as another dimension. Nearly as much thought on this had to be placed on testing the fringes of the current dimension, as the professor had hypothesized that matter could be rearranged at a dimensional fringe. As he thought on this point, Kronius looked to the professor and nodded in confidence. He then offered the book back to the professor.

Necnea and Vincent were still discussing the possibilities of another dimension. They were getting to be quite annoying as they discussed the same points back and forth. "Vincent, there is nothing else that could be conceived as a dimension," continued Necnea, persistent. "Why do you not understand that?"

"Necnea," answered Vincent, "as much as you may be an expert on time and space, I doubt in the context of the poem that an opening to another realm is as simple as..."

"Enough!" interrupted Kronius, himself annoyed by the discussion. "We will find out what the poem means by a dimension soon enough. Maybe it is more, maybe it is less; we cannot know until we find out."

Immediately, Necnea and Vincent stopped. There was an awkward silence for a moment.

Sarah Haughton took a breath. "Anyway," she continued, "the rest of the poem seems to forecast what must be done to prevent this. The symbols are a little abstract, and unfortunately, how this is established is unclear."

Professor Magnon feared what this might mean for his daughter if it were really true. It overcame his sensibilities on the falsehoods of supposed prophecies. He was already deeply concerned for her. She had been brought to so much emotion and mental fracture already, but the professor was sure, as he thought on the subject, that the poem forecasted more. His daughter was going to be hurt more. That is, if she did not die first. There was a greater deal of resolve in the professor over this. The professor was very defensive of his daughter, and would not allow any harm to her, no matter what.

"There is little more I can tell you," continued Sarah. "Any other meanings that might be hidden in the lines, I cannot give you a certain definition."

Professor Magnon nodded solemnly. "Then let us continue," he said. "Let the gods work out what they can about this poem. We must focus on Setadev, as is our task."

"We know he has a connection to a group called the Enlighteners from the Shadows," added Necnea, making mention of the fact directly to Sarah. "As a matter of fact, we think it is his group. I understand you are quite bureaucratic and know much of politics and history; might you know something about them?"

For just a minute, silence filled the air, as Sarah Haughton thought very hard about what she knew. It was a long minute for everyone.

"A little," answered Sarah, as she leaned onto the podium on the professor's desk. She was trying to recall as much as she could. "Aurana has had some trouble with them historically before, but nothing ever severe enough to warrant significant action. The most they have ever done here in recent years have been semi-violent demonstrations in Atwals, and those were put down easily when it became clear that they intended to become violent."

Kronius started pacing. "Surely Aurana has some files on them somewhere," he said. "Aurana tends to be very good with its record-keeping, if I remember right. Would one of those pinpoint locations they would occupy?"

There was a slight pause. "No," said Sarah. "Like I said, there has not been a need to pursue them, so they have not been thoroughly analyzed. Chances are, no one has a file on them here in Aurana."

Necnea shook her head. "Lovely," she said, in a tone of sarcasm. The frustration in the air was palpable, almost tangible. Still, this had only been step one of the trip in the mortal realm, after all.

"I do, however, have a suggestion," Sarah added.

Everyone only looked at Sarah. They were ready to listen with intent, and Sarah understood the cue.

"It is a little bit of a longshot," she began, "but rumor has it that some of those book-burners may be hiding out in Cornelia. Needless to say, that city is very torn by war, but there is nowhere better to hide anything than in pure chaos."

Vincent Stryker nodded. "Now that is an excellent point," he said. "When all else fails, start with the fire and move to the ice."

Awkward silence filled the air for a second as everyone stared at Vincent Stryker. Then, the professor understood it. "Ah!" he began. "Interesting use of an idiom, but quite appropriate indeed. Start where there is the most chaos, and work your way to the most order."

"It's an old Scurnian saying, James," chuckled Vincent, who was raised and had spent most of his life in Scurnia. He referenced his days in the Scurnian military by adding, "One of my favorite stratagems, at that."

Kronius raised an eyebrow. The idea of using stratagems interested him, as he took a quick glance at the book the professor had handed him. It was still in the professor's hands. The messenger god nodded and added, "That is an interesting thought. Perhaps this is less of a search and more of a competition of wits with Setadev. Strategy will be important in what we can find, since there is little to go off of to begin with."

"Then let us be off," acknowledged Necnea. "The more time we waste here, the more time Setadev will have to counter our strategies." There was a pause in the room. Necnea was certainly eager to be done with this as soon as possible.

Finally, the professor nodded. “Indeed,” he said. “However, I see no reason why we should not wait until tomorrow morning to depart. I am sure that our searching through Cornelia will be much more fruitful during the daytime than at night.

Necnea thought about it for a moment. “Very well,” she finally answered. “In that case, we might be best served to continue studying through the night here in your office. We can allow Vincent Stryker to rest while we do.”

Professor Magnon looked over to Vincent. He nodded as well.

“Then that is what we will do,” acknowledged the professor.

Kronius also nodded and placed the *Stratagems* book on the podium. “Perhaps this would be a helpful reference as well.”

“As I am sure,” chuckled Sarah, who had seen the title of the book on it before Kronius set it on the podium. Then, she turned to Professor Magnon, and whispered, “Would you come and walk with me for a moment?”

The professor looked down at Sarah for a second. He nodded and followed her out the door. The others thought little of it, knowing that the professor’s business was his to know and his alone.

After all, there was work to be done. Vincent walked over to a comfortable chair in the professor’s room and settled himself down to get some sleep. Necnea and Kronius, being immortals that did not require sleep, started going through the poem and the books on the professor’s shelves. Kronius made sure to point out to Necnea what the professor had showed him about dimensional space theory, stirring her interest.

Outside, Sarah and Professor Magnon were walking together down the empty halls of the Bladinstar School. “Might I ask what you wanted to talk about?” asked the professor, after they were several steps away from his office. “I can tell that as much as you have tried to show your confidence and resolve, something has frightened you.”

There was a pause, as Sarah took a breath. “You are as sharp as ever,” Sarah nodded. “James, despite as long as we have known each other, all of this new knowledge frightens me. Are we really so out of control of our own world that little-known prophecies and powerful immortals control us?”

Tyrinion wrapped his arm around Sarah's shoulder. They walked together through one of the doors to the outside of the building. "No, actually, I would say not. This one immortal we call Setadev, he is an anomaly, a danger that has been building silently for five thousand years, without any of us knowing." He paused for a second. "Yet Sarah, if anyone is in control of this world, it is you. That is to say, yourself and the rest of the mortal. This world here, what the immortal call the mortal realm, is all yours. We did not create any of this. We do not continue to shape it, either."

There was a slight pause. Sarah closed her eyes.

Reaching down, Tyrinion grabbed a handful of dirt and picked it up. "This soil, and all of the living creatures it supports, are here because of nature. This society you see around you was built by your contemporaries. The peace here is because you choose to live in peace. I did not determine that for you."

"It is just…" she began, finding difficulty in making the right words come out, "for decades I assumed you were just a magically gifted professor, and now I know you to be so much more. There is so much my old mind is still trying to process here."

Seeing that he needed to restore Sarah's confidence, the professor responded, "I believe you are doing well. You have been quite helpful tonight. Because of you, we know more about what we are doing."

Sarah only shrugged. "I know what you are trying to do," she said. "Still, it is hard to feel as though I have any significance anymore, James. I used to believe that I was doing something important by running this school, and now I do not believe that I have even that to fall back on anymore."

"Do not even dare to think that!" the professor nearly exclaimed.

All Sarah could do was listen. She had stimulated something within James Magnon.

Needing to calm himself down, the professor took a breath. "Sarah, you have helped to inspire a whole new generation of magic casters and preserved our way of life," he continued. "In many ways, you have done more than I could ever do." Sarah tried to respond with her disbelief in this, but the professor pre-empted her. "I can only do so much, Sarah. So can Necnea, and so can Kronius. The same is true of all of the gods, as well. We are not omnipotent. I may be immortal, that is true. But Sarah, that does not mean your existence is meaningless or any less significant than mine."

Drooping her head, Sarah answered, "I wish I could believe that…"

Again, Professor Magnon put his arm around his former student. He was trying to be as reassuring as possible to Sarah, who he realized was definitely having a crisis of meaning. What she had learned in the last few days had instilled a fear in her.

And that was exactly why mortals were not supposed to know about immortals. That was why the gods had picked a minimalist approach to affairs with the mortal, and why they were not more interventive. Professor Magnon had told Sarah in confidence about his identity because he was sure that if anyone could understand and bear the burden of the knowledge in a responsible manner, it was Sarah Haughton, Headmistress of the Bladinstar School of Wizardry and Sorcery.

To an extent, he was wrong. What the professor had failed to realize is that even the strongest of wills can be felled by meeting someone who they identify as a deity. Regardless of the fact that Sarah was not suddenly in a position of inferiority sheerly by learning of the professor's true identity, she did feel insignificant, as though she were only a pawn in the world instead of being a figure of inspiration, as she was to her students at the school and to those she spoke to during her days in bureaucracy with the Aurana Department of Magic Affairs.

Though the professor knew that he and his fellow gods did not identify themselves as being omnipotent or holy, he saw now that even mortals in a relative position of power would not see it that way.

Sarah turned her head away. "I know what you are trying to tell me, and I appreciate it" she said meekly. "Professor Magnon, I wish I could share with you how honored I am to have been your student since I was young."

"It is nothing," responded the professor. "Learning is an important thing, after all, regardless of who you learn your knowledge from, as long as it is correct."

Gently, Sarah nodded. She then lowered her head. "I know now," she said. "At least now, I know the real you."

Chapter 21

Lady of the Metoi

Caitlin was still distraught. She tried not to show it.

For the past couple of hours, she had been traveling through the Wastes by herself. Though it was winter, the wastelands were still very warm, in part due to their dry and arid conditions all year round. Had the Wastes been a more survivable region, those factors might be a little more pleasant as a retreat from the winter.

Earlier in the day, Arthur and Rachel had wished her their most sincere goodbyes. Unusual as it was that they seemed without objection to her wish to continue on alone, Caitlin reasoned that they had to know how important this was to her. She should have known that that could not be the case, but in her frustration over the whole situation it seemed like the best explanation.

Following Rouge and Resa's directions had led Caitlin to this place, the remains of Metoi Village. Though the sight was still horrifically devastating, it appeared that some cleanup had taken place. Nearby was a mass grave, freshly dug and filled for the Metoi who had lost their lives to General Sayo's tragic actions. Their names were not noted, save for that of Chief Aspectra, and one marker was placed at the site. Ashes still covered much of what was once the village, but many of them had blown away in the wind, meaning that the ash density was much less than it was when Kevin had walked through this village. Remnants of books were now visible in the ash piles, some of which may have been intact enough for survival. Sadly, however, many of the records kept by the information-keeping Metoi tribe were now lost forever.

Considering all of this brought Caitlin even further down than she had been lately. Still, she pressed on for one reason, and one reason only. She had a friend she had to save. And by saving him, she could prove wrong all of those doubts in her mind.

As Caitlin looked out among the remains of Metoi Village, she sighed. Such destruction was senseless. So much death, so many losses, so many Metoi people left homeless, and all of it so Setadev could get a hold of Kevin. Now, all that remained were piles of ash. If only this destruction could have been avoided, Caitlin thought to herself.

Then, a voice came from behind her. "I see you stare upon the tragedy of the Metoi," said the voice.

Caitlin turned to see a middle-aged woman standing next to her. She was medium-skinned with dark hair, typical of people of the savage tribes of the Wastes. She was clothed in a long piece of brown fabric fashioned into a plain dress, and on one of her arms up by her shoulder was a tattoo of a spiral with five points projecting from it. There were smaller tattoos on her arms and across other visible portions of her skin, symbols of love.

Seeing Caitlin's reaction of unfamiliarity led the woman to answer, "Oh, I am sorry. Forgive my intrusion."

Caitlin shook her head. "No worries," she said as she extended her hand. "I'm Caitlin. Caitlin Amelia Magnon."

The other woman shook Caitlin's hand. "Marilynn, Lady of the Metoi."

"So, am I to presume you know something about what happened here?" asked Caitlin.

Marilynn let out a deep breath. "I do, too well," she acknowledged. "May you be blessed that you did not have to witness it." She paused again, for only a moment, as she and Caitlin continued to stare out onto the ashes of what once was Metoi Village. "Forgive my intrusion again, but what brings you to this place?"

Could Caitlin trust Marilynn? For a second, she pondered this question until she realized that she was speaking to the former wife of the Metoi chief, Aspectra. Caitlin recalled the story of how the wife of the Metoi chief had returned to Seta Archa to spread word of the plight of the Metoi people to General Sayo.

Though Caitlin had never been to the Wastes, she had been well educated on many areas of the world by her father, including cultures of the tribes of the Wastes. The way Marilynn had introduced herself as

Lady of the Metoi to Caitlin was not in a way to indicate she was a Metoi female; it was a title. Females of the Metoi tribe did not typically have the ability to receive titles, but as the chief's wife, Marilynn would have been granted that privilege as the representing female of the tribe.

"I'm here looking for a friend of mine. He walked through here a few days ago and disappeared."

"Ah, the one referred to as Kevin," acknowledged Marilynn.

Instantly, Caitlin snapped her head to look at Marilynn. "How did you…"

"The Vanguards, Rouge and Resa, told me of him," nodded Marilynn, who did not turn. She instead looked down, and closed her eyes. "Your friend has quite a reputation, I hear. In the short time that I have known the Kirkwood sisters, never before have I heard them speak highly of anyone other than him. He seems to have created an impression with them that they are much better people for knowing him."

Caitlin could not resist a chuckle. That's my Kevin, she thought to herself. Or at the very least, that *was* her Kevin.

The duality of her thoughts was quite stressful to Caitlin. She had not ever thought so ill of Kevin before, even though she loved him. Not even before she had been set free of her emotionless roadblocks. Not even with the lack of progression of their relationship since the end of the conquest. Not even despite his choice to go on without her, resulting in his capture. Still, something told her there was a possibility that what Setadev had told her when he shattered her mind were true. There were signs. He had wanted to go off alone, she felt things had been slowing between the two of them… and there had always been some doubt in Caitlin's mind. Maybe it was because these emotions were such new concepts to her, or maybe it was because there was something there to be afraid of. Caitlin could not be sure. She had already broken her promise never to doubt Kevin ever again.

"You must think highly of him as well, judging by your reaction," commented Marilynn.

Caitlin lifted her head. "Not exactly in the regards that Rouge and Resa do, but I do have quite a bit of care for him."

"I see," nodded Marilynn. "Your friends have told me that he proceeded to the east from here. In the same direction as Sayo's men, I believe."

"He was tracking them, is my understanding," answered Caitlin. "Seeking to put down Sayo before he did any more damage out here."

"So he was," Marilynn whispered. Tones of sadness were in her voice.

Caitlin nodded. "Sayo will be brought to justice, some way or another. What we see here..." emotion was starting to leak through Caitlin's composure as she continued, "should never happen again."

Marilynn sighed. "It never should have happened in the first place. The emperor promised us peace and sealed it with the law that troops were not allowed in the Wastes without permission. Had that law been enforced, Sayo would not have killed my husband and burned our village down."

There was a pause in the air. A tear dripped from Marilynn's eye. The wind started blowing. It howled across the land of the destroyed village. Marilynn could not hold back her crying any more. Some of it became audible. Having heard the story of what had happened at Metoi Village, Caitlin could now see that Marilynn was still in deep mourning over the loss of her husband. She did not want to push the issue, however. She did not want the wife of the Metoi chief to hurt any more.

"All will be well, I know," cried Marilynn quietly, as she wiped her eyes and tried to calm herself. "The Metoi are a strong people. We will rebuild our nation as we always have, and the emperor has shown us support in the aftermath. The empire protects us for now, but we will only need them for so long until we can reemerge a stronger and better tribe."

Caitlin nodded.

There was another long pause.

Marilynn then addressed Caitlin. "If you are going east in pursuit of this boy, there are some things that you should know. The first is that if you head too far east, you will enter the lands of the Aequina. Of all the tribes in the Wastes, they are one of the most savage and primitive, and they despise the Metoi. I can't promise you will be safe if you enter their lands."

"I understand," nodded Caitlin. "I will keep that in mind."

There was a pause, as Marilynn took a breath. "Bear this in mind too," Marilynn added. "The Aequina are the descendants and relatives of the Daritel tribe, the ones Seta Archa citizens refer to as the 'savages' that controlled the city nearly twenty years ago."

Suddenly, Caitlin's eyes widened. "Are you serious?" she asked in shock. "You know who was responsible for the war twenty years ago? They're not extinct?"

There was another long pause. Marilynn was reluctant to answer. "I swore to my husband that I would never share this, but you need to know," the Metoi woman continued. "Yes, I know that the tribe never truly died. They merely became a new one under new leadership."

"Then why does no one else know?" Caitlin asked forcefully.

Again, Marilynn shook her head. "I mean no offense by this, but the issue has always been a wasteland issue. Tribes of the Wastes often do not consider outsiders as being important in our societies, and admittedly we oftentimes withhold information of each other for our own safety. Perhaps we are xenophobic in this new society we live in as members of the Solunar Empire and of its government, but it is our way."

Caitlin only looked away. She was not in any mood to talk about the withholding of this. The Alliance-Daritel War had, after all, been the starting event that had initiated every major world event of the past twenty years. It had long been believed after their defeat that they were simply no more, because they were given nowhere to run and were thought to be completely annihilated. The more Caitlin thought about it, the more she realized it was a foolish thought, even for the governments involved, to believe they had wiped out every last Daritel.

Still speaking, Marilynn continued, "For the most part, we have kept away from the Aequina because they practice human sacrifice of their prisoners, and they tend to be very hostile. That said, they have not declared war on any other tribe in two decades, so we have been content to leave them be. The odd thing is, though, that while the Metoi do not interact with the Aequina because of their violent tendencies, we have had some interactions with a few Aequina tribe members, and those Aequina noted to us that the chief who led the Daritel to Seta Archa started acting very weird in the days of the Daritel's departure. One of them noted that the chief's eyes seemed to flash red every now and then during the departure phase. An odd irregularity of magic, do you think?"

Flashing red eyes. Tracer magic. Setadev? Certainly not beyond his capabilities, Caitlin thought to herself, as few would be capable of such a powerful spell. Perhaps it was that which was Setadev's first move in the mortal realm, after waiting for five thousand years to make his move. Even knowing this, Caitlin shook her head no. She did not want to let Marilynn know she knew, because tracer magic was very dangerous stuff.

"Anyway, it is irrelevant now," continued Marilynn. "The Aequina are much weaker now than they were as the Daritel, but they have rebuilt and are still very formidable, so be careful when you head to the east."

Caitlin nodded. "I will do that," she said.

"And bear one more thing in mind, too." Again, Marilynn took a breath. "If you are in pursuit of Sayo and find nothing, I suggest that you head north, through the lands of the Toronaga. They are our allies, and will protect travelers if you can identify as someone who knows the Metoi."

Passively, Caitlin nodded, unsure as to whether or not that would be necessary. "All right," she acknowledged. "But why should I head north?"

Marilynn sighed. "Because if Sayo is not out there," she continued, "he will have headed for the fortress."

"Fortress?"

"Yes. The Fortress of Da Leval."

Caitlin looked at Marilynn, slightly confused. "What interest does Sayo have in such a fortress, and how do you know about it?"

Marilynn paused. "The fortress is a sacred place to a legacy society of Seta Archa. And, as we Metoi are the information keepers, we know much of it."

Gesturing, Caitlin indicated for Marilynn to continue about the fortress.

"Well, this fortress is supposedly made of all white stone, and it has a wall surrounding it. Word has it that this society from Desolunar runs their operations out of there; it's a group of people who wear red robes and golden chain necklaces, that like to destroy information. Much as Demonicus used to be"

The Enlighteners from the Shadows.

Caitlin knew exactly who Marilynn was describing, and understood why Marilynn was suggesting it. It was quite likely for them to be involved with the general. Or with Setadev, for that matter, considering it was his group.

"And where exactly is this fortress?" asked Caitlin. "North of the Toronaga, I understand, but can you be more specific?"

"Of course I can." There was a bit of despair and vengeance in Marilynn's voice, reflecting how upset she still was. "We Metoi are the information keepers, after all; we know much of the old Desolunar top-level knowledge. This bit, I know in my head, and I am sure that until General Sayo is brought to justice, it is a location I will not forget where it is."

"So where is it?" asked Caitlin.

Marilynn said the location.

In response, Caitlin shook her head. "Really?" she asked. She then put her face in the palm of her hand. "If that's the case, and Kevin is there, then this just became a lot more difficult, and a lot deadlier."

"I would recommend you go there now," continued Marilynn. She then briefly gave Caitlin directions on how to get there, before continuing, "I doubt that Sayo and his men could last so long out there in the Wastes without resources. I believe you are more likely to find him at the fortress."

"Thank you," nodded Caitlin. "However, I will start with following the trail first. If it leads to Kevin, then that is the way I would prefer to go."

"Very well," nodded a somber Marilynn. "If you do find this boy, I ask that you do me a favor. Send him my deepest thanks for thinking so much of the Metoi as to risk his own life for us. Even as an outsider, and even though he has gone missing in the line of duty, he deserves our honor and respect for it."

Caitlin's eyes nearly shed a tear. Then, she nodded.

Though she had doubts about Kevin, Caitlin could always respect his kind nature and the fight he had for those in need. He had a good heart, that was for sure. As long as he actually cared about her.

No. Caitlin tried not to think of that. No matter how convincing Setadev's words still rang in her head. She kept trying to remind herself that that was a message deliberately placed in her head alongside a shatter spell. It was not real. It could not be real.

Together, Caitlin and Marilynn spent a few more moments before Caitlin decided to part. She explained to Marilynn that time was of the essence and she had to keep moving. Marilynn agreed, and both women shared a goodbye before Caitlin continued to the east. Coming from this meeting, Caitlin felt more as though she had met someone she could trust. Marilynn had been someone whom she had approached with skepticism at the start, but she had demonstrated her credibility as the course of the conversation had continued. She seemed to care, to want to help as much as she could, and she seemed implicitly to trust Caitlin, as well.

Yet as Caitlin continued on past the destroyed village, her thoughts of her meeting with Marilynn resonated in her mind. There was something about the wife of the deceased Metoi chief that reminded her of herself. It was a side of herself that Caitlin did not want to remember, at least not as a dark time. Marilynn had seemed, except when she shed tears for the loss of her husband, to be holding herself together with all of the discipline she could muster. Clearly, she had been hurt and hurt badly, and it reminded Caitlin of a time when her discipline had been her entire persona.

There was something different about Marilynn, though. It was as though the pain of losing her husband had caused Marilynn to shut off connections to herself. The pain had numbed her, and turned her into something that she was not, something that she never was, and something that she should not have to be. That became quite visible as they talked.

Nor was it something Caitlin wanted herself to become. That was her one major fear, that she would become something that she did not want to be. She loved the feelings that came with connecting with

Kevin almost as much as she loved Kevin himself. Something strong came with that power. That power being love might have been an oversimplification, Caitlin reasoned. Then again, maybe it was not. It was hard to say.

Still, the thoughts of the situation at hand resonated in Caitlin's head, as she continued on to the east. There was little that she knew for sure, but she did know she was following Kevin's trail. At the same time, she was following her own path of self-discovery. In the time since she had regained her emotions, Caitlin had been learning a great deal about herself that she had never known before. She was learning more about what she liked and what she did not, more about human emotions and triggers, and how certain sights can inspire deep sensations. And since she had lost Kevin, she was re-learning about independence and self-reliance, about how to survive without him, about how to be the hero herself, much like the heroine in *Tale of the Valkyrie*, a novel that both Kevin and Caitlin enjoyed and over which they had bonded.

She was going to be Kevin's hero. She could not wait for that moment. Provided he had not betrayed her.

Again, Caitlin had to force that thought out of her head. It was still such a prevalent afterthought that she grew to fear those moments. Each time it had sent a shockwave up her spine. Beyond all hope, she hoped it was not true.

As Caitlin pondered all of these thoughts, distance continued to go by as she continued to the east. Though the weather was still hot, as it was commonly in the Wastes even in the winter, Caitlin's perseverance kept her going. Periodically, she would take a drink from a canteen that she took with her from Seta Archa. It was the only object that she carried with her, hung around her shoulder by a sling, with a small pouch with some food rations.

Nearing the end of the day, the setting sun gleamed an obscure light. All across the Wastes, the barren ground gleamed a dark red color. The heat was still prevalent for now, but Caitlin knew that it would be getting cold very soon after the sun set.

And Caitlin was absolutely exhausted.

Her dress was soaked in sweat from the long, hot walk. Quite a few of her muscles were extremely sore. She had sores on her legs and feet from walking so far. Her long and straight red hair was now a jumbled mess. It had been the most exhausting day she had in a long time, as she had pushed herself to keep walking further and further.. So badly she wanted to rest, now more than ever.

In order for her to rest, though, she needed to find shelter. Out here in the Wastes, many dangers lurked in the night, from wild animals to the dangerous Aequina tribe that controlled the lands in which she was standing, to the possibility of any of Sayo's men still lingering in the area from which Kevin disappeared. Come to think of it, Caitlin could not be sure just how far she had to go in order to find where Kevin disappeared. She may have passed the location already, or she may have a couple more days to go. Regardless, she believed for now that she had to keep going until she found some sign of where Kevin was.

Up ahead, Caitlin saw an embankment in the soil. It was a curious geographical feature. Carefully she approached, wondering what was behind it. Could it be an Aequina structure?

As she neared the embankment, Caitlin leaned forward. Upon reaching it, she stretched out to look over the steep mass of ground.

On the other side was a sharp drop, with a cliff face dropping down the embankment by the height of a couple of stories. Below, a few black tents stood in no distinct pattern, but the looks of things appeared to show a great deal of movement down there recently. Many footprints were still present in the dirt, suggesting that this may have once been a larger campsite that was recently packed up. Large enough for a military unit, given the range of the prints visible.

This must have been where Kevin was, Caitlin reasoned. The ledge had given just enough shade to preserve the prints in damp soil, made so by water used by the soldiers. It took Caitlin several minutes to walk around the edge of the embankment and down to the ground below. The whole time as she did so, she kept looking for any of Sayo's men, worried that any of them might still be around. Even as tired as she was, Caitlin was smart enough to know to show precaution as much as possible.

When she finally reached the bottom, Caitlin started in toward the cliff face, looking for any remnant of what remained. The tents were rather barren from appearance, made of black fabric with little more than the stakes sitting atop them. It appeared that they were simply left behind, maybe to mark the spot or maybe simply because they were not needed. It was hard to say for sure. Beyond the shade of the cliff, there were not any more footprints. The dry sand and high winds in the surrounding area had erased any traces left behind. That meant that Caitlin had come to the end of her travel to the east. She had nowhere further to go in this direction.

For now, though, despite the risks around staying here, the remaining tents would have to work as shelter. They were the best shelter possible in the middle of the Wastes. There would be no other functioning shelter nearby, especially while in Aequina territory. Plus, the sun was setting very quickly, and it would not be safe to travel in the cold, dark night.

Caitlin continued on to the nearest tent, knowing it would be the safest place to be for the night. It would also be a welcome opportunity to rest. The sun was almost completely blocked out by the black fabric of the tent. As Caitlin entered the tent, only darkness was present. She could not see much of anything in the tent at all. There were no candles, no torches, no potential light source of any kind. Even if Caitlin lit a fire with her magic, she could not keep one sustained all night without a fuel source. Still, she did light a spark in her fingers for just a moment, to give her some time to look around in the tent.

It was empty, completely unloaded. Though the tent had been left behind, the insides had been cleaned out and all of the resources taken. No more water to be found. For now, though, it was going to have to do. Even though the ground was full of loose dirt, Caitlin set herself down and covered herself with a piece of a torn-down tent. She was very tired, exhausted, and needed to relax her muscles. As desperate as she was to find Kevin, she knew she had to stop to rest.

It was not going to be an easy night for her. Still, she tried hard to get some sleep. After all, the days ahead were bound to be long, as Caitlin returned back to the west. With traces of Sayo having been here, and no sign of which way they went, it only made sense to her to take Marilynn's advice and follow the way to the Fortress of Da Leval.

It seemed like a logical next step in the search for Kevin, especially with no other leads. Coming back to the west would get her safely out of Aequina territory before she headed north.

Soon enough, the wear of the day had caught up to Caitlin. She fell asleep within a few moments. Thoughts of Kevin were still very much in her mind as she fell asleep.

And as she was asleep, she started to dream.

Chapter 22

Human Emotion

Caitlin was standing in a gigantic meadow. Only she was subconscious. Her hair was clean and straight, her clothes were fresh and not dirty, and the world around her was much different from the Wastes. The wind was blowing, but only lightly, and the air carried a scent of fresh flowers.

Ahhh… this was the best, she thought to herself. Everything was lovely. So awe-inspiring, so emotionally empowering.

For several minutes, Caitlin in her dream took in the experience of being in such a beautiful meadow. It almost looked like Aurana east of Rikleifer, where the sprawling meadows expanded in all directions. The natural sights could have been inspirational to all poets and authors around the world. As lovely as it was, though, it seemed a little empty. As though there was no companion with her, when there should have been. No person, no animal, no nothing. The serenity was beautiful, but if this were her life, she would feel very alone.

So you do miss him after all, don't you?

A hand touched Caitlin's shoulder. She flipped around to see a surprising, yet all too familiar sight.

"I should have known this was your vision, Amelia," Caitlin responded. "I have not had such a vivid dream since the last time I saw you."

Dressed in a plain black dress and looking exactly the same as Caitlin, stood Amelia. Named for Caitlin's middle name solely to separate herself from whom she called "the real Caitlin", Amelia was representative of what Caitlin used to be: cold and nearly emotionless, highly disciplined, but not without concern. They had met in a dream before; when awake, Caitlin had reasoned this vision was her mind trying to sort itself out.

"Indeed," answered Amelia, in her normal tone without

emotion. "You have not needed me for a while, Caitlin. However, I sense that you may have some doubts as of late, and I think that it is time we have another discussion."

Caitlin stood, looking puzzled at the representation of a fragment of her mind.

"You cannot hide it from me," continued Amelia. "Caitlin, I am surprised that you do not wish to speak with me on this matter, even after you realized you were only talking to yourself by doing so. I brought you here in your subconscious so you could seek solace in this communication, not to frustrate you."

The face on Caitlin was a distraught one. "I'm not sure I want to talk to you again, Amelia," she said. "We are one, you and I. Yet I know that you aren't real, so if I listen to you, then I'm really crazy…"

"Am I really not real?" interrupted Amelia, unwavering in her tone, "or is the mere fact that I am a part of your mind and not with a physical form or consciousness make me not real? Ask yourself that question carefully, Caitlin."

Shaking her head and turning it, Caitlin answered, "I know what you're getting at. But how can I call you real, when you are only the representing member of the inner voices in my head? You are what I once was, yes, but you are not me anymore."

There was a slight pause. "You are missing something," responded Amelia. "I am not only what you once were, but you might become me if you are not careful."

Caitlin snapped. "How could that be? Tell me!" In just a few words, Caitlin had gone from reluctance to stun.

"I see I have touched a nerve," Amelia continued. "Perhaps now you will listen to my words and consider them with caution, for if you don't, you may become me once again."

Absolutely in disbelief, Caitlin shook her head and put her eyes into her hands. She mumbled to herself, "Gee, was I really like that before?" She paused. "Just get to the point," she eventually said, starting to become impatient with herself. "You know already that I don't like this game that you're playing."

Amelia nodded. "Indeed," she said. "He who has taken Kevin away from you also plays such similar games with the psyche. And the more you let him, the more things he will take from you, until you are left with nothing."

"So you know," commented Caitlin.

"Of course I do," responded Amelia. "I am you and you are me, remember?"

Caitlin nodded. "I know that," she said, trying not to get too upset with Amelia. After all, Amelia was only trying to help. "But what do you mean by that?"

There was a long pause. Then, Amelia started to pace in front of Caitlin. "When Setadev attacked, he played his game, and won. He convinced you that not only had he captured Kevin, but that Kevin cared not for you. Forget about the shatter spell. There is no evidence of Kevin abandoning our love, yet even with your mind intact you still cannot shake it."

"Amelia, I would really rather not talk about this…"

"And I know why," interrupted Amelia. "You have been hiding doubts lately, Caitlin. And yet you're too afraid to admit it, even to yourself. That is why you can't bring yourself to talk to me instead of having me tell you everything you already know. You are so afraid that it might be true that you have let it paralyze you."

With that, Caitlin stopped trying to argue. She stopped where she was and looked Amelia directly in the eyes. Now, Amelia had Caitlin's full attention.

Carefully, Amelia took a breath before continuing. "Caitlin, why do you continue to let these doubts take hold of your mind? You promised to Kevin a few months ago that you would never doubt him again, and yet you continue to do so. I fail to understand why you allow yourself to feel any doubt, especially since he has done nothing that we know of, for certain, to hurt you."

"You know something, Amelia?" began Caitlin, a little hostile in her tone. "That is part of why I don't want to talk to you about this. You don't understand because you don't have emotion and humanity. That is the price you pay for your excessive restraint. I would be talking to you in very much the same way if the roles were reversed and I was how I was a year ago."

Suddenly, the roles were indeed reversed in a different way.

Amelia was now speechless and listening to Caitlin, as she began to explain.

Caitlin let off of her eye contact and lightened her tone. "It's not as though I hate you, or anything like that. Yet you just cannot understand that my doubts cannot be explained. They are there, and they are just the way they are. I cannot simply get rid of them or the fears just by saying I choose to get rid of them. I have to work through them."

"Then explain to me this," responded Amelia. "At least allow me to expand the depth of my knowledge on human emotion. Why is it that you have had building doubt? Have things with Kevin not been great as of late? Have not the two of you taken care of each other well and has not your love been strong?"

Dropping her head, Caitlin sighed. She took a moment to think. "They have been fine," she finally answered. "Sometimes, though, 'fine' is not enough when one talks about love. Kevin has done a lot to take care of me, and I have done a lot to take care of him too, but lately it had seemed like things were stalling out. We have been together for several months now, but for the last three months or so, we haven't really grown much closer than we were. I know we moved quickly and became emotionally close in a short amount of time, but I almost wish I could advance things further myself, but it's so difficult… I'm not even sure I know how." She was revealing the truth in saying so.

"If I may," stated Amelia, having listened intently before, "I wonder if you have considered the possibility that Kevin also wants to advance, but doesn't know how to do it, either."

Caitlin raised an eyebrow. "What do you mean?" she asked.

"I mean this," responded Amelia. "It is true that you lack experience with situations of love and emotion, and I understand why things are difficult from your perspective on advancing your relationship with Kevin. However, what are the odds that Kevin himself does not know how to proceed, either? After all, we do know he had issues with trying to have a relationship before he met you. The road that you two are traveling is just as new to him as it is to you." Amelia then paused for a minute. "I understand your frustration with me, and that I cannot have the understanding of emotion that you can.

However, I can only hope that you won't forget the lessons that having that discipline taught you as well."

Shaking her head, Caitlin said, "I think I get what you're saying. Kevin grew up too, but on the inside, he's still going to be nervous and afraid like he was the first night I met him." Caitlin stopped, on a point of realization. "He even had a lot of trouble trying to tell me how he felt the first time."

"You remember," said Amelia. "Very good. That is all that I wanted to pass to you, Caitlin. I hope you have not been offended by my intrusion of your subconsciousness or my attempts to interpret your emotions. I can only hope that which I have shared with you will help you to figure it out yourself, before you are overwhelmed."

There was little Caitlin could do to argue that. Amelia was right, and she knew it. In retrospect, Amelia had actually been quite helpful, not in trying to help directly, but by helping to highlight some things for her to think about. Maybe Kevin was nervous about pushing things forward as well. Maybe he was not a traitor to their mutual trust, but instead just a victim of this whole thing. Maybe she had never understood his nerves about things as well because she was so nervous about it herself. It just might have been true. Of course, it would not be that easy. Not until she knew the truth for sure.

In respect, Caitlin gave Amelia a hug, even though she knew Amelia could not feel an emotional connection back. "Thank you," she said. "It means a lot to me that you care so much for my well-being."

"I always will," commented Amelia, "for as long as you need me."

Caitlin nodded as she hugged Amelia tightly. Amelia had always been so helpful, if rather unexpected at times.

Then, Caitlin's arms slipped. She fell forward onto the ground.

As she picked herself up, she saw that Amelia had disappeared.

Wake up! Wake up! A thunderous cry stormed across the landscape. Then, the meadow began to disappear.

Caitlin's eyes snapped open.

She was being jabbed in the side by a spear. "Now, stand up!" yelled a loud voice.

Quickly, Caitlin flipped around and stood up. There was a spear pointed right at her neck. She raised her hands in surrender.

In front of her was a man with a dark tan and many tattoos on his body. He wore only a loincloth around his waist. Several scars also were visible on his body, including one large set across his chest in the shape of a square with extended tails on the lines at the top right and bottom left corners.

That scar indicated exactly where he was from, and Caitlin knew it. He was from the Aequina tribe. And now, she was his prisoner.

"Easy," said Caitlin. "I'll cooperate."

The angry look on the Aequina man did not ease up. He kept his spear pointed directly at Caitlin's neck.

Clearly, negotiation was not going to work.

Thinking quickly, Caitlin unleashed a ball of air magic from her hand, shoving back the Aequina man. She then charged up more air magic, preparing to fire a beam once the man stood back up.

Yet as Caitlin took aim at the Aequina man, he scampered backward and out of the tent. That was a rare move for someone of the Aequina to retreat. Fearing that this may be a dangerous situation, Caitlin kept air charged in one hand while she carefully pulled back the tent flap with the other and stepped out into the night.

Suddenly, she found five spears pointed at her neck.

There were nearly twenty Aequina surrounding her. Far too many for Caitlin to be able to take them all. She raised her hand in surrender again, and this time, she knew there would be no negotiation.

One of the Aequina males then stepped behind her and grabbed her hands. He then pulled her arms down and tied her hands behind her back. At the same time, another Aequina applied a pair of shackles to her ankles, placing a short chain length between them to obstruct her ability to run.

This was a horrific situation. It was happening so fast that Caitlin almost could not believe it. Though she showed a strong persona to her captors, she was terrified inside. She knew of what the Aequina did, and how they treated prisoners. They were cruel, not beyond the concepts of torture.

And what they did to women… that might have been the

scariest thought of all.

The same Aequina man she hit with an air blast earlier then stepped up to her. He said, in a firm tone, “You are our prisoner.”

Caitlin lowered her head. Then, someone jabbed her in the back with a spear.

It was time for a forced march, to the Aequina village. As she was led away, a tear came to Caitlin’s eye. Now, she might not see Kevin ever again. She might not even live to see the sunrise.

Chapter 23

Ghosts of War

The nation of Nuve rests between Aurana to its west, the Solunar Empire to its south, and the Peaked Mountains to the east, with Scurnia lying further beyond to the northeast and Gardolk to the southeast. Its lands once originated around the city of Cardol in the south, but since had expanded very far north into the tundra, where all civilization began to fringe off as the climate became colder. Three rivers define the land shape of Nuve: the Aurun River on the west border, the Calphos River on the south border, and the Rhonean River, which runs from the Abyss of the Royal Sovereign south to the Calphos River, dividing the southern areas of the country into two parts.

For hundreds of years, the rule of the country has been under the Raijin family, currently under King Raijin Lester and his immediate family. His younger brother, Raijin Shane, serves as the Vanguard of Nuve. The current capital rests in north-central Nuve, in the city of Nuvenia, on an island in the Abyss. Accompanying the royal family's rule is that of the Collective Council, which serves as a check on the king's power.

There was, however, a brewing civil war in Nuve. Two factions stood in opposition to Nuve's government, and both controlled pieces of the kingdom. To the very far north in Tundrosa and Soverenia provinces resided the Demonstrative Organization of Northern Nuve, also known as Demons for short. They sought a government rule that is less powerful and grants more power to the people, and often operate with stealth tactics and intelligence operations; however, they often fought only in defense. Another group, the Cornelia Chimeras, possessed a great amount of Cornelia Province in southwestern Nuve, and maintained a much more militarily active state.

The land of Nuve is divided into five provinces: Tundrosa to the far north, Katalina to the central-east, Soverenia to the west and central areas of the country, Cornelia to the southwest, and Leticon to the southeast.

Leticon Province to the southeast was among the most unique of land areas in the entire world. As was most of Nuve south of the tundra, much of the province was grassland and only mildly fertile. Exceptions to this were to be found south around the Calphos River, where the flowing water provided life to the lowlands in the area and formed a meadow-like land similar to much of central Aurana. Cardol sat just southwest of Leticon Province on the Calphos, itself being so close to Cornelia Province and the border with the current-day Solunar Empire as to be significantly different from Leticon. The foothills of the Peaked Mountains to the east also made for lush land, perhaps the most fertile lands in all of Nuve. At the very southeast corner of the province was a valley where the Calphos River passed through the Peaked Mountains, into the kingdom of Gardolk. Because it was seldom traveled, much of its beauty was preserved.

Despite this lush land around the Calphos, Leticon was very sparsely populated. Though it was territory that belonged to Nuve, the nation's grip on Leticon was very weak and one who could travel through Leticon would likely be able to travel through it unnoticed.

It was often said that Leticon was haunted by the ghosts of war, and it was for that reason that many people chose not to live in Leticon. The province had seen quite a bit of action in the previous two wars, including Nuve's drastic loss of their own capital to Desolunar at the Battle of Cardol. In each case, it was Leticon's border with its southern neighbor that had been the cause of the bloodshed, and in each case Leticon was almost constantly in a state of chaos as ownership passed from one nation to the other, and back again.

This alone, though, was not all of the history that Leticon had had; after all, the neighboring province of Cornelia had suffered the same fates and people still chose to live there. Unlike Cornelia, however, Leticon had historically been a sight of many battlefields over the course of human history, all across the grasslands. It was not uncommon for one to walk across graveyards without realizing what they were walking over, and rumors of the entire province being haunted were not uncommon at all. Very few towns still existed in

Leticon, and so much of the land was empty, uncolonized space that one would wonder if they were even in civilized lands at all. In fact, many who went deep into Leticon's empty plains off the known routes never returned, nor were heard from again.

All of this made much of Leticon a very lawless place, even if there were few to be found in the province. There was no provincial government at all, no occupied major cities, and little to be shown that this territory actually belonged to Nuve or to any other nation in existence.

It also made hiding something in Leticon very possible. For instance, a large fortress that no one in Nuve knew of.

Standing a few charnas north of the Calphos River, and set in the grasslands just a few days west of the valley passage of the river through the Peaked Mountains, stood an ancient and gigantic fortress. It was surrounded by a wall of stone and stood several stories tall, in a very plain design with little stylistic touch.

It had been over a week since Setadev, General Sayo, and the rest of the army Setadev had termed "the remnant of the fallen" had departed their camp in the Wastes. Now they were across the Calphos River, and the fortress was within view.

"Welcome to my fortress," said Setadev to Sayo.

Sayo only stared at it in awe as he continued walking. He tried, however, not to show any reaction to his boss walking next to him.

"Miraculous, is it not?" continued Setadev. "This fortress has stood here in Leticon for a few thousand years. It has been rebuilt several times as war has ravaged this province, but while this land has been under the control of Nuve since the era of the superstate kingdoms began, this place has become only a lost memory."

Glaring at the fortress, Sayo said, "You were not joking."

"No, I was not," answered Setadev. "You will find as you travel with me, that very little that I say is a joke, my general. After all, I do back up everything that I say."

Looking away, Sayo said, "I know."

"Good, my general," continued Setadev. "Now, allow me to properly welcome you to the Fortress of Da Leval, the relay point of the Enlighteners from the Shadows. It is my home away from home, of sorts, and perhaps the one building in this entire realm that I would slightly mind if it were destroyed. Surely, they are expecting us."

With that, Sayo glared at Setadev. "We sent no message of our forthcoming arrival," he noted.

In response, Setadev rolled his eyes. "Ah, my general, you do not see how the game is played. You should know me well enough to know that I have other methods of communication than physical ones. I am, after all, more powerful than any figure, mortal or immortal, to have ever existed. And once my power has been fully reawakened, none shall even hold a chance in preventing me from my goals."

Sayo only nodded.

The Fortress of Da Leval appeared rather docile amidst the barren landscape it sat on. No snow was on the ground at the moment, revealing dead grass and infertile dirt, with no hint of a road to be seen. It was built of white stone, a much rarer material in the modern day than in the past. This showed to Sayo, at least, that Setadev was telling the truth in that the fortress was indeed quite old. It had been a few thousand years since white stone was common in architecture.

Suddenly, Setadev raised his hand in command. "Let us stop here for a moment."

Everyone stopped. Even the troops behind Setadev and Sayo stopped.

Setadev then turned around and looked directly at the two Enlighteners who were carrying the box that contained an incapacitated Kevin Trent Stryker. He pointed at them and said, "Take him into his special chamber in the tower. Make sure to use the wall shackles."

The two men took heed to their command, grabbed the box tighter, and went on ahead with some troops. General Sayo and Setadev stopped for a moment, as the troops passed them and headed toward the fortress. Then, Setadev asked the question. "Do you know why Leticon has the reputation it does today, my general?"

"Only on the basis that it has been the subject of many wars," acknowledged the general.

"Ah yes, that is true," answered Setadev, "but that is only half of it, my general." He waved to the general to continue forward, and he and the men all continued along the road. "To tell you an absolute truth, we are responsible for at least part of the reputation of Leticon. People disappear here without ever returning, and that is because they have stumbled upon the fortress and we must kill them to keep our secret safe. In that sense, the curse of the fortress that we have created has in effect contributed to the curse of the entire province."

Sayo crossed his arms. "The legends work in your favor."

"Exploiting them enhances the power of what we have done," Setadev commented. "By the time of my fall from the Realm of the Angels, Leticon had already been a particularly bloody region. The area was under the control of at least ten individual kingdoms at any given time, as kingdoms would rise and fall in the area. Recorded history has noted at least fifteen hundred individual kingdoms in the last ten thousand years, including Nuve, which technically claims control over the province today. Each one fought for their land, and in turn had to defend it. There was almost always constant war, without a moment of peace, until Nuve unified the province a couple of hundred years ago." He paused. "We showed up about five thousand years ago, and constructed the Fortress of Da Leval to be the strongest possible castle in the region. Heh… amazing what hiding amidst chaos will do to keep you secret until you are strong."

Sayo nodded.

"Anyway, keeping ourselves isolated allowed us to maintain our secrecy, and our ways of ridding ourselves of strangers kept them from coming to us. In time, the Enlighteners were able to spread, with the fortress still as a relay point. Yet despite the globalization of our secret group, we kept this place as our one source of visible danger, surviving even through Nuve's unification."

"And by virtue you have made your Enlighteners a part of legend," commented Sayo.

Setadev nodded. "A side effect of our influence," he said. "I need none of it, but the power of fear can still be quite the motivation. In the situation we are in now, no tool could be more useful."

"I see," said Sayo.

There was a pause in the air. Only the sound of footsteps continued, as soldiers continued marching into the Fortress of Da Leval.

"Come with me," Setadev finally said. "I wish to show you

something."

Sayo only acknowledged by nodding, and did as he was told. Into the fortress the general and the fallen deity went together. They proceeded straight through the middle, through the outer gate and down the hallway. Then, they climbed several flights of stairs, and traveled around a circular hallway.

Setadev then opened a door to a room in the center of the building, about halfway up the center section of the building. He invited Sayo to come in.

Following this lead, Sayo entered the room.

Torches lit the entire room, but the inside of this room was not white stone as was the rest of the building. It was gray stone, instead. A workbench sat on one end, but little else was present. The room was fairly wide and quite long, but otherwise empty. "This is my own private workspace," Setadev said as Sayo admired the room. "The door is magically locked to the touch of the founder of the Enlighteners from the Shadows. As that is me, of course, the door opens for me and only for me."

Slightly doubtful, Sayo reached for the door handle. The second he did, an insurmountable pain shot up his arm and shoved him back. Perhaps Setadev was not embellishing at all. It would certainly be a way to prove to the Enlighteners that he was the real founder and not an impostor.

"Just had to see for yourself?" asked Setadev, noticing Sayo's reaction to grabbing the door handle.

Sayo said nothing. He only looked at Setadev to respond.

Setadev shook his head. "Anyway, Sayo, what do you know of women?"

"Of women, sir?" asked Sayo.

"Yes, of women," answered Setadev. "We are going to be building one today, so certainly you must know something about them, or else you will not be helpful."

Sayo was confused. What was Setadev getting at?

Again, Setadev shook his head. "Let me explain to you how the game is played, General. As you are quite aware, the pure one is being locked up in the dungeon right now, and is being administered the aphrodisiacs, as ordered. The next step in my plan is to break his spirit by breaking his connection with that pathetic half-immortal girl who dares to calls herself an angel. I have started that process by shattering her mind. However, to truly make this break complete and real on both sides, I will make this division a reality. And to do that, I need to create a companion for him while under the control of the aphrodisiacs. Then, he will fall to temptation, and after he has, I will gain his cooperation before I end his life."

Suddenly, Sayo's eyes widened. "I see why you wanted the aphrodisiacs," he said.

"Correct," nodded Setadev. "And now you see how the game is played. When the pure one's self-control is lost, it will only be a matter of time before he falls to temptation and betrays everyone he knows, including his love."

Looking a bit reluctant, Sayo asked, "Could not your powers accomplish this, as you did with the girl?"

Setadev laughed briefly. "I like the way you think, Sayo, but no. Tracer magic could allow me to possess him, or a shatter spell would allow me to break his mind. However, as it turns out, the pure one's sword seems to have protected him from tracer magic, even when it is away from him. Perhaps Vinz Larinion's sacrifice was not quite so futile after all, in that it has protected this boy, but it is no matter, for I had not wanted to use that magic to possess him, anyway. My revenge is to truly break his spirit, and simple possession tricks would not do that. So, I will use more intricate methods, and I will reserve a shatter spell for when I feel the time is right, as I would delight to see this betrayal happen organically and honestly. And to do that, I need someone who can work on that in a much more feminine nature than I can; one who can seduce him and make him forget all about his past life is the type of individual I need. So, naturally, I will make one."

Sayo was confused. "How?" he asked.

"In the same way I made myself," answered Setadev, with a chuckle. "I made myself using divine power from my original form, and gave itself a conscience all its own, which I took over after my own body's downfall. Using what I have left, I will do it again now. Though it will take more effort since I do not have quite so much power, I still have the technique."

Then, Setadev closed his eyes. He started to float off of the ground. He was powering up, and channeling all of the energy he had in his current form.

"So, am I to presume that now is the time?" asked Sayo.

Setadev said nothing. He focused his power, and a form appeared a few steps away. Slowly, it began to materialize from the bottom up, and was completed in only a few seconds. "Answer your question?" Setadev finally asked.

Silently, Sayo nodded. He then stepped up to the form, and began to observe it with a cautious and critical eye. Though he did not know at all what the form looked like at all, the form was that of Caitlin Amelia Magnon. It stood silently with eyes open, and appeared motionless and without conscience.

Continuing to stay energized, Setadev said to the general, "This is where I need your assistance, Sayo. Look well upon this form, for it is that of the half-immortal girl that I mentioned before, at the same age as she is now—sixteen, the age of adulthood. Red hair, just as her mother before her, and deep blue eyes and a nose that come from her father. While tricking the pure one into thinking this copy is her would be nice, I believe that he would not fall for such a trap, even on aphrodisiacs, because he is aware of where he is. Therefore, knowing that the pure one has some attraction to this exact female form, I suggest we make small changes that will enhance the way the pure one sees her. As I have little interest in pursuing desires of the flesh, however, this is one task for which I do not have the appropriate knowledge." He paused, as he focused on Sayo for a moment. "So, what assessment do you make?"

There was a moment's pause, as Sayo looked over this figure. He began to do what he was told. "I would at least start by making the dress black instead of white. Our aphrodisiacs work partially by sensory inhibition, but a white dress would gleam very brightly in such a dark room like the dungeon that that effect would be weakened."

"Excellent point," nodded Setadev. "However, my general, that is not why I am having you inspect the model for this individual we are creating. I am already aware of such effects, and such are already in my consideration of the final design. What I need from you is to dig down and draw upon your most carnal male instincts to determine what improvements need to be made in order to make this individual more attractive than this demonstration."

For several minutes, Sayo had no response as he inspected the model. He was being asked to be a pig, and he knew it. Still, this was the command of his leader. Still, Sayo was finding this particular task difficult. He had, after all, not seen very many women during the course of his military journey, and he was definitely quite a bit older than the figure in front of him, but after close observation had some ideas for changes. He put his hand to his chin and stepped next to Setadev to share his findings.

"She is cute, but there definitely is room for improvement, from the perspective which you have asked me to analyze," Sayo finally stated. "Overall, somewhat attractive, but for absolute carnal attraction, I can recommend some changes."

"Proceed, general."

"For starters, although she has a lovely face, it does look a little unbecoming of an attractive woman. It looks more like a cute one, like one might see on a younger person than she is. I might suggest you add a little bit to the maturity of the face, and smoothen things out to make her look as though she is more fully developed. Keep the appearance youthful, but slightly more like she is fully in her prime."

"Good, Sayo! Now keep going."

"The eyes are lovely as they are. Color of sapphires, and shaped well. The hair. however, I suggest a completely different look. The most popular among my younger soldiers are ladies who possess blonde hair instead of the red, and with some curls in it, too, though not too curly."

"Very well."

"Lastly, the body shape is decent, but there is work that can be done. I suggest that you cut the weight down by a little bit to make her very skinny in the abdomen, and enhance her chest size and hips a bit more. I would also give her a slightly more tan complexion, as though she has enjoyed a bit of sunshine in her life. The current model color is nice, but it is just a little pale for most attractive females."

Suddenly, Setadev let up the energy. The figure disappeared.

"My, General Sayo," continued Setadev, "I had no idea how much of a carnal pig you really are on the inside. You have quite the critique for the appearance of a sixteen-year-old girl, but you have done what I have asked of you. Well done."

Sayo put a fist to his chest. "I have only done as you requested." In reality, Sayo was disgusted on the inside. That was not something that he wanted to do. He felt it was not his place to be critical of female appearance, especially in an individual much younger than him. In all actuality, it was not a topic that mattered to him, as he felt as though he would be as obliged to perform duty in defense of any of his people, regardless of their appearance. However, this was the price to serve Setadev; to do what he himself would not necessarily like and sound shallow, was critical to keep Setadev satisfied.

"Now, then," continued Setadev, "we must configure a personality for our doppleganger. I would not be in control of this figure unless I fell in this one, just as how I displaced Pseudo when I fell in my own. Therefore, we must tailor this person to sway the heart of the pure one. She should be seductive and pushy just enough to take a hold of the pure one's interests."

"Perhaps we should also ensure she is loyal," commented Sayo, "and strong enough to take on someone like this half-immortal girl that you describe. One can never have enough weapons at their disposal, after all."

Setadev nodded. "An excellent suggestion," commented the fallen deity. "Perhaps she should be loyal enough to be my left hand. You are, after all, my right."

Sayo said nothing.

"Very well, then," continued Setadev. "I think we have enough to make this creation. Now, stand back, general, for you will now see how the game is played." Setadev's tone had become quite dark at the end.

Again, Setadev began to float as he powered up again. Loud cracks rippled through the air as energy continued to build. Then, across the room, the new individual was beginning to be rendered. The assembly started at the bottom, and Sayo could see the black dress and leggings assembling. There was both red and gold trim on the dress, but in no spots were the trim colors next to each other. The skirt bottom also went quite a bit shorter than the initial developmental model that Setadev had first put together. Setadev was indeed quite devoted to making sure this new model would be quite a bit more attractive.

Rendering continued upward, and more of the dress became visible. Though the dress's basic design was similar, many of the angles on the dress were shaped differently. Still, the dress was long-sleeved and form fitting around the abdomen and sleeves. Then, the head began to be developed. Setadev had taken all of the suggestions Sayo had made, and crafted blonde hair with some curl as part of the form. The face was a little similar to the other model, but quite different because Setadev had implemented all of the suggestions into the design. The upper chest was more voluptuously designed, and the entire body had a curvature applied to it that was not there before. Some weight was trimmed off of the body, as well.

By all means, this was a very attractive female. She could definitely pass for eighteen or nineteen in age, and would turn heads anywhere she walked.

As the final rendering was completed, Setadev fell to the floor and collapsed to one knee. He put his hands over his chest, as Sayo looked over and witnessed the event. It was the first time that Sayo had ever seen Setadev show any weakness.

Slowly, Setadev began to regain his composure. He took some time to get back to his feet, which appeared as almost a painful experience. As he finally stood up, Setadev said in agony, "I hate this body. Had I had my original body, I would not have had any problems at all in generating the power to complete her."

Sayo finally saw even the slightest glimpse of Setadev's motivation for re-powering himself. Before, it had always seemed that he already had a great deal of power, but finally Sayo had seen Setadev hit a limit.

"And now to give her a name…" Setadev finally continued. "In the interest of keeping the pure one interested, she should have a true feminine name as well. Then, all will be ready to begin the procedures."

Sayo had nothing to say.

"Any suggestions, Sayo?" asked Setadev.

That was the last thing Sayo wanted to hear. "Not at all," commented Sayo.

"If you say so," answered Setadev. "If that is the case, then I believe I will name her for the *rengan* word for seductress. After all, that is what she will be."

Suddenly, Sayo had to interject. "Have you no respect for women, Setadev? That sounds incredibly disrespectful."

"What reason would I have for that?" Sayo answered back. "I have respect for no one, Sayo. Neither men nor women. When the world is mine, the only one to be respected will be me."

That made Sayo quite cross, but he said nothing.

"Besides," continued Sayo, "you may find that the *rengan* word for seductress is quite an interesting one indeed in the tones of the current language. The word is *satiana.* Now, that is a name that in our modern language does sound quite becoming of a female. Satiana. I like it. It is the perfect fitting name."

Again, Sayo rolled his eyes. He made sure Setadev was not watching him.

At that instant, Satiana's eyes opened. "I am Satiana," she acknowledged.

"Yes, you are," answered Setadev, as he turned to Satiana and walked over to her. "Welcome to the remnant of the fallen."

"It is a pleasure, my creator," acknowledged Satiana as she gave a curtsey. She then looked at General Sayo. "You are not his creation. Who are you?"

Before Sayo could answer, Setadev did for him. "This is General Martin Sayo, the head of my forces. He is my second in command, and my right hand. He is the only full human that I trust to execute my plans."

"I see," acknowledged Satiana. "So, am I to be your left hand?"

Setadev nodded. "You know well," he said. "You will also find that you have been imbued with a great amount of my divine power. Though you may not yet be aware, you have both the power and the skill to use this energy."

Satiana raised her hands, and began to look at them. "Interesting," she said. "I do sense that power." She then turned and looked at herself in the mirror that was in the room, and nearly jumped backwards. "Wow…" she said in amazement. A tear nearly came to her eye.

"Yes, indeed you are a very attractive female, Satiana," commented Setadev. "The features you have physically are very important parts of your design. However, if you see fit, then you should feel free to use your appearance to boost your self-image. It will be necessary for the task you will be assigned."

That made Satiana turn back toward Setadev. "And what task is that?"

A laugh came to Setadev. "There is someone in this building whose heart I am looking to derail. Your main task will be to seduce him, break apart his relationships, and get him to fall for you. Feel free to use any tactic you see necessary, as long as you get the job done. Do so, and you will be well rewarded when the world is mine."

"Understood," nodded Satiana. "I am, after all, a fragment of you."

Sayo was disgusted. He still did not say anything.

"Hold on," commented Satiana, as she raised her hand. She then walked over to Sayo. "Do you have a problem, general? You seem to be disturbed by what you are seeing in me. I wonder why."

General Sayo shook his head. "I just find your character somewhat unladylike, Satiana. Please take no offense, but I doubt any female, promiscuous or not, would merely jump to an assigned task of seduction so quickly after being told. Most women and girls are more reserved about such behaviors."

There was a slight pause. Then, Satiana smacked the general upside his face.

"You listen here, General," she said sternly. "You may be my superior, but I am a fragment of my creator. I am part of Setadev, too. I will listen to him, and to you as well, but you do not tell me how to be what I was created to be!"

Sayo took one step back and did not respond.

"You still have a problem?" asked Satiana, more aggressively as she raised her hand again.

"Down," commanded Setadev.

In response Satiana lowered her hand.

"It appears you may have inherited some of my more aggressive and risk-taking aptitudes," continued Setadev. "Unintentional, but I like that. However, Satiana, I want you to understand that General Sayo speaks only to those he respects. And for the moment, he does have reason not to respect you for making such a move, so consider it a compliment that he respects you enough to speak to you. In this case he is right; your conduct so far has been reasonably unbecoming of a lady. Be more polite and respectful to begin, and then you can transition to the aggression if provoked."

Satiana put a fist to her chest, in salute. "Affirmative," she said.

Finally, Sayo put his hand up to his face. That smack still stung.

"Sayo, perhaps you should get some rest," stated Setadev. "It has been a long march here, indeed, and all mortals do need rest. I have some private briefing I must conduct with Satiana. Perhaps in the meantime you would enjoy your quarters across the hall. They are quite lavishly decorated."

In response, Sayo nodded and exited through the door.

What was he doing? Sayo could barely even talk to Setadev now. Every action was becoming more and more inhumane, more disturbing, less rational and more personal. The reasons for Sayo's joining with Setadev were starting to become less and less clear.

After Sayo made it to the door of his quarters, he opened it and entered his room quickly. He then threw down his sword that was fastened to his belt and flopped down onto the feather bed in the room. He was absolutely exhausted. Yet there was much going on in his mind. He still had thoughts of desertion, although he wanted to be certain before he made such a drastic move. Not to mention, of course, that trying to desert in the middle of Leticon would not be a smart idea. The ghosts of war were not exactly friendly with travelers, after all.

If he did, though, he thought of cutting the pure one free as well. The innocent boy did not deserve what he was getting right now, or what he was about to receive from Satiana. Sayo felt very bad inside for that, and was already guilty of victimizing him.

Sayo knew, though, that the penalties for deserting now would be extreme. His odds of success were not great for escape from where he was, and Setadev would certainly turn his attention to the general at some point if that happened. And even if Sayo made it out and managed to evade Setadev, the Solunar Empire would want him for treason, murder, and other crimes. All of the other kingdoms—save for maybe Gardolk, who might capture and extradite him to Solunar—would want him for war crimes for his service with Desolunar.

Yet Sayo could not stay here, either. So much was wrong with this situation. What could he do?

That was the question that would take a long time to answer. For now, Sayo rolled himself over to sleep, knowing that he had to rest.

Several hours would pass, as Sayo slept. His army was setting up their operations in the fortress, although little was left to them for now except to set up fortifications and run guard shifts. There was plenty of room in the fortress for all of the troops, as the fortress was quite spacious.

A few hours later, there was a knocking on Sayo's door. Then, the door opened.

Sayo rolled over in the bed.

"Time to get moving again, general," said Setadev. "We have some business to attend before we set this plan into motion. And make sure you have that vial of aphrodisiac with you." He then proceeded back into the hallway.

As he wiped his eyes and swung himself around, Sayo grabbed his old Desolunar military jacket and followed his master through the fortress. It was not far to where they were headed.

Chapter 24

The Prisoner

The Fortress of Da Leval contained a thick-walled dungeon, nestled in the core of the building. Encased in the building's central support around the middle height of the structure, the dungeon was the darkest place in the entire building. An iron door served as the entrance, and no windows or bars were present in the room. Its cells were arranged vertically, with a prison room on each floor. The top floor contained his most valued prisoner.

Attached to the walls were shackles, chained with anchors that were built into the stone. Though the chains had been changed periodically during the building's history, the lead anchors that were meshed into the stone had not been replaced since the construction five thousand years ago. Despite this, the anchors were still quite strong, as Kevin Trent Stryker had discovered firsthand.

For the last few days, Kevin had been trying very hard to work himself loose. There was no success to be found. Those anchors were solid. If only he could have pulled his sword to him, he might be able to work his way out of the chains with its power. Unfortunately, his ability to call his sword to him only worked over a short distance. He had never really tried it before except for once or twice. Instead, all he could do was remain seated on the ground and think. Though things were tough now, he had only to endure until he could make his move. He had too many people out there caring for him for him to just give up.

Already in his mind, he knew that he had to give many apologies to Caitlin. She was probably worried sick about him by now, and likely upset that he had left on his own. He thought he was doing the right thing trying to stop General Sayo as soon as possible, and he turned out to be wrong, instead falling into an insidious trap. Needless to say, when he could figure his way out of this, he would owe her the biggest bouquet of flowers that he could afford to purchase.

Would she even know why he bought flowers for her? Granted, Caitlin would know the reason in her mind, but would she feel it in her heart?

So many times, Kevin had to reason out how Caitlin would react to certain emotional situations. Some things, he had had completely wrong, like the idea of taking Caitlin to the Rikleifer Rangers dangerball game on a cold winter night just before starting the journey that ended up with him locked in here. Though it ended pretty well and the two of them went home that night holding hands, Kevin could tell Caitlin had little understanding of the tradition of the game and felt little reason to understand it. She also took little enjoyment from the event's cold weather and made Kevin reconsider doing it ever again.

This did not frustrate Kevin, though he was an adamant fan of dangerball and loved the sport in the wintertime, but it did make him quite nervous. Even if Caitlin was very heart-set on Kevin, he was still quite nervous about making sure Caitlin liked him all the time. Maybe it was something new about being in a relationship, but the whole experience was still scary. If he did something he feared would make Caitlin uncomfortable with him, he would be rushing to make amends and pretend the incident had not happened.

He really did not want to lose her. Caitlin was his whole world right now. Maybe his nerves made him the worst boyfriend to have a girlfriend like her. Yet he was not just her boyfriend. He was her guardian, her protector, and her defender. He was teaching her everything he could about the world, and was giving as much to her as he possibly could to make her happy.

Maybe that was the wrong way for him to be approaching it. After all, Caitlin was also strong and independent. At times she was a bit fragile emotionally, since handling her feelings were a new experience for her, but she was still the strongest person he knew. And yet Kevin still felt the need to be chivalrous and think he had to be the one to keep her safe, not the other way around.

Kevin had hoped that what he had done had not taken her strength away from her. Sometimes, Kevin wondered if he had done more harm than good for Caitlin. What if she was better the way she was before she had ever met him? Just because he believed that humanity made him stronger did not mean it would do the same for Caitlin. Or, furthermore, if humanity really did make him stronger, he wondered.

As Kevin pondered this, the door swung open. In marched Setadev and General Sayo. They shut the door behind them, and simply stood in front of Kevin, silent. Frustrated and rebellious given the circumstances, Kevin said, "Are you two going to just stand there, or are you here for a reason?"

"Oh, no reason at all," stated Setadev, calmly. "I am only here to take in my last looks of you as you are. Sayo is here to be my witness."

"Before what? Before you break me?" asked Kevin pointedly. "Because if that is your intent, you'll have to kill me first."

Setadev shook his head. "So eager to die, are we? I guess you really do not care for those who you claim to love."

Kevin only growled back.

"It is all fitting, regardless," continued Setadev. "Do you not see the world I am trying to build, Mr. Stryker? It will be a unified world, where all war will end. What could be so bad about that?"

Taking a breath, Kevin said, "Nothing. But your means to that end are wrong."

"Oh, is that what you believe?" commented Setadev as he stepped closer to Kevin. "You just do not see how the game is played, do you? A unified world under me will be a peaceful one, pure one. It will be a utopia for all, and all I ask is that you bow to me. What could be so wrong about that?"

Instantly, Kevin pulled his chains out as far as he could, pulling himself as close to Setadev as he could. "Then maybe you don't see how the game is played!" he screamed, turning the common phrase of Setadev against him in frustration. "Maybe the people don't want your rule. They want to rule themselves and do as they see fit. You can't break the resolve of the people; they will fight you with all of the spirit they have until you realize you can't rule them!"

"Such an interesting person to claim being the voice of the people," said Setadev as he shook his head. "I wonder why I do keep you alive, Kevin Trent Stryker. I swear, some days I do." He knelt down next to Kevin. "So enigmatic, yet so deluded. You are far too prideful, pure one, and that is why you fail. Do you even know what you fight for? Clearly it is not for your own life or for your friends, since you seem so willing to die and hurt all of them. Even that pathetic angel you call your girlfriend, you would not even mind dying even if she ended up heartbroken permanently from it?"

"I would die to protect her," Kevin said firmly as he glared into Setadev's eyes.

"And if you did that, then how would you defend the people?"

Kevin had overstepped, and Setadev had caught him. He sat back down against the wall.

Setadev then prompted for Sayo to hand him something. "Do you see now?" he asked Kevin, handling the vial that Sayo had handed him. "You have no idea what you are fighting for. Instead, you are just a pathetic and weak man who is lost in his own desires and responsibilities so much as to realize he fights without any real purpose." He then turned and prompted for Sayo to step forward.

"Do you know what you fight for?" Kevin then asked.

That made Setadev stop in his tracks. He extended his arm to stop Sayo, as well.

As a pause set in, Kevin continued, "If I am so weak to you, then why do you have me locked here in this room? Why have you formulated such a scheme just to keep me here, restrained with these chains? Is it only because you hate me, or is it something more?"

Setadev scoffed. "Do not flatter yourself, pure one. You will know how serious things are soon enough." He then directed Sayo to continue.

The general approached Kevin with a firm attitude. He then looked down at Kevin, who stared into his eyes. There was no fear there, no worry. For someone who was as weak as Setadev claimed to be, he certainly did not have that appearance.

Then, Sayo pushed back on Kevin's forehead and lowered his jaw forcefully with his other hand. Setadev then stepped in and poured the contents of the vial into Kevin's mouth. Once the contents were poured in, Sayo moved his left hand off of Kevin's chin and over his mouth to keep the pure one from spitting out the contents.

Kevin tried to keep himself from swallowing, but Sayo then plugged Kevin's nose, forcing him to swallow. Sayo then removed his hands, having to wipe the left one to remove the liquid on it that Kevin had tried to spit up.

What was it? Poison? A paralytic? A drug of some type? Why did Setadev force Kevin to drink it?

"Now, Kevin, I hope you will enjoy this 'special blend' that we put together just for you," continued Setadev. "Please enjoy this little taste of my utopia while it lasts, because the good times will not last forever for you."

Then, he and Sayo turned and exited through the door.

As they left, Kevin sighed. He looked down at himself in the darkness, wondering what kind of inner strength he really had. At times, Kevin took the philosophy of his inner strength, when he had questioned it before, from how he would be remembered historically in Aurana.

King Andrew II of Aurana had declared that it may be said of Kevin, "the heart of the dragon, the spirit of the phoenix, the strength of a warrior together united". It was the way that Andrew had seen Kevin for having the confidence to overcome everything he had lost and risk even more to aid in the overthrow of King Arnold IX. Kevin faced no consequence from the events because Arnold eventually did turn over power peacefully to his son Andrew, and in fact he was rewarded with the rank of Vanguard of Aurana. Eventually, Kevin became curious about what the saying really meant, but he finally came to an understanding that the saying was all about his inner strength. Yet if he really had inner strength, then why did he not have the right answers to Setadev's questions? He did not have the mental fortitude to stay ahead of the fallen deity and was made to look like he did not know what he was talking about. And, in some ways, Kevin was not sure if he did know what he was talking about anymore.

It would be rather selfish to Caitlin if he died a senseless death. Setadev was right. He would not be able to fight for her or anyone else if he perished.

As Kevin looked toward the door, pondering these thoughts, his vision started to become a little fuzzy. Mentally, he was beginning to feel more fatigued than ever, even more so than his continued fight with the chains in the prison cell had done.

What was it that Sayo had made him drink? What did Setadev mean by a piece of utopia? Something was going on. Kevin's body temperature was also starting to heat up, and his fingers were becoming twitchy. Still, he had his consciousness and his focus.

Then, the door opened. Two guards had escorted someone into the cell, then shoved her inside and slammed the door again. Instantly, she turned and started banging on the door. "Let me out! Let me out of here, you bastard!" she screamed.

"That won't do you any good," said Kevin, from the other end of the room. "The group here won't listen to your pleas."

The girl then dropped her hands. "It's no good," she said. Then she turned toward Kevin.

She was the prettiest thing he had ever seen with his eyes.

Her hair was long and golden, and with just a couple of curls in a very stylish manner. She wore a black dress with a short skirt. Her skin was tanned slightly as though she spent her summers outside, and her body shape was perfect—voluptuous in the right areas and slender in others for the perfect female shape. The eyes… those looked familiar.

As she turned, the girl's eyes widened. "Oh, I'm sorry," she said. "I should have greeted you if we are to be cellmates. My apologies."

Amazing. She was simply amazing.

Wait, where were these thoughts coming from? Certainly there were amazing people around the world, but none were more amazing than Caitlin. Or were there? Kevin blinked his eyes a couple of times, finding it harder and harder to keep them open and focused. "It's no trouble at all," he smiled awkwardly. "What are you here for?"

"I wish I knew," answered the girl, as she shook her head and walked across the room to Kevin. She then knelt down. "Why are you here, and why are you all chained up?"

Kevin's memory was gone. The circuits in his head were not connecting. He was not able to remember anything or think logically.

All that was left was desire. "I wish I remembered," he said. "I'm not sure I know anymore." His vocal tone was incredibly bright, despite the fact that the material he was speaking on was very grim. It would have been an indicator to any sane person that something was not right here, but Kevin could not recognize that because of his delirium. Then, his voice perked. "If I may say so, you are the prettiest girl I have ever seen in my life."

The girl's eyes lit up. "You really think so?" she asked, smiling. She sat down next to Kevin, placing his arm across her shoulders. "Well, to tell you the truth, I know we just met, but I think you're really cute, too." She started curling up beside him. "We're going to need each other if we're going to survive in this cell."

The emotions in Kevin's brain were spiraling out of control. Everything was flushing out of his brain, and only the girl next to him was on his mind. He started leaning in closer to her. The rest of his mind was vacant, as an effect of the aphrodisiac he had been forced to drink.

"My name's Kevin," he said. "What's yours?"

The girl looked at him and smiled. "Satiana," she said.

Chapter 25
Sacrifices

Caitlin's eyes popped open. She found herself tied to a pole.

Earlier, she had been led to the Aequina village and away from her campsite in the leftover tent. Then, she recalled being blindfolded, but there was little more than that that she could remember. Her blindfold had been removed a couple of minutes ago, but Caitlin wanted to wait for silence before she opened her eyes again. The fear was rippling through her veins, in an almost paralyzing sense.

Around her, she could see a bunch of torches lining the walls of the room. The entire room appeared to be lined in gold and silver, with a thick stone construction. She seemed to be in the middle of the room, although she could not look behind herself to be sure.

This was a shrine.

The Aequina were known to practice human sacrifice, especially on younger girls and women, and they often did more than simply cut out one's heart. The place where she was seemed to be indicative that this was to be her fate, as well.

Caitlin managed to look down, and saw that she was not wearing part of her dress. Someone had removed the top piece that normally rested on her shoulders that covered part of her chest and draped over her dress down the sides past her waistline. It looked like a lot of the dress had been dirtied more than it had before. As she tried to keep moving her head, she realized that someone had cut her red hair, too. It was now cut above her neckline. That made her feel quite violated—that was *her* hair and no one else's to determine for her, and nowadays she kept it long because she liked it, as did Kevin. More important on her mind was what was becoming painfully and frighteningly obvious from this situation.

She was being prepared for a ritual. That much seemed apparent now. Why else would the Aequina go to such lengths? With her hands tied behind her back, there was little she could do with magic.

Come to think of it, the Aequina had tied her hands with actual rope, not like the shackles they placed on her legs, she realized. If she was very careful and could get her hand into the right position, she could light a spark of fire and torch the rope.

A creaking noise came from the far end of the room. Someone was opening a door. The sound was behind Caitlin. She must have been facing the rear of the room. As the door then shut, a voice echoed through the hall. "Our preparations are soon to be complete for the sacrifice. We are quite fortunate that we found her when we did, or else we would not be able to finish the ceremony."

Both of the Aequina stopped. Neither one stepped in front of Caitlin.

The second individual, from the speaking voice Caitlin could guess was an Aequina female. "Excellent," she said. "Then we will make the remaining preparations. Our warning to outsiders will be complete soon, and our expression of dominance will be ready."

There was a moment of silence. Caitlin was terrified.

The Aequina female chuckled. "The tribe leader will be quite pleased," she continued. "On the eve of war, it is important that we complete our sacrifice and strike fear into our opponents before we begin. Of course, I am sure that the Metoi already have quite a bit of fear struck into their hearts from whatever destroyed their village, but they will soon learn that the Aequina have no mercy for them."

That was why she was to be sacrificed. A pre-war ritual before an attack. Worse yet, it was on the already weakened Metoi. Marilynn and the Metoi tribe were in danger. If Caitlin were to go back now, if she could get free, she had to warn them.

If she had the energy to get back. Caitlin was dehydrated and thoroughly exhausted. If she managed to get free from the Aequina, she would have to find water and shelter, and fast.

"Interesting taste," continued the Aequina female. "Your men have quite the taste in sacrifices. She looks to be from Desolunar in heritage, from her hair color and general appearance. Probably adult age, but very young if that. I am sure that the land will be pleased with this sacrifice."

"Yes, High Priestess, I agree," acknowledged the Aequina male.

Something the high priestess had said had made Caitlin think something was very wrong with this situation. The "taste" comment seemed off-color, but that was not it. And interestingly enough, the priestess actually had a good pinpointing on Caitlin's heritage. Though she lived in Aurana and was born and raised there, her father was five thousand years old, and her mother was from Seta Archa. A tint of red hair was actually known to be fairly common of ancestral descendants of Seta Archa residents in the former city-state that became the capital of Desolunar.

Desolunar. That was it. The Aequina had no idea that Desolunar had collapsed and the Solunar Empire had taken its place. They were completely oblivious to the world around them. Still, in retrospect that changed little given the circumstances. It was likely that the Aequina would not change anyway. After all, the entire area of the Wastes was under very little control by either the past or present government, both of which allowed the Wastes to govern themselves for the most part. Human sacrifice was technically banned under both Desolunar and Solunar Empire law, but Desolunar had turned a blind eye, allowing the Aequina to continue to practice it.

"Then let us prepare the altar," continued the high priestess. "By dawn, we will burn this girl at the stake, and the smoke will carry her soul as a warning to all tribes of the Wastes that the Aequina are the dominant tribe."

Caitlin's eyes widened. Those were haunting words.

Though stories of the Aequina tribe were common in the Solunar Empire, few understood how their society worked. For the most part, this was because they were very isolationist except when they were warhawking. Even the Metoi feared the Aequina, and the Metoi were normally one of the stronger tribes in the Wastes.

Suddenly, Caitlin heard the doors slam behind her. The high priestess and Aequina male had left. Still tied to the pole, Caitlin thought of where she was at and how she ended up in this predicament. She had never really been put in this kind of situation before, where she was a prisoner. She was finding herself more frightened than she had ever been before. Fright was still such a new emotion to her that it paralyzed her from her neck down her spine, making her forget that she had to escape.

Was this really what she was without Kevin? He had invested quite a bit of time into her to show her all that life had to offer, and all of the emotional surges that came with them. Happiness and the feeling of being loved, Caitlin had to admit, were quite worth all of that time. However, Caitlin also realized that she only had those feelings when she was with Kevin. Essentially, Caitlin had become dependent on Kevin for much of her inner strength and the gifts of being a person who could embrace being a unique individual instead of one who had no care for individuality and human emotion.

At least in one way, Setadev had been right. Caitlin was codependent on Kevin's desires to be closer to her and his dependency on close interactions with her. That also explained why she was worrying so much about her relationship with Kevin slowing down as time passed. Kevin had put forth so much effort into being with her when they started out, and she knew that he needed the closeness as much as she did. However, in the last three months, their relationship had slowed advancing, and Caitlin started to feel the sensations of an addict deprived of her fix. It was not that the love was not there, but the rapid advancement they had, slowed down. They were little further than where they were after the Battle of Seta Archa—in love, but still holding back from taking the next steps.

The relationship was the addiction. She wanted to be closer to him. In more ways than one. Oftentimes, she wondered if Kevin had thought the same thing. Yet her personality had developed a shyness in that since she was still trying to learn all of the sensations of emotion, she was afraid to talk to Kevin about those feelings she had that he could not see from the outside.

If Setadev was really right about codependency, though, was he also right in saying that Kevin did not actually care for her? The more and more she thought of it, the more and more Caitlin was afraid that that possibility might be true.

Suddenly, something snapped outside of the building. Members of the Aequina tribe were headed back toward the shrine. Caitlin's head snapped out of these dreary thoughts for the moment, as she started to fathom her escape. Her adrenaline started flowing, her senses were raised, and her magic was at the ready. She was back to being focused, ready to make her escape.

As carefully as possible, Caitlin managed to get her right index finger and thumb together on the outside of the rope binding her to the pole. Then, she snapped her fingers, lighting a spark that started to burn the rope.

The fire burned fast, scorching through the rope in a minute. Then, with her hands free, Caitlin bent down and spread a wave of darkness magic across her shackles, targeting specifically the anklets. Slowly, the darkness began to dissolve the entire shackle set as Caitlin continued to focus, wearing down the metal at an even rate. She watched as the shackles immediately rusted over and faded into dust with the destructive force of darkness.

She was free. Seeing the top piece to her dress in the corner of the room, Caitlin quickly ran to it and set it on her dress, not even bothering to fasten it together for the moment. When she turned back around toward the pole, she saw that the pole was now on fire. It must have ignited from the burning rope.

Then, the doors at the other end of the room opened.

Caitlin could not let the Aequina capture her again. She had to gain the upper hand on them, by any means necessary. Now, she was the huntress.

Using air magic, she fired a beam of air straight through the burning pillar towards the door. The strong wind force brought on by this shot dragged the fire of the pole with it, blasting the individuals in the door with a rushing force of fire. The Aequina tribesmen there were forced out of the doorway and thrown to the ground with severe burns.

The blast had also lit the shrine on fire all around. The walls had caught fire and quickly the shrine was becoming an inferno. Already, the entire entrance to the shrine was encased in flames, preventing any exit. Caitlin had to get out before the fires grew higher and the smoke became lethal.

Moving fast, Caitlin turned to the back wall and began casting an even larger spread of darkness. She focused all of her energy into it, looking to take out the entire wall. Within one minute, the wall had disintegrated.

Quickly, Caitlin prepared to hop out of the burning shrine, right into a large group of Aequina who had the building surrounded. This time, they would not gain the upper hand. Summoning as much energy as she had, Caitlin put all of the force of the element of earth that she could into her right fist. As she leapt from the shrine, Caitlin prepared one of her most powerful attacks that she had in her repertoire. Combining earth and darkness, Caitlin hammered down against the ground with all of the force she could put into one shot.

The powerful force impacted into the ground launched almost all of the Aequina into the air, as the ground below shattered into pieces. Many were launched into the air, some to a substantial height, before falling back to the ground.

Caitlin stood up and saw the damage she had done. In realization, her hand came to her mouth, which was hanging open. Those were not simply Aequina men. They were women and children, too. They had been waiting to celebrate the sacrifice.

How many of them had she seriously injured?

No time to think about that, though. Aequina soldiers were approaching, quite angry with the attack that had just happened. Caitlin was tired and out of energy, but she had to keep fighting if she wanted to make it out alive.

One of the Aequina soldiers made it to Caitlin very quickly and stabbed at her with his spear. Having seen it coming, Caitlin dodged it and smashed a small fireball into his face, blinding him temporarily and putting burns on his face.

Next one up tried to swing his spear in a slicing motion toward Caitlin's neck. As she stepped back to avoid it, she struck back with a lightning whip attack. She was effective, putting a giant scar across the Aequina soldier's chest and throwing him backwards.

Another one came up and swung at Caitlin. As she tried to sidestep the spear, though, he changed his move into a stab and struck Caitlin in the left shoulder.

Aaaaaaaaaaaaahh!

Instantly, Caitlin stepped back and shrieked loudly in pain. Quickly, in fury, she blasted the stabber with a fire spell, knocking him over. Then, she grabbed her shoulder with her other hand.

That hurt.

The path behind her was clear, so Caitlin had to flee and flee quickly. Enough Aequina had suffered from her attack. If she could simply break away, that would be a victory for her. In that way, she could protect the Aequina as well as she could herself. And once she managed to get free, she could try to find shelter, food, and water.

That was a desperate proposal, however. The Aequina lived in some of the harshest terrain of the Wastes. All around were some of the driest areas in the entire world, due to very dry clay soil and few plants in addition to the normal hot and dry conditions of the Wastes. The village of the Aequina, in fact, was located where it was in order to take advantage of an underground well that supplied enough water for the village. For food, the Aequina tended to be a hunter-gatherer society that perused the lands east of their village, but the animals out there were of many varieties and quite a few were either poisonous or capable of seriously injuring someone with large fangs or horns. And furthermore, the Aequina had taken whatever supplies Caitlin had left behind in the tent. She could not make it away like this.

After she had made it far enough away, Caitlin stopped and fell to her knees, clutching her injured shoulder. She had to take a few deep breaths. Not only was she severely tired, she also had used up a good majority of the magic energy she had saved. Every shot she had fired, every attack that she had mustered, had sapped her strength and energy, but also drained her magic. Without time to absorb more energy into her body, she might run out of magic if she had to defend herself further.

In an effort to regenerate her magic while she was resting, Caitlin set herself down facing toward the village, and let her legs drape along the ground. She kept her shoes on, in case she had to get up and run again, but she did remove the top piece, pull up her skirt, pull down her leggings, and pull up her sleeves. The more skin she could expose, the quicker that her magic would recharge. Of course, however, she was not going to completely expose herself in the open, even if that would have allowed the fastest recharging. Then, she began touching up her shoulder wound with light magic, slowly but surely alleviating the pain and repairing her body injury.

A view from above revealed the structure of the Aequina village. The shrine from which she had escaped was towards an edge of the small town. There was some gold plating on the side, but most of it was constructed of wood. Also unique about the shrine was that it was the only building that was elevated a short distance off the ground by supports, as the rest of the homes and constructs sat on the ground directly. The homes themselves had some elegance to their stylings as well. Many had pitched wooden roofs that were quite different from the thatched roofs of kingdom villages. From the appearance of the color, though difficult to make out by firelight, the wood appeared to be from dead trees. How the Aequina had acquired such wood was a mystery, since the Wastes provided little of that type of material. Little more sat in the town other than the shrine, a mishmash of homes scattered in no particular pattern, and a very large wooden stake that rose as high as two Aequina homes, with a pile of kindling around it.

That was going to have been where she would be burned at the stake, as part of the Aequina ritual.

For a couple of minutes, Caitlin sat watching the chaotic village below her from the embankment she was sitting on. The shrine was completely in flames, lighting up the night sky. All around down there, it appeared that the wounded were being treated and the shrine was being isolated to prevent other buildings from catching fire.

Yet what damage had been done to the Aequina people? There was certainly a distinct possibility that Caitlin had killed quite a few of them. As she thought about this, Caitlin crossed her arms and set her head in them.

She could remember watching Kevin kill his first person. For him, however, the experience was terribly traumatic. This was for several reasons other than just being the first time; naivety and immaturity were certainly part of it, but more so was the fact that the man was an innocent who Kevin did not mean to kill. Though it took Kevin quite some time to get over, and a little help from Caitlin's father, the experience had become a part of the fabric of Kevin, and made him decisive when the moment came for him to make the serious kill. That would come over a month later, in a decisive battle with Pseudo on the

Cliffs of Vallia. Or at least, it should have been decisive. In retrospect, it was no longer that way.

In terms of the battle with the Aequina, Caitlin did have a reason for doing what she did, in that she was acting to protect her own life. She knew, as well as anyone in Solunar knew, that her life was in distinct danger. Even to those who had not witnessed her escape, simply being in the presence of the Aequina usually meant one's life was about to end. Still, on a moral level Caitlin did feel a lot of remorse and regret. If she had ended even just one life of an Aequina, then she had done something very gravely wrong. No Aequina needed to die for that, no matter how desperately she needed to escape. Yet she had snapped quickly to using fatal force in order to get away. Why?

Caitlin placed her hands in front of her and looked at them. Was she really a killer?

A tear came to her eye. She needed Kevin to put this into context for her, but he was missing as well. Who knew what kind of lives had been lost in that village directly because of her?

Regardless, Caitlin was not going back to find out. The Aequina were still too dangerous. Plus, she would need to find water and shelter fast. No amount of apologizing would get her any good graces with the Aequina, especially after an attack like that. There had to be some way through the Wastes that would lead to such resources. Tribes did live out in this wasteland, after all. Maybe the way to Kevin would take her there, if she could only find which way that was now.

Quickly, Caitlin's eyes widened, and she rapidly began shuffling through the removed top piece of her dress. She had just now realized that she was no longer wearing the pink heart key necklace that Kevin had given her three months before. She rifled through the folds of fabric, trying to find it as desperately as she could. She had to have that key. It was the only reminder of Kevin that she had left, and it was a very special one at that.

As she did, someone pointed a dagger at her neck from behind. "Stop moving," demanded a female voice.

Caitlin stopped dead in her tracks.

She was absolutely shocked and frightened.

The woman then spun around, revealing herself to be an

Aequina female dressed in very elegant garb. Her clothing was mostly of a bright purple color, with many pieces of gold and gem jewelry decorating her body, including a tiara, rings, necklaces, and bracelets. "Take a look at what you have done, and tell me why I should not kill you now."

Instead of answering, Caitlin drooped her head. She was too tired to let anyone intimidate her right now.

Seeing this, the woman lowered her dagger. She then turned toward the village, looking the same direction as Caitlin was facing. "Awful lot of damage you have done to our village. Our people are quite afraid of who or what you are. I, however, am not."

Still, Caitlin said nothing.

"And to think," continued the woman, "all you had to do was participate in a little ceremony of ours, and the only life lost would have been yours. Instead, you had to cause all of this destruction, and show yourself as a monster. What do you have to say for yourself?"

Caitlin glared up at the woman. Now, the switch was flipped. "Is that how you treat outsiders, to sacrifice them?"

"That is how we treat trespassers!" screamed the woman, as she threw her dagger at Caitlin. She had not even attempted to aim her shot, however, causing the dagger to fall next to Caitlin and stick in the ground. It was not an attack, but an intentional warning. "You should be honored to be a sacrifice for the mighty Aequina! Instead, now you are a source of dishonor. I should tear you apart for what you have done to my people."

Suddenly, Caitlin stood up. There was a new look in her eye, one of both weariness and also of fury. Though she did have regrets, they were quickly disappearing as her disposition became stronger. "And what have you done to my people?" asked Caitlin strongly. She pointed a finger to the village. "How many outlanders have you kidnapped from other tribes and sacrificed? How many innocent people have you murdered?"

"I have murdered no one," snapped the woman, as she pulled out another dagger. "I am the High Priestess of the Aequina, after all. Murder, I do not commit. Offerings and signals of power to our people, I do accomplish."

"Tell me how many you have killed!" responded Caitlin angrily.

The priestess flipped the dagger around in her hand. "Too many to count," she said. "That is, not counting you as of yet."

"What you are doing is murder!" exclaimed Caitlin. "Solunar law protects travelers through the Wastes and makes your sacrifice acts illegal. What you are doing is not defense, but cold-blooded murder, plain and simple." She then ran her fingers through her hair; her short, freshly cut hair. "Not to mention the sick and twisted violations you committed to my body. What else did you and your people do when you knocked me out besides cut my hair?"

"We did not assault you or violate you, if that is what you are implying," continued the priestess. "You are a true monster if you are committing such accusations without proof. How dare you defame the Aequina like that?"

Caitlin was deeply offended. "Your people have been murdering others for years and years, and I am the monster?"

Pointing her dagger at Caitlin, the priestess answered, "And how long have you been murdering others? For someone who is quite critical of the Aequina ways of killing, you have developed quite the skill for that yourself in your powerful magic. It is a trait that many of our people have never seen, and never have any seen it to the level you have. You have invoked much fear in them, but I have no fear for you." She then flipped the dagger again, this time showing Caitlin the side of the dagger. "Do you know what this is?"

Black splotches were present in the dagger's iron sides. Recognizing them, Caitlin instantly took a step back. "Antite," she said. "A weak alloy of iron and antenz that can disable one's magic." She could deeply recall having been struck by it a couple of times before, and that it was a favored tool of Demonicus a few months before.

"You know your metals well," replied the priestess. "This was a gift from the ruler of Desolunar, proof that I am the authority out here. I decide what is moral and what is not, and I hereby decide that you have committed a violent atrocity by attacking the Aequina people. You are hereby sentenced to death." She pointed the dagger again at Caitlin's neck.

This time, it was for real.

Thoughts of everything in her life flashed through Caitlin's head. Then, an image of Kevin. She had to fight for him.

An idea came to her head.

"Any last words?" asked the Aequina priestess.

Quickly, Caitlin formed a lightning whip in her hand and smacked the side of the priestess's wrist, knocking the dagger out of her hand and causing the priestess to reach down at her wrist in pain. Then, Caitlin hammered her in the head with a shot of fire.

The Aequina priestess fell to the ground. After a second, she popped back onto her hands and knees, and turned to look at Caitlin.

"Yes," answered Caitlin, "I do have something to say. Next time, walk the walk before you talk the talk. I'm done here."

As she said this, Caitlin turned and walked away. She wanted nothing more to do with this, or with any of the Aequina. She stopped only to pick up her dress's top piece, placing it in her left hand to carry.

The priestess, however, was not done. Her face was burned and her body was in pain, but her anger was unrestrainable. Furious, she picked up her antite dagger and let out a scream, charging to stab Caitlin with it. She kept her arm up and away from her body as she ran and yelled at the top of her lungs.

Quickly, Caitlin flipped around. "You fool!" she screamed as she blasted a beam of darkness into the stomach of the priestess. She poured all of the energy she had left into that shot.

It was a direct hit.

Instantly, the priestess shrieked in pain and dropped the dagger. She continued to scream as Caitlin's blast lasted a few seconds, and her body began to disintegrate. By the time the beam had ceased, the priestess was completely disintegrated.

Caitlin stared blankly for a moment, realizing what she had just done. She wanted so much, despite the hatred burning inside her, to have spared the life of the Aequina priestess. Immediately, she felt guilty and started to hurt inside.

She had killed someone for certain now. Nothing could have hurt more than that thought. No time for that thought now, though. She had to get out of here, and fast. Using whatever she had left, Caitlin fled from the village, heading directly away from the burning fires of the shrine. Though she was not quite sure which way she was running, she knew she had to get as far away from the Aequina village as possible.

What have you done, Caitlin?

A voice echoed in Caitlin's head. It was Kevin's. Caitlin's subconscious was using it to tell her something. Still, she kept on running.

Why did you have to kill her, Caitlin? Why did you have to hurt all of them and destroy their sacred building?

'No, I had to kill her,' Caitlin consciously thought to herself. 'If I hadn't, she would have killed me first.'

You didn't have to kill her, Caitlin. You could have merely used another spell. You didn't need to use deadly force. Her blood is on your hands now.

"No!" screamed Caitlin aloud as she continued running.

Yes. And you expect to save me when you are showing yourself to be no better than Setadev? I was right to ditch you after all.

Caitlin kept running. She had to try to push this nightmare out of her head.

You cannot resist me, for I am nothing. And now you see how the game is played.

The voice, it was all fake.

'Setadev,' Caitlin responded in her head. 'What do you want from me?'

You know what I want from you, Caitlin Amelia Magnon. I told you to stay out of my business. But, if you really feel that you want to come and see your boyfriend again, and see the traitor to your trust that he really is, then allow me to invite you to come and see us, and witness it for yourself. He will be much happier now that he is away from you.

'Where are you, you sick son of a…"

Now, now, there is no need for such language, angel. If you want to see the boy who has destroyed who you are and continues to hurt you, you may come and visit us. We will be waiting for you in the Fortress of Da Leval.

'Then I will see you there, and I will prove you wrong!'

That is, of course, if you can survive this far. You may not even survive this night. You have no food, no water, and no shelter. The conditions in the Wastes will kill you.

'Try me. I will survive as long as he needs me.'

Oh, young angel, you do not see how the game is played. You will see soon enough, however. And do mind the security if you arrive; I will not inform them that we are expecting company. I would not want to get their hopes up, after all.

Caitlin continued running. 'Then we will see, soon enough.'

For a long time, Caitlin kept going and going. She had to keep going. Nowhere was there water or shelter to be found. Only wasteland surrounded her.

Then, she had to stop. Her body would not carry her any further. As soon as she did, she passed out.

Only wasteland surrounded her. The wind blew across the wasteland, howling with the sound of death.

Chapter 26

Neutrality's Consequence

Southeast of Rikleifer, sitting on the east side of a bend in the Aurun River, the city of Cornelia sat alongside the riverbanks. The largest city and capital of Cornelia Province in Nuve, Cornelia represented nations of pride.

The main source for Cornelia's size and business was trade. River access made trade to northwestern Nuve, Gardolk, and the east side of Aurana possible, and even to the Solunar Empire if the city were interested. There was at least one direct access road that led to Rikleifer, Aurana, and another to Nuvenia, Nuve. As such, Cornelia was Nuve's chief market town and the city was full of shops and street-peddlers. Much of the interest in the city focused around the harbor on the Aurun River, though the city was fully developed all around and contained gray-stone buildings and roads. In some ways it appeared very much like Nuvenia's cold stone walls, except the weather was often more tame and the city more open to the air than Nuvenia. Also distinctive were the thatching on the tops of houses that stood in contrast to Nuvenia's complete stone construction that included tiled ceilings.

As for Cornelia Province, the land sat to Nuve's southwest. Because of its chaotic location, bordering Aurana to its west and Solunar to its south, Cornelia was a wartorn land. It had been conquered three months before by the former nation of Desolunar, until the Battle of Seta Archa destroyed Desolunar, and since then it had been rebuilding slowly. It still held a large population overall, sustained by the Aurun River to the west, the Calphos River to the south, and the

Rhonean River in the east side of the province.

Cornelia was not extremely well known as a location for its history, but it had struggled through the Triple Alliance war with Desolunar, of which Nuve was a part of the former. Most of Cornelia had been taken over by Desolunar in that war. Two keystone battles marked Cornelia's fall. The Battle of the Aurun River Delta, at the location where the Aurun merged into the Calphos River, was a catastrophic loss for Nuve that resulted in Desolunar's control of the Calphos River waterway over a decade ago. Only six or seven months ago, the Battle of Cornelia was a chaotic affair that saw the city of Cornelia be conquered, if only for a short period of time.

In part because of the war, but also from a perceived ineptitude of Nuve's government over Cornelia, a factional group known as the Cornelia Chimeras had emerged from the province. Their mission was simple; independence of Cornelia Province from Nuve was their sole goal. It was a movement that had been gaining steam, and was still growing as Cornelia was being reassembled. Their inspiration was the chimera, a predator of two known morphs—brown and black—that resided in many forest and meadow settings of the world, including areas of Cornelia. Chimeras were known to be very persistent in their pursuit of prey, traveling for days if need be, to pursue their desired prey. The movement had taken this behavior as perseverance rather than persistence, and used the symbol of the chimera as one of never relenting.

For now, the movement and the Nuve government were at peace as they worked together to rebuild Cornelia. However, it was clear to those that lived in Cornelia that the Cornelia Chimeras would not accept anything less than autonomy and independence once the nation had been reassembled. Perhaps it was the foreshadowing of the end of the era of superstate kingdoms. Others, however, saw it as insignificant on the whole of the world. In any regard, it was likely going to be bloody. Some blood had been spilled before in incidents between the Cornelia Chimeras and the Nuve government. Though recent months had seen some temporary peace between the sides, it was clear to many in the province that the Chimeras would surface once again, and their determination would not rest until Cornelia was independent.

Standing in the middle of the town during an overcast day, Professor James Magnon stood next to Necnea near a town fountain. They were a few blocks from the river. It had only been a couple of hours that they had been in Cornelia, and already the pessimism was starting to set in. "Surely I have never seen a city as bleak as this," commented Necnea. "Everything seems so dull and lacking in life, including the people."

Professor Magnon shook his head. "If you think this is a bleak city, perhaps you had better walk a couple of weeks to the north and see the town of Venarose, also on the Aurun River. That town is so run-down that it is a safe haven for criminals of all types."

Necnea shook her head. "Pity. I would hope we would have guided the world to be better. Seeing scenes like this are depressing reminders that we have failed to do that."

"If I were you, I would not wish that," miffed Vincent Stryker as he walked by Necnea and stepped forward. "What you see before you is what makes life worth living. The air has a staleness, and the city is full of action, but the excitement of it all gives energy to our lives and makes every day an adventure."

Necnea rolled her eyes. "And at what cost does that excitement come with?"

"Oh, I'm not saying that our world is perfect," said Vincent, "and I'm not saying that there aren't those who would agree with you. But I will tell you, it is the fact that life isn't dull that makes it worth living."

"Surprising words from a man who lived in a cave for years," commented Kronius.

In response, Vincent laughed. "Oh, I still had my adventures when I lived there," he said. "Every day, Sammy and I would take a trip into the valley on the other end of the caves, where the Grandiose River ran through the Peaked Mountains. We had the adventure there of living off the land, and we saw and experienced something different every day. Would a mother and her children share that kind of enjoyment? No, I'm sure not, but still I am sure they would enjoy something that isn't routine every day if they had the opportunity, and those that do live in routines always enjoy the breaks that come in between."

Suddenly, the sound of an explosion ripped through the air.

Vincent, Professor Magnon, Necnea, and Kronius all turned around, seeing a large fireball and smoke cloud in the air. "You were saying about breaks in routines?" asked the professor, pointedly.

Kronius immediately pulled back his robes, preparing to run toward the explosion. Before he could, however, Necnea seized him by the arm. "What is wrong with you?" she asked. "We cannot reveal ourselves here, even if there are injured. Do you want Setadev to find out we are on to him and have him turn our attention to us? If we die, many more will die."

Immediately, Kronius turned and growled, but eventually settled down. He knew Necnea was right. Taking a rash action now and potentially saving lives now could have even worse consequences later for the world. Best intentions, in this case, could possibly end up with the worst results imaginable.

"Must be the Cornelia Chimeras getting into it with the Nuve army again," remarked Vincent. "It's probably an armory or something that was destroyed."

"So, whose was it and who destroyed it?" asked the professor.

Though Vincent was sure the professor already knew the answer to that question, he was willing to answer it, seeing that the professor wanted Kronius and Necnea to learn something here. "Probably the Chimeras destroying a Nuve armory, or whatever they managed to get their hands on," he remarked. "Such a violent technique is characteristic of them. Nuve's army usually doesn't do that; they're more likely to take the traditional routes of most modern-day forces and raid an enemy armory to confiscate the weapons inside. Destruction is not a priority of theirs."

"In which case, this situation is likely not related to the Enlighteners, since they operate in secret," commented Necnea. She turned to see the professor nodding in agreement.

All of a sudden, yelling cries of "Give way!" echoed down the street. Quickly, everyone on the street hurried to the sides, next to the buildings. Within a few seconds, a horde of Nuve soldiers in blue uniforms were running down the street, in the direction of the explosion. The brigade continued to hurry down the street, but one soldier near the back began to slow down, eventually stopping in the middle of the road. He looked around carefully, and after observation pulled his sword out. There was an odd quiet among the scene.

Silence filled the air.

Then, fifty men in red robes jumped out of a house behind the man. Instantly, the soldier turned around, raised his sword, and gave chase. "Stop, criminals!" he yelled, vehemently. A very thick Soverenian accent was in his voice, indicating his upbringing in west-central Nuve.

The men in red did not stop. They ran very quickly, quicker than the soldier could run. Seeing this, Vincent also began to give chase. Knowing that there would be no end to this situation that would result in the best circumstances, Professor Magnon aimed toward the men in red robes and raised his right hand. Suddenly, an orb of darkness magic appeared in his hand, which he quickly launched at the feet of a man in red robes. The blast took out the road underneath him, causing him to trip and fall.

The soldier, without question, took advantage of the situation. He sheathed his sword and whipped out a short piece of rope from his belt. Once he arrived at the fallen man, he grabbed the man's wrist and began to tie it. He then tied the rope to the man's other wrist. "In the name of the statutes and laws of the glorious Kingdom of Nuve, by the authority of the crown and the scepter, I hereby arrest thou on charges of treason against Nuve, destruction of crown property, and theft."

It was at that moment that Vincent Stryker arrived and grabbed the man by his ankles to make sure he did not run off. Then, he pulled out a piece of rope he carried himself and tied the man's ankles together.

"Thanks for the help," said the soldier, looking up. Vincent managed to get a good look at him this time. The soldier was middle-aged, in his forties or so, with black hair and a complementary mustache and beard, all of which were well-trimmed. He wore several medals on his uniform, which was blue with white trim. Most recognizable and notable on his uniform was a patch in the shape of a triangle on his arm, which was a red triangle with a black one inside of it. Just like the one Vincent's son Kevin had on his uniform.

Vincent recognized this man. He made eye contact then, and said, "No problem."

Suddenly, the soldier's face brightened, and a smile cracked. "Well, I must admit I am surprised that thou are here today, much less that it was thou who assisted me. Vincent Stryker, the legendary Vincent the Pure One himself. It is an honor indeed."

"Says you," answered Vincent. He then moved around to grab the man by the arm to lift him up, as the soldier moved to the other arm. "I would consider it an honor, and also quite funny, to see you here as well, Raijin Shane."

Then, Vincent and Shane lifted the man, who appeared to be unconscious from his fall. "Merely doing my duty," he answered. "I have been here since before I was recalled to pacify Nuve and deal with Desolunar, to ease tensions between Nuve and the Cornelia Chimeras. Cornelia has really been where I have been living for the last couple of years or so."

"Good to hear," acknowledged Vincent. They had the man lifted and were holding the man up by his arms, using his legs and feet to support his weight along the ground. "Wait a minute," Vincent said as they straightened the man. He then reached over and grabbed the man's necklace from around his neck and pulled the end out of his robes. Attached to it was a tag with the letters "WN" etched into it.

Vincent dropped the tag and cursed under his breath. Realizing that Vincent knew something about this person, or at least something of the group the man belonged to, Shane mentioned, "I have been trying to drive these men out of Cornelia for the last few months now, it seems. They continuously steal our supplies, and are quick to jet out of here after pulling some guerrilla tactic. Then, they come right back."

As Vincent and Shane approached Professor Magnon, Necnea, and Kronius, the professor asked, "Enlightener?"

The only response Vincent gave was a nod.

Shane continued, "Thy friend here is likely one of those responsible for the attack that resulted in the explosion." He and Vincent then set the unconscious man down on the ground next to the building where everyone was standing. Then, he continued, "That building over there is actually a Cornelia Chimeras armory. It was unlawfully entered a while ago."

"Is not the whole building unlawful?" asked the professor.

Shaking his head, Shane responded, "Technically it is illegal for the Chimeras to have an armory, yes, but Nuve has turned a blind eye to such issues since the armistice was signed half a year ago. More important right now is the fact that someone else, another outside group, has been stealing and destroying the lives and property of both sides. Our investigations have turned up little so far about them."

There was an interruption before Shane could continue, however. Two men had arrived behind Shane, wearing Cornelia Chimeras uniforms: light blue with gold trim. They both saluted, and one said, "Vanguard Shane, is everything all right over here?"

Shane turned and saluted back. "It is," he said. He then indicated to the man on the ground, who was still unconscious. "If thou could, please take this man to the law enforcement office. He is arrested for treason, destruction, and theft, in correlation with the situation happening over at the armory."

The two men saluted again, and promptly picked up the man and walked off with him. After they were a significant distance away, Professor Magnon continued, "It seems as though relations with the Cornelia Chimeras are good if you trust them enough to handle a prisoner."

"That is only an illusion," scoffed Shane. "The armistice keeps us at peace and lets us work together for the moment, but there is still so much disrespect because we will not grant independence to Cornelia Province. Notice how they referred to me as 'Vanguard Shane'? They will not speak my family name because my brother is the king of Nuve."

Kronius was miffed. "I am sorry, but I do not believe we have met properly before. You are?"

"Oh, but of course," commented Shane. He extended his hand to the professor, who was standing slightly in front of Kronius and Necnea. "I am Raijin Shane, Vanguard of Nuve. My brother is Raijin Lester, the king. And who might thou all be?"

Professor Magnon returned the handshake. "James Magnon,

wizard and professor at the Bladinstar School. Perhaps you remember me from the planning for the Battle of Seta Archa, about three months ago."

"I do," nodded Shane, "just as I do Vincent Stryker. The other two, however, forgive my intrusion, but I have yet to make thy acquaintances."

"Ah, very well then," acknowledged the professor. "To my left is Kron Kalavere, my assistant."

Though he rolled his eyes, Kronius accepted the fact that this was to be his character for the moment. "Pleasure to meet you," he said cordially as he shook Shane's hand.

The professor continued, "And to my right is Necana Larin, a mystic and a well-learned scholar."

"A pleasure," said Necnea, as she offered a curtsey. Handshakes between men and women, even in a business environment, were still considered quite taboo in Nuve, and Necnea was smart enough to recognize this.

Shane bowed in response. "Naturally," he said.

"Allow me to ask," continued Necnea, "how did you know those men were in that building when you stopped following the men headed toward the explosion?"

A snicker came to Shane's face. "Cornelia changes people," he answered. "Among our men and the Chimeras, citizens who support either the country or the faction and thou never really knows which one, traders from Aurana who have their own views of the situation here, and these new men in red who are stealing our resources, one develops very sharp senses in the fear of being ambushed. Only the citizens, those who are not viewed as a threat, are really considered safe. I would be worried about your own safety while you are here."

"And your point?" asked Vincent.

"Let me put it this way," responded Shane. "Thou must develop a great sense of hearing in order not to be ambushed in the city of Cornelia. Walking or running by and hearing fifty people or so in a building trying to be quiet or contemplating an escape is not so hard to hear if thou knows to listen. Still, even I was surprised by their numbers."

Vincent just shook his head. "Figures," he said. "Enlighteners will run and hide like the cowards that they are."

This made Shane raise an eyebrow. "Pardon?" he asked. "Thou knows who those men in red are?"

Nervous, Vincent looked over at Professor Magnon, afraid he may have said something too revealing. However, the professor responded with a confident nod, informing Vincent that this was a subject he did not mind talking about. *Go ahead*, the professor then projected with thoughtspeech into Vincent's head. *He and the rest of Nuve deserve to know who they are fighting.*

"We do," Vincent continued confidently this time, with that reassurance in mind. "Those men, they are called the Enlighteners from the Shadows. Despite their name, though, I doubt if there is anyone in this world they have actually enlightened."

"Interesting," commented Shane. "So thy enemy has a name, and consequentially so does mine. What more do you know of them?"

"Not as much as I would like," answered Vincent. "We do know they're book-burners. They have existed for centuries, albeit normally in silence and they're not normally this active; when they are, however, they try to destroy knowledge. We were actually looking for them ourselves."

A strange look came to Shane's face. "What wrong have they done to thou?" he asked.

"They kidnapped my son," remarked Vincent.

Suddenly, the strange look on Shane's face turned to stun. "Thy son..." he stammered, trying to put the things he already knew together. He started pacing as he did so. "They have the Vanguard of Aurana, and a good friend of mine." Then, Shane looked up at Vincent. "What would they want with thy son Kevin?"

Vincent glared at Shane for a moment, bothered by knowing he could not explain everything here. "The Enlighteners have a strong connection with the old Desolunar. Demonicus, as it turns out, was one himself. Naturally, they know Kevin brought on the downfall. I fear that something sinister may be in the works."

"Oh dear," said Shane. "I am sorry for thy loss, Vincent. Do thou know if he is still alive?"

Tilting his head down, Vincent continued, "It is hard to say. It would seem that that is the case for now, but we must find him soon if we are to assure his safety."

"I see," nodded Shane somberly. "Then thou are here in search of him, and thou are following the Enlighteners."

"That's right," acknowledged Vincent. "We heard through a friend of ours that there may be Enlighteners making a ruckus here. Might you know where those men that we chased out were headed?"

James, Necnea, and Kronius held their breath for a moment.

"Unfortunately, I do not," answered Shane. "We did not even know who they were until thou explained only a moment ago. They steal our supplies, then they retreat. Otherwise, we know little."

Vincent started pacing, shaking his head. How was he going to find his son now? The one lead he had had just ended in a dead end.

"Pardon me," interrupted the professor, directing his comments to Shane, "but which way were those men headed when you chased them out of town?" He pointed in the direction. "Where does that road lead?"

Shane looked over in that direction. "That road travels through several towns in Cornelia, across the Rhonean River, and all the way to Cardol," he said. "It used to be quite the major thoroughfare when Cardol was the capital and largest city of Nuve, but such is not the case anymore. Nowadays, it is merely another road that leads into the cursed province, haunted by the ghosts of war."

"Cursed province?" asked Kronius.

"Leticon," Necnea answered to Kronius. "It is just east of here. Rumors of the entire region being haunted go back as far as when I was a little girl."

Shane chuckled. "Much longer than that, Ms. Larin," he said, not knowing that Necnea was as old as she actually was. "Even before Leticon was a province in Nuve, it has been considered to be haunted. Nowhere can thou walk in Leticon without being within spitting distance from an old battlefield or a military gravesite. No small town in Leticon is without its secrets, for this reason, and no major cities lie within the province's old borders for the same reason."

Catching the reason for the remark, Necnea merely looked

away. She knew that her identity had to be protected first and foremost, as was traditional deity policy.

Professor Magnon's attention, however, could not have been more focused. "Where in Leticon could they be headed?"

Upon hearing this, Shane looked around. He kept examining all of the city around him. Then, he leaned in, and said, "We had better go to the strategy center, and fast."

Although not knowing what he meant by that, Vincent, Necnea, Kronius, and Professor Magnon nodded and agreed. Then, they began following Shane.

The streets of Cornelia were not in the best of maintenance. Destroyed buildings were everywhere to be found along the roadsides, and the cobblestone streets were chipped and broken. Many houses were missing a roof or had large chunks missing out of their sides or tops. Street signs were missing from every corner.

"Must be the poor side of town," commented Kronius.

"On the contrary," responded Shane, as he continued to lead the way. "This used to be the wealthy side of town, actually. Most of the traders lived in these homes when they were actively trading that week or month. And do not be fooled by their small size; these homes were only temporary homes for the very wealthy. The poorer people, such as dockworkers and peasants, lived closer to the port on the river so they could be nearer to the market and the port to acquire their small amounts of money."

Kronius kept looking around that the broken buildings. "I am still so surprised seeing this," he said. "I can barely believe it."

"Welcome to the wartorn Cornelia," answered Shane. "This damage is not from the 'Enlighteners' that Vincent described. This is from the Cornelia Chimeras. They use such violent tactics that could be called terrorizing, that it is such a wonder that they have the support of the people that they do."

Kronius glanced back. He then dropped back and let Vincent walk with Shane a few steps forward of them. Then he asked the professor and Necnea, in the ancient tongue of *rengan*, "*How much of that is believable?*"

"*Enough, trust me,*" said Necnea in *rengan* as she looked at the buildings.

"*Can we really believe it, though?*" asked Kronius. "*He is the Vanguard of Nuve, after all. What we see here is a borderline civil war being held together by a fragile armistice, and Shane all but directly stands on one side of that, with his home country and his brother, the king. That being said, how much of this damage is really his and that of his Army of Nuve?*"

Professor Magnon looked at Kronius. "*It is hard to say for sure, but I would almost have to estimate about seventy-five percent is Chimera destruction. The rest is Nuve aggression.*"

"*That is a higher figure than I see,*" said Necnea. "*Are you seeing something here that I am not seeing?*"

"*Perhaps,*" answered the professor. "*Look around. A lot of these buildings are destroyed in groups, in rows. That would be consistent with mass striking, a lot like what the open rebellion of the Cornelia Chimeras would be aiming to create. The ensuing chaos is what they would need to drive the people in their direction and panic the Nuve forces. Destroying such buildings in a wealthy area would also motivate the poor who see the rich as their oppressors, and the Chimeras would take the position of their saviors. Some of these, though, you can see are buildings that are destroyed individually, with the others around left intact. This indicates selective attacks, likely because someone was hiding there or conducting an operation there. Since we know as well that Nuve has official offices and such here in Cornelia, as this is a provincial capital, we know they would not hide their command centers and armories. Therefore, we have to conclude that they were Chimera storehouses and that Nuve likely destroyed them.*"

"*Hmmm... I see what you mean now,*" noted Kronius. "*Yet what do you see as well, Professor? Shane does not seem to have any fear walking through this neighborhood. He does not appear to be afraid to walk through here even if there are attacks that happen here. Perhaps what we see is not quite so obvious as we might think, and perhaps we do not see the actual motivations and therefore not the actual situation.*"

The professor contemplated this for a moment. "*You may*

actually be right on that one, Kronius. Congratulations, you may have a valid point here."

"*Spare me the insults*," answered Kronius.

At this point, Shane opened the door on the next building, and invited everyone in. Vincent was the first to enter the large building, which was about three times as large as the nearest house. The professor looked up and read the sign above the door before going in, which read "Central Operations Relay Station". Inside, there was a secretary behind a desk, who said nothing when she saw Shane with a group of individuals, as they walked right past her. Shane then led the professor and the others through a couple of rooms, into a map room. Then, as everyone entered, he locked the door behind him. He reached into a shelf and pulled out a map, which he then set out on the table. Everyone gathered around to look at the map.

"This station is well equipped with much of the intelligence that Nuve carries about the area," Shane explained. "It serves to keep military operations out of the capital building." He then pointed to the map. "The map on the table is one of Leticon Province. As thou can see, there is a lot of empty space, yet one could chart all of the battlefields and graveyards if they desired. Thou should see about twenty small towns and villages marked in the province, perhaps the most notable being Kinsmoor in the north-central area. That said, even Kinsmoor has little more than a hundred or so people in it and its surrounding area. Needless to say, only the very brave live there, or anywhere in Leticon Province."

Vincent nodded, then asked, "What about to the south? The road the Enlighteners were on led toward Cardol, which should suggest they're not headed to northern Leticon. It's not the right angle for them to run to the Solunar Empire, either, since it would take them smack dab into the Wastes. What's in the south of Leticon that makes it so special?"

Sighing, Shane answered, "Not much. Aside from Cardol, which would be too near to Cornelia or to the Solunar Empire to avoid detection as they have, there is little. As you can see, the Calphos River runs along the southern border, but there is really quite little in the area. Past it, though, is the valley passage into Gardolk, the so-called

‘Southern Pass’ through the Peaked Mountains.”

“Might they have some connection in Gardolk?” asked Kronius.

“It’s hard to say for sure,” commented Vincent. “We don’t have any evidence for that yet. In any case, if they had connections there, then why would they go so far to steal from Cornelia?”

“Could be because it is easier to transport those weapons and such down the Calphos River, as opposed to up it,” added Shane. “The quickness of using the river would help them escape undetected into Gardolk’s less populated areas if they could make it that far through Cornelia Province without detection. They could then unload somewhere in the metroplex, provided they also had a means to transport it across the ground to their destination, wherever it was in Gardolk.”

“I doubt that,” Vincent responded. “If that were the case, then why not load the weapons up here at the port? Why not escape down the Aurun River and then head into the Calphos at the delta? It would be much quicker.”

Shane nodded. “I do have yet to see them take off on a ship from the port,” he acknowledged, “but all boats here are registered with the dockmaster and inspected thoroughly before being allowed to depart, so that and the checkpoint down the Aurun River near the delta may be their deterrents. Little else remains in southern Leticon, though, and Gardolk’s dockmaster system is a notorious joke. I would guess that about all there is that is left to do is to follow that route, see if there is something in Cardol that they are up to, and if nothing is found, take the river down into Gardolk. There is little else I can recommend for thou.”

Vincent looked up at Professor Magnon. “Do we have a choice?”

The professor shook his head. “It would seem to be the only choice left.”

Lowering his head, Vincent sighed. His head hit the table.

“Vincent, what is wrong?” Shane then asked.

Slowly, Vincent raised his head. “I just don’t think my son is in Gardolk,” he said. Then, he pointed to the map. “My gut tells me he’s here somewhere, in Leticon. He’s in here somewhere, and I bet the

Enlighteners have some kind of operation post out there. I think that's where they're keeping him."

Shane just shook his head. "Leticon is a big place, Vincent. Unless thou have a closer lead, I think going to Cardol is probably your best bet. And if he's not there, then the only lead thou have is to head down the river to Gardolk. I know thou spent years trusting thy gut, but this time I think thou have to go with what the evidence says, if thou want to save thy son."

Professor Magnon took to Vincent's side, and said, "Shane is right. This is the best lead we have. If we do not follow it, we may not get another chance at it."

Again, Vincent lowered his head. He still did not like the idea. The man was heartbroken, and that was for sure. He missed his son dearly, despite the persona of confidence he had been attempting to display. Not only was Kevin his son, but Vincent had only known Kevin for a very short time. To lose him now would be for Vincent to lose everything in his life that he had left to live for.

This time, Necnea gave Vincent some reassurance "We will find him, I can assure you that. To do that, though, gut instinct is not enough. We have to use the evidence we have. You know, as well as I do too, that there are numerous places to hide in the kingdom of Gardolk just as there are in the province of Leticon." She paused for a second. "Let us follow the road to Cardol, look for leads on our way, and then follow the trail from there. If it leads to Gardolk, then we will go there, and if it leads anywhere else, we will go there instead."

Suddenly, there was a banging at the door. Vincent nodded to Necnea while Shane walked to the door. "Must be the secretary," he explained, a few steps from the door. Without concern, he did not stop as he approached the door and opened it.

And then, there was a sword pointed straight at Shane's abdomen. Completely caught off guard, Shane instantly raised his hands and backed up. Upon seeing this, Vincent instantly raised his hands, and so did the three gods.

Ten members of the Cornelia Chimeras, dressed in full light-blue uniform, walked into the room. All had swords or crossbows drawn. Clearly, the armistice between Nuve and the Chimeras was going to be null and void after this.

Then, in walked a man dressed in a trimmed Cornelia Chimeras uniform, with a great deal of medals and ribbons pinned to his jacket. Another one trailed him in. The first man then stated, "Shane, I am surprised. It was easier to get thou to surrender than I thought."

Shane spit at the ground. "Arsuf Maxwell, leader of the Cornelia Chimeras, and his brother Zachary. I will be damned, indeed." He looked over at the trailing man.

"That thou will," responded Maxwell. "Thou know how this will end, Shane. I am sure thou know all of the facts already and what is going to happen to thou."

"Facts? What facts?"

"Oh, come now, Shane, you need not deny it any further," answered Maxwell. "I knew from the day that I saw thou in the armistice hearing that I could not trust thou after all. Thy words were tainted with the voice of thy powerful family. I wonder how much thou had to pay to get the Vanguard of Aurana to come and assist thou with those negotiations, so thou could sabotage us."

Shane scoffed. "I came with thou from Cornelia to Nuvenia to discuss it, remember? I never paid the Vanguard of Aurana, either. He approached us all by way of the Demons office in Nuvenia, and through their organization."

"I am sure thou would like me to believe thou, but I will not," commented Maxwell. "Unfortunately, thou has been caught. That man in the red robes that thou gave us? He spoke, and he told us all that we needed to hear. He told us of thy schemes and how thou has been faking destruction of thine own buildings while stealing from ours to depower my army. Now, thou will face the consequences."

"That is a boldfaced lie!" yelled Shane.

The man holding a sword to Shane's abdomen raised it to his neck. This was a sign for Shane to be silent, knowing that his arguing would not get him anywhere now. No one in this room was going to listen to him.

Maxwell, however, laughed. "How typical of a Raijin," he said. "Thou and thy family have been doing this ever since thou inherited the Nuve monarchy hundreds of years ago. Thou should consider thyself fortunate that thou had me duped for a few months; I chose to abstain in the armistice voting because I believed the Demons and King Lester would decline, and that my Chimeras would be morally superior for deeply considering the options first. When the Demons and Nuve accepted, however, thanks to Steffen Robert's speech, I was forced to accept or my Chimeras would appear to be insensitive. Now, I know of thy ploy, and must now believe that the Demons are in cahoots with thy family."

"Why do you do this?" interrupted Vincent, instantly drawing a Chimera soldier to point his sword at Vincent. Still, Vincent continued courageously, "Your paranoia is causing you to react this way without evidence, and you're listening to a man who has done damage to you that you have seen. On what grounds do you really have the evidence for this?"

"And who might thou be?" asked Arsuf Zachary, stepping forward. "Thy uniform is Scurnian, yet quite torn up as I can see. Might be time to have thy government replace it, if thou ever sees thy government ever again."

"That would be your last mistake," answered Vincent, "because you're talking to Vincent Stryker, Vincent the Pure One. If my blood ends up on your hands, you can guarantee that you will have the ire of the rest of the world."

Though Vincent used an angle he disliked, he had hoped to draw Maxwell's sensibility by formally presenting his identity and consequences. Yet Maxwell was unfazed. "Not when it is revealed that thou are a Nuve conspirator," he said. "I have discovered thou with the Vanguard of Nuve. I believe in this case I have the evidence to say that."

Vincent growled. Nothing he could say now. It was clear that Arsuf Maxwell was going to put any spin on this that he wanted.

Maxwell then turned back to Shane. "Now, I hereby convict thou, Raijin Shane, of war crimes against the Cornelia Chimeras. I shall have thou taken to the gallows, to face execution by hanging, in the public square of Cornelia."

There was a long pause. Shane nudged his right arm a little bit.

"But before I do," interrupted Maxwell, "I think I will take my forces directly to Nuvenia, and see that I kill your brother and his wife and children first."

No!

Instantly, Shane swung his right arm at the man in front of him, catching the man's sword with his Nuve stealth bracer that he was wearing. Shoving the man's sword arm back, Shane then kicked him, and fired the bracer's hidden dart launcher, shooting a poison dart into the man's neck.

Five Chimeras with crossbows then stepped forward and shot directly at Shane. All five of them hit him: four in the chest and one in the neck.

"No!" screamed Vincent.

The Chimeras then turned to where Vincent, Kronius, Necnea, and Professor Magnon were standing. As the professor looked down, he charged earth energy in his fist. Then, he slammed it to the ground, throwing up a thick cloud of dust into the air, making it impossible for anyone to see.

"Now, Necnea!" he screamed.

Suddenly, the dust stopped moving. Time was standing still.

Necnea was the goddess of time. This was one of her powers. Only Vincent, Necnea, Kronius, and Professor Magnon were conscious of what was going on.

"Let us get out of here," called the professor. He and Kronius then exited through the door.

Necnea started out, but then turned to see Vincent kneeling over Shane's body, with a somber expression. Upon noticing that she had stopped, the professor and Kronius leaned in as well, to make sure Vincent would be all right. Though Shane had not been a close friend of Vincent, they had served together and fought side-by-side in the Battle of Seta Archa. That made Shane's death mean so much more to the old general.

And yet, the gods were just ready to leave without empathy. He looked up at Necnea, with a tear in his eyes. "You could have done that the minute they walked in. You could have saved him. Why did you have to do that now instead of then?"

Bowing her head, Necnea said, "We have to remain neutral,

Vincent. Though we are here now, we cannot intervene in the affairs of man. That is one of the strongest rules the gods have. You know that as well as I do."

Vincent shook his head as he looked at Shane somberly. "It's because of us that Shane is dead. He's hit in the artery on his neck and once in his heart, and no healing can cure that. And it's all our fault because we stopped the Enlightener and took him prisoner. We interfered already and caused this."

Sighing, Necnea took a few steps toward Vincent. "It would have happened at some point or another," she commented, adding some more emotion to her voice and a more supporting tone. "Whenever one of them would have captured an Enlightener, they would have told the authorities the same story. We only accelerated the inevitable, and had we not, we would not have a lead to the pure one now."

A tear fell from Vincent's old and tired eyes. "He was a strong man, and a good one," he said. "I will miss him, as will Nuve."

"This could shake things up in Nuve," added Kronius. "The peace here is now strongly disturbed. With this, it is likely that the armistice holding the peace between Nuve and the Chimeras will likely fall apart, and civil war will break out."

While Kronius said this, Vincent had pulled out his katana, called the *Lavinia*, and put it to Arsuf Maxwell's neck. Frustration was welling up in his veins. He wanted to kill Maxwell for what had just happened.

With time frozen, it was the perfect opportunity.

He raised his sword and took a swing at Maxwell's neck.

Suddenly, the professor caught him as the old general pressed his sword, ready to cut into the flesh. "No, Vincent," exclaimed the professor, throwing him back gently, but to the ground, with a wind spell. The impact was so fast that it knocked Vincent off of his feet.

Stunned but unharmed, Vincent picked himself up from the ground. "What was that all about?"

The professor continued. "To kill Maxwell now would be no better for intervention in man's affairs. I understand you want revenge, but now is not the time. The world will change from these events, for certain, as Kronius just said. However, that is neutrality's consequence.

Remaining neutral in world events means that some things will change, and not always necessarily for the better. Still, that is the natural order of things, and overall the natural order is the best path. That is why we must do what we do."

Vincent pulled himself up, as he sheathed his katana. It did not feel right, but he had no choice. Professor Magnon would not allow him to take the action he felt was warranted.

"Can we get going?" Necnea suddenly exclaimed, her eyelids moving like crazy as her eyes were closed. She was struggling. "I cannot keep the time pause going for very much longer."

"Very well," nodded the professor. "Let us walk out of here, then. We will return to my home in Wyntrail to rest and regroup, then search the road to Cardol before we head there." He then opened up a teleportation gateway and passed through it. So did Kronius.

As Vincent headed through the gate, to be followed by Necnea, he could only think of Shane and of his own son, who was still missing. How much more sadness must he and this world endure? And what would become of Nuve now?

Chapter 27

Realizations

A fireplace burned, blowing heat up a stone chimney in a wooden shack. Outside, there was the sound of rain falling on the roof, creating a series of tapping noises that echoed throughout the room. The ground was dusty, but the wooden plank floor kept most of the dust of the ground away. It was very comfortable and cozy in the room. The shack served as a perfect retreat from the freezing rain occurring outside. So too did the animal skin blanket, which was perfectly warm in the cold winter weather.

The feeling of warmth was so good in the winter weather that Caitlin wanted to stay under the blanket forever. As she slept, she started to feel her body strengthening, regaining its energy. The warmth reminded her subconscious of Kevin and of the warm feelings that she felt whenever he was around.

Wait a moment... This isn't right. Caitlin's eyes suddenly popped open in realization of this, and she sat up and looked around to see where she was. She saw the shack in all of its coziness and everything in it. How did she end up here? That was the prevalent thought in her mind.

Where was she?

Suddenly, Caitlin's eyes locked with those of a man and woman in the corner of the shack. They were clearly of a tribal people. The woman, seeing that Caitlin was looking at her, said, "Ah, you're awake," and walked over to Caitlin. She then knelt down and said, "I hope this is warm enough for you. If it's not, I'm sure we can find one more blanket for you."

Trying to wipe her eyes so she could see clearer, Caitlin answered, "It's fine, thanks. I'd just like to know where I am, if you could tell me."

The woman nodded. "Oh, but of course," she said. "You're in

the Toronaga village. You should really consider yourself very lucky for being where you are now. It's pretty likely you would have been dead by now, otherwise."

The Toronaga. She was safe here. "What happened to me?" asked Caitlin.

Quickly, the woman turned and grabbed a wooden cup with water in it. She then offered it to Caitlin, who took it and started drinking. "Some of our tribesmen were out late on a hunting trip, and they saw the fire from the Aequina village. On their way to investigate, they found you passed out on the ground, in a position as though you had been running as fast as you could away from that village. And in fairness, I wouldn't blame you for running from there. I can only imagine what they might have been intending to do to you."

Silently, Caitlin nodded. Then, she continued, "They were intending to use me for a sacrifice. I fought my way out of there."

"Consider yourself fortunate," answered the woman. "Very few ever escape the Aequina. Many Toronaga have been killed simply for feathering near our territorial border with them. Every day, our men must be prepared in case the Aequina decide to attack us again, and for that reason we train our martial arts and war tactics frequently."

Upon hearing this, Caitlin sighed, knowing the warning that she had to give to the Toronaga. "Then I guess I need to let you know of something," she said. "The Aequina are planning an assault on the Metoi, your allies to the south. I am not sure if you've heard or not, but the Metoi are very weakened right now because their village was destroyed and their chief was killed. My sacrifice was supposed to be a statement of power before they began their invasion."

Roused by this, the man came over and spoke in the woman's ear. They then conversed for a second before he stepped back over to the corner of the room and had a seat at a table there. "It will be some time before the Aequina are ready for that," continued the woman to Caitlin. "As I understand it, much of the Aequina village has been destroyed by fire. They will not be ready to carry out an attack on the Metoi."

Caitlin turned her attention to the man to respond, recognizing that these facts were something the man had just said to the woman and were not her own words. "And what if they do?" she asked.

Instead of responding, the man only turned his head and glared at Caitlin.

Quickly, the woman turned back toward the man and started waving her arms. "She doesn't know, she doesn't know our ways."

With that, the man nodded and turned back.

The woman then turned back to Caitlin and explained, "I'm sorry, but please, let me shed some light for you. The Toronaga are very deeply rooted in tradition and in our ways. In our culture, only the men talk with men and only the women talk with women. The only communication between genders that occurs is between a husband and a wife, from the day that they are first betrothed by their parents as arranged for marriage."

Silently, Caitlin nodded. She remembered in that moment that Rouge Kirkwood was half Toronaga, having been fathered by a man from Seta Archa. She wondered in that moment, briefly, other than her martial arts skills if she knew anything of the ways of the Toronaga. Certainly a woman such as herself would never accept being arranged to be married, Caitlin thought to herself. It led her to a comment that she felt she needed to share with the woman in front of her. "You do know that the new Prime Minister of the Solunar Empire is very big on spreading women's rights throughout the Wastes and all of the empire, correct?"

"I do know that," answered the woman, "but also, they accept our customs. We honor the government in Seta Archa as long as they honor ours. That has always been the way that life in the Wastes have worked since the institution of kingdoms and dictatorships there, although being a part of their government has only started recently with the Solunar Empire. They allow us to keep our culture, and it is by that which we live our lives."

Again, Caitlin nodded in understanding. She was not in agreement with this idea that Toronaga culture had, but she did get the idea and would follow its premises while she was staying here with them. "So, the man is your husband, then?" she asked.

"That is correct," nodded the woman. "Our marriage was arranged by our families since the day of my birth. He is a Toronaga warrior, and I'm his wife. He is the one who found you, actually, and that is why you are staying with us. Our chief granted us permission to take care of you for a few days, if need be."

Caitlin took a breath. "I'm honored," she said. "And thank you and your husband for saving my life. I am very grateful."

"Well, you're certainly welcome," smiled the Toronaga woman. "My name is Kana, and my husband over there is Tangu. I'm a seamstress here, and my husband is a warrior, as you already know. What's your name?"

"Caitlin Amelia Magnon," answered Caitlin. "I'm from Aurana, and I'm a wizardess."

That word put a thought squarely in Kana's head. "Wizardess?" she asked. "Is that another term for a witch?"

Taken aback by this response, Caitlin said, "Well, sort of. 'Witch' is really sort of a word with a negative connotation, though, which is why 'wizardess' is more common."

"Then it was you who set fire to the Aequina village," stated Kana.

Silently, Caitlin looked away for a second before looking back. "That's right," she said. "They had me tied to a pole in their shrine. It was everything I could do to escape from them. I did feel bad for doing it, but I couldn't let them sacrifice me."

Surprisingly to Caitlin, Kana responded, "Understandable. Your hair tells me that they did indeed capture you. Surely a lady such as yourself does not cut your hair so short as to have the appearance of a young man's."

Caitlin reached up and ran her fingers down her hair. It was a little longer than where the Aequina had cut it, which she attributed to her recovery from the amount of magic she had used against them. As she recovered, her hair grew quicker because of the amount of element that her body was absorbing to compensate for how much it had used in the magic spells. Still, it was very short, indeed shorter than she would ever cut it. How would Kevin react if he saw her like this?

"And that does make me wonder," continued Kana, "what would you be doing so far out in the Wastes in the first place?"

There was a long pause. Taking a deep breath, Caitlin

answered, “I was looking for a friend of mine. He was following the trail of an old Desolunar general who massacred the Metoi. He was last seen heading east from the Metoi.”

Kana set her hand on Caitlin’s shoulder. “If that is the case, then I am sorry to report that he is most likely dead. Whether by this general, or the Aequina, or the environment, it is not likely that he could have survived.”

“No,” stated Caitlin as she shook her head. “I know that he was captured by the general. That much I do know, though I can’t tell you how, and I’m sorry I can’t. The general and his men had been camping out somewhere on the edge of the Aequina lands, as far as I can tell, but it appears they have been gone for some time now.”

“Indeed, we have noticed,” added Kana. “Come to think of it, I can recall seeing the men march by. We Toronaga watched as the men marched across the edge of our lands, just a few days or so ago. At first we wondered what they were doing in our lands, since the new Solunar Empire has laws that prevent that, but we decided to let them go anyway because they stayed so far from the village and in an area which would not disturb our activities. They were heading north, without stopping, all the way toward the river.”

“To the river...” Caitlin stammered, in realization. Her eyes widened. “They must be headed for the fortress, then.”

“The fortress?” asked Kana. “I don’t know where or what that is, but the way they were headed, they were definitely heading into Nuve, right into the area of Leticon Province.”

Leticon. The haunted province. The home of the Fortress of Da Leval. “Then that is where I need to go next,” Caitlin stated with confidence. “Marilynn was right, then. She said that if I did not find what I was looking for in the Wastes, that I need to head to the fortress to find him. It seems that she was right all along.”

Kana nodded. “Marilynn, Lady of the Metoi, is quite wise indeed. I am sure that she will be an excellent leader for her people until a new tribal chief is named. The Toronaga will help to keep her and her people strong until they can rebuild, although I am sure that it will take help from Seta Archa to fully rebuild and restore the information and records that they are so well known for in the empire.”

Caitlin nodded. After her meeting with Marilynn, she could not agree more.

"Now, then," continued Kana, "if you are heading to Leticon Province, you can head north from our village. That will take you to the old Nuve capital of Cardol, just across the river and only a little ways across the border our lands share with Nuve. You will know you have crossed into Nuve and are near the river when the lands become lush with life, supplied by the river's endless supply of water. From there, I'm not sure where to tell you to go, only that that is the quickest way into the province."

"I know where to go," said Caitlin, remembering the directions Marilynn gave her. She was going to go east on a small dirt road from Cardol, deeper into Leticon. From there, she had the pattern of turns she needed to take in mind, to get right to the Fortress of Da Leval along the dirt paths of Leticon. "I can make it there on my own."

Kana reached over and straightened Caitlin's blankets. "Now, now, I would wait until tomorrow morning until you leave," she said with a level of comforting in her voice. "You've been asleep for nearly a day now. Before you leave, you should let us take care of you and make sure you are well."

Caitlin leaned back and set herself back down on the floor. "Thank you, Kana," she said. She then enunciated, knowing she was not likely to hear any response to this comment, "And thank you too, Tangu." Then, she put her voice back to normal. "I'm glad to have met such kind people as yourselves."

In response, Kana nodded. "You are very welcome. It is a Toronaga custom to show kindness to the weary. Now, get some rest. We will take care of you until you are ready to leave."

With that, Kana walked away and back toward her husband.

Caitlin leaned all the way back to the floor again, and ran her fingers through her hair again. She hated it. She could recall, just a few days ago, sitting in the castle at the center of Rikleifer and twirling her long red hair. She kept thinking about the different things she could do with it, and what Kevin might think of what she would do with it. Losing most of it was not what she had in mind. Granted, her hair would grow back faster just by using magic, but to regrow all of that hair would take a lot of energy expenditure for several weeks in a row.

Though the blanket was warm, Caitlin's shoulders were still cold. This was because she was not wearing the top piece to her dress. Without the top piece, Caitlin's shoulders and uppermost section of her chest were exposed, in what was another feature of the dress for the magically-inclined to open more skin for magic energy generation. Caitlin knew that she wanted to regenerate her magic, but right now warmth was most important to her. Having spent most of the day sleeping and resting, she would likely be fully regenerated by the time she woke up the next morning anyway.

Reaching over to grab that top piece, a little pink key fell out of the folds of fabric in it. Seeing it, Caitlin dropped the top piece and grabbed the key by the cord it was hanging on, and looked at it for a few minutes. Rounded in shape and dyed a light shade of pink, with a heart-shaped head and a standard key-shaped peg, this was to be symbolic of the effect termed in the lore as the "Key of Hearts", something that by this point meant so much to both Kevin and Caitlin.

This was the key that Kevin had given her a few months ago. He had gifted it to her a few months after they saw it in a store in Aurana City together, and he saw her admire it. Though not a real object of magic, the term "Key of Hearts" had been referenced in a prophetic poem once before. It was actually a folklore term, referencing the betterment of one individual by affection for another. No better was that reflected than when Caitlin was able to make a transformation into her angel form by the sensation of affection and a strong connection to Kevin. By the same token, Kevin claimed he was able to fight harder and be stronger whenever Caitlin was near him. He said he felt a need to protect her, and that made him stronger. Likewise, whenever she needed to protect him, she was stronger, too. They were supposed to be there for each other.

Kevin had given her the key a little over three months ago in what was supposed to be a romantic moment on a log near Caitlin's house. She had taken him to see a place where she would sit and think from time to time, and it was there that he presented her the key. In response, Caitlin was so overcome, but felt she had to tell Kevin the truth about all of her worries and fears, and how she loved Kevin but did not want to be a traditional wife someday. Kevin reassured her that he loved her for her and did not need a wife if it meant not having her.

In the months since that day, Caitlin had never taken off her key. She kept it underneath her dress's top piece and above her dress, with the desire to keep it as close to her heart as possible. The cord it was attached to only showed a little bit by hanging it like this.

Looking at the key reminded Caitlin of so many things. She kept remembering all of the good times that she had spent with Kevin. She remembered fixing the roof with him, and going to a midwinter game of dangerball with him. The more she looked, the more that one particular incident about a month ago came to mind...

"Do you remember this meadow, Caitlin?" Kevin had asked.

"Sort of," answered Caitlin. "We walked by here on our first trip together to Rikleifer."

The setting was a meadow just off of the road south of Rikleifer, a short distance from the city limits. Quite a bit of snow was on the ground, and the snow was falling from the sky, as well. Kevin was wrapped up tight with a few layers of clothes on under his Aurana military jacket, while Caitlin was still wearing her dress, but with insulated layers of clothing underneath. Both were also wearing knitted scarves, hats, and gloves. The weather outside was particularly cold this day, after all, and for what Kevin had planned, he wanted them to be prepared and as warm as possible.

"That's right," Kevin answered. "It's a nice, open meadow. Very tranquil in the summer, but maybe even more so in the winter with less travelers on the road nearby."

Caitlin just shook her head. "I'd find that hard to say," she said. "It kind of seems like the bitter cold would ruin that tranquility."

Kevin gave a slight nod. "True, but that's just to us," he said. "Look at the snow, though. All of it is fresh and none of it has been disturbed. The meadow itself is at peace." He then reached down.

Confused, Caitlin responded, "Okay... but what's your point? Why did..."

Whack!

A small pile of snow hit Caitlin in the face. Kevin had thrown a snowball at her. Angry, Caitlin responded in a very irate tone as she wiped the snow off of her face, "What the hell was that for?"

"Hey, relax," Kevin answered. "It's just a snowball fight, Caitlin. It's something kids and some young adults do for fun here. They'll throw snow at each other because it doesn't hurt too much to get hit by, but it is fun to throw and cover whoever you're playing with with snow."

There was a pause. Caitlin was still trying to understand it.

"Here, now you try it," Kevin finally said, as he stood firmly and spread his arms.

Reluctantly, Caitlin reached down and grabbed a wad of snow. She then rounded it into a ball shape and threw it at Kevin.

Kevin stepped a step to the right, dodging the snowball.

"Hey! No fair!" exclaimed Caitlin. "You're not supposed to dodge it!"

Laughing, Kevin responded, "It's all part of the game, Caitlin. You can dodge, you can throw, just anything. There's no rules, no turns, nothing. It's all just a lot of fun."

Caitlin rolled her eyes. Now she had an idea on how this worked. "Oh, really?" she asked as she bent down and picked up another wad of snow. "Then let's see how you like this." She stood back up and fired another snowball.

Quickly, Kevin jumped, but the snowball hit him in the chest anyway. He came to the ground and picked up one to throw back. As he did, Caitlin kept picking up more snowballs and kept throwing them at Kevin, as Kevin threw back from the ground. They were both laughing the whole time.

It was so much fun. How something so simple and so unorganized, and also seemingly violent from an outside perspective, could be so fun seemed so bewildering to Caitlin. Yet, in a scary sense, it was almost exciting. Caitlin had never had so much fun than she had at that moment.

Then, Kevin stood up and continued to pelt Caitlin with snowballs. As Kevin stood up, though, Caitlin started running toward him while still throwing snowballs at him. Eventually, they were within point-blank range and laughing. Kevin then took a huge scoop of snow in both of his arms and dumped it on Caitlin while she reached down. That made her laugh even harder.

In response, Caitlin grabbed a huge amount of snow in her arms, but seeing that Kevin was standing to throw a snowball at her, she slammed the snow and herself right into him, tackling him to the ground. They were both laughing the whole way down, and for a moment as they lay on the snowy meadow together.

Then, there was a long moment as they looked into each others' eyes.

That was a fun day for sure, Caitlin remembered. However, nothing ever happened after that. Though they had kissed a couple of times before, Kevin and Caitlin did not kiss after that moment. As a matter of fact, Kevin was hesitant to do anything after that moment except gently move Caitlin off of him. That was a point where there was plenty of room for their relationship to advance. Kevin had taken her out there that day as part of his attempts to show her the better parts of life with emotion, and it had certainly worked that day. Caitlin had a lot of fun that day and learned how something so simple like a snowball fight could be so enjoyable.

At the same time, why could not she and Kevin take their relationship a step further that day? Caitlin could count the number of kisses she and Kevin had shared on her hands. It should have seemed like an opportune moment for that, and yet it did not happen. She could recall looking into his eyes and feeling very nervous, but in her defense she was hoping he would make the first move. After all, did not boys usually make the moves on the girls in traditional culture?

Maybe Kevin was still a little nervous. Maybe that was just an excuse at this point. Still, little had happened for Caitlin to be proud of on that front. It was part of why the doubt had perturbed her emotions so much. With the ties of love seeming to be fading despite all of the time that they had spent together, the idea that Kevin may not actually care for her that way was a sincere concern. She would have to work hard and prove she could do it on her own, to discover the truth about the boy she cared so much about.

And that was exactly what she intended to do. She would

destroy Setadev and prove him wrong. She would silence the dark voices that he was sending to her. She would make sure that General Sayo was brought to justice for the slaughter of the Metoi, and that Setadev would not be able to carry out his vengeance.

In the mean time, she put the Key of Hearts back to her chest, fastened the top piece to her dress, and went back to sleep, knowing only that she had another long day ahead of herself tomorrow. Every day would be a long day until she made it to Kevin.

If only she could have seen what was waiting for her at the Fortress of Da Leval. Maybe then she would know of her newest adversary, who threatened to take Kevin away from her for good.

Chapter 28

Accept Inferiority

The next morning, Caitlin shared her goodbyes with Tangu and Kana, grateful to have been saved by them and to have had their help. It was time for her to head off if she wanted to save Kevin. The fortress was looming, and the path to it headed into Nuve, and the southwest region of Leticon Province. From there, the pathway would head east, through the dirt roads and frozen plains of the haunted province.

Southwest of Leticon sat the grandest city of them all. Often considered the most beautiful city in the world in terms of design and the most culturally significant, the city of Cardol sat on the Calphos River, a couple of days east of the Rhonean River delta. Once the national capital of Nuve, Cardol was very large in size and each of its buildings and homes were carved of glimmering white stone, a unique sight in the world.

The only problem was, all of those buildings and homes were vacant. During the Triple Alliance war with Desolunar, the citizens of Cardol were forcibly evacuated from the city by the Nuve government, in order to avoid the destruction of the city when it became clear that the advancing Desolunar forces were not going to be able to be stopped. Most were evacuated to Nuvenia, the new capital city in northern Nuve, but others emigrated to areas of Cornelia, Soverenia, and Katalina provinces. Of course, few left to head into Leticon.

Despite the reputation of Leticon for being a cursed province and being so near to the capital territory of Nuve, Cardol was relatively unaffected by the rumors over the course of its history. In most of its existence, Cardol had been charted as its own independent district in order to keep the city out of Leticon or Cornelia, which it somewhat sat between.

Before the wars, Cardol was the most prosperous city in the world. Sitting on the Calphos River, just a few hours' walk east of the

Rhonean River delta, Cardol was a city based both in the past and in the present. Walking into the city would give one a sense of antiquity based on its ancient style, but the society and technologies in the city were anything but ancient. Knowledge ran rampant in the city, and a thirst for education and a savvy society rarely seen in Nuve's spartan culture existed in Nuve's former capital city. Cardol's library was extensive, its university was among the best in the world and the best overall in Nuve, and its businesses were fairly prosperous. City morale and standard of living were higher than the average, although the city did, like most cities, have slum areas and problems with taking care of the poor.

All of that was before the vicious Battle of Cardol during the most recent Desolunar War, which ironically did not take place in Cardol itself, but instead in proximity to the former Nuve capital. In the areas surrounding the city over a decade ago, the forces of the former kingdom of Desolunar were working off of previous success at the Battle of the Aurun River Delta to capture the entire length of the Calphos River from Aurana across to the Peaked Mountains. As they continued to advance, it became clear to the Nuve government that Cardol was in serious danger of capture. It was then that the forced evacuation took place, leaving Cardol completely undefended and giving Desolunar no reason to overrun and destroy the city. In some ways, it was brilliant; in others, it was devastating.

Regardless of the many perspectives on Cardol, lives were saved by evacuating the city. The one word that would describe it now, however, was "forsaken". Despite being given back all of their lands up to and slightly south of the Calphos River, Nuve had not repopulated Cardol or placed any government forces there. The internal conflict of the nation prevented that.

As Caitlin walked through the city, the emptiness echoed throughout the main boulevard. The howls of the winter wind flooded between the buildings of Cardol. No snow was falling at the moment, but the biting winter cold was certainly more prevalent here than it had been in the Wastes in the previous few days. Whether or not this was due to the Wastes' desert-like wasteland climate or just because the weather had been warmer at the time she was there, Caitlin was not sure. However, it was not an issue that concerned her. Weather conditions did not matter to her as long as she had to continue forward.

Still, she did wish it was warmer. The last day or two of traveling had been very cold, and Caitlin had been shivering the entire way. The cold was not going to stop her, but even the most well-wrapped person would likely struggle with the cold weather on this journey. She let out a sigh as she looked upon the forsaken city. Her breath was visible in the air. The Toronaga had left her with a special pair of animal fur earmuffs to keep her warmer, but the temperature in Cardol was so cold that the earmuffs made little use. Without her hair, her neck and head were much colder, too.

It was getting colder outside as the sun set, and Caitlin knew that she had to get to someplace warm soon. The temperature was dropping, and fast. Also, despite being supplied with some foodstuffs from the Toronaga for her safe journey, they could only afford to give her a couple of days worth. She would need to find some more. Fortunately, there were some to be found in a storehouse nearby. Caitlin had to plug her nose as she walked through the storehouse since most of the food in there was rotten from the abandonment of the building, but there were some preserved foods that were still in edible condition. She felt bad for taking the food, but she hoped that if anyone questioned it, that he or she would understand.

Because of the smell, however, the storehouse was a bad place to stay a night, so Caitlin tried to find another building that might be cozy. She found one in a small house with a fireplace that was left open and unlocked. Knowing that this house belonged to somebody, despite the fact that it had been abandoned for ten years like the rest of Cardol, Caitlin was at first hesitant to stay in the house. However, deciding that she needed to rest and that it was unlikely anyone else would be in Cardol anytime soon, Caitlin decided to walk in.

Dried wood was still in the fireplace. Perfect, Caitlin thought to herself. She would be able to light a fire that sustained itself for a little while. Using just a little bit of fire magic, she lit the logs on fire and started warming herself to it. She also took the opportunity of the fire and the solitude to remove her dress and wash herself with a piece of cloth and a bucket of water. It was the best she had felt in a long time.

Before going to sleep, Caitlin decided to warm herself by the fire a bit more. While she did, she noticed a desk with a chair in the room, and upon it was a book. Curious, she walked over and read the cover of the book. It was called *Immortality is a Truth* by Setaeus Demota.

Setadev. Caitlin had seen translated pages from this book before, but never the whole thing. Why was this here? This was a very old and ancient book, and although at least one copy was known to be in Cardol's library, none others were known to exist in the mortal realm. Perhaps the library actually had two and the person who lived in this house had been a librarian or a scholar of some kind.

Wondering if she might be able to find out more about her enemy, Caitlin carefully opened the cover of the book and started to read. The book was in *rengan*, the ancient language, and contained no translated pages. Caitlin could read some *rengan*, although she was not particularly skilled with it. She flipped through several sections, hoping to find something that might be helpful to her that she could read. Unfortunately, she was unsuccessful, with the most she could find being a section on how to control people. It spoke to Setadev's personality, at least, that he would want everyone else to accept they were inferior to him. Ready to give up trying to translate any of the text having not recognized anything she might find helpful, Caitlin stepped away from the desk and went to the fire to warm up more before retiring to the bed for the night.

Then, as the darkness settled in overnight, Caitlin curled up in the bed and covered herself with a quilt she found in the house. Certainly, she would have to leave a note of gratitude here in the morning for whomever owned this house. As she fell asleep, however, the only thought in her mind was Kevin. She was so close now, she could feel it. She could be there by the day after tomorrow. Her eyes closed and her subconscious took over. Though peaceful thoughts floated in her mind, anxiety did as well. Still, the weariness from her travels had overcome her, and she was so tired that sleep came easy.

The next morning, Caitlin put on her dress and took a piece of wood with her. She then used darkness magic to remove some of the excess and shape it into a torch. Now she could keep herself warm and keep a light burning as she traveled through Leticon.

Leaving a thank-you note on the door as she left, in case whoever owned this house ever did return to Cardol, Caitlin closed the door and breathed a sigh of frustration. There were still a couple of days to go to reach the fortress, and she was so anxious to get to Kevin. She ran her fingers through her short hair, which once again had grown just a slight little bit, but was still very short. Then, she gathered herself and walked to the east, along the road that would take her in the direction of the fortress. Within an hour of traveling, Cardol was completely out of sight.

Again, silence befell the forsaken city. Evermore would it be barren, evermore would it be silent. It was doubtful that Cardol would ever be more than a ghost town. The ghosts of war, the ghosts of Leticon, were claiming Cardol as their own now.

Two days later, however, the silence was interrupted, as a teleportation gate opened in downtown Cardol. From that gate walked Professor Magnon, Necnea, Kronius, and Vincent Stryker. Together, they had been searching for evidence along the road between Cardol and the city of Cornelia for the past couple of days, looking for any evidence of where the Enlighteners from the Shadows were headed or where they may have gone. None was found, and now the frustration of the failed search was on the faces of the searchers.

"Stay sharp, everyone," warned Professor Magnon as the group came out of the gate. He then shut the gate and destroyed it. "Cardol may be vacant as a city, but it would be an interesting hideout for the Enlighteners, at least as a relay point." Professor Magnon started leading the group to walk in a certain direction through the streets of Cardol.

Vincent Stryker shook his head. "I still don't think my son is here, James. I swear that something tells me he's deeper in Nuve."

"If he is, then we have little chance of finding him," Kronius gravely nodded. "Still, if he is there, then we do need to follow the trail of the Enlighteners, because they will eventually lead us to him."

That made Vincent drop his head. "Is there not a clue as to where he may be?"

Professor Magnon looked away. "Not as far as I know," he said.

"We have had a poem that some believe may be a prophecy, and a hint that Setadev's group is stealing supplies from Cornelia and headed this direction."

"And even if the prophecy is real, it has a high likelihood of not being true," added Necnea with a little bit of a frown. "About nine and a half percent, or nine and three quarters, have ever been deemed accurate. We usually call it ten percent is a good estimate."

Again, Vincent shook his head. "I understand that," he said. "I have known of the gods for twenty years, and even Vinz Larinion told me of such when I first visited the Realm of the Angels twenty years ago when he told me of the conquest prophecies." He turned to Professor Magnon. "With such a high rate of falsities, though, I can only imagine why you're skeptical about it."

The professor stopped, stopping everyone else as well on the city street. He rolled his eyes briefly. "I am not skeptical. I outright deny that prophecy is real." He paused for a moment. "There are literally thousands of volumes of prophecies in the library in the Realm of the Angels. Most prophecies are written in fairly bold, clear, and elegant language, and most tend to be written in the ancient language of *rengan* as well. They tend to be presented well, but one cannot call a bit of flowery language to be forecasting the future if the accuracy is not there."

"Then why are ten percent true?" asked Vincent.

Necnea looked at Professor Magnon. She was a believer in the reality of prophecy, as were most of the gods. She was interested to hear the professor's answer.

"Any claims made in publication, even the most inaccurate ones, are based around some level of truth," answered the professor. "Most especially when they are very general and generic. Claiming a prophecy about the formation of large kingdom from smaller ones, for instance? Anyone who knew anything about world events could have seen in the Third Era that was the direction things were going. Some guesses will be easy. Others are more bold and, therefore, are very unlikely to be correct." He paused for a second. "The two poems of the 'Letters to the Adventurer' by Clavius Lekion Stryker Dominous are both this way as well, if one really wants to try and deem them prophetic."

"I would say based on the events you have described, that they appear to be that way," interjected Necnea, continuing the explanation. "We gods have done studies on this for years, and yet we have no explanation on prophetic inaccuracy, either, other than that many who have claimed to be prophets simply are not. If we believe one to be true, we therefore must take it seriously until it can be vetted."

Kronius, who was somewhat in between on whether or not to believe in prophecy, added, "The only way we are really likely to understand why prophecies have such uncertainty is if we can ever come to understand where prophecies originate. Some in history have believed that the Great One, a deity that is far older and lived either before us or lives currently in a different dimension, sends prophecies to the mortals and immortals here. Yet we cannot even be sure of that, nor can we confirm or deny the possible existence of the Great One. King of gods Ralios Larion is certainly receptive to the idea, although even he is skeptical as to whether or not it has any merit."

Vincent just shook his head. All of this sounded like babble to him now. He somewhat regretted provoking this conversation.

"Professor Magnon makes a good point, though," Kronius then continued. "He has convinced me to examine this subject with a more skeptical eye than simply what I have been taught prior."

The professor nodded. Necnea said nothing, feeling not particularly sour but not interested in debating the topic.

"All right then," shrugged Vincent after a moment's pause, not interested in hearing any more. "Let's not completely ignore why we're here. This city is large, but it's empty. Maybe we can find an Enlightener presence here, or perhaps some other hint of where they may have taken my son."

There was an extended pause. Then, Professor Magnon finally answered, "Agreed. I have an idea where in the city I would like to look. Necnea, Kronius, do you two agree this is the best course of action?"

Almost immediately, Necnea nodded. "It is a good idea to make proper use of our time and location," she said. She turned to see Kronius also nodding.

"Then it is agreed," acknowledged the professor. "Come and find me when the sun lines up with the horizon this evening. Though it is overcast today, there should still be some daylight and it should be noticeable." With that, Professor Magnon turned and headed down one street.

Necnea, Vincent, and Kronius turned the other way and began to search the town. As they took their first few steps, Vincent only shook his head. Noticing this, Necnea put her hand on Vincent's shoulder and said, "I know how you feel, but I promise you, he does care about your son. Tyrinion can get a little distracted when he has a passionate argument."

Vincent only nodded. "I know," he said. He sighed. "I've known James for a long time. I wonder if it's a defense mechanism for him. After all, his daughter is doing what she has to do by going after Kevin herself." He paused for a second. "I can see where his daughter obtained her all-business mentality that Kevin claimed she used to have."

"Very much, it is apparent," added Kronius, who had known quite well of Caitlin's previous mentality. "The more that we see Tyrinion this way, the more we can see how Caitlin used to be." He paused for a second, remembering something. "Tyrinion did mention to me once before that he regretted never letting Caitlin be a child when she was growing up. He must have been working day by day on solving his own treason case and isolating Setadev as the traitor to the gods and the conqueror who sought to control the realms. What must a child see in that, unable to grasp such understanding?"

Necnea lowered her head. "Only pain," she said. "At least, to begin with. Children are so full of happiness, it seems, yet the unhappiness of those who raise them will reflect greatly on their personalities as they grow older. Then, they develop a new normal and grow numb to what they used to feel."

Letting out a sigh, Vincent added, "I only wish I knew how my son grew up."

Kronius answered with confidence, "He grew up well. I think you can see that in his personality today."

Vincent Stryker nodded. "He had a great mother." He sighed as he looked down at his sword, a katana which he named *Lavinia*, after Kevin's mother.

Nowadays, Vincent was once again a somber man. Despite the opportunity to be on another adventure, the thing he enjoyed most in life, he was once again struggling with frustration and a feeling of helplessness, just as he had been before he met his son. It was true that he was feeling some personal frustration from missing his son and having to go through such an ordeal once again. That much was evident in the tone of his voice and the expression on his face. Plus, to top things off, Vincent's back was acting up again and reminding him why he quit this kind of lifestyle.

Some time later that day, as the sun was falling to the horizon and the sky began to darken into dusk, Vincent, Necnea, and Kronius regrouped and sought out the professor once again. Despite a broad search of the entire city that included aerial viewing by Necnea and Kronius, no evidence of any Enlightener activity was turned up. There was no evidence of the theory that Enlighteners were taking boat rides from Cardol through Nuve into the kingdom of Gardolk, either. With this in mind, Vincent Stryker hoped that the professor had come up with something from his work.

By luck, they found the professor a few minutes later standing by a house. He was staring at the door. "What's going on?" asked Vincent, breaking the silence.

The professor turned. "It appears that my daughter has been through here," he said. "She left a note on the door of this house. The ink is still quite fresh, as though it has only been on the paper for a couple of days, and the handwriting is very distinctively hers."

Carefully, Necnea stepped up and examined the page, without removing it from the door. "Very nice handwriting," she said, noting that Caitlin had a very elegant writing style. "I must ask, though, what brought you to this house?"

The professor chuckled a little bit. "It is mine," he said. "While establishing my human identity, I did live in Cardol for some time, and this was my home. I've kept this house and used it from time to time as a quiet place to work. It is quite a coincidence indeed that my daughter found her way to this house, and was here so recently. She may be on to what we are looking for." He opened the door to the house and walked in.

"Let's hope so," commented Vincent, as he followed the professor in. Kronius and Necnea followed suit.

It was evident that someone had been in the house recently. Some fresh ash was in the small fireplace and the professor had noticed a few logs were missing. Also, a book on the professor's desk was opened. And Kronius recognized it.

"Is that *Immortality is a Truth*?" he asked the professor.

"It is," acknowledged the professor, "by Setaeus Demota, of course. "Setadev's manifesto, or at the very least his brainstorming journal on how to conquer and rule over everything. This may be the only copy of this book left in existence, aside from the one in the Realm of the Angels, of course."

"Why do you know where it is, then?" asked Vincent Stryker.

"Full of questions today, are we, old friend?" returned the professor. "If you must know, I put it in Cardol's library years ago. It is a dangerous book, but if the library in the Realm of the Angels were somehow to be compromised or destroyed, where better would be a place to hide it than among the largest collection of books in the world? Then, Arthur and Rachel found it, and I decided it might be best to study it further." He looked down at the book. "Caitlin knows how to read a bit of *rengan*, but I doubt she could read something as complex as this. An interesting page she has open."

"Hm?" asked an interested Kronius.

Stopping for a moment, the professor gestured for everyone to gather around as he read aloud the words of their enemy in its original *rengan.* As he did, Necnea translated aloud for Vincent Stryker to understand.

"The first keys to society's acceptance of our new ways of life will be to accept that the mortal will be inferior to the immortal," Necnea translated. "Therefore, their acceptance of immortality as a truth and that they are not able to be granted immortality will lead to the most stable society in these circumstances. Only those who have been selected to be immortal should be made as such. Those individuals should be responsible, powerful, and ambitious, yet compassionate in a modest amount. To be too compassionate would risk compassion taking over one's decision making. To the extent of ensuring society's acceptance, information needs to be kept out of their hands. Though it would seem like a tragedy to intentionally stunt the growth of our race by limiting their knowledge, the idea that the masses are stupid on a whole has proven time and time again to be quite accurate and therefore proper responsibility for the powers of immortality cannot be assured. Of course, however, society will not be so willing to simply accept inferiority without a little guidance. Therefore, a network of immortals devoted to this guidance is the simplest answer. They will be gods among men, ruling from beyond the reach of the mortal. Until that day comes when this can become a truth in itself, however, fellow mortals of the selected type will meet together and discuss our plans."

The professor shut the book. "That is from the thirtieth chapter of the book, titled 'Acceptance'," he continued in the modern language. "In it, he details his plans to control the mortal by use of the immortal, his fellow 'gods', the very same you know today."

Kronius widened his eyes.

Necnea picked up where the professor left off, "Initially, that was what we were meant to be there for, I am sure. Had my husband, Vinz Larinion, not cast out Setadev, it is likely we would see a much different world than we do now."

Nodding, the professor continued, "When this section of the book was written, Setadev had not yet figured out how to activate the Stripe of Life, the item that makes mortals immortal, one of the Seven Stripes of the Elements. However, he did have it, and believed in what it could do. From this, he wrote parts of *Immortality is a Truth* and completed it shortly after he had established the gods in the Realm of the Angels, having achieved his own immortality and those of the original gods by that point."

"That is correct," acknowledged Necnea, addressing her comments directly to the professor. "When we all started together, Setadev was very ambiguous as to what he wanted the gods to be. We used to meet in his fortress every day, and eventually we all stayed there on an extended basis until we made our ascension to the Realm of the Angels."

"Fortress?" asked Vincent.

Again, the professor nodded. "Indeed. The Fortress of Da Leval," he said. "Named for the ghost town that the fortress was built over, Setaeus Demota had it constructed with all of the wealth that he had. He descended from aristocracy, after all, and sold all of his possessions to afford it. He made sure it was of the absolute best construction possible for the era, in white stone and with fortifications."

Vincent had a feeling. "Is this fortress still around, then? Five thousand years is a long time, but if it was made of stone…" He paused, not completing his thought.

Necnea chimed in, "As far as I can recall, it stands to this day. Usually, however, there is no activity to be monitored, as none has ever been found and the fact that it stands in Leticon suggests it is unlikely to ever have significant activity again."

"Though it seems that now that analysis may be inaccurate," countered the professor, as he put the book down to his side. "My daughter has been through here, and we left her last in Seta Archa." He glanced over at the note on the door for another moment. "She also stayed here on the north side of town, not at all near the river. I know for certain as well that I never did tell her about this house, so she chose to stay on the north side for another reason. This suggests that she may be on to something, and whatever it is is likely to be deeper in Leticon. Coincidentally, that is where the fortress is. If she managed to get directions there by someone who knows the modern paths, she is smart enough that she would have stayed a night close to the road to save her travel time the next day."

Vincent felt relieved. "If she was here a couple of days ago, then she has a headstart on us," he commented. "I would be willing to bet my life that she knows where Kevin is, and that she is headed to him now."

The professor answered, "She does have the head start. In fact, she may already be there, or perhaps she has already been there." He paused for a second, as he closed the book. "I suggest we proceed straight to the fortress, and find out if it holds any secrets. Let us find out what my daughter knows."

Confidently, Kronius nodded. "No objections from me," he

said.

"Nor from me," commented Necnea. "It is a sound idea."

Vincent Stryker agreed very firmly. Heading to the fortress meant heading deeper into Leticon, but he did not fear it. His gut feeling told him that it was possible his son was there.

If only he had known that he and the gods were already too late, he may not have had even that slightest bit of optimism.

Chapter 29

The Fortress

The pathways were clear. And here was where they had led.

Caitlin had followed Marilynn's directions perfectly, and thanks to the Toronaga helping to keep her alive, she could now see something in the distance. Perhaps it was this fortress, the rumored Fortress of Da Leval, which Marilynn had referenced.

As she looked around, Caitlin was very well aware that she was now in Leticon Province in Nuve. A couple of days ago, she had crossed the Calphos River and entered the kingdom, as she followed the trail that was used by Sayo's army. Though she was familiar with the rumors of Leticon Province, and she knew her life was in danger if she continued to go after Setadev, she kept going on anyway. If this was the way that led to Kevin, this was the way she had to go.

It was a cold winter day, and the snow was just starting to fall in the Leticon grasslands. For now, it was only flurries, but all signs from the clouds to the west were that the snow was going to get worse very soon. Caitlin was shivering. The weather was still very cold outside, and though she was wearing a dress with long sleeves and had leggings on underneath to keep her legs warm, the cold still penetrated through her dress. Her mental focus was keeping her going, but perhaps if she would have had the discipline she used to have, she might not be struggling with the cold right now. The thought of that had crossed her mind, but Caitlin knew that the strength she had being herself far outweighed that of her former discipline.

As she stared at the fortress, Caitlin started looking all around. It was curious that, if this fortress was as old as Marilynn had said it was, that Nuve had not picked up on its presence. After all, even though this was Leticon Province, this was their territory and surely they had well mapped out their provinces.

Better yet, why had no one discovered and annihilated this

fortress in its entire history? Around the time when this fortress was supposedly built, the entire world had been much more divided, and many smaller kingdoms and feudal systems existed. Yet despite the wars each waged and the many shifts of power over the years, especially in Leticon where war had been especially bloody, this fortress had somehow evaded notice of all of them. The era of the superstates of Aurana, Nuve, Scurnia, and Gardolk had only existed for a few hundred years now, which meant that thousands of years of feudal rule of various kingdoms and several hundred years of Nuve rule over the area had yet to turn up or raise attention to this fortress.

Its owner was Setadev, and its inhabitants were the Enlighteners from the Shadows. Caitlin did not want to face any of them; she knew they were strong with magic and exerting the effort to defeat one would merely waste time and energy. Not to mention, of course, that getting surrounded would likely mean failure and capture, just like Kevin. And there was no way the strategic side of Caitlin would allow that to happen. She knew that would get her no closer to Kevin. Setadev would not allow that if he captured her.

Over the top of the fortress, a watchtower stood tall. Caitlin had to be careful; she knew it was likely that she could be spotted. The snow was helping her in this case; because her dress was mostly white, save for the red trim, she blended in well with the snowy setting. It would also make breaking in that much harder just to get through it to the fortress; with time being so crucial, any hindrance was going to hurt her attempt.

There was still quite a distance to the fortress. Knowing that now was the time for her to begin the break-in, Caitlin took a moment and pulled the Key of Hearts out of her dress. It was still hanging from her neck. She lifted it in front of her eyes and looked at it carefully for a moment.

Kevin, if you can hear me, I'm coming for you. She spoke with her mind magic, unsure if she was close enough to Kevin for him to hear her, much less be conscious and able-minded at the moment to listen to the message.

I wish you could see everything I've seen without you. I've done so much to find you, and I think you would be proud of me. I've seen beautiful sights, like the ones you wanted to show me all along. I've fought hard battles against Setadev and the odds, and so far I'm still alive. I'm missing only one thing right now, and that's you beside me.

She paused for just a quick second, as she pondered the key.

Whenever I look at this key that you put around my neck, I think of you, and I know that you would never betray me. I feel much better about my doubts when I see this key that you gave me. It reminds me of every experience we've shared together, and how our lives are better with each other. It reminds me of how I am who I am today because of you, and how much happier that has made me.

Caitlin then sighed. She realized Kevin probably could not hear her.

Stay safe. I'm coming to get you. Then, she tucked the key back in her dress and clenched her fist. Now was the time for action.

Before she could go in, Caitlin had to evaluate the fortress carefully from a distance. Making the wrong entrance move could get her captured or killed. Even so, there were no guarantees that any move once she made it into this monstrosity of a construction would keep her safe, especially since she could not plot out her moves once she made it inside. From an outside view, the fortress appeared to be circular in basic shape. Two cylinder shapes made up the fortress's base, one on top of the other, with the tower appearing to be off-center from its base. Another wall appeared to be in front of it, but for some reason this did not appear to be simply a wall. Caitlin could not put her finger on it, but something about the way it was shaped seemed different.

No time to think about it. The doors were open. Some soldiers in black were moving supplies out through the gate. Now was the time to advance. Carefully, Caitlin slunk across the snowy meadow, being careful not to get too close to the men. Every movement was well measured. Every step was cautiously made.

As Caitlin made it close to the door, she had to distract the soldiers in order to make it past them and into the fortress. This one, to her, was going to be the easiest part of this whole intrusion. She stood low to the ground, and charged fire magic in her left hand and light magic in her right. Then, she smashed them together while keeping the energy in her hands, and in doing so formed a magic exploding shot.

Then, she launched it a moderate distance away from the door.

A large visible explosion and a loud noise accompanied the shot. In response, almost all of the soldiers turned their heads and began running to the location of the explosion. This allowed Caitlin to run up to the door and sneak in.

It turned out that this was not a wall. Inside the entrance was a long hallway. It was the pipelike entrance into the fortress itself. No matter. As long as no one caught her in the hallway, it made little difference as to how the fortress was designed. She was still going to make it to Kevin.

Quickly, she made it down the hallway and around the next corner. There was an intersection here. For a moment, Caitlin debated which way to go but eventually settled on the right, seeing that the way left was not lit and fearing that heading straight down the middle would lead to more guards. The hallway wound around in a circular path, and there were no windows to show any sigh of light from outside. Only torches lit the path.

Suddenly there was another hallway heading toward the building's center. Caitlin had to seize the opportunity to get closer to the building's middle. She was sure that Kevin had to be in the middle somewhere. Surely Setadev would be keeping him in the highest security area in the building.

As she made it down the hallway, Caitlin saw a flight of stairs. They went up. If Kevin were being kept prisoner here, however, it would be more likely that he was in the basement. Still, Caitlin knew she could not assume as much and that she had to keep moving forward, so she snuck her way up the stairs and onto the next floor.

First guard at the next corner on the second floor. He was guarding an iron door. Iron door. Like a prison door.

Was she already this close?

Kevin! Kevin, can you hear me? Caitlin was frantically sending the message through her thoughtspeech.

There was no response. Though Kevin was not trained with magic and could not submit his own thoughtspeech, he was able to think out his responses and let Caitlin read his mind. If she were this close, he should have been able to hear her. Maybe she was wrong.

This may not have been it after all.

As Caitlin stepped forward, she saw that the next door was also iron, and was guarded. Perhaps it would not be so easy to identify where the prison cells were, after all. Certainly, they would not simply be behind one iron door in the middle of nowhere. There would almost have to be more than one, to keep the security higher.

Suddenly, one of the guards noticed her. He pointed his spear at her, also drawing the attention of the other guard by doing so. "Freeze! Drop to the ground!" he yelled.

The second Caitlin heard the guard yell, she instantly took to action and fired a blast of darkness magic right at the guard, throwing him hard into the wall. She did not use enough force to disintegrate the man. Then, the other guard started charging Caitlin with his spear. She hit him with the same spell, again taking care not to use too much energy. She did not want the same debacle with the Aequina to happen here.

Still, she knew she had to proceed quickly and with care. The tower guards would certainly be alerted very shortly, so she had to move on. As cautiously as she could, she continued past the guards and into the next hallway.

Nothing here, just more doors. To the left, there were more guarded doors, and to the right was a staircase. Caitlin chose to continue up the staircase, trying to avoid the guards as much as possible. As she climbed, she sent her mental signals again, trying desperately to call for Kevin and get him to respond.

She still could not find him. She could not sense him.

Where could he be?

On the next floor, there was a large room that lacked any hallways at all. However, there were stacks of weapons all around. Every type of weapon imaginable was there: swords, pikes, spears, axes, halberds, longbows and old Desolunar prototype longbows like the one owned by Rachel, crossbows, at least one quarterstaff, and lots of arrows and bolts. On the other side of the room appeared to be crates of foodstuffs and other supplies. "Nuve" was printed on a few of the crates. Clearly, this room was a makeshift armory and storage facility. What could the Enlighteners be doing with all of these supplies and weapons?

Then, the sound of footsteps clicked down the stairs at the other end.

Quickly, Caitlin ducked next to the crates beside her. She had to hide.

The careful and deliberate pace of footsteps crossed the room echoed through the air. It made Caitlin very nervous as she sat, crouched behind the crate. She was very paranoid. Whoever was walking was walking in such a way that they were suspicious.

Curses, Caitlin thought to herself. Maybe she had walked into the room without watching the volume of her steps enough, and was heard.

The sound of a sword being drawn from its scabbard rang through the air. Caitlin's muscles tightened. She started charging another blast of darkness in her hands, just in case she needed to counterstrike. No chances could afford to be taken. Not with being so close to rescuing Kevin.

Suddenly, the footsteps stopped. Right next to Caitlin.

Caitlin held her breath. The wait seemed like forever as only silence came from the other side of the crates. Someone was waiting on the other side. Someone was looking for her. Please don't find me, Caitlin thought to herself.

Then, the steps continued. Caitlin breathed a sigh of relief, unable to hold her breath any further.

That was when the figure walked around the crates and saw Caitlin.

Instantly, she blasted him with her darkness magic, throwing him against the wall.

The man slumped to the ground in pain.

Though Caitlin had never seen him before, she recognized the uniform he was wearing as being an old Desolunar uniform. It was very heavily decorated, with many medallions and ribbons scattered all over it. There was no way his rank was anything less than General, and he clearly had not been back to the Solunar Empire capital of Seta Archa to get a new uniform in the new imperial style.

"General Sayo," said Caitlin, confidently. She started charging fire magic this time.

The general rose slowly, grabbing his abdomen the entire time, right where he had been hit. He stared at Caitlin in horror, recognizing her from the modeling he had done with Setadev only a few days before. He remembered being warned that this was the form of the half-immortal girl.

"The angel?" asked Sayo, in pain.

"Spare me that," answered Caitlin as she approached Sayo. She put her hand, engulfed in the flames of fire magic, up to Sayo's head before he could raise his sword. "You tell me where I can find my Kevin, or your head will start to get very hot."

Sayo said nothing. He then pointed to the left, as if to signal something. Instantly, Caitlin turned her head to see where he was indicating.

Then, Sayo kicked her in the stomach.

Caitlin fell to the ground in severe pain. Sayo had kicked her hard, as if he had not pulled any strength back at all. She hit the ground with a heavy thud, and the stone floor only made the impact that much harder.

Going for the surrender, Sayo then brandished his sword. He was going to make sure Caitlin was subdued. Whoever this girl was, she was a threat to Setadev. Yet she too, much like Kevin, was young. Was this really the kind of world he wanted to live in, where those who had just come of age were really the villains?

Hesitantly, Sayo stabbed downward. Quickly, Caitlin rolled to her side, dodging Sayo's sword strike as fast as she could. As she swung to her side, she formed a lightning whip from pure light magic in her hands.

Then, Sayo raised his sword to try and stab her again. Perfect opportunity. She swung her lightning whip at General Sayo, catching him by the ankle and knocking him off his feet. He tumbled to the stone floor, while Caitlin pulled herself up. She raised her hands and was ready for Sayo to try and stand up again.

Sure enough, he did just that, leaving Caitlin ample opportunity to hit Sayo in the arm, forcing him to drop his sword. Then, with the sword clear, Caitlin smashed him with a huge blast of wind magic, pressing Sayo against the wall in a slumped-over position.

As Caitlin let down her blast, a sound of slow applause came from down the hall. Caitlin turned quickly, with eyes wide open, to see Setadev in his deformed Pseudo form, applauding. "Well done, angel, well done," he said. "For you to make it this far impresses me."

Caitlin started walking toward Setadev. He was the last person she wanted to see, as his face struck her with true fear, unlike any fear she had ever felt before.

"However, this is where I must stop this game. I have allowed you to come this far, but now it is time for this to end. You will not kill General Sayo, and you will not find the pure one here."

Getting defensive, Caitlin tensed up and responded, "Really, Setadev? You actually care about someone for a change? What an oddity, indeed. I would have thought you to believe he's expendable."

By this point, Sayo had retreated behind Setadev and continued past him. Setadev took notice of this and said, "He is expendable. As a matter of fact, I would not be the slightest bit bothered at all if you took his head off of his shoulders. However, I would rather deny you the sensation of victory than to give you any hope."

Sayo heard that, turned his head, then turned back and continued walking off.

"Have it your way, then," remarked Caitlin, as she charged fire in her hands. "We can do this the easy way or the hard way. You can either tell me where I can find my Kevin, or you can burn. Your choice."

Setadev laughed. "*Your* Kevin? My, what a feisty one indeed! You are quite aggressive when confronted, angel. How does the pure one put up with you, indeed? Oh, I am mistaken; he does not, because he does not care about you."

"You're a liar! You take that back!" exclaimed Caitlin.

"Am I really?" answered Setadev almost immediately, in a suave yet cocky tone. "Obviously you believe me to some extent. Otherwise, you would not be behaving as you are. When provoked, your responses become childish."

Caitlin stepped back in frustration. She started to enhance her fire magic, in anger, preparing to unleash it on Setadev. She was angry.

Anger. Another new emotion for her. Now was not the time to think about that, though.

"So, I am right, then," continued Setadev, noticing her reaction. "You do believe what I have told you, after all. Your actions show that you cannot deny the possibility. Face the reality, angel. You are not getting him back."

At that moment, Caitlin unleashed the full extent of her fire magic in a beam shot. Setadev needed only to hold up one hand to deflect all of it. Eventually, Caitlin had to stop. She knew she was not damaging Setadev.

"Pathetic," Setadev finally commented as the beam dissipated. "Do you not remember, angel? You cannot defeat me, for I am nothing. If those words will allow you to see how the game is played, then I will allow you a minute to let that soak in if need be. However, I see that as being of little value. I wonder why you came out here so far, and sought out my fortress, when you knew that you could not defeat me and that Kevin never really cared for you to begin with. Why did you, then?"

Caitlin said nothing. The fury was in her eyes.

"Oh, did I touch a nerve there?" asked Setadev, mocking Caitlin. "Are you having problems believing that he would always be faithful to you? Or is it that you came here following your wild hopes, just wanting something so strongly from him? Your emotions have taken full control of you, angel, and yet you simply will not give in and admit that."

Clenching her fists tightly, Caitlin only intensified her rage.

Setadev shook his head. "Pity," he said. "However, I must say I do admire your resiliency. You are quite pesky, in many senses. Yet, speaking to you from person to person, as I did before in informing you of the pure one's deceit of you, your resiliency is futile. Do not let me be the one to tell you he betrays you."

Fire materialized in Caitlin's fists as her energy continued to charge. "If you are so determined on that fact, then why not let me see him for myself?"

For a second, Setadev was silenced. Then, he raised his hands, and took on a stance for magic casting. "I have my reasons," he answered. "After all, I only desire to humor the both of you for the same reason."

"And that would be?" asked Caitlin.

Gaaaaaaaaaah!

In response, Setadev blasted Caitlin backward into the wall with an air spell. As she hit the wall, Caitlin let out a bloodcurdling scream.

The force had shot her so hard that she was stuck in the wall, unable to free herself. It was likely that the impact would have killed her had she not been half-immortal. Never before had Setadev used so much force on Caitlin all at once, even if he had smashed her into objects before. This one was different.

With an evil laugh, Setadev reached into his robes and pulled out an arrowhead. It was covered with black splotches and had been sharpened. "You still do not see how the game is played," he said as he took the arrowhead to Caitlin's hand and scratched her skin with it, just lightly enough to draw some blood. "As I have told you several times already, you cannot defeat me, for I am nothing. It was pointless for you to charge your magic. Yet you entertain me with your futile efforts, your pitiable attempts to defeat me, and that is quite enjoyable. I must admit, I find you quite an amusing character, angel."

Still in great pain, Caitlin struggled to stay conscious. She realized that Setadev had scratched her with an antite arrowhead, disabling her magic.

"For now, however, you have made me tired of dealing with you. Though I have been hesitant to rid this world of you because you are the first angel born in any known era, I believe I do not want to see you again. Since you will not stop bothering me, however," he said as he pulled her out of the wall, "perhaps it is time for me to end your life now."

Then, Setadev raised one finger. Something lit up at the tip of it. It was divine power, raw, and never seen before. He gripped Caitlin by the front of her dress with one hand, and pulled back his other hand with the intent of launching it into Caitlin.

Unable to defend herself after being beaten senseless and drained of her magic, Caitlin only rested with her fate soon to come upon her.

I'm sorry, Kevin, she thought to herself, even though she knew Kevin could not hear her. *I'm so sorry for everything. I let my doubts control me and because of that, I couldn't save you. I'm so very sorry.*

Nothing she could do. Setadev had won this battle. She had failed. And now she was going to pay with her life.

Suddenly, there was a burst of noise as someone came running up the stairs. "My lord! My lord!" exclaimed a voice. As the voice approached the top, the figure of an Enlightener appeared, nearly out of breath. "There is an army outside! Dressed in black and orange, at least several hundred. I think they mean to attack us!"

Setadev powered his energy down. "You are lucky," he said to Caitlin. "If I kill you, I am going to enjoy it." Then, he threw Caitlin to the floor and turned to the Enlightener. "Bind her hands and take her to a cell. I will address this concern personally."

The Enlightener put a fist to his chest. "Yes, sir," he acknowledged, as he pulled out a short rope from his sash. Meanwhile, Setadev turned and proceeded up the next flight of stairs, with no sense of immediate hurry. Such behavior was rather typical of Setadev. Whatever the distraction was, it was merely that: a distraction. Little could unnerve him, even if his fortress had somehow come under attack.

After Setadev had disappeared, the Enlightener bound Caitlin's hands with the rope and picked her up by her arm. "Let's go," he commanded, in a stern voice, leading her back down the stairs.

Her face was beaten. Her short hair had been dirtied. Her dress had been torn and was stained in her own blood in various places.

At the bottom of the stairs, another Enlightener grabbed her other arm as they continued to lead her through the fortress. As they did, Caitlin started to regain her consciousness. She was grateful to have been left alive, but knew she had to seize her opportunity, and fast. Without magic, that would be a difficult prospect.

In their red robes, the Enlighteners were quiet and firm with their hold. There was no way to break free without her magic.

Around the corner, there was a cell without guards. One of the Enlighteners opened the door, allowing the other to push Caitlin inside and close it. With her hands still tied, she made her way to a wall near the door and leaned back against it, trying to maintain her consciousness and energy.

She had to figure out a way out of this. She just needed a couple of minutes to catch her breath and get herself together again.

The cell she was in was pitch black and allowed in no light. Feeling around a bit, she found the edge of the wall, near where the door was. The corner there was sharp, at least somewhat. If nothing else, that stone lip might be able to cut the rope. It was likely to be her best bet at the moment.

As Caitlin started rubbing the rope bind against the stone corner, she thought about Kevin and how close she had come, only to fail. Caitlin knew that if she were to escape, she would have to cut herself free, recover her magic, and try to remove the door with her magic. That might take a long time, especially since the magic-draining effects of antite tended to vary. Setadev had clearly demonstrated that he had a supply of antite somewhere, and there was always the possibility that the doors or walls were laced with the anti-magic material, which would obliterate her one chance entirely.

Even if she could escape, how could she save Kevin? Could she save herself? Setadev had caught her the first time; maybe his powers were so sharp that he could track her down. She could not beat him.

Caitlin gasped.

Those were the same doubts that were holding her back now. If there was one thing that Kevin had that carried him through his trials, it was optimism. Maybe Kevin was an idealist, but that was part of what Caitlin liked about him to begin with. He knew some things to be impossible, yet continued to do them and showed that they were not impossible at all. For example, he led the Battle of Middle Aurana without any military experience at all and providing what was a winning strategy, even if the battle ended up being a losing affair. Caitlin always admired Kevin for the things that carried him through the toughest tasks imaginable.

It was something that she wrestled with herself in her new experiences with emotion. Doubt was proving to be a new feeling that was difficult to overcome. Had it been any other time, Caitlin might have been fine with wrestling with such emotions and learning how to cope with them, even if it meant a few challenges with Kevin. Now, however, was far from an appropriate time. As a matter of fact, it was the worst. Now, it would cost them both of their lives, and endanger the realms again.

Yet as Caitlin pondered this, another realization hit her. What could be attacking this fortress and threatening Setadev's operation?

Chapter 30

Confrontation in the Plains

Outside the fortress were several thousand men in black uniforms, with orange accents. This was the might of the army of the Solunar Empire, standing without fear in the heart of Nuve's Leticon Province. Amidst the ghosts of war, in foreign territory without permission, not a soul stood in fear of the fortress or what might be beyond its walls.

Standing at the gates of the fortress stood their indomitable leader. "I don't think they're taking us seriously," Arthur Falchor said to an officer standing next to him. "Tap the gate with the ram a little harder. Let them know we're here."

The officer saluted and then delegated the command. A ram was being pushed into the entrance into the fortress. From the building above, Enlighteners and soldiers merely looked down upon this, unsure what to do and lacking any specific orders. Such an offensive out here was quite a surprise.

"Are you sure this is a good idea?" asked Rachel Reinhart to Arthur.

"Of course it is," answered Arthur. "Our people are in there, after all. Those soldiers are our fellow countrymen. We need to show them who we are, and what better way to get their attention than to knock on the door?"

Rachel rolled her eyes. "I didn't mean just that," she said. "I mean all of it. This is Nuve territory, after all, even if it is Leticon. We're invading the legal boundaries of another nation. Is that really a good idea?"

Arthur shook his head, still a little skeptical himself on that one. "I've thought about it for the last week or so," he said, "and I guess I've come to the conclusion that though this is legally Nuve, we can definitely make an argument that this area and all of the area we have traversed through on this side of the line is really under the control of the Enlighteners from the Shadows, and we have a justified reason to be here on that account." Then, he gave Rachel a little more direct look. "Of course, you do know that as prime minister, you may have to defend that point if Nuve starts to question us about it."

Rachel responded with a nod. "I do," she acknowledged. "To be honest, I'm not sure we'll have the chance to defend ourselves, anyway."

"Do you mean physically here or in a Nuve court later?" joked Arthur.

In response, Rachel turned and gave Arthur a light hit in the arm. "You know exactly what I mean," she laughed.

Laughing as well, Arthur had to straighten himself up. "I suppose I do," he chuckled, as his laughter faded. "It's doubtful that they even have a court out here in the Nuve plains, anyway. Forget that this is Leticon; the land all around since we departed from the river is as dead as a rock, even underneath the snow."

"As is much of southern Nuve," interjected Rouge Kirkwood, the co-Vanguard of the Solunar Empire, stepping into the conversation as she flipped around a dagger. "The land is relatively dry here. It's a little better in Cornelia than it is in the middle of Leticon, though."

Arthur nodded, not exactly needing the geography lesson. "So I know," he said, with some sarcasm in his voice. "Rouge, I could use a brief defense evaluation. They're clearly not listening while we break their door in. What do you make of what they could be doing?"

Rouge stopped flipping her dagger and thought for a moment. "We think they only have a few men from Desolunar, less than five hundred or so. As to what they're doing, your guess is honestly as good as mine," she said.

"How about I tell you in person?" yelled a voice from above.

Arthur, Rachel, and Rouge looked up to see Setadev, in his Pseudo form, standing on the top of the battlements above the gate with two Enlighteners and several soldiers in the old Desolunar uniforms on the platform behind. Though he looked much like Kevin still, the scars and physical deformities made it clear, even from a distance, who was actually present.

Looking up, Arthur and Rachel only stared in horror. They had yet to meet Setadev himself, but had met Pseudo in person before knowing he was a fragment of that fallen deity. Rouge's mouth dropped open, having only heard of Pseudo's demise but now seeing him alive.

Setadev merely shook his head at this. "What a shame," he said. "A waste of a perfectly good gate, and also of an army and a ram."

"Hello, Setadev," Arthur called upward toward the battlements.

Almost taking a second deliberately to ignore Arthur, Setadev then looked down and said, "Ah, well, I must be gazing upon the new Emperor of the Solunar Empire. What, may I ask, brings you beyond your borders here to me?"

As Setadev said this, Arthur drew his Sword of Corruption. "You already know the answer to that question," Arthur yelled back. At the same time, Rachel pulled her bow off of her back and nocked an arrow from her quiver, while Rouge pulled out a dagger and started flipping it around again. Rouge also whistled over to her sister Resa, and had her join them as well.

Noticing this, Setadev's gaze became fixed upon Arthur's sword. It turned into a dark-colored energy of magic in the young emperor's hand, before shooting out of it and up into Setadev's hand. Arthur grabbed his hand in pain in response, then looked up to see the sword completely formed in Setadev's grasp. "Another pity," remarked Setadev as he examined the blade.

"Hey! Give that back!" Arthur called up to Setadev.

"And why should I do that?" Setadev immediately responded. "It is mine; not yours. I created it, or do you not remember?"

Arthur scowled.

"Shameful, though," Setadev continued, as he still examined the blade. "It is in many ways like that cursed Sword of Purity, but it has far lesser power and ability. A failed experiment, in many ways. Hmmph..." Setadev finally scowled. "I wonder how that incompetent known as Demonicus failed to use it to take you under his wing."

"So much for speaking highly of your son," commented Arthur as he rolled his eyes.

"He is not my son!" exclaimed Setadev. "He is an incompetent, nothing more. Another failed experiment, and just more proof of the limits of the mortal."

Arthur could not believe a thought was coming to him sympathizing with his own father, Demonicus. Not after what he had done, even if Setadev was worse. Yet it did bother Arthur to know Setadev had shunned the former dictator of Desolunar so easily.

Then, Setadev lifted the Sword of Corruption again. "Just as this sword is incompetent," he said, as he examined it very closely. "Even with my ability to split my divine power into multiple bodies and add some into this sword, it still lacks power." Raising his free hand, Setadev placed it on the tip of the sword. Then, he pressed his hands together, and the Sword of Corruption disappeared between them.

Arthur's eyes widened. His sword had dematerialized.

Setadev shook his head. "Good riddance to a piece of junk, indeed," he said. "Then again, I think the same could be said for all of my plots without myself here personally in the mortal realm, so I will proceed with myself present from here on out. If you want something done right, you must do it yourself." Then, he looked down at Arthur. "Is that why you are here, Emperor? Are you here to stop me yourself?"

"I believe you know why I am here, Setadev," Arthur called back. "This may be Nuve territory here in Leticon, but the people inside are my people. I will take them home with me. All of them."

There was a pause. Then, Setadev began laughing hard.

Rachel nocked an arrow in her bow and pointed it above Setadev, as if to aim at him. Quickly, however, Rouge put her hand on the bow and pulled it down, shaking her head to tell Rachel that was not a smart idea yet.

"You really do not see how the game is played, do you not?" Setadev laughed. "The people here were never your people to begin with. They were always people of Desolunar, and before that, they were of their own lands before Desolunar came into existence. Never were they people of your pathetic Solunar Empire, nor were they ever followers of you."

Arthur groaned. "They have families in my empire," he answered. "They are still my responsibility, and I will not abandon them."

"No, of course not, and that is why you are here," responded Setadev. "However, surely you know that your efforts are all for not when it comes to why you are *really* here. Even if you believe your army can get into my fortress, I won't be surrendering my... shall we say, prized possession, to you. The pure one will not be escaping this place."

That angered Rachel to hear that. "Oh really?" she asked loudly as she raised her bow again. This time, Rouge could not stop her, as she released the arrow. Up into the sky it went, following a perfect arching trajectory for such an upward shot.

At the top of the wall, Setadev took two steps back. The arrow fell right in front of him and bounced off the floor.

Rachel cursed under her breath.

Setadev stepped back into his position. "Very well placed," he said. "You possess the accuracy of the legendary amazon. Had I not stepped out of the way, you would have hit me in the side of the neck. A good shot."

Frustrated, Rachel nocked another arrow. "Next one's coming right for you."

"I think not, Prime Minister," interrupted Setadev. "Unless, of course, you would like me to kill your angel friend as well."

Suddenly, Rachel gasped. She immediately lowered her bow, as Rouge and Resa lowered their weapons as well and Arthur took a step back. "What have you done with Caitlin?" Rachel asked desperately.

"Oh, nothing much," answered Setadev, almost passively. "I caught her snooping around in my fortress, so I locked her in a cell." Then, Setadev paused, as he briefly looked back at the fortress before looking out to the Solunar Empire's forces. "It seems quite humorous to me that everyone seems to want to rescue the pure one. Every one of you seems to want to go to such ridiculous lengths, even as far as risking war with uninvolved nations, just to rescue this one person. Yet, how many times must I remind you people? You cannot defeat me, for I am..."

"Vulnerable!" Arthur yelled up to Setadev, interrupting him blatantly. "You're in a weakened state, Setadev, and I know it. For once, you don't hold all of the cards in this matter. If you want to claim that we can't defeat you, then why don't you prove it?"

Setadev scoffed. "Do not underestimate my power, mortal. Even in this form which looks much like your friend, I am still Setadev, and I am nothing. However, if you think that you can best me out of my fortress, then all you have to do is make the first move. I will be waiting." Then, Setadev turned away and walked back inside the fortress.

Too easy. It could be a trap. Then again, Setadev tended to be overconfident, at least in appearance from their encounters with him.

Arthur turned to Rachel. "Let's do it," he said.

Rachel nodded confidently. She turned to the Solunar Empire forces and commanded, "You heard him! Prepare to advance!"

Quickly, Rouge flipped out one of her knives. "Archers to the ready! Advance the ram to breach the gate. Ladder units to the ready!"

As the commands were issued, archers in old Desolunar uniforms appeared on top of the wall and aimed their bows down at the new Solunar Empire troops. Arthur's soldiers prepared to return fire.

"Hold!" commanded Arthur. "Prepare to fire, but do not do so until my command!"

The troops did as they were commanded. The ram was ready to advance again, as foot soldiers waited behind it to storm the castle. Archers had their arrows aimed up at the archers on the wall, and more men were ready with long stick ladders, preparing to set them up to scale the wall. The men were listening intently for Arthur's command.

Quietly, Arthur leaned in to speak to Rachel, Rouge, and Resa. "Notice someone missing?" Arthur asked.

"Yeah," nodded Rachel. "No General Sayo to be seen."

"The general's probably inside or something," commented Resa.

"Maybe," Rouge responded, "but that's pretty unlikely, Resa. He's in charge of the troops, but the troops are out here without him. Everything we know about the general suggests that he should be out here."

Arthur nodded. "Indeed," he said. "In fact, I wonder if their troops have any will to fight their fellow countrymen without the general here to give orders." And on that, Arthur turned and issued a loud verbal command to his troops, one that he knew the soldiers on the wall would hear. "Do not engage any Desolunar troops unless they engage you first. Any and all Enlighteners, however, should be engaged immediately."

Immediately, there seemed to be confusion on the wall. Troops were talking to one another, asking what to do. Certainly, Arthur had caused a stir by making such a comment. Then, moving for the ultimate equalizer, Arthur yelled up to the soldiers on the wall, "Former soldiers of Desolunar, we are the Solunar Empire! You are among friends and family. Those who surrender will be offered complete amnesty and will have the opportunity to go home and be with their families."

Silence filled the air. Then, Rachel turned and made the next command. "Advance the ram!" she yelled.

The ram started moving forward. As it did, arrows started flying down from the sky. They were aiming for the ram and for the men pushing it forward. Immediately, Solunar Empire soldiers began firing back. Though there was still a rain of arrows to fight through, it was lighter than Arthur and Rachel had initially expected. Some of the soldiers above had to have been moved by what Arthur had said; fighting for a lost purpose, the desire to go home was a strong one for some.

The volleys of arrows continued to fly. As the ram started beating at the door, Rachel ordered for the ladders to come to the wall. Immediately, three ladders were advanced to the wall, and the men were leaning the ladders as they were taught in the empire: base away from the wall to make the ladders harder to push down.

Suddenly, a shot of fire came down from atop the wall and torched one of the ladders. The troops putting it into position had only an instant to scamper away. They were lucky to escape with their lives, as the ladder was destroyed in an instant.

There had to be Enlighteners on top of the building. Though

Desolunar forces had had mages in their ranks before, Arthur was fairly certain he still had all of them in the Solunar Empire, if his previous documents were to be believed.

"Where is he?" Arthur yelled over to Rachel, as another volley of arrows had been launched up the wall. "I don't see an Enlightener. Where did that fireball come from?"

Rachel shook her head. "I can't see one, either," she called back.

Another ladder was coming into position. It had to be defended. As the ladder came into place, Rouge flipped out both of her daggers and took a poise. "I'm going after him, wherever he is. Cover me, Resa."

Arthur and Rachel looked over, giving a nod of confidence in the talented former assassin.

Resa nodded too. "I'm on it," she said, charging light magic in her hands.

Then, the ladder locked into place at an angle, as two Solunar Empire soldiers held the base of the ladder tight. As they did, another shot of fire came down toward it. Quickly, Resa lined up her shot of light and fired it, intercepting the fire blast and causing a minor explosion in the place the two shots intercepted. The explosion created smoke, serving as the perfect distraction.

Immediately as the smoke rose and clouded the top of the wall, Rouge ran as fast as she could up the ladder, using the moderately shallow angle of the ladder to run and skip every other rung on her way up the wall. She was agile and quick, and never faulted as she stepped lightly on the ladder and over the battlements.

It turned out the "wall" was quite wide indeed, with its top surface stretching all the way back to the central tower. It was not actually a wall at all, but the ceiling of the fortress's first section. At the top, Desolunar soldiers started fleeing in fear at the mad rush of Rouge. Some even recognized her as Demonicus's former master assassin, and were instantly frightened. One archer in particular, however, stood cold and steely-eyed. He nocked an arrow and took aim, just as Rouge leapt over the battlements.

Almost without hesitation, Rouge flipped her dagger upward as soon as she touched the floor and deflected the arrow. Then, she charged that archer without fear. The archer had no time to nock another arrow or to draw a sword. Quickly, Rouge tossed the dagger in her right hand up in the air, caught it, and threw it at the archer.

The dagger hit him right in the eye. He fell over instantly, dead.

At this moment, several Desolunar troops began charging Rouge, as if inspired by the death of the archer. Carefully, Rouge began backpedaling as the soldiers advanced, right into her own soldiers. Several Solunar Empire soldiers had climbed the ladder and were establishing a position on the wall. Two more ladders had locked into place, allowing more troops to advance up the wall, and Rouge's sudden appearance had allowed them to advance without being attacked. Still, many of the Desolunar soldiers stuck their ground, while others retreated. Now, the close combat had begun.

As the troops of each side started to fight, Rouge saw a man standing further down the wall, dressed in red robes. That was the Enlightener. The only one.

He was staring her down. Now, she had to make her move. Behind her, Resa was starting to climb the ladder. There was no time to wait for her, though. That Enlightener could kill her and a lot of soldiers if she did not draw his attention. The Enlightener then raised his hands and pointed them at Rouge. The former assassin flipped her dagger in the air and said to herself, "Well, let's just see how quick you are, then."

With incredible agility, Rouge caught her dagger and leapt onto the battlements, as she started to run down them. Despite the gaps and the narrow edge she was running along, she ran with precision and accuracy. After passing the troops, she hopped down and grabbed her other dagger from the deceased soldier without skipping a step. She flipped them both into the air and charged the Enlightener at full speed, leaping and bringing her daggers down at his neck.

At that moment, the Enlightener blasted her in the chest with a fire spell. Rouge was thrown back quite a distance across the wall, skidding as she hit the floor.

"No!" screamed Resa as she stood on the top of the wall.

She had seen the whole thing from the ladder top. Her sister was the one person in her life who meant the most. Resa had never spent a day in her life without her sister by her side.

As the men in front of her continued to fight, Resa stepped up onto the battlement and looked very closely at the Enlightener. A stare down then occurred as the Enlightener returned the look, resulting in their eyes locking on in glaring hatred.

Resa glanced over to see her sister Rouge still on the wall, but still down. No matter how extensively she was hurt, Resa was not going to allow this Enlightener's attack on her sister to go unpunished. The men continued to fight behind her. Resa stepped down off of the wall and glared at the Enlightener, who was glaring back. Now was the time for war. By no means was Resa a master in magic, but she was infuriated, and that made her dangerous.

Carefully, Resa started walking back and forth across the wall, staring down the Enlightener. As she did, the Enlightener did the same, revealing a deep gash across his cheek. Rouge had injured him after all; she came very close to striking him down.

Fury glowed in Resa's eyes. Fire energy glowed in her left hand, as light energy glowed in her right. She slammed them together in her hands to create her most dangerous technique, a magic exploding shot. The forceful combination of fire and light magics were very unstable, turning into an immensely powerful blast that could be fired as a shot. As Resa was incapable of using magic beams, this technique was a favorite of hers.

In response, the Enlightener began charging darkness magic.

There was a long pause. A very long pause.

Then, Resa fired first. The Enlightener fired a second later.

Resa's shot fell low and impacted the wall floor about halfway between herself and the Enlightener, throwing up smoke and damaging a sizable chunk of the wall. The Enlightener's shot disappeared in the smokescreen, beyond where he could see whether or not he hit his target.

Only silence filled the air. The darkness spell did not sound as though it had hit anything. Baffled by this, as the shot should have hit the wall, or the men behind, or anything, the Enlightener walked toward the smokescreen to investigate.

Swish!

It was the perfect move. Using the smokescreen as cover, Resa had kneeled down, grabbed one of her sister's daggers, waited for the Enlightener to approach, and stabbed the Enlightener in the heart. As soon as she did, the Enlightener disappeared and only a red robe and a gold necklace were left behind, falling to the ground in a small pile.

He was gone, for now at least.

Clutching her shoulder, Resa turned around and ran back to where her sister was. Resa had been hit by the darkness spell that the Enlightener had cast, but she had braced for it. Still, though Resa had some level of healing spells, she did not use them on her shoulder. She was saving all of the energy she had left for her sister. Finally, upon reaching Rouge, she managed to see the extent of Rouge's injury.

Rouge had been hit square in the chest with a very powerful fire spell. Her uniform was singed over a large area of her torso and her skin was badly burned. She had also been knocked unconscious as well, and Resa worried deeply that she may have more internal injuries. Then, Resa looked up toward her sister's head to see a pool of blood flowing heavily from it, likely from the impact of hitting the floor.

Resa had to act quickly. She put herself to work on Rouge's head injury as best as she could. Unfortunately, the most she could do with her magic was just enough to keep Rouge alive; the damage was so extensive that it would be fatal if she did not do this.

Down the length of the wall, the Desolunar troops were falling back as the Solunar Empire soldiers established their position. Many in the Desolunar archery unit had willingly surrendered right away, taken with Arthur's offer of amnesty and the opportunity to return home. There was a lot of community healing to be done in Seta Archa and the entire nation of Solunar, and now they would have the opportunity to be a part of that process.

As business was being taken care of and the troops were working on securing the perimeter of the fortress, Arthur and Rachel began racing up the ladder as well, confident in the security of that section of the wall. When they reached the top, they saw Resa leaning over Rouge's body, and immediately rushed to the side of their friends.

"What happened?" Rachel immediately asked as she knelt down next to

Resa.

"The Enlightener was waiting for my sister and slammed her with a powerful fire spell," Resa answered, as a few tears fell from her eyes. "She's hurt badly."

Carefully, Rachel looked over Rouge's injuries as Resa cast her healing magic. As she examined the injuries, Rachel saw the charred clothing and deeply burned skin, and gasped. Then, she looked up to Arthur. "Rouge has serious burns," she said, a tear coming to her eyes too. "As deep as these burns look like they are, she may have some significant internal injuries to her heart and lungs that we're not seeing."

Arthur's eyes became more serious. "Can you heal her, Resa?" he asked.

Resa kept focused on what she was doing, but more teardrops dripped from her eyes to the ground. "I can't do it," she finally said. "I'm not strong enough to heal all of her injuries. It's taking everything I have right now just to keep her alive."

Rachel called aloud for a medic.

Wiping his brow, Arthur responded confidently, "Come on, Resa. I know you can do it."

Another teardrop fell from Resa's eyes. "No, you don't understand," she cried. "I'm not a strong enough spellcaster to be able to heal someone, and confidence isn't the issue. I can't generate the magic power and I can't manipulate it well enough to heal significant injuries like this. I'm just a low-level mage, that's all."

At that, Arthur was left speechless. No wonder healing magic was not so well used in war, if it took such rare strength to heal severe wounds. To Arthur, Resa was very strong in her magic skills, yet it was turning out in the end that despite outward appearance, she was not so strong in it at all. Now, he worried gravely that Rouge was going to die. Resa was the only magic-capable individual he had brought with him to this battle, and there was no amount of medical supply and treatment that could treat the deadly woulds that Rouge had suffered.

In the months since meeting the sisters who became two of his best friends, Arthur had come to know both Rouge and Resa Kirkwood quite well. Most of all, however, he knew that Rouge and Resa depended on one another, since for so many years they had been each other's only safety net and best friends. No bond of sisterly love could be stronger than theirs. Now, as a deep friend himself, Arthur tried his hardest not to cry as he watched Resa work desperately to keep Rouge alive. It appeared, though, that it would be all for not.

"Wait a minute!" exclaimed Rachel, popping up to her feet. An idea had hit her, and she turned to Arthur to share it. "If what Setadev said is true, then Caitlin is inside this fortress, too. She's a high-level sorceress, and we know what she's capable of in terms of magic. If we can raid the fortress, free her and Kevin, and bring her here to heal Rouge, she might have the magic power to make that happen."

That was it. The perfect answer. Maybe it was fortunate that Caitlin had beat them to the fortress after all, if Setadev was to be believed. Confidently, Arthur nodded. He grabbed Rachel by the shoulder and gently pulled her up. "Then let's go forward," he said.

Rachel nodded in acknowledgment. She pulled her bow out again and nocked an arrow.

Arthur leaned over the battlements. "General, how is the progress on the door coming?" he yelled down to his troop leader.

As Arthur looked down, waiting for a response, he noticed that the ram that had been pounding the door had been pulled back. Many of his men were now on standby. The general that Arthur had called to took a few steps forward and yelled back, "The door is far too sturdy, sir. It must be a reinforced door. It is so strong that it has actually cracked several beams in our ram from the recoil of us pushing it forward and hitting the door."

No way in through the bottom. That being said, Setadev had to have an entrance on this level. Otherwise, he would not have been able to make it out to the wall from inside the fortress. Arthur turned and looked back toward the center of the fortress to see a door right behind him. It was not a large door at all, which meant it had to be easier to breach. He and his men were going to force their way into the fortress one way or another.

Seeing this door, Arthur leaned over the battlements again. "General, divide your men!" he commanded. "I want them divided into three forces; one force is to secure the fortress perimeter, another is to secure the top of the wall, and a third is to help us advance into the fortress and capture it."

"Sir, that will divide our forces quite thin," the Solunar Empire general called back up to Arthur. "We do not have a large number of troops with us."

There was a slight pause, as Arthur considered this. "That is quite all right," he said. "I think we should be okay even if we divide up the forces that thin. Once we breach the fortress, our numbers will matter little anyway because of how narrow the passageways will be. We will be thin on the outside and the wall, but we will have to live with that."

Without question, the general saluted. "Yes, my emperor," he acknowledged, as he proceeded to divide his men.

Arthur nodded and turned back toward the wall, as the sound of clashing swords continued to ring through the air. While Resa was still doing everything she could to keep her sister alive, Rachel was now speaking with a Solunar Empire soldier. Before Arthur could get over to her, however, he was stopped by another soldier of his, accompanied by a soldier in the old Desolunar uniforms. He was one of the captured prisoners who had surrendered. "My emperor," began the Solunar Empire soldier, "pardon me for interrupting, but I have brought for you the lieutenant commanding the archery unit that was defending this wall."

The lieutenant then knelt before Arthur. "It is an honor to serve you, my emperor."

Though Arthur felt as though he had no time for this, especially while in the middle of a secured area on an active battlefield, he could not advance anyway until the reinforcements he needed were on the wall and in position to breach the door into the fortress. That would take a little bit as the men had to climb the ladder to reach the top of the wall. Recognizing this, Arthur knelt down and raised the lieutenant's head. "There is no need for such formality," he said. "We are the same, you and I. We are men here to defend what is best for our country, the same country." He rose, and brought the lieutenant with him. "I am Arthur Falchor, the heir of Desolunar and the Emperor of the Solunar Empire."

"The heir?" asked the lieutenant, his eyes widening. "We had been told that a traitor to Desolunar had usurped the throne. We had no idea that Desolunar had come into the hands of its heir."

Arthur took a breath. If that was the explanation for all of this carnage and why these men had followed General Sayo, it would be sad. Still, that was not completely an inaccurate story. In many ways, Arthur actually was a traitor to his own throne because he had overthrown his father with the help of Kevin Trent Stryker. For that he had to have an explanation for the lieutenant that made sense and did not distort the truth. He thought about what Kevin might say, reasoning that his best friend might suggest that the whole controversy might simply be a matter of perspective.

"It all depends on the way you see it," Arthur answered. "I am the heir of Desolunar, the natural-born heir, that is true. That being said, I did help in the downfall of Desolunar, I cannot lie. However, I did so not to destroy Desolunar, but to help it and its people. The Solunar Empire, which I now command, defends the rights of the people who live there, and we're no weaker a people because of it." Arthur then paused, seeing the speech was likely not to help against any preconceived notions. "What is your name, lieutenant?"

"Lieutenant Desoto, sir," acknowledged the lieutenant.

"Even if you do not believe me, Lieutenant Desoto, and I can certainly see why you would not at this moment, I do encourage you and your men to return home to Seta Archa," continued Arthur. "Admittedly, the city is struggling at this moment with the winter, but I think that you and your men will find a whole new social structure and families that are reunited with each other. Our people, when we get through this winter, will be a better people for it. I want only for you and your men to join us and see what the Solunar Empire is before you judge it for yourself."

Lieutenant Desoto nodded. "Fair enough," he said. "I am sure my men and I look forward to the opportunity."

"I'm proud to offer it," said Arthur. Then, realizing that the lieutenant might know some things, he asked, "Do you know where the prisoners are kept in this building?"

The lieutenant stopped to think for a few minutes. "I believe most are held in the center of the tower," he said, pointing the the cylinder-shaped center of the fortress. "However, I do know that Lord Pseudo has a special prisoner he keeps in a reinforced dungeon cell on the top floor. Supposedly it's some young man who wronged him before. He says he has something very special planned, but he has not said yet what that might be."

Kevin. He was here after all. Caitlin was on the right track.

"Then there is little time," Arthur said. He then turned to his Solunar Empire soldier. "Captain, please escort the lieutenant and his men off the wall. We will regroup at the end of the day down the road from here."

"Affirmative," saluted the captain, as he then proceeded to lead the lieutenant to the ladder. The lieutenant offered a salute to Arthur as well, grateful for him and his men to be left alive, much less with a chance to return home.

As quickly as that was over, Arthur ran back to Resa, as soon as he could. Rachel was still leaning over Resa, offering her support as she continued to try and treat Rouge's injuries. A medic had finally arrived as well, and was wrapping her injuries as much as possible. Resa stopped for just a second to pull up her dress above her knees and roll up her short sleeves, to maximize her amount of open skin to let her channel more energy. She did so despite the cold air of the winter day in the plains. Behind Arthur, more and more Solunar Empire soldiers were arriving behind him. It was time to advance.

Arthur leaned down to Resa. "How long can you keep her alive if the medic comes to bandage her up?" he asked.

Already, Resa was looking exhausted. Another tear fell from her eye. "Not long," she said. "I don't know how long I can keep restricting her injuries like this."

"Then we don't have much time." Arthur looked over to Rachel. "Let's go," he said.

Confidently, Rachel nodded as she stood up. She nocked an arrow in her bow and prepared to move in. About thirty Solunar Empire soldiers were lined up in front of the door on the wall into the fortress. Rachel and Arthur both stepped behind them. Though unarmed himself since Setadev had destroyed his sword, Arthur stepped next to Rachel. "Ready?" he asked.

Rachel nodded. "Ready," she said. Then, she turned to the troops. She called out, "Breach the door and advance!"

At that order, two Solunar Empire soldiers approached the upper door with sturdy metal rods and began prying at the door, near the lock. A man with an ax was also hacking away at the door, focusing around the lock area to loosen it. Within a moment, they had the door wide open, perhaps even easier than they could have breached the lower door with the ram.

Immediately, several soldiers charged into the building to start clearing the area. Arthur and Rachel were not too far behind, and they ran up to the door together. Without a sword and without wanting to take one from any of his soldiers, Arthur was going to need to trust Rachel with his defense going into the fortress.

Arthur looked out briefly beyond the wall. Since there were no enemy troops on the ground because the fortress was supposed to be secret, securing the perimeter would not be too challenging for his soldiers. Then, he looked over to Resa, who was doing everything she could to keep Rouge alive. He turned his head and looked up the side of the fortress tower, knowing that Kevin and Caitlin were in there and needed rescue. Finally, he turned again and looked at Rachel, who was looking at him, almost with a slight smile. He had no time, though, to question what that was about.

For Rachel, she knew what she had to do, and what she was fighting for. Her friends Kevin and Caitlin, and Rouge and Resa too, all needed her to be strong for them. Arthur needed her to be strong for him, too, and it was very important for her to be there for him.

After looking around and then at each other for a minute, the call came from the hallways, "All clear, my emperor!"

Arthur motioned to Rachel. "Let's go," he said.

Chapter 31

Risky Decisions

Having been under the influence of aphrodisiacs constantly and without pause for days on end, Kevin was still chained in his cell in the Fortress of Da Leval. He could not hear what was going on downstairs. He could not hear Caitlin being locked into a cell below him, and he could not hear the advancing forces of the Solunar Empire making their way into the fortress. Such would have been a sign of hope for him, yet he could not hear them. His ears were losing sensitivity. His vision had not been clear in three or four days. All of these were side effects of the prolonged use of the aphrodisiacs that were being administered to him. Even if he had his senses, though, Kevin was almost to the point of being brainless, unable to connect his thoughts or remember where he came from.

Next to Kevin, the unchained Satiana was laying next to him. She was curled up next to him, stroking him softly. "I'm so glad I was paired with you," she said quietly and sweetly to him. "You're so sweet, you know that?"

There was only a blank look on Kevin's face. His lack of self-awareness left him without thought or reflection on what Satiana was saying. It was as though he was completely zoned out beyond any sense of acknowledgement of the world around him.

Satiana began to pull herself even tighter to Kevin's side. "You know, I'm not sure what I'd do in here without you, my love," she continued. "If we're destined to be in here forever, I think I'd be okay with that, as long as I get to spend it with you."

Still, Kevin was unresponsive. Something in his mind was trying to connect the dots and realize what the situation was. He had not been administered a dose of the aphrodisiacs in quite a while, and their grip on his mental state was starting to loosen.

Suddenly, the door on the cell slammed open. A rush of cool air flooded the room, as airflow had been quite limited into the cell while the door was closed. The colder air jolted Kevin, stimulating his nerves and raising his awareness slightly. It also alerted Satiana, who stood up next to Kevin as soon as the door was opened. In the doorframe was General Sayo, saluting as he stood in the doorway.

"General, this is important work," Satiana immediately told the general. "You know that Setadev ordered you not to disturb us unless..."

"We are under attack," interrupted the general. "They are through the front wall."

As Satiana listened to the general, she brushed the dirt off of her dress. "Fantastic," she said. "General, your men must be terribly inept if they could not maintain the defense of the wall. This is a strong fortress; no matter how few your men are, they are always in the advantaged positions."

Sayo said nothing.

After a moment of silence, Satiana sighed. "Then I suppose that the Enlighteners and I must take up the defense inside the building. Are you asking for my help with your job, General?"

There was a pause. Then, Sayo said, "Yes."

Satiana groaned in response. "Fine," she answered. She then stepped up to the general. "If that is what you want, then you will have to stay here and watch him. Even while he is chained to the wall, he is overdue for his next round of aphrodisiacs and coming into his own recognizance, and Setadev demands that he needs to be guarded if he ever regains full consciousness." She then paused for a moment and let Sayo take a step back out of the threshold, as she stepped past it. "You should know that I will make sure Setadev knows of your ineptitude," she stopped to say. "Regardless of what he who I am fragmented from may believe, I have always thought that you and your men are worthless to our cause. For now, however, you will be an adequate guard while I clean up the mess you should have had no problem handling." Then, Satiana stormed off down the hallway, leaving Sayo where he was standing.

Sayo glanced down the hallway, then turned and walked back through the doorway. Satiana was gone now. This was the time to carry out his real plan.

As he walked up to the chained Kevin, he shook his head. This boy was going through something that no one should ever have to go through. He knew of the chemicals being put into Kevin's body and he knew of what Satiana was doing to him. All of it was terrible.

Tired and drained, Kevin slowly looked up at the general. "Who are you?" he asked.

That was a sign something was wrong. The general knew that Kevin knew who he was. He had made remarks about the general before.

Feebly, Kevin continued, "I feel like I used to know you from some place."

The general nodded. He then knelt down, and pulled a vial out from his jacket. "Drink this," he said as he offered the vial to Kevin. "It is an antidote to the aphrodisiacs you have been given. It will counteract their effects very quickly."

Exhausted and very thirsty, Kevin reached out and grabbed the vial. He did not even know if it would quench his thirst, but he knew it was a liquid and that was what mattered. He still lacked the cognition to realize that he was drinking a potion and not a beverage. Very quickly, though, that would change. Kevin felt his mind starting to clear, and his senses starting to return just a few seconds after drinking the antidote. As he started to regain his mind, Sayo took his set of keys and started unlocking Kevin's shackles.

After the general had Kevin's legs unshackled and his left arm, Kevin had his mind back. He stated in surprise, "General Sayo! What the hell are you doing?"

Quickly, Sayo shushed the young pure one. "Keep your voice down," he said, as he unlocked Kevin's final shackle. "If you want to get out of here alive, you had better come with me."

"Is that a threat?" asked Kevin, who upon being free instantly leapt up and stepped back.

The general put his hands up. "Easy," he said, as he pulled a scabbard off of his belt. There was a sword in it, the Sword of Purity. He presented it in front of Kevin. "I believe this is yours."

Skeptical, Kevin extended his right arm, and called the sword to him. It transformed into energy and rematerialized in his hand, just as it should have done. He then grabbed the scabbard out of Sayo's hand, and strapped it to his own belt. "You'll forgive me if I am wary of you," he said as he swiped the sword around a little bit. "I don't trust you, or anything that you have planned."

Sayo nodded, his hands still up. "That is fair," he acknowledged. "You do not have any reason to trust me at this point."

Kevin looked carefully at his sword, just to be sure it was his. As he examined it, he saw the familiar glow of the sword's venation, which represented the sacrifice of an immortal in the blade. That part could not be faked for certain. "Then answer this for me," he continued. "Why have you set me free?"

There was a slight pause, before Sayo said without wavering, "I need your help."

Confused, Kevin asked, "What?"

The general nodded. "I have set you free because I need your help. We need to get out of here together if we want to keep Setadev from accomplishing his goal."

There was another pause, as Kevin was still confused. He pointed his sword at Sayo. "You had better start making sense right now, or I won't hesitate to cut you down," he demanded. "You're working for Setadev. I know you."

"Then at least allow me to explain to you everything that has brought me here to freeing you," Sayo answered, "but not here. We have to get moving now. We will not have long to try and escape from this place."

"And what place is this?" asked Kevin, raising his sword to Sayo's face. He was making it clear that he was not going anywhere with Sayo without some explanation.

Sayo raised his hands higher, realizing that he had to stop and slow down before . "It is the Fortress of Da Leval, deep within the province of Leticon in southeastern Nuve. It is a meeting point for the Enlighteners from the Shadows."

Kevin took a step back. He was starting to put the pieces together of where he was and where he had been before. "I knew the Enlighteners had to be involved in all of this 'remnant of the fallen' business," he said, as if in realization. "What's the plan here? What's Setadev got in mind for all of this?"

General Sayo shook his head, realizing Kevin would not let this go until he had some level of understanding. "I do not know for sure," he answered. "Pseudo originally convinced me that he wanted us to take back Seta Archa and restore Desolunar. Despite my personal distaste for him even when we worked together in the Desolunar military, Lord Demonicus had placed him second in command of Desolunar, making him my superior officer. Therefore, to obey him was to be my directive." The general then paused. "I really must insist, if you want to hear more, that we get moving. If we stay here longer, we may be found."

Shaking his head, Kevin lifted the handle of his sword higher. "No," he said. "I don't believe you, Sayo. You're more clever than that. You have something up your sleeve, and I know it." His voice started to raise. "Now, do you want to tell me what it is, or should I start taking your limbs off one at a time?"

Instantly, General Sayo hushed Kevin. He then paused and started whispering, as he shut the prison door next to him, "I do have something up my sleeve, but it is not against you. It is against Setadev." He leaned in closer, and looked around for a moment almost in paranoia before continuing, "Your friends in the Solunar Empire are here to rescue you and bring down this fortress. I have ordered my outer defense troops to defend in a weak strategy entirely from the outer wall, and to surrender once their position is taken. If you want to leave this fortress alive, now is the time."

"And what do you have vested in me?" asked Kevin.

There was a moment of silence, as Sayo lowered his hands more. "If there is one thing I know, it's that you are the only true opposition to Setadev. If all of this is going to be fixed, you're the one who can do it."

Briefly, Kevin considered this. His mind was coming back, and these thoughts just did not add up. Sayo was not supposed to be like this. He was supposed to be a cold, heartless man who was a traitor to his homeland and as loyal to Setadev as Demonicus himself. In what world would he see something in Kevin, aside from the fact that

Setadev had some vengeance plan involving the young pure one?

That might be it in itself. Sayo did know how far Setadev went seemingly just to set up a trap for him. Even so, what proof did Kevin have that he could trust Sayo? He might be able to find out about that by leveraging the issue of trust.

"Do you even know who you are dealing with?" Kevin asked pointedly, his grip tightening on his sword. "I don't mean Setadev. I mean me."

Silently, Sayo said nothing. He seemed baffled.

Kevin had him. Unknown to Kevin, Sayo was putting his life in Kevin's hands, and to cause Sayo to second-guess his thoughts of who he was freeing had stunned the old general. With this leverage in hand, Kevin continued, "Do you see the jacket which I am wearing? I am the Vanguard of a nation which you have betrayed. I came out to the Wastes to destroy you. Does none of that bother you?"

The general stood stoically. He answered, "No."

After a slight pause, Kevin started shaking his head. He was not expecting such a simple answer. Reluctantly, he lowered his sword and placed it back in his scabbard. "Very well," he said, knowing that to continue to argue would be futile. For now, he would have to trust the general, without much choice if he wanted to get out alive. He took a couple of steps back, indicated his left hand toward the door, and said, "Lead the way."

Without hesitation, the general walked over and opened the door. "As you wish," he said. "Follow me." Then, he walked out the door, with Kevin following him closely.

Outside, the hallways were made of plain white brick. What was this place? Kevin could not remember how he had arrived here or where he had been taken to. All he knew was that this was, according to General Sayo—whose trustworthiness was questionable at best—the "Fortress of Da Leval", in Leticon Province of Nuve. Having been educated on the rumors surrounding the province while in school at the Rikleifer Academy, Kevin was well aware that Leticon Province was supposedly feared to be haunted and had a very dark past. Appropriate place for the Enlighteners from the Shadows to be based out of, for sure.

As he followed the general through the seemingly endless stone hallways of the fortress, Kevin tried his hardest to recall how he arrived here and what had happened. He could barely remember anything leading up to this point. In his earlier rage against the general, he had not asked how long he had been in the cell. While his memory was still very blocked, the antidote was taking effect, clarifying his memories and shedding light into what had brought him here.

He remembered leaving Seta Archa, heading east for the Metoi village that General Sayo had destroyed. Earlier that day, he had said goodbye to his best friends Arthur and Rachel, and to his love, Caitlin. It had been an unusually hot day in the Wastes, but it could have simply seemed to be that warm because the arid lands of the Wastes were not affected by the cold winter, in contrast to the rest of the world. Rouge and Resa had gone with him to check out the village and look for clues to where Sayo may have gone. The Sword of Purity had pointed him east, away from any sustenance whatsoever. It had made little sense to Kevin as to why Sayo would run that direction. Then, the Sword gave him a warning, before seemingly countermanding it.

No. That second voice had to be Setadev. Somehow, some way, it had to be his voice.

Later that evening, Kevin had found Sayo, but had been trapped. Setadev had him, and explained that burning the village and camping his troops to the east had all been an elaborate snare. Then, Setadev knocked him out. Anything that had happened in the cell, how he got there, and how long he had been there, was still blank. He could not remember any of it, not even the last few minutes before being given the antidote. Whatever he had been given before that the antidote was now removing, had given him a severe case of amnesia.

Down a flight of stairs went the general, with Kevin close behind. As they reached the bottom, Kevin asked, "Tell me, general, how long was I in that cell?"

The general seemed confused, but kept moving as Kevin kept following. "Probably a few weeks? I'm not sure exactly how many days."

Suddenly, Kevin's eyes widened as he kept running. "A few weeks?" he asked. "I've been in that cell for weeks?"

Without stopping, the general nodded his head. "Don't you remember? You and Satiana kept a counter on the wall of how many days you had been together in that cell. Every day, the two of you would count how many marks you had made on the cell wall."

That baffled Kevin greatly. Who was Satiana? Kevin did not remember any of that. Boldly, he asked the general, "And just who the hell is Satiana?"

"She was your cellmate," answered the general. "I'm surprised you still don't remember, especially considering all the things you two did together."

Kevin stopped in his tracks. A few steps later, the general noticed that Kevin had stopped, and quickly halted himself. As the general turned back to face him, Kevin demanded, "Tell me what you mean by that. What the hell has been happening to me that I can't remember? In fact, what was that antidote for, and why can't I remember anything?" His hand was hovering over the crossguard of his sword, as if he were ready to grab it and strike Sayo down at a moment's notice. Never before had Kevin been so upset in anger.

Again, the general put up his hands. "Look, Kevin, we don't have time for this," he answered. "I promise I will explain everything once we're out of here. If we want to rescue your angel friend and get out of here alive, we have to keep moving."

Angel friend. Caitlin.

She was here!? And Sayo knew where?

Immediately, Kevin charged and blasted General Sayo into the wall, pressing his sword flat against the general's chest. "Where is she?" he demanded loudly. He then pushed harder and screamed, "Where is she?!"

The general was stunned. Kevin now had the sharp side of the sword under his chin. Something about this angel friend of his made him even more determined than worrying about his own life. Slowly, the general put his left hand on top of the blade, and motioned as if to push it down gently without touching the blade, as the frustrated Kevin eased back as well. "Easy," he said. "I know you want to save her, and I will lead you to her. I need you to trust me."

Knowing that he was not going to get anywhere without the

general, Kevin took a deep breath as he pulled his sword back. "I'm sorry," he said, as he placed his sword in his sheath. "You are right, General. I won't stop you anymore."

General Sayo nodded. "That is all right," he answered, lowering his arms. "Once we are out of this place, I will explain everything to you. I am sorry, too, that I have not had the opportunity to explain all of this yet and left you in confusion."

Not as sorry as you will be, echoed a voice from down the hall.

Kevin and the general sharply turned. Down the hall, walking toward him, were Setadev and a group of about fifteen Enlighteners. Turning the other way, Satiana was now blocking the other direction with about fifteen Enlighteners of her own.

They were stuck. Captured again.

Sayo growled as he pulled out his own sword. "You want to say that again?" he stated to Setadev forcefully. Very rarely before had Sayo shown such a furious demeanor.

"Hmmm, I find you quite intriguing, General," responded Setadev casually. He started pacing in front of his group of Enlighteners back and forth across the hall. "However, you have unfortunately proven something I have known for quite some time; you do not see how the game is played."

Again, Sayo groaned, as Kevin pulled his sword out as well.

"I am nothing, Sayo, or did you not remember that? Did you not think that I had realized you would betray me at some point? I am well aware that about half of your men outside were given the instruction to surrender, and that the Solunar forces are entering the fortress. In fact, I had planned on it."

Suddenly, Sayo's eyes widened.

Kevin was finally putting the pieces together on the general. He was honest about trying to escape, after all. "I'm sorry, Sayo," he said, feeling like his stalling may have contributed to their recapture.

"It is not your fault," answered Sayo. "They were waiting on us."

Satiana then picked up the speech. "And now, the two of you will never see the light of day again," she said, picking up Kevin's attention and causing him to turn toward her. "What a shame. You could have shared in our glory, Sayo, and the pure one could have lived in eternal bliss forever, but now you have destroyed all of that. Think of what you could have had, and think of what you will have now."

Sayo said nothing.

Kevin, however, started glaring at Satiana. She seemed oddly familiar, but Kevin could not place from where. As he briefly looked her over, he was attracted to her form, as any young man his age would be. She looked to be his age, with long blonde hair that was just a little bit curly. She had almost the perfect shape for a woman, and was attractively dressed in a long simple black dress with red and gold trim. Certainly, she was the type who would instantly be in the consortium of aristocrats and royalty, desired by all no matter what life she came from. More attractive than Caitlin? Perhaps to most men, but not to Kevin. Sure, Caitlin was not as shapely as this girl, and more cute than attractive in her appearance. Maybe her straight red hair and appearance would be perceived as less attractive to most, but to Kevin, she was perfect.

Raising his sword and pointing it at Satiana, Kevin inquired, "And just who are you supposed to be?"

A strange smile came to Satiana's face as she started walking up to Kevin. "Why, don't you remember me, Kevin, my dear?" she asked with a much lighter tone. Then, she started gently stroking Kevin as she walked around him. "I'm crushed. After all, we've had such great times together that I'm surprised you're not begging for me now."

"What do you mean?" asked Kevin, confused.

There was a slight pause. Then, Satiana started chuckling, much to Kevin's surprise. "You really don't remember, do you?" she asked, almost mocking in her tone. "I guess the drugs you've been on have blacked out your memory." She then laughed, as her tone became more seductive and she gently stroked Kevin's shoulder, "Not to worry, you'll remember me soon enough."

Almost immediately, Kevin shoved Satiana off of him. "Get off of me," he said, as he pointed his sword at her again.

Satiana chuckled. "Now, now, there's no need for that, especially if you don't know me," she said

"I know enough to see you're in with Setadev and his

Enlighteners, which means you're my enemy," Kevin answered confidently. "Don't even try to play games with me."

Rolling her eyes, Satiana snapped, "Oh really? Pretty funny that you say that, coming from someone who..."

"Enough, Satiana," interrupted Setadev, with force in his voice.

Immediately, Satiana silenced herself. She took two steps back.

"So, then, what do you two have to say for yourselves?" Setadev continued to Sayo and Kevin. "General, you could have been the ruler of the world. The people of this world could have been entirely under your command, and you could have been able to see every nation unified under your rule. All that you want this world to be could finally come to be true, and the only rule you would have to serve is mine. Why would you throw that all away?"

Sayo glared at Setadev, making direct eye contact. "I would rather die," he stated.

There was a slight pause. Kevin turned his head toward Sayo, in stun. Then, he turned back to make sure Satiana did not make a move. However, the thought was clearly in his head. Working for a world under Setadev was not what Sayo wanted. That was clear now.

"And what of you, Kevin?" Satiana then asked. "You could have had a life of eternal bliss. You could have had the love that you've always wanted."

Confused, Kevin pulled down his sword slightly, as Satiana started pacing in front of him. "I already have that," he stated boldly. "She happens to be the greatest girl in the world."

"Oh, is that really the case?" Satiana probed. "That's awfully funny considering the things you've told me." As Kevin flinched, Satiana continued, "You see, I know that you have your doubts about your relationship with her. I know you worry that she will not be the right person for you. I know you worry that she will someday believe that you are not the right person for her, and that her relationship with you is just because you showed her how to have emotions. I know that you think about it daily and that you often wonder if she really loves you or not."

Kevin's eyes widened. Somehow, Satiana knew his innermost thoughts. Who was she, and how did she know all of this?

"What a shame that you could not see how the game is played," began Setadev, causing Kevin to spin around. "Our lovely girl Satiana here could have been a great person for you. Do you find her attractive, Kevin?"

Saying nothing, Kevin tightened his grip on his sword. He felt very uncomfortable right now, but could not show it.

Then, Setadev shrugged. "Ah, do not worry about answering, for I already know that you do. She is quite an attractive young woman, is she not? In many ways, I would say the she is the perfect specimen for a human female."

"Get to your point," interrupted Kevin, not wanting to put up with the taunting.

Again, Setadev shook his head. "Very well, then, ignore the thoughts of what you could have had. Unfortunately for you, and for the general, I no longer feel the need to keep you in comfort, just as I no longer need the general or his forces."

Kevin's grip tightened on his sword.

"However, I do have special plans for the two of you," Setadev continued. "You see, pure one, that I did not keep you alive just to torture you by separating you from everyone and everything that you know. Within a few days, I will be completing my rebirth into my actual body, with my full power and the world in my grasp." He then paused and stepped back. "I can honestly say that I do not admire this mock-up of your own form. You are quite fragile, unshapely, and thoroughly imperfect." Then, Setadev ran his hand through his hair, including the grey streak that spanned from the front of his head to his back. "I am actually quite surprised that you and your friend who runs the Solunar Empire could cause such damage to my creation," he continued. "I have decided not to address them because they serve to remind me of what I owe you."

Setadev just made a severe mistake. In his careless comment, he had just implied that he was currently vulnerable. Even if Setadev had some other form he could leap to upon the death of Pseudo, to kill him now would collapse the operation around him and wreck his current plans.

Gently, Kevin kept a grip on his sword but loosened his grip, allowing the tip to rest just above the floor. If he were to get out of this situation, he would need to separate himself from the pinch he was in between Setadev and Satiana, and the Enlighteners they had with them. Kevin heavily doubted he had any chance while caught between two forces in the hallway, essentially between a hammer and an anvil.

There was one chance that he was sure Setadev would not have foreseen. Chances are, it was likely going to hurt. And, Kevin was not going to be able to take Sayo with him. He would have to come back for the general.

Still, it was his only shot.

"Am I boring you?" Setadev then asked pointedly, catching that Kevin's mind was elsewhere. Then, he extended his arm, and channeled some divine power. "Here, please sit down."

Suddenly, a very painful shock came over Kevin and the general. Sayo had fallen completely over and appeared to have been knocked unconscious. Kevin had caught himself and collapsed onto one knee, leaning over his other. His sword was still in his hand, with its tip leaning right across the ground. Time to make some risky decisions.

Stepping closer, Setadev started looking down at Kevin. He then knelt down directly in front of the pure one, and said, "Now, you are going to pay, Kevin Trent Stryker. Put down your sword; you already know that you cannot defeat me, for I am nothing."

Again, Kevin gripped his sword tighter. He did not look up to look into Setadev's eyes.

Setadev shook his head. "What are you going to do, Kevin? Are you going to hit me with your sword?" He stared even harder. "Try me. I dare you. Then, you will see how the game is played."

Kevin glanced up, with a smile on his face. "I think I already do," he said. He swung his sword in a full circle around him as the tip dragged on the ground, cutting through the floor.

Crash! Kevin landed on the hallway below, dirty and in pain from the impact he had just taken. Debris from the chunk of stone floor he had cut through were scattered all around him, and a cloud of dust had kicked up into the air. Though Kevin was mildly injured and was feeling pain, his strategy worked to success, and he chuckled a little bit as he stood up and took off down the hallway. Setadev had anticipated that Kevin would strike him, and although it was tempting to do so, Kevin knew that Setadev was not anticipating an escape attempt by having the floor sliced open using the bright blue magic of the Sword of Purity.

He had to find Caitlin, and he had to find her fast. He was not going to leave this fortress without her.

On the next floor above, Setadev stared down through the hole in his floor. He knew, at that moment, that Kevin had figured out just how vulnerable he was, and instead of striking and being blocked, Kevin had done something he did not anticipate. "Well done, pure one," he finally said as he and Satiana looked through the gap. "So, you finally have seen how the game is played."

Satiana looked over at Setadev. "You're not going to let him get away, are you? I still want to keep my favorite toy."

"Not to worry, Satiana," answered Setadev, as he jumped down through the hole. He then called back up, "The thrill, after all, is in the hunt."

Further down the hall, Kevin was running as fast as he could. Though he was not sure where to go, he had to keep moving. He had to find where Caitlin was in this building. She had to be here somewhere. The more time he spent in the fortress, the more likely he risked recapture, even if Arthur and Rachel were here as the general had implied. He had to move quickly, but he was not going to leave Caitlin behind.

As he kept running, he raised his sword. "Please, if she's in this building, show me the way to her," he pleaded.

The Sword of Purity flashed briefly.

Then, it tugged at Kevin, pulling him forward. Kevin picked up his pace, trying to keep up as best as he could. If there was something that Kevin had always been sure of, it was that he needed to trust his sword. Somehow, it had deep intuition, and if it knew where Caitlin was, Kevin had to follow it.

At a four-way intersection, the sword pulled him to the left. Kevin followed it confidently, hoping he would not run into any Enlighteners on his way. Any delays, any at all, might keep him from getting to her.

The next hallway took him down a flight of stairs and into a large empty room full of crates. Weapons of all types sat around. As Kevin approached the other end of the room, there appeared to have been crates that were knocked around, as though there had been a scuffle here today. Probably not too long ago.

Then, Kevin saw the imprint in the wall that was human-shape.

Memories of being slammed into a pillar by Setadev three months ago resonated through Kevin's mind upon seeing this. He only survived because Setadev did not want to kill him at that moment. This same slam must have been done by Setadev, Kevin reasoned. The shape of the figure in the wall was fairly short, and if anyone was going to survive that blow, that person either must have been spared by Setadev intentionally trying not to kill them, or the person who was shoved into the wall must have been immortal.

Caitlin. The figure was Caitlin's height. Even if she had survived the hit, chances are that she was hurt.

More reason to pursue Setadev after he had time to escape with Caitlin and regroup. No one was going to hurt her while he was around. Why was she even here? Either Setadev captured her too, or she came here in search of him. Maybe she was here to rescue Kevin. He could not put that out of his mind, knowing that she cared so much for him that that was actually quite likely, that he had possibly been the reason she had been captured.

No time to stop and think about it. Down the next flight of stairs Kevin went, continuing to follow his sword. In order to stay ahead of Setadev, if he were pursuing, Kevin had to keep moving. On the next floor, there were more iron doors, much like the floor he had just escaped. If this was a detention level, maybe Caitlin was on this floor.

Next floor was full of hallways again. At the next intersection, the sword pulled him to the left again, and again Kevin followed. There appeared to be another corner at the end of the hall, turning directly left. The sword was glowing brighter, perhaps to indicate that he was almost there.

I'm sorry, Kevin, echoed a voice in Kevin's head.

It was Caitlin's voice! Maybe she was projecting her thoughts in the hopes that he would hear her somewhere in the fortress.

I'm coming, Caitlin, Kevin thought to himself. He was hoping Caitlin could hear him, if she was trying to listen and hear if he was thinking a response.

Then, Kevin reached the corner. When he did, Setadev zapped him with the same power he used to knock Sayo unconscious. This time, Kevin completely fell over, caught off guard. Setadev had been waiting for him here the whole time.

As Kevin's consciousness started to fade, Setadev looked over him and said, "I guess I was wrong. You really do not know how the game is played. Did you not think that I would anticipate you would come after your little girlfriend?" He paused for a moment. "Let that soak in, that it is your fault that you could not save her. Instead, now I will have to implement an even deeper torture for her, when the time is right. For now, however, it is time for us to leave."

From downstairs, the thunder of footsteps roared through the fortress. As Kevin lost his consciousness, he had only one thought: I'm sorry, Caitlin.

Then, he blacked out.

Once the pure one lost consciousness, Setadev created a teleportation gate by blending light and darkness magic in a specific way. Then, he picked Kevin up and took him through. After he proceeded into the energy, the gate collapsed with a loud bang.

Chapter 32

Avoidance Maneuver

"What in the world was that?" asked Arthur, holding up for a moment.

A loud bang had shaken the ceiling above the heads of Arthur, Rachel, and several soldiers of the Solunar Empire. Dust fell from the stone bricks above, as well as down the hall. Something had exploded somewhere in the tower, although where exactly it was, neither was sure.

"Whatever it was, it doesn't sound good," commented Rachel.

"Yeah," nodded Arthur. "Neither is the fact that we haven't ran into any Enlighteners in here yet at all. Something's not right here."

"Agreed," Rachel acknowledged. "We'd better find a set of stairs and check out that loud bang. I have a feeling that has something to do with it."

In agreement, Arthur nodded.

The floor Arthur and Rachel were on was somewhat of a maze. From the door they had entered on the second floor of the tower, they had so far been unsuccessful in figuring out the layout of this building. None of the Solunar Empire soldiers also infiltrating the building had reported back with any locations yet, either. In light of the absence of any Enlighteners and the seemingly instant surrender of any former Desolunar soldiers they were finding, Arthur's troops were conducting a room-by-room search of every space in the tower, looking for Kevin and Caitlin, or any other prisoners in the building.

Nearly three minutes later, a soldier finally reported to Arthur and Rachel that he had found a flight of stairs that seemed promising because it had dust that was stirred up, a sign that someone had been there recently. Not wanting to waste any time, Arthur immediately directed the soldier to gather up some men and begin to canvas the upper floors. Still, as Arthur issued these commands, something seemed strange about the floor he was on. Iron doors were all around, and the corridors seemed quite complex. The building was supposedly over five thousand years old, which meant that it may not have been constructed in typical designs of the current day. Maybe this was a detention level, and not the basement.

A detention level on the second floor, with a door that led to the outside? Granted, that door led to the wall of the building and not directly to the ground, but still, it was a strange construction. Unusual, perhaps, but for what purposes did the Enlighteners use this building over the years?

Or was detention organized completely differently here?

"Damn," cursed Arthur quietly, as he stood in the hallway with Rachel. "What I'd give to have the Sword of Corruption with me right now."

"And why's that?" asked Rachel, as she peeked through the iron bars of the windows in the doors, looking for Kevin and Caitlin.

Arthur shrugged in frustration. "Something feels very wrong about this place. I could really use the weapon, and a magic sword would make me feel best."

Rachel nodded. "That would be nice if Setadev hadn't destroyed it," she answered, as she hurried to the next door and looked.

"Yeah," said Arthur, as he rolled his eyes. Always the skeptic in her tone, he thought to himself. Then again, she was right. No reason to linger on the thought now that his sword no longer existed. Aside from the fact that it was a strong magic sword and might be useful to guide him, Arthur had little reservations about the Sword of Corruption being destroyed. It was another connection to his father that he did not want to think about.

He kept standing still, pondering this as Rachel moved from door to door, looking for any sign of Kevin or Caitlin. Thoughts of his father and of his heritage always seemed to bother the young emperor, who had reluctantly followed in his father's legacy to lead a country that had never been his home before. The Solunar Empire, having given back all of the lands that Desolunar had previously taken, was less than half the size of its predecessor, but it had needed a leader to guide it out of the period of the warring land that it had been.

Wait, what was Arthur doing? Rouge was dying outside, and Resa was doing everything in her power just to keep her sister alive. Kevin and Caitlin were still missing. He could not just stand still, no matter how deep his mental scars were.

Before he could move, however, Rachel called to him. "Arthur! I've found Caitlin!" she screamed.

The sound snapped Arthur out of his funk. Immediately, Arthur started running toward the door.

As quickly as she could, Rachel grabbed the door handle and turned it. The prison cells were unlocked from the outside. When the door opened, however, Rachel and Arthur saw a horrendous sight.

Caitlin had been badly beaten, and was covered in bruises and cuts. Her dress had several tears in it, and was filthy beyond compare. Blood stains were included in the many particles of dirt and debris on the dress. Furthermore, someone had cut Caitlin's hair above her neckline and around her ears, at a level very close to her scalp. Her longer hairs were trimmed above the lower cut, but never came any longer than to the tips of her ears. Rachel knew very well, as Caitlin was her best friend, that she would never cut her hair this short. She sat on the ground, her hands bound and her eyes half open, only semi-conscious from the beating she had taken.

Someone had assaulted her. She could not even turn to see who was looking for her.

Rushing in, Rachel fell to Caitlin's side. "Caitlin, are you okay?" she immediately asked, as she put her hands on Caitlin's arm.

Caitlin was barely able to roll her head to look at Rachel. "I... think... so..." she answered in a weak tone. "I'm... I'm hurt... badly..."

At the door, Arthur let out a loud whistle down the hall. He was signaling for two men who were canvassing a section of the hall further down from where they were. Given Caitlin's heavily weakened state, Arthur needed them to get her out of the building as soon as possible.

"It's going to be okay," said Rachel, trying to keep Caitlin calm. "We're going to get you out of here. Everything's going to be all right."

Leaning up a bit, Caitlin started to hack and wheeze. She was having trouble breathing because of her injuries. Then, she turned her head toward Rachel. "You have to find Kevin," she said, as she coughed again. “Don’t worry about me. He’s here somewhere and he’s in trouble; you have to find him!” She was getting worked up.

“Easy, Caitlin,” said Rachel as she repositioned her hands to settle Caitlin back down. “We have men doing that already. We brought an army out here, and they’re canvassing the building to find him.”

Gently, Caitlin let out her breath. She did not understand a lot of what was happening at this moment, but she was relieved to know that Kevin would be found. “You were right about one thing, Rachel,” she said. “Maybe it was a bad idea for me to try to do this on my own."

As two men entered the room, Rachel said reassuringly, “Yeah, but we all do stupid things for the ones we love.” The men were Solunar Empire soldiers. Working together, they walked in and gently lifted Caitlin by her shoulders. Carefully, they stood her up to carry her. “Let’s get her out of here,” commented Rachel, also helping to lift her up. She then looked toward Arthur. “Can you keep looking for Kevin?”

Arthur nodded. “Already on it,” he said as he nodded and ran off down the hallway. He was gathering up his men and checking their progress on the building search.

With Arthur gone, the two men and Rachel helped to carry Caitlin out of her prison cell. Even though Rachel had ran so fast and so frantically through the tower’s mazelike structure and had forgotten her way back to the wall, the supporting soldiers knew where to go.

Suddenly, the fear of Rouge dying outside came to Rachel’s mind. Only Caitlin’s healing abilities could save her now. Could Rachel really ask the severely beaten girl to save Rouge’s life? Of course, Rachel knew that Caitlin was also a friend to Rouge and her sister Resa, but at the same time Caitlin appeared to have nearly been killed herself. Would she have enough energy left to be able to save Rouge’s life?

They had to move quickly. Outside, Rouge Kirkwood was dying from internal injuries to her chest. “Caitlin,” Rachel began, awkwardly, “I need to ask you for a huge favor. When we make it outside, there is someone that needs your help.”

“Who is it?” Caitlin asked, with a weak tone of voice.

Rachel paused for a second. "It's Rouge," she continued. "We fought hard to capture the fortress wall in order to get here, and Rouge was the first one onto the wall. She lost a fight with an Enlightener and took a hard fire blast to the chest. Resa is doing everything she can out there to keep her sister alive, but she's not strong enough to heal Rouge."

Silently, Caitlin looked aside as she was still being carried down the halls. Rouge was a friend of hers too, and she had been seriously injured. Caitlin wanted to do anything she could to help Rouge, but she knew something very bad that Rachel did not. She took a breath before telling her. "Rachel, I don't have any magic right now," Caitlin informed her friend. "Less than an hour ago, Setadev scratched me with an antite arrowhead and threw me in this cell."

Confused, Rachel looked at Caitlin. "Antite?" she asked.

"Antite," reiterated Caitlin. "Antimage metal, as it's otherwise known. Coming into contact with it can disable a spellcaster's magic for days."

Rachel was stunned. "Wait a minute," she exclaimed, as she kept moving down the hall with Caitlin and the soldiers, "are you saying there's absolutely nothing you can do for her?"

There was a moment's pause. The last thing Caitlin wanted to do was to be the death of Rouge for giving up so easily. She started thinking of any solution possible. Within a minute, a technique her father taught her recently came to mind, but she would have to have some access to magic to use it. Gently, she looked down and tried to energize a bit of magic in her fingertips, but could not. It had not been long enough for her to have a little bit of access to her magic just yet.

Outside, Resa did not have the power to heal her sister. However, Resa might be able to perform the technique to unlock Caitlin's magic. To do so, Caitlin knew, would be to risk her own life, but that was the only answer. Turning back to look at Rachel, Caitlin finally answered, "There might be something I can do. We have to hurry."

Beside her, Rachel nodded confidently. Together, with the soldiers carrying Caitlin, they raced through the halls and out the doors on the second floor. There, Caitlin finally had the chance to see what

Rachel was talking about.

Resa was kneeling over Rouge's body. Medics were currently wrapping her wounds, having applied salve in order to treat her burns. Still, Resa was working very hard to keep casting her healing magic, pressing on no matter how weary she was becoming from the effort. As she kept putting everything she had into keeping Rouge alive, Resa looked up and saw Rachel, with two Solunar Empire soldiers, bringing Caitlin to her.

"Caitlin!" exclaimed Resa.

Carefully, Rachel and the soldiers set Caitlin down. "Hi, Resa," Caitlin said as she came down to her knees. Her voice was very weak.

"You have to help me," Resa began, frantically. "Rouge was hit hard by a magic fireball. I can't heal her. Please, you have to help..."

"Slow down," interrupted Caitlin, as she gently put her hands on Resa's face. Even as defeated as she was, Caitlin was maintaining her composure and control of the situation. "Listen to me very carefully, and very closely. I need your help if you want me to save Rouge."

Resa's eyes locked onto Caitlin's. She was focused and would not say anything, intent on listening to Caitlin in order to save her sister.

Seeing that she had Resa's attention, Caitlin continued, "Now, here is what I need you to do. Are you able to form a spark of magic, half light and half darkness?"

Slightly confused, Resa answered, "Maybe, I think so, but why?"

"I've been in contact with antimage metal within the last hour," answered Caitlin. "There is a technique that can counteract this, but I will need your help. In order to unlock my magic quickly enough for me to save Rouge, I need you to take a spark composed of light and darkness magic, exactly half and half of each, and use internal sight magic to guide you to touch all of the abnormalities within me with the spark directly."

There was a slight pause, as Resa shook her head. "Caitlin, I can't use internal sight magic," she said, deeply worried. "It's not something I'm capable of."

Aside, Caitlin cursed under her breath. Internal sight magic was a very advanced technique, and she remembered in that moment that all of Resa's training in magic had been to be an assassin and was focused on attack and stealth techniques. Then, she straightened herself up, knowing what had to come next despite how much more dangerous it was. "Then we'll do it blindly," she said. "As soon as I have a little bit of magic control, I will try to help guide you."

"I don't know," Resa started shaking, realizing what was being asked of her. "I don't know if I can do this. If I'm off by just a little bit one way, I could paralyze you or kill you. Caitlin, I can't..."

"Yes you can," interrupted Caitlin, moving her hands to Resa's shoulders. "Just trust me, and go slowly."

There was another moment's pause. Then, Resa let out a sigh. "All right," she said. "I'll try." With that, she closed her eyes and created the spark on the end of her fingertips.

Though Caitlin would not tell Resa, she was nervous about doing this as well. Her father had taught her this technique, based on his research after she told him about being scratched by an antite arrow at the Battle of Middle Aurana, but she had never used this technique herself. Now, she was entrusting her life to Resa with this technique, without the aid of internal sight magic, in order to save Resa's sister.

Cautiously, she closed her eyes as well, placing her trust in Resa.

Carefully and slowly, Resa advanced the spark to Caitlin's chest and away from her fingertips, and into her body. She moved very slowly, not wanting to take any chances. Gently, she started where she began, working around in a circle at a slow pace. Resa was nervous to advance in any one direction.

"Stop," Caitlin said quietly, causing Resa to stop moving the spark. "I'm starting to see some of the patches; you must have hit one already and opened up enough for me to use internal sight. Adjust the spark to move upward and to your right just a little bit."

Silently, Resa did as she was told. As she was still working blindly, she continued to move slowly, advancing the spark in the direction Caitlin requested. It took several seconds for her to move it across Caitlin's body, making sure not to hurt Caitlin. All the while, Rouge was slowly dying.

Another minute went by, as Resa worked in a circle around the next spot. "Excellent," said Caitlin, as she felt the abnormality disappear. "One more to go; head straight for your left. Move quicker this time, because we don't have much longer we can leave Rouge like this."

Responding as she was told, Resa slid the spark to her left, going for the last spot. She trusted Caitlin and moved faster, although not too fast. There, she began working the spark again, using all of the mental concentration she had left to alleviate Caitlin's magic block.

She worked at it for another couple of minutes, in silence.

Suddenly, Caitlin started demanding, "Dissipate it! Dissipate it!"

Resa did as she was instructed. As she did, Caitlin opened her eyes and positioned her hands above Rouge's body, releasing a large swath of light magic. It was healing magic.

Immediately, from a short distance away, Rachel could see the power of her best friend and just how much difference the energy that Caitlin could use when compared to Resa. Before, when Resa had been trying to keep patching up her sister, the appearance of light magic appeared to be directly under her hands and very dimly lit. Caitlin's magic, however, spread farther than the width of her hands and glowed much brighter, indicating the amount of energy she was capable of using in her healing spells.

Several more tense minutes passed, as Caitlin continued to work on healing Rouge. Though their friendship had initially started very roughly with Rouge trying to kill her, Caitlin and Rouge were now friends as well, as was Resa. Each would die for the other if need be. For now, though, the battle was about preventing death, so that Rouge may live to fight another day.

Another minute passed. Resa kept watching on in agony, nibbling at her fingernails in anxiety. What was going on? Only Caitlin really knew, as she used whatever energy she had to continue working.

Then, the glow faded from Caitlin's hands. She fell back onto her heels, letting out a deep breath. "Rouge will be okay," she said weakly. "You did good work, Resa. You kept her alive and kept her from bleeding out long enough that this would work. She needs to rest now."

In excitement, Resa leaped over and gave Caitlin a big hug.

"Hey, easy now!" interrupted Rachel, as she walked over to Caitlin and Resa. "Caitlin's not in such great shape herself."

Caitlin looked over to Rachel. "It's okay, Rachel. Let her have her moment," she said.

From behind her, a voice said, "I don't think that's a good idea."

Everyone turned, including the Solunar Empire soldiers, to see the emperor standing nearby. He had just exited the fortress.

Rachel looked at him for a second. "What's going on?" she asked.

Arthur shook his head. "Nothing good," he answered. "Do you want the bad news or the even worse news first?"

"Might as well start with the bad news," Rachel muttered, in her normal cynical voice.

"This is serious, Rachel," Arthur responded, hearing Rachel. "The men have canvassed the fortress, but there's no sign of Kevin anywhere. In fact, there's no sign of Setadev, General Sayo, or any of the Enlighteners either. It's almost as though the soldiers we engaged out here were defending an empty fortress."

Rachel's eyes widened. "How can that be?" she asked. "Caitlin was here. We saw Setadev and we know that he was here, and we also defeated at least one Enlightener and know they were here. Where could they have gone?"

"Who knows," Arthur answered. "There's nothing here, either, to say whether or not Kevin was here."

Letting out a sigh, Rachel said, "Well, at least it could be worse. At least Caitlin's all right, and Rouge will be, too. Tonight we can keep searching the building for clues as to where they have gone, and we can spend the night here and rest without being spotted in Nuve."

"And that's the even worse news," said Arthur. "It looks like before he left, Setadev sabotaged the building's structural integrity. Our engineer predicts that the fortress will collapse in on itself in the next few hours, which means it's unsafe to occupy."

Stunned, Rachel shook her head. "Why the hell would he do that? This fortress has stood for five thousand years, and now he wants to destroy it?"

"I wish I knew," answered Arthur. "I would guess it's because he doesn't want us to find out what he's up to and what he and Sayo have planned for Kevin."

"But here's the thing," countered Rachel. "With his troops and his Enlighteners, it's actually pretty likely that he had the upper hand on us, even once we did get onto the wall. Why execute an avoidance maneuver and delay us instead of fighting back and destroying us?"

Arthur shook his head. "Only thing I can figure is that there's something here that we're missing."

"We know he's vulnerable, even if he's still mighty," added Resa, still on her knees by her sister's side. "Maybe he's not as strong as we think he is, or perhaps he does not have nearly the control over his force that we think he does."

Briefly, Arthur considered this. "It could be possible, but there is a way to know for sure," he said. Then, he looked behind him, saw one of his generals, and commanded, "General, fetch Lieutenant Desoto from the surrendering forces for me. I have some questions to ask him."

The general saluted and turned and walked away, doing as he was instructed.

From a short distance away by Rouge's body, Caitlin said weakly, "There is another possibility." As she started, Arthur and Rachel turned toward her and walked over. Caitlin continued, "While I was working my way up that tower, I found a very large room full of supply crates. A lot of these looked like weapons and food crates, enough to fuel an entire army. The thing is, though, that these crates weren't Desolunar crates. They were labeled as Nuve crates."

Rachel leaned down next to Caitlin. "They've been stealing from Nuve?"

"Sure looks that way," answered Caitlin. "He had all of the supplies his forces could need. They were stored on the next floor above where I was being kept." She paused for a moment. "I had a fight with General Sayo in that room. He would have gone down, had Setadev not intervened."

"Is Setadev the one who injured you?" asked Rachel.

Caitlin turned her head toward Rachel. "He nearly killed me," she answered. "I think he still has that power, and he would have had you guys not knocked on the door out here and distracted him."

Rachel was shocked. "He nearly killed you?" she asked. "You're sure?"

Exhausted, Caitlin nodded. "I'm sure," she said. "I'm not sure if he would have wanted to kill me, but he at least made it clear he could if he wanted. He charged something in his fingertips with the intent of slamming it into my head. It didn't look like any magic I know of, though. I think it was raw divine power."

At this point, however, Caitlin and Rachel were interrupted by Arthur briefly shushing them. Lieutenant Desoto had been brought into Arthur's presence, and for the moment Arthur's question to him would take precedence.

Arriving in front of the emperor, Lieutenant Desoto knelt down and bowed his head. "You have called for me, my emperor?" asked the lieutenant.

"Indeed," nodded Arthur. "I want to ask you a few questions. Be honest with me, for I know now that there are no troops inside that building. Why is it that you and your men surrendered to us so easily?"

Lieutenant Desoto let out a sigh. "If I may be honest," he answered, "though not everyone in our forces were willing to comply with this order, we were given the order to surrender. Those that engaged were the ones that were not willing to simply give up."

"And who gave that order? Pseudo?" asked Arthur.

The lieutenant shook his head. "No, it was General Sayo," he answered. "The general gave this order to his lieutenants directly, and in confidence. He would not say why, but he made it very clear that we had to do this. He told us it was likely that he would not make it out alive, but that he would try to join us after he did something."

Arthur was confused. "And did the general say what that something was?" he asked.

In response, the lieutenant lowered his head. "He did not say. He only said that it would be for the better of all of us and our families."

The emperor let out a sigh. Why would General Sayo tell his men to surrender? Clearly some of them had not heeded the order, which would only be natural given the bizarre circumstances. Given the lack of Enlighteners present and the one that attacked and nearly killed Rouge, the general must not have had command over them. Perhaps Sayo was not truly Setadev's right-hand man.

Maybe Sayo had had second thoughts about this whole ordeal and decided to give up his goal of restoring Desolunar. This was not a completely ridiculous idea given that Sayo himself was not a native of Desolunar, and was an Auranian from the city of Atwals who had joined under the banner of Demonicus after his hometown was captured. And if Setadev had known about this and found out that Sayo had second thoughts, it would explain why Sayo guessed that he may not make it out alive, if the lieutenant was to be believed. That in itself, however, was also reason for the general to continue his pursuit given the fall of Demonicus, and the timing made little sense after the attack on the Metoi and the retreat to the Fortress of Da Leval. Certainly as well did the risks of following Setadev outweigh the rewards, especially since Sayo likely wouldn't know that Setadev was a fallen god with the history he had. To him, Setadev would merely be Pseudo, a powerful general of Desolunar who was a look alike for Kevin Trent Stryker with a few cosmetic defects.

Perhaps it was another trick Sayo and Setadev had up their sleeves. Wherever they and the Enlighteners had gone, they had taken Kevin with them and sabotaged the fortress. With the supports in the basement severely weakened, it would only be a few hours at most until the core of the building collapsed on itself.

What was the plan here? What was really going on?

With that, Arthur politely dismissed the lieutenant and thanked him for his information. For now, there was no more that could be done here. With the fortress collapsing and no leads on where to go next, the only move was to retreat, rest the men, and regroup his forces. After days of long marches to reach Leticon, his forces needed to be rested.

Knowing this, Arthur gave the order for his men to fall back from the fortress. There, they would set up camp for the evening. Where they would go next, however, Arthur was not sure. His only hope was that Caitlin knew a little bit more about Setadev's plan and could say more once she had rested.

After he had given the order, Arthur walked over to Caitlin to help her up, along with Rachel. Resa joined with two other soldiers to carefully lift her sister and take her down the wall. As they walked over to the wall's edge, Arthur looked over to see all of the soldiers moving. They were regrouping and reassembling their formation to prepare for the retreat. It would take a little while until they were ready.

Then, all of the motion below stopped. Everyone froze in place.

Surprised, Arthur turned his head. All of his men on the wall were frozen in place, too. In fact, it seemed like only he, Rachel, and Caitlin were aware of what was going on.

"What the hell happened here?" screamed a voice from the ground.

Arthur leaned over and saw some familiar faces moving through the still crowd. "I might ask the same question, professor," he answered. "What's with all of this?"

Looking up, Professor Magnon stepped in front of Kronius, Necnea, and Vincent Stryker, and answered, "This is a time stop, courtesy of Necnea. What are you and your men doing at this fortress?"

Without hesitation, Arthur responded, "Come up here and I'll explain. There's someone up here who I think you'll want to see."

Responding to this, the professor turned and nodded to Necnea, who was using her power to maintain the time stop. Then, the professor jumped into the air, using his divine power to fly up and onto the wall. There, he saw as Arthur and Rachel were supporting his daughter, who had been very badly beaten.

Stunned, the professor reached out to hold his daughter, who collapsed into his arms. She simply had no more energy left. Carefully, the professor knelt down while holding Caitlin, getting her back down to the ground, as Caitlin lost consciousness. Then, he glared up at Arthur and Rachel while kneeling, and said, in a stern tone, "Explain."

Almost too nerved by the professor's fear-invoking attitude, Arthur had trouble making any words come out of his mouth. He understood the professor's demeanor, however; he loved his daughter greatly and seeing her in such a shape had hurt him deeply. With himself unable to speak, Arthur motioned to Rachel, who nervously began to explain, "We were out here in pursuit of General Sayo, following a tip given to us by Demonicus on where this force that attacked us, the 'remnant of the fallen', would have ran. We arrived today, but instead were greeted by Setadev, who informed us that both Kevin and Caitlin were taken prisoner here."

"You let her go off on her own without any escort?" asked the professor angrily.

Rachel was shaking, but she stepped forward. "She told us that her search for Kevin was something that she had to do on her own. She was headed for the Wastes, and we trusted her safety there because the Toronaga and the Metoi in the west would protect her, and only the Aequina further in could be any threat."

Seeing Rachel so nervous and feeling the same himself, Arthur said, "It was my decision to let her go on her own as she wished, and after finding out from Demonicus about this fortress, we came here to put a stop to the general and the Enlighteners."

There was a long pause. The sound of steps on a ladder echoed through the air as Vincent Stryker was using one to scale the wall. Then, the professor sighed. "As I figured she might desire," he said. "And what happened? Your men are in a retreat, but at a calm pace."

"Where is my son?" came a voice from the edge of the wall. It was Vincent Stryker, the legendary original pure one himself, dressed in his old, tattered, and faded Scurnian uniform from his war days. As he made it to the top, he hopped over the battlements and ran over to the professor's side.

At the same time, Kronius and Necnea each flew up the wall to join their companions. Arthur gave a brief wave to Kronius in recognition, and Kronius returned the wave. Now was not the time for catching up, though. As he and Professor Magnon were working together on the same side, Arthur knew it was vital to tell the professor everything.

"When we arrived, we set up a ram and started to work on the front gate," Arthur began. "As we did, Setadev made his presence known at the top of the wall, at which point he took and destroyed the Sword of Corruption that I kept on my belt. We exchanged words and taunts briefly, but instead of taking part in the defense itself, he went back into the fortress. At this point, seeing the number of old Desolunar troops on the wall, I called out loud enough to inform all of them that if they surrendered, I would take them home for them to reunite with their families and hold no punishment to them."

"A noble proposition indeed," interrupted Kronius. "You must make for an excellent leader of your people."

Arthur only nodded, himself a doubter of that principle. In his serious state, no witty sarcasm came to mind. He continued, "After that, we advanced the ram for another attack on the gate, but the archers on the wall proceeded to fire back at us. I will say this, though; the rain of arrows that resulted was certainly lighter than I would have expected. Without the high ground, though, the ram attack was faltering after an Enlightener made an appearance and shot fire at our unit. So, we began a siege ladder assault, and Rouge led it with the goal of taking out the Enlightener. Within about fifteen minutes we had the wall, but at a terrible cost: Rouge was severely injured in the attack, and nearly killed."

"Is she all right?" asked Necnea, in her usual sense of concern.

Rachel answered, "She will be okay." Then, Rachel looked over to the professor. "She's still alive thanks to your daughter. After we captured the wall, we saw a door on this level and breached it. Inside, we began our search and found Caitlin in a locked cell, in the condition she is in now, but conscious. Immediately, we escorted her out and brought her out here to heal Rouge, which she did marvelously."

"And yet now they're both unconscious," added the professor, as he held his daughter. "After the beating she took, I am surprised that Caitlin had the energy to perform such drastic healing measures on what could have easily been a fatal injury." He glanced over to Rouge, who was frozen solid by the time stop, along with her sister Resa and two other men carrying her body. "I would not be surprised if it is some time before either of them wake. Even in the course of healing magic, such severe injuries often require much rest which magic cannot provide."

Briefly looking around again for a second, Rachel asked, "Was freezing Rouge and Resa really necessary? They know about you guys and who you are."

Necnea shrugged, as her face started to show signs of struggle.

"I did not have time to try and find and separate them out in this time stop," she answered. "Now, can we move this along, please? I will not be able to hold time in place for very much longer."

"And what of my son?" Vincent then asked again, with desperation starting to show in her voice. "Where is he?"

"He's not here," answered Arthur.

Vincent Stryker looked down. He was upset. "Then what happened to him?" he asked.

Silently, Arthur took a breath. Then, he continued, "I wish I knew, Mr. Stryker. When we searched the building, we found it completely empty. No Setadev, no General Sayo, no Kevin, and no soldiers or Enlighteners at all. In fact, it seemed deserted altogether, except that the pillars in the basement have been sabotaged and this building will likely collapse in a few hours."

Unhappy, the professor shook his head. "So, Setadev has skirted off and taken the pure one with him. Whatever it was that he was planning here, he has done his best to make sure we will not find out."

"Except he missed something," said Rachel, as she stepped forward again. "Caitlin mentioned just a few minutes ago that while on her way through the fortress herself, she saw a large number of crates, which were labeled as being from Nuve."

Hearing this, Vincent Stryker cursed under his breath. "That explains where the supplies the Enlighteners stole from Cornelia went to," he said. "Wherever Setadev and his Enlighteners ran, that must also be where the stolen supplies are."

"The question then is, where?" asked the professor. "I have not the answer to this one. From tracing the supply lines and the Enlighteners from the Shadows to Arthur's leads from Demonicus, everything we had led to this fortress. It would seem, however, that we have somehow fallen for a decoy. The men were real, the forces were real, and the supplies were real, but the intention to use this place was false."

"I have to wonder what Caitlin saw in her travels, then," commented Rachel. "She never did manage to catch us up on everything that she found on her way to finding Kevin."

There was a sigh. “Likely no more than we did,” answered Necnea, who had been the one to sigh. “If I know anything about Setadev, it is that he does not leave loose ends on anything. He ensures that everything is complete.”

“Well, what else could we be missing?” asked Kronius.

A silent minute passed. Necnea winced, signaling that she was very close to being unable to control the time stop anymore. Then, Rachel said it. “Wait a minute, why are we approaching this whole thing backwards?” she asked.

Kronius was confused. “How do you mean, Arthur?” he asked.

“Think about it,” answered Rachel. “We came out here looking to stop Setadev in order to stop a revenge plot on Kevin and to bring General Sayo to justice for the attacks on the Metoi village. What we haven’t even really considered, though, is what is Setadev up to? We know he is weakened in his current form; should we not be focusing on that and on what he’s doing to fix that? And, frankly, if he just wanted revenge on Kevin, why keep him alive? Why not just kill him and have that be the end of it?”

Another silent second passed. “Very wise,” commented the professor. “Rachel, Prime Minister of the Solunar Empire, you are quite the bright one, indeed.”

Rachel blushed briefly at the compliment.

“Can we be sure Kevin *is* still alive?” asked Kronius. “I very much know Kevin to be resilient and would hope he would find a way to stay alive, but in the face of our enemy, I do not know.”

Almost immediately, Necnea shot that down. “He almost certainly would have taunted us if that were the case,” she said. “Setadev celebrates his victories. He would not let us go without knowing if he accomplished that.”

Silently, Kronius nodded. That made sense. It also reassured Arthur and Rachel, who were worried by the thought for a moment.

“We must find out how Setadev plans to revive himself,” the professor continued. “In some way, he knows how to bring back his full body and his full form, but how that is possible even I am not certain. I am sure, however, that he has been planning this for some time now and knows exactly what he is doing.” The professor paused for a moment. "I would imagine he would need to find a way to intersect his body with a powerful source of immortal energy without killing himself, and become one with the energy."

From his pocket, Vincent pulled out a folded piece of paper. "Might this have some bearing on it?" he asked. He then read it aloud, "A source of power has emerged, a powerful gate from the seven powers' disintegrated fate. Another dimension is open somewhere, and if he crosses the rift, all will despair. Ancient weapons are all abound; he knows them all, and will search 'til they're found. Those who watch from above, overhead, will not be able to rest in their beds once the truths of all are revealed, and the Great Conqueror returns completely healed." It was an excerpt from the second poem of the *Letters to the Adventurer* by Clavius Lekion Stryker Dominous.

"Is that some kind of prophecy?" asked Rachel. "It's an interesting-sounding poem."

Necnea answered Rachel. "The professor and I differ on this. I believe it may be, but the professor dismisses the notions of prophecy altogether."

"Even if it were not, could that be it?" continued Vincent. He looked at the professor. "Perhaps your theories on dimensional space theory that you proposed in *Stratagems* are not so farfetched after all."

The professor appeared deep in thought. "A rift where dimensions twist could be the way Setadev could merge himself with more immortal energy, given the absence of the Seven Stripes, particularly the Stripe of Life. But we have not yet seen evidence that Setadev has such a dimensional gate." He paused for a second, and then speculated, "It could, however, be possible that all of the material acquisition Setadev has done is in service of locating and protecting a gate."

"But where would he have gone?" asked Arthur.

Rachel sighed, an unpleasant thought coming to her mind. "Does anyone know if Setadev has teleportation magic?"

There was a slight pause. Then, Kronius nodded. "Likely so," he said. "If that is the case, then he and his men could be anywhere by now. It would explain how everyone disappeared, especially if he had all of this planned out. The only problem with that is that means he could be anywhere by now, whether near or far."

Arthur was frustrated. Had he brought his men out here and violated the boundaries of another nation only to come away empty handed without even so much as a lead as to where to pursue Setadev and General Sayo? Though few lives were lost in the quick battle, were the men who had taken injury here really worth the reward? Setadev and the general were still free to wreak havoc on the Solunar Empire as they wished.

He looked down at Caitlin, who was still unconscious. She had paid the cost of falling for the decoy, too, and also came away with nothing. What had seemed like an easy victory and the capture of the Enlighteners' fortress was actually a defeat, and a chance for Setadev to escape and continue his plans without any pursuit following him. Now, Arthur had to be careful. His men were a long way away from home, in foreign territory, and were tired from days of marching. He had to make sure his men would survive their rest before returning home and hope no one attacked them. Worse yet, the empire was without its leader for the time being. He and his men had to return home.

Suddenly, there was a slight flinch from everyone around. Necnea was losing her grip on the time stop. Seeing this, the professor said, "There is little more we can do without a new lead. The gods and I will return to the Realm of the Angels and assist Lord Ralios Larion in his search through the library there. Hopefully we may be able to find something on what Setadev could be looking for, and where it would be."

Arthur nodded. "Then we shall return to Seta Archa to regroup," he answered. "The sooner we are out of Leticon, the better. In the meantime, we will continue to seek leads to Kevin and see if we can find him."

"Very well," nodded the professor. "If that is the case, then you will undoubtedly pursue Setadev and General Sayo if you do find such a lead." He looked briefly at his daughter, stood her up, and placed her back in Arthur and Rachel's arms. "I ask that you take care of her too while you are gone. If you do pursue Setadev, then you will need her in order to stand a chance of surviving, and you are already aware that though you are Kevin's best friend, no one wants to rescue him more than Caitlin does."

Without hesitation, Arthur nodded. "I am aware," he said. "Thank you for placing your trust in me, and in Rachel as well."

Rachel looked at Arthur and gave a nod as well. She was glad to be trusted with this.

Then, Vincent Stryker looked toward the professor. "I think I would like to go with them," he said. "I won't be much help in the Realm of the Angels, but I can help them down here."

The professor turned to see Arthur and Rachel both nodding in agreement. Vincent Stryker was a legendary general and an excellent military strategist, in addition to being Kevin's father. Beside him, Kronius and Necnea also agreed, knowing that that was likely the smarter move to take advantage of Vincent's talents.

Then, the professor looked straight at Arthur. "Then let it be so," he said. He then turned to look at Vincent. "It will appear awfully suspicious if you just showed up here during a time stop, or were anywhere near here. Therefore, I think it best if we dropped you off near Cardol and had Arthur's retreating forces pick you up there."

"Agreed," nodded Vincent Stryker. "While I wait, I can continue to search Cardol for any hints, for which we did not have time before."

Again, the professor nodded, as Kronius and Necnea grabbed Vincent Stryker by his arms and prepared to lift him. "Arthur Falchor and Rachel Reinhart, take good care of my daughter for me." Then, he and the gods lifted into the air, taking Vincent with them. "Until we shall meet again, take care."

In an instant, the gods were gone. The time flow began to resume, and everyone started moving again. The professor was actually not so confident, Arthur realized to himself. As a matter of fact, neither was he.

It would be a long way back to Seta Archa, and a dangerous trip.

Chapter 33

The Elegant Land

To the east of the Solunar Empire and Nuve, and to the south of Scurnia, was the kingdom of Gardolk. Known as “the elegant land”, Gardolk had been ruled by Queen Mildred for the past few years, and during her rule, a land that had formerly seen much conflict with its northern neighbor had finally progressed toward peace and prosperity.

Much of Gardolk was lush, as the land sloped lower and lower as one continued to the southeast. The Calphos and Grandiose Rivers supplied much health to the land, which grew food that could not be found anywhere else in the world. Also supplying a unique flair to the cuisines from Gardolk was the Great Sea at the very southeast of the kingdom, which hauled in a great deal of fish that could not be found in the rivers of the inland kingdoms. Added to these trades were tracts of precious metal reserves to be found in the mines at the western edge of the kingdom. The southeastern region of the Peaked Mountains was much thinner across than the range further north, but on the Gardolk side of these mountains, gold and silver had been discovered in several areas. Likewise, ancient artifacts from past civilizations were also to be found in the western end of the kingdom.

All of these made Gardolk the most elegant of the world’s kingdoms. Their isolationist policies on external affairs added to this by keeping the kingdom out of the business of the rest of the world. Save for war with Scurnia over the northern border of Gardolk, the elegant land had seen little war in its history.

In fact, Gardolk’s superstate kingdom was established in peaceful settings, as well. Nearly twenty smaller kingdoms in the southeast region of the world joined together by the power of the Contract of Gardolk, named for the city of Gardolkia where it was written up. Together they unified under a single monarchy, which remained intact to the present day. Their unified flag was purple as a background, with straight lines of gold creating a flag five squares wide by four squares high, representing the twenty kingdoms.

In the same vein of Gardolk's diverse origins, the regions of Gardolk varied quite a bit based on their heritage, and twenty regional houses existed which represented the twenty Royal Families. Divided into twenty provinces, each local government was named for and ran by one of the Royal Families, with one house also controlling the crown. Periodically, when succession was in dispute, rulership of the country would pass to another house, and the current ruling family was of the province of Renaud, in east-central Gardolk. Culturally, those of the northern edge of Gardolk were a harder-edged people whose culture was quite similar to the roughneck lifestyles of Scurnia with a distinctive flare of elegance, while the southwest was a very distinctive region altogether with some of the oldest cultural traits in the mortal realm. The southeast, however, was the heart of Gardolk.

The twin cities of Gardolkia and Beralinchi accounted for more than two-thirds of the kingdom's population. Between the center of Gardolkia—at the delta where the Grandiose River merged into the Calphos River—and the edge of Beralinchi where the Calphos fed into the Great Sea at Gardolk's southeast corner, there was little to tell where one city ended and another began. Perhaps the only notable differences in the metroplex were that there were two city centers—one at the Grandiose River delta and one at the Calphos River delta with the sea. These belonged to Gardolkia and Beralinchi, respectively. As the metroplex expanded, small towns and village were absorbed into the new metropolitan area, forming a few minor suburbs and neighborhoods with their own names.

In their origins, Gardolkia and Beralinchi had started as two separate city-states. Over time, these cities developed into full kingdoms. After the signing of the Contract of Gardolk, Gardolkia became a hotspot when it was established as the capital of the new nation, attracting many new citizens and becoming a renaissance area of sorts. When the Royal Palace burned down a few hundred years ago after being struck by lightning, a new one was constructed in Beralinchi where there was much more room for construction and a view of the Great Sea. Likewise, citizens and businesses moved with the palace to their new capital city; however, Gardolkia was not abandoned or left to rot. The latter remained a flourishing city of innovation, and as more citizens came to the area, the distance between the two cities began to disappear. Now, no distance was left.

The Calphos River ran through the center of the entire metroplex on its slow trek to the Great Sea. By this point, it had already collected the waters of the Aurun and Grandiose Rivers, as well as the tributary that ran through Nuve's Abyss of the Royal Sovereign via the Rhonean River. This made Gardolkia and Beralinchi popular trade cities for rare goods and wares from nearly every known corner of the mortal realm. The entire business made trade the driving force behind the economy of Gardolk's two largest cities, and added to their abundant natural resources to make the land one of the wealthiest in the world.

The fact that they were an isolationist nation, however, made for some difficulty for outsiders. Though the passage of the Calphos River through the Peaked Mountains allowed for some transit and communication between Gardolk and lands to the west, the fact that the river on the other side of the mountains ran through Leticon Province and just north of the Wastes kept all but fast-moving traders out of Gardolk. Likewise, the rough plateau of Scurnia and war with that nation over the ill-defined border kept many from Gardolk from associating with Scurnians.

Perhaps the most isolating feature of Gardolk, however, was the predominating attitude of elegance also made many in Gardolk pretentious. The entire concept of Gardolk being known as "the elegant land" came from the culture they had built in one of the civilized world's most lush areas and the wealth that had come to the royal families as a result. All twenty of the royal families lived very well off and firmly believed in the superiority of their people to others, and influenced their citizens to hold the same beliefs. For the citizens of the metroplex, however, pretension and elegance were merely an afterthought. They were simply looking to make the best of their lives.

Along the Calphos River just northwest of Gardolkia, a boat had arrived at a warehouse. It was a typical wooden supply transport boat built specifically for travel on the river, and would carry up to two people and a fair amount of cargo. This particular boat's cargo had been covered by a cloth. It was parked at a dock for unloading cargo that would be taken further inland.

As soon as the boat was tied to a stake on the riverbank, two men were instructed by their supervisor in the warehouse to begin unloading it. Desiring to be paid and have money to take home to their families, the two men proceeded outside to begin unloading the boat. Their first step would be to secure the boat by its other side and tie it to the riverbank as well; then, they would be able to unload the boat's cargo without risk of it moving.

"You want to steer the boat while I get the tie line ready?" asked the first worker.

The second worker nodded, and then took a step onto the boat with a pole in hand. He planned to plant it in the riverbed and push off of it to bring the boat's end to the shore. As he walked onto the boat, he made a passing comment. "So, I heard there was some attack over in the wastelands across the mountains a few weeks ago. Supposedly there might be some civil war breaking out over there."

"Yeah, I heard about that," responded the first worker. "Guess the 'Solunar Empire', or whatever it's called now, ain't so strong. Figures, you overthrow one dictator, and whatever's remaining can't even stand on its own two feet just because one person is gone."

Pushing on the planted pole to get the other end of the boat into position, the second worker answered, "I guess. I thought their new emperor was supposed to be the son of the dictator, or something like that. Wonder how they let that fly."

"Meh, people are like that," said the first worker. "They'll take every hit from someone and choose not to learn their lesson. It's kind of all over the place, from as far away as Aurana all the way here to Gardolk. People just don't stand up for themselves and say that enough is enough. Instead, they still bring about those who have hurt them before, and keep wanting more."

"I ain't so sure about that," interrupted the second worker, as he continued to push the boat's end to the first worker. "Then again, I've never been a political man."

The first worker chuckled, as the boat's end came close enough for him to grab it. He started to tie it off, as he responded, "Which of us has? Politics are all for those who claim to have power. We the people are just so stupid to believe it that we let them have it." He paused for a second, as he checked his knots. "'Course, we don't have too much of that to worry about here in Gardolk. The current house has been ruling for a couple of generations now, and look at Beralinchi. We're doing okay in money and making honest livings. Now, there's no war, either."

"Still a huge city, though," commented the second worker. "Lot of problems here too."

"Hey!" interjected the first worker. "It's no different than any other metropolis." He finished tying off the boat. "Now, give me a hand with that cloth," he continued.

The second worker, not wanting to discuss politics any more, said nothing but took a position on one side of the cloth. The first worker did the same on the other side, and together they flipped a side of the cloth over on top of the cargo, revealing what was underneath. Several large crates were stacked together, at least a dozen. On each crate, the word "Nuve" was stamped in large letters. The next side of one of the crates read "Property of the Nuve government. If found unsecured, please return to the nearest government office."

The eyes of the first worker widened. "Hey Tony, you'd better get John out here," he said. "I ain't touching this stuff until we find out what the hell is in these things."

Nodding in full agreement, Tony, the second worker, ran toward the warehouse. He was gone for several minutes, until he returned with an older man. This was the supervisor at the warehouse, who was responsible for all unloading and operations of the facility. His hair was gray and he wore a beard, a sign of his age and experience.

"Mark, what do you have for me?" the supervisor asked.

Mark, the first worker, shook his head. "Take a look for yourself, John," he answered, as John walked up toward the crates. "These are Nuve government crates. I ain't touching these until I know what's inside them."

"Did you read the manifest?" asked John.

Looking aside, Mark scoffed. "You don't need to read the manifest to know this is bad news, John. I can all but guarantee you this is illegal cargo aboard this boat. If we unload it, we're contributing to illegal activity, and I ain't going to be a part of that." He paused for a second. "You can't get a hold of these even with a prosperous civilian business. Only the Nuve government can legally hold these crates, which means that these are stolen."

Sighing, John reached over to the cloth and pulled the boat's manifest out of a pocket. He unfolded it and began to read it over. Within a minute, he said, "These are medical supplies, Mark. Says they're for transport up north as part of Nuve's relief assistance for Tron, to help in the aftermath of the war with Scurnia. The boat driver and his accompanying representative also mentioned they were emissaries of Nuve."

"Yeah, well, you know something?" asked Mark. "I still ain't unloading this boat. I don't believe that their manifest is right, not with these crates."

John rolled his eyes and shook his head. "Do you want me to grab the boat drivers and ask them what's in the crates?"

"No, I want you to open these and prove that I'm right," Mark snapped back. "This just ain't even right, and you know it, John. I guarantee you that if we open these crates, we'll find weapons or military supplies, or something of that sort."

There was a pause, before John answered, "You're full of it, Mark." He then turned to Tony. "Start unloading this boat."

"Tony, you'd better not unload the cargo," Mark snapped. "If you do, we're all in serious trouble."

"Hey! What's going on out here?" yelled a voice from behind the three men.

John, Tony, and Mark turned to see two men watching them. They were dressed in red hooded robes, with their hoods up. Little else was visible except that each one was wearing a necklace with what appeared to be a gold tag hanging at the end. After another pause, one of the two men continued, "Gentlemen, why is our cargo not being unloaded? We have provided our official manifest and have explained our destination and intent. This is more than what is necessary to have a boat unloaded."

Glaring at Mark, John continued, "He's right. Now, get this

boat unloaded."

Mark stared coldly at John. "No," he said.

"Do it or you're fired," responded John.

With this, Mark stared back at John for a moment. Then, he threw his hands in the air and stepped off the boat. He began walking back toward the warehouse.

"Hey, where do you think you're going?" asked John.

"I quit!" interjected Mark. He kept walking away.

John sighed. He was not going to stop Mark from quitting. However, Mark had been one of his best workers for years. Clearly he was quite upset by this whole situation, and understandably so, but John was not going to lose business just because the crates were official Nuve government crates. The manifest documents checked out, and that was all he was legally obligated to check.

He turned to Tony. "Go ahead and unload the boat."

Not wanting to be fired, Tony proceeded to begin unloading the boat.

As Tony began to work, John approached the two men in hoods. "My apologies, gentlemen," he said. "It's quite unusual that we have that sort of thing with one of our workers. We will have your cargo unloaded and ready for you to transport very shortly."

"Thank you," nodded one of the men. "We are on a tight time schedule, so please have it ready for us as soon as possible."

John nodded, and then walked away. Such was typical of business in the elegant land.

After John walked away, the other of the two men pulled down his hood and pulled out a map. He unfolded it to reveal a map of Gardolk. On it was a thick red line, with one end at the Calphos River in Beralinchi. The other end did not stretch north to the border. It went west, across the heart of Gardolk, all the way to the Peaked Mountains.

"We must make haste," he said. "Master Pseudo is waiting for us at the mountain."

Chapter 34

Designs

Within Angel Tower, the sole building within the Realm of the Angels, rested the largest library in the known universe. For the past five thousand years, the gods had been collecting written works to form a gigantic database of information, fiction, prophecy, and lore. In addition, they contributed their own works from their years of study.

The gods were very devoted individuals when it came to study and research. Since the early days of Vinz Larinion, the major philosophy of the gods was one of minimal interference in the mortal realm. Contrary to the desires and beliefs of Setadev, who sought total conquest and the formation of a utopia, Vinz Larinion maintained a firm dogmatic view of neutrality and non-interference when it came to the affairs of the mortal. He dictated that to interfere with the mortal would be to keep them from being able to stand on their own, and their eventual reliance on the immortal would lead to social decay and the end of human advancement. Therefore, the gods as they were should interfere at a minimum at most and should never reveal themselves as immortals in front of the mortal. For the gods, this was a tough edict to begin, as all of the original deities began as mortal humans themselves, but such eventually became their mantra universally. It became one of their core values.

As a result, Vinz Larinion dedicated the work of the immortals, who would otherwise have a lot of time on their hands, to lives of study. The gods would work hard on learning of all subjects, from literature to mathematics, from technology and the sciences to humanities and the arts, from swordplay and archery to magic and experiments with divine power. This was their devotion, and in the last five thousand years, it had been the never-ending task of the gods.

However, the gods had long suspected that they were not the first immortals ever to exist. While they had in many ways taken on the role of the "nameless ones" in modern religion, and stories left behind of them inspired anonymous polytheism which much of the mortal realm now observed, they were far from the only immortals in lore. One such figure in lore was that of the Great One, a mighty independent immortal who supposedly led and commanded everyone and everything. Where he was, who he was, if he had existed anymore or ever at all, was entirely unknown. Artwork and stories of his activities, however, had survived for thousands of years, predating even the gods themselves.

Other figures and concepts existed in the lore as well. Angels, magical objects and energies, phantasms, theories, all sorts of ideas could be found in lore that predated the gods. They had named their realm for the concept of the angel, but knew little about angels or possibilities of their existence except for what was in their lore. Prophecy was also stored within the library, though the gods had exhausted years of study only to never definitively prove prophecy was factual, and even so at its best over ninety percent of vetted prophetic passages considered possibly authentic were completely false.

The library itself ascended for stories and stories. Naturally, holding more than five thousand years of books required a large amount of storage space and a detailed organizational system, which the gods had implemented. Studying literature was but one learning method of the gods, but one they valued.

While studying in the library, king of gods Ralios Larion sensed a disturbance. Someone had just arrived in the Realm of the Angels. With a feeling as to whom had arrived, Larion stopped his research and headed for the entrance to the tower, at the very bottom floor.

He had been right.

Arriving back in the Realm of the Angels, Professor Magnon, Necnea, and Kronius proceeded up the stairs into Angel Tower. On the walk, the professor began to change over his appearance again, taking a slightly younger look with his hair tied back, changing his robes to purple, and adding a centerpiece onto his chest. This was the appearance of the god he was, Tyrinion.

"Let me ask you something, professor," began Kronius. "If you so detest your current appearance as Tyrinion, then why do you persist in maintaining this appearance here? Why not simply appear as you are?"

Tyrinion shook his head as they walked. "It is not my preference, Kronius. However, as our peers identify me as Tyrinion and not as Professor James Magnon, an appearance change is only appropriate in this case. Here, where appearances are matters of accolade and esteem, it will do better for any arguments I must make if I appear as I was when I was held in the highest regard here."

"You are still held in such a regard," echoed a voice from down the hall.

Tyrinion, Necnea, and Kronius stopped in their tracks. Approaching them was Ralios Larion, dressed in his royal red robes and sporting an elder appearance. Though he was himself a younger god of only three thousand years, Larion took upon an older appearance to earn respect, especially in his current position as the handpicked king of gods, as well as the god of light. Selected by the noble Vinz Larinion to rule, his name of "Ralios Larion" was a combination of his immortal-born name of Ralios, and a shortened version of Larinion.

Tyrinion, however, was not so impressed by Larion's comment, and was still trying to get used to the idea of Larion being the king of gods, having never lived in the Realm of the Angels under his rule. "If you would say so, then I will believe that is your perception," he answered. "However, I do not perceive it in the same light that you do."

"Oh come now, Tyrinion," answered Larion. "As I have told you before, you are welcome to return here whenever you wish. I would not have said such things if I did not truly believe that you are a god and should be respected as such. Five thousand years of tenure is more than enough when compared to the few years that you have spent running to deflect a lie."

"Enough of this," interjected the professor, who was clearly miffed with Larion's take on the issue. Though Kronius and Necnea both knew that Larion took every matter quite seriously and was one of the most diligent gods around, the professor did not see the same in Ralios Larion, with whom he had had very little acquaintance. It was clear that Tyrinion was still uncomfortable being here and held onto his shame, whether or not that shame was just. "We have run out of leads to follow in the mortal realm, and Setadev has disappeared. The pure one is still his captive, as well. Unless we can pin down where he is heading, we will not be able to stop him."

Larion nodded. "I worried that this might happen," he said. "What happened?"

Tyrinion shook his head. "I am not sure," he answered. "We followed the trail of the Enlighteners all the way to the Fortress of Da Leval, which was where Setadev had gone. By the time we arrived, though, the Solunar Empire had already stormed the fortress. They were being led by Emperor Arthur and Rachel Reinhart, two of Kevin's best friends. Together, they managed to rescue my daughter, who was also being held prisoner there after being captured while trying to save Kevin, but Setadev escaped with Kevin and also sabotaged the fortress so it would collapse a few hours after he left. He left no leads, no trail, and nothing else to follow to indicate where he might be headed."

"Cold," scoffed Larion. "Setadev runs, takes the pure one and all his evidence with him, and leaves your daughter. Wherever we have to follow him, I sense a trap."

"As do I," nodded the professor, "but I have faith in my daughter." He paused for a second. "Have you made any progress on the research?"

Larion lowered his head a little. "There is little we have found of what Setadev could be doing to try and revive himself without the Stripe of Life." He paused for a second. "Additionally, we have been conducting as much research as possible on all aspects of the poem almost around the clock, in case it is a true prophecy, but we have found little so far. As it would turn out, you would happen to be the foremost expert on dimensional space theory, Tyrinion."

"Then there are no true experts," commented the professor. "My work on dimensional space theory was little more than stating the possibility, and has been that way for five thousand years."

"As I am aware," nodded Larion. "Nothing in our lore has given us any clue, and we have all but a section or two of the library left to canvas."

Tyrinion took a step back and let out a sigh. He cursed under his breath. “So, maybe the knowledge of what Setadev is after is truly lost after all,” he said. “Only he knows what he is doing, and only he knows where he is going.”

Shaking his head, Larion agreed. “It seems that way,” he said.

Aside, Kronius was getting frustrated. He could not believe that both Larion and Tyrinion seemed to simply be giving up. Normally a bit timid, he knew now that he needed to say something, and change the course of this discussion.

“No!” exclaimed Kronius, stepping forward. He placed himself directly between the professor and Larion in the hallway. “If there is one thing my travels with Tyrinion have taught me, it is that the answers to every question are available somewhere. There must be enough out there for Setadev to know.”

“Then the question is, where?” asked Larion, directly to Kronius. “I trust your words have plenty of merit, but we have not the solution. Might you have an idea, Kronius?”

For just a second, Kronius hesitated. He was still a bit nervous, but he had time to think on this, and an idea had come to mind. The Fortress of Da Leval was Setadev’s design, as was the city of Seta Archa. Setadev, as a mortal man, had designed a great many things and was excellent at thinking through all of the possibilities. What if this were thought out, too?

“Maybe,” he finally said aloud. “The professor and Necnea know better for sure, but I have read of Setadev. The man himself, Setaeus Demota as he was known, supposedly ran many experiments; his trials with the Stripe of Life to discover immortality is one of them in itself. If what we are looking for has not been indicated in the literature, then perhaps what Setadev is going after is something that he was previously involved with himself. Since he was hiding in the realm below for five thousand years and spent only a few short weeks as king of gods before that, it could be something he worked on during his mortal life.”

Necnea had a skeptical look on her face. “It is a solid idea, Kronius, but Setadev always kept very good documentation of all of his experiments and constructions, and we have them all. Even during his mortal days, he made sure to take down notes on everything he did. If it were something he did, he would have noted it."

Kronius thought on this for a moment. Necnea had a good point, but in that moment, something occurred to him that may be the answer. "Have you read his studies, Necnea?" he asked. "I have read all of them, and in each one, he is very successful at what he sets out to do. However, what if what we are looking for is not a success, but a failure?"

"A failure?" Tyrinion inquired. "You think Setadev might be going after an experimental failure as part of his plan?"

Nodding, Kronius acknowledged with confidence. "I may have been naive to his intentions before, but I know more about the man now than I ever did, and I think we could say from his kidnapping plot of Kevin Trent Stryker that he is quite the sore loser. If this were a failed experiment he were going after, what reason would he have to write about it?"

"There is more to be learned from failure than from success," stated Larion.

"But not to him," realized the professor out loud. He looked at Kronius briefly, realizing how right he was. "Setadev was not the type to acknowledge failure, ever. At the very least, I agree with Kronius that we should at least explore the possibility."

"If it were a failed experiment, though," began Necnea, "then why would Setadev pursue it now?"

Turning to look at Necnea, Kronius responded, "Five thousand years is a long time. Maybe something has changed that could alter the experiment."

Nodding in agreement himself knowing the strong validity of Kronius's argument, the professor looked toward Larion. "Perhaps we had best call a special session of the gods, those who knew Setadev before we became immortal. If Kronius is right, then there is a possibility that somebody knows something."

"Whether or not by mistake, irrelevance, or hiding," noted Larion. "Well done, Kronius," he stated. "We may finally have our answer at last."

The professor, Necnea, and Kronius nodded.

Chapter 35

The Experiment

Within half an hour, word of the meeting had been spread around the tower. Another half an hour later, it was cancelled.

After the announcement of the meeting had been made, many of the gods had begun speaking with one another, knowing what they were scheduled to discuss. In chatting with his fellow deities, Chatka, the god of peace and war, and one of the original twenty gods, had found one of his peers who had an idea. He informed Larion of this, who then cancelled the full assembly in favor of a small meeting with Forrestren.

Forrestren, the god of technology, was one of the original gods who followed Setaeus Demota into the Realm of the Angels. Several inventions were credited to him during his time as a mortal, and he became internationally renowned as a technology expert. This also led the power zealot Setaeus Demota to recognize his intellect. Upon the formation of the gods and the discovery of the passageway into the Realm of the Angels, however, Forrestren's talents of invention were less necessary thanks to the new energy of divine power that was discovered alongside immortality. Dressed in green robes with silver trim, Forrestren had served as god of technology since his arrival.

"My lord, I think I might know of what you seek," Forrestren began, in the meeting room with Larion, Chatka, Necnea, Tyrinion, and Kronius. I know of a secret device that Setadev was working on before he brought us to the Realm of the Angels."

"Tell us what you know, Forrestren," responded Larion. "What do you know of this secret device that Setadev built?"

Forrestren sighed. He was about to recall a story he wanted only to forget. "It started about fifteen years before Setadev brought us here," he began. "At the time, Setaeus Demota was pondering a theory being developed by Tyrin Amtensen, or as we better know him, Tyrinion. He termed it 'dimensional space theory', the idea that there may be different dimensions out there that exist on the same plane and not on different planes. At the time, it was just a thought that Tyrin Amtensen was only developing, but Setaeus Demota wanted to try and draw open a portal to it."

Necnea then rose. "Not even Vinz Larinion had any knowledge about that. Why is it that only you have any knowledge of this?"

Again, Forrestren sighed. "It is something that Setaeus asked that I keep secret, because he was not able to open up even so much as a dimensional rift, much less a portal to another dimension. Only he and I worked on it, and after our ascension into the Realm of the Angels, it became merely an irrelevant mistake. It was never functional, and Setadev never could make it operational no matter how much he tried. For him, it was just a failed experiment, and it was to myself, too."

Larion only shook his head. Such secrets were exactly why it seemed he could never find the information he needed, despite the massive library present in Angel Tower. He was an advocate of documentation for that reason. Reluctantly, he sighed and said, "Continue about this device."

Forrestren nodded. He started using hand gestures and explained, "It was a large ring on a pedestal, with six spaces in the ring itself, one for each of the six types of magic not counting life. Though Tyrin Amtensen had not postulated this, Setadev believed, as he usually did, that anything could be accomplished if enough force were placed into it. As we already know, one can travel within a realm via teleportation gates, created by spinning light and darkness magic in just such a way that it creates a rift within the realm. He believed doing so with all of the kinds of magic might create a dimensional rift."

Aside, Professor Magnon cursed under his breath. From looking at the structure and hearing what Forrestren was describing, he could see where this was going. He was surprised, in fact, that he had not thought of the idea first.

Continuing, Forrestren explained, "While the four lower elements of earth, ice, fire, and air cannot be manipulated in the same ways that light and darkness can, Setadev believed that adding in these four elements, with each element's opposite across from one another to create three separate sets of poles, could potentially create so much instability in the realm that it would form a gate powerful enough to open a rift in the dimension itself, at a deeper level than merely a teleportation gate. Stone was used as its main composition, and brass and iron were used as a core of the stone structure in order to sustain the gate without continuous magic casting. Needless to say, it was very difficult to construct and craft, and would be extremely difficult to replicate."

"So, why was it deemed a failure?" asked Larion.

Forrestren shook his head. "Setadev never could open a gate to another dimension, or even a rift," he answered. "He could never get the power high enough. Still, Setadev himself was convinced that he could open this gate, and that the reason he could not was not due to power alone, but due to some powerful source of magic and divine power in the world that caused interference to opening a rift."

This stirred up some discussion amongst the gods. Quickly, Kronius took out a piece of paper and started reviewing it. As Larion called for silence again, Kronius pulled Necnea aside, and pointed to a line on the paper. "A source of power has emerged, a powerful gate from the seven powers' disintegrated fate," he quoted from the second poem of *Letters to the Adventurer*. "Maybe the Seven Stripes of the Elements served to block a dimensional gate?"

Necnea nodded slightly. She responded quietly, "Possible, but we should not theorize on that yet. We really do not know, but I appreciate your smart thinking."

Kronius nodded, and tucked the paper back into a pocket in his robe.

Larion was speaking aloud. "Forrestren," he began, "could Setadev be able to open this gate now?"

There was a moment's pause. Then, Forrestren shook his head. "Even if Setadev believed that some other source of feedback kept him from opening a gate to another dimension, I studied his technique and I could not see how he could ever generate enough force to do it. The clashing magic energies just keep canceling each other out as more force is added, and I believe he would need an exponentially greater amount of force to get close to opening one, if his theory were correct on this structure."

"Then what danger is there in this gate?" Necnea then asked.

For this, Forrestren had no response. He seemed to be caught off his guard with knowing exactly what it could do.

The professor, however, had an idea. He stood and continued, "Even if a gate to another dimension could not be opened, it is certainly possible, provided Setadev's concept was valid, that he could force enough power into the gate to open up a minor dimensional rift. Such a tear in the dimension could have the potential to reorganize the matter and energy of anything that passes through it."

There was a collective gasp.

"If what you are saying is true, Tyrinion," said Larion, "then that means that if Setadev could power this gate, and he passed through this rift with some new source of divine power, he and this source of divine power could be combined into one form, which essentially would mean..."

"That Setadev would be revived," interrupted the professor. Before the crowd could get involved, however, he continued, "Before we get too worked up on the concept, let us consider what this means. With such an influx of divine power, Setadev would have all of the power that he had before, but the only way he could do so is with a source of divine power equivalent to a god. No such source exists, however, since the Stripe of Life which gave us all our immortality exists no more."

"So, then, to do so would be pointless," commented Necnea.

A look of horror came to Larion's face. He had just realized something.

Noticing this, Chatka turned toward the king of gods. "You know of such a source, my lord?"

Silently, but shaking, Larion nodded. "I do. We created it."

There was a huge clamor again in the room. Necnea called for silence.

"My lord," said Chatka, "you would not be suggesting the Sword of Purity, would you?"

Larion nodded. "I would," he said. "Vinz Larinion's sacrifice went right into the blade. Essentially, it contains an immortal's divine power. All Setadev would have to do would be to intersect himself at the rift."

The professor gasped in realization. "That must be why he put so much effort into this revenge scheme with Kevin. By taking Kevin captive, he would keep the Sword of Purity close to him. Even Setadev would not have the ability to overpower Vinz Larinion's blessing that locks the sword to the pure ones. He needs one of them to manipulate the sword, and taking Kevin gives him the added disguise of vengeance." Briefly, the professor shook his head. "Kevin would never willingly help Setadev, but if the poem holds true and Setadev needs the energy from the Sword of Purity to restore himself, then it would only make sense that Setadev would keep Kevin alive and try to break his will."

"That must be it," acknowledged Larion, frustrated. "We have to find this gate; it is the best lead we have to Setadev's new home base." He looked to Forrestren. "Do you know where Setadev hid this gate?"

Reluctantly, Forrestren shook his head. "I only wish I did," he answered. "All I know about where it is is that Setadev and I built it in an underground cavern."

Chatka then picked up the conversation. "That means that realistically this cavern could be anywhere. There are caverns all over the mortal realm, and it stands to reason that we only know of a small percentage of them. It also indicates to me that Setadev was crafty enough to hide his gate somewhere he knew only he knew of. Nowhere else could he say that."

Larion carefully considered this for a moment. "Yet, while I can say for sure that I have not ever met Setadev myself, from his teachings and his past works I cannot honestly believe that he would not have documented all of this. Location, information… anything at all."

Hearing this, Tyrinion turned to Larion. "Setadev did not acknowledge his failures, and that is why we do not have information," he answered. "If there is one thing that those of us who came to know Setaeus Demota learned, and as I am sure the pure one has learned, it is that Setadev is notorious for his ego and believes that he is incapable of error. I am sure he has made plenty of them and will acknowledge a 'mistake', but he would never acknowledge a 'failure' outright."

"Setadev did use the word 'failure' to describe this gate once," added Forrestren. "He asked me never to speak of it again after that, and we buried it."

Tyrinion glared over at Forrestren. "You buried it?" he asked.

"Yes," acknowledged Forrestren. "It is so well buried, I would presume, that not even a teleportation gate could take one there. Knowing where exactly to place the gate so as not to end up buried oneself in the middle of the earth would be downright impossible, for how deep it is buried under the earth of the mortal realm."

Suddenly, Larion raised an eyebrow. "That would eliminate many underground caverns in the world if that were the case." Briefly, Larion paused. "We are likely to see Setadev beginning an excavation sometime soon, right where this gate is. If he is heading for the gate, then where he begins his dig is where we need to be to intercept him."

Necnea shook her head. "Still, that does not solve our main problem. In order for us to prevent Setadev's revival, provided this is his strategy, we have to find him *before* he gets to this gate. If Setadev has had this planned for a while, then he has likely already started his excavation and is on his way to the site with the pure one in tow. Unless we can find where it is, and soon, we will be too late."

Larion nodded. "My decision, then, is made." He paused and stared directly down the table, gathering everyone's attention. "We must go out into the world, and walk among the ranks of the mortal. We must see if we can discover anything, anywhere, any place at all, where there is an excavation in progress, and see if we can find this digsite. It may be disguised as a mining operation, a historical preservation, a scientific study, a construction project, or anything at all. We must spread, research, and discover." He paused for a moment. "Daily, we shall convene here at sunset in the mortal realm in order to review the day's findings and explore any leads."

Quickly, Kronius and Necnea looked over to Tyrinion, expecting him to flinch at this call. Silently, however, Tyrinion had no reaction. He merely crossed his arms and lowered his head. This was the right decision logically, and he knew it. Everyone would have to partake in order for this strategy to be effective.

"Are there any questions?" asked Larion.

Only silence echoed throughout the room. The direction was clear.

"Then our pathway is clear," continued the king of gods. "Let us find this gate, and destroy it before Setadev can activate it. There, we are likely to find the pure one as well."

With that, the gods dispersed. They had their assignments to begin, and other gods to inform of the direction.

Tyrinion, however, stayed back to ask a question to Larion. Noticing this as the gods left, Larion asked, "You have something to inquire, Tyrinion?"

"I do," nodded Tyrinion. "The decision you have made is the right one, but how much do you measure into stopping Setadev from reviving himself, and how much do you measure into saving the pure one?"

Larion bowed his head. "A great deal to both," he answered.

"And yet you do not show that," responded the professor. "It seems to me that we are all guilty of such an infraction. We place so much value into defeating the man that has tormented us for the past twenty years that we forget to rescue the one who saved us a few months ago. I will admit that at times I am just as guilty of it, as are Necnea and Kronius, I am sure, as we all are here. Are we all so shallow and so focused that we forget about him?"

With this, Larion sighed. "I think of him every day, and what he embodies," he answered. "Some day, I do hope we can properly thank him, and your daughter as well, for everything they have done." He paused for a second. "I can only think of what she is going through right now."

Tyrinion nodded. "A lot," he answered. "A lot more than any girl her age should have to go through."

"Her strength must be remarkable," said Larion. "Never let it be said that she is not a hero in herself, for everything she is doing, as well."

Tyrinion nodded. She had become so strong, he had realized at that moment. She was fighting for him almost purely; that was her motivation. Maybe, all in all, she was the only one who had that thinking and would never forget what she was fighting for.

Chapter 36

Fangs of the Chimera

A full retreat had been the only option for Arthur, Rachel, and the Solunar Empire forces. Already in foreign territory without permission, being spotted in Leticon would be quite hazardous to the new nation of Solunar. Though Arthur had considered that risk when leading his troops to the Fortress of Da Leval, he had considered the potential benefit worth it. Without rescuing Kevin and capturing Pseudo and General Sayo, however, Arthur was returning home empty-handed. He felt like he was failing.

Walking next to him, Rachel felt she was the same way. Arthur had shown the most physical signs of pressure, but she too had been putting herself under stress. As the prime minister of her nation, she was taking under a large amount of responsibility and was Arthur's primary advisor.

Silently, Resa walked alongside them, with a somber expression. The thought of her sister, behind her, was deeply on her mind.

Behind Resa were two tented carts. One was carrying her sister Rouge, and another was carrying Caitlin. Both were unconscious, resting in the carts as the men carried them across the land. Neither were medically in good shape, and neither had regained consciousness in the last couple of days since the retreat began.

From the silent plains of Leticon, the city of Cardol became visible. Ever silent, ever abandoned, ever as it was and always would be. Even with the defeat of Desolunar, the new border with the Solunar Empire was just south of the Calphos River, of which Cardol rested on the north side, and paranoia and chaos still rocked Nuve. Haunting memories of Cardol were likely to shake Nuve's foundation for years. Now, it resembled much of neighboring Leticon.

"Are you sure you want to take us through Cardol?" asked Rachel.

Next to her, Arthur nodded.

"It sort of makes sense," added Resa. "The city would be a good place to stop and rest the men for a little while. There'll be some shelter there and the rivers with water."

Silently, Arthur leaned his head down. "Even so, we will still have to be careful," he said. "We went around Cardol on our way to the fortress in order to avoid being seen. We'll run the same risk going through it on our way back. I think we'd best stay on our guard." He paused for a second. "Still, it's a few more days to Seta Archa from here. Our men would do best to rest in the city."

Rachel nodded. "I only hope nothing more bad happens," she said. She then looked back at the two carts behind her. "They could use a little peace and quiet for some time."

It was getting tough to stay positive. As much as they had thought they were winning the battle at the Fortress of Da Leval, the escape of Setadev along with Kevin had turned it into a large defeat. Now, with nowhere to go and with friends close to death in the middle of a land where they were not supposed to be, there was not much optimism to be had.

Though this trip was not supposed to be fun, Rachel had enjoyed that part of this experience. She was getting to travel with her friends Rouge and Resa, all to save her friend Kevin and protect her best friend, Caitlin. Traveling around with Arthur was so enjoyable, although she would never say it out loud. For now, though, it would not matter much until Kevin was rescued.

From behind them, Vincent Stryker approached, having caught up from Cardol just a little while ago. "We would do best to leave as soon as possible," he said. "Staying in Cardol is not a bad idea given that we do not have enough time to get the men out of Nuve before darkness sets in, but we will want to get an early start and get into Solunar territory as soon as possible."

"Agreed," nodded Arthur, as they kept approaching the city. "I doubt the men have ever seen a city as lovely as Cardol. Provided Nuve has still not reclaimed the city with an actual population as of yet, we should be safe." He looked over to Rachel.

In response, Rachel nodded. "It is," she said, herself being the prime minister and thus the newly trained expert on diplomacy for the empire. "Nuve still considers it a hazardous zone, and with the threat of the Cornelia Chimeras right across the Rhonean River, that likely won't change until Solunar is established as a peaceful nation and the internal conflicts plaguing Nuve are settled."

By this point, Cardol was in clear view, as was the road straight to it. The snow-covered ground was pure white all around, almost appearing to absorb the white stone city of Cardol into it. As the army came closer to the city, however, barely visible against the horizon of the day and the ground, was a line of blue.

"Arthur, you had better hold your men, right away," directed Vincent Stryker firmly.

Not wasting any time, Arthur immediately turned and gave the order to halt. Resa assisted in ensuring the men came to a vigilant stop. Then, Arthur turned to the old Scurnian general. "What's going on, Mr. Stryker?"

Vincent pulled out his sword, a katana he called *Lavinia*. With the sword in hand, he pointed out toward Cardol. "Soldiers," he said. "It would be unlikely if they haven't spotted us already with their scouts."

Arthur rolled his eyes and put the palm of his hand over his face. "Great," he said, sarcastically. "Just what we needed."

Seeing what was going on, Resa stepped up to Arthur and whispered something in his ear.

In response, Arthur nodded. "Do it," he said quietly. "I would rather make the first move if we have to, anyway."

Resa nodded and scampered away. As soon as she did, Rachel stepped up and asked Arthur, "What was that all about?"

"We may need to move fast," he answered. "I'm having the men prepare for battle. We can't get caught off guard here."

"You do know that making the first move would be an act of war, right?"

"I do," nodded Arthur, "but regardless, us being here is already one. We can't be in any worse shape if we are prepared."

Next to him, Vincent nodded in agreement.

Rachel rolled her eyes and stepped a couple of steps away. She understood what he was saying, but did not want to accept that answer.

As the men unsheathed their weapons and prepared for combat, a few men on horses came up from the marching men in blue, reaching the Solunar forces in a short amount of time. Soon, however, it became clear to Arthur, Rachel, and Vincent that this was not going to be a simple incident to handle. The uniforms being worn by the approaching men were not simply blue. They were light blue, with golden trim. These were not Nuve soldiers; they were Cornelia Chimeras.

Immediately, Arthur turned around and called for a sword to be passed to him. Without his familiar Sword of Corruption at his side, he wanted a weapon just in case things spiraled out of control. After catching one that was passed to him, he turned around and prepared for the encounter ahead.

Three men on white horses stopped in front of the young emperor and dismounted. The leader, dressed with more decor on his uniform than the others, began with a pompous air, "Well, well, well, is this not an interesting situation? A foreign army, dressed in orange and black, walking around in Nuve territory? And in Leticon, no less. Thou must have some guts, indeed."

Arthur was very bothered. "Who the hell are you supposed to be?" he asked.

"That does not concern you," responded the man, instantly. "My question is, who the hell are thou, and what are thou doing in Nuve? From the look of the uniforms of thy men, I would presume thou are of the Solunar Empire. Scouting ahead for another invasion, perhaps?"

Finally, Vincent Stryker had the opportunity to step up. "You don't need to tell me who you are, Arsuf Maxwell, you murdering scumbag."

Maxwell stepped up. "Well, well, well, isn't this a pleasant surprise? Vincent Stryker, thou traitor to Nuve. Thou denies it, yet thou are clearly aligned with the Solunar Empire and are plotting the next invasion to threaten this land. Must thou always be so obvious?"

Before Arthur could interject, Vincent started yelling. "You fool!" he exclaimed. "Would you shut up and listen for a minute? I'm not here to start a war; I'm here to prevent one."

Scoffing, Maxwell responded, "Just who do thou think thou art fighting for, Vincent? Thou were originally a general of Scurnia, then thou retired. Lately, thou wore thy Scurnian colors when the Triple Alliance pounded Desolunar, then thou moved to Aurana. Now, thou art in the presence of the Solunar Empire soldiers, walking alongside them in Nuve territory. Explain thyself."

Calmly, Arthur raised his arm. "Hold!" he commanded. Then he leaned next to Vincent. "You don't have to do this," he said. "I don't expect you to explain yourself to him, whoever he is."

Vincent gently shook his head, as he responded to Arthur, "He is the leader of the Cornelia Chimeras, a former Nuve general named Arsuf Maxwell. He was some young hotshot Nuve general during the Alliance-Daritel War, and was brutally aggressive and forceful with his own men. He also murdered Raijin Shane, Vanguard of Nuve. Let me handle him; I know him."

Arthur nodded and turned away. "Suit yourself," he said. "It's your call."

Immediately, Rachel scowled at Arthur. "What's wrong with you?" she asked. "This is about more than personal pride; it's about us and our people who we take care of. If you let Vincent just have his way here, he may do something that will put the empire in danger."

With a confused look, Arthur responded, "You do know this is Kevin's father we're talking about, right? Not to mention a highly experienced general."

"Still, Arthur, we have to be extremely careful," Rachel answered. "He already called this guy a 'murdering scumbag', if that doesn't say enough there."

Reluctantly, Arthur nodded and turned around again. Rachel had a point, and he knew it. Sometimes he was glad just to have her along as his voice of reason, even if he did tease her periodically for being cynical. Even so, he was going to let Vincent handle this, trusting him to de-escalate the situation.

Vincent continued, to Arsuf Maxwell, "Does not the incident in Cornelia bother you? The forces behind such a move, the Enlighteners from the Shadows, were hiding out here in Leticon. They are enemies of the Solunar Empire as well. As I followed them out here, the empire did the same, without any harmful intent toward Nuve or toward the Chimeras."

"Thou expect me to believe that, really?" asked Maxwell. "How dumb do thou believe me to be? I know thou to be a traitor. I know thou to be fully well against me and my men. And now, I have caught thou trespassing in Nuve with Solunar Empire soldiers."

"Max, open your eyes for a second!" Vincent screamed back. "Can't you see the bigger picture here? You had goods stolen from you by men in red robes, the Enlighteners. They, including the one you interviewed in Cornelia, have been feeding you false information on who your enemy is. I've never fought against you; we've always been on the same side, even twenty years ago."

"And even then, as thou are now, thou were a chastising piece of garbage," responded Arsuf Maxwell. "Thou have no right to call me a 'murdering scumbag' when thou look at thyself. The death of Raijin Shane was warranted; he had been a dictator-in-waiting for some time and he did not deserve to live." He then raised his sword. "And thou, sir, are next."

"Hold!" commanded Arthur, stepping forward. Though Vincent was angry, he had no choice but to take a step back. "If you assault Vincent Stryker, you declare war on the Solunar Empire. I will have no choice but to pursue annihilation of the Cornelia Chimeras if you do."

Arsuf Maxwell scoffed. "And who the hell might thou be, again?"

"The name is Arthur Falchor, Emperor of the Solunar Empire," responded Arthur. "Vincent Stryker is a guest general of mine. An attack on him will be treated as an attack on the empire, and you will suffer the consequences as a result."

Cocky as ever, Arsuf Maxwell rolled his eyes. He chuckled awkwardly. "Well, Emperor Arthur, I can see you are fairly young and naive. Have you not realized that you have already done the same by bringing your men into Nuve?"

"I brought them here for exactly the reason that Vincent has already explained."

"Without seeking Nuve's permission first? Leticon is, after all, Nuve territory."

Arthur paused. "Had we done that, we would have lost the trail of the Enlighteners, so pardon my informality," he answered. "As I listen to your voice, though, I seriously doubt that you give a damn about Nuve. I think you're looking for an excuse to pick a fight."

Maxwell glared at Arthur.

"You need not hide it," added Vincent Stryker. "I'm well aware of what you and your Cornelia Chimeras seek. You want your own land, and you have no problem taking Cornelia Province with you to cripple your main rival, the land that you deem did you wrong by not giving you the power you wanted."

"And so it may be, but I would like to see thou prove that to the people," Maxwell fired back. "Thy reference to my desire to be named regional governor to Cornelia several years ago will hold no weight when thou discuss said incidents to the government of Nuve." He pulled up his sword and shined it a bit with the cuff of his light blue military jacket. "That is, if thou ever get to see the government of Nuve in their capital city again."

Vincent clutched his sword tighter. Arsuf Maxwell was taunting him at this point. Still, Vincent had to hold himself back. He remembered what Professor Magnon had said about not altering the destiny of Nuve.

For a moment, Arsuf continued to shine his sword, as everyone looked on. Then, he continued, "Tell me, Vincent, what does your son have to do with all of this?"

"Excuse me?" asked Vincent, surprised.

"Thou heard me, plain as day," commented Maxwell. "Thou see, I know thy presence in Nuve is not for what thou claims it is. Thy son, the Vanguard of Aurana, is here in Leticon, is he not?"

"And what business is it of yours?" Vincent asked back pointedly. He did not like where this was going, and was highly suspicious.

Maxwell scoffed. "Answer the question. Is the Vanguard of Aurana here in Leticon?"

Quickly, Vincent was growing angrier. Arthur, however, stepped forward. "He was here, a prisoner of the Enlighteners," the young emperor answered. "They've since departed and retreated from the province, with him still their captive."

Vincent rolled his eyes. Arthur was still naive as a leader.

"Oh, really?" asked Maxwell pointedly. "That is not what I hear. And now, thy presence here with the Solunar Empire and the emperor's answer has just confirmed it for me."

That caught Vincent and Arthur's attention. They were listening intently.

"How humorous," began Arsuf Maxwell. "Thou, 'emperor', has just shown me that thou knows the Vanguard of Aurana personally. Did thou think thou could pull a double move on me by getting Aurana involved in an alliance between thy nation and his in a conflict against my forces in Cornelia? Thou will not get away with it, and I will see to that myself."

"Are you insane?" Vincent responded sternly. "You've been brainwashed by listening to the Enlighteners! Can you not see what threat they cause to all of us?"

"Stop trying to change the subject," said Maxwell. "On behalf of Nuve, and of the Cornelia Chimeras, I hereby arrest thou for conspiracy to attack Nuve." He raised his sword. "Prepare thyselves, if thy seek to defy me."

There was a momentary pause. Then, Arthur leaned his sword down, pointing it into the dirt. "I won't fight you, Arsuf Maxwell," he said. "It matters not what you claim to do." He then turned to his forces. "Prepare to move out!" he called, as he started walking away, angling toward the flank of his men.

"Are thou not listening to me?" Maxwell yelled, offended. "Then thou will die!" He started charging toward Arthur, sword up.

Vincent and Rachel tried to jump in his way, but the two Cornelia Chimera soldiers with Maxwell blocked their paths. Before any Solunar Empire soldier could respond, Arsuf Maxwell was closer than they were to the emperor. He had an open path to kill Arthur. And Arthur was completely oblivious.

Whish!

Suddenly, Maxwell fell to the ground. As he did, the two Cornelia Chimera soldiers ran to him.

Arthur turned around to see what had happened, not expecting anything behind him. For a second, as he realized what had happened, his life flashed before his eyes.

There was a knife in Maxwell's chest.

Everyone looked over to the direction from where the knife had come. Leaning out of her cart, wrapped in bandages from her chest down, was Rouge. She was conscious, and was climbing out of the cart, with her other dagger in her hand.

"Rouge, you're alive!" yelled Resa, excited. She immediately ran and hugged her sister.

Though she let her sister hug her, Rouge had no reaction. She raised her other hand with her one remaining dagger, and started flipping it in her hand. She was staring directly at the two Chimeras, who had stopped in their tracks, as Arthur, Rachel, and Vincent merely stared on in utter stun.

"Now, boys," she began, "which one of you wants to be next?" She looked over at the dagger she was flipping in the air. "Or, maybe, I could kill both of you with the same dagger on one throw."

Immediately, the men scurried off, back toward the Cornelia Chimeras forces.

Arthur looked at the body of Maxwell in stun. He knew now that Maxwell had just tried to kill him, but the Chimeras general was now laying dead at his feet, thanks to some quick thinking from Rouge. Unfortunately, it was too quick thinking.

As these thoughts ran through his head, Vincent walked up to join him, while Rachel ran up to Rouge. "Glad to see you chose the right time to wake up," Rachel said to her. "Enjoy your nap?"

"Not really," shrugged Rouge, as she flipped her dagger back into its sheath on her belt. "How long was I out?"

Rachel looked up at the sky for a second. "Oh, just a couple of days," she said. "Actually, you have Resa to thank for keeping you alive."

In response, Rouge popped an eyebrow. "Really?" she said. She looked down at her sister, who was still hugging her. "Thank you for saving my life, Resa," she said. "Some days, I wonder what I would do without you."

Resa smiled, but took a step back. "Don't thank me," she said.

She looked over to the cart where Caitlin was still unconscious. "Thank Caitlin. I kept you alive, but she's the one who really saved you."

Rouge looked over at the cart. She stared for a long moment. "Is she okay?" she finally asked.

Nervously, Resa began, "Uhm, well…"

"Resa! Get over here now!" Vincent yelled over to her. "Run!"

Immediately, Resa bolted off, following Vincent's direction. Though Rouge was stunned, she was worried about Caitlin and persisted with her question to Rachel. "Is Caitlin okay?"

Letting out a sigh, Rachel responded, "We think she will be. We found her in the fortress, but Kevin was long gone, and so was Setadev. She was so badly beaten, and so depleted, that it took her everything she had to save your life."

Rouge bowed her head. Then, she and Rachel both turned to look at Arthur, Resa, and Vincent having a discussion over Maxwell.

"Can you save his life?" asked Vincent.

In response, Resa said nothing but crouched and pulled back her sleeves. The wind all around began to pick up as Resa pushed her healing magic out of her hands above his chest wound. The dagger was very close to the center of his chest.

As she did, Arthur looked point blank at Vincent. "Why?"

"He was looking for an excuse to kill you, from the first moment," acknowledged Vincent. "If I had to guess, he wanted to pick a fight with you and accuse you of starting it."

Arthur shrugged. "I didn't mean that," he said. "I'm all for less people dying if at all possible, but our reaction was appropriate. He made the first move, and we responded. If he dies today, he dies because of his own stupidity, and his death would likely be of a net benefit to the empire and the world if it keeps the Chimeras from making advances on Nuve or on our northern border."

"Except the world won't see it that way, Arthur," responded Vincent. "Those men that fled from us will carry the message that says how this event went down. They will tell the world that they were investigating an invader's presence in their homeland, and their leader was killed by an assassin from the Solunar Empire. It doesn't matter whose intention was what. We're in Nuve illegally, and they know that."

Pretty soon, Arthur was cursing under his breath. He did not like politics like this.

Vincent sighed. He continued, as he gripped his katana tighter, "Professor Magnon had to stop me as well, when I tried to kill him. I wanted so much vengeance for the death of Raijin Shane that I would not have given a second thought to taking his head off of his shoulders."

Arthur cursed, starting to understand the situation fully. He knew little of Raijin Shane, but based on his experience at the Battle of Seta Archa a few months ago knew that the man was the Vanguard of Nuve and the brother of Lester, King of Nuve. The fury built up in Arthur's veins. And yet, if he wanted to protect his people, he had to hope that this odious ruler of the Cornelia Chimeras had not suffered a fatal injury. He and Vincent both looked down at Resa.

Sighing, Resa let off her power, and stood up. "It's no use," she said. "Even Caitlin wouldn't be able to cure him, I'm sure. That dagger was so precise that it must have hit him square in the heart. I couldn't heal his wounds fast enough to keep up with the bleeding."

Silently, Arthur lowered his head. "So he's gone," he said.

Resa nodded, and then lowered her head. "I'm so sorry, Arthur," she said.

"What's going on over here?" asked Rouge, catching everyone's attention as she started walking toward the body with Rachel following her. "Is he still alive or something, so we can probe him for information?"

Arthur sighed, as he turned to answer Rouge. "He's dead," she said.

Once she was right next to Maxwell's body, Rouge reached down and pulled the dagger out of his chest. "So what's the big deal, then?"

Vincent looked up at Rouge, and shook his head in disbelief. "This was the Supreme Leader of the Cornelia Chimeras, Arsuf Maxwell. You killed him."

"I know that," nodded Rouge, as she flipped the other dagger in the air a bit and then sheathed it. "He tried to kill Arthur. I wasn't going to let that happen, and it was just as I was peeking out of the cart for the first time, so I didn't have any time to do anything but react."

"The consequences may be severe," noted Rachel to Rouge. "It's certainly possible the Chimeras, or maybe even all of Nuve, might declare war on Solunar now. The Chimeras were still protected under an armistice with the Nuve government, even if Mr. Arsuf was disloyal and distrusting of it. We're not even home yet; we're just north of Cardol."

Rouge paused Rachel from continuing by raising her hand. Her mind was full of thoughts.

A moment went by, as the winter wind started to pick up. The sun was beginning to set over the horizon, reflecting a swath of orange light across the white landscape. In the distance, the Chimeras force appeared to be retreating. Snow started to fall again, in the form of flurries. Soon, the winter night would be upon them. Still, the original plans for camp had to be scrapped now. There was too much to hazard by camping anywhere within Nuve. It would take at least another few hours to get out of the country entirely, but now it had to happen, and it had to happen fast.

After this pause while everyone was speechless, trying to comprehend what to say and do next, Arthur finally stepped up. "We have to get out of Nuve, and right now. Let's take the men south of the river and across the border. We can set up camp when we're back in the empire, and we can plan out what we want to do from there."

Rachel, Rouge, Resa, and Vincent all nodded. The direction was clear. Though she was still injured, Rouge immediately set to issuing the command to the troops, as did her sister. Vincent Stryker, wary as he was, kept his sword out as he began walking with Arthur in a southernly direction at the front of the men. Periodically, he would reach and clutch his back, sore from all of the travel and from his lingering medical conditions.

Soon, the three ladies caught up with Arthur and Vincent, as the men continued marching to the south. They were traveling east of Cardol as they continued, allowing the troops to see the white stone structures on the outskirts of the city. Walking past it would take some time, but at its southern edge was the Calphos River, and the ill-defined border with the Solunar Empire just beyond it.

"So now which way do we go?" Rachel asked, as she caught up with everyone. "We'll have a bunch of affairs to settle back in Seta Archa, and I'm sure that the council might be getting a little restless without us there."

"Not to mention the hell there'll be to pay if Nuve decides to ally itself with the Chimeras and believe their story," commented Arthur.

Vincent nodded. "It only figures that such may have been their plan all along, Arthur. Ridding themselves of Raijin Shane in a private environment meant that they got rid of the one officer who was the most suspicious of the Chimeras' true intentions. Now, they've managed to find an opportunity to start an incident while pointing the finger at us. Maxwell likely did not intend to die in the attack, but we may have lit the fire in his brother when word reaches him."

"What do you mean by that?" asked Resa.

"I mean that Maxwell was bad, but his brother is worse," he said. "It's said that among the Arsuf family leading the Cornelia Chimeras faction, Maxwell is the claws while his brother Zachary is the fangs. As vicious as Maxwell is, his brother is completely unhinged." He paused for a second. "I had the unfortunate pleasure of meeting him once, during the war. He wasn't at battle age just yet, but one could tell he was going to be a dangerous person, and something seemed very off with him."

"That figures," commented Arthur. "If it isn't one thing, it's another." The frustration was visible on his face, and his sarcasm was turning into a dark seriousness.

Rachel put her hand on Arthur's shoulder. "Easy, now, Arthur," she said. "We don't want to antagonize and make the situation any worse."

A little surprised at having Rachel's hand placed on his shoulder, Arthur turned his head and gave her a strange look. Immediately, Rachel retracted her hand, suddenly appearing a little nervous.

Next to her, Rouge nodded. She looked across at Arthur and said, "Rachel's right, you know. In retrospect, the last thing we need to do is get punchy about this. We have to be really cautious and use some diplomacy if we want a peaceful resolution."

There was a slight pause.

Then, the unexpected happened. Arthur started laughing. "Rouge suggesting diplomacy for once?" he began. "Don't get me wrong, you're exactly right, but…" He started laughing again. "… but, of all people, you suggesting diplomacy is the most hilarious thing I think I've ever heard in my life."

"I don't see what's so funny about it," commented Rouge.

Even Rachel and Resa could not resist a snicker. "It's because you're so take-action all of the time," chuckled Resa. "You're not the type to suggest a peaceful solution."

"Hey!" interjected Rouge, bothered. "Just because I have quick reaction times doesn't mean I'm not all about patience and peace."

"Funny you say that when your eyes glow at the thought of a fight," joked Resa. "I've seen you, Rouge. You almost get a smile to your face when you get to attack, even when we were assassins and not Vanguards."

Suddenly, Vincent clapped his hands together. "Children, this is no time to ramble on," he interrupted with force, grabbing everyone's attention. "This is serious, and we need to make some decisions."

There was a brief silence, but the first to respond was Rachel. "Agreed," she said, switching back to her standard realism. "But where can we go? We now have an issue to deal with, absolutely, but we have to keep trying to find Kevin." She took a look back at the covered cart which was carrying Caitlin. "For all of us, we have to find out what Setadev is up to, and put a stop to him before he resurrects."

Vincent nodded. "I do have a suggestion for you," he said.

"And what's that?" asked Rachel.

Bringing his head back to level, Vincent answered, with a heavy sigh, "Before we arrived at the fortress, the gods and I had followed a lead that the Enlighteners might have an operation going in Cornelia, which is where we had met with Raijin Shane, and where he would be killed by Arsuf Maxwell later on. We were looking for some lead to where they may be going, especially when we found out they were stealing supplies out of Cornelia."

"Like the ones Caitlin said she found in the fortress?" asked Arthur.

"Quite possibly," nodded Vincent, "although it would seem by their quick disappearance and the abandonment of the fortress that those crates were a decoy as well. The Enlightener operation in Cornelia was not exactly silent, so the discovery of those crates would be a perfect end-of-the-road indicator if the gods and I had beaten Caitlin to the fortress. A perfect double-decoy trap set in the fortress, Setadev had either one of us captured if he wanted us. If I had to guess, though, I don't think he anticipated your arrival."

Arthur nodded. "I called him out on his vulnerability back there at the fortress," he said. "Setadev wouldn't let that happen if he'd planned it out, I wouldn't think."

"Likely not," acknowledged Vincent. "Regardless of the ploy, though, Shane believed that the Enlighteners were heading somewhere else. Rather than going deeper into Leticon, he thought that the thieves might have headed southeast to Cardol, as they would have to go to the fortress, but instead of proceeding into Leticon they grabbed boats at Cardol and took them down through Nuve and into Gardolk. This way, if they were hiding their actual base in Gardolk, they could avoid dockmaster searches in Cornelia and a checkpoint at the Aurun River delta where it flows into the Calphos. He was never sure of a connection to Gardolk, but the culture there tends to be to leave people to their business with minimal questioning, so it would serve as an ideal place to hide a base."

Very carefully, Arthur had to consider this. "Sounds to me like it'd be worth a look," he said, "but it would mean another illegal trip into another nation. We've already caused enough trouble here. Still, if it leads to Kevin, it'll be worth it."

Beside him, Rachel nodded. "Normally I would say it's a bad idea with little to really go off of, but we have to find him, and that's the best we have."

"We do need to stabilize the situation, though," commented Resa. "Much as my sister and I want to save Kevin, too, I am a little scared what will happen to us if we don't fix stuff with Nuve. She and I have already lived through a lot of war, and no one in the empire wants to see more."

Again, Arthur nodded. "Agreed. Suggestions, anybody?"

He paused for a second, as no one answered.

"Seriously, guys, I would really like to have some suggestions here. I'm not really sure what to do next."

There was a long pause. No one had any ideas.

Arthur turned to Rachel. "You're my prime minister, Rachel," she said. "You're my top advisor. Tell me, what should I do?"

Rachel stammered for a moment. "Please don't stick this all on me," she said. "You're the emperor; isn't it your decision?"

"It is," Arthur nodded, "but I count on you for your advice. I'm not asking you to make the decision for me, but I want to know what you think is right. What is the right course of action here?"

For another moment, Rachel clammed up. She felt like Arthur was sticking the whole Solunar Empire and the futures of their friends on her back. Still, if she could not come up with at least some type of suggestion, then she would be asking Arthur to do the same. Right now, she could be considered the second most powerful woman in the world, even at just eighteen years old. It was time for her to make the same kinds of tough decisions that people in similar positions of power did.

"Arthur," she began, slightly nervously, "do you want to abandon Kevin? I want to save him, but we may lose more than him if we go after this lead into Gardolk. I mean, I still want to save him too, but…"

"But nothing," interrupted Arthur. "That one is not negotiable. Kevin's our best friend, and he went so far to save both of us before. Not to mention as well, of course, that Setadev is weak right now. He's bigger than our empire and whatever conflicts that play in, Rachel. If we have a clean shot at him and can bring him to justice, it's worth whatever war that starts as a result."

Unfortunately, Rachel had to agree. She did not like the idea of ditching Kevin, either, but from the position of her duty as prime minister to manage the affairs of the empire, it had seemed like the best answer. Arthur, though, had more than valid reason not to go back and abandon their operation. If the trip to the fortress had done anything at all, it had revealed that Setadev was vulnerable, that he did indeed have Kevin, and that he was up to something. Still, what would happen now with the war? Even though going back to Seta Archa was a necessity to regroup the men and ensure the empire remained strong and ready to deal with the threat, someone would have to have the gall to explain all of this to Nuve. Dealing with the Chimeras would be one thing, but if it incited all of Nuve into war, the Solunar Empire would be annihilated easily in its weakened state. There were, after all, no hard feelings with Nuve.

A plan seemed clear now, and Rachel had an idea who she wanted in each role.

"Then let's do this," she began to suggest. "Let's divide into three. As the prime minister, external affairs and diplomacy are my responsibility. So let me go to Nuvenia, to smooth things over with Nuve and maintain the peace with them. Arthur, you can go back to the empire and see to the recovery taking place. Then, to continue on our lead, Rouge and Resa can proceed into Gardolk and lead the charge against Setadev, as well as the rescue of Kevin."

Arthur considered this briefly. He stopped in the snow, causing everyone with him to stop momentarily as well.

His hand went to his chin, as he considered the options carefully.

"A good plan," he finally acknowledged. "However, I would much rather have it so Rouge and Resa went to attend to the empire, while I went to seek out Kevin. He is my friend, and Setadev and General Sayo are my responsibility to defeat, not theirs."

"Arthur, it's not their responsibility to run the country in our absence," responded Rachel.

Suddenly, Vincent Stryker stepped forward. "No, that is the responsibility of your Imperial Council," he said. "Rouge and Resa's job is to serve as the figurehead forward guard for the troops, which is a role they can serve in Seta Archa while they keep your empire from splitting itself apart."

"So you actually suggest sending Arthur off into Gardolk by himself looking for Kevin?" exclaimed Rachel in surprise. "He's the emperor. If Gardolk were to capture him, do you know what they would do to him?"

"No worse than what Nuve would do to him for coming here," commented Vincent. "And I'm not suggesting that he go alone." Vincent reached back and clutched his shoulder. "My body's not what it used to be," he continued. "Though I want nothing more than to save my son, my body just cannot hold out for another battle at the front lines. I would be better served by going to Nuvenia myself, and sharing with them what I have seen. I can tell them of the plight of their Vanguard, of the king's brother. I can share with them Maxwell's scheming, his plans and what his forces are trying to do to the kingdom." He paused for a second. "And that would leave you available to accompany Arthur into Gardolk, to see to his safety and protect him."

Rachel's eyes widened. She turned and looked at Arthur.

"Deal," nodded Arthur confidently. "Mr. Stryker, we'll send you with a horse and some supplies, as it'll be a couple of weeks to make it to Nuvenia. Rouge and Resa will take the bulk of the troops home, and we'll take a contingency force along the river by boats. This way we can save our men the marching and move quicker to find Setadev and his encampment."

"Whoa, wait a minute, are you sure about this?" Rachel asked in surprise.

Again, Arthur nodded confidently. "Absolutely."

Beside him, Rouge also nodded. "It would be best if Resa and I took the troops to rest," she said. "I am still in no shape to fight. Perhaps we are best served in that role, then."

Though appearing disapproving, Resa also nodded to indicate she would be willing to accept this. Rouge could tell that Resa really wanted to go with Arthur and Rachel, but knew she had other responsibilities. "This isn't our fight," she finally said, "but it is yours. Just make sure you give the general a good smack across the lips for me."

Arthur chuckled. "Will do," he said. He then stopped chuckling as he looked back at the cart carrying Caitlin. "I wonder what we should do with her."

Rolling her eyes, Rachel reached over, grabbed Arthur's

shoulder, and shook him. "We should take her with us," she said. "No one wants to save Kevin more than she does, and if she recovers soon, she may be the best chance we actually have of defeating Setadev. Not to mention, of course, that she's our best friend, too."

Silently, Arthur nodded. He knew as well as Rachel did, too, that his half-sister would just come running after Kevin once she found out even if they sent her with Rouge and Resa. Still, he did worry for her safety, even if the professor himself would trust him to take her into Gardolk.

"Then it's settled," Arthur finally said. "Let's get back to the other side of the river and rest the men. After that, I have a feeling that we still have a long way to go."

As Arthur finished his sentence, and the men continued forward, Arthur looked up for a second. The snow was starting to fall faster and heavier. As it did, he hoped that Kevin was still safe for the moment.

Chapter 37

The Conqueror's Plan

Western Gardolk is often known for its mining areas. Along the kingdom's mountainous border with the Solunar Empire, the Peaked Mountains range is noticeably less wide than it is between Nuve and Scurnia; however, the rough terrain still makes the range very difficult to cross. Those who have been willing to cross the lush fields and foothills have found that the mountains in this area often carry wealth deep in their cores.

Gold and silver mines dot the entire range from northwestern to southwestern Gardolk, running through three of Gardolk's twenty provinces. Numerous mining towns exist along the foothills of southwestern Gardolk, and several active mining camps are in operation at any given point in time, even in the middle of winter. Despite the wealth to be had in these mining towns, the harsh conditions and terrain mean that only the bold in Gardolk's elegant society pursued their fortunes in the mountains.

Little did those in Gardolk know, however, that hiding in these mountains was a secret. Just south of the valley passage where the Calphos River ran through the Peaked Mountains, beyond a couple of peaks, was another mining camp nestled in a small reach. In this reach, there was an abandoned gold mine in the very back. The reach itself was filled with the khaki tents of a mining operation from Gardolk that had long since ceased operating. At least a hundred or more tents were still pitched and set up in the reach. Since its abandonment, however, the encampment had been claimed.

It was here that Setadev had his operations in play. In the midwinter, snow covered the mountaintops and coated the ground. Though the climate in Gardolk tended to be a bit warmer and more hospitable than other nations, the winter is not so forgiving in the mountains. Cold air whipped between the peaks and the wind was sometimes unforgiving, especially at altitude.

Camps that operated in the winter needed to have a constant supply chain, including warm clothing and survival gear. Despite the distance across the country, most of these supplies for the mining camps came from the metroplex of Gardolkia and Beralinchi because most of the industries and commercial development of Gardolk was localized there. That made transit across Gardolk far less suspicious than from the edge of the valley passage in itself, despite the extra distance to travel. Gardolk also lacked any port cities other than Gardolkia and Beralinchi with the capability to process cargo, making the metroplex the prime location for almost any goods to be processed.

The tents themselves were never very warm during the winter. Oftentimes extra layers of fabric were added to keep the cold air out. Those who stayed in the camps tended to become very demoralized after a short period of time, making camaraderie an important factor in the success of mining camps in the winter.

In one of the larger tents in Setadev's mining camp, Kevin Trent Stryker and General Sayo were tied to poles supporting the fabric layers. They were prisoners, now stuck together in the same area and with their fates now inexplicably tied to one another. Having been beaten to the point of exhaustion at the fortress, Kevin spent a lot of his time cursing under his breath. There was little he wanted to say to Sayo, whom he blamed for a large part of this incident.

A few days had passed since then, mostly in silence. There was no sign of Setadev, nor any sign of Satiana. The only other presence in the tent was the periodic arrival of an Enlightener to feed the prisoners, and he never said a single word to either of them. Kevin had previously thrown complaints to the Enlightener, but Sayo said nothing.

The only comfort Kevin had for the moment were his thoughts. After he was out of here, he was going to return to Caitlin. He would visit with Arthur and Rachel, and with Rouge and Resa, too. He would come back to destroy Pseudo. Maybe in exchange for trying and failing to break him out, he would arrest Sayo and attend the treason trial to follow instead of killing the general. Then, the world would be set at peace.

As he thought about it, all of that seemed shallow. At this point, though, Kevin was okay with shallow. He was so mentally and emotionally wrecked by Setadev's drugging and imprisonment that such a blunt assessment of how things would be seemed rational.

Memories were the only tie to his sanity he had left.

He had one such memory on his mind right now. For the three months between the Battle of Seta Archa and the beginning of this whole incident, Kevin lived with Caitlin in his home in Rikleifer, and they exchanged letters constantly with Arthur and Rachel in the Solunar Empire. It would take about a week for messages to reach back and forth, with letters being sent by trained falcon between mail stations in each major city.

On one such occasion, Kevin had been at a meeting with a military official in the city castle for an hour during the day, as one of his military duties as the Vanguard of Aurana. While he was away, the mail had come in, and Caitlin had been very excited to get the new letter. Upon his return, he had found Caitlin reading it already:

The door shut tight as Kevin came into his house from the icy cold outside. He walked inside and took off his military jacket, then walked toward his bedroom. Inside, Caitlin was lying on his bed, resting on her stomach with the letter in her hands. She had her head up and was reading it.

"Hi, Caitlin. New letter from Arthur and Rachel?" he asked.

"Yes," she answered. "I'm glad you're back; we can read it together now."

Kevin chuckled. "I think you've already got a jump start on me on that one," he said. "What's new with them?"

"Oh, not much, it seems," Caitlin answered, a smile on her face. "Of course, they're missing us, and they say that Rouge and Resa do, too. Rachel decided to send me a new poem she found in their library in Seta Archa. She thought I might like it."

That made Kevin raise an eyebrow. "Oh really?" he asked playfully. "May I read it?"

Lifting herself up to a sitting position and spinning around, Caitlin passed a page of the letter to Kevin. "Check it out," she said.

With a smile, Kevin took the letter. "Gladly," he responded, as he unfolded the page. He had read quite a few poems before, but he knew that Rachel was the most poetic of his friends and she often had quite an eye for poetry. As he took a look at the page, he saw the header noted the poem's title was "Written in the Stars". He began to read to himself:

Your name is written in the stars
By the nameless ones above.
They toiled hard, all day and night
To position every individual light,
To show you all their love.

I watched them work, and saw them put
Together each and every part.
I dreamed of that whose name I could see,
Wondering what to you I could be,
So around your name I drew a heart.

Sometime, somewhere, I do know
That you will see it too.
You'll know then that you'll be okay,
For always someone will be there and stay
To ensure a great life for you.

But I wonder, will you see the heart
That I drew around your name?
Will you know who sketched such emotion,
A symbol of true devotion,
And not just someone's claim to fame?

Ah, but your heart has been latched
Onto someone else, I know.
It's locked in place by a strong hope
That holds tighter than a rope;
With every day, your heart will brighter glow.

Yet every word you say for your loved one,
When I hear, I'm sad inside,
For every word I hear you say,
Almost each and every time and day,
I've said myself, and sometimes almost cried.

So I hope you will see the heart I drew,
And be truly happy, don't pretend.
And whether or not your emotions defect,
Understand that you I will always protect,
And continue to fight for and defend.

For I have faith in my heart;
And everything will work for the best.
My heart in the sky around your name,
Whether or not you think it's all a game,
I hope you'll see it apart from the rest.

Your name is written in the stars
By the nameless ones, in part.
Yes, I am certain, honest and true,
For I have faith in my heart, it's you
Whose name in the stars I'll circle with my heart.

"This is wonderful, Caitlin," Kevin finally said aloud when he had stopped reading. "It almost reads like a love letter, and yet it still seems so artistic."

"It does," Caitlin answered. "It kind of reminds me of when you and I got to know each other on our travels before we had that night out on the bridge north of Nuvenia. We were so taken by each other, but could never tell each other how we felt."

Kevin nodded. Then, he gently reached around and put his arm on Caitlin's shoulder, holding her close, too. "I'm just glad you're past it and now you're a part of my life," he said.

He expected that to be a nice comment. Instead, Caitlin let go of him a little bit and seemed shocked by it for just a brief second.

"What's wrong?" he asked.

"It's nothing," Caitlin answered quickly. She then took a second to breathe, and let her emotions relax as she put her arms around him again. Knowing that she would only make things worse by not telling him, she began, "It's just that I'm really not past it, I guess. I still worry about us in the future, if we'll still want each other."

With care, Kevin leaned over and brushed his other hand across Caitlin's cheek. "I'm sure you'll get to make all of your dreams come true, one way or the other." He tried not to sound glum, brought down by the doubt Caitlin was expressing.

There was a slight pause, as Caitlin leaned in closer. "I don't want to think about that right now," she said. "Right now, I have you with me. What that means now and what that may mean in the future doesn't matter for the moment. It just means I get to be close to you now, and that's all I really want."

Sometimes, looking back at that, Kevin had wondered if he had not done enough in that moment. If there was one struggle that Caitlin was having since regaining her emotions, it was her issues with her self-image. By all means, Caitlin was more cute than attractive for her age, but Kevin liked her no matter what she looked like, even if she had not brushed her hair or chose to put on comfortable clothes instead of her dress. Caitlin, though, did not see it that way. Ever since regaining her emotion, she had doubts about herself, about the way she looked, about how she behaved in public while she learned to embrace her emotions, about her dreams and if they were incompatible with his, and about how she could keep herself from losing Kevin.

Coincidentally, Kevin was not the most confident in his self-image, either. Ever since he was young, he never liked that he was not athletic, not popular, not confident in social situations. In some ways, he was a bit of a recluse too, and he never thought he could end up with a girl as special as Caitlin in his life.

Even after Kevin helped Caitlin to overcome her hesitations that kept her from being happy while being with him, she still had times she doubted herself, that she needed to have more to make sure she would not lose everything. He wanted to show her that everything would be all right no matter the situation, but for right now, that certainly did not seem like the case, anyway.

He was still tied to a pole somewhere in the middle of nowhere, as far as he knew.

Silent moments had continued to pass. A fire crackled inside the tent, in a contained steel pot to keep the tent from combusting. The frustration was getting to him. For a moment, Kevin looked down and cursed under his breath again. Then, he said, "You know, if I ever get out of this situation, I'll skin you alive personally with my sword."

There was a long pause. "If you keep that attitude up, we'll never get out of this situation at all," Sayo finally responded.

Kevin scoffed. "You try getting set up and lured into a trap, kidnapped, and drugged, and tell me if you would feel any different toward the person who set all of that up."

Sayo lowered his head. "I regret that," he said.

Trying to be mindful that Sayo was the one that set him free in the fortress, Kevin answered, "I'm aware of that. Your regret, though, is far too late. The damage has been done, and I have no desire to cooperate with you."

"You need not have one," commented Sayo. "I can understand your frustration."

Again, Kevin looked away. He wanted nothing to do with this. He was upset, beyond solace. At his age of sixteen, who could blame him?

Looking aside for a second, Sayo sighed. He knew he had to relate with this boy, or else neither one of them would ever make it out of this situation. Teamwork, as he knew from his many years of military service, was going to be paramount. "My name is Martin; you can call me Marty if you like," the general began, modestly, hoping that being willing to open up about himself might get to the pure one. "I am forty-eight years of age, and I hail from Atwals, Aurana."

Don't do this, Kevin thought to himself. Still, for some reason he could not bring himself to say that out loud.

"From a young age, I wanted to be a soldier," continued Sayo. "As soon as I was eligible, I enlisted in the Aurana military and started making my way through the ranks. Eventually, I became a commander, just in time for the savage war to begin. It was on that assignment that I met a Scurnian general…"

"Don't even finish that," Kevin interrupted. "I know your story already, General. You met Vincent Stryker and joined his attack against Seta Archa. After that, you returned to your hometown and defended Aurana against a Desolunar invasion at the Battle of Atwals, at which Atwals was destroyed and you were defeated. You joined Demonicus after that and became the second highest ranking general in his army, until you were defeated at the Battle of Seta Archa by Vincent Stryker and Auranian officers John Bryant and War Commander "Ironman" Eukert. From there, you retreated east of the city."

Sayo's jaw dropped a little bit. "Astounding," he said. "How do you know all of that?"

Reluctantly, Kevin rolled his eyes. He knew what he had to do now. "My name is Kevin Trent Stryker," he said. "I'm sixteen years old, soon to be seventeen, and I'm from Rikleifer, Aurana. I am the son of Vincent Stryker."

For a second, there was a pause. "That explains a lot," he acknowledged calmly, trying not to let his true surprise show. "It explains why your sword looks so much like Vincent's old one; because it is." He paused for another second. "Does it explain why Setadev wants to torture and destroy you?"

"Possibly part of it," Kevin answered, "but there's much more to it than that. My best friend is the heir of Desolunar, and I followed you out to the Wastes on his request."

"Your best friend?" asked the general.

"Yes," Kevin nodded. "He's the emperor of the Solunar Empire, now. He is the son of Demonicus."

"Amazing. And he became your best friend?" the general asked.

"Yeah, he grew up down the street from me."

"Incredible," said the general. "What an amazing coincidence."

"Just the way it happened," answered Kevin. "We had never known about our destinies before we became friends. Arthur is my best friend, and always will be. We won't ever let anything tear apart our friendship."

General Sayo nodded. “I see,” he said. “No wonder the Solunar Empire are your friends, and they tried to rescue you at the fortress.”

“Had you not tried to free me earlier, they may have made it to me,” commented Kevin.

There was another awkward pause, as the general sighed again. “Kevin, I sincerely doubt that would be the case,” he said. “Setadev gave up his fortress willingly; it is likely in a pile of rubble now because he sabotaged the structural supports.”

Kevin’s eyes widened. He knew Caitlin was in that fortress; he had been captured again trying to save her.

Yes, rather intriguing, is it not?

The voice came from outside the tent, as a figure stepped in. It was Setadev.

Instantly, Kevin’s fury started to leak into his voice. “I swear to you, if you so much as laid a finger on Caitlin, I’ll…”

“You will do what, exactly?” Setadev asked back. “From the look of things, you are in no position to make threats. As I told you, I have no desire to kill the world’s only angel. She is alive and with your friends in the Solunar Empire; I will take her when I have a containment structure befitting of her, and not before.”

Kevin breathed a sigh of relief.

“I would not be so calm if I were you,” Setadev quickly responded. “It was fun luring your friends out into Nuve and giving them nothing to show for it. The men they captured…” Setadev turned his head toward the general, “…your men, General Sayo…” he turned his head back, “are no longer of any use to me. All of the supplies we need have been routed through the fortress and down to this digsite. My Enlighteners are now the only forces I need, and I have all my equipment and supplies here.”

“So you say, but my friends will find you,” said Kevin. “Wherever we are now, they will chase you down and destroy you. I know as well as you do that you’re weak right now. Otherwise, you’d be letting me run free because you’re so arrogant that you wouldn’t care.”

Setadev’s fingers twitched for a second. “Did you not forget that I am carrying out my revenge on you?” he asked. “I would prefer to keep you as my pet for the moment, and let you observe my revival before I destroy you."

"You can have my body, but you can't have my mind," Kevin snapped back. "When Caitlin finds you, she's going to turn you into dust."

Suddenly, Setadev started laughing. "Do you really think that?" he asked. "Let me ask you, Kevin. Why do you think she would care about you when you are willing to cheat on her with another woman?"

"That's a lie!" snapped Kevin. "I would never cheat on Caitlin!"

Again, Setadev began chuckling. "What an interesting defense, because you will," he laughed.

A confused look came to Kevin's face.

"And now you see how the game is played," Setadev chuckled. "Why else do you think I would want to drug you? It allowed me to capture your mind, to decide for you what you were going to do. And I decided for you that you were going to cheat on your little girlfriend. Although the timing of our interruption at the fortress was quite unfortunate, I will yet make sure that not only will you lose your inhibitions, that you will do it in front of the angel."

Kevin dropped his head. Tears were coming from both of his eyes. He was legitimately brokenhearted by this. Setadev was trying to tear Kevin's life apart, more so than just taking him prisoner.

"Now, she will be as powerless as you are," Setadev continued. "Once I am revived, I will come back for her and place her somewhere upon which I can view her at my leisure."

"You underestimate her strength," Kevin responded, without lifting his head. "She is far more powerful than I am, and she has still come for me regardless of whatever you've told her. She will come for me again, and next time she will see to it that you can't come back to life again."

Setadev chuckled. "Trying to be overconfident, are we?" he asked. He chuckled again. "I suppose that you have a point," he continued as he started to walk around Kevin. "I was rather surprised indeed that she had come all the way out to the fortress after I shattered her mind. And though I did not kill her there, I did have a lot of fun beating her and coming within a few seconds of taking her life. Much as I would not have liked to end her life, I am sure I would have enjoyed it."

Kevin started breathing heavier. He was getting angry.

"How did you enjoy Satiana's company, by the way?" asked Setadev. "Is she not quite beautiful indeed? You could do better than that angel girl, anyway, and our lovely Satiana is certainly an example of that. She is so much better for you, anyway."

Kevin scoffed.

"In fact, we designed her based on your angel's design and making her more beautiful," continued Setadev. He then turned to Sayo. "Is that not correct, general? After all, I relied on your advice to make it happen."

Suddenly, Kevin's eyes shot over to the general. He lifted his head.

"You made me do it," responded the general. "I felt very disgusting for that."

"Or so you say, but I know how it appeases to the carnal instincts of any man," laughed Setadev. He turned his head. "Of course, you already know that, Kevin."

Spitting at the ground in disgust, Kevin said, "What did you make me do with her?"

A wide smile came to Setadev's face. "I made you do nothing. I have only facilitated it by administering some aphrodisiacs to let your inhibitions go. Even when you are out of your mind, you are surprisingly resilient, but I will be upping the ante very soon."

Looking away, Kevin was cringing. He did not want to imagine that. This whole matter was so disturbing, and Kevin was disgusted by the way he was being used. Now he understood why.

"Now, if you would be so kind, I have matters to attend," Setadev continued after a second's pause. "As lovely as it would be to continue this taunting session, whether to torment the pure one for his betrayal of his friends, or the general for his attempted but futile betrayal of myself, business must come before pleasure, after all." He walked toward the tent flap. "Enjoy your time here, as short as it may be," he said, as he departed.

The fire still crackled quietly. All else had grown silent.

A long minute passed.

Then, Kevin broke the silence. "If we get out of here together, general, I will be willing to cooperate with you until we escape. Then, we can go our separate ways."

Sayo looked away, himself a little disappointed that he could not gain forgiveness from Kevin, despite trying to rescue the young pure one before. "What will you do, Kevin?" he then asked. "Will you return to your friends?"

Another second passed. "Maybe," commented Kevin, "but not until I destroy Setadev."

"I don't think revenge is the best course of action here," responded Sayo.

Kevin sighed. "It's not that," he said. "He is too dangerous to be left alive. Regardless of how much you understand of gods and deities from what he has told you, general, he is still very strong and still wishes to control the world." For a second, Kevin looked around. "If I could only find my sword…"

"He probably has it somewhere where he knows you can't get it," said the general.

Again, Kevin scoffed. "There is nowhere I can't get it if I know where it is," he said.

Instead of questioning or making a comment, the general just shook his head. Still, neither one seemed to be understanding the other, except that they did agree that Setadev needed to be stopped.

Then, Kevin broke the silence again. "Why'd you change your mind, general?"

"Huh?"

"I asked you why you changed your mind. Why did you decide to help me? Setadev could offer you much more than I can, and now you're a prisoner like I am."

The general merely turned his head aside. "Much as you may believe so, I am not completely heartless."

Kevin rolled his eyes. He did not want to hear this now. He was likely to find disgust with the answer, no matter what it was. Instead, he lowered his head and let himself relax in the silence again.

The general also said nothing more, not wanting to continue this antagonization.

Outside, the temperatures were dropping as the evening was falling rapidly. Setadev, still in his guise and form as Pseudo, was now over by the entrance to the abandoned mine. An Enlightener was there, alongside himself and Satiana.

Setadev was not in for good news.

"The rock is proving more difficult than we thought to excavate," the Enlightener was commenting. "Even with the new shipment of hand drills and picks, we are having a hard time carving this mine deeper. It would seem to explain why this particular mine was abandoned."

That made Setadev's eyes go cross for a minute. "Then we will have to dig harder," he demanded. "Double the staff on all shifts. I want that chamber found within the next couple of days."

The Enlightener nodded and walked into the mine.

"The next shipment of supplies is expected to be here tomorrow morning," Satiana told Setadev. "We are expecting it from the eastern roads."

"It is not soon enough," Setadev responded. "I told those men that after the deliveries are made in Gardolkia, they are to have the supplies loaded up immediately and start on the road right away, not spend a night in the city. Otherwise, the time delay to travel across Gardolk undoes the benefits of not unloading at the mouth of the Southern Pass. Avoiding detection from irregular behavior is pointless if we take so long to restock our weapons, mining equipment, and supplies through the more common route."

"They are men, not immortal as you are," responded Satiana. "Driving them so hard will only lead to them being less productive and unable to complete their tasks at all."

That caused Setadev to shoot a glance at Satiana. He snarled for a second. "Comments like that make me wonder if you are truly a fragment of myself or not."

Satiana nodded. "I am who I am: a piece of the great deity Setadev, but an independent consciousness all to my own. As your creation, I am merely telling you what I see."

"How you are acting is weak," Setadev snapped back. "If you wish to live, and not be reabsorbed back into myself when this is all done, you will have to be stronger than this."

For a moment, Satiana appeared miffed. She was almost stunned.

Suddenly, another Enlightener came up to the cave entrance from outside. Immediately, he bowed before Setadev, indicating that he requested an audience with the fallen deity. Setadev turned to acknowledge the Enlightener. "Rise," he commanded. "Tell me what news you have."

Doing as he was instructed, the Enlightener stood up. "My lord, our scouts in the Southern Pass have reported back. They have spotted Solunar Empire forces entering the mouth of the pass by boat. The emperor and prime minister appear to be leading the forces."

After a second's pause, Setadev rolled his eyes. "Persistent, are they not?" he asked aloud. Then, he directed, "Prepare a contingency force to defend this place, to annihilate them when they arrive. Satiana and I will execute the next phase of our plan there."

Without another word, the Enlightener bowed again and walked away.

"You have a new strategy?" asked Satiana.

"No," answered Setadev. "We will merely be using every tool at our disposal to complete our objective. You will be an integral part of it, my dear. So will the pure one, as a matter of fact. And this time, we will break their spirits for good." He paused for a second. "Start by giving him all of the aphrodisiacs we have left. All of them."

Satiana's eyes widened a little bit. That was overdose, on the borderline of homicidal. Even she had a heart of some kind. She was not Setadev. Like Pseudo before Setadev's downfall three months before, she was merely a creation using a fraction of his power. Still, this was the purpose for which she was created. "Very well," she finally nodded. "What else?"

"I will explain the rest later," Setadev responded. "However, let us say for now that tomorrow morning, the Solunar Empire will no longer have any reason to pursue us when they see what has become of their hero."

Satiana saluted, and then walked out of the mine.

She stopped by a tent near the mine and grabbed all the remaining aphrodisiac. There was only two doses left, but distributing them at the same time would likely cause a psychotic reaction beyond normal brainwashing. It was a perfect pairing to the tormenting Setadev had just performed.

Suddenly, she felt guilty. Still, this was her job, after all. She had work to do, and she had a good idea what Setadev was planning. It was time to take Kevin's false affection for her to the extreme, for all the world to see. And the idea did sound fun, even if the methods were irrational. The easiest way to defeat an enemy is not to kill them, but to make them lose the will to fight, whether by demoralization or loss of cause. Such tactics were favorites of Setadev over the course of time.

With the aphrodisiac in hand, she stormed into Kevin's tent, where he was still weary, tied to the pole. As she walked in, Kevin spit at the ground. "What do you want?" he asked firmly.

A wide smile came to Satiana's face. "Oh, do you not enjoy my company anymore?" she asked with a snide tone. She lifted up the bottle to show it to Kevin. "Shameful, indeed. Maybe it's because you haven't had any of this to enjoy recently. Oh, how much it sets the mood; a sip of this, and suddenly you're in love with me."

Kevin's eyes widened. That was the drug he had been put on, the aphrodisiac. Even though he realized that, he asked aloud, "And what the hell is that?"

Satiana laughed. "I thought I already told you what it was…"

From behind Kevin, Sayo interrupted, "It is a drug called 'blue soup', made from a combination of several rare plants found in lush areas of Gardolk. It is designed to inhibit the senses, obscure the mind, and escalate emotions at the most primal levels."

Rolling her eyes, Satiana looked up. Sarcastically, she stated loudly, "Thank you, General Sayo, for the lesson on potions. Now, if you wouldn't mind shutting up for a while, I have business to complete."

Sayo said nothing in response. None was warranted while he was in such a helpless position.

Slightly, Kevin shook his head. "So, we're back to this, are we?" he asked.

Again, Satiana laughed. "Oh, pure one, how you amuse me," she said as she popped the top of the bottle off and plugged Kevin's nose, forcing him to open his mouth. As she poured in the entire bottle, she said, "Tomorrow morning, you will give me what I really want."

As the last bits of the potion fell into Kevin's mouth, Setadev then entered the tent. "Amazing how your brilliant sword is able to protect you from allowing me to possess you," he said. Light magic appeared in one hand while darkness magic appeared in the other, as he put his hands to the sides of Kevin's head. "This, however, I think you will find works differently. And if you angel can experience a mind shatter, then you can, too."

Chapter 38

The Valley Passage

A gentle rocking sensation was felt quietly in sleep. It felt so comforting, so peaceful, as if the world itself were otherwise at pause. For some reason, there was an odd sensation of tranquility accompanying it, like nothing could ever ruin these moments.

Peacefully, Caitlin opened her eyes. She was in a tent somewhere, and the rocking was real. How did she get here? She could not remember much, only that it had felt as though she had been asleep for ages. Her head was still in pain, but otherwise she felt relatively normal. She could tell she was still pretty scuffed up, but she was awake and moving around normally.

She looked down for a moment to realize that she was not wearing her dress. Instead, she was in a Solunar Empire standard issue uniform. Black pants, a black button-up shirt, and orange trim all over. She did not remember putting that on. Quietly, however, she put this to the back of her mind and knew that the answers would arrive as soon as she poked her head out of the tent.

The second she did, someone said, "Hey! Caitlin's up!"

Immediately, Caitlin looked around. Her friends Arthur and Rachel were in front of her.

"Where are we?" she asked.

Rachel looked down at Caitlin and smiled. "We're on a boat on the Calphos River," she said. "I'm glad to see you're okay; you've been asleep for quite some time."

Quietly, Caitlin gave a slight nod. "It feels that way," she said. "How long was I out?"

"Probably close to a week," answered Arthur. "You've been unconscious ever since we left the fortress."

There was a second's pause as Caitlin took a couple of deep breaths. "I remember that," she finally said. "And where are we now?"

"We're on the way to Gardolk," Rachel answered. "Right now, we're traveling through the Southern Pass. There's a valley passage in the mountains where the Calphos runs through the Peaked Mountains. Vincent Stryker informed us that the Enlighteners from the Shadows may be stealing Nuve supplies and smuggling them into the country, so we are going to investigate with a small force."

Caitlin shook her head lightly. "Another illegal invasion of a country, I guess?"

Arthur and Rachel looked at each other for a second, awkwardly chuckling. Then, Arthur looked back at Caitlin. "I guess you could call it that," he said, "but if Kevin's here, then we're going to find him."

"Not to mention Arthur's doing some scouting," Rachel chuckled. "He spotted an old arena on our side of the river that we went past, and now he wants to build a city there. He thinks it can be a trading post and a site for a world competition of sports, or something. And if anyone in Gardolk asks, that's what we were doing and we accidentally drifted too far down the river."

A slight smile came to Caitlin's face. She was so grateful to have such great friends. For a second, she looked down at her clothes, then looked back up and asked, "What's with the uniform?"

An awkward look came across Arthur's face. "Well, you see, after what happened at the fortress, your dress was torn up pretty badly. The only other clothes we had were spare uniforms, so I grabbed one in your size and had Rouge and Resa dress you in them while you were unconscious. I hope you're not too upset."

For a second, Caitlin paused and took a breath. "Not really," she finally answered, "as long as you guys didn't lose my dress."

"Don't worry about that," responded Rachel, as she reached under her bench on the small boat. She picked up the dress, revealing several tears and stains, and some areas where new thread was present. "While you've been sleeping, I've been trying to sew up all of the gashes and holes in your dress. I'm trying to be very careful since I'm not a very talented seamstress, so it will be a little while until I can have it all put together again."

Caitlin nodded. "Thank you," she smiled. She then looked down briefly at herself again, knowing this was a man's uniform she was wearing. After all, as military customs across the world still only allowed men to participate, the only people wearing military-style uniforms made specifically for women were her friends Rouge and Resa Kirkwood, the two Vanguards of the Solunar Empire. Naturally, then, the empire's forces would not have any spare female uniforms around. Then, she ran her fingers through her short hair again, missing the hair that she had spent years growing out. Never before she had met Kevin did she care so much about it. She knew he liked it, and the more she was experiencing the new sensations of emotions that she was learning, the more she became proud of it, as well.

Noticing Caitlin's odd behavior, Rachel asked, "What's up? You're acting kind of weird right now."

"Hmm?" asked Caitlin. "Oh, I guess I'm just kind of feeling down is all."

Silently, Rachel nodded. "Missing Kevin?" she asked.

"A little," Caitlin answered. "It's better than it has been because I know we'll find him soon. I can feel it."

Arthur smiled. "That's a refreshing burst of confidence," he stated. "That's something we haven't had around here much lately."

Caitlin nodded. "I know the feeling," she said. "And I know that after all we've been through already, we have to be close. Still… I don't know how to put it."

Lowering his head, Arthur answered, "It has been such a long trip, and so far we have nothing to show for it. This isn't like our journey a few months ago, at all. This hasn't really been at all like we were hoping."

Next to him, Rachel nodded. "Kevin told us when we were at the Battle of Middle Aurana a few months ago that winning the little battles was important. He even professed it during the briefing before the battle. We did that some when we traveled before, but this time we haven't won any at all. Is that it, maybe?"

However, Caitlin shook her head. "It's not that, either," she said. "It hasn't been easy, but that's not it."

"Well, why don't you catch us up?" Arthur asked, with a polite inflection. "I'm sure Rachel and I would love to know how in the world you ended up in the fortress."

"Me?" asked Caitlin, stunned. "I'd like to know how you and the army ended up there, too. Were you following me to try and keep me safe?"

Rachel shook her head. "No," she said. "Arthur let you go on your own on the condition that we were going to help you, but not by following you. We went and spoke to Demonicus, who was himself an Enlightener, and he told us about the fortress buried in Leticon. It took us a little while to mobilize the army, but we proceeded into Leticon and headed straight for it, with the intention of overrunning it, taking down Setadev's plans, and hopefully rescuing Kevin if he were there."

Caitlin sighed. "But you didn't find him," she said. "You found me instead."

"And that's why we're on the boat now," answered Arthur. "We're not giving up, and we're hoping you haven't either."

"Of course not," Caitlin snapped back. She then stopped for a second, allowing herself to relax. "I just wish you would have rescued him instead of me. He's probably suffered enough by now."

With that, Rachel shifted herself across the small boat to put herself next to Caitlin, and hugged her. "There's no need to bargain your own life for his," she said. "We want both of you to be safe."

Before Caitlin could respond, Arthur then jumped in. "Why don't you tell us where you've been and how you ended up at the fortress?"

There was a moment of silence, as Caitlin gathered herself. "All right," she said, reluctantly. She paused again to gather herself, with the pain of her experiences still weighing heavily on her mind. "When I left Seta Archa, I headed straight for the Metoi village. There, I met Marilynn, Lady of the Metoi, who was surveying the damage again, herself. She and I talked about it momentarily, and she also gave me a warning about the nearby Aequina. She also told me that she knew the Daritel tribe twenty years ago were associated with the Aequina."

"They were?" asked Arthur, his eyes widening. "Who did she say they were?"

Caitlin nodded. "Supposedly Marilynn said their leader's eyes were glowing red the day of the first attack."

Arthur looked down and rolled his eyes. "Tracer magic.

Someone was controlling him just to start a war? Could that have been Setadev as well? Or maybe…"

Rachel reached over and tugged on Arthur's arm. "We can talk about this later. Shouldn't we let Caitlin talk about her experiences?"

Looking over at Rachel, Arthur gave a short nod. He then looked back at Caitlin. "I'm sorry," he said. "Please go on."

"It's okay, Arthur," acknowledged Caitlin. "In any regard, Marilynn warned me about proceeding too much further east, but I knew I had to go to where Kevin was kidnapped in order to find my answers. It was a long day, but I finally found the abandoned campsite, on the opposite end of an embankment. It was really late by the time I made it, though, so I had to stop for the night. A couple of tents were left behind from the old forces, and that seemed like as good a shelter as any. While I was sleeping, though, a few Aequina soldiers came by and lured me out of the tent. I tried to fight one off, but then I was surrounded quickly, and had to surrender."

Rachel shook her head. "That explains the hair," she said, as she hugged Caitlin a little tighter. "I'm so sorry."

"Huh?" asked Arthur.

In response, Rachel sighed. "Do your research on your own people, Arthur," she said. "The Aequina practice human sacrifice. One thing they do with any females they sacrifice is cut their hair above the neckline, sometimes even higher like in Caitlin's case here. They believe it's a message to their captive of the sacrifice the prisoner is about to be for their cause."

Arthur lowered his head. He had tried to study all of the customs of his many peoples and nations as best as he could in his short few months as emperor. His feelings on that matter, however, were mute compared to the empathy he felt for Caitlin, who by now he realized was a victim of an attempted human sacrifice.

Silently, Caitlin nodded. "I was lucky to get away," she said. "They left me alone in their shrine, and tied my hands behind the support post of the building. Their mistake, though, was leaving my fingers free. I was able to light a spark and ignite the rope, then escape the building and a horde of anxious Aequina." She paused, deciding that she did not want to tell them of the Aequina she had killed in the burning village. "I ran, as far away as I could, until I passed out. I woke up the next day in the home of a Toronaga family." She paused again for a second, trying to gather herself. "After recovering from my ordeal with the Aequina, I knew where I had to go. Marilynn had given me one additional option for where Kevin might be: the Fortress of Da Leval, located in southern Leticon a couple of days east of Cardol. And…" she paused for a second, "Setadev dared me to come there to find Kevin."

"So arrogant, as always," commented Arthur.

Caitlin nodded again. "I thought so, as well," she said. "Still, it was the best lead I had, and I had to go to Kevin if he was there." She put her hands over her heart. "It took me a few days to get there, but I managed to sneak in pretty quickly. While there, General Sayo found me, and I would have killed him had Setadev not intervened. That's when he beat me and nearly killed me, stopping when he heard you guys were there with the army."

"Pardon me for asking," interrupted Arthur, "but how did he nearly kill you? How *could* he kill you? Aren't you immortal?"

Weighing this in her mind, Caitlin answered, "Well, I really don't know that for sure," she said. "But, I do know that's what he was intending to do, or at least show me he could if he wanted. He charged a spark on the tip of his finger, but it was not magic. It was divine power, in its most raw form, and I'm certain of it. Had he impacted me with it… I can only imagine what would have happened. I could have exploded, I could have disintegrated… I really don't know for sure."

"Well, let's step away from that," began Rachel, trying to redirect the conversation to ease Caitlin's mind. "That's when we finally caught up with each other, and you had to save Rouge."

Caitlin nodded. "Where are they, anyway?" she asked.

"Oh, we sent them back to Seta Archa, along with about half of our troops," answered Rachel. "Someone has to run the country while we're gone, after all, and Rouge isn't really in any kind of good shape right now." She paused for a second. "I still have to wonder how you keep so much grace under pressure. You've gone through so much and you're still going."

For a second, Caitlin lowered her head. "I guess that comes

from all of the discipline I put myself through over the years," she said. "Kevin's taught a lot to me about emotion and living with happiness, but I'm still me and I still have all of the lessons I had before."

Arthur nodded. "I get that," he said. "I still don't get what makes you feel so weird."

There was a long pause. Caitlin looked up and around at her surroundings.

After progressing so far into the Southern Pass, the land all around the boat was lovely. Mountains dotted each side along the pathway of the Calphos River, which ran smoothly in the valley passage all the way along. The water was very clear here, and the valley was quite lush during the warmer months. Had it not been for the series of boats traveling down the water, numbering about fifteen, traveling through the passage would be quite peaceful and quiet indeed.

Then, Caitlin looked down at herself again. "I'm really not sure," she said. "I mean, there are a few things." She looked over the side of the boat, at her reflection in the river. "For starters, I look like a boy. For some reason, that bugs me more than I think it should."

"And why's that?" commented Arthur. "I thought you wouldn't have cared too much about your appearance."

Immediately, Rachel reached over and smacked Arthur's arm. "Arthur, let a girl be proud of herself," she said. "Caitlin's lost her identity with her hair cut and being dressed in a military uniform. It's not like her, and she knows it."

Arthur scowled. It did not quite add up to him, thinking Caitlin's serious mentalities would have prevented that issue of self-image.

"I guess that's the case," commented Caitlin. "I mean, I really don't know what it is for sure, but I have always worn a dress and had long hair. After I met Kevin, I was surprised a little bit that he liked those features about me so much, and I really tried to keep my dress neat and my hair straight and long when I wanted to share some special moments."

"You're not afraid he won't like you when he sees what you look like now, are you?" asked Rachel.

Caitlin shook her head. "It's not that, either," she said. "Maybe that's a little bit, but it's not quite all of it. I feel like, though, that something's wrong. I mean, more than just where we're at and what's all happened so far."

For a second, Rachel frowned, a little confused. "You don't think you might have inherited your father's foresight of the future, do you? He does always seem to know what's going to be coming before we do, and knows where we'll be before we know."

That gave Caitlin a chuckle. "You make it sound like you think he's psychic," she said. "He's not, really; he's just very sharp and observant. As a god, he can sense differences in things such as energy and time, and he has a high level of intuition and five thousand years of experiences. When he seems to have us beat, he has evaluated that which he can sense and used his best judgment."

Arthur also chuckled. "I'm sure he acts on his hunches."

"Yes, he does," nodded Caitlin, smiling with the fond memory of her father.

Even Rachel had to chuckle a little bit as she leaned back. "Well, maybe my fears were misplaced, then," she said. "We'll be at the Gates to Gardolk tomorrow morning. I'm sure we'll find what we're looking for in the elegant land."

Caitlin bowed her head. "I sure hope so," she said.

As the evening passed, Caitlin had valuable time to catch up and enjoy a little time with Arthur and Rachel. Even though he was her half-brother, Caitlin could not see Arthur as anything different than one of her friends. Rachel, definitely, was her best friend aside from Kevin, who she was with in a much closer nature.

Still, Caitlin felt very uneasy. Her nerves had not calmed over the evening. Something still did not feel right. Perhaps she was having premonitions. Perhaps it was just a matter of having gone through so much already. She had felt like she had lost her identity and her humanity through all of this.

However, it did not seem like any of that was the case.

Night fell and the winter breeze blew violently as a snowstorm started to set in. Fortunately, the troop boats were all stocked with blankets and low tent canopies, helping to keep everyone warm and protect them from the elements. When Arthur had sent for the boats, he knew of the unique equipment Desolunar had had for their forces and thought the small, canopied boats designed for distance travel would be perfect for this operation.

In the night, Caitlin slept quietly. Despite the worries, peace was finally setting into her mind. For the first time in a while, she could be at ease, if only for a little bit.

Still, something kept nagging at her across the whole night. Why did Setadev leave her alive, aside from his fancy with an angel? And what was scaring her so badly right now? She missed Kevin, and missed him badly. Still, her gut feelings were telling her that it was not a good idea to keep going. What was going on?

The next morning arrived, cold and quiet. Above, the sky was gray, covered entirely by clouds. The wind whipped through the valley passage, and the snowfall was beginning to pick up. It was becoming more difficult to see, as a blizzard was setting in. Caitlin poked her head out the side of the boat to see where they were and what was coming up. Just ahead, the tall Peaked Mountains seemed to be coming to an end, and a pair of tall pillars stood on either side of the river, decorated in various colors. A pair of flags stood at the top of each one: purple with gold trim, and gold grid lines separating the flag into twenty individual squares, five wide by four high. This was the flag of Gardolk.

This area was known as the Gates to Gardolk, the passage from the Southern Pass into the elegant land, and the primary trading route for the little business between it and Aurana, Nuve, and the Solunar Empire. No port town existed near the passage, representative of the isolationist nature of Gardolk. Though a few towns existed along the Calphos River, the only port capable of cargo handling and mass shipping was down the river in the Gardolkia and Beralinchi metroplex. Cargo unloads at any point up the river were usually seen as suspicious by local citizens for this reason.

Around that time, Arthur and Rachel also woke up. Quickly, they readied themselves for what was coming up. A few minutes had elapsed, allowing everyone to be fully conscious and alert. Arthur had pulled up a horn and sounded it back toward the trailing boats, signaling for his troops to be up and ready to move out.

"There it is," commented Arthur, as he turned around and put down his horn. "The Gates to Gardolk are just as I have been told. Impressive, but silent and unwelcoming." He reached over and grabbed a pole out of the boat to start pushing it on the riverbed toward the southern edge of the river.

"Onward," added Rachel. "It's the passage to our next destination, wherever it may be in this country." She stopped for a second as Arthur beached the canopy boat on the southern riverbank. She then turned to see the troops beaching theirs as well along the banks at the gate. Then, Rachel turned to look at Caitlin, who had a hand up trying to block the wind from her face. "Kevin will be here too, you know," she said.

"I hope so," said Caitlin, as Arthur and Rachel disembarked the boat and assisted her as well. As she stepped off the boat, however, the wind started picking up.

"My, the wind's awfully heavy today," commented Rachel. "You can barely see for all the falling snow, too."

Arthur raised a hand up to his eyes. "It's too easy to go snow-blind in this blizzard, even in the light of day. We may have to build camp here and wait until the storm passes to continue on."

The wind blew even harder for a moment. Then, it turned sharply and started blowing in a different direction. It was a crosswind.

Caitlin's eyes widened. "Oh no," she said, in realization. Then, she started yelling. "Everyone, look out! He's here!"

Suddenly, a strong voice echoed through the air, *I was wondering how long it would take for you to know I have been waiting for you.*

Chapter 39

Elegant Tragedy

Out from the blizzard emerged two figures, as the winds started to calm. The snow, however, kept falling hard. One figure looked familiar, almost like Kevin but covered in scars and dressed in black, and the other was a very attractive girl in a black dress.

Instantly, Caitlin started charging magic in her hands while Rachel pulled out her bow. Arthur, still without a weapon all his own after his Sword of Corruption was destroyed, took the steering pole from the boat and lifted it up in a defensive stance. "I thought something was wrong," Caitlin commented. "I hate it when I'm right, sometimes."

Setadev started chuckling. "Your sense of humor amuses me sometimes, angel. Something the pure one taught you, no doubt?"

That made Caitlin cross. "Your sense of humor amuses no one but yourself. Either tell me where I can find Kevin, or I will destroy you."

Arthur and Rachel looked over at Caitlin with wide eyes. She was serious and hellbent. This was a side of her that they had not seen before.

In response, Setadev put his face in the palm of his had. "Oh, angel, how much you do amuse me. Still, you do not see how the game is played. Why do you think I would tell you where he is, or think that you can destroy me when you have been thoroughly unsuccessful up to this point?"

Caitlin clenched her fist in frustration. Arthur, though, stepped forward to keep her from getting too angry. "Don't patronize," he said. "I already know you're vulnerable. You're in no position to make any threats."

"Or what?" asked Setadev. "Or you will hit me with the pole in your hand? Hah!" He started laughing.

Arthur clutched the pole tighter. This time, Rachel stepped forward to calm him down. "Just tell us why you're here," she said. "Clearly you don't have an ambush, as you would have had a better chance at that in the middle of the valley, not here. You're not here to destroy us yet, because you could have done that in Leticon. What business do you have?"

Setadev chuckled. "Oh, plenty," he answered. "I thought I might introduce you to someone while you are here. Please, allow me to introduce someone to you all, but particularly to Caitlin." He stepped back and placed his arms to the side. "This is Satiana, my new right hand in all of my operations."

Satiana stepped forward.

Arthur's jaw dropped a little bit. Caitlin's and Rachel's eyes widened in a bit of jealousy.

She was absolutely gorgeous. Satiana was dressed in an elegant black dress trimmed with red and gold, somewhat similar but distinctly different to Caitlin's white dress. She had a lightly tanned skin tone that perfectly matched her long blonde hair, which had a few curls. Her eyes were the color of sapphires, similar to Caitlin's. In terms of shape, she was slimmer than Caitlin, but shapelier.

By all means, she was an attractive young lady. She stepped forward with a smile, almost like the kind Caitlin would give to Kevin. "Pleased to meet all of you," she began, with a curtsey. "My name is Satiana."

There was an awkward pause. Neither Caitlin, nor Rachel, nor Arthur had any response to this surprising presentation. She seemed sweet, pure, and extremely beautiful. How could she be allied with Setadev? For a moment, Arthur's jaw stayed hanging open, as he had not seen such an attractive young woman in a long time. "She's so pretty," he said in awe.

In response, Rachel turned and hit him hard in the side of the arm.

Immediately, Arthur reached up and put his free hand on that spot. "Ow!" he exclaimed, more in surprise, than in pain. "What was that for?"

"Just who are you staring at?" asked Rachel.

"What does it matter to you?" Arthur asked back. "It's not like you're my girlfriend, or anything. Even if she's the enemy, I can look for a minute."

Rachel looked away and to the ground for a moment. She was hurt and felt like Arthur was a selfish pig. He was not acting any differently than any other young man his age, but he did not realize he was being more hurtful than he thought.

Caitlin, though, had no reaction to the joking. Her eyes were focused, and her glare was stern. She would not buy the perception of beauty and niceness that Satiana was projecting. Something about her seemed familiar in a weird sense, and Caitlin could sense Satiana's power. It was almost immortal, as if Satiana were another piece of Setadev.

After another moment of glaring, Satiana stepped up to Caitlin. "You have a problem with me?" she asked, getting an attitude in her voice. She started getting in Caitlin's face.

"Not at all," Caitlin coolly responded. "I'm not fooled by you, though."

"Oh?" asked Satiana. "So you won't be surprised when I teach you to respect me." She lit up her right fist in fire and tried to punch Caitlin in the stomach.

Catching the move at the last second, Caitlin extended both of her arms and formed a panel shield out of light magic, protecting her as Satiana tried to punch forward. Forcefully, Satiana continued to push forward, as Caitlin struggled to keep her shield up. Satiana's power was massive, shaking the foundation of Caitlin's resistance.

Who was this girl?

Sensing that Caitlin was in danger from this attack, Rachel drew her bow and aimed it directly at Satiana. She fired, only to have Satiana duck her shoulders low enough to dodge the arrow, without stopping her attack. Before Rachel could have another arrow nocked, however, Satiana ceased her attack, and Caitlin lowered her shield.

Caitlin started breathing heavily. "You're strong," she said.

"Well, maybe you shouldn't have glared at me," answered Satiana. "Do I need to teach you some respect?"

"What's your problem?" Caitlin snapped back. "Are you just

looking to pick a fight?"

"My problem is you," Satiana responded, as she physically shoved Caitlin back. "Why are you even here?"

Tbat made Caitlin confused. "Huh?" she asked. "We haven't even met before just now. What problem do you have with me?"

"Just look at yourself," Satiana answered. "Short hair and a man's military uniform. What kind of woman are you? You're underpowered, weak, and pathetic. You have no right to exist in this world."

Caitlin clenched her fists. She was furious.

At this point, Setadev stepped forward. He called to Satiana, who turned back and looked at her master. "Show a little more respect for the world's only angel," he said. "She is, after all, unique to this world. There will be a place for her in our new world."

"As what? Your showpiece?" commented Rachel back to Setadev as she listened.

For a second, Setadev considered this. "In a manner of speaking, I suppose you could call it that," he responded. "I am sure, though, that she might serve a fitting role in my services and the utopia while I will create."

Whatever it was, it sounded disgusting.

"You take that back!" screamed Caitlin, as she fired a beam of darkness at Setadev. Satiana made no move. Setadev merely raised one hand, and diverted the beam around him. Within a second, Caitlin stopped powering the beam, realizing that she was acting in futility.

"Oh, my dear angel, so feisty, are we?" Setadev then asked. "Relax; you will come to know your role soon enough." He then turned to Arthur and Rachel. "As for you two, you have no role in my new world, but I would love nothing more than for the two of you to witness the downfall of the world and the failure of your best friend. That, to me, would be satisfying."

Arthur was furious. Rachel, though, extended her arm to hold him back. Fighting Setadev would give no benefit at this point. "Tell us, then. What kind of world are you trying to create?"

In response, Setadev chuckled. "Ah, so finally someone is bright enough to question my motives. Well played, my dear girl, well played. You do not see how the game is played, but you at least hold some idea of the rules."

It was hard for Rachel not to pull up her bow and take a shot at him. Setadev's cocky attitude made him an infuriating person to deal with.

"I seek a utopia, a paradise," Setadev began. "I have, ever since I founded the gods five thousand years ago, and such was to be their task and purpose. And all I asked in return was that I was to be the one who controlled it, who had the power to make its decisions and direct it. All would bow to me, but such is the way that rulers control the respect of their people."

"And it just so happens under your utopia that you are the ruler," commented Arthur. "Your so-called 'utopia' makes everyone accountable but you. You've shown in your history that you don't have any qualms with using corruption and manipulation in order to achieve your goals." He raised his pole. "On that statement of fact, I challenge your utopia. That is the reason that no one person should rule the world."

Setadev started chuckling. "And why would I place any value in the words of a seventeen-year-old illegitimate emperor of an illegitimate nation?" He scoffed sarcastically at Arthur. "Besides, you forget one crucial fact here, young emperor. I am not a man. I am a god. I hold more power than the gods that watch from above, only pathetically observing and making their small changes and influences. They are not truly gods, for they lack the ambition to control their world and seize the opportunities their ambitions afford them. Only I am a true god, and it is only fitting that the world in turn be ruled by me." He paused for a second, almost for dramatic effect, ever the showman. "For five thousand years, I have waited to begin my conquest and seek my revenge on those who exiled me. You will not be any interference in my plans."

"And yet, we have interfered," pointed out Rachel firmly. "Take a look around you, Setadev." She paused, as she looked at the mountains behind. "Where is your next ambush? Why not ambush us there? Why have you not ended us yet? You pulled a fast one on us at the fortress, but you did so because you knew you could not beat us and our army. Your powers are strong, but they are limited, and you know it."

"That will be rectified soon enough," responded Setadev. "Yet, minister, if I am so powerless, why don't I end your life right now?"

Rachel's eyes widened as Setadev charged light energy in his hands. Then, he fired it in a beam.

She was frozen, stunned by this sudden turn.

"Caitlin!" yelled Arthur, as he began charging toward Setadev.

In a split second, Caitlin jumped in front of Rachel, with her arms crossed and a shield of light around them. She managed to get into position just in time to deflect the beam off her shield and into the sky. It was taking all of her effort to block the attack.

For a moment, Rachel stood stunned as Caitlin kept blocking the beam. "What are you doing?" Caitlin finally yelled back at Rachel. "Get out of here! Now!"

Still hesitant, Rachel stepped out of the way. Noticing this, Caitlin started to push forward through the beam, holding her shield up the whole way. She was pulling all of the strength she had to force her way closer to Setadev.

As she did, Setadev flinched just a bit. Arthur caught this on his charge. He was not anticipating Caitlin to have so much strength left. This was the opportunity.

Seizing it, Arthur swung his pole and caught Setadev by the back of the head, where he was not expecting to be hit. Stunned, he fell forward, as his beam continued and cut into the ground before he hit it. As Arthur pulled his pole back for another hit, Satiana grabbed the back end of the pole and tugged Arthur, with enough force to throw him backwards toward his men, who were completing their disembarking of their boats.

Rachel pulled up another arrow, this time reaching for one with an antite arrowhead from her quiver. She nocked her bow and took aim for the fallen Setadev. Despite having just been caught off guard a little bit ago, she kept herself in check and her focus clear. She took aim with her keen eyes and let her arrow fly. It was right on target, as Setadev began to stand up again.

Quickly as he could, Setadev reached up and grabbed the arrow by the shaft in midair, keeping it from hitting him. Before he could get back to a defensive position, though, Caitlin hit him hard in the face with a blast of darkness energy, knocking him to the ground.

In response, Satiana jumped in front of the fallen Setadev and began forming a shield of light herself. Arthur and Rachel backed off and took up position next to Caitlin, who was charging for another attack.

From behind Satiana, however, Setadev started laughing as he stood up again. "I suppose you three have grown somewhat," he said. "That, I will admit, was fun." Satiana then stepped aside and lowered her shield. "However, as always," Setadev continued, "your efforts are futile." He dropped a fist to the ground, unleashing a powerful earth magic that created a fissure in the ground.

The resulting earthquake was powerful enough to knock Caitlin, Arthur, and Rachel to the ground forcefully. Behind them, the disembarking men had to pause to deal with the tremors of the earth below them, shaking them vigorously.

A gap was created in the earth below, too wide to jump. It went all the way to the mountainside, making the only way around the side that Setadev was on. Caitlin was isolated on the south side, away from the river. Arthur and Rachel were now stuck on the north side, with the men behind them.

"Perfect," chuckled Setadev.

As Caitlin stood up, she brushed herself off and saw she was isolated. "You guys okay?" she called out, looking over to where Arthur and Rachel were struggling to stand.

Hesitantly, Rachel stood in soreness. "Yeah, I think so," she said. As she rose, she clutched her forearm. "I think I may have sprained my wrist in the fall, though."

Within another second, Arthur also managed to make it to his feet and started brushing himself off.

Without a moment's pause, Satiana began walking over toward Caitlin, away from Setadev. She had a look of determination in her eyes, as if she were out to kill somebody. At the end of the fissure, Setadev stood calmly, as though he knew what were about to happen.

Satiana walked straight up to Caitlin and slapped her hard across the face. Anger was in her eyes. “You don’t deserve to exist,” she said. “He may want to keep you, but I would like nothing more than to destroy you.”

Cautiously, Caitlin raised her head. There was a red mark on her face, the size of Satiana’s palm. “Why do you hate me so much?” she cried lightly, with pain stinging her face. “What have I ever done to you?”

Spitting at the ground next to Caitlin’s feet, Satiana said, “You’re nothing but a stupid little…”

Furious, Caitlin lit her hand up in fire magic and decked Satiana across her face, interrupting her sentence. She was hit so hard that she fell to the ground. “You take that back!” she screamed to Satiana. “You don’t even know me!”

From across the gap, Arthur yelled, “Yeah, Caitlin! Beat the snot out of her!”

Rachel grabbed him by the arm. “Arthur!” she said. “Have some respect, would you?”

“But that was awesome!” he commented back to Rachel. “She insulted Caitlin, so Caitlin knocked her out cold. Satiana just got leveled!”

Caitlin looked over and smiled at her half-brother, surprised by the compliment to her strength. “Thanks, Arthur,” she said.

In response, Rachel just stared at Arthur, with her jaw hanging open. That was so unlike a typical Caitlin response, although admittedly a bit less inappropriate for the moment.

Then, Caitlin turned back to Satiana, who was standing up. “I don’t know who you think you are,” she said, “but you will not get away with that. Tell me, what do you really want with me? Why are you here?”

“Why am I here?” asked Satiana, as she brushed herself off. “I am here to tell you who I am,” she said, an awkward smile coming to her face. “I’m Satiana, the right hand of Setadev,” she answered. Then, she walked another step closer to Caitlin. “I’m the one who’s here to take your boyfriend away from you.”

Suddenly, Caitlin’s eyes widened.

“I do find it so funny,” Satiana continued. “Setadev has told me all about you, you know. He says that you are strong, but that all of your powers beyond your magic skills are dependent on another. You, of all people, have the most trivial weakness of any individual with power, and yet also the most poetic." She looked around for a second. "It is only fitting that we should have this meeting in Gardolk," she continued. "Such an elegant tragedy could not play out in a more elegant land."

Steaming, Caitlin lowered her arms and started charging her energy cautiously. "How can I believe you with your attitude?" she asked, pointedly. "For all I know, you may only be telling me what you know will hurt me."

"My, so full of questions, are we?" Satiana asked pointedly. "Now, would you keep asking that question when I take Kevin away from you?"

Kevin. She said his name.

Immediately, Caitlin hit Satiana with a blast of darkness, catching her by surprise and knocking her off her feet. Caitlin then continued to throw darkness blasts, screaming, "You can't have him! He's my Kevin! You'll never have him!"

After a few seconds, Satiana rolled over and shot a blast of ice at Caitlin, causing her to stop. She was hit square in the chest and thrown back. As she struggled to stand up again, Satiana walked over to her. "*Your* Kevin?" she asked. "Is that what you think, really?"

At this point, Arthur signaled to several of his men and began rushing toward the end of the fissure where Setadev was standing. Before he could get anywhere, though, Setadev pushed back with a heavy wind spell, keeping Arthur and his men from advancing, no matter how hard they tried to run. He shook his head at Arthur, indicating that he was not going to allow Arthur or his forces to interfere with what was going on on the other side of the fissure.

Rachel tried to nock an arrow in her bow and take a shot at Satiana, but it hurt her too much to pull the string back to fire. Her sprained wrist was making it impossible for her to make a shot. It would effectively be only Caitlin and Satiana on the other side of the fissure, with no one else involved. They could only watch.

This was a trap, Rachel realized.

Caitlin was breathing heavily. Especially in the cold winter, ice blasts tended to cause frostbite. As she stood up, trying to shake off the pain of a strong shot that was not quite point blank, crystals of frost were visible on her Solunar military jacket. Still, she was determined, and she stood to face her aggressor. “I don’t ‘think’ it,” she answered. “I know it. He is mine as much as I am his.”

Satiana rolled her eyes. “Do you really think that you are his?” she asked. “Can you be certain? Or are you merely reciprocating that which you wish to believe, because you want it to be true and fear the opposite?”

“Don’t listen to her, Caitlin!” Rachel called out. “This is all a trap! She’s trying to set you up for something!”

For a moment, Caitlin stopped in her tracks. Rachel had a very valid point. Yet secretly, those words still nagged at her, too. She had come this far to save Kevin, but what if the worst were true? She looked over and gave Rachel a slight nod. Satiana’s words would not do the same.

“Oh, would you stay out of it?” Satiana called back to Rachel. “This has nothing to do with you.”

“Nor does it have anything to do with anything you have to say to me,” Caitlin shot back, drawing Satiana’s attention again. “If you want to try me, you had better say it with your magic. I want nothing to do with your words.”

Satiana started glaring at Caitlin. Her eyes were fixed, her gaze was firm. “Is that how it is to be, angel?” She started charging energy in her hands. “Then, let us speak in a manner traditional of the past.” She took a battle stance.

In response, Caitlin did the same, as she charged darkness magic in both of her hands. Despite the close hit of the ice blast, she was still ready to go. Today was the best she had felt physically in a long time. It was time for a showdown, a formalized start to a fight between two individuals. As soon as one flinched, that would signal the beginning.

Caitlin and Satiana stood silently, with their glares fixed upon each other. Neither one would make a move. A minute passed by, as the breezes picked up slightly.

Rachel and Arthur watched intently across the gap. Arthur shot a glance over to Setadev, who was staring intently. If only he could get around the chasm and over to his sister, he could help her out. Setadev, though, would certainly not allow that. Rachel stared, with her eyes fixed open in stun at what was about to unfold. She kept envisioning herself pulling up her bow and taking several shots at Satiana, none of which she knew she could make because of her sprained wrist. For a moment, Rachel thought about having the twenty archers she had in her hundred troops behind her take aim and fire, but she took a look down at Setadev, knowing he could counter that. Setadev was weak, but the only way they stood a chance against him was with Caitlin assisting.

The wind whipped in the air, as snow continued to fall. Caitlin and Satiana were both frozen in place, motionless. It was cold, so cold that it was tough to focus. Caitlin was having a tough time concentrating.

She flinched.

Satiana jumped on the opportunity and flung a scattershot of light magic at Caitlin. Quickly, Caitlin countered by crossing her arms in front of her face and energized a shield of light to bounce the shots off. With this, Satiana seized the opportunity to roll to the side and do the same attack, at another angle.

It was now too wide for Caitlin to block. She dropped her shield and fell to the ground as quickly as she could. When she did, she took several hits to her body, but she knew the hits would come and was ready. They were unavoidable and painful, but could have been more so had she not dropped to evade most of them.

As soon as the shots passed, she rolled on the ground to her right a few times before standing up. She snapped up as quickly as she could, raising her hands in a defensive stance. She looked all around. She had to locate Satiana as quickly as she could, before she could be hit with something more severe.

"Caitlin! Behind you!" called out Rachel.

Too late.

Satiana jumped and smashed Caitlin in the head with her knee. She was driven to the ground with force, pushing snow all over herself.

Standing up from the attack, Satiana stood up and looked over Caitlin, who was reaching to clutch the back of her head as she slowly leaned up. "Pathetic," she said. "You're not so witty, are you?"

There was no response from Caitlin as she slowly pushed herself off the ground and to her knees.

"As I thought," commented Satiana. "Far too easy. You could not hurt me if you tried."

Furious, Caitlin said nothing. This fight was far from over.

Instead, she reached over, grabbed Satiana by the ankles and pulled them up as she stood up. Satiana was caught by surprise, sliding in the snow and falling to the ground. As Satiana's head hit the snow, Caitlin stood over her with an orb of earth in one hand, and fire in the other. She smashed them together to create a giant blast of molten rock and slammed it into the ground where Satiana was, as forcefully as she could.

The resulting burst knocked Caitlin back a bit and shot Satiana back against the snow with force. As soon as Satiana stopped sliding, she immediately began rolling in the snow to ease the burning from such a powerful shot.

Caitlin thought about it for a second, as she raised her hands again. She really did not like that particular combination. A molten lava blast from earth and fire combining was a painful and destructive attack, almost too cruel even for Satiana.

Still, she was surprised when after a minute of rolling, Satiana rolled over onto her back and propped herself up on her arms. She looked a little scuffed up, but her clothes were not damaged at all. Her skin was visibly undamaged. She should have been injured much greater than that. She was, however, breathing heavily. Maybe she had been injured after all.

"I would suppose I spoke too soon," commented Satiana, still breathing heavily as she held herself up by her arms. "I was not anticipating that."

"There's more where that came from, if you want," Caitlin responded. She began charging darkness magic in her hands, preparing for another attack.

Satiana lifted herself off the ground and stood back up, charging light energy. in her hands. "Then show me!" she screamed as she fired a beam of light at Caitlin.

Caitlin responded by firing a beam of darkness.

Across the chasm, Rachel had little time to grab Arthur and pull both of them down to duck.

Boom!

The two blasts intercepted each other and created a loud noise. Light and darkness usually cancelled each other out, allowing the energy to dissipate itself. In this case, there was so much force behind each beam that the energy could not dissipate quickly enough. The resulting explosion shook the ground, throwing up a cloud of snow.

For a minute, everyone was snow-blind. The wind picked up the snow and blasted it around the field, making it difficult to see. As the snow settled back to the ground, the result started to become discernible.

The resulting explosion had knocked both Caitlin and Satiana backwards against the ground. Their shots at each other had essentially been a draw, as both were incapacitated from the blast. A pair of tracks in the snow were visible, each leading to the two ladies, where they had slid in the snow from the explosion.

"Caitlin! Are you okay?" Rachel yelled across the chasm.

Slowly, Caitlin started to move from the spot she was in. Her hands went up to her head as she started to ease herself up. She was covered in snow, and her short hair was caked in it. She looked to be very badly scuffed. "I think so," she finally answered, as her left hand kept clutching her head. "That, however, did hurt."

Satiana was standing up from her spot. "Impressive, angel," she said. "I see now why Setadev and the pure one value you so much. Or, should I say, how much the pure one pretends to value you."

Finally, Caitlin was making it to her feet and trying to brush off all of the snow. "You keep saying that," she said, still clutching her head lightly. It was clear that she was very sore all over her body. "I won't believe anything you say. Not for a single minute."

"Oh?" asked Satiana. "Is that the case?"

For a second, Caitlin took a breath, trying to catch it. "You can keep saying it all you want, but I know my Kevin. He cares about me. He always has, and always will."

There was a slight pause.

Then, much to Caitlin's surprise, Satiana started chuckling, in the same awkward way that Setadev did. What was she up to?

"Well, then," Satiana began, "why don't I let him show you himself?"

Caitlin gasped. Behind Satiana, a small teleportation gate had formed, and collapsed quickly. Then, Satiana stepped aside.

Someone was standing in that place now. Someone with short brown hair, looking down. His shirt was red, and his pants were dark green Auranian military trousers. The figure raised his head, revealing his face.

Caitlin's eyes widened. "Kevin," she whispered.

Across the chasm, Arthur and Rachel's jaws each dropped. "He's here," said Arthur in stun.

"I don't believe it," commented Rachel. Then, she yelled over to Setadev, "What manner of trickery is this? Are you expecting us to be fooled by whatever mock-up or illusion you're presenting to us?"

"Oh, this is no mock-up," responded Setadev. "Be patient, minister. You will soon see how the game is played."

Rachel was stunned. Setadev was known to use deception before, but his words seemed frank. Whatever this was, it was too suspicious to trust. If Setadev and Satiana's arrival here were really a setup and actually well-planned, this may have been what they were actually looking to accomplish: whatever was about to happen.

Satiana stepped up next to Kevin, who was utterly motionless. "Don't you like my new friend, Caitlin?" she asked. "I believe it has been quite a while since you have seen him."

Slowly, Caitlin started walking toward him. "Kevin," she whispered again, so surprised to see him. She extended her hand, as if to reach out and touch him while trying to walk to him. "Is that really you?"

Kevin said nothing. His eyes were wide, his mouth gaping open slightly.

Upon seeing this, Caitlin's eyes lit up. She could tell it was him and did not see the look of his face. She was just so happy to see him. She wanted to touch his face, to know that he was real, then to hug him and take him home with her.

Tears came to her eyes. She broke into a run and wrapped her arms around him.

In response, Kevin turned away, toward Satiana who was now standing next to him. Surprised, Caitlin slid and fell in the snow. She fell against the ground, but caught herself on her hands and did not fall all the way back.

Rachel and Arthur looked on with surprise. They glanced at each other briefly, sharing the same stunned look from what they just saw.

Suddenly, Caitlin's eyes shot up to Kevin. Satiana wrapped both of her arms around him and hugged him tightly. She looked up at him in shock while Kevin's eyes were cold and forward, pupils widely dilated but not glowing red. He did not even bother to look down at Caitlin.

Another tear fell down Caitlin's cheek, but this time from sadness instead of happiness. "But Kevin," she asked, "why?"

"I would not ask him such questions," Satiana laughed, staring down at Caitlin and pointing at her in jest. "He's a little bit different now, you see? He is the man that he has always wanted to be. All he needed to do was release the one thing that kept him weak, which was you."

Caitlin stared up. Her face was turning red, as she was trying her best to hold back her tears. She wanted to cry so badly. "No," she answered, as she tried to hold back her crying, "I have to hear it from him." She lifted herself off of the ground and back to her feet. "I love you, Kevin. You've told me before that you love me. Don't you love me, too?"

Kevin's gaze stayed locked forward. He said nothing

It was getting tougher for Caitlin to hold back her crying. "Kevin, just tell me the truth…"

At that moment, he and Satiana shared a kiss.

Shocked, Caitlin's eyes widened. She collapsed to her knees. She could not hold back her crying anymore. "No!" she screamed aloud. "No! No! No! No! No!"

Reluctantly, Kevin turned and directed Satiana to do the same. As they turned away, Satiana created a teleportation gate.

Still crying, Caitlin reached a hand out. She was desperate, screaming, "No! Please, don't go! Please, Kevin, don't go! I love you!"

Across the chasm, Rachel and Arthur were brokenhearted. Tears were coming from their eyes, too, as they watched their friend betray another close friend. They turned to look at their observing troops, several of which were also starting to tear up a bit at what they were witnessing in front of them.

Kevin stopped in his tracks, without taking his hand off of Satiana's shoulders.

Breathing heavily, Caitlin cried again. "Please, don't leave me!" she screamed. "Please, Kevin, don't go with her!"

A moment of silence echoed through the air as Kevin and Satiana disappeared through the gate.

Setadev then walked over, and placed both of her hands on the side of the distraught and distracted Caitlin's head. "This time, you will not be coming back until I am ready for you." Light magic energized in one hand, and darkness in the other.

The silence echoed through the stillness of the day, as if a great shattering had occurred. A shattering of a mind.

Into the air, Caitlin burst out a terrifying scream. The screaming continued for at least a full minute before Caitlin fell silent, collapsing into the spot where she was kneeling.

As quiet fell, Rachel stared over directly at Setadev. "You!" she screamed. "This is what you had in mind all along, wasn't it? This is why you're here!"

Setadev started chuckling. "I felt the need to share it with you, and now you see how the game is played. With the angel fully incapacitated, I think you will find that you do not possess anything near what you need to defeat me before I complete my revival. Beware," he began, as he opened a teleportation gate himself, "you may find my operation if you keep looking, as I fully expect you to do. I will not be disguising myself this time behind a false army and a meaningless fortress. However, should you choose to follow that path, you will only find your deaths. As you have provided me some amusement for the day, I will allow all of you to live for now." He stepped into the gate. "Take care of the angel for me. I will be back for her when I am ready to put her on display." As he went through, the gate disappeared.

With Setadev gone, Arthur and Rachel ran to where he was as quickly as they could. They rounded the edge of the fissure in the ground and headed straight to Caitlin, who had her face down in her knees, kneeling on the ground. She was still crying. The snow provided an appropriate background for the events that had occurred. Shattered glass rains from the sky. Shattered glass, it rains so dry…

Immediately, Arthur and Rachel put their hands on Caitlin's shoulders. Both of them were tearing up too at the betrayal of their friend, but neither was crying like Caitlin. "I understand," said Arthur. "I understand your pain."

"There, there," said Rachel, holding Caitlin a little tighter. "We'll get through this together, I promise."

For another minute, Caitlin kept crying. She was inconsolable.

Then, there was silence. Caitlin tried to stand up. Arthur and Rachel let go of her, allowing her to do so. As she did, though, the look on her face was not what either one of them expected.

She was quiet, at peace. Her face showed no emotion, no sign that she had been crying save for the frozen tear drops. Then, she started screaming again before Arthur and Rachel started walking her back toward the boat.

Arthur looked straight at Rachel. "Do you know what's going on?" she asked.

Silently and somberly, Rachel nodded. "I think so," she said. "Caitlin described to me what it was like when Setadev shattered her mind before. I think he has done it again."

Arthur clammed up. He really hoped that was not it, but it appeared to be. His half-sister's psyche was shattered again, with the image of Kevin betraying her.

Carefully, Arthur and Rachel led Caitlin to a boat, and gave her to a couple of the soldiers to guard. She was to be kept inside a canopied section to keep her as warm and protected from the elements as possible. As the soldiers put her in the boat, the screaming intensified.

Rachel let out a long sigh. "We need to be there for her," she said. "We have to try and find Professor Magnon; if he put her mind back together once, he can do it again."

Arthur appeared reluctant. "I just don't know," he said. "I'm just so bewildered by what I just saw. I need to decide in light of these events what we should do."

Sighing, Rachel looked over at Arthur. "I think it's fairly apparent," she said. "We lost here, and our primary objective is no longer worth pursuing. Your empire is also losing control step by step, and it would be for the best if we returned now to stabilize it." She paused for a second. "I hate to say it, but we're not in good shape, Caitlin has been beaten badly again, our forces are small and tired, and the Solunar Empire needs us. There's no point to rescuing Kevin anymore, and our opportunity to defeat Setadev has closed. We can't do it without him, and let's face another fact here, too: all of our power to rescue him was banking on Caitlin's strengths. Without either, we don't stand a chance."

Arthur shook his head in frustration. "I don't think so," he said. "I know Kevin; he's been my best friend for years, and I know he would never do what we just saw. We know he wasn't possessed because his eyes weren't glowing red, so he must have had some reason to do what he did. He acted a little forced, too."

"Are you insane?" Rachel shot back at Arthur. "Granted, I haven't known Kevin nearly as long as you have, but what he just did was a betrayal! Look at what his actions did to your sister! I'm not just referring to how he just destroyed Caitlin's mind, but he's now on Setadev's side! Who knows why he decided to join forces with that evil jerk, but now he is a traitor regardless."

"And again, I wonder about that," commented Arthur. "I think there's something we're not seeing here. Maybe he was doing it to protect us from something, or maybe he has a plan, or maybe he was made to do it. Let's face a fact here; Setadev came here to show us that, and we fell for the trap. He's been known to deceive before. Whether or not he wanted to show us something real or not could easily still be up in the air."

Rachel sighed again. "Fine," she said. "You're the emperor, so it's your decision. As always, I will follow you wherever you need to go. However, I want you to know that I don't agree with this at all."

Lowering his head, Arthur said, "Very well. I will accept that for now. I know you're not happy, but I still believe it to be in the best interests of the empire that we wait here a few days and discuss this further. We don't even know where to find Professor Magnon at the moment, so we would be best to sort this out and not make a hasty decision."

There was a moment's pause, as Rachel turned and took a brief look at the Gates to Gardolk. "If I may make one recommendation, though, I would suggest we go ahead and set up camp immediately."

That, Arthur could accept. "I agree," he said. He then turned, and issued the orders to the men.

For a couple of hours, the men of the Solunar Empire worked hard on setting up their tents and a campsite next to the gates. Afterward, they took the time to prepare food, get social with one another, and rest up. Arthur and Rachel spent their day with Caitlin, trying to help her with everything that had happened. Even so, Caitlin would alternate between periods of appearing blank in her mind, and screaming. She said no words at all.

The night came peacefully, as the snow from the day finally stopped. Arthur and Rachel had their tents placed near Caitlin's, at an edge of the campsite. Neither one could sleep well.

Caitlin had started screaming in her sleep.

Chapter 40

Sunken Fangs

Within Leticon are very few towns. Due to the province's reputation, no provincial government exists and very little law is in place. Across the plains in Nuve's southeastern province were large and open tracts of land, where the faded yellow grasses seemed to extend for long distances in each direction. Of the towns and villages in Leticon, most were spread out long distances from each other and few were much larger than several homes. Many of the villages were only a tiny square with houses surrounding it, with no other streets aside from the road they sat on.

The largest town in Leticon, with little doubt, was Kinsmoor. Nestled deep in the north side of the province, Kinsmoor was about the equivalent size of Venarose, a town in western Nuve at its border with Aurana. It measured only a few blocks on a small road that led from the south end of the Abyss of the Royal Sovereign, wound through Leticon, and led ultimately to Cardol at the border of the kingdom. To reach Kinsmoor, that particular road tracked a moderate distance east of the Rhonean River.

Much like the rest of Leticon, Kinsmoor too had its secrets. Several times the center point of various kingdoms, possession of Kinsmoor had changed hands at least fifty times in recorded history. It was the bloodiest point in the entire world and had often been a heavy point of contention. This was due to the accidental discovery of an expansive vein of gems in the grounds all around the town. Its initial location was right on the border of a kingdom, and thus became the focus of attention of many nations because of the wealth it could bring. By the time it had fallen under the control of the expanding kingdom of Nuve, as did all of Leticon, the gem vein had dried up and so did the region's wealth. Thus, Kinsmoor became a town of desolation, destroyed by its own industry and the wars for control of its business.

Locally, Kinsmoor was now a lawless city. Order was held by vigilante residents, but no government existed at all. Because of this, Kinsmoor was also a hub for organized crime, the largest of which was a group known as The Syndicate. However, as the region was poor, few actual activities of crime aside from muggings occurred in Kinsmoor.

Like most of Leticon, ancient battlefields and graveyards were all around. At Kinsmoor, they were numerous and visible everywhere. One, however, was very well known; in the center of Kinsmoor itself, taking up one of its few city blocks, was the Heroes' Resting Place. Known as a cemetery for revered individuals, it served as the final resting place of great influencers of the world from past and present.

Having trotted his horse for nearly a week, Vincent Stryker was starting to clutch his back with every step. The old horse Arthur had given him, unfortunately, was simply not up to the task; it was all Arthur had to spare for the moment. Additionally, Vincent was in poor health for a fifty year old man, even if he tried to hide it as much as possible when in combat. Even with the ride, he was having to go slower than he desired. His days with the Scurnian army seemed so distant from now.

As did his son. He had only known his son for a few months now and missed him so much. When he first found out that Kevin had taken up the Sword of Purity, Vincent was very upset and did not want Kevin to experience all of the potential consequences such as this that would come with it. It was his willingness to let his determined son continue that allowed them to reconcile their father-son relationship. Watching what was unfolding right now was making him reconsider that decision, but he understood why his son wanted that. He fully supported his son in all of his endeavors.

Approaching Kinsmoor, Vincent immediately took to cautious behavior. He took off his Scurnian military jacket and turned it inside out before putting it back on, refusing to button it this time. The last thing he wanted was to be recognized as an outsider in Kinsmoor. The citizens in Leticon's largest city tended to be highly suspicious of those not from the area.

Carefully, Vincent walked up to the first building and pulled himself as close to it as possible. The more he could stay out of sight, the better. All around, he saw the houses and a couple of small buildings in the tiny city, but saw no people. That was unusual, Vincent reasoned to himself. Despite being in Leticon, Kinsmoor was still not a ghost town. It made little sense in the middle of the day for there to be no one there.

Vincent continued to the next block, where there was a cemetery honoring great warriors. Once he saw who was in there, he ducked behind the corner of the building. It was the most unexpected sight.

Almost all of Kinsmoor was in attendance, about two hundred citizens. There was a coffin on a stand, and three men in uniform were making a presentation to the people in attendance. The uniformed men were not wearing navy blue Nuve uniforms. They were wearing light blue Cornelia Chimeras uniforms.

The Cornelia Chimeras were not supposed to have any influence across the Rhonean River in Leticon. Why were they in Kinsmoor? With a nonchalant approach, Vincent casually walked toward the cemetery and joined the crowd. He was interested in what was happening.

"It is for this that we honor his last wish, to be buried in the Heroes' Resting Place here in Kinsmoor," the most decorated Chimera was saying as Vincent walked up. "Arsuf Maxwell was a great man, indeed. His death has been a tragic one, and he will be remembered deeply by all of thou who cared for him so much."

Maxwell? His body was already here? He and his followers had to have arrived by horseback on a different route; it was the only way they could have made it to Kinsmoor before Vincent himself arrived. The old general had taken the shortest route to Kinsmoor but was not riding at full gallop. The Chimeras must have had access to horses and rode at full gallop all the way here.

Better question: why was Maxwell being buried in Leticon? Granted, the Heroes' Resting Place was legendary in terms of cemeteries for its reputation of holding ancient warriors. Even so, would Maxwell not want to be buried in Cornelia for all of his efforts there?

The man speaking was a younger man, and his uniform was very decorated. Only Maxwell himself ever wore a uniform with more accolades than that. He kept a neatly-trimmed haircut and thin facial hair, in a dark brown color. His blue eyes were full of fury. "Of course, very few people in Cornelia or Leticon realize that Maxwell himself was from Leticon," the man continued. "He may have had a passion for Cornelia and for freeing it from the tyrannical rule of Nuve, but his heart was always with his true hometown of Kinsmoor. He was always grateful for the support his people gave him, and knew that Leticon would stand fully behind him."

The corruption of Cornelia ran far deeper than Nuve's second largest city, Vincent Stryker realized in that moment. Arsuf Maxwell had no fear of Leticon; in fact, he was from it. Perhaps that was the reason after all that he did not send forces into the province. He had it under lock and key already. He did not fear the ghosts of war. He embraced them.

If Nuve knew, this would be a huge conspiracy that would make the Cornelian crisis much worse. That meant that the Chimeras had influence over the entire southern half of the country. Should the Chimeras take full control of Cornelia and Leticon in the south, and with the Demonstrative Organization of Northern Nuve already controlling the cold province of Tundrosa in the north, Nuve's two remaining provinces of Soverenia and Katalina would not have enough strength to resist attacks from both sides.

This was a rather complex issue. Worse yet, it placed Aurana, Scurnia, and the Solunar Empire on notice. Aurana and Scurnia each had formal alliances with Nuve, and the Chimeras were perfectly positioned to endanger both Aurana and the Solunar Empire if they chose.

"Maxwell stood firmly for the principles we defend in both Cornelia and Kinsmoor," continued the man. "He subdued the vicious Vanguard of Nuve, Raijin Shane, who was found to have organized an assault on a Chimera armory. As such, he brought an end to a cornerstone of Nuve's corruption."

Vincent was furious. He knew Raijin Shane to be a good man, a respectable person who took care of his country. The Chimeras' perspectives seemed slanted to him.

The man then bowed his head. "His end came too quickly, at

the hands of the Solunar Empire who were scouting illegally in Nuve. For that, we will bring justice upon them in the short future."

As Vincent was afraid of. However, that was also part of why he was traveling to Nuvenia.

Then, the man raised his head. "I will remember him best, however, as my brother. He was a special individual to me, and I will always be proud the he wanted me to be a part of his organization and thus his dream. Soon, very soon, we will fulfill that dream when we march on Nuvenia and oust the Raijin family and the Collective Council."

The Chimeras were going after all of Nuve? It was stunning. They did not want independence. They wanted domination.

He had to warn the king of Nuve, Raijin Lester. The more he stared upon the man who was making the eulogy, the more he began to look familiar. His facial features looked very similar to those of Arsuf Maxwell himself. Remembering the incident in Cornelia, he recognized this individual as Arsuf Zachary, Maxwell's unhinged younger brother and second-in-command of the Chimeras himself. Zachary, the fangs of the chimera, was prepared to sink them into the flesh of both Nuve and the Solunar Empire. Perhaps this was Maxwell's strategy if he were to perish in leading the Chimeras. He would die a hero and allow his more aggressive younger brother to lead the charge to their ultimate goal.

Suddenly, as Vincent was watching the ceremony, Zachary's eyes caught his. He turned away and trotted his horse off, hoping that he would evade Zachary's attention. Sure enough, Zachary seemed not to notice and allowed the funeral to continue.

Shortly, Maxwell's body was being lowered into the ground, as he was given full funeral rites and ceremony. As this occurred, Vincent took the chance to slip away. Though he was originally planning to stay in town to rest up before continuing, the last thing he needed was to be in the same town as the new leader of the Cornelia Chimeras. After all, Arsuf Maxwell had branded him a traitor. Zachary would surely not have any remorse for the old general. That was why Vincent Stryker retreated when Zachary's eyes locked onto his.

Darting away toward the north, Vincent made it to the next

block and slowed up. He had to put his mind at ease. If he were to get too panicked, he would be likely to make a mistake and alert the Chimeras of his presence, or end up in the wrong place. For a moment, as he slowed down, he started to reconsider staying in the city. Kinsmoor was the only real rest stop on the road between Cardol and Nuvenia, especially since most travelers heading for the south of Nuve preferred to head in the direction of the province of Cornelia instead. He needed to restock his traveling supplies here, and might as well take the opportunity to rest. If he could do it with caution, there would be no need to panic and run off.

As he looked around where he was, Vincent noted the structures around him. At the next block was a small inn, two stories but likely only big enough to hold four or five guests at most. However, it was the only inn in Kinsmoor, which made Vincent worry that the Chimeras might be staying there. Around the next block to the right, there were some stables. Rare as horses were, there were a few in the hands of private stables and not under the control of governments. As Nuve had no official government hand here, this was likely to be a private stable.

Vincent headed that direction in order to check it out. As he approached, he noticed a sign that said "Horse rental for travel: Kinsmoor to Nuvenia and Kinsmoor to Cornelia routes available. Single horse express ride: 2 pieces of gold. Twin horse and carriage rental: 5 pieces of gold. Rider assumes all liabilities and will pay for neglect of horses."

Perfect, Vincent thought to himself. He was sure that Arthur would understand if he could not bring this horse back to the empire, but right now, time was of the essence. If he could shave off a couple of days by getting a different horse, it was worth it.

Reaching into his pocket, Vincent grabbed out a couple of gold coins. He then approached a man who was washing a horse in the stables and said, "Excuse me, I would like to rent a horse."

The washer immediately stopped and turned to face Vincent. He then gave the general a strange look. "You look like you already have one," he said.

Vincent nodded. "Unfortunately, I need a fast horse," he said. "This poor old horse is not going to get me there fast enough. I can let you have her if I can get a ride."

It took the washer a few moments to consider this. "You can leave your horse here, but I still must charge you for the ride and emphasize you are only getting a rental."

Knowing he had to increase his speed, Vincent nodded. "I am okay with that." He dismounted the old horse.

"Very well," acknowledged the washer. "We only offer two routes," he answered. "Are thou heading to Nuvenia or Cornelia?"

"Nuvenia," nodded Vincent. "I have business there which I must attend to."

The horse washer nodded as he walked to a desk on the end of the stables. He could not have been more than twenty-five years of age, but it seemed as though he were the only one here. "Excellent," he said, as he reached down and grabbed a set of reins from under the desk. "Understand that thou must return the horse to the South Stables within Nuvenia when thou have arrived at thy destination. Fail to do so within the next few days, and we will have our 'friends' take care of thou. Is that clear?"

Vincent nodded. Reading into the situation, he could tell now that this was a stable operated by The Syndicate. He would have to use caution when proceeding forward, or else he would have an organized crime group following him and hunting him down. However, such were the risks for any service in Leticon, knowing that The Syndicate had control of most regional industry in the area.

"Very well," nodded the young man. He withdrew a piece of paper and a feather quill from his desk. "I will need to take down thy name and primary place of residence, as well as thy ultimate destination and business."

That was the last thing Vincent needed. The Syndicate would use that information to help track him down. As much as it was the Chimeras that he needed to hide from, The Syndicate would be equally dangerous if they had reason. Lying would go further; The Syndicate would still try to track him down and deliver an even worse punishment. However, a thought came to his mind. Vincent reached into his pocket and pulled out six more pieces of gold. He put them directly in the young man's hands. "Perhaps we can forget the name and business. My destination is Nuvenia, where I will return the horse."

For a moment, the young man stared at the gold in his hand. Then, he tucked it into his trouser pocket. "Very well, we will forget the name." He looped his reins around a black horse next to him. "This is Thunder. He is a quick horse; perhaps not my fastest, but he will get thou to Nuvenia reliably." The young man then glared at Vincent. "Thou had best make sure to return him to the South Stables in Nuvenia, or thy head may come off thy shoulders."

Vincent nodded, as he grabbed the reins to his horse. "I will bear that in mind," he said. Then, he started walking the quick horse away, toward the inn. As he stepped away, he saw someone else approaching the stables.

It was Arsuf Zachary and his men. What were they doing there?

Quickly, Vincent pulled his horse to the side of the street. He started looking over the horse, keeping his eyes away from Zachary. However, he was listening intently to what was about to be discussed behind him.

"Do thou have our horses ready?" Zachary demanded.

"Indeed," nodded the young man. "Three horses for Nuvenia, my fastest."

Suddenly, Vincent's eyes widened. He would have expected Zachary to return to Cornelia. Why was he headed for Nuvenia?

"Excellent," Zachary acknowledged. "We will come and pick them up tomorrow morning. Would thou be willing to place the billing for this on our tab? Our previous business with thy organization has always been good."

Behind Vincent, the young man shook his head. "The Syndicate honors thy brother and respects thy loss. He was a good business partner. Per the boss, I have permission to grant thou free use of these horses for this trip, as a show of support."

Zachary nodded. "With gratitude, we will accept thy gift. Have them ready for us tomorrow at the crack of dawn; we have a meeting with the king for which we cannot be late."

Almost as immediately as he heard that, Vincent hopped up onto his horse and started off. He knew that Zachary and the Chimeras would see him, but would be very unlikely to recognize him or reason that his activities were irregular. He took a right at the intersection with the main road, and continued north as quickly as possible.

"Who was that?" Zachary asked.

"Just the last customer," answered the man. "He rented my fourth horse."

For a moment, Zachary glared into the distance. He then turned to his fellow Chimera soldiers, and said, "We will still go according to plan, but let us keep an eye out for him as we head to Nuvenia."

The two soldiers saluted in acknowledgement.

Already a short distance down the road, Vincent was leaving Kinsmoor as quickly as he could. He flipped his jacket back around as he continued to flee north. There would be no opportunity to stay the night in town. He had to beat the Chimeras to Nuvenia, and if the stable man were correct, they had quicker horses than him.

What did Zachary want with the king of Nuve? To tell him about his brother's demise and to place the blame? To kill him? There were any number of possibilities, and Vincent was not about to allow any of them to come to fruition.

No matter how sore he was, Vincent pressed on as quickly as he could. He had had no chance to replenish his foodstuffs or get any rest, but he had to make it to Nuvenia as soon as he could. Somebody had to know about the Chimeras, their association with The Syndicate, and their acceptance in Leticon, and it could not be Zachary who told the story first.

Chapter 41

Breaking Free

A sick feeling was in Kevin's stomach.

He was regaining his consciousness, tied to a pole in a tent somewhere. For some reason, he felt very queasy, and he could not recall what had happened over the past few hours. His last memory was being tied to this very same pole, but he had no idea how he had lost his consciousness. This was not a good feeling.

Slowly, he opened his eyes to get a good look around. He was in a tent with General Sayo tied to a pole next to him. He was in the same spot that he remembered, at least. Nothing appeared any different.

"You're awake," said Satiana, who stepped around the pole so Kevin could see her.

Kevin raised his eyes, and glared at Satiana. "No thanks to you, I am sure," he said as he spit at the ground. "What did you do to me? Why do I feel like there's a gap in my memory?"

In response, Satiana laughed. "I wanted to play with you," she said. "Of course, you never seem to want to play with me unless I give you some blue soup, so that's exactly what I did."

"You didn't…" snapped Kevin, knowing she was referring to the aphrodisiac.

"I did," Satiana giggled. "Of course, you're difficult, so I had Setadev shatter your mind so I could make sure you played. We played a really fun game, too. We spent a lot of time together and we went on a little trip, and Setadev put your mind back together when you came back."

"And where did we go?" asked Kevin. He had no idea what "shattering a mind" had to do with anything, unfamiliar with the concept.

Satiana paused, then laughed again. "Oh, come now, Kevin. If

I told you everything, what fun would there be in that?"

Kevin spit at the ground. "You're sadistic," he said.

"I try," Satiana laughed again.

Then, General Sayo spoke up. "Don't let her get to you, Kevin," he said. "You know she's just trying to get under your skin."

"Silence, general," directed Satiana.

No, by all means, general, please keep going.

It was Setadev. He walked into the tent, along with two Enlighteners.

Satiana seemed to flinch in surprise. Kevin caught this, but was more captivated by Setadev's entry. "What the hell was that for?" Kevin asked aloud, quite frustrated. "Setadev, you were standing right there. Why do you need to keep sending your initial message mentally when you're just out of sight?"

Setadev laughed. "It is one of my trademarks," he said. "And, furthermore, it is my right in my world." Then, he turned to the general. "Continue, Mr. Sayo. Tell me what my lovely right-hand is trying to do with Kevin."

Sayo said nothing. He no longer respected Setadev; there was no need for any more comment. There was a moment of silence.

"I see that this discussion is over," Setadev finally commented. He then turned to Satiana and snapped his fingers. "Take the general to another tent. I want to speak with the pure one alone."

Satiana nodded and walked over to the general. She cut loose the ropes looped around the support post. As she pulled him off, the two Enlighteners grabbed him by the arms. Slack rope that had been looped around the support post fell slack, but the general's wrist and ankle ties remained intact, keeping him tied up. Then, the Enlighteners walked him out of the tent, and Satiana followed behind. She stopped to turn and look at Kevin, winced as if knowing what was about to come, and then walked away.

For a second, Kevin looked on in disbelief. What was that all about? Satiana's behavior there was a little odd; if she were a fragment of Setadev and shared such ties with him, and were his right hand, then why would she wince as though sympathetic? Something about the situation was curious.

Interrupting his contemplation, Setadev snagged his attention. "Look into my eyes," he commanded. "We have much to discuss, pure one."

Disgusted, Kevin shrugged as best as he could. "We have nothing to discuss," he said. "I'm presuming that you used those aphrodisiacs to make me do something with Satiana again and then decided to go and tell Caitlin and all of my friends? They must be on their way here, aren't they?"

"Oh, worry not, pure one," Setadev answered. "Even if they keep coming, I will not mind, for I have given them their last warning that they will meet their deaths if they advance any further. I have no fear of them, and have only allowed them to live because their interference has been minimal at best. The Solunar Empire is no danger to me; they may interfere with my operations, but soon my work will be complete, and my revival will be done. No one, whether your best friends or their military leaders, can endanger me."

Kevin looked up into Setadev's eyes. "Caitlin can," he said. "I think you fear her. I think that's the real reason you've been drugging me and telling her all about the results."

Setadev chuckled. "It is quite humorous you said that," he said, "because during this last trip, I let *you* tell her that you did not love her anymore."

Instantly, Kevin's eyes widened.

"You what?"

"Exactly as it sounds. You did not need to say much; all you did was kiss Satiana. And I let you do it in front of your friends from the Solunar Empire, too."

In response, Kevin let out a horrific scream. Then, he started yelling at Setadev. "How dare you! Stop trying to control me!"

Again, Setadev chuckled, but glared into Kevin's eyes to show that he was being truthful and frank. "Pure one, you have not been under the control of tracer magic at any point since I captured you. All that has been done is that your inhibitions have been let go with the effects of the aphrodisiac, perhaps with a bit of magic to reduce your resistance, and you spent a long amount of time with Satiana. In no way have I ever controlled you, which means that those actions were your own."

Kevin dropped his head. He had no response to that. How could he do such things? Was he that willing to break his relationship with Caitlin when he was not in complete conscious control of himself? If he did do that, did that mean that he did not truly love Caitlin from the bottom of his heart?

Of that last question, Kevin told himself there was no way he did not, even if he asked himself questions about it periodically. He felt disgusting. He doubted Setadev was lying about this; though he had never been under the control of tracer magic, he knew that Setadev liked to gloat. That made it very unlikely that the fallen god was lying.

"I can see I have evoked some response," Setadev continued in his normal cocky tone. "This is the way things are to be, pure one. Welcome to the beginning of my world. And now that I have humbled you, I am ready to discuss business with you."

Kevin lifted his head slightly. "Just tell me what you want," he said.

"As you wish," answered Setadev. He paused for a second to remove the Sword of Purity from his side. It was still in its scabbard, allowing Setadev to safely transport it, but he was very cautious not to grab it by its handle or crossguard. "I put your mind back together from the shatter spell for a reason, so that we may have a discussion. Let us face some facts, Kevin. You have now lost everything you have ever had. You have no friends, no love, no family. Did I mention that your father was not with your friends on the way to see you?"

Kevin was too upset to contemplate that.

"You visually betrayed the trust of your friends in front of them, and they now believe that you have joined me," Setadev continued. "Should I let them return, eventually word will also travel to Aurana about this, and you will be branded a traitor there as well. So, Kevin, what do you have left aside from your virtues? I would say nothing."

Kevin dropped his head. How could this all be so bad? What could have gone so wrong? Was this Setadev's real torture? He had broken Kevin by inflicting pleasure, not pain; by twisting thoughts, not body parts. Now, Kevin was broken. He had little will to fight. He had nothing to fight for. He had been defeated in battle before and thought that he had lost more battles than he had won. However, this was the first day he felt truly beaten by an opponent. He lowered his head, overwhelmed and tired.

Setadev chuckled again as he observed the defeated Kevin. "Allow me to offer you an alternative to your fate," he said. "Surely you know why I cannot let you go free; your virtues and your pure aura have made you too much of an annoyance for me to wish to deal with anymore. However, you have done something that no other individual, mortal or immortal, has ever done. You scored a small victory against me a few months ago. For that, I would be willing to offer you a place in my utopia, but it will come with a cost."

Without lifting his head, Kevin asked, "And what is that?"

"I need you to surrender your sword," he said.

Taking a breath, Kevin scoffed. "You already have it," he said.

"But not its control," Setadev answered. "I care not about controlling the Sword of Purity on a regular basis, nor do I look to having you as a fighter on my side. I have no need of such things. However, I do want the power of the Sword of Purity." He lifted the sword to show it to Kevin with more prominence. "It is useless in its scabbard; even I cannot withdraw it from its sheath. If you are willing to give me its power as its operator, I will ensure that you are well taken care of in my utopia. It is the least I can do for the most worthy adversary I have."

Kevin took another deep breath. "You must be slipping, Setadev," he said. "I thought that you told me that I don't see how the game is played, and that you don't fear me. Yet I am the most worthy adversary you have?"

"Indeed you are," Setadev nodded, "just as how you do not see how the game is played, and just as how I do not fear you. You have not placed any challenge on me, but neither has any adversary I have ever faced except for Vinz Larinion, and he is long gone. In your sword is the proof that he has already been defeated. Even if you prove no challenge, you could have a role in my utopia after all as a sign of human resilience. Let your continued struggles here mean something."

Pity? That was completely unlike Setadev. Kevin had an idea where this was going. He spat at the ground. "Nice try," he said.

"Even if you have me, and even if you kill me, the power of this sword will never be yours. You can try this stunt on my father and he won't break. You will not get me to relinquish its power, no matter what you do."

Suddenly, Setadev threw the sword and its scabbard to the ground. "You might want to take some time to think about it," he said back to Kevin, "because you do not see how the game is played." He then stepped back. "Be warned, Kevin. I will make your life much longer and much more torturous if you choose not to cooperate." He then stepped out of the tent.

As Setadev left, Kevin let out a sigh. How could things be any worse?

He just wished he could go back and fix everything. He wished he could tell Arthur and Rachel where he was and what had happened to him, and he wished he could tell Caitlin that none of the things she had seen and heard were true. He wanted to get out of here now, to try and fix everything. Setadev's offer was not an option.

How could he escape? He had been pondering that question for weeks now when not drugged up on the blue soup. The ropes were tight agains the pole. He could not move his hands, nor his legs. No one was around to help him. Nothing had changed; the only things different in the tent right now were the absence of Sayo and the presence of the Sword of Purity where Setadev had thrown it in frustration.

The sword. That was it. Kevin had told Sayo before that if he knew where the sword were, there was no place he could not escape.

Closing his eyes and opening his hands tied behind his back, Kevin focused hard on the sword. He had to call it to him. If it was in his hands, he could break free. He concentrated hard, thinking of Caitlin and of what he had to do if he could just have it in his hands.

Please come to me, he thought in his head. *I need you in order to fix all of this.*

Another second passed.

Then, the sword began to dematerialize in the scabbard. It broke down into its natural elements and shot out, reforming in its entirety in Kevin's right hand.

Perfect.

Immediately, Kevin proceeded to find the serene place in his mind and light the sword up in its bright blue power. Then, he carefully cut through the rope binding his hands to the pole. He swung his arms free and flipped his sword down to cut the rope binding his ankles.

He was free! The next question was, how could he get out of here?

Quickly, Kevin closed his eyes and lifted his sword. He had to slow himself down. He took his time for a moment, knowing that he had to make his next decision wisely. If he were to leave in the wrong direction, he could get lost and walk right into a group of Enlighteners. He had to trust his sword, knowing he had no idea where he was.

He closed his eyes and asked his sword where to go, leaving his arms loose. Silently, he waited for over a minute, until he felt his arms being pulled in a direction. It happened to be north, although he had no idea that that was the direction. That was the way to go, one way or another. His sword had led him into a trap before, but he had to believe that he could trust it.

Silently, Kevin slowly opened the tent flap and looked around. He saw two Enlighteners on either side of the tent, and tucked his head back in before they could notice. If there were two there, he was not going to escape so easily and may be caught by Setadev before he could get so far.

Another strategy came to mind. Kevin positioned himself between the two tent posts holding it up and started yelling out, "Hey! Let me out of here! So help me, I will kill everyone here!"

Though the yelling actually meant nothing, it did make the two Enlighteners at the flap turn and walk into the tent to find out what was going on. When they did, Kevin took a full circle swipe of his sword, cutting both posts at the same time and collapsing the tent instantaneously. As the tent fell on the Enlighteners, Kevin slashed upward with his sword fully lit, opening a gap for him to escape through. Once the tent had fully collapsed, and Kevin found himself on the outside of the tent, he took off toward the north.

Quickly, he tucked around the next tent. He knew the collapsed tent would draw attention, so he had to move quickly and stealthily. He snuck across the road to the next tent, looking for a way out.

Looking all around, Kevin saw only mountains to the north, west, and south. Though the east was open, the sword had pointed him north. Many more tents were to the west, and a few more were to the east, north, and south. There had to be a few hundred people here, and if they were all Enlighteners, Kevin was in big trouble.

He looked back down where he came from to see Enlighteners swarming the area. They were trying to figure out what had happened, and without a doubt Setadev would know very shortly as well. He had to escape, and escape quickly. There was no time to go back for the general, wherever he was. He did not particularly care for the general anyway, and any opportunity for that had already eluded him.

Knowing he needed to make sure that he was not caught, Kevin started darting from tent to tent, watching for Enlighteners as he made his way north. Several times, he had to pause between tents to avoid passersby. As much as he could, he tucked himself into tents under their long edge in order to dodge traffic. He was lucky not to end up in any tents with Enlighteners in them.

After about ten minutes of negotiating his way through the tents, Kevin arrived at the edge of the camp and ran up the hillside at the end. He then looked down to see the group of Enlighteners at the tent trying to figure out what was going on. Then, he held his sword out, allowing it to guide him again. It pulled to the northeast, where Kevin looked to find what appeared to be a road into the mountains. Wherever he was, that had to be the escape from the camp that the sword wanted him to head for. He started running in that direction, heading up and into the rougher terrain that followed along the road.

Kevin had to keep moving, in case the Enlighteners were following him. He was not sure where he was, but he was very glad to be out of the camp. For now, he had no time to figure out where he was or where he was heading. He had to keep going down this road and get as far away from Setadev as possible.

He had to find his friends, and he had to find Caitlin. He had to fix everything that happened, whatever it was even though he remembered none of it. When he was able to reconnect with them, he would use his freedom and approach to gain the upper hand on Setadev.

For now, though, he thought only of the people he loved.

You are wasting your time, echoed a voice in Kevin's head. It was Setadev. *You can prolong this if you like, but it will only result in the same thing.*

"Shut up!" yelled Kevin out loud as he kept running.

The mountain road went straight up into steep terrain. It was long and high, but fortunately it did not lead directly over the summit of any mountain. Instead, it ran between two mountains, although at a slightly high elevation. The terrain through here was forested in coniferous trees, in contrast to the desolate clearing he had just escaped from. Though he was not exactly sure where he was, Kevin knew he was in the mountains now. This section of the Peaked Mountains through Gardolk tended to be covered in life from the nearby Grandiose River valley, and creeks from the mountains flowed down into the valley.

All Kevin could keep in his mind was to keep running. He tired quickly but he had to keep moving if he wanted to escape any pursuit. Setadev would not be pleased when he figured out that the mistake was his and not that of his guards. Before Setadev had the chance to rectify this, he had to get away as far as possible. He had to find Caitlin, and all of his friends. He had one chance to fix everything, and then he could either return home with them or pursue Setadev with their support.

Quickly, however, the evening fell. Kevin had walked all day and was exhausted. As the evening fell, he considered himself lucky to find one of the many streams running through the mountains. He spent the night there and took the opportunity to get a fresh drink of water. He did not have any of his provisions with him, so for now this was how he would have to live, and he would have to find food soon.

Underneath a tree by the stream, Kevin was shivering in the cold as he prepared to settle in for the night. To keep warm, he put together some sticks that had fallen off of nearby trees, piled them together, and lit a fire. At this moment, he felt very fortunate to have taken classes on survival skills while at the Rikleifer Academy a couple of years ago.

With the Sword of Purity, Kevin scraped as much snow as he

could off of a space so he could lay down. He took off his jacket and rolled it into a pillow for his head. As he lay in that spot next to the fire, he could not help but think that even in such a discomforting situation, he had not been this comfortable in such a long time.

He had to hope that he could survive the trip down the mountain road without provisions and could find his friends.

Chapter 42

Betrayal

The foothills of the Peaked Mountains were very lush lands in the summer, and so were the mountainsides in this area. During the winter, the numerous coniferous trees in the highlands provided shelter to local animals of all kinds. Tributary creeks to the Calphos River ran down several mountainsides in the area. This was the province of Frera, one of the twenty of Gardolk, and it was a region known for its unique culture. Three provinces had their border lines drawn against the national border at the Peaked Mountains, and from north to south Frera was the middle of the three. A few pathways led into and through the east side of the mountains within the borders of Gardolk, and it was along one of these roads that Kevin was running along. He was proceeding north along the road, which ran up and between a couple of mountains while angling to the east to come around the north side of the smaller mountain to the east. He had been at it for a day, though the road had not come to an end as of yet. Still, he had to persevere and continue. He had to find his friends, and he had to escape from Setadev before he was caught.

Following a different road running in a valley between the foothills and the mountains, Arthur, Rachel, and the Solunar Empire detachment unit were continuing southward. More or less, they were heading this way because it seemed like a logical place to hide since the terrain became more flat and open the more one headed east. They could not stay at the Gates to Gardolk in care trading boats came through the Southern Pass, and needed to be somewhere they could exit to Solunar when that was decided. While Leticon was a province where something could be hid in plain sight in the open, that would not be possible in Frera or any of the Gardolk provinces. An added benefit of this route was that in case an emergency evacuation were needed, Arthur could lead his forces across the mountains back into Solunar, although the trip to Seta Archa would be very difficult and long.

It had been a few days since the event at the Gates. Next to Arthur and Rachel, Caitlin was still walking on. She was still wearing a men's Solunar Empire uniform and her hair was still very short. She was being kept in a tent by herself, still bouncing back and forth between dead silence and screaming.

Both Arthur and Rachel were extremely worried about her. It would be easy to say they needed to find her father, but he could be anywhere in this moment.

In the early afternoon, Arthur's men had found one of the tributary creeks. Along the waterway were growing hardy plants unique to the Gardolk foothills that could be used as a food source. In the middle of winter, this was the best possible discovery for Arthur's small army. Because of this, Arthur decided to have his men set up camp along the creek. Though he was in a rush and did not have time to dawdle, Arthur decided that he could use the opportunity to rest his men for a few days in order to rebuild morale after all of the long trips.

He still had a lot to consider. He was still thinking about going back home with his forces and calling off the advance. He knew Rachel thought that that might be the best action, and it did seem difficult to pursue knowing there was little that could be done against Setadev without Kevin there. And there would be no rescue of him anymore.

With the setup in place, spirits around the camp were warming up with the opportunity of rest. Even though this was an entirely volunteer force with Arthur, even they missed their homes in the Solunar Empire. The chance to take some downtime, however, was reinvigorating to them even in the cold of winter.

In the evening, Kevin spotted the Solunar Empire encampment, using the Sword of Purity to guide him. A pathway ascended a foothill near the camp, taking Kevin just out of the way of the encampment but overlooking it at a small ledge. Kevin felt he needed to make sure his friends were here before he came down to see them, just in case the Solunar soldiers saw his Auranian uniform and assumed he was an enemy.

After a short while, Arthur emerged from a tent. Rachel walked out with him, but Caitlin was nowhere to be seen. Kevin went to leave to walk down the path and toward the encampment, but he felt the Sword of Purity push him back. It did not want him to go down there. Unsure why this would be, Kevin decided to heed its advice, still feeling he had to trust his sword whenever it gave him direction.

"Any word from the scouts yet?" Arthur asked Rachel, who had sent a couple of men further south to check the area.

Rachel nodded. "Yeah, but it's not much," she said. "The terrain gets a little rougher further south. There's a fork in the road ahead with one that branches off into the mountains, but it looks to be pretty steep. No sign of activity from Setadev or anything like that, though."

"Great," said Arthur sarcastically as he shook his head. He then knelt down next to Rachel. "I'm thinking of turning back," he said.

Interested, Rachel gave him an odd look. "Why is that?"

Arthur shook his head in response. "I guess it just feels like a futile battle after all," he said. "You were right. There's just not any reason to be out here anymore, and with the situation in the empire getting worse, we're needed there."

Kevin, who was listening in, was surprised. They came this far and now they had no reason to be here?

For a second, there was silence as Rachel thought about her answer. "Are you sure you want to do that?" she asked.

Puzzled, Arthur responded, "Why would you ask that? Wasn't it your idea to go back?"

"It was," acknowledged Rachel, "and call me a cynic again if you must, but it's not like you to go back on your decisions."

Lowering his head, Arthur said, "I'm just not sure anymore," he said. He seemed to be retreating in his mind.

Rachel's eyes widened. "Don't tell me we're going back to this again," she said, recalling Arthur's attitude just a few weeks ago while he looked upon Seta Archa from the top of the city pyramid. "Arthur, I do think we should just go home, you're right. But not like this. I can't support you when you're like this, making decisions just because you're demoralized."

For a moment, Arthur seemed lost and confused. Now he did not know what to do.

Picking up on this, Rachel said, “Just think on it some more. The men could use some more rest before we march back, and there’s enough resources we can hold out a few days. When you’re actually ready to acknowledge that Kevin has betrayed us and we are best to go home and see how things play out, come and tell me it’s time to go back.”

Arthur lowered his head. “I still don’t believe he did,” he said.

Again, Rachel shook her head. “Believe what you want to believe,” she responded, as she walked away, “but I know what I saw.”

For a moment, Arthur looked away. He simply could not bring himself to believe what he had seen, too. He knew what Rachel was getting at, but she seemed so cruel to simply cast Kevin aside after everything that had happened. He too had seen what Rachel had seen. There was no hint of red in Kevin’s eyes, no sign of his actions being determined by tracer magic and possession. What Arthur had experienced that Rachel had not was several years of friendship. Rachel and Kevin were friends from school at the Rikleifer Academy, where Kevin had a crush on her but never really expressed it. Arthur, though, had been friends with Kevin since they were kids. Kevin was not capable of betrayal of his friends; he simply valued his friendships with others too much.

A shocked Kevin sat up on the small ledge, listening to everything he could hear. It hurt him greatly to hear he was being accused of betrayal. No wonder the Sword of Purity did not want him to go down there. He did not want to leave; all he wanted to do was to listen, to try and understand what had happened to make them feel that way. He could not confront them now.

Looking up, Arthur pondered his next move. He looked into the western sky, above the mountains. Above, the sound of something cutting through the air echoed across the mountains.

“What could that be?” he said loudly to Rachel, pointing up and grabbing her attention.

A little surprised, Rachel reached over and grabbed a torch from a nearby tent. Holding it up, she looked through its light at the figure as it closed in. “Looks like a gryphon,” she said. “Maybe one of our troops. Could be a messenger.”

Slowly, the gryphon began descending just west of the campsite. As it came closer, Arthur and Rachel could make out a person on top of it. Rachel was right. It was a Solunar Empire messenger. Only their troops used gryphon transport, a remnant of the Desolunar era. Quickly, they ran over to the troop's landing spot to rendezvous with him.

As they arrived, a soldier dismounted the gryphon, dressed in a black uniform with orange trim. "Good evening," Arthur said as the soldier stepped down. "What's your business?"

The soldier immediately bowed. "My emperor, I am honored to make your acquaintance," he said. He then rose and grabbed an envelope out of his jacket. "I have a message for you from the vanguards."

Arthur nodded as he accepted the message. "Thank you," he said. "If you would like, feel free to rest at the camp. It is quite late."

The messenger nodded. "Thank you, my emperor," he said, as he took the reins of his gryphon and began walking toward the camp. He had done his duty and earned his night of rest, in the eyes of Arthur.

With the soldier walking away, Arthur and Rachel were left alone where they were. As Arthur opened the envelope, Rachel asked, "Rouge and Resa sent this? I wonder what's up in Seta Archa?"

Sighing, Arthur said, "One way to tell," as he removed and unfolded the letter inside. Its handwriting was simple but well-written, definitely Resa's:

Dear Arthur and Rachel,

On behalf of Rouge and myself, we hope your trip is going well so far. We know you will stop Pseudo and bring Kevin home to us soon.

Arthur and Rachel stopped reading at this point, having reached the same phrase simultaneously. They looked at each other awkwardly for a moment before they continued reading:

As we have recently come back to the city, we thought you might want to know what has been going on in the empire while we've all been away. To put a long story short, though, not everything has been the best. Fortunately, our return here may have helped with that, although we're really not sure what the extent of everything is just yet.

It looks like we made it back in the nick of time. The Imperial Council has not been content with their emperor running around the land and taking their army into foreign countries. That being said, they were pretty satisfied that we brought back quite a few troops. Most of the fight came from the Seta Archa representatives, and the wasteland tribes didn't really care since the army doesn't have any soldiers from the Wastes and we're going after someone who assaulted the Metoi. Since we've come back, we've managed to keep the frustration down for a little bit.

The Aequina have registered a formal complaint with the council. It seems they're claiming that a girl of Seta Archan descent annihilated their village with fire and earth spells. I'm presuming this might be Caitlin? She does have a "Seta Archan" appearance, not just in her lighter skin but also her hair color, and her mother was from Seta Archa if I'm not mistaken. The complaint doesn't appear to be taken very seriously by anyone on the council, however, given the Aequina's known past of human sacrifice. Since the force that hit them was supposedly one person and not an army, a lot of the Seta Archa representatives and most of the wasteland tribes are simply presuming the Aequina messed with the wrong person.

Unfortunately, the winter has not been kind to Seta Archa, either. Food and water have been a big issue while we've been gone. We placed the returning soldiers, including the surrendering Desolunar forces, on rest while the remainder of the army is working on civic duties to help provide for the people during the winter. Those few troops you have left with you are the only troops out on defense or fighting at the moment, so we had better hope that we do not see any attacks anytime soon. It will be some time until we are able to protect our empire adequately, and according to the military advisor will likely take a few years for us to properly rebuild our forces. He is also concerned about our political situation and that we may not be ready for an attack from Nuve or Cornelia, much less Gardolk.

For some happy news, Rouge is doing better, too. She still has her chest fully wrapped and bandaged, has some breathing trouble every now and then, and it's likely she'll have some scars when all is said and done, but she is recovering well and is grateful to be alive. She sends her deepest thanks again to Caitlin for saving her life, as do I.

We wish we could be out in the field with you, but know why we can't. Still, we wish you the best, and hope you will bring Sayo and Setadev to justice for their crimes. Kevin brought us all together, you know. It would make him happiest if we could return the favor and save him the same way he saved us.

Sincerely yours,
Resa Kirkwood, Vanguard of the Solunar Empire

Arthur and Rachel were stunned silent.

Finally, Arthur broke the silence. "Well, at least they're all right," he said. "It sounds like Rouge and Resa are keeping things together."

"Isn't this more encouragement for you to turn our forces around and head for home?" Rachel asked in response. "We have problems at home and little to gain here. Why do you intend to keep this going on?"

Arthur glared back. "You know why," he said. "How come you're so willing to give up on a friend who has been willing to sacrifice himself for us?"

Rachel shook her head, as she started to walk off. "Tell that to your sister," she said. "And tell it to all the men who saw him walk away with them." She stopped after walking a few steps and turned around. "And tell it to me," she said, revealing the tears that had built in her eyes, before she turned back around and continued walking.

Surprised, Arthur just shook his head and turned around. Sure enough, it was affecting Rachel. She did care. But Arthur just could not give up on his best friend, not yet.

Another shriek echoed throughout the air, followed by loud coughing. It had come from Caitlin's tent.

That sound grabbed Kevin's attention. What was that? He could tell it was Caitlin. Instinctively he snapped up and looked toward the tent. He was about to run down to her, until he saw Arthur and Rachel running that way, along with a medic. Arthur and Rachel both looked in the tent, as the medic ran in to make sure Caitlin did not injure herself in her screaming fit.

Rachel yelled at Arthur at this point. "Do you see what I mean? Your sister had her mind shattered and her whole world destroyed, and all because Kevin abandoned her for that fragment of Setadev! He made this happen to her!"

Immediately, Kevin became extremely upset. Caitlin was broken, and they thought it was all his fault? Was it?

He couldn't take this anymore. Without anyone noticing, he ran off down the road as far as he could.

Kevin ran for five minutes before stopping at the fork in the road. He could not believe what had just happened. He felt like his world was crumbling around him, and now he realized, whether true or not, he was considered responsible for the destruction of Caitlin's mind. She was evidently now a shell of herself, and it was all his fault. Frustrated, he took out his sword and started swinging it around, looking for any way to let out all of his stress.

How could his best friends in the world just abandon him like that? Why could they not understand that he was not under his own control? After all he had done for them and was continuing to do, and the suffering he had gone through, how could they just turn their back on him like that? Could he have been the one to do so much damage to Caitlin, and why would they not let him try to fix it?

He realized they would not listen to him. Not now, anyway. Even Arthur seemed like he had not made his mind up about Kevin, and trying to get around Rachel to get to him would make things worse.

Was this Setadev's true revenge? Was this how the game was played?

Never more before now did Kevin feel like his spirit had been broken. He was tired of fighting, tired of the torture. He wanted so much for things to go back to the way they were just a few months ago. Now, aside from his father wherever he was, he had truly lost everything.

Frustrated, Kevin withdrew his sword. It was the source of all of his frustration right now. Setadev wanted its power, for what reason he did not know. Since picking up the sword, he had faced so much more than any human being should face.

Despite being broken, he was true to himself and true to his heart. He hated Setadev and knew what would happen if the fallen deity were to regain full divine power. All he had left were his virtues, and he would not let those go, no matter how easy it would be to do so.

Even his life meant little at this point. His virtues would vindicate him, even if no one else would.

He flipped his sword around in the air, then held it in front of himself. "Please," he said to his sword, "let them remember me," he said tearfully. "Let them know the true Kevin Trent Stryker, and remember me as I am instead of what they perceive." He lit his sword up and flipped it over, sticking it into the ground. Then, he let go of the sword and left it in the ground.

Kevin began walking to the south, back along the mountain road. He would prove to them his virtues, and he would do so without his sword, even if it cost him his life.

Chapter 43

From Both Sides Now

Three different organizations were in control of segments of Nuve. Despite claiming official legal jurisdiction over all of the kingdom, the official government of Nuve only held total control over the provinces of Soverenia and Katalina, respectively. The province of Leticon had no true controller given its reputation, and even Nuve did not bother to enforce a provincial government due to its status and emptiness in the plains. To the southwest, the Cornelia Chimeras controlled much of the province of Cornelia, despite Nuve's continued insistence that the provincial government there was still in control of the area. Oftentimes, it was falsely believed by outsiders that another group, the Knights of the Dragon, controlled areas in the far eastern sections of Katalina, but both Nuve and the Knights of the Dragon denied this. Instead, it was merely an area where the Knights had some influence and where they conducted activities, but they did not seek any control.

In the northern province of Tundrosa, another organization had a firm hold of that area. This group was the Demonstrative Organization of Northern Nuve, also known as the "Demons" for short. The shortened name came solely from their lengthened name and not from their reputation or from any outside influence or connection. Their take on ruling philosophy was the key dispute they had with the government of Nuve: Demons leader Steffen Robert was a firm believer in a more libertarian form of rule, with minimal control from leadership and more freedoms allocated to the people. Nuve's laws were not terribly restrictive, but were slightly more so than any of the other kingdoms in the realm.

Tundrosa was so named for its tundra-like climate. Much of the northern province of Nuve was very cold almost all of the year, and snow tended to fall more often there than in other regions. During the summer, Tundrosa was usually only mild at best. Several small towns were scattered across the province, and all were very close-knit, as teamwork survival was imperative to the continued existence of these towns in the tundra. There was also one significantly large city in the province, and that was Edenbrook.

Situated a few days almost due north of Nuve's capital city of Nuvenia, Edenbrook was quite modestly sized. It was currently Nuve's third largest city by population, well behind Nuvenia and Cornelia. Though Nuve maintained a token government presence in the city, as well as an official provincial government office, it had realistically conceded all control of Edenbrook and almost all of Tundrosa to the Demonstrative Organization of Northern Nuve. Flags in Edenbrook's business district and city center flew everywhere, with most flying the Demons flag of a diagonally bisected rectangle with crimson red to the left and top and black to the bottom and right. The only Nuve flag, bearing a blue field with white trim and a gold letter N in the middle, flew from the official government office of Nuve.

Though Edenbrook was the third largest city by population, and was quite a bit smaller than both Nuvenia and Cornelia due to its cold climate, the Demons organization was still quite a bit larger than the Cornelia Chimeras to the south. This was because the Chimeras were centered around the city of Cornelia and not pervasive throughout the city or the province, but the Demons pervaded every end of Tundrosa, from all of Edenbrook to the villages and towns throughout the tundra. Most in the north were believers in the philosophies of the Demonstrative Organization of Northern Nuve, and many flocked to their leadership.

Underneath the political aspects, Steffen Robert had a deep reputation of being an honest man, as well. He had been present himself at the armistice hearings and spoke on behalf of the concept of peace. Very much he had tried to keep the Demons from public confrontation with Nuve's forces, although the Demons did raise military forces. Proactive in the Demons organization, however, was an undercover operations network that performed espionage and gathered intelligence. The Demons did not work only on Nuve's government itself, however; they also performed such activities on renowned criminal organization The Syndicate, as well as on the Cornelia Chimeras and in some Nuve civilian matters.

It was a snowy day in the cold city as Larion and Tyrinion walked around the city's main thoroughfare. Tyrinion was in his form as Professor James Magnon, which he preferred as his main identity. Larion looked no different than he usually did, though his royal red robes stuck out just a little bit. Having taken the same initiative as the direction they gave to the fellow gods, they were traveling together while looking for clues to Setadev's dimensional gate, presuming their hypothesis was correct.

Larion loved to walk among the mortal. It was not an opportunity he had very often, given that he was the king of gods and had responsibilities to attend. Tyrinion was long used to walking among the mortal, given the one hundred and fifty years he spent in hiding while being mistaken for Setadev and falsely persecuted. The latter aspect was a subject as Larion and Tyrinion talked while they traversed the main street in Edenbrook.

All around, fires burned in torches and the city appeared all lit up. Banners with the colors of the Demons were hanging all across the buildings and strung across the streets, as the city remained vibrant even in the depths of winter. Although Edenbrook was very cold, the warm glows from the windows and the lights and decoration made the city an attractive place to visit.

"I have never understood one thing," Larion said to Tyrinion, as the two walked along the street together, having spent a while talking about Tyrinion's past exile. "Why is it that you have resented your past identity? You seemed quite content with it for the past five thousand years, up until recently."

"It is as I am," Tyrinion answered with confidence. "I would suppose I have two reasons why I prefer to be 'Professor James Magnon' as opposed to Tyrinion. The first reason is the scars I still carry from exile." He paused for a second. "You have no idea what it is like to be forced out by those for whom you have given the most, only because you were trapped and everyone believed a lie for a hundred and fifty years."

Nodding, Larion answered, "I can only imagine. And the

second?"

Tyrinion looked over to the king of gods. "My daughter," he said. "To her, as I am now, as James Magnon, I am her father. Though I may be the same individual, Tyrinion is not her father. The god of darkness is not her father. Her father is a professor of magic. And being her father means more to me than anything else in the realms anymore."

Larion nodded. "I understand," he said. "I believe I do now more than I have before."

"You see things from both sides now, and because of that, you know," Tyrinion answered. "Being a god is something that is superficial, only a title for which I no longer fit the role. Being a father, however, is something no one can take from me."

"Indeed," acknowledged Larion. "I am quite excited by the fact that your daughter means more to you than anything else. It shows the kind of father that you are."

Quietly, Tyrinion closed his eyes and nodded. "Or at least the kind that I want to be," he said. "I worry often that I am not the kind of father that I should be; nor was I ever, for that matter. I should be a more active part of my daughter's life; I cannot recall a time I ever was."

"You have seemed to me that you have one," commented Larion. "If you do not, then why do you spend all of your time among the mortal?"

Then, an unexpected reaction. Tyrinion looked away. He had no response.

Always ready with an answer, however, Larion did. "It is because by being here, you are remaining a part of her life," he said. "You are letting her live her life and make all of the discoveries she needs to make on her own, yet still you are here to watch her grow up and be a part of her experiences and source of support."

Tyrinion shook his head. "I do not think so," he said. "If that were the case, I would have never let her go on her own. Not then, when I had her travel with the pure one on their trip to stop the conqueror months ago, and not now…" A tear started to come to his eye.

Catching this, Larion raised an eyebrow. "What did you see?" he asked.

Taking a deep breath, Tyrinion said, "I saw her nearly killed. She had been beaten badly by Setadev, assaulted to the point that no one should ever have to go through. And it is all because I allowed her to go on her own, and I let her friends take her along while they continue to search."

"Tyrinion, you cannot supervise her forever," Larion commented. "We can discuss 'what if' statements all of the time, but the truth is that you cannot be your daughter's protector for the rest of her life." He paused for a second and noted Tyrinion's lack of a reaction as they continued walking on. "Think about it this way, if you will," he continued. "Had you not let her go on her own the first time, she never would have had the chance to become good friends with Kevin Trent Stryker. In turn, we would have never discovered that she is an angel, and she would have never awakened to her true potential. Because you had her go with him, your daughter is the person she is today."

"That may be, and for that I am proud," Tyrinion answered, "but had I given her that kind of care much earlier, she may have never become emotionless to begin with. Her past state was my responsibility because I encouraged her only to be focused on her studies, and never on being herself." He raised his head. "Do not misunderstand me, my lord; I am proud of Kevin Trent Stryker and I am very happy that he and my daughter are together. Very much I believe that I am among the truest judges of character and I have a belief that I could never see that boy as being dishonest."

Again, Larion nodded. "Let us hope it remains that way forever," he said.

The snow was starting to fall a little bit heavier. Suddenly, a sharp gust of wind started to blow into the town. It was buffeting, pushing strongly and throwing snow into the eyes of everyone in Edenbrook who stood outside. "A snowstorm is picking up," said Tyrinion, as he pulled up a side of his red and black robes to protect himself better from the blowing snow. "We had better find shelter."

Quickly, Larion shot a glance over to a nearby tavern, which had a glowing window. "You never know who you will find in a pub," he said. "There may be something useful for us there, and we can pass the time."

Agreeing, Tyrinion motioned to Larion toward the tavern, As quickly as they could, they hustled over to the door and entered the pub, just glad to find shelter from the snowstorm. For now, this would be where they would hide out.

Inside, the tavern had a warm feeling. Demons flags hung all over the inside of the pub, as well as a painting of Steffen Robert. It would had to have been a commissioned work, Larion reasoned. This particular tavern had a fairly open design and had plenty of space to walk around. Plenty of kegs sat behind the bar itself, and each was labeled with a different type of ale. This was one of Edenbrook's prime pub locations, known simply as "The Place to Be".

As they walked in, Larion and Tyrinion both proceeded to the bar. They were shaking their robes off as they approached, trying to brush off as many snowflakes as possible. Taking a seat at the bar, Larion said to Tyrinion, "This might actually be a lucky break for us. So much social activity happens at pubs that we may be able to find out some more information."

Reluctantly, Tyrinion nodded. "If this had to happen at some point, I would suppose this would be the time," he said. "I have often had some discomfort in these places."

"Is that because you are trying to hide that you are antisocial?" asked Larion.

Tyrinion raised an eyebrow. He had never been called out on that fact before. Of course, Tyrinion did have his connections and was able to approach others with a calmness and a cautiously managed approach, but he hid his shyness with social situations well. "You seem to be able to tell more about me than even I am willing to admit, Larion. Now, you are taking my role that I am accustomed to."

"Oh, it is nothing," commented Larion. "As with all of the gods, I believe that it is for the best that I am observant of the people they actually are and understanding them. In your case, I have spent probably more learning about you than I have any of the other gods since I took the role of king."

“You have? May I ask why?” asked Tyrinion.

“Because I want you to feel welcome to come home,” Larion answered.

Surprised, Tyrinion was having difficulty coming up with the words to respond.

As they sat there and Tyrinion was deep in thought with what to say to Larion, a female bartender approached the two from the other side of the bar. “Hello, gentlemen,” she said in a very polite voice. “And who might thou be?”

This was typical for Edenbrook, a cultural trait of northern Nuve to always make formal introductions. Tyrinion looked over at the woman and said, “A pleasure to meet you. I am James Magnon, a professor in magic education from Aurana.”

“And my name is Raleigh Lawrence, of the town of Venarose,” Larion then said, inventing his own identity on the spot. “We are here together on business.”

For a second, the woman looked intrigued. “An Auranian and a Nuvenian working together in business… interesting.” She paused then before saying, “My name is Martha, and I will be thy waitress this evening. Can I interest thou in a drink?”

The professor thought for a second. “Just water would be nice,” he said.

Larion then said, “I would love a nice glass of ale. Something from the local area would be good.”

Martha then nodded and proceeded to start getting drinks for the two gods.

Then, Tyrinion leaned in and whispered in Larion’s ear. “She must be affiliated with the Demons,” he said. “They are nice people, but they tend to work in secrecy and they are highly suspicious of outsiders.”

“Interesting,” commented Larion back, quietly. “Perhaps we can get some information from her, then.”

A slight frown came to Tyrinion’s face. “Possibly,” he said, “but even if she were a Demons operative, which is certainly possible, it would be difficult to get information from her. Operatives are very well trained, and even loyalists alone tend to be very protective.”

As Martha walked by, she placed the drinks on the bar. Then, she walked over to serve more customers.

Larion took a big drink from his glass. "Seems quite unusual for an organization that claims to promote libertarianism to have such a detailed undercover network for intelligence and operations."

"As some have said in history," commented Tyrinion, as he drank from his water glass, "certain things are only a means to an end. Whether or not the Demons will eventually give up their networks is something for them to decide someday, and will likely determine whether or not they are true to their words. They at least paint a brighter picture than the Cornelia Chimeras to the southwest do, and have brought hope to the people of Tundrosa. Although it is difficult to know for sure as well, rumor has it that they would be content with just possession of Tundrosa if they could gain independence."

Shaking his head, Larion took another sip of his drink. "Whether or not that is the truth, we cannot be sure. In some ways they seem so calm with their peaceful encouragement, and yet in others they seem so deceptive with such organization."

"Are we any different?" Tyrinion asked as he took a sip from his water glass.

"I would suppose not," said Larion, as he put his glass down. "Here we are, conducting operations in territory that is not our own, to end a war. Elsewhere in the world, our fellow members are working in pairs searching in various parts of the world. Kronius and Necnea are working together in western Gardolk, for instance. Datyrios and Chatka are serving as our coordinators in the Realm of the Angels, collecting our information and reports."

"We are as we are," commented Tyrinion, "just as the Demons are as they are. That being said, they have no relevance to Setadev's cavern." He paused for a moment. "Let us face a fact here. We have been searching Tundrosa for days, but there is no sign of there even being the existence of a known cavern here. Quite frankly, it is too cold here to dig for one, and the people up here have similarly never desired to invest time in the cold digging, either. As we are so far away from the rest of civilization as well, no information on a potential hit has come this far."

Reluctantly, Larion nodded. "I agree," he said, as he drank the rest of his drink. "After this snowstorm subsides, perhaps we are best to head south into Soverenia, then. There is more likely to be accessible caverns there, or perhaps more knowledge of them from someone in the city of Nuvenia."

"A good plan," nodded Tyrinion. He then finished the rest of his water and then asked, "I realize that I am the supposed expert on dimensional space theory, but how do you suppose Setadev is planning to revive himself? Do you really think the Sword of Purity is key to his plan?"

Larion nodded. "I do," he said. "I think Setadev knows that he needs the power of a god infused into himself to regain his power."

"It is the only thing that would, with the Stripe of Life no longer in existence," noted Tyrinion in agreement. "With the Seven Stripes of the Elements destroyed, restoring his divine power to full strength would mean taking it from another source, and a dimensional shift would let him infuse it into himself."

"Exactly," said Larion. "That is why I believe it must be the Sword of Purity that is the power source. It is the only raw source of divine power available in the universe."

"A solid point," acknowledged Tyrinion. "Should he try to take something like a god, I could only theorize he would be forced to share a consciousness with that god, as well." He paused for a second. "I cannot even imagine what would happen if two whole individuals went through a dimensional rift together."

In agreement, Larion nodded. "The possibilities there seem unique, do they not? The idea that two people could be combined, share the same thoughts and powers, and essentially become one individual… it is an astounding possibility. It is also exactly what Setadev would want to avoid. He would not want another conscience to struggle against him."

"Which is why he needs raw power," completed the professor. "Even so, I cannot imagine that the sword itself would work. We still have no idea what is entirely in that sword aside from metal and divine power." Having difficulty, Tyrinion pressed forward. "Maybe there is more of Vinz Larinion in that blade than we know. I doubt that Setadev has not considered this possibility, either."

Considering this point for a second, Larion said, "Maybe." He then paused for a second, as he leaned his glass in and allowed Martha to refill it. Then, he took a sip and set his glass down. "I still think much on immortal death. We have witnessed and heard of it twice, and twice alone. We have come to conclude that only disintegration into raw elements will kill the immortal, dividing their life energy with it and allowing it to scatter. When Vinz Larinion died in sacrificing himself to create the Sword of Purity, he ensured that his energy was channeled into the sword, but still the method was a form of disintegration." He paused again. "That is why I believe the only thing Setadev could use is the sword."

Tyrinion nodded. "Bear in mind that Setadev disintegrated as well," he reminded Larion, "although his survival was only because he had fragmented himself and had constructed an escape route for his consciousness. In that case, Setadev was killed by trying to hold in too much energy all at once when given the Seven Stripes of the Elements." Tyrinion paused as he started to put the math together in his head. "It may very well be that the Seven Stripes of the Elements had no special feature to their combination within one individual after all. Perhaps a sheer overload of divine power, within a god, is all that is needed."

For a moment, Larion's eyes widened. "I have a feeling that the Sword of Purity would be capable of that. It contains the divine power of one of the strongest immortals and can penetrate an opponent by a stab or impactful slash. If that works, all Kevin would have to do to accomplish a disintegration would be to figure out how to unleash all of that energy into the blade at once."

"And I am sure that Vinz Larinion knew this," nodded Tyrinion. "This serves as the explanation for why he would be willing to sacrifice himself, and chose a mortal to wield it. He created a weapon for the mortal to be capable of killing the immortal."

"A curious choice," nodded Larion, "but one that makes sense. He did create it to kill the conqueror, after all."

Tyrinion rolled his eyes. "You mean me," he said.

"Actually, I do not," reversed Larion. "Vinz Larinion, contrary to the rest of us, never said that out loud, at least. He did admit that he had lost his faith in you, and was quite surprised that you had turned on us, but never said he was making the sword to kill you, specifically."

Reluctantly, Tyrinion looked away. He still had no desire to think of his exile, regardless of all of the recent apologies. "We have to fear that Setadev may have that power, as well. Even if he has not used it yet, he has certainly teased that he can."

Larion nodded, as the firmness in his eyes began to waver. "I fear as much, as well." He paused. "I have often had visions, believing that someday I will be in a fight with Setadev. I cannot help but feel that my life would end at that point."

"Do not write your own death sentence, my lord," commented Tyrinion.

Taking a sip from his glass, Larion said, "I am certain I do not as of yet." He then drank the rest of his drink and set the glass back down. "Death is not a fear of mine, in any regard. Perhaps we are growing too old, after all."

Confused, Tyrinion said, "I am two thousand years older than you are, and you are saying you are too old?"

"Only in metaphor," responded Larion. "I am a rather thoughtful individual, you will find, professor. Three thousand years, while a shorter lifespan than yours, is still longer than the lives of any of the mortal you will find. Setadev has the same problem in a sense; had we been allowed to die, then the world would keep moving. Instead, it stays stagnant as we continue to watch on, as war after war constantly breaks out. Are we the problem now?"

Pausing and shaking his head, Tyrinion looked away and said nothing.

Silently, Larion took a breath. "I believe we are," he said. "The war has ravaged us because some of us refuse to allow old wounds to heal. If my understanding is right, Setadev still holds a bitterness of five thousand years, and an ambition that he will not allow to rest. If only this world were willing to let the old pass and allow the new to take the reins, such events may never have happened, and I think will be the only way this situation will ever be truly resolved."

"Are you suggesting that gods should not exist?" asked Tyrinion.

“No, of course not,” the king of gods quickly countered. “However, every now and then an era simply needs to turn over. We have many young gods who would be perfect to be the new blood that lead our universe.” He paused for a second. “Take Kronius, for example. In many ways, he is full of unbridled energy and represents a hope for us.”

Reluctantly, Tyrinion nodded a little bit. “I can certainly see part of your point,” he said. “Kronius is a brilliant individual at his roots. He lacks the experiences that you, or even I, have had, but he has shown a developing sense of logic and intuition.”

“He does,” said Larion. “Chatka, the peace and war god, has been his friend for the longest time, and I am sure both you and I hold his word in the highest regard. He has all of the faith and confidence in the realms for Kronius’ potential.”

“Having worked and traveled with him, I can say the same, even if I did not feel that way initially,” nodded Tyrinion. “I understand that part, Larion. However, the part I do not understand is why you believe that we are antiquated in our age. I do not consider this an issue of the old not turning over into the new; it is a matter of one man who will not put down his ambition for the sake of the realms and the people who live in them.”

“And yet our existence and his are symbiotic and symbolic of a stagnant world,” Larion answered. “It is all right if you do not agree with me, Tyrinion. Perhaps it is only the deluded vision of an old man.”

Again, Tyrinion rolled his eyes, “I am older than you are,” he stated again, a little disturbed by Larion’s repetition of this fact. This behavior did not seem like Larion’s normal demeanors. Knowing that gods were not capable of being intoxicated, he asked with a certain sense of sarcasm, “Are you sure you have not had too much to drink?”

Larion chuckled. “I am sure of that,” he answered. “Still, at the end of this whole thing, I want you to know one thing, Tyrinion. For the longest time, I have believed that my reign as king of gods will be short. I have seen myself in a confrontation with Setadev himself, and I believe that I will lose. The pure one and your daughter, however, I am more hopeful can defeat him.”

Tyrinion stood up, as he reached in his pocket to grab out some bronze coins and set them on the bar, enough to pay for the drinks. “You are writing your own death sentence, then.”

As he stood up, Larion shook his head. “Perhaps I am, after all,” he said. “However, if we are heading for the province of Soverenia, I might recommend we stay in town until the winter storm dies down.” He paused for a second. “And, I would recommend that you take your original appearance.”

Reluctantly, Tyrinion shook his head. “Always the same argument with you, is it?”

Chapter 44

Last Resort

Another night had passed since Kevin had turned around from the Solunar Empire encampment. Still, he was in disbelief over everything that had happened.

This was Setadev's revenge, for sure. Kevin was bright enough to recognize that this had to be one of the purposes of all of the drugging and torment over the months. While it may have seemed so petty, it had the potential to tear apart everything that he had worked for. Not only that, but it could also tear apart his friends' accomplishments as well. Could the Solunar Empire survive without a liaison to the other kingdoms that could vouch for its goodness? That was a role that Kevin played as the Vanguard of Aurana and the best friend of the emperor of the Solunar Empire. Was it selfish to think of himself as that?

What damage it could have done to Caitlin, however, Kevin feared the most. For all he knew, she could be a different person entirely. He knew she tended to be sensitive to change on an emotional scale right now while emotion was still new to her. He had recognized that while she was living with him, and had tried to be careful as a result. Certainly he had his doubts about their future together, as would be typical in any new relationship for someone who had been so unsuccessful about it before, but he would never desire to bring harm to Caitlin whether by intention or not.

There was little he could do about it right now, though. It was evident from that Arthur, Rachel, and Caitlin were not willing to talk with him right now, if Caitlin even could. Because Kevin did not remember exactly what had happened in front of them and had only heard secondhand from Setadev himself, he had no idea what they had seen and experienced from him.

As Kevin thought on this on his travel back across the mountain road, it did occur to him that he may have been able to escape because Setadev allowed him. It was certainly possible that Setadev wanted him to hear from his friends as an effort to break him. That would certainly explain why his sword was left in the tent, even if it appeared to be in frustration.

What did Setadev want with the Sword of Purity, anyway? Leaving it planted in the ground would hopefully keep it out of his hands given what Kevin was about to do next, but that was not the full reason why he had done so. He felt compelled to leave behind a message to his friends, that he was going back on his own and he was not going to betray them and give Setadev that power.

What he was going to do was going to be his last resort. He was going to free his last ally, General Sayo, and figure out what to do from there. As he had told Setadev before, he was only the man who sought the downfall of the conqueror, and nothing more. Now, he had to prove that without his greatest tool and without his friends.

By the end of his second day heading back on the trail, night had just fallen when he came within sight of the encampment. The night was cold in the winter, but the breeze was light, making it more bearable. Looking at the camp and analyzing it for the first time, he saw just how large it was and its unique shape. The camp was built into an indent in the mountain range, at the back of which there was a mine. Kevin was not sure himself what the purpose of this specific camp was, but he knew that Setadev was here. No fires were burning in the camp at all; it would be very easy to miss in the dark.

Before advancing, something caught Kevin's eye above in the skies. He looked up at what he thought was a shooting star, but then turned to face away from the camp as he followed the object in the air. It was hard to see in the dark, but against the outline of the night sky, it vaguely appeared to be a person. It could not have been Caitlin in her angel form, though, as her wings would have glowed bright enough to be seen.

Maybe it was a god, from the Realm of the Angels? One way or another, it was too high to yell to and draw its attention. To do so would likely alert the camp below and not who or whatever was above. If it were the case that the figure above was a god, however, maybe

Kevin could figure out a way to light up the night sky at the camp and draw their attention. It was just another consideration to be made on this venture.

Turning back around, Kevin stared upon the camp. He had to squint to see it clearly due to the darkness all around. On the plus side, it would offer a significant amount of cover. He was dirty and tired, but knew this would be his opportunity. Preparing for his silent advance, Kevin reached over and pulled back his left sleeve, unveiling his Nuve stealth bracer, a past gift from Raijin Shane. It gleamed slightly in the moonlight as it was trimmed in silver, shining against the blue paint and the gold-painted letter N on the palm piece. With confidence, Kevin then flipped the guard open, revealing the stealth bracer's inner workings where it contained a small dart launcher with poison-tipped darts.

Gently, Kevin wound back the tensioning cable to arm the dart launcher. He then pulled a dart from the bracer's small storage area and set it on the line. He was hoping that maybe he could disable someone who had a sword and take it. He flipped down the bracer plate and headed off.

Heading toward the camp was a slope where cliff ledges wrapped around the perimeter of the indent. Kevin proceeded past these and headed directly for the tents at the bottom. At the bottom of the hill, he slowed down to make less noise, and began to sneak around the camp. The main question in his head was the location of the general, knowing that it was likely that he had been moved.

Quietly, Kevin snuck into the camp. He knew, as he ducked behind the first tent he found, that it was likely he was not leaving this camp alive tonight. He would very likely be captured or killed, but he had that mentality coming into this situation already.

If Sayo were in a tent, he had to be in one that had a center pole within it, and it had to be a thick one. This would prevent him from being able to escape, and would be ineffective otherwise. That meant Kevin had to look for a larger tent that had a substantial support holding it up. It would be the most likely that the general was there.

Carefully, Kevin ducked and pulled up the side of the tent, rolling underneath it and inside. He stood up cautiously, trying not to make any noise. It had turned out he was right to be as silent as possible; inside this tent was a man sleeping on a cot. Kevin could hear him breathing, and knew he had to avoid waking the man. Against a tent side, Kevin could see the outline of a cloak hanging on a hook.

This was an Enlightener cloak. A perfect idea, Kevin realized. Gently, he tiptoed over to where he saw the cloak, trying not to trip on anything or make any extra noise. With care, he made it over and pulled the cloak off of the hook. Quickly, he flipped it over himself and pulled the hood up. Then, he very carefully exited the tent. As he did, Kevin breathed a huge sigh of relief, knowing he was fortunate not to have had an encounter with that Enlightener.

Armed as he was, Kevin still wanted to avoid confrontation at all costs. Now, however, he was in the disguise of an Enlightener. Kevin kept his hood up, hoping to hide as much of his face as possible. At least for now, he could walk freely amongst the camp. As he toured the area, he kept trying to reason where Sayo could be. Even in the middle of the night, he had to reason that Sayo was in a guarded area. Therefore, he had to find a tent that had a guard in front of it.

Walking around through the camp at night, Kevin tried to keep as quiet as possible. Where could Sayo be? There were a reasonably large number of tents in the camp, which meant that Kevin had to walk through them looking for a guarded tent. He had to be very quiet even in disguise, as it was quite unlikely that many Enlighteners would be awake and he did not want to draw much attention to himself.

Passing through the camp, he found one tent large enough to have such a pole for Sayo to be tied to. Carefully, he lifted the side of the flap and looked inside, only to find he was wrong. However, what was inside that tent was a large amount of explosives. Now that would be something that would create a flash large enough to alert anyone watching in the skies. As he put the tent flap back down, he made a mental note to come back to this tent later on in the night.

After twenty long minutes walking through the camp, he found what he thought was the tent. One Enlightener stood at the front of the tent flap, while the tent itself was supported by a heavy post in the middle. Kevin had been lucky not to walk across the side of the tent with the guard, and thus had the upper hand. He had a plan in mind.

Calmly, he walked up to the guard. "Shift change," he announced in a low voice. "You can take the rest of the night off; I'll take over."

The Enlightener pulled his hood down and frowned. "Strange," he responded. "I do not recall being notified that I would be getting relief from guard duty tonight."

Kevin nodded, keeping his hood up. "Special arrangement of the administrator," he said. "He wanted you to have time to rest this evening for something tomorrow."

This time the Enlightener turned to face Kevin. "That makes no sense," he said. "The administrator has already told me I am only to be on guard duty until…"

Before the Enlightener could say more, Kevin reached up and shot him in the face with the stealth bracer. The Enlightener fell over, dead from the poison on the dart, and disappeared as the cloth and necklace he was wearing alone fell to the ground. Truly, Nuve poisons were quite deadly. As expected, though, the Enlightener had disappeared upon being supposedly killed.

Without hesitation, Kevin then quickly moved inside the tent. He was right. Inside the tent, asleep and tied to the pole, was General Sayo. There was little time to waste, however. He walked up to the general, tapped him on the face, and said, "Hey, general! General!"

Sayo nearly jumped. "Huh? What?" he snapped as he awoke, surprised.

Immediately, Kevin shushed him as he pulled down his hood. "Please be quiet," he whispered. "I'm here to get you out."

Straining to get his eyes in focus, Sayo looked up. "Kevin? Is that you?"

"It is," whispered Kevin, as he circled around to the back to start undoing Sayo's knots, starting at the ankles. "Stay quiet; we won't be able to escape unless you do."

"Gotcha," Sayo whispered back. "How did you get free?"

"Long story," answered Kevin, as he shifted up to the knots binding Sayo's arms to the pole. "I managed to escape shortly after you were escorted out of the tent we shared. I came back to rescue you."

A confused look came to Sayo's face as Kevin worked on his

knots. “Why?” he asked.

Kevin took a deep breath. “Because,” he answered, “I forgive you.”

In response, Sayo nodded, as Kevin finished untying him and his hands and ankles came free. “Thanks,” he said as he gripped his wrists, “but I’m not sure I deserve it.”

“Regardless, it is there for you,” Kevin responded, “provided you will do me one favor.”

Sayo nodded. “Name it,” he said.

“I need you to get out of here,” answered Kevin. “To the northeast, there is a mountain road that leads across the side of a peak and around to a valley road. You can cross it in a day if you keep moving. The Solunar Empire was there. If you can find them, you need to bring them here, and show them this encampment. If we’re to bring it down, we need their help.”

For a second, Sayo rolled his eyes. “You know, they may not be willing to listen to me,” he said.

Suddenly, a loud horn blasted across the camp. They were found out!

Kevin cursed under his breath, but quickly regained his focus. “Just do the best you can. They’ll listen to you more than they’ll listen to me,” he responded, as he flipped up the side of his bracer and rearmed the dart launcher. “I will cover you to help make sure you escape. Swear to me that you will find the emperor and the prime minister, and Caitlin.”

Again, Sayo nodded. “That I swear,” he said. “You’re not coming along?”

“I’m not,” Kevin answered. “I have something I have to do first. I believe someone is in the area looking for this camp, and I plan to let them know where it is.”

Though skeptical, Sayo nodded. “I understand,” he said, as he stretched his legs out a bit. “I’ll be ready to run.”

“Good,” nodded Kevin. “Get going. What I’m about to do should serve as a distraction so you can escape.”

In acknowledgment, Sayo nodded one more time as he walked out of the tent. Fixing his bracer, Kevin put his hood back up for one more trick. He headed back toward the tent full of explosives, knowing that if he could set it off, it would likely let whoever was flying in the air know where the camp was. He just had to hope it was a god that he saw. If nothing else, the explosion might have a chance of being visible from where the Solunar Empire forces were, if it could go high enough. Grabbing an unlit torch from the side of another tent on the way there, he prepared for war.

All around, Enlighteners were scampering, searching around the camp. They knew the horn was the sound for an escaped prisoner. Though Kevin was in disguise, he had to act quickly if he was going to keep General Sayo from being discovered.

In front of him, an Enlightener stopped and stared at Kevin, as if recognizing he was unusual. Without time to react, Kevin reached up and shot his dart launcher again, making the Enlightener disappear as his robes fell to the ground.

At the explosives tent, Kevin stopped. He reached down, scraping the torch against the ground. The match head design of the torch allowed it to be lit this way. Then, Kevin threw it at the tent and began running to the west. Immediately, the explosives tent caught fire. It quickly engulfed the entire structure, lighting up the area. Many Enlighteners started fleeing from that section. Utter chaos was sweeping through the entire camp.

Then, the explosives ignited.

The loud bang that resulted echoed throughout the air. A massive fireball shot into the air, lighting up the night sky. Enlighteners ran for their lives as the exploding tent shattered the silence.

As it happened, Kevin ducked behind another corner behind a tent. As he did, someone grabbed him by his neck and lifted him into the air. "You disappoint me, pure one," said a dark voice.

"As do you, Setadev," Kevin answered back. "Really, you and your forces couldn't stop me from blowing up your camp?"

"Very funny, but you do not see how the game is played," Setadev said firmly. He looked down for a second, then looked back into Kevin's eyes. "Where is your sword, pure one?" he asked.

Kevin chuckled. "Wouldn't you like to know?" he asked.

"Yes, I would very much so," demanded Setadev. The anger in

his voice then escalated. "Where is it? Where is it?"

Though Setadev's grip was painful, Kevin laughed in his face. "I see perfectly well how the game is played," he said, using ironic repetition.

Setadev scoffed as he threw Kevin to the ground. Several Enlighteners arrived as well, surrounding the pure one. "Quite," answered the fallen god. He then turned and looked at his Enlighteners. "Rough him up, then tie him up in a tent. I want full guard on him, all of the time, until I say otherwise."

Doing as instructed, two Enlighteners reached down and picked up Kevin by his arms to carry him off. Dirtied and beaten, Kevin chuckled a bit knowing he accomplished three things.

Setadev wanted the Sword of Purity, and Kevin denied him of it.

Sayo was headed for the Solunar Empire force.

And maybe, just maybe, if that were a god in the sky, maybe they saw the explosion.

Chapter 45

Subconscious Awakening

In the middle of a cold winter night, Rachel and Arthur sat next to each other on the edge of a creek. The troops were camped out along the valley road that ran next to the water, taking advantage of the slightly more lush climate of the valley to rest comfortably. The command tents were set and guards rotated shifts of protecting the camp, but the emperor and prime minister were sitting away from their men on the riverbank.

So much had happened in the past days. It was as though everything they had known had been turned upside down. A few days had passed since encountering Setadev, Satiana, and Kevin at the Gates to Gardolk, and still the empire's forces remained where they were, a short distance away from the gates into the foothills of the Peaked Mountains. They had neither advanced nor retreated, unable to decide what to do.

Arthur looked up as Rachel was sitting down next to him. She began, "I finished sewing up Caitlin's dress. Not sure if it'll help her or not, but I left it in her tent for her. If we get her back, I think she'll want it."

Nodding, Arthur then changed the subject. "I've decided we should just go back home tomorrow morning," he told her. "Back to the empire. With Kevin gone forever and no real reason to keep following Setadev anymore when we clearly can't beat him by ourselves, I don't see another option other than just to pack it up and go home."

Carefully, Rachel nodded and adjusted her dress as she sat next to Arthur. She agreed with him, seeing he had finally made his decision carefully, but seemed to have quite a bit on her mind. "Did you ever think things would be like this?" she asked him. "I mean, all of this?"

A moment passed, as Arthur gave a long sigh. "No, honestly, I didn't," he said. "I'm still in shock that things have turned out that way. What are you supposed to do when your best friend betrays everything you know and stand for?"

Rachel nodded, silently. "I guess I still just can't figure out how or why he went to Setadev and got with that lady in his encampment. It just doesn't make any sense why he would do either of those things." She looked briefly over at Caitlin's tent. "He loved Caitlin, and his cause was pure and for the right reasons against Setadev. Why would he defect?"

Arthur shrugged. "I don't understand it. I know he wasn't possessed by tracer magic, but I still feel like somehow he was not in control of himself. He wouldn't do that."

"Are you still trying to defend him?" Rachel asked pointedly. "Arthur, I know he was your best friend, but he's betrayed us! Don't you get that? Everything about his demeanor at the time says that. He was too afraid to say anything to us, the coward."

Turning away, Arthur shrugged again. It was hard not to snap back at Rachel for calling Kevin a coward, but she had a point based on what they had seen. "I don't know. I just don't know," he said. "I want to believe him, so badly."

Gently, Rachel relaxed her demeanor. She could see that Arthur was stressing out about this, and why would he not? Kevin and Arthur had been best friends for most of their lives, after all. It would only be natural for him to take this hard. She put one hand on his shoulder and said, "We're all human. We are all capable of deception, of betrayal, and of manipulation. It applied to General Sayo, and it applies to Kevin, and to you and me as well if we chose to pursue those routes."

Arthur only shook his head. Then, he turned and looked toward the small personal tent where Caitlin was staying. "She hasn't said a word since that day," he noted. "She's been alternating between quiet and screaming. I only have to wonder what's really going on in her head, with her mind being shattered."

Rachel sighed. "I hope this isn't for good," she said. "When we go back, we need to find her father. We'll accept whatever punishment he decides to give for letting this happen to his daughter, even if that means we never see Caitlin again."

"Let us hope not," said Arthur. A tear came to his eye. "I've already lost my best friend and many good soldiers on this campaign. I don't want to lose my sister, too."

Quietly, Rachel put her arm across Arthur's shoulders. "Me neither, Arthur. Me neither."

And as strange as that was, Arthur turned and hugged Rachel in response. To him, it was all about how much both of them cared for Caitlin. What could she be going through since the events this morning?

The night was getting late, and everyone was turning in, except for the night watch. Inside her tent, Caitlin was as silent as ever. She was resting with only a blank stare on her face. The shatter still being in her mind, she could not formulate a complete thought, but surges of emotions kept running through her. The last thing she saw, the image of Kevin kissing Satiana, was the one thing that stuck in her head.

Such cruelty. She had lost him forever. Tears were still falling from her eyes, even when she was not screaming.

Quietly, the night was passing by. As she slept, Caitlin began to dream, as her subconscious remained intact. She was standing in a meadow, alone. The skies above were dark red, littered with black clouds. A few lightning bolts struck across the sky.

All she could think about was how much she missed Kevin, even though he had betrayed her. They would never be together again. He was her one source of happiness, the one thing that made life worth living for her. So much came out of their relationship, and with only a few months together they had already explored so much of who each other truly was.

After looking up at the sky in thought, Caitlin looked back down. Ahead of her, facing away, was Kevin. Immediately, she started calling his name.

At the first call, Satiana arrived, next to her. "Do not be so surprised if he does not answer you," she said. "After all, he's mine now." Then, Satiana ran off, grabbed Kevin by the hand, and kept walking.

"No, don't!" screamed Caitlin from her spot. "Don't go with her!" She started crying. "Kevin, don't go, please! I love you! Don't go with her, please!"

Within a minute, both of them were gone.

Caitlin fell to the ground, crying. Another crack of lighting crashed across the sky.

Suddenly, everything changed in Caitlin's dream. She found herself standing in the middle of a vortex of energy, but it seemed as though everything had stopped around her. Nothing else appeared above or below her. What was this? All her subconscious could think was that this was very unusual.

She felt something oddly familiar yet different on her back. She reached behind herself to feel hair dangling down her back. Hers. Her hair was back, and it was ever so slightly longer than it was ever before. Then, she looked down to see her clothing gone, and a long white cloth wrapping around her body. As she turned her head to follow the cloth, she also saw translucent wings appearing from her back.

She was now in the appearance of an angel, as depicted in ancient lore. There had to be some significance to this, somehow. Still, there was no one else present. "Amelia, if you are here, I request that you reveal yourself," she stated aloud. She recognized she was in a dream, and suspected her alternate subconscious personality.

There was a slightly cheerful voice responding. "Of course," she said, causing Caitlin to turn around.

Amelia was not in her black dress that Caitlin had worn before ever meeting Kevin. She was dressed in the white wizardess dress with red trim that she had worn since getting closer to him.

"I don't understand," Caitlin said. "You are Amelia, aren't you?"

Amelia laughed a little bit, with a big wide smile. "As we've discussed before, we are both Caitlin Amelia Magnon. We are just reflections of one another. I am the one finding my way through all of the new emotions Kevin has shown me."

Caitlin took a step back. "That's not right," she said. "It was the other way around. You were the emotionless one and the one who represented what I was, while I… I…"

"See, you don't even know," responded Amelia, giving Caitlin a hug in support. Caitlin could not even raise her arms to return the feeling. "My personality is whichever one you need to see when you need to see it, and you need a reminder of who you are."

Caitlin looked down. Was she Amelia now? "Explain the clothes," she then requested.

Amelia chuckled. "Not my idea this time," she said. "The one who has brought us here together tonight suggested it to remind you of who you are, while he repairs your mind. After he is done, you will never need me again."

"Never need you again?" Caitlin asked. "Then…"

"Then this is farewell," said Amelia, as she started to fade. "With his help, we will become one again as your mind heals and becomes as it should be." Her voice started to become more distant. "Listen to your heart, and listen to his words."

Caitlin reached out, as the last bit of Amelia disappeared. She vanished out of sight. "Amelia?" Caitlin asked in stunned surprise. "Amelia, are you here?"

There was no response for a moment. Then, a flash of light appeared directly in front of Caitlin. The light of the flash was so bright that Caitlin had to raise her arm to prevent her eyes from going blind. Then, the figure of an older man with a darker skin tone, dressed in robes of silver and blue trim, walked from the light. "She is not here," said the man, "but I am."

Caitlin's eyes widened.

In an instant, the light faded out, and the older man stood in front of Caitlin. "I apologize for the surprising imagery, but I thought this might help you to remember who you are."

"And who are you?" asked Caitlin, without emotion.

The gentleman bowed. "Forgive my intrusion," he began. "My name is Vinz Larin, although I am sure I am remembered better as Vinz Larinion."

Vinz Larinion. The departed five thousand year king of gods. Exactly as he had been pictured in the Realm of the Angels, and exactly with the physical form that Tyrinion had described to her. Immediately, Caitlin fell to her knees. "How could I see the great king of gods in my dream?" she asked herself quietly.

"Oh, this is no dream," Vinz Larinion answered, despite how quietly Caitlin had asked herself the question. "This is a vision you are having. You are seeing it because I want you to see it."

Slowly, Caitlin's head rolled up. "How could that be? You died a little more than twenty years ago."

Nodding, Vinz Larinion answered, "So I have heard. However, if the truth must be known, I did not truly die in the conventional sense when I created the Sword of Purity. No longer do I exist in a corporeal form, but I continue to live on within the sword. I have given it a life of its own, directing the pure one where he needs to go and giving him my power through his sword. The skill is all his, but the divine abilities of the sword are mine."

Caitlin gasped. No one would have ever believed in the twenty years since he had passed on that Vinz Larinion would still be existing in some form, much less within the sword that he had forged with his own sacrifice.

A smile came to Vinz Larinion's face. "I must say that for the daughter of Tyrinion, you have grown to be quite a lovely young woman," he continued. "I know of your ancestry, and that you are the first angel ever born from the gods as we know them. In many ways, I would say that you make us proud."

Just as her father had described to her before, this image of Vinz Larinion was very kind and friendly, it seemed. This was, according to her father, part of what drew the gods to Vinz Larinion and made him so likable as the king of gods for five thousand years. At least whatever vision she was seeing was accurate in that extent, as was his appearance. It was said that Vinz Larin was initially born to parents from the tribal nations in the predecessor to the modern-day Wastes in the Solunar Empire, and that he had left them as a young adult to pursue a life exploring the world. He grew to be a knowledgeable man and an academic scholar, but never lost himself in elitism and maintained his self-image very well as he made himself wiser. He was also the first recruited by power zealot Setaeus Demota and became his right-hand man when he saw the utopia that Setaeus wanted him to see. During this time he had also met and married a mystic named Necana, better known now as the goddess Necnea. By the time Setaeus led his followers to the Realm of the Angels, Vinz Larin had become an older man and had decided to keep this appearance even when he was able to change it with divine power. This also matched what Caitlin was seeing.

Still, how could it really be him?

Then, Vinz Larinion started chuckling. "You still do not believe I am real, do you?"

A look of stun came across Caitlin's face. Something seemed intimidating about that now, but still she nervously pressed through to say, "I'm not sure I know how I can believe that you are here before me. Please forgive me," she said.

Calmly, Vinz Larinion walked over to the kneeling Caitlin and put his hand on her shoulder. "Please feel free to rise," he said. "You need not show such formalities to me. I want to be able to see you on the same level, and not from a higher one."

Gently, Caitlin raised her head, but did not stand up. She looked directly into the eyes of the kind king of gods whom she saw plain as day. His dark skin and white hair and beard made his silver robes seem to shine even more, as if to reflect light into her soul. She could see now, from his kindness and respect, how the gods that she had come to meet and respect had developed their immense kindness and desires not to be thought of as elite. Their much-beloved king exemplified that same spirit of respect and equality.

"Now I know you believe, at least a little bit," continued Vinz Larinion, as he stared into Caitlin's eyes. "By the end of this vision that I am showing you, you will believe, and you will know. That, I can promise you."

"Answer me this, then," Caitlin asked. "If you are real, then why have you waited until now to talk to me? Why not get in touch with me earlier?"

There was a slight pause. "I do apologize that I could not get in communication with you earlier when you needed it most," continued the former king of gods, "but this is the first time I have been able to do so. My life energy is tied into the Sword of Purity, and I do not have any power away from it. I can only contact you now, and heal your mind in the process, because the sword is within proximity of here and it is unsheathed."

Caitlin raised an eyebrow. "It is?" she asked. "Is Kevin somewhere near me?"

"He is not," answered Vinz Larinion. "He abandoned the Sword of Purity in a road near here. Kevin overheard Arthur and Rachel blame him for your condition." He paused for a moment. "Kevin was so upset by the situation that he did not even approach them to talk to them. He spiked the Sword of Purity into the ground near here and left it in its place. He then took off and headed back for Setadev's base of operations, alone."

"Then he is a traitor," said Caitlin. "He is abandoning us."

"No, he is not," answered Vinz Larinion. "Kevin left his sword in the hopes that you might find it soon and know that he meant true enough to leave behind his most valuable tool and show you that he was not taken in by its power. He wanted you to know that there was more to him than what Setadev could ever offer."

Caitlin was stunned. These realizations were hitting her hard, and she was struggling to understand what she was seeing. "How do I know you're not just a dream of mine trying to make things better for me?" she asked. "I don't see how I can trust that what you are telling me is true, if you appear only in my mind like this."

Vinz Larinion bowed his head. "That is why you are consumed with your doubt now," he answered. "Kevin has often had the same thoughts himself, and I can feel those within him every time he grabs the handle of the Sword of Purity. He has always been afraid that you might not actually have those same powerful feelings for him that he has for you."

"Kevin has no feelings for me anymore," answered Caitlin. Though she tried to maintain her mental discipline, a tear fell from her eyes. She could not hide the sadness as she had done for the last couple of days. "He made that very clear to me about a week ago." Another tear fell from her eyes.

There was a momentary pause. Then, Vinz Larinion shook his

head. "If you truly believe that from your heart, then we have no reason to continue," he responded. "If that is indeed what you truly believe, then you have fallen for Setadev's scheme just as he wants. Do not be fooled; it is an illusion and nothing more."

Caitlin was confused. "An illusion?" she asked. Then, she slowed down, taking a second to do so. "With respect, my lord, I saw him with my own two eyes give a passionate kiss to a lady named Satiana, and he left with her."

"Yet behind the marionette, the puppeteer is still pulling the strings," mentioned Vinz Larinion. "I believe that you have used that expression yourself when describing how Demonicus was controlled by Setadev as well in that sense."

The puppeteer is still pulling the strings. Caitlin's eyes widened. That perked her interest. She pulled herself up straight and asked, "Do you know what happened?"

Again, Vinz Larinion nodded. He stepped closer to Caitlin and put his hand on her shoulder. Suddenly, two chairs appeared next to her and to the former king of gods. "Please, let us have a seat. This will take some explanation."

As she wiped her hand across her eyes to dry them, Caitlin did as she was asked.

Vinz Larinion also took a seat. "Now, this may be tricky to explain, but please, listen closely," he began. "While Kevin was placed under a different sort of control than Demonicus was, Setadev was still the puppeteer, just as he has always been." He paused for a second. "Kevin never meant to betray you. When he arrived at the Metoi village, I warned Kevin through the sword that continuing to pursue General Sayo was a dangerous idea, but Setadev must have detected my interference and also sent a message to Kevin at the same time to tell him to go after Sayo. He presumed it came from his sword as well."

"So, Setadev encouraged him to go off on his own! And he thought it was you," realized Caitlin. Her eyes opened wider.

"That is correct," nodded Vinz Larinion. "It had been Setadev's plan all along. He wanted two things. One of these was revenge on Kevin and on you."

Caitlin nodded. "Right. I know that," she said. "That's why I don't understand why he has Kevin on his side."

"We will get to that," noted Vinz Larinion. "Setadev was well aware that Kevin would find the way to Sayo's camp along an embankment in the Wastes, and so when he arrived, Setadev immediately captured him and started to move Sayo's unit to the Fortress of Da Leval. There, Setadev locked him up in chains, in a dark cell with little to no light. He was unable even to stand up and walk, much less move around."

Caitlin's eyebrows raised. This was starting to sound disturbing, more so than she had known. "Then how does Satiana play into this picture?" she asked.

Shaking his head, Vinz Larinion began, "Before I tell you, let me warn you that despite as sadistic as this plan sounds, what you are about to hear is even more disturbing." He paused for a moment before continuing, "Setadev needed someone for Kevin to be drawn to, because he ultimately needed Kevin's cooperation. He chose to make someone, by making another fragment of himself, but in an attractive female form and again with an independence of thought."

Immediately, Caitlin looked down at her hands. How could Setadev's strategy involve trying to attract Kevin with someone prettier than her? It was disgusting. Truthfully, although Caitlin would not admit this aloud, she had had some issues with the way she saw herself. At sixteen years old, she had wanted like many girls her age to look beautiful, but was able to look in the mirror and point out all of her imperfections, even if Kevin did not see or acknowledge them. These issues were even worse after the Aequina had cut all of her hair off. To lose Kevin to someone who was deliberately made to be prettier than her hurt her deeply. Still, Caitlin kept looking at herself while Vinz Larinion gave her a moment. Her appearance as an angel did make her feel beautiful, even if her face and her body was the same. It made her feel a little better.

"I see how you admire the form you are in now," noted Vinz Larinion, causing Caitlin to suddenly look up at him. "What you are seeing now is you, plain and simple. The only thing in your form in this vision that is not you as you are is the cloth you are wearing, but that is only to remind you of what you have lost, and who you can be."

He paused for a moment. "You need only fight your own self-doubt and Setadev's manipulations to see who you really are on the inside."

Caitlin looked up. She had never really seen herself like this before, and it made her feel much better. "You mean my angel form," she said.

"That is only part of your identity," Vinz Larinion continued. "You are a strong, smart woman amongst the most powerful people in the world, and perhaps as powerful as the gods. Since you are only half-immortal, your access to divine power is limited. However, when your nerves start to excite in just the right way, you gain more access through the stimulation of these emotions, which in turn are connected to the release of your divine power." He paused for a moment. "As I am sure you have come to realize, stimulating emotions such as anger, hate, fear, and frustration do not cause this reaction. Even happiness, as powerful an emotion as it is, is not the trigger. There is one feeling, however, that is strong enough."

"Love," interrupted Caitlin, in realization. "Every time it's happened, it's always been for love or for fear of losing the one I love." She reached to her chest, forgetting she was in a vision, to feel for the key that Kevin had given her. Surprisingly, she reached to her chest and found it, hanging tied to her neck just as she normally wore it. She looked at it for a minute and thought of Kevin.

"That is correct," nodded Vinz Larinion. "It is for that reason Setadev tried to break apart your relationship with Kevin. I would not be surprised if Setadev actually fears you and is not strong enough to contain you as of now. He had to make sure as well that you were subdued, but if I know his strong sense of curiosity, I do not think he ever intended to destroy you."

Caitlin threw her hands down. "Why not?" she asked, confused. "I don't understand. Killing me would be the best way to make sure I stayed out of his way, and would have absolutely crushed Kevin if he still loved me. He even tried to kill me before with his divine power, but was interrupted before he could."

"Perhaps," acknowledged Vinz Larinion. "But more likely, by doing so, he instilled fear within you."

Lowering her head, Caitlin sighed. "You're right about that," she said. "That was the first time I was ever really afraid for my life."

Vinz Larinion nodded. "Exactly," he stated. "As my old mentor would put it, 'now you see how the game is played.' Setadev's most overused tactic has always been the weapon of fear, just as it was five thousand years ago and just as it is today." He paused for a moment. "Kevin was and still is susceptible to that same weapon as well, but he no longer fears death. Although he feels a responsibility to defend other people, what he fears most is losing you, or any of his closest friends."

Caitlin looked away. Right now, she was still having a hard time believing that.

"That same weapon, Caitlin, has been used on you," continued Vinz Larinion. "It has left you without your strongest power, that which might be able to defeat Setadev once and for all. The design of Satiana was for exactly that purpose; she was to make you believe from the bottom of your heart that Kevin had betrayed you, when in actuality he never had. At least not willingly."

Suddenly, Caitlin's ears perked up. She looked straight into the fallen deity's eyes. "Not willingly? Are you saying Kevin was possessed?"

"No," answered Vinz Larinion, calmly. "I protect him from that." He paused to gain his composure. "Instead, Setadev formulated an even darker plan. He began to administer aphrodisiacs to Kevin, but I do not mean the various scents of perfumes or anything of that sort which can stimulate the senses. These were mind-altering, sensory-inhibiting chemicals that made Kevin lose total and complete control of himself. He had lost memory of who he was, what he was doing, almost everything while under the influence of these drugs. While locked in the Fortress of Da Leval, Kevin had been drugged heavily with these chemicals, leaving him in a state without self-control." He paused again. "But Kevin resisted as hard as he could, so when Setadev was ready to confront you at the Gates to Gardolk, he drugged Kevin as hard as he could and shattered his mind to make Kevin unable to resist any longer. The things that you heard, and the things that you saw, were all because Setadev wanted you to hear of and see these things."

Quickly, Caitlin stood up from her chair. "Hang on," she said. "If what you're telling me is true... if what you're telling me is true..."

Caitlin struggled to make the words come out as her vocal tone shallowed out, "then that means..."

"It means that Kevin is innocent," answered Vinz Larinion. "He still loves you, and he needs you."

Immediately, Caitlin's hands fell to her heart. It hurt, and it hurt badly. Despite what she had seen, she felt bad now for ever doubting Kevin. After everything they had been through together, how could she have lost her faith in him? They had been together for almost a year now in absolute time. Together, they had fought through so much. And it was all the villain who they had spent so much effort fighting against that had caused her to doubt him.

Still, how could she have doubted him again, when she promised him she never would? Now, if she could only believe that this vision was true, that this really was Vinz Larinion and she was being told the truth.

"And that leads to the second reason Setadev did this," Vinz Larinion continued. "He needs the Sword of Purity to revive himself, but he needs Kevin to manipulate it for him because he cannot touch it. Recruiting Kevin to his side would allow him to have it, but Kevin continues to resist. That is why he left his sword near here, but he did not know doing so would let me reach you."

Caitlin fell to her knees. She was crying, feeling a complex mixture of happiness and sadness. Things were not as they seemed to be, and she felt sorry for falling apart. Yet she could still fix this, and the opportunity to do so was before her.

Quietly, Vinz Larinion then stood up from his chair, and the two chairs vanished into thin air. "It is time for me to depart now," he said. "Caitlin, daughter of Tyrinion, the future lies in your hands. Kevin's future is in your hands as well. It will be up to you to save him."

Caitlin's eyes widened. "Save him?" she asked.

"He will be waiting for you as a prisoner," answered Vinz Larinion, "and when you wake, you will know for sure that what you have seen and discussed with me tonight was not merely a dream, but the truth." He turned and started walking away.

"But when will we see you again?" asked Caitlin, as if desperate.

Vinz Larinion stopped. "I live on as the Sword of Purity," he answered without turning. "You will see me when you find it." He then paused for a moment. "Tell your father that I am sorry we persecuted him falsely, and tell Necnea that I love her."

Stunned, Caitlin stood and watched as Vinz Larinion took a few steps and disappeared into the air. What he had said, if he was really truthful in this supposed vision, made her wonder what the days in the Realm of the Angels must have been like under his rule. More than that, however, she was now missing Kevin again.

What did the old king of gods mean when he said that she would have to save Kevin?

Suddenly, her heart started racing as it came together. Kevin was in trouble! Vinz Larinion said Kevin went back to Setadev's encampment, alone, without his sword. There was no way he was going to win that battle alone. What was he thinking?

It was a suicide mission. One way or another, he was going to prove he was loyal and true to his cause, even if it cost him his life.

She was the only one who could save him.

In that moment, Caitlin's eyes popped open. Awake now, with her mind fully intact and healed, she was in a cold sweat with such dark fears running down her veins. Even in her tent, she could feel the wind feeling even colder across her skin, over her chest and back, and around both sides.

That didn't make any sense, Caitlin realized. Unless...

She turned over. Indeed, she was floating a short distance off the ground. Then, she turned her head to see a translucent angel wing coming out from behind her right shoulder. She looked the other way to see another one as well. In her spark of fears for Kevin's life and the feelings of love she felt for him again, she had transformed into her angel form in her sleep. She had not been in this form in quite some time.

As she saw this, Caitlin ran her fingers through her hair. It ran longer than she remembered. In fact, it ran all the way down to where it had been before the Aequina had cut it off. Her healed mind was proof that she had seen Vinz Larinion for real, and her hair was how Vinz Larinion had helped to restore her self-image that her journey had taken away from her.

Quickly, Caitlin peeked outside. The sun was just coming up over the eastern horizon. Looking for her clothes, she found her dress was in the tent. As fast as she could, she put it on and raced outside, not even bothering to lower her angel form. She had to hurry as quickly as she could if she was to save Kevin.

He had spiked his sword into the ground. Only he and his father could pull it out. However, if Vinz Larinion was the Sword of Purity now, and had projected a vision to Caitlin, then perhaps it would listen to her.

It was the only shot she had, at least.

As fast as she could, she raced out of the encampment and headed south, still floating as she did. She had to find where Kevin had left his sword. Right now, it was the only clue to where he might be headed, as well as where Setadev was located.

Frantically she kept searching further and further down the road, moving as quickly as she could as her angel powers accelerated her. Minutes were passing by, and she was getting further and further away from the camp. At the fork, she headed up the mountain road. If Vinz Larinion had truly appeared to her, then Kevin's sword had to be here. She was sure of it.

She kept going. Around the next bend, she found it.

Immediately, Caitlin stopped and dropped to the ground. Sure enough, the vision was right.

And standing in front of it, looking at it, was General Sayo.

Chapter 46

Angelic Revival

Sayo's eyes locked onto Caitlin's. For a moment, they looked at each other in stunned silence, each surprised to see the other there.

After almost a minute, Sayo raised both of his hands to the level of his eyes, with his palms out to show he was unarmed. "I surrender," he said.

Caitlin only looked at him in a confused state, wondering if this was a trap. She remained vigilant. "Tell me why you're here," she asked.

In response, Sayo lowered his arms but kept his hands out to show he still intended to surrender. "I need the help of the emperor and the prime minister," he answered. He then paused before continuing, "And you, I need your help as well."

"And what makes you think I will help you?" asked Caitlin.

Again, Sayo paused for a second. "I need your help to rescue Kevin and put a stop to Setadev," he answered. "We do not have much time."

Rescue Kevin. Just as Vinz Larinion had said.

Still, this was General Sayo. He could not be trusted. This was the man who had assaulted her, who had tried to kill her. Even if he could not kill her, just trying to attack her before was a sign of his intent. The murder of the Metoi tribe was also at his hands, and so was Kevin's kidnapping. She was so angry at him.

Anger. Her emotions were restored.

Walking up to him in fury, Caitlin smacked the general as hard as she could across his face. "And why should I believe you?" she asked. "You killed a large number of innocent people. You kidnapped Kevin in the first place. You've tried to kill me before. I should kill you where you stand for what you have done."

Sayo lowered his head. "I wouldn't blame you if you did," he said. "However, I made a promise to Kevin that I would at least try to find you. He made me swear, that if I ever did one more thing in my life, that I needed to find you, and the emperor and the prime minister, as well."

Infuriated, Caitlin clenched her fists tight. Then, she hesitated.

Vinz Larinion, in the vision, had said that she would have to rescue Kevin. What Sayo was saying was consistent with that. Angry as she was and untrusting of the general, she had to at least consider the possibility. She had to slow down and try not to blow up. Gently, she lowered her arms. "All right," she said. "Start from the beginning." She paused for a second, to slow herself down. "I promise you, as long as you tell the truth, I won't hurt you."

Quickly, Sayo took a step back. He was a little unnerved by such a move, but was able to maintain his composure. He paused, before beginning his explanation, speaking slowly and with a cadence to ensure Caitlin would not kill him, "I do not profess my innocence to you. I admit to the things I have done. I sent men in to burn the village of the Metoi and kill Chief Aspectra, to lure out Kevin Trent Stryker. I took him with myself and Lord Pseudo to the Fortress of Da Leval. I helped to administer aphrodisiacs and mind-altering chemicals that placed him in an altered state of thinking."

There was a pause. Sayo was confirming what Vinz Larinion had said in Caitlin's vision from last night. Caitlin responded, "Thank you for your honesty. Go on."

Cautiously, Sayo proceeded. "At the Fortress of Da Leval, I began to have a change of heart. Pseudo started to seem rather demented, and his objectives were clearly not the goal of restoring things to the way they were under Demonicus' rule in Desolunar. He promised me the world, but I could not buy it under him. I knew of who he really was; he told me the name Setadev and explained everything to me about his existence as a fallen god, which I did not believe at first but came to realize as I saw what his power could do."

Caitlin nodded in acknowledgment, continuing to listen.

"As I grew to fear him, I came to see hope in Kevin Trent Stryker. I knew as well that if Setadev were so committed to this young boy, he must have been capable of great things, and clearly Setadev treated him as a threat. He had to be a source of hope, and as time passed, I felt quite guilty about all of this." He paused for a moment. "At the fortress, I gave the orders to my men to begin a retreat back to Solunar, and to surrender to Solunar Empire forces if we ran into them. I convinced them that that was the best action for us, but that I myself would stay behind to accomplish an unfinished task: freeing Kevin from his prison."

Caitlin nodded. "And that's when we fought, isn't it?" she said. "I was there to search for Kevin and set him free. You would have been a dead man right there if I would have had my way, had Setadev not intervened and saved your life. Instead, I ended up beaten, nearly killed, and thrown in a cell below there." She wanted so badly to spit at the ground in disgust. She had spoken her peace in telling Sayo that she had wanted to kill him.

However, if what Sayo were saying were true, then she assaulted the general as he was going to save Kevin. What could have been had they not run into each other? Would Setadev had known she was there in the building at that time? Regardless, it was a moot argument at this point. There was no way Caitlin and the general could have worked it out. Caitlin's rage would have kept the general from being able to reason with her, and the general's fear for his own life meant that he would have had to fight back. Such was human instinct, especially for a man so well trained in warfare.

"I do apologize for that, and wish I could express to you my sorrow," Sayo continued. "I recognized you because Setadev showed me a model of your figure and asked me to make improvements on your physical features in order to help him create Satiana. It was one of the most mentally disgusting tasks I have ever been asked to do."

Caitlin said nothing in response. She wanted nothing more to do with that which had violated her self-image, especially not after the inspiring words of Vinz Larinion had pierced her soul.

After a moment's pause, Sayo continued. "As Setadev kept up with what he was doing, I proceeded up the stairs and toward Kevin. Little did I know, though, that the Solunar Empire would arrive at that moment to search for Setadev and myself, to bring us to justice." He paused. "I hope my men are safe."

Gently, Caitlin let out a breath. Here, she could empathize. "Some were killed on each side," she answered, "but I was told that losses were minimal. The emperor, Arthur, however, was pretty upset about any loss on both sides."

General Sayo sighed and had a tear come to his eye. "Such is always the case with war, and the part of it I hate the most," he answered. He wiped his eyes before continuing, "As the battle began, I went into Kevin's cell and told Satiana that we needed her assistance on the wall, feigning weakness. When she left, I set to work to free Kevin and administer antidotes. He too, like yourself now, was hesitant to receive my help, and kept resisting me as we tried to escape together. As we tried to make our way out, however, we were pinned between Setadev and Satiana, who had figured out that we were trying to leave. I thought at that moment that I was dead and that I had failed."

"And you did fail," Caitlin noted.

Sayo nodded. "The next thing I knew, I woke up chained to a post, next to Kevin. Setadev continued to threaten and torture us, but this time he kept Kevin off of the drugs. Instead, he continued to torment Kevin, intentionally, to frustrate him. Then, a couple of days later, he told us he had big plans for Kevin, and removed him from the room. What he did, I only wish I knew."

Caitlin looked aside scornfully. A tear came to her eye. She vividly remembered the incident at the Gates to Gardolk. Only Kevin would really be able to tell her what happened.

"Then," continued Sayo, after letting his previous sentence soak in with Caitlin for a moment, "last night, Kevin came back, alone. Setadev did not have him captive, somehow. He came to set me free, then told me to run and find the emperor, to bring him to Setadev's encampment to destroy it. Meanwhile, he would proceed to try and stop Setadev himself."

Caitlin's eyes widened. Kevin was on what was sure to be a suicide mission. At the very best, he would be recaptured, and at the very worst he would be killed. No success could come of that. Curse the pride of men, Caitlin thought to herself. Still, she felt responsible for that. No time to fret, though; she had to stay focused. She had to know if Sayo was telling the truth or not. She refocused her eyes into a glare. “Show me where this encampment is,” she said, calmly but with determination.

After a second’s pause, Sayo bowed his head. He pointed to the first mountain behind him, directly southwest. “Behind that peak, there is an indent in the mountain range. It used to be a set of gold mines, but has long been abandoned. Whatever Setadev has been looking for, he has been looking for in there. For no other reason would he be there.”

Briefly, Caitlin looked up. That would likely be a march of a few hours for the army. However, she had the good fortune of being an angel, of being capable of levitation and flight. Her translucent wings were still glowing bright, a sign of her power as a half-immortal. “Let’s go have a look for ourselves, shall we?” she asked, not looking down.

“Can’t we go grab the emperor first?” asked Sayo. “I mean, it will take a while…”

Before Sayo could finish his sentence, Caitlin grabbed him by the wrist and took off toward the mountain’s peak. Sayo was caught completely by surprise, and he exclaimed as Caitlin carried him away, “Who or what are you?” He had no idea what an angel actually was.

Caitlin glared back at him, her sapphire eyes glowing with divine power. “I’ll tell you when I know I can trust you,” she answered.

Sayo looked away for the moment. He was only along for the ride here, and he knew it.

It only took Caitlin a few minutes to reach the peak of the mountain. Upon arriving, she carefully set Sayo down. Around her, she saw the Solunar Empire forces back on the road just northeast of her. To the south, she could see the inlet that Sayo was referring to.

From the high point, Caitlin could see everything around. Sayo pointed to a small campsite against the edge of the mountains in the inlet. “What we are looking for is down there,” he said. “Though my troops were left behind at the fortress, Setadev still has a few hundred or so Enlighteners guarding the entrance to the mines.”

Caitlin nodded, and looked directly at Sayo. “So, Kevin is down there as well?”

“Indeed,” acknowledged Sayo. “He should be in one of the tents toward the middle section, although which one exactly I am not sure.” Then, Sayo pointed toward the mountain behind the inlet. “The mine is over there, and that is where Setadev has been excavating. Whatever he is after is down there."

"Good," said Caitlin. "Let's go!" She started leaning forward, as if to take off again.

Immediately, Sayo put his arm out in front of her. "Not yet," he answered. "It may not appear so, but because of the Enlighteners, I guarantee that Setadev has the place heavily defended. If we're going to raid this place, we're going to need that army that the emperor has brought with him."

Frustrated, but knowing that Sayo was right, Caitlin stopped. She took a second to breathe, realizing that she could not let her newfound desire to rescue Kevin get in the way of working logically and keeping anyone from getting captured. "You're right," she said. "Let's head back down the mountain. We can plan out a strategy."

Sayo nodded, as Caitlin picked him up again and started flying down the mountain.

As she flew, Caitlin thought about what she almost just did. She wanted so badly to see Kevin one more time, and to save him, that she nearly flew straight into the inlet knowing that Setadev and Satiana were there. She had tried once before to go it alone, and had been captured herself.

She needed to pace herself and not be too hasty. That had been Kevin's mistake as well as hers. The army could be around and into the inlet by early in the afternoon. Now, she would have to convince Arthur and Rachel to conduct this assault.

Another thought came to Caitlin's mind. Already she was halfway down the small peak, flying as fast as she ever had before, while she had questions to ask. Carrying Sayo down the mountain, she asked him, "Tell me something. Why did you partner with Setadev, and why did you change your mind?"

There was a long pause as Caitlin continued down the mountain. Then, Sayo let out a sigh. "Like any man, I only desired to protect that which I valued. When Atwals was destroyed by the Desolunar forces, many of my fellow citizens in the region were taken captive by Demonicus. My decision to become a part of Desolunar's army and use my talents in the service of Demonicus saved their lives; they were spared because I promised they would become a part of the new kingdom and would not start any uprisings."

Caitlin was unsure whether or not she could believe this, but if it were true, it would mean that Sayo had more decency than anyone had credited to him.

He continued, "When Demonicus was defeated, I fled with my men after the Battle of Seta Archa to protect them from what the allied forces might do to them. We ran to the Wastes, and there we found Pseudo, who was Demonicus's declared right hand man. It was then he revealed to me in confidence alone that he was actually a god. It seemed unlikely until he demonstrated his powers, and it was then that the Enlighteners from the Shadows became a part of our group. The attack on the Metoi, it was done on his orders, but I will admit I did not question them. I simply executed."

That in itself made Sayo a war criminal regardless. He admitted to what he had done to the Metoi. However, despite her frustration and memories of seeing Marilynn's tears, Caitlin decided not to object yet, knowing that what Sayo had to say next would interest her the most.

"Beyond that, it's exactly as I said earlier. After we had trapped Kevin, I wondered what Setadev could want with this boy so badly. The more I thought about it, the more I realized that whatever he had, he was a danger to Setadev and the elaborate precautions and revenge schemes set up were planned with such deliberate actions because Setadev knew it. I gained my skepticism as well on whether or not I had made the right decision to follow Setadev as his behavior seemed to become more irrational. Eventually, he made me feel so sick to my stomach and so degraded by his actions that I decided to rescue Kevin and leave the remnant of the fallen."

Suddenly, Caitlin stopped, landing on the road behind a rock at a bend, still a short distance from the Solunar Empire encampment. She saw the Sword of Purity, and it reminded her of something. She asked Sayo, "So how did Kevin get his sword near the Solunar camp?"

"Kevin broke out," he answered. "Actually, he did it at the Fortress of Da Level the first time; we were confronted by Setadev before we could get free. Kevin didn't trust me the whole time, and he actually ditched me during the escape. Later on he wouldn't tell me why he left me there, but he was very upset when I told him you were in the fortress, and threatened me for your location. When he ran, I believe he tried to find you." He paused. "He did it again from the encampment a few days ago, but he came back to free me, saying that the emperor and the prime minister would be more willing to listen to me than to him.

Immediately, Caitlin's hands fell to her heart. If Sayo was right, then Kevin had been true after all, and Arthur and Rachel were not willing to talk to him over everything that happened. She remembered everything.

At this moment, a voice echoed from the north. "Hey Caitlin, where are you?" It was Arthur's voice.

"I don't know where she could have ran," quieter echoed a voice from Rachel. "All I know is she took her dress and ran off."

Quietly, Caitlin looked at Sayo and said, "Stay here. They will snap to judgment if they see you first and may try to kill you."

In response, Sayo shook his head. "I have no fear," he said. "I deserve whatever I receive on that front."

There was a moment's pause. Then, Caitlin nodded. "Very well," she said. She then jumped up into the air above the rock, letting her angel powers levitate her. She looked to the north and waved, and said, "I'm over here!"

Arthur and Rachel were just on the other side of the bend. They looked up in surprise, not expecting to see Caitlin, with her mind fully intact again, in her angel form. She had her long hair back as well, and was dressed in her white wizardess dress. "Whoa!" Arthur exclaimed as he stopped where he was, which Rachel did as well.

With her translucent wings shining, Caitlin settled down on the other side of the rock, as General Sayo began to step around the other end of the rock. Seeing this, Arthur almost instantly put his fists up, but Caitlin placed herself between him and the general, with her hands forward. "Settle down, Arthur," she said. "The general has come to surrender to us."

Almost immediately, Sayo dropped to his knees and bowed down. He had no spirit left to give. He was only relieved to be away from Setadev's camp.

Rachel shook her head for a second, but then walked up to Caitlin and gave her a quick hug. "I'm so glad you're back the way you were," she said, "but I am so confused as to what's going on."

Behind her, Arthur nodded. "As am I. Care to explain?" he asked.

Caitlin nodded. "Of course," she said. "I don't think, though, that you'd believe me if I told you." She then proceeded to explain about how Vinz Larinion had invaded her dreams last night and explained everything with Kevin, and how he was fixing her mind with his power because the Sword of Purity was exposed so close to the camp. She explained how in turn she woke up with her hair at its original length as proof that what had happened was real. She then explained running south on the realization that Kevin was in danger, and bumping into General Sayo, who wanted to surrender to her.

Arthur and Rachel looked at each other for a moment, almost surprised. Though there was no absolutely certain way to confirm Caitlin's story, the evidence of her in her angel form with her hair the proper length seemed to confirm it. They shared a feeling of guilt for expressing such negative attitudes about Kevin and, not knowing he was there, making him leave his sword and run off instead of being willing to talk with them.

Looking directly into Arthur's and Rachel's eyes, Caitlin spoke with confidence. "I don't know about you guys and if you still want to go back to the empire," she said, "but I'm going after Kevin. I have to see him again, and I have to help him prevent Setadev from reviving."

Again, Arthur and Rachel looked at each other. They nodded, knowing what had to happen. Arthur looked back at Caitlin and said, "I think we agree," he said. "If nothing else, we have to see for ourselves."

Rachel nodded in agreement.

"Then it's agreed," Arthur acknowledged. "I had better go and direct the men to prepare to head south instead of north today. I have a bad feeling that we will be in a battle here very soon."

"You will," stated Sayo from his knees. "I can take you to where they are. It is Setadev's encampment. What he is doing there, I don't know, but he is carrying out some operation deep within the mines there. This one, I am sure, is no fake."

For a second, Rachel looked down at Sayo and stared. Then, she looked up at Arthur. "Let us go and prepare the men," she said. "I believe we are best to trust Sayo's word for the time being, and prepare for battle."

With confidence and receptiveness, Arthur nodded. He then proceeded north, as Caitlin and Rachel followed with the general.

Within the hour, the men had the camp packed up and were ready to move out. They were ready to depart in the opposite direction as they had planned before, and were headed south. General Sayo was guiding Arthur and his forces, as they marched on to what would be their biggest battle of this campaign, in just a couple of days. This would be the end of the operation. Though they were unsure if they could bring Setadev to justice, they knew they had to try.

At the fork, Sayo directed everyone up the mountain road. He explained that at the other end of this road was an indent in the mountain range, where there was a mine and an old mining camp which was now being run by Setadev. This was Setadev's base of operations.

A short distance up the road, however, something was sticking out of the middle of the road. Something very familiar.

"Is that the Sword of Purity?" asked Rachel.

Caitlin nodded. "It is," she said. "I knew it was here and I had already seen it, just as Vinz Larinion told me it would be here."

"He did?" asked Rachel. "Why would Kevin leave this here, though? Without it, if he were really going to stop Setadev, it would be suicide. He doesn't stand a chance without it."

Sayo bowed his head. "He didn't," the general said. "Kevin was recaptured again when he broke me out. I was very lucky to escape."

Arthur nodded. "At least he wasn't killed," he said. He then started walking past the sword, looking at it planted in the ground. "With this sword, he may have had a chance to avoid that, though. Even if he were friends with Setadev, that jerk would only want Kevin along with the sword. So, why then would he leave it behind?"

"Because he was trying to tell us something," Caitlin answered, gathering the attention of everyone around her. "Vinz Larinion told me last night that Setadev needs this sword for his revival, and that's why he wants Kevin on his side. Kevin left the sword to let us know that he was not tempted by its power and was keeping it out of Setadev's hands."

Rachel let out a deep sigh. "I can see that," she said. "Regardless of how accurate that may be, the next question is, what do we do with it?"

There was a slight pause. "We take it with us," nodded Caitlin. "Even if Setadev needs it, so does Kevin." With caution, she approached the planted Sword of Purity. Arthur, Rachel, and Sayo stood back as she did. Everyone knew what would happen if they grabbed that sword. It would not be a pleasant experience, knowing that the sword was locked. The two individuals that could wield it were Vincent Stryker and Kevin Trent Stryker.

Now, Caitlin was about to try and pull it out of the ground. She had tried to grab the sword by its hilt before, with equally painful results.

Quietly, Caitlin began talking to herself, as if to address the sword and Vinz Larinion. "I hope you were right, and that you were real," she said. "I need your help. Kevin is in danger. He needs you to be there for him. You have always guided him right in the past. Now, I need you to help me find our way back to him." She closed her eyes and reached for the hilt.

She touched it with her fingers. It instantly sent a shock up her arm, causing her to withdraw in pain. Arthur and Rachel each gasped.

Undaunted, Caitlin extended her arm again. "Please listen to me," she said quietly, as she closed her eyes again. "Please listen. I beg of you. Without your help, Kevin will no longer exist. Please listen, and please guide me to him." She hesitated for another second. "If you are in there, Vinz Larinion, I want to believe that you are really in there. I know you want to help him too. Please let me use your power to help him."

Then, she reached forward again and put her fingers on the hilt. This time, there was no shock.

She reached forward and grabbed the sword firmly, yanking it out of the ground. As she lifted it, the sword lit up at its tip and pulled in the direction of southwest, right along the mountain road. She turned to Arthur and Rachel, and waved to them. “Let’s go,” she said.

Confidently, Arthur and Rachel looked at each other for a second and nodded. Sayo nodded as well.

Chapter 47

Perspectives

It had taken Vincent Stryker quite a bit of time to reach Nuvenia. At the source of the Rhonean River was the Abyss of the Royal Sovereign, a wide and deep lake that was at its narrowest point nearly two charnas across. Within it rested Nuvenia, a stonewalled city on a large island in the middle of the lake.

Constructed as a fortress city during the formation of the superstate kingdoms, Nuvenia was a fairly new city in terms of age when compared to other modern large cities, but was by no means brand new. The city was named for Nuve, which built it in its modern era, in contrast to the city of Gardolkia, which lent its name to the country of Gardolk. Nuvenia's location on an island made it extremely difficult to build, with construction taking years to complete. In all, the city was entirely walled around the island in stone that stood four stories high and wrapped all the way around the island, save for the two gates at the north and west ends of the city.

Though boat travel was still common given the presence of a small unwalled beach on the west side of the island, two bridges were constructed at great expense to provide land access. These bridges were at the north and west sides; the famous north bridge was fully solid and constructed of wood, considered an engineering marvel for its length and rigid structure along its entire length to the north shore, while the longer western bridge was a high quality suspension bridge that rested on the surface of the water, held afloat at all times by the tension in the ropes holding it up.

Nuvenia itself was a very compact city. It held approximately a third of the population of the province of Soverenia, the most populated of Nuve's five provinces. Most of the city streets were quite narrow with the exception of those that led to the bridges, meeting at a town square where those roads intersected. Homes and businesses were jammed into the city walls, and the color of weathered gray stone was apparent everywhere. The climate of Soverenia tended to be very rainy, but was only modestly lush due to the thick cloud cover that rarely ever lifted. This climate contributed even further to the weathering of Nuvenia's walls and buildings, although they were new enough not to be at risk of destruction due to the erosion continuing to occur or due to the city's low upkeep.

Inside the high walls of Nuvenia rested a royal castle where the King of Nuve, Raijin Lester, and his family resided. It also served as the center of government operations of Nuve, which was by far one of the most militaristically complex nations in the world. This unique system was a necessity due to modern Nuve's history of suffering at the hands of attempted conquests and internal strife.

Riding as quickly as he could, Vincent Stryker pushed his horse on. He had crossed into Soverenia two days before on horseback and had continued at a breakneck pace. He was racing Arsuf Zachary to town, even though Zachary had no idea that this was the case. Vincent was not entirely sure how he would get an audience with the King of Nuve, but he had to make an attempt to do so.

Having approached from the south, Vincent had to swing around to the west side of the Abyss of the Royal Sovereign, which took quite a bit of time. No connections to Nuvenia existed to the south and east due to the island's location nearer to the northwest corner of the lake. Once he reached the suspension bridge, Vincent rode his horse as quickly as he could. The jaunt across the shaky bridge still took a few minutes due to the width of the Abyss.

The gates to Nuvenia were always left open, let only to close in case of an emergency. Despite its appearance as a giant fortress from the exterior, Nuvenia was very much the capital city of Nuve as well as the provincial capital of Soverenia. Though Nuve was more culturally restrained than either Aurana or Gardolk, it did take pride in its traditions and stylings, and Nuvenia was the current center of Nuve culture ever since the evacuation from Cardol two decades before.

As long as Nuvenia itself were not endangered, it would remain an open city to all. Tucked away in Soverenia, it was a fair distance from both the Cornelia Chimeras to the southwest and the

Demonstrative Organization of Northern Nuve—also known as Demons—to the north, as well as several days from Aurana or Scurnia and a couple of weeks from the Solunar Empire or Gardolk, placing it in relative safety.

Entering the city through the west gate, Vincent slowed his horse down, not wanting to cause any injuries by riding through town too fast. He kept the horse moving at a modest trot as he headed toward the city's central square.

At the city's center, the castle was just to the east. Deciding it would be a better idea not to have The Syndicate after him, however, Vincent turned south and found the stables two blocks south on a side road. Though no one was there at the time, Vincent decided to hitch up the horse to a post outside the stables instead of waiting, and then proceeded to walk back to the castle.

In the city square, he stopped for a moment. He was not sure if he had beaten Arsuf Zachary here, but regardless he needed to discuss matters with the king. Now, the question would be, how easy would it be for him to get an audience with the king? Vincent really hated leveraging recognition of his actions in the Alliance-Daritel war, but it had proven to be a most effective tool. It would have to work again.

The castle in Nuvenia stood almost as high as the walls surrounding the city itself, and were just as badly weathered. Surrounded by four towers and composed in a square shape, it was the center of all of the government of Nuve, as well as the residence of the king himself. Courtrooms and governmental business areas filled the first floor, while the second consisted of government offices, including for city and national functions, liaisons to the provincial governments, foreign affairs, and regulations. The third floor was the residence for the king and his family, but the entire castle lacked a throne room.

Though Nuve was a monarchy, its leadership was more focused on ruling than on glamor. A large part of this came from Nuve's unique government structure. Though Aurana, Scurnia, and Gardolk were traditional monarchies with provincial governments managed by members of their respective royal families, and the Solunar Empire was ruled by an emperor with a council of members of its many individual nations, Nuve's government had been restructured centuries before to include a check on the king's power. This body, known as the Collective Council, shared responsibility with administration of the country and had the ability to reject any decision the king made so long as three quarters of the council agreed. They also could make their own decisions and implement them at their will, but the king in turn held a check on them in that all appointees to the council had to have his approval. Frequently the king and the Collective Council would be at odds and would make countermanding decisions, and both sides were frequently accused of corruption. Which one actually was corrupt was anyone's guess.

For a second, Vincent stopped at the door that led into the castle. He took a look down at his sword, a katana he called *Lavinia*. It was named for Lavinia Trent, the one great love of his life and the mother of his child. In the same spot that sword was in now, he used to carry the Sword of Purity twenty years before, which was a straight-blade longsword. His son carried that now, and it was for his son that Vincent was doing everything he was doing.

Looking up with confidence, Vincent walked into the castle. He knew exactly what he had to do.

Inside the castle's first floor was a giant room that served as a reception and information area. Without permission, this was the only area the general public was allowed in, and guards were posted all around to enforce this. The stone walls were plain along all sides, and the floors were tiled in alternating black and white stone. Hallways were marked at all ends of the room, with one marking the passage to the Great Hall. At the far end was a desk with an attendant, along with several other reception areas along the sides of the building.

Vincent walked to the far desk. There, a female receptionist asked, "May I help thou, sir?"

"I need to see the king at once," Vincent answered with a bit of force. "It is an emergency."

"I'm sorry," responded the receptionist, "but thou will need to make an appointment for that, and it will have to be reviewed by the king's advisors for relevance to determine whether or not a meeting is necessary."

That was the response Vincent was expecting. He responded

firmly, "Tell him that Vincent Stryker is here."

"That will make no difference," began the young receptionist. "Thou must still…"

She was interrupted, though, by an older receptionist who walked over. "Hold thy grip," said the older woman, who then turned to Vincent Stryker. "I will be happy to escort thou to the king's office."

Nodding, Vincent stepped aside as the older receptionist directed him. Knowing he would not be permitted to keep his sword with him, he removed the sword and scabbard from his belt and set it down on the reception desk.

The older woman then led him to a staircase behind the desk and proceeded upward, heading up immediately and quickly. "Thou will have to forgive my coworker," she said to Vincent as she proceeded up the stairs. "She is young and does not know who thou art."

With a slight chuckle, Vincent responded, "It's quite all right, I'm sure."

"It is not, actually," responded the older receptionist without laughing. "The king declared that thou would be granted a visit at any time should thou desire. I thought thou knew this and that is why thou arrived today."

"Actually, I wasn't aware of it at all," answered Vincent. "However, my visit is most urgent indeed, so it is quite convenient."

"I understand," said the receptionist as she reached the top of the staircase. They had gone past the second floor and reached the third. Then, the receptionist led Vincent down the hallway and knocked on a door. "Thy Excellency, thou has an emergency visitor, permitted by thy declaration."

A muffled voice echoed from the other side. "Enter," it said.

In response, the receptionist opened the door and stepped back. "You may proceed," she said to Vincent, signaling for him to step forward.

Doing as he was instructed, Vincent entered the chamber. The door closed behind him. Inside was a very regally decorated office, colored in navy blue and white with some gold trim all the way around. A desk sat in a corner, but before Vincent was a clean-shaven gentleman with a full head of gray and brown hair who appeared to be in his fifties. He was dressed in a very regally decorated Nuve military uniform, covered in medallions. This was a royal uniform. A crown was atop his head, and a set of blue robes hung from a peg in a corner of the office.

Immediately, Vincent bowed. "Your Majesty, I am honored to make your presence."

Surprisingly, a smile came to the king's face. "The pleasure is mine, I am sure," he said as he stepped forward to shake Vincent's hand. "I recognize who thou art. Thou art Vincent the Pure One, hero of the Triple Alliance."

"And you must be Raijin Lester, King of Nuve," Vincent answered, shaking the king's hand.

Raijin Lester nodded. "Indeed," he said. "I understand thou has an emergency to discuss with me?"

"I do," acknowledged Vincent. "Has Arsuf Zachary come to see you yet?"

The king shook his head. "He has not spoken with me for several months," acknowledged the king. "Neither has his brother, Arsuf Maxwell, for that matter. We have not met in person since the Battle of Seta Archa, where Arsuf Maxwell served as one of my lead generals. Tell me, what is going on?"

Needing to slow down, Vincent placed his hands in front of himself. "I need to tell you something," he said. "There is very bad news from Cornelia." He paused and took a breath. His face turned pale, as if he had seen a ghost. "Raijin Shane is dead."

Instantly, the king's face turned pale as well. "He what?" he asked in stun, raising a hand to his head. He paced around for a few steps in total surprise. That was the king's brother, and the Vanguard of Nuve. Then, he looked into Vincent's eyes. "Who did it and why?"

Vincent took a breath. "Arsuf Maxwell," he said. "I was in Cornelia on business when I bumped into Shane and helped him capture someone who attacked a Chimeras armory. He turned the prisoner over to the Chimeras and invited me to a military station to help me with my business."

"And what business might that be?" inquired the king.

"My son was captured by a rogue group known as the

Enlighteners from the Shadows, operating out of Leticon at the time," he said, "although I believe they have fled since then. Shane was trying to help me chart where they might have gone, when Arsuf Maxwell arrived and accused him of being a traitor to the armistice. Shane fought until the end bravely, and I was lucky to escape with my life."

Silently, the king nodded. "I see," he said. He looked toward the ceiling for a moment. "My brother was a great man, deserving of much respect." He paused for a long moment.

Vincent Stryker bowed his head, knowing he needed to give the king a moment to process everything.

The king then raised his head. "Much like thy son, Vincent Stryker. I too respect him for his willingness to go into unknown territory and help us in Nuve to put our differences aside for a few moments before we were conquered by another foe. Have thou found him yet?"

"No," answered Vincent, as he shook his head, "but it has to do with what I need to discuss with you next."

Raijin Lester took a breath. "Very well," he said, still appearing to have difficulty processing the death of his younger brother. "Proceed."

Vincent nodded. "Your Majesty, I have come to request your forgiveness for an act on Nuve soil. I have come here on behalf of the Solunar Empire and its new leader to explain a situation."

The king gave Vincent a strange look. "Interesting," he said. "Thou run with an odd pack indeed nowadays."

"Not really," answered Vincent. "The heir of Desolunar became the emperor of the Solunar Empire. He is the best friend of my son and a good young man who wants the empire and consequently the world to see peace. It is for that reason that I am here representing him today."

Though confused, Raijin Lester stated, "Proceed, then."

Again, Vincent nodded in acknowledgment. "While I was in Cornelia, the emperor of the Solunar Empire took another route. Knowing the amount of time it would take to come to Nuvenia to ask permission to enter Nuve and the even longer amount of time it would take to gain such approval, he took his forces on his own into Leticon toward the headquarters of the Enlighteners. A mistake by a young leader, but one with good intentions." Vincent was telling an equivalent story knowing the Enlighteners left on their own during the battle, but did not want to explain all of the complex stories surrounding the entire truth. "He drove the Enlighteners out of Nuve. Solunar never intended to endanger Nuve in any way, but acknowledge they were trespassing. I bumped into them on the way back to the empire, but so did Arsuf Maxwell. He threatened war on the empire as a result."

"An understandable reaction for a loyal Nuvenian," stated the king, "but curious for him, given his standing."

"Seemed more or less an excuse to start a war," said Vincent, "although they were in the wrong place to begin with, admittedly. It was there that Arsuf Maxwell made an attempt on the emperor's life, but one of the two Vanguards of the Solunar Empire killed him before he could do so."

The king bowed his head. "So, Maxwell is dead as well."

"He is," acknowledged Vincent. "But his actions were less than honest; he saw it as an opportunity to start a war between Nuve and the Solunar Empire, and then to have the Chimeras capitalize on it. Now, he is a martyr for their cause, and I think he planned for that possibility. I didn't really understand why until I started my trip here to explain everything to you."

Raijin Lester frowned at Vincent. "Not that I doubt thy story at all, but I too do not understand. Maxwell had everything to gain by staying alive, and nothing to gain by his death. What would becoming a martyr now do for him when Cornelia is not independent?"

"More than either you or I realized," began Vincent. "On the road north, I went through Kinsmoor. There, when I arrived, Arsuf Zachary was eulogizing his brother as they placed Maxwell in the Heroes' Resting Place. He mentioned a connection that the Chimeras had to Leticon: Maxwell himself was from Kinsmoor. Zachary spoke very highly of the Chimeras' relationship to Leticon, implying that the Chimeras had more influence there than most believe."

Shaking his head, the king started pacing around his office. "I know not whether to believe thou at this point," he said. "So much I want not to. All of it sounds so false, yet if it is true, then Nuve is in much worse shape than we originally feared."

"You may believe as you will, but I will speak what I believe and know," Vincent answered. "And you may want to be cautious. Arsuf Zachary is on his way now, and is not too far behind me. He intends to oust your family and take the whole of Nuve."

King Lester breathed heavily for a minute. Then, he said, "As I feared, almost exactly. While Maxwell was well-reasoned if not a bit feisty and vindictive, I have met Zachary before and he is extremely ambitious."

"And by becoming a martyr against the Solunar Empire, who were caught in the wrong place at the wrong time, he could maintain his illusion of being loyal to the armistice of Nuve," stated Vincent.

"And that is the part that thou has yet to prove to me," returned the king. "It would not seem so logical then for Zachary to come after myself and my family." He then glared a little deeper at Vincent. "How do I know that thou have not come to me first in order to get me to take more immediate action against the Chimeras?"

"Your Majesty, I am only asking you to show some understanding to Solunar given the circumstances," answered Vincent calmly. "Action against the Chimeras is your prerogative if you so choose."

For a moment, there was silence as the king appeared very cross. He had a lot of information to process.

Then, the door flung open. Suddenly, Arsuf Zachary stomped in, with his eyes glaring. Behind him, in the hallway, a receptionist was yelling, "Mr. Arsuf, wait! Thou cannot go in there!" Zachary, however, slammed the door behind him, silencing her.

"What is the meaning of this?" demanded the king.

"Thy Majesty, we need to speak, and now," Arsuf Zachary responded forcefully, with a great deal of anger in his voice. He then pointed to Vincent Stryker. "This man is a traitor to his alliance. He accompanied the Solunar Empire on an unsolicited invasion into Nuve territory, seeking to conquer all of us from the south yet again." Zachary clenched his fist. "And he stood by and did nothing while my brother was murdered."

"Your brother was killed while trying to assassinate me, Zachary," Vincent interjected. "And we gave our explanation as to why we were there to him. It was not an invasion."

"Thou lies!" Zachary yelled back at Vincent.

"Silence!" exclaimed the king.

Vincent Stryker had to catch himself. He was getting frustrated at Zachary's unfounded insinuations, but could do little. If he were to persuade the king, he would need to maintain his calmness and present his points well. Blowing up at Zachary now would do him no benefit, although the old general was fuming so much that he felt like challenging Zachary to a showdown duel.

Beside him, Zachary had no reaction.

King Lester then stepped over and grabbed his robes. As he put them on, he said, "Now, does either of thou have any proof of what thou have told me?"

"Him being here already is my proof," snapped Zachary. "Great as he may have been, why does Vincent Stryker need to be here? He beat me here to tell thou his story first so that thou, Thy Majesty, would believe it. He wants thou to believe his lies."

Carefully, Vincent shot a glare over at Zachary, but said nothing and held back.

Lester looked up at Vincent. "Might thou have something to say?"

For a moment, Vincent observed Zachary. Something was not right, and he knew it. It was typical of everyone in Nuve to be allowed to carry their weapons everywhere as Nuve was a war-driven nation, but even so, something was amiss with what Zachary was carrying. He then responded to the king, "Is it not castle policy that those entering the castle cannot carry a concealed weapon?"

"It is, to prevent assassination," commented the king. "No weapons, actually, can be carried past the reception desk. Why would thou ask such a question?"

Immediately, Vincent pointed at Zachary's lower right leg, where he had noticed a bulge. "Because Zachary is carrying a dagger in his sock," he said.

Zachary reached down and grabbed the dagger.

As he grasped it, Vincent Stryker grabbed him by the arm.

They struggled over the dagger. Vincent would not let go,

knowing what Zachary's intent was. He and Zachary wrestled for a solid minute as King Lester stepped back in horror.

Suddenly, Zachary tried to fling his arm upward to withdraw the dagger. Still, Vincent would not let go. The dagger flew out of Zachary's sock into the air.

It stuck in the ceiling, between a pair of bricks.

Vincent let go, relieved that the dagger had not caused any harm. He knew exactly why Zachary had a dagger in his sock. All he would have had to do was sneak the dagger out of his sock and throw it or thrust it the right way, and he would have killed the king without screaming or resistance.

"Thou vile beast!" exclaimed King Lester, pointing directly at Zachary. "It was thy men who killed my brother, was it not?"

Instead of responding, Zachary spit at the ground. "Curse thou, thou Raijin scum!" he exclaimed, as his temper finally claimed the best of him. "Long live Cornelia, and long live the Chimeras!" He lunged for the king, an older man than him.

The king was helpless. He had nowhere further to back up.

Quickly, Vincent stepped in front of the king, crossing his arms into a defensive stance. He and Zachary shoved hard against one another, each trying to impose their will on each other.

Leaning in, Vincent was trying to make his old body push harder. His back was letting him know how unhealthy he really was. Still, sheer willpower kept him from giving up.

They pushed and pushed at each other.

Zachary tried to throw punches. Vincent focused on dodging as many as he could. The struggle was on. One for the future of Nuve.

Vincent managed to grab the dagger and swing it very close to the Chimera leader's neck. Suddenly, the advantage was his, as his slice was dead on at the neckline.

Immediately, Zachary ducked it and bolted for the window on the other side of the office.

Before Vincent could catch him, he jumped out of it headfirst.

Quickly, Vincent and King Lester rushed over to the window and looked out of it. In front of the castle was a cart full of straw, where Zachary had landed. It was attached to a horse, and was already departing, accelerating to a quick speed through Nuvenia's city streets.

"Damn," cursed Vincent under his breath, as he reached to clench his back in pain. "He had an escape plan all along."

King Lester looked up to the dagger, still sitting in the ceiling. He then looked down to Vincent. "I owe thou a great deal of gratitude," he said, calmly. "It surprises me that Zachary would come to Nuvenia himself to kill me. I would suppose that goes to show that thou were telling the truth."

"I have," nodded Vincent, as he sheathed his katana. "And Zachary would likely tell you the same; it is all a matter of perspectives." He then turned to the king. "Will you take punishment upon the Solunar Empire as a result of their actions?"

The king thought it over for a minute. "I would have to consider it," he said. "I have no choice. At the very least, however, I would ask thou to take a message to the new emperor and tell him that he must meet me in person for a diplomatic summit. It, along with the growing issue of the Cornelia Chimeras now showing influence in the entire area of the south of my nation and just north of their border, are things we must discuss."

Vincent nodded. "I can do that," he said. He then shook the king's hand and thanked him greatly for his time. In return, the king thanked Vincent for saving him from assassination and praised the timeliness of the visit. Lester also suggested to Vincent that they should get together for a more formal discussion at some point in regards to the war and catching up on past and present events.

With that, Vincent departed the castle. For a moment, he paused and looked up into the sky. Raijin Shane was heavy on his mind, but he was thankful for the sacrifice that Shane had made for him. Without Shane, he would not have uncovered the conspiracy in Leticon, nor would he have found out what had happened to his son.

On that note, he had no idea where his son was or where Arthur and his men were at. Reuniting with them was not an option at this point.

Exiting the castle, Vincent looked around the town square. It was busy and full of motion, a typical working day in the city. Amidst the central square, there was a lot of hustle and bustle all around. As part of Nuve's restrained culture, the people of Nuvenia had a working mentality and tended to be driven toward industriousness over expression.

He looked up toward the sky. As was typical of Soverenia, the skies were heavily overcast. The light gray of the clouds contrasted well with the darker stone of the city. Looking back down, the city seemed so bland. Even in the busiest areas, the energy seemed so muted.

Knowing there was little he could do, Vincent walked over to a nearby tavern, known simply as the Pour House. It too was relatively busy, but at least Vincent could get a nice drink there. For now, there was little else that he could do. He had not been to a pub and enjoyed a drink in a long time.

Walking into the small building about a block away from the central square, Vincent looked around to see the bustling tavern covered in wood from its walls to its benches and tables. As he looked around, he was fortunate enough to get a booth to himself, upon which a waitress offered him a beer. He was more than glad to partake.

At peace with himself, Vincent took a drink of his beverage. He then held it out in front of himself and considered it for a second. In the postwar years he had spent in solitude, living as a recluse in western Scurnia, he had not had the opportunity to have a drink. He was never a heavy drinker, desiring not to be a drunk, but did enjoy one or two every now and then. It used to be in the days of the Alliance-Daritel war that General Stryker, a Scurnian field unit leader, and his Auranian friends Commander Martin Sayo, Commander Milton "Ironman" Eukert, and Knight John Bryant would get together and share some beverages while they worked out the strategies to win the war.

Nowadays, he looked around and saw no friends with him. He had not even had the chance to share a drink with his son for the first time yet.

A pair of individuals walked up to Vincent in the busy tavern. "Pardon us," asked an older gentleman wearing elegant red robes, "but may we sit here? It is quite busy in here and we cannot find any other available seats."

Vincent looked up. "Sure," he said. Promptly, the two

individuals sat down at the bench on the other side of the booth, but something seemed strangely familiar about them to Vincent. The older man had gray hair and a full beard, and his red robes seemed almost royal in appearance. Next to him was a slightly younger man with long blonde hair tied into a small ponytail in the back, in purple robes with a large black centerpiece covering his chest.

The waitress appeared, but both men denied any drinks. That seemed unusual to Vincent. Shrugging to himself, he took another sip and then asked, "So tell me, why nothing to drink?" He paused for a quick second to sip again and continued, "Even those who come in here to socialize…"

"Usually order at least a glass of water," smiled the older man.

He finished Vincent's sentence perfectly. That was exactly what he wanted to say, to the letter. Suddenly, he placed his finger on to whom he was speaking. "Ralios Larion, king of the gods themselves," he said aloud but quietly.

"Well done, Vincent Stryker," Larion responded.

"Why do you have to do that?" asked the man next to Larion. "Your habits seem to be quite illogical, Larion. Is it necessarily so bright to keep going on finishing everyone's sentences all of the time?"

Raising an eyebrow, Vincent asked, "Professor Magnon?"

The other man rolled his eyes. "Not in this form," he said. "Dressed and shaped like this, I am Tyrinion, the god of darkness. I am in what I suppose is my true identity at the moment." He glanced over at Larion. "It is his idea whenever we meet, that I be in this form and not my identity as Professor James Magnon."

"I see," nodded Vincent, himself knowing who Tyrinion was and being a friend of Professor Magnon for some time. Knowing they were one and the same, he had no qualms about seeing the professor like this. "Have you found me to check in with my progress?"

Larion shook his head. "Not at all, actually, but we have much to discuss. Necnea and Kronius spotted an explosion in the mountains, and Enlighteners were spotted there. I think we may know where your son is, as well as how Setadev plans to revive himself."

Chapter 48

The Convergence

The last advance was ready.

A day and night after starting down the mountain road, Caitlin, Arthur, Rachel, General Sayo, and the Solunar Empire forces were standing at the other end, looking down upon a large encampment in an indent in the mountain range. The morning sun was just rising to the east in the cold winter morning, and the troops were rested after camping out on the road during the night. They were ready for battle today.

Below, the mountain road sloped down into the indent, while a pair of rock ledges were on either side about halfway down the slope. There was an opening to the foothills to the east, while only mountains surrounded the other three sides. At the back of the indent, in the west, was a hole in a mountain which looked to be an abandoned mineshaft. There was some damage around the eastern side where an explosion appeared to have previously taken place.

"This is it," said General Sayo, as he stood at the high point on the road. "I would presume that Kevin is being held down there in a large tent. It is about the only place that he could be kept tied up." The general then paused as he turned to point toward the mine. "Over there, Setadev has some project going on. After we rescue Kevin, I would not be surprised if we find Setadev over there."

Caitlin nodded in confidence. "Then we will go there when we are through," she said.

"Now, hang tight here, Caitlin," said Arthur as he stepped forward. "I don't know if we have enough here. We only have about a hundred men or so, and I have a feeling we will run into some Enlighteners down there."

"There are only Enlighteners down there, and not anyone else," acknowledged Sayo.

"Exactly," responded Arthur. "And they won't be easy to overthrow. Given the size of that camp, there must be a few hundred of them."

Rachel stepped forward and put her hand on Arthur's shoulder. "We'll never know if we don't try," she said.

Arthur thought this was a weird reaction from Rachel, but did not say anything.

"It is doubtful that all of the Enlighteners are well versed in magic and combat," Sayo then added. "We cannot presume so just because Setadev has selected a few for certain aspects of defense. Certainly magic is a part of their arts, yes, but I would doubt that so many have a wide range of talent and have gone undetected for years."

"Possibly," nodded Arthur, considering the possibility. He was deep in thought.

A frustrated look came across Rachel's face. She looked as though she had an idea but was debating over the details. "It's almost ideal," she said. "I see a critical flaw in this encampment."

"What is?" asked Arthur.

"A fire attack," answered Rachel. "Look around. Even though it's snowy all around and cold, the encampment is relatively sheltered by the mountain range all around, which means it's reasonably dry. The tents are close to one another, so catching one on fire should start a chain reaction that ignites them all with some time. There's just one problem…"

"We have to rescue Kevin first," interrupted Caitlin.

Rachel nodded. "Exactly," she said. "And given that we are likely outnumbered several times over, we're not likely to be able to attack successfully and extract him safely." She took another detailed look over the camp. "Even if we started the fire in a corner, presuming we could find him quickly, it looks as though there are enough tents for some five hundred Enlighteners, at least. They may not all be skilled warriors or magicians, but I have a bad feeling there will be a significant number."

"A good point," acknowledged General Sayo. "Then in order to win, proper tactics will have to be used. A strategy needs to be placed in order to neutralize their advantage, and one in particular comes to mind."

Arthur stroked his chin. "So, then, what's the easiest way to overcome being outnumbered by a force several times larger than ours and potentially with far greater power?"

Suddenly, Rachel looked up, in realization. This was something they had used before a few months ago, personally. "You funnel them through a narrow passage, so they can't use their numbers against you," she said.

Caitlin looked over at Rachel. "Fantastic idea!" she exclaimed. She then calmed down before asking, "Where should we pull them through?"

Sayo's face was beaming with confidence, as his military prowess was coming to use once again. "It is an old military lesson," began Sayo, picking up the response, "that whenever available, one should always use the high ground in order to leverage the advantage of gravity on your opponent."

Reacting to this comment, Caitlin, Arthur, and Rachel all looked down at the sloping mountain road as it descended to the valley. They also looked at the cliff sides next to them, which could be walked upon a short distance before dropping off. If they were to use these tactics, this was the place to do it.

"All right, let's do it," commanded Arthur. He then turned to General Sayo. "Can you lead the men?"

A confused look came to Sayo's face. "I can, but why would you have me?"

"You are a skilled military leader, general," answered Arthur, "far more skilled than I. My best friend Kevin would tell me that I have to trust you, so that is what I will do." He then waved his arm in front of his men. "They too will place their faith in you, but you had best not let them down."

Sayo bowed, then gave a traditional salute. "I understand," he said. "Command me."

"Very well," nodded Arthur. "Set up ten archers, five on each ledge. I want them to be supporting fire while the remainder of the men engage near the bottom of the slope."

With a nod in acknowledgment as a response, Sayo then turned to the men, raised his hand, and pointed his finger down the road. "Begin setup for a passage defense," he said. In response, the hundred men proceeded down the pathway, as Sayo followed and started giving specific instructions on the way to the bottom.

As Sayo was beginning the setup, Arthur then looked over to Caitlin. "Rachel and I will help up here to try and keep the Enlighteners away from the camp, and keep them distracted. If we give you this opportunity, can you find Kevin and get to him quickly?"

Without any doubt in her demeanor, Caitlin lifted the Sword of Purity a little bit. "I can," she said. "Just give me whatever time you can, and I will find him. Be warned, though, that Setadev or Satiana could come out and mess with everything at any given time. We will have to be very careful about that."

"We can do that," nodded Rachel, expressing no fear in her voice, as Sayo was approaching the trio by himself. "Once you have Kevin secured, you should set the camp ablaze. That should give us the momentum we need to destroy their morale and drive them out. After that, we can advance toward the mine and see what Setadev has planned."

Arthur then looked over to Caitlin. "Do you think you can call the Enlighteners out for us in a proper fashion?"

In response, Caitlin nodded confidently. With a tranquil demeanor, Caitlin reached into her dress and pulled out her necklace. She looked in her hands and stared at the Key of Hearts, the little pink heart-shaped key that Kevin had given her. As she closed her eyes, she grasped the key tightly. It was symbolic of her reason to fight. Slowly, she floated higher, ready to head to the top of the mountain to begin the distraction.

Beside her, Arthur and Rachel were surprised. She had full access to her angelic power, showing she really was all the way back. "Awesome, Caitlin!" Rachel exclaimed. Next to her, Arthur nodded.

Sayo's jaw dropped in awe. "I have been meaning to ask," he began, trying to keep his discipline visible. "Who are you?"

This time, when asked this question, Caitlin looked straightforward but was willing to give an honest answer. "I'm an angel," she answered. "My father is an immortal, just like Setadev. My mother was a mortal human."

Taking a deep breath, Sayo answered, "I see. I also see now why Setadev obsessed over you, as well."

In response, Caitlin shot a glare down to Sayo. "Don't remind me," she said. With that, Caitlin took off up the side of the mountain to the west.

"Good luck," Rachel called up to her as she left.

Caitlin did not turn around. She proceeded straight up the side of the mountain, ready to create the diversion. Right now, she knew she had to save Kevin. This was her opportunity. As she flew up, she pulled the Sword of Purity in front of her. "Great Vinz Larinion, if you're still in there, I hope you're right about this, and that you can take me to him."

The Sword of Purity flashed briefly. Its venation glowed brightly.

Within a moment, Caitlin reached the peak, the same one to which she had been with Sayo the day before and from which she had first seen the encampment. Settling herself down on the peak, she started charging a powerful blast of darkness magic. In the light of the morning, darkness would contrast greatly against the background, and would reach all the way to the ground as long as it did not hit anything on the way down. She had to aim carefully from this distance, as magic was not the most accurate skill in general, but she was not trying to hit a target. She needed to miss the camp and miss the forces below, and place her shot between the two.

Fully charged to the most force she could muster, Caitlin launched a beam of darkness at the ground below. It was well placed, almost perfectly, and it reached down to the ground. From the ground level, it was extremely noticeable, making some of the Solunar Empire troops flinch a little bit in surprise.

Over a minute passed in silence, as the men on the ground stood waiting for action. They were in position, fully blocking the mountain road, with archers placed on the ledges. Arthur then looked to Rachel. "Do you still have that collection of antite arrows in your quiver?"

Rachel nodded, as she pulled one out and nocked it in her bow, a prototype from the old Desolunar forces. "I do," she said.

"Good," said Arthur. "Be ready; if we see any Enlighteners who can shoot magic, you're the one who has to take care of it."

Stepping over to a ledge, Rachel kneeled down and took aim toward the ground. "Will do," she said firmly.

Then, the sound of a horn echoed through the air. The Enlighteners were alerted.

Suddenly, Rachel turned up and looked to Arthur. "Stay with me, please?" she asked.

Arthur walked over and kneeled down next to Rachel. "Of course," he answered. "I won't leave your side, Rachel."

A smile came to Rachel's face. "Thank you," she said. She then hesitated before continuing, "When this is all over, I want to tell you something."

Confused, Arthur responded, "And what is…"

Boom!

A blast of fire impacted the ledge just above where Arthur and Rachel were crouched. They were lucky not to be injured. Down below, a few hundred Enlighteners were rushing toward the mountain road in a mass mob. There appeared to be more than there were Solunar Empire soldiers. Sure enough, they were alerted exactly as expected. The Solunar Empire was not trying to hide. They were attempting to be visible to create the necessary diversion.

Quickly, Arthur pointed out the particular Enlightener who fired the shot. In response, Rachel aimed her arrow cautiously and true, hitting that Enlightener in the shoulder from long distance. The antite in the arrowhead disabled his magic, preventing him from shooting again.

Below, at least two hundred Enlighteners charged at the ninety Solunar Empire soldiers at the base of the mountain road. Sure enough, Sayo had been right after all. These men were attacking with swords and spears in their hands, not with magic.

The Solunar Empire forces stood without fear, and Sayo stood without motion or reaction at all. The terrain was providing an enormous advantage, as the Solunar forces held their line. From above, Arthur was hoping that none, or at least very few, of his men would be killed in the fighting. He knew the Enlighteners would disappear if a fatal blow were delivered to them. Below, the line was holding on the incline, using the ledges next to the road to restrict the number advantage of the Enlighteners. As long as the lines held, the Solunar Empire would have the tactical advantage.

Below, Arthur spotted another Enlightener stepping back to fire magic. Immediately, Arthur pointed him out to Rachel. "There, there!" he exclaimed. "Go for that one!"

Rachel was working on nocking another arrow. Before she could get it fully ready to launch, however, an incoming shot of light magic was headed right for her. Quickly as she could, she stood up and bolted further down the cliff, with Arthur close behind. The shot was so powerful and so close that the force of its impact threw Arthur and Rachel to the ground.

From the ledge, archers were raining down arrows upon the advancing Enlighteners. However, they could not seem to hit the magic caster on the ground. As Rachel reached another clear spot on the ledge to take a shot, Arthur lined up beside her to call out information that would help Rachel with her shot, such as wind direction and speed.

Below, the troops were fighting on. Not choosing to advance, Sayo held his troops where their numbers would not be at a disadvantage. They held the high ground on the road, while the aggressive Enlighteners continued to advance. Only the magic casters were proving dangerous to the troops.

Rachel had to aim, and aim fast.

"East wind is light," commented Arthur, acting as Rachel's spotter while she started to aim the next shot. "Watch for him to jump backward; he sees us."

Too late.

Another blast was shot before Rachel could get lined up and her arrow nocked. There was no time for Rachel to react. Quickly, Arthur leaped and shoved her out of the way, knocking her to the ground.

A loud explosion sound occurred. The blast struck the ledge.

Dust was kicked up everywhere. Stunned that she had been pushed, Rachel leaned up and tried to see through the dust. There was a large hole in the ledge.

The Enlightener's blast had hit the end of the ledge path below

Arthur and Rachel, destroying that section of the cliff. Arthur was nowhere to be seen.

"Arthur!" screamed Rachel. "Arthur!"

There was a pause. It was the longest second of Rachel's life, as she anxiously waited for any response at all to tell her that Arthur was okay.

Then, she heard coughing. "Over here," a voice responded faintly.

Quickly, Rachel scrambled over to the edge of the blast zone, where the dust was finally starting to lighten. She managed to see a pair of hands hanging onto the edge of the damaged area of the road. "Are you all right?" Rachel asked, as she rubbed her eyes to get the dust out.

"Yeah," coughed Arthur, as he clung to the lip of the cliff. "I just thought I'd do some hanging around, that's all."

Almost relaxed a little bit by Arthur's comment, Rachel rolled her eyes as she grabbed Arthur by the wrists. "Sarcastic as always, are we?"

"If you only knew," laughed Arthur, as Rachel started to pull him up. Before she could get him very high, however, another blast rocketed through the air.

Rachel had nowhere to go. The blast hit low on the cliff, shaking the whole rock face. More of the side of the rock shook off, throwing Rachel off the edge. She screamed as the impact shook her off.

She was lucky. She caught herself by her feet, dangling by the edge of the broken area. Arthur still had a hold of her wrists, and was dangling from her as they held onto each other.

However, she was struggling to hang on, and was slipping fast.

Below, at the bottom of the cliff, death stared her in the eyes. Tears started coming to Rachel's eyes. "Arthur, I'm scared," she cried. "I don't know if I can get back up onto the cliff again."

Arthur looked up into Rachel's crying eyes. A look of fear was in his own, beyond anything he had ever felt before. "Let me go," he said. "Save yourself. One of us has to take care of the empire and rescue Kevin, and that's you."

"No!" Rachel screamed back at him. "I won't ever let you go! How could you even suggest that?"

Breathing heavily, Arthur responded, "Rachel, it's no good if we both die."

"But don't you see I can't live without you?" asked Rachel without thinking. She was speaking entirely from her heart, as she cried and yelled at Arthur.

Eyes widening, Arthur was listening intently. He was stunned.

"We've been traveling together for a long time, and I realized you were good the more time I spent with you," Rachel began, fearing this would be her last moment to tell him. "I was so taken when you asked me to be your prime minister in Solunar that I came there just to be with you. I care about you so much more than I ever told you…"

Suddenly, Rachel was interrupted as more of the ledge began to fall, and her grip started slipping from the rock face. "I love you, Arthur!" she exclaimed in surprise. "I love you!"

Arthur was completely shocked.

Then, the ledge gave way.

Rachel shrieked.

Within a second of slipping, Rachel felt someone pulling her by her ankles, slowing her descent. Arthur was still holding onto her, not letting go. It took less than a second for Rachel to figure out what had happened.

"Caitlin!" she exclaimed.

A smile came to Caitlin's face as she heard her name called. She was holding Rachel by her ankles, slowly floating down to the ground where the ledge was still intact. "You didn't honestly think I was going to let my best friend and my half-brother die, did you?"

"Way to go, Caitlin!" Arthur called up to her, in excitement. "I knew you wouldn't let us down!"

Politely, Caitlin smiled again as she set Arthur and Rachel down at the ground. As she set them down, she said, "You guys had better stay down here and take shelter until we're ready to light the camp on fire."

She was interrupted, however, by the approach of the Enlightener who had been shooting spells. He fired a massive blast of flames right at the trio.

With only a slight bit of opportunity, Caitlin formed a shield of light between her hands and held it up, pushing back against the fire burst.

"Rachel! Shoot, now!" she exclaimed.

Rachel nodded in confidence. She nocked her arrow and aimed it upward at a projectile angle, guessing where the Enlightener would be for a drop shot. Taking great care and half a minute to adjust, she let the arrow fly over Caitlin's shield.

The feathers of the arrow fluttered in midair as the shot flew in an arc. It was a beautiful shot, one that the Enlightener never saw coming. The shot came down perfectly into the side of his neck, causing him to disappear instantly.

As the flames disappeared as well, Caitlin turned to Arthur and Rachel. "Well done; that was a perfect shot," she told Rachel as she tapped her best friend on the shoulder.

In response, Rachel leaned in and gave Caitlin a full hug. Arthur eventually joined in within a few seconds as well. Their embrace lasted for a few seconds.

When they broke apart, Caitlin said, "Stay safe, you guys," as she lifted the Sword of Purity in her hands. "I have to go now." A smile came to her face. "Besides, it sounds like the two of you have some things to talk about."

For a brief minute, Arthur and Rachel looked at each other. Then, Rachel looked away and started blushing. "Go get Kevin for us," Arthur finally answered, breaking the silence. "Bring him back so we can all be friends again."

Caitlin nodded in confidence and immediately began running into the camp with the Sword of Purity in her hands. As she did, Arthur and Rachel stayed against the ledge, watching the battle from a distance away as Sayo and his men started to push back against the disheartened Enlighteners, who had just seen the core pieces of their attacking strategy removed by the defeat of their magic casters.

Meanwhile, at the mouth of the inlet, a teleportation gate opened. From it emerged Vincent Stryker and Ralios Larion, along with Tyrinion, Kronius, and Necnea. Immediately as they exited,

Larion turned and closed the gate, preventing it from being seen or being used again.

"We're too late," Vincent Stryker commented, as he looked into the inlet. "A battle has begun. The Solunar Empire is already here."

As soon as he heard this, Larion jumped into the sky and levitated higher, to get a better look. "It appears as though we were right, however. The encampment is here."

"My lord," began Kronius, "shall we proceed?"

Larion, in response, looked to Tyrinion, who shook his head. Larion then responded, "I think not." He then pointed over toward the mountain path, where he saw the troops and formations of the combatants. "It looks like the Solunar Empire is doing fine. Once they are clear, we can advance as a group and gather with the pure one and his friends. Then, we can make a unified approach."

Understanding this and placing his impatience aside, Kronius reluctantly nodded in agreement. "Should we bring more gods, then?"

"If we do that, we run the risk of exposing ourselves, or worse, endangering their lives as well if Setadev can kill immortals as we believe he can," Tyrinion answered. "We are best to assist the pure one ourselves, and trust that our power can do it."

Again, Kronius nodded. He looked over to Necnea, and saw that she nodded in agreement as well. This was the decision they had made.

Within the camp, Caitlin was running frantically. There were some Enlighteners still there, and Caitlin would have to make her way through them. She kept moving at a high speed through the camp, desperate to find Kevin.

At one intersection, an Enlightener took a shot at her with a blast of fire.

She ducked quickly and shot one back herself, hitting the Enlightener square in the chest.

The Sword of Purity started glowing brighter and brighter. She was getting closer. She could feel it in her heart, as well. He had to be close.

Suddenly, she stopped at the next intersection. Six Enlighteners had her surrounded. Two more came up from behind, blocking her exit.

Caitlin had to stop herself and spin around to analyze the whole situation. There were now eight Enlighteners around her in total. Simultaneously, all of them began to charge magic in their hands, of various elements. They were planning to attack her all at once.

She ducked to the ground, put her hand down, and unleashed earth magic with all of the might she could muster.

The shaking earth shook the Enlighteners off balance. The ground was shaking and breaking apart under the spreading force of the earth magic. Then, Caitlin commenced an angel rush straight ahead, blasting the two Enlighteners in front of her aside. She moved so quickly that the disoriented Enlighteners could not keep up with her or track where she was heading.

Glowing brightly, the Sword of Purity was guiding her, taking her where she wanted to go. Kevin had to be here. She had to trust that his sword would take her to him. After making a turn, Caitlin kept going straight, not slowing down for an instant. She was flying just above the ground as quickly as she possibly could, anxious to see him. This was what she had spent so long trying to do, had suffered through so much pain and torture to accomplish. She was so close to having him back again.

She stopped suddenly in front of a tent. The sword stopped here. No guards were watching it, likely having been pulled away by the diversion. As she looked at the sword, which started to fade, her breathing became heavy. Slightly nervous, she pulled away the tent flap and stepped inside.

There he was.

Inside, Kevin was tied to the tent support post in the middle. He appeared to be badly beaten, as he was bruised and had several scarred cuts in his skin. His arms and ankles were tied tightly to the post, and his head was down as he was worn out from the beating.

"Kevin," she said, as she rushed over to start cutting his tie ropes, "I'm here for you."

There was a slight groan from Kevin. He barely turned his head, grimacing in pain. "Caitlin," he began, with great exhaustion and despair in his voice, "I… I'm sorry."

"Don't be," answered Caitlin, as she cut through Kevin's

binding ropes and set the sword down as she looped around to grab the exhausted Kevin by his front to help keep him upright. "I'm just so glad to see you're still alive."

"But Caitlin, I…"

Suddenly, Caitlin leaned in and kissed Kevin on the lips. Kevin responded as well, wrapping his arms around her as they shared a long kiss. As she held him, she started releasing healing magic, which showed as Kevin's scars started to fade and the discolored bruises on his face disappeared. Finally, Caitlin let go of him. "You're here with me at last," she said, "no matter how much Setadev and Satiana tried to break us apart."

A smile came to Kevin's beaten face. "Caitlin, you figured it out," he said tiredly. "You realized I would never betray you."

In response, Caitlin smiled as well. "With a little bit of help," she answered. She then pointed to the Sword of Purity, which Kevin stepped over to pick up. "You may not believe this," Caitlin continued, "but I think Vinz Larinion, the five thousand year king of gods, is still alive within that sword."

Feeling a bit reinvigorated, even though he was worn down, Kevin replaced the Sword of Purity in his ornately decorated scabbard. "Somehow, I would not be surprised by that," he said. "I've often thought this sword had a conscience, more than the magic and divine power infused into it. And now I know," he continued, as a tear dripped from his eye, "because it let you hold it while it guided you to me."

Caitlin walked up to Kevin and grabbed his hand to hold it. "Come on, let's get out of here," she said. "Arthur and Rachel are here as well. They miss you too, and I think they want to apologize to you."

As they walked toward the tent flap, Kevin answered with a smile, "I'm not sure I need to hear them apologize. They came here for me; that's all I want."

Giving a nod in acknowledgment, Caitlin signaled to Kevin toward the exit, to where they both headed. Quietly, as they looked at each other, Caitlin and Kevin pushed through the tent flap, exiting together. Suddenly, something had their attention. Their eyes widened, surprised to have this happen.

Someone was waiting for them.

Chapter 49

Dance of Courtship

"Hello, Caitlin," came the shocking voice of Satiana, who was standing in front of everyone, accompanied by several Enlighteners. "I have been waiting for you."

For a second, Caitlin gasped in surprise. Then, she glared directly into Satiana's eyes. "You," she said aloud. "Do you know how much I want to bash your face in right now?" She started charging magic in her hands.

Snow was starting to fall in heavy flakes. The breeze was starting to pick up. Sweetly, Satiana crossed her arms. "I can't imagine why that might be," she laughed.

"I don't find your sarcasm funny," responded Caitlin. "You know exactly what you've done, what you've been doing." Her voice then turned more serious. "And now I know exactly why."

"Do you?" asked Satiana, coyly.

"I do," said Caitlin. "You're a creation of Setadev's. He designed you, based on my own figure, in order to attract and seduce Kevin while under the influence of aphrodisiacs to incapacitate him and show me things to break us apart."

Next to Caitlin, Kevin's eyes widened. That was the full extent of the scheme. That was who Satiana was and what made her who she was.

In response, Satiana laughed. "Oh my, that's very well worked out, Caitlin," she said. "But it sounds like you only have half the story." She waved the the Enlighteners, dismissing them. As they departed in various directions, Satiana continued, "I am more than just his creation. Setadev bestowed upon me a piece of his full power and his immortality. I am a piece of him, a part with my own consciousness, just as Pseudo himself was before Setadev became his consciousness."

Immediately, Kevin drew his sword. "So, then you are a fragment of Setadev, just as Pseudo is. If we don't kill you, then defeating Setadev as he is now will only let his mind jump to you, and he lives on." Kevin tapped his sword against the ground. He looked over to Caitlin, who looked at him as well and nodded in confidence. He then turned back to Satiana. "That means we can't allow you to run free."

"Don't leave anything behind," Caitlin told Kevin. "We have to disintegrate her. It's the only way to make sure she doesn't come back like Pseudo did."

"Who said anything about running?" responded Satiana, chuckling as she turned. "Kevin Trent Stryker, for someone who loved me so much I find your attitude quite hurtful. I have no intent on running," she smiled. Then, she took a step back. "This time, I plan to show you my full power." As she spoke, Satiana began to lift into the air. She was surging with energy, the power of Setadev's almighty divine power radiating from every corner of her body. The back of her dress seemed to explode as a pair of wings, solid and black, emerged. She was a false angel. "Behold the power of the true great one, the great lord Setadev!" she exclaimed.

Kevin stared in awe. Caitlin, however, was unfazed. "I already know you were designed based on me," she said confidently. "Just because you have your own set of wings does not scare me. You're not me and you're not an angel. You are only a terrible fraud and a horrific individual."

"Your pitiable insults have no effect on me," laughed Satiana. "Once I defeat you, despite Setadev's desire to keep you around, I will make sure that your existence comes to an end." She started glaring. "And whether or not you are mortal or immortal, I can assure you that I fully have the power to do that."

Caitlin clenched her fists. Her determination made her float a little higher and made her energy radiate even more.

Satiana then looked down at Kevin. "And after that," she continued, "I will take you back with me and ensure you never want to leave my clutches again. Perhaps it would be best if you considered this battle our dance of courtship, as it will be the final thing you witness before you become mine once again."

Furious, Kevin raised his sword and pointed the blade directly at Satiana. "Not on your life," he said. "I will never submit to you."

"You won't have a choice," laughed Satiana. "In fact, just to prove that point, you're going to have to watch this whole thing from the ground." Suddenly, Satiana started raising higher, a great distance into the sky. Then she blasted a strong force of darkness magic straight at Kevin.

Kevin stood dumbfounded, unable to react quickly enough.

Immediately, Caitlin bolted in front of him and turned her charging magic into a shield of light. She managed to block it at the last possible second, right above him. Caitlin had her arms bracing the shield as she pushed back, while darkness magic dispersed off of it and into the ground. "Leave her to me!" Caitlin called out to Kevin. "Get yourself to safety."

"But, Caitlin…"

"Just do it," Caitlin interrupted. "She's making it clear she wants a fight in the sky to keep you from joining in."

Before Kevin could answer, Satiana stopped blasting. Immediately, Caitlin shot upward to meet her in the air, leaving Kevin on the ground to watch. At this point, whether or not the Solunar soldiers saw anything meant little, as Satiana was not going to hide. However, Caitlin still hoped in the back of her mind that she would not stand out fighting Satiana in midair above the mountain peaks.

Higher and higher she went. Satiana was going incredibly high into the sky, above the clouds, beyond where Kevin or anyone else could see. Caitlin followed in close pursuit, all the way until Satiana suddenly stopped. Quickly, Caitlin stopped as well.

"Why did you come back?" Satiana then asked. "You've seen what he's done to you. You know he doesn't love you anymore."

"And that's where you're wrong," Caitlin shot back at Satiana. "I know he does love me. I also know that you are a massive liar who drugged him to take him away from me."

"Is that so?" asked Satiana. "Then why don't we prove, right here and right now, whose love is stronger?" She raised her arms into a defensive stance, suggesting that she wanted a one-on-one duel, in showdown format.

Caitlin was more than glad to oblige. She placed her arms up, choosing more of an offensive stance to have the first attack.

Both remained still, sustained in the air. The wind flapped each of their dresses around, but no other motion was occurring. Whoever flinched first would be the first to be struck down, or at least the first to take a hit. In her mind, Caitlin was formulating her strategy, figuring that Satiana had to have a reason to take the battle so high into the air, and that she had to counteract it by bringing down Setadev's fragment to the ground. It was likely that Satiana had full divine power, even if in a limited capacity to immortals, which made her very dangerous. Caitlin herself had angelic power, so unknown yet comparable and different to divine power. Both also had extremely strong magic skills.

Over a minute passed. Neither was willing to flinch. A determined glare was in Caitlin's eyes. Her mind was disciplined from the years of training she had done. Even with her emotions in full force, she was still very focused as an individual.

Suddenly, the breeze in the air turned, blowing Caitlin's long hair into her eyes. Despite her focus, some of her hair hit her open right eye directly, causing her to flinch.

Immediately, Satiana fired a shot of light. Caitlin was quick enough to move out of the way by ascending.

Satiana started placing multiple shots of light blasts in various spots. Caitlin was darting around in all three dimensions cautiously but quickly, making Satiana's shots futile. Still, she kept firing in order to try and hit Caitlin, even placing some shots where she predicted Caitlin might be. Caitlin's reaction and response time, however, was just too quick. Her years of training in magic skills had honed her dexterity and quick decision-making, and her angel powers allowed her to execute them.

Frustrated, Satiana screamed into the air, as she raised her arms up. A wave echoed from her in all directions. This was not a wind wave; it was a force shockwave created by divine power.

From this, Caitlin had nowhere to evade. She was impacted and shaken up for a minute. She stopped and placed her hands on her ears, impacted by the wave and its painful effects.

With Caitlin temporarily immobilized, Satiana started charging divine power in her hands, in a pure form. After charging for several seconds, she fired it directly at Caitlin.

In the nick of time, Caitlin put her arms up and formed a shield of light. Still, the blast was very forceful. Caitlin was barely holding on, only just managing to block the attack.

Very soon, her shield was going to fail. She was already feeling weak trying to hold back so much force. Once the shield failed, she would be impacted by the full force of an obliterating raw divine power blast. Inside, Caitlin was fearful. She did not want to let Kevin down, but she was scared of Satiana's raw power.

I'm sorry, Kevin, Caitlin said in her mind, echoing out in a way for Kevin to hear in his head. *She's just too strong.*

From below, all Kevin could see were flashes. Still, Caitlin's message echoed through his head. She kept projecting.

I just... I can't do it... She's too strong...

You can do it, Caitlin. Push through her attack.

Kevin? You can hear me projecting my thoughts to you?

Of course, I remember how this works. I love you, Caitlin.

Love. It was a powerful thing.

Caitlin knew what she had to do. Her wings started to glow brighter; her energy seemed to radiate brighter. Kevin's connection had sparked her heart again and had given her the support she desperately needed. Now, she was going to push through Satiana's attack.

Putting every bit of her energy into her shield, Caitlin shot forward with an angel rush, using her angelic power to propel her. Against the force of the blasting divine power, she was moving slowly but was able to move. She kept going as hard as she could, pushing against the blast and advancing closer to Satiana.

The gap between Satiana and Caitlin was starting to close. Satiana tried to force more and more energy into her blast against the advancing Caitlin, but Caitlin kept coming closer. Within a minute, she was right against Satiana, scattering the power against the shield of light. Then, Caitlin pushed even harder, slamming her shield directly into Satiana. Satiana was knocked off balance, and her blasting of divine power ceased. Caitlin was exhausted, but this was her opportunity.

Flying above her opponent, Caitlin then charged raw power. With all of her remaining might, she unleashed the blast directly down at Satiana, towards the ground.

Satiana had nowhere to go. She had no way to defend herself.

Caitlin hit her squarely, forcing her down. Refusing to let up, Caitlin continued forcing her angelic power blast until Satiana fell to the ground.

A loud crash was heard from Satiana hitting the ground, as the blast finally disappeared. Immediately, Kevin rushed over to where Satiana had fallen. A short distance away, Caitlin was coming down, having succeeded in her attack. She was exhausted, having used all of her energy, and was not able to fight any more. As fast as she could, however, she made it over to Satiana as well, on the opposite side that Kevin was.

There, Kevin stood over the fallen fragment of Setadev, sword in hand. He appeared a little confused, staring at his sword for a moment while also glancing over at Satiana. Thoroughly defeated, Satiana pulled herself up by gripping onto Kevin's legs. "Please save me," she begged in a delicate voice.

Kevin said nothing. He stood like a stone statue, unmoving. Even Caitlin was unsure of what he was going to do, and was afraid of what was going to happen. What was really going on in his mind? Though she could read it if she wanted, she had made the promise to Kevin never to invade his private thoughts. Respect for him would mean never violating that promise, nor her morals.

Tired and taking heavy breaths, Satiana pulled herself a little higher. "Help me, Kevin," she said faintly. "She'll kill me if you don't." She paused for a second. "Was everything between us all fake? After all the time we spent together, you still really don't care for me?" She paused again. "Please, just give us one more chance. Help me. Save me."

Slowly, Kevin lifted his sword. He then leaned in and put his head next to Satiana's, as he wrapped his free left arm around her. "I'm sorry," he said.

Then, he stabbed her in the chest, running his sword completely through her.

Across from him, Caitlin's eyes widened in surprise. She was not expecting him to do that. She started walking over to where he was standing, nerved by just how easily Kevin had been willing to run Satiana through.

Stunned and in great pain, Satiana leaned forward and placed both of her hands on the blade of the Sword of Purity. Instantly, her hands were shocked from its effects. Tears started coming from her eyes, as she cried. Kevin looked down into them, surprised to see that her eyes had sincerity within them. He kept his hands firmly on the sword's handle.

"Thank you," Satiana said quietly. She looked up. "Thank you both." She then coughed, as she struggled to take in air as she spoke her last words. "I am a piece of Setadev, and if he dies, his consciousness will come to me. But I am not him," she paused.

Caitlin and Kevin were both listening intently. This was not the reaction they were expecting to hear.

Satiana continued, "The truth is, even I am not completely heartless. I do sincerely like you, Kevin, even if I joke about making you my plaything." She then coughed again. More tears started falling from her eyes. "I'm sorry to both of you for all of the pain I have caused to you. And I thank you both," she gasped for one last breath, "because you have set me free and kept me from becoming him."

Silently, a deeply thoughtful Kevin bowed his head down and lit up his sword. He unleashed its full divine power by focusing it, knowing he could not make the same mistake he did with Pseudo that left Setadev with a way to stay alive. Though not knowing if what he was going to do would work, Kevin had to make sure Setadev's transfer of conscience could not happen again.

Caitlin took a step back and watched on, not knowing how to feel.

With all of the focus he could, Kevin unleashed the divine power of the Sword of Purity through the blade and into Satiana's body. She disintegrated all at once, vaporized into dust which the breezes of the cold winter day swept up and into the air. No part of her was remaining or was anywhere to be seen.

The wind howled through the air as the last bits of dust disappeared into the sky.

"She's gone," Kevin finally said, quietly, as he sheathed his sword.

Silence filled the air. The wind whipped as the snow fell, and a sharp breeze crossed the camp. With a strong feeling, Caitlin reached around Kevin and hugged him from behind. "I can only imagine how hard that must have been," she said, "even knowing who she was."

"Yeah," answered Kevin reluctantly, as he lowered his head. "I have to wonder, though, if we could have saved her somehow. She seemed so regretful in the end, unlike Setadev himself…"

Inside, Caitlin felt a little hurt by that. Still, she knew Kevin regretted every life that he had to take. It was not a pleasant feeling, and Caitlin felt the same way during the times she had done so, as well. So easy it was to forget sometimes that everyone was a person, regardless of how they were born or where they were from. Both Kevin and Caitlin had learned that by now, and both were more conscious to that fact than either one was willing to reveal.

Suddenly, Caitlin remembered something. She immediately let go of Kevin. "I almost forgot," she said, as she looked over to where the Solunar Empire forces were, directing Kevin's attention that way as well. "Are you ready to run?"

"What do you have planned?" asked Kevin, slightly confused.

Caitlin winked at Kevin. "Just watch," she chuckled, as she lit a spark of fire in her fingers and threw it at the nearest tent. It was engulfed in flames just a few seconds later, seemingly unaffected by the cold weather and the snow.

Quickly, Caitlin started running to the west. Kevin followed right behind, and asked, "What's that all about? Why are we burning the camp?"

"It'll destroy the morale of the Enlighteners," Caitlin answered. "Within a few minutes, this entire camp will be up in flames. The Enlighteners will have no choice but to either retreat or surrender."

As he kept running, Kevin nodded. He understood the strategy now.

Chapter 50

At the Brink of Reality

Sure enough, Caitlin would prove to be right. Within just a few minutes, an entire swath of tents were aflame in the camp. The winter breeze was helping to spread the fire around the camp; while several Enlighteners struggled to try and put it out, the wind carried it faster than they could work on it. The tents were proving extremely flammable as the fire kept spreading. In less than an hour, the fire had engulfed the entire mining camp, and Enlighteners were fleeing in all directions. Even the forces trying to fight off the Solunar Empire troops were backing down, seeing they had nothing to defend anymore. None were willing to surrender, but many did start retreating. Within another few minutes, the Enlighteners were defeated and had all retreated from the indent.

While the fires were burning, Kevin and Caitlin fled to the north side of the indent away from the camp to wait out the action. After the Enlighteners had all fled, they headed toward Arthur and Rachel, near the mountain road.

Immediately, there were group hugs around Kevin, as he was finally reunited with his friends. “It’s good to see you again, my friend,” said Arthur.

Rachel then said, “We’re sorry we ever doubted you. Can you forgive us?”

Tears of happiness were in Kevin’s eyes. “Of course,” he answered, as the group hug split up. “How could I ever be upset at you guys?”

“Good,” smiled Arthur, as he stepped back and grabbed Rachel’s hand. They stood next to each other, holding hands just as Kevin and Caitlin were.

That caught Kevin’s attention. “Arthur, what the hell are you doing?” he asked as he pointed it out.

"Oh, this?" he asked as he lifted Rachel's hand in his. Next to him, Rachel smiled and giggled a little bit. "Well, it's a long story."

In response, Kevin raised his free hand and put it over his eyes as he lowered his head. Then, he shook it and started snickering. "Congratulations to you guys," he answered. "I'll be honest; I never saw that coming."

"Oh, you'll get used to it soon enough," responded Rachel with a smile. "After all, we're actually just getting used to it ourselves."

Their discussion was interrupted, however, by the arrival of General Sayo, along with several troops. He immediately saluted and said to Arthur, "Pardon me, my emperor, but I have my report on the battle ready for you if you are ready to hear it."

Before Arthur could say anything, Kevin responded, "Ah, General Sayo, I'm glad to see you found the empire's units." Looking around, as he saw Arthur unflinching and listening intently, he said, "I can see as well that Arthur has offered his forgiveness to you."

"Please," nodded the general, "in your case, Kevin, you may call me Marty if you so choose."

Kevin nodded, but said no more.

Arthur decided to pick up the conversation at this point. "Proceed, general," he commanded.

Sayo saluted. "The Enlighteners have entirely fled the area. Our men have suffered many injuries, but there appear to be few casualties thanks to your efforts to suppress the magic casters. There are at least fifty hooded cloaks scattered across the ground, telling us we have taken out at least fifty Enlighteners."

"Excellent," nodded Arthur. "Then all that's left is what is in the mine." He looked around the area for another minute. "Setadev is nowhere to be seen. I am willing to bet he is waiting for us in there."

"I concur," nodded the general. Looking around, it seemed that Arthur, Rachel, Kevin, and Caitlin all had the same idea. That was where they needed to go. They had to bring an end to Setadev. It was time to take him out.

"Then we will take to action," Arthur responded confidently. "General Sayo, from here we must go it alone; your men will be of little benefit to us here. Have them set up camp here and fortify our position in case Gardolk forces find us and try to find out why we're here. We're not out of the woods yet just because the Enlighteners have been removed."

Without questioning, Sayo saluted, and then turned and walked back toward the men. Arthur, Rachel, Kevin, and Caitlin began walking the other way together, toward the mine. They had a mission to complete, and this time they would do it together.

"You seem to have some trust in the general now," commented Kevin to Arthur.

"Perhaps a little," Arthur answered. "I still don't trust him personally myself, but I have no choice but to put a little faith in him at this point." He paused for a second. "It was actually Caitlin who suggested I should trust him to start."

"Oh, really?" asked Kevin, as he turned his head over toward Caitlin.

Surprisingly to Kevin, Caitlin nodded. "He told me he needed our help to rescue you. After a little bit, I got him to tell the truth, including admitting to the horrible things he's done over the years, including the attack on the Metoi. Once that was out, it was evident he was not the same General Sayo who had been our enemy."

Kevin nodded. "I see," he said. "I'm just so glad you guys found me and have trust in me again."

Rachel bowed her head. "To tell you the truth, we never should have lost our trust in you at all. We all fell for their trap. Had Arthur not insisted we wait, had you not left your sword close enough that it could send messages to Caitlin, and had it not told her the truth and led her to find your sword and General Sayo, we would never have come back for you. It's only because all of that happened that we were able to find our way to each other again."

"In any regard, it happened," smiled Caitlin.

Briefly, Kevin looked and smiled at Caitlin.

Within a few moments, the group was in front of the mine entrance. It was quite inconspicuous, little more than a hole in the mountain. Nothing appeared to be lit within the mountain, though, meaning the cave inside was likely very dark. "Here we are," sighed Kevin. "Anyone want to be the first to go in?"

"You're not volunteering?" asked Arthur, sarcastically.

Shaking his head, Kevin responded, "I'm sure I would normally. In this case, though..."

Suddenly, a voice interrupted Kevin. "In this case, though, you are unsure since little of this has been your journey in itself and you do not know if you deserve to go first."

Kevin turned, and saw several individuals standing together. "Ralios Larion?" he asked, surprised at the older man in royal red robes.

Larion nodded. "That is correct," he answered. He then stepped aside to give way to two other individuals: Vincent Stryker and Professor James Magnon.

Almost immediately, Kevin and Caitlin's eyes teared up. They each ran to their parents, filled with joy to see them.

"Dad!" exclaimed Kevin, as he ran up and hugged his father.

Energetic, Caitlin jumped up into the professor's arms. "Father!" she exclaimed.

Both Vincent and Professor Magnon were pleasantly surprised by the reactions of their children, and each returned the hug. In Vincent's case, that hug came with a little bit of pain as his old injuries to his back were acting up. It had been so long since the children had seen their fathers that the ecstasy in their emotions were exploding. Truly, they were two proud fathers. Each hugged and held his child for over a minute, saying nothing but letting their emotions say every word possible.

Likewise, Kevin and Caitlin could not have seen anyone that would have made them more happy than to see their fathers. They had gone through unimaginable horrors in the last few months, and the comfort of family was deep for both of them.

"I am proud of you, my daughter," the professor said to Caitlin, setting her back down. "You have accomplished so much, and your bravery is so remarkable. I could have never asked for a better daughter."

"Thanks, father," smiled Caitlin.

A few steps away were Kevin and Vincent. "My son, I've missed you," said Vincent as he hugged Kevin for a minute before letting him go. "I hope you're okay."

Kevin nodded. "I am now," he said. "Thank you for coming here."

"I would go anywhere for you," acknowledged Vincent. "I didn't come here alone, though." He looked over at Caitlin. "Your father helped me most of the way," he said. "As did Necnea and Kronius."

Suddenly, Kronius approached Kevin and Caitlin, having not been seen by them yet. "How could I not be involved with protecting my friends after all they have done for me?" he asked.

Having grabbed their attention, Kevin and Caitlin then ran over to Kronius and hugged him as well. It had been a long time since either one of them had seen their mutual friend. For Kevin, Kronius would always be Kron Kalavere, the god in hiding that found him and asked for help getting home.

"You made it!" exclaimed Caitlin, as she hugged Kronius.

Awkwardly, Kronius chuckled a little bit as Kevin and Caitlin held him tight. "Of course I did," he said. "I had to make sure I saw the two of you together again."

A hesitant thought came to Caitlin's mind. One she tried to stifle.

"It's good to see you too, Kron," said Kevin.

In the meantime as Kevin and Caitlin visited with Kronius, Arthur addressed Vincent Stryker. "Any luck in Nuve?" he asked, as he held Rachel's hand.

"Some," Vincent responded. "It's a more complex situation than we thought. I'll have to explain later when we have more time. I have a feeling we will be moving quickly here very soon."

Sure enough, he was right. Necnea then stepped out in front of the crowd. "I hate to cut things short here," she commented, "but I sincerely doubt that Setadev will be waiting long for us. The more we wait, the more chance Setadev escapes without us catching up to him, or finds another way to complete his revival."

Having let go of his father, Kevin turned his head to Necnea. "Another way?" he asked.

At Kevin's opposite side, Kronius picked up, "We think Setadev may have a dimensional gate in this mine. With it, he may be attempting to open up a dimensional shift. Then, with the power of your sword, he could siphon off raw divine power and infuse it into himself at the shift to reorganize his physical form and truly revive himself in full."

Kevin walked over to Kronius, more surprised than anything. "Is that what he wants with my sword?" he asked. He then reached down with his left hand and clutched the crossguard. "Because if that is the case, he will never get it out of my hands, and he will never have my hands to place it in his device."

"And what exactly is this plan?" asked a curious Rachel. "I'm still not sure I understand what you mean by a 'dimensional gate'."

"I am not sure we know, ourselves," Larion answered to Rachel. "It is only all theoretical at this point, but everything we have seen so far seems to suggest it." He paused for a moment. "We have not shared it with everyone here yet, but we found another prophetic poem."

Suddenly, Kevin flared his eyes in surprise. That was just great, he thought to himself. More interference from prophecy and its glaring tendency to be inaccurate. Keeping his curiosity and frustration contained for the moment, he continued to listen.

Professor Magnon then picked up the response. "Whether or not they actually are prophecy, we found out something curious about the two we have found so far. They are part of a series called the 'Letters to the Adventurer', and were written only a few hundred years or so ago, by someone named Clavius Lekion Stryker Dominous."

That made Kevin look puzzled. He looked at Caitlin, who looked confused as well.

"In any regard, we discussed inventions that Setadev had created before his five-thousand-year exile, which a god known as Forrestren suggested a past failed project by Setaeus Demota before he gained his immortality and became Setadev. Very little work has been done on different dimensions and examining that possibility, but we think a shift opening in it might allow Setadev to reorganize the matter and power of his body."

"Yet he's not as strong as he was," noted Arthur. "He's still really strong, but we've seen how he's vulnerable."

"Indeed," acknowledged the professor. "Logic would then dictate that he needs a divine power source, and the previous source, the Stripe of Life from the Seven Stripes of the Elements, was destroyed when Kevin and Caitlin caused the disintegration of the realm below after the battle of Seta Archa. We have reasoned that Setadev wants the Sword of Purity as his source of power."

"So he set his trap to get Kevin, who can control the sword," added Rachel. "It would not be the first time he has done so." She looked into the mineshaft. "This too could be a trap."

Arthur nodded. "In which case, however," he said as he looked toward the mine entrance, "we have no choice but to spring it."

There was a unanimous nod of agreement.

Within a few moments, everyone had regrouped. Vincent and the professor had had the opportunity to get to talk briefly with their kids, and Arthur and Rachel had the chance to talk about the incident up on the ledge. The gods had the chance to catch up with everyone and thank Kevin, Caitlin, Arthur, and Rachel for all of their efforts. However, sharing the full stories of their individual adventures would have to wait. That would take too long. For now, they had business to attend, and with that in mind they joined together to proceed into Setadev's cavern, with as much caution as possible.

Inside the abandoned gold mine, darkness was everywhere. Only Caitlin's wings served as a light source, as Kevin and Caitlin led Arthur, Rachel, Vincent Stryker, and several gods through the mine. Regardless of how far they had to walk inside the mountain, they remained committed to what they had to accomplish: the destruction of Setadev, once and for all.

It was clear that the mine had been stripped to its fullest. Small tunnels seemed to go in all directions, dead-ending while searching for more gold veins. Quite simply, no more was available. The tunnels wrapped in all directions and the main line serpentined around, showing the continued search for the gold and the lack of success that was brought to the miners before. Some wooden braces were still in positions, but most had long since fallen apart, leaving only an artificial cave as the structure of this hole in the mountain.

About ten minutes' walk through the warped and curving tunnels, Kevin stopped at the edge of a pit. It was at the very end of the main tunnel, which went no further, and it looked more freshly dug than the rest of the mine system. "It looks like we go down from here and find out what lies beneath," he said.

"This must be Setadev's access to the cavern," Professor Magnon stated, stepping up next to his daughter. "From our best guess, he must have had this camp here to drill access into his project site. This is where he plans to carry out his revival."

Kronius stared over the pit, which seemed to have a strange yet ominous feeling to it. "It feels as though we are at the brink of reality," he said, "when we consider what Setadev has planned down there."

Larion nodded. "I only wish we knew exactly what he has planned." He paused. "We have a good guess, but all of it is based on theory. We have no true idea as to what he really has planned to do, or how he plans to implement it."

"Aren't you guys as smart as he is?" Arthur asked to Larion. "I mean, I know we all know how strong he is, but wouldn't the minds of all the gods combined be able to surpass the wit of one who's lived as long as each of you has?"

The professor lowered his head. "Unfortunately, Arthur, the real world does not work that way. While Setadev is about as old as myself, or as Necnea, he is extremely cunning and a very formidable planner. Truly, he is a unique talent that history will likely never see again, and that is the exact reason that he is dangerous as an immortal."

"And even more dangerous with his power," commented Necnea. She looked over at Kevin's sword, which was resting in its scabbard on his belt. "Had he not been, my husband would not have needed to sacrifice himself in order to create the Sword of Purity."

Kevin looked down at his sword, spurned on by the glance of Necnea. "Without it, I wouldn't be the individual I am today," he said. He then looked up and stepped over to Necnea. "I don't think I've had the chance to do this formally, so let me do it now." Firmly, he stepped up to the goddess of time and looked at her firmly in the eye, as she waited in curious anticipation. With a kindness in his eyes, Kevin said, "Thank you for the sacrifice of your husband." He paused for a second.

"I will not allow his sacrifice to be in vain."

In response, Necnea started shedding tears. She was deeply moved by the humility of the young pure one. Though she did not make any crying noise, her eyes showed all of her emotion. She looked firmly at the young pure one and nodded, unable to say more at the moment.

A few steps away, Caitlin could not help but watch and think about the kindness of Vinz Larinion and Kevin's humility that he had just displayed. When this were all over, she would have to tell Necnea about speaking with Vinz Larinion himself. And after all that Kevin had gone through in the last few weeks, Setadev had never truly broken him or changed him, after all. He was still the same kindhearted individual that she had fallen in love with months before.

Yet another thought was also on her mind as well, and it pervaded into her innermost feelings…

"There's something here I don't understand, though, on the topic of the Sword of Purity," commented Rachel. "If there's a possibility this plan involves Kevin's sword, why didn't we leave it outside?"

With that comment, Kevin started pressing up on the crossguard of his sword with his left thumb. "I didn't leave the sword because even Setadev can't use it without control of me," he answered. "He clearly can't control me, or else he would have done so instead of drugging me. He also can't touch this sword. Only my father or I can do that."

"Are you confident in that?" Rachel asked.

In response, Kevin nodded, as he stepped to the edge of the pit. "I am," he answered. "Shortly before I left to find you guys, Setadev made his first offer for me to serve him. He had my sword in his hands, but in its scabbard. He wanted me to do it for him."

The professor nodded. "It is very good, then, that we managed to make it to you."

Caitlin lowered her head, as she stepped closer to the pit. Her eyes were burning with fury from the memory of what Setadev had done to Kevin and to her. "He did try, father," she said. "We'll have to tell you the story after this is over."

Professor Magnon and Vincent both nodded, curious in this fact.

Then, after a moment, Caitlin asked, with a passion in her voice as she grabbed Kevin's hand tightly, "Shall we proceed? If anyone wants to back down, now's the time to do it."

Silence filled the air.

Then, Rachel stepped forward. "For our friends, my bow is always at your service," she answered.

Arthur then stepped up. "How could I miss this?" he joked. Then, his tone of voice turned more serious, as he glanced at Kevin and then at Caitlin. "My best friend and my sister need me. I will always be there for both of you."

Confidently, Kronius took a step forward. "How you four have grown up," he said. "You are all like the children I never was able to have with my wife," he said.

In response, Arthur shot Kronius a glance. "Really?" he asked. "That's how you think of us?"

Kronius chuckled. "In a better way than I think you think I think of you all," he answered. "I had always imagined that someday I would get to have children of my own before my wife passed away and I became an immortal." He paused for a second. "I did not have that opportunity, certainly, but in many ways being able to travel with you four has given me an insight into what that may be like, and I mean that with the most sincere feelings." Again, he paused. "If I had had children, I could only wish they would turn out like you."

"Well, thank you," responded Kevin. "You're certainly a part of our family too, Kronius."

Nodding, Kronius then said, "So you will know, then, that I must be counted in, no matter what Setadev has planned."

In response, Caitlin nodded, as if knowing that was for sure before Kronius ever said anything.

Necnea then stepped up to Kronius's side. "My powers are at your command," she said. "I will be here."

Then, the professor stepped forward. "As would I wherever my daughter goes," he said.

Caitlin smiled at this comment.

"And I would for my son," nodded Vincent as he agreed, as well.

Larion then stepped forward. "From the day we first brought Vincent Stryker to the Realm of the Angels, through the day we found Kevin, to today, I have always believed that someday there would be a final confrontation that would bring peace to the realms." He paused, as he considered his thoughts for a moment. "It came later than I expected, but that day is today, and I could think of no one better that I could accompany on this journey."

Everyone was together on this. Caitlin then looked to Kevin, who was still holding her hand. "We started this together," he said. "Let's finish it together."

Suddenly, a voice pervaded the air, speaking to everyone standing around the pit. *Please come in. We have much to discuss about the way the game is played.*

It was Setadev.

With confidence, Caitlin looked over to Kevin again. "This time, you're not going it alone without me," she said. "You don't have a choice."

Kevin nodded. "I agree. This time, we'll do it together." He then looked around at Arthur and Rachel, Vincent, Larion, Kronius, Necnea, and the professor. "With all of our friends," he continued.

No one in the group flinched. They all knew that this was the path they had chosen.

Simultaneously, Kevin and Caitlin turned toward the pit together. They were still holding hands, as they prepared to go together. With a confident jump, they leaped together into the hole in the ground.

Chapter 51

Remnant of the Fallen

The slide seemed to last forever until everyone hit the bottom of the pit. It was a terrifying few moments as the steep tunnel led downward and downward. No one was sure just how far underground they were heading.

Suddenly, the bottom came up quickly. The tunnel began to shallow out toward the end, making for an easier approach. As Kevin and Caitlin climbed out of the tunnel end, waiting on the others to reach the bottom, they saw a sight that was absolutely unbelievable at the bottom.

They were in a cavern chamber, underground. It was a natural phenomenon, previously without access before Setadev's tunnel, where the ground split open and formed a pocket of air surrounded entirely by rock. To Kevin and Caitlin, it did not appear much different than a space between realms to which they have been before, but this was in their realm. Though it was by all means a natural and common feature, discovering one was extremely rare, and this one was pristinely smooth across its sides.

In the center of the cavern stood a giant stone ring on a pedestal, at least three times taller than Kevin himself. It was covered in markings and *rengan* text, that of the ancient language used centuries ago but one the gods were all fluent in. Six slots were present in the ring structure, equally distant from one another.

As the gods arrived at the bottom, Larion's jaw dropped. "So it is true," he said. "Setadev's gate really does exist."

"It is quite an astounding sight," commented the professor. "It would be amazing if it turns out to function. What a shame that such ambition was hidden away from the world for thousands of years."

Yes, what a shame it has been.

There was no surprise there. Kevin drew his sword and Rachel nocked an arrow in her bow. Everyone else prepared to be on the defensive.

With a twisted laugh, Setadev walked around from behind the gate, still in his Pseudo form. "Five thousand years of my own ambition has been kept silent by you fools and your lack of vision to see how the game is played."

No one moved. Everyone was silent.

"You may be the worst hypocrite in this room, Tyrinion, and your new appearance as a human professor does not fool me," Setadev then said, looking directly at the professor. "Do you not remember that it was your actions that contributed to Vinz Larinion and the original gods kicking me out of the home that I created for you? I taught you all the things I knew and gave all of you power and immortality. And this is how you repaid me?"

"I still stand by my decision," the professor rebuked, sternly. "While it is a shame that five thousand years of ambition have gone to waste, your ambition was and still is far too dangerous for the world to bear. I stand by the same words that Vinz Larinion told you when he expelled you from the Realm of the Angels: no one man should ever rule the entire populace."

Setadev rolled his eyes.

"You knew this before you ascended to the realm," Tyrinion continued. "Vinz Larinion warned you of what conquering the world would do, and why he could not allow that. The world cannot go forward under one ruler. The people will fight and continuously rebel because no one ruler can satisfy the needs and desires of every person. Some needs and desires will come into conflict with those of others. And when they rise up and you resist them, they will be such a thorn in your side that you will destroy them. More and more will rise to their cause, sickened by your rule, and you will continue to destroy them. Then, eventually they will run through their strength and be so worn down and decimated that they will be destroyed entirely, whether by your hand or by their own in their efforts to bring you down."

Setadev scoffed. "Oh come now, Tyrinion, and you believe you and your precious gods can be different?"

Larion then interjected, as he stepped forward, "That reason is exactly why the gods have tried to avoid direct intervention at all costs. It is just as Vinz Larinion guided us five thousand years ago, and we have maintained that philosophy. The world may have consolidated somewhat, but it is still keeping the same spirit that he embodied."

Then, Setadev started chuckling. "And just who might you be, naive one?" He stepped up straight to Larion, showing no respect in his approach. "Your appearance is old, as are the regal looks of your dark red robes, and I can clearly see you are a divine immortal one, yet you are not familiar to me. Instead, you must be a younger immortal, one of the ones I have heard was brought in by abuse of the Stripe of Life."

"You are wrong," Larion stated back firmly. "I was born in the Realm of the Angels to two immortals, three thousand years ago." His eyes showed a strong confidence in resistance to intimidation. "I am Ralios Larion, god of light and the king of gods."

An evil laugh came from Setadev. "So, you are Vinz Larinion's successor." He then chuckled again. "I highly doubt that when Vinz Larinion chose to sacrifice himself to make that wonderful sword on the pure one's belt that the gods would together elect you to be their king for as young as you actually are. It then stands to reason that you were hand-selected to be the next king. Might you be his son?"

"No, he is not," interjected Kronius, coming to the defense of his king. "He is the son of Trenos and Delineas, born as Ralios. He has no relation to Vinz Larinion himself; he took the name Larion in tribute of the former king."

Setadev shot a glance over at Kronius. "And you must be a newer one, too." He looked over Kronius's robes. "White with gold trim, and green and blue stripes. And a young face at that. You must be a lower god, near the bottom of the ranks, and yet you walk here with the higher ones who came to seek my defeat." He then laughed for a second, turning to Larion. "Are you losing followers so quickly?"

Before Larion could say anything, Kronius responded. "I happen to find you rather intriguing as well, Setadev."

Raising an eyebrow, Setadev asked, "Oh, do you, now?"

"I do," nodded Kronius. "When I first began this journey, when we all assumed Tyrinion and not you were the entity responsible for the conquest of the realms, I looked up to you as an inspirational figure.

Your knowledge, your power, all of it was grandiose and I admired your feats. Then, I heard more and more about what you did, and how you went about your feats, that your ends were more malicious than first thought. Seeing you now and hearing from you now, I cannot see you as being any different than that: a villain who only seeks his own selfish conquest."

Chuckling, Setadev said, "You do not see how the game is played," as he walked over to Necnea, with her long black hair, middle-aged appearance, and purple robes. "And let me guess, Necana Larin, that you are here to seek revenge because you blame your husband's death on me?"

"No," Necnea answered firmly. "My husband did what he did of his own volition; his sacrifice was his choice. However, you do bear some of that burden from my mind as the cause for him to make that decision."

"Bear it not anymore; he had the option not to do so but chose to do so, anyway," Setadev commented. Then, he walked over to Vincent Stryker. "You, I did not expect to see here. What happened to you, pure one? Did we not have an agreement? You put down your sword and I would stay away?"

Vincent glared at Setadev. "You violated that first," he said. "Furthermore, I made that deal believing you were Tyrinion, not Setadev."

Setadev nodded. "True, but you are still pathetic," he said. "Why is it not you who carries the Sword of Purity? And do not make an excuse such as your back; that is not something that would hold you back."

"My back is not what holds me back," Vincent Stryker responded. "I did put down the sword and have not picked it up again. It rightfully belongs to my son now."

Shaking his head, Setadev said, "You still have so much potential, yet you cannot defeat me, for I am nothing. I find your attempt to throw away what you have remaining to let your son take the effort upon himself quite amusing." Calmly, Setadev then walked over to Arthur and Rachel. "And what do you two have to say for yourselves? You would risk your empire for me?"

"We would do anything for our friends and for our future," Rachel answered. "If you knew what honor and love meant, maybe you would realize that."

Again, Setadev laughed. "Honor and love are weak human concepts," he answered. He then looked to Arthur. "I could be construed in a sense as your grandfather, you know. Does that not bother you?"

"You are not my grandfather," Arthur answered back. "I'm sad to admit I actually feel sorry for my father, Demonicus, that he has to listen to your voice."

"Funny," said Setadev, unbothered by the response by the emperor. "At least I know I have no reason to keep you alive." He then walked over to Kevin and Caitlin. "As for you two, I despise you the most. Despite all that I tell you and all that I have tried to keep you kept out of danger, you continuously refuse. Angel, I have told you that you have a place in my utopia and that I would rather not destroy you, yet you seem to continuously seek it." He looked to Kevin. "And you… I gave you the opportunity to live a content and happy life. I gave you someone to live it with who could have made you happy, and I offered you a place in my utopia in exchange for your cooperation. Why have you consistently denied it?"

"I denied it because I didn't want it," Kevin answered. "I don't want something fake and artificial. I have someone real who I live a content and happy life with, and I believe in the world being run by its people and kingdoms. Let us figure out how we want to run our world; we don't want your interference."

"And if you're looking to keep me under glass as a showpiece, I would rather die than do that," commented Caitlin. "I am not yours to own."

Setadev shook his head. "Pity," he said. "Very well, then. You both will meet your deaths in due time. However, I am most desirous that you witness my revival, along with everyone here."

"You do know that we cannot allow that," Kevin commented back, as he raised his sword. "We will ensure that. You will never take this sword from my hands, and you will not use it to revive yourself."

"And had you come down here alone, that would have been

exactly what I would have done," responded Setadev. He started looking around. "But now that I see that all of you have come down here together, I have another option." He looked toward the gods. "The question is, which one of you wants to die?"

The gods all looked stunned. "What do you mean?" asked Kronius.

In response, Setadev said nothing. Instead, he just laughed. "Just watch and learn," he said as he jumped back and high into the air. In the top of the gate was a slot in the ring. He positioned himself directly above it.

On the ground, Kevin lit up his sword. Caitlin prepared for battle as well.

Before they could go, however, Larion lifted himself into the air. "I won't let you open the gate!" he exclaimed. He rushed Setadev, charging divine power in his right hand.

Setadev lit up a shield, made of raw divine power, between Larion and the gate. Not anticipating it, Larion ran square into the energy, bouncing off of it with a thud. He slammed into the ground, where Necnea immediately rushed to his side, but appeared unhurt.

"Just for that, it looks like you will be the first to die, king of gods," Setadev continued, as he put his hands into the slot. Light magic started to emanate, collecting in the space. He then slid down one of the sides, energizing fire and air and placing respective magics in identical slots down the sides.

Immediately, Kevin started running up toward the gate, with sword in hand. Quickly, however, Setadev created his projected shield again, bouncing Kevin off and sending him sliding against the ground. Caitlin ran to his side immediately to take care of his wounds.

Without a comment, Setadev dropped off to the bottom of the ring and energized darkness magic into it, directly across from the light pole on the other side of the ring. Then, he skipped over to the opposite side and energized ice and earth magic into two more slots. Now, all six elements were present in the gate, at opposite ends of each other.

A loud, twisting noise rang through the air as the poles were energized.

Everyone could only watch on as the gate began to energize,

lighting up in a swirl of color. Setadev would not allow them to get near it while he was powering it up. Suddenly, it began to ripple and make an even more horrific noise before falling silent. Around, energy was visible coming from the slots. Within, a swirl of color indicated what had happened.

"Behold, a dimensional shift!" exclaimed Setadev. "Behold the greatness and glory of the almighty conqueror! I am the Great One himself!" He moved behind the gate.

Tyrinion looked over to Necnea. "Stop time, right now," he said. "We have to destroy this gate."

"I cannot," Necnea responded, as she stared at the gate. "I already tried a few seconds ago."

"Hmmph, you did not think that I would not have figured out how to counteract your temporal abilities, did you?" Setadev responded directly to Necnea. "I also happen to know that because you spent so long focusing your divine power on how to learn to control time, you have no ability to fight in any other way."

Necnea scowled at Setadev. Still, she could not say anything because he was right.

Rachel nocked an antite arrow and aimed it at Setadev. She did not fire yet, knowing that she had to wait for her opportunity.

Back on his feet, Larion started charging at Setadev again, as Kronius and Tyrinion prepared to go next. He was unfazed, even knowing whose eyes he was staring into. "You will not be revived! I will not allow it!" he called out, as he accelerated to full speed. He was preparing to level Setadev with the most magic and divine power he could muster.

In waiting, Setadev stood in front of the gate, while Kevin stood up finally next to Caitlin a little ways away. Suddenly, the pieces started to come together in Kevin's head. Setadev told Larion that he would be the first to die, and that he had a way without using the Sword of Purity to repower himself. Each god was an immortal and a source of divine power. And the gate Setadev needed to recombine the energy was right there, and it was active. Setadev knew this, and was holding back that he knew how to separate Larion from his power, permanently.

"Larion! It's a trap!" screamed Kevin.

That drew the attention of everyone standing near Kevin.

For Larion, it was too late.

He charged, attempting to slam Setadev with a hand full of divine power in a raw form. As he neared the gate, Setadev grabbed his wrist and threw him into the gate. Then, with his fist fully charged with a massive amount of divine power, he punched clean through Larion, disintegrating him in the gate's energy.

"No!" Necnea screamed.

Everyone else could only watch in horror. Larion was gone.

Stunned silence filled the air of the cavern.

Setadev, without hesitation, then jumped into the gate himself. Suddenly, there was a bright flash that lasted for several seconds, as the gate emanated a brilliant energy. Within a moment, the flash finally dissipated, as the gate returned to its normal coloring but remained energized. From it stepped out Setadev.

He was back.

In his revitalized form, Setadev appeared as he had before. He had short brown hair and golden robes, was young in appearance, and was quite tall. He appeared very divine, well sculpted, and quite muscular. Caitlin's eyes widened in surprise. It was plain to see in his aura how much power he had again.

"You pile of divine garbage," Kevin said up to Setadev, as he stepped forward and recognized perfectly his former and current foe. "You killed Larion to steal his divine power and combine it with yours to revitalize yourself. You will pay for what you did!"

Laughing, Setadev said, "You still do not see how the game is played, do you? This is *your* fault, Kevin Trent Stryker. When you destroyed me a few months ago, you also destroyed the Seven Stripes of the Elements. By doing so, you in turn allowed me to do this. The dimensional gate could not function before due to interference in the universe from the stripes, and by destroying them with me in the realm below, you allowed this gate to function." He then pointed to Kevin. "Place the blame on yourself, pure one!"

Suddenly, Setadev was struck by a blast of divine power. Setadev was knocked over, but picked himself up quickly. He looked to see where that attack came from.

It came from Tyrinion. He and Kronius flew up and positioned themselves in front of Setadev. "This game is over," he said. "We cannot allow you to live any longer, Setadev."

"Still bitter for revenge, are we, Tyrinion?" asked Setadev. He looked down for a second. "I do not know which will be more fun: destroying you, or killing your daughter and making you watch me do it."

"How dare you!" exclaimed Tyrinion. "You lay a finger on my daughter, and you will suffer the most painful death imaginable!"

On the ground, Caitlin looked up, in concern. "Father…" she said, faintly. It seemed like this situation was making him someone that he was not. He was serious, but furious and angry, too. That was not like him at all.

Setadev chuckled. "So be it," he said. He vanished in front of Larion and Tyrinion's eyes, almost as if into thin air.

"Where did he go?" asked Tyrinion.

"I do not know," Kronius answered, "but I have a bad feeling about…"

"Watch out!" exclaimed Tyrinion, as he jetted toward the professor, pushing him out of the way. From above, Setadev came down and blasted Tyrinion in the back with divine power, slamming him down into the cavern floor. He hit the ground with a hard impact.

Immediately, Setadev descended to the ground and lit up his fingers in raw divine power, the same technique he tried to attack Caitlin with at the Fortress of Da Leval. He was ready to blast it into Tyrinion's skull and kill him. Not even the immortal were truly unable to die.

With fury in his eyes, Setadev slammed the spark downward.

Caitlin, too far away to help, could only watch what was happening to her father.

Cling!

Rushing to Tyrinion's side, Kevin caught the spark with his lit Sword of Purity. He started pushing back against Setadev's efforts, fighting against the divine power wielded by his adversary.

As Setadev pushed back, he said, "Persistent as always, pure one?"

Kevin's eyes became firm, as he saw Tyrinion gaining conscience below him. "Always," he said. Then, he yelled, "Now, Caitlin!"

Setadev seemed caught by surprise as Kevin ducked. A blast of darkness came from the opposite side. Quickly, Setadev formed a shield of light with his opposite hand, as he pushed Kevin with his attacking spark. The darkness blast from Caitlin, shot from a few steps away, was merely deflected off of the shield. "Really, now, pure one," Setadev answered, "you did not expect such a simple stunt to work, did you?"

Another blast, this one of divine power, came down and leveled Setadev in the back. He was shoved into the cavern wall. As the blast dissipated, its launcher spoke. "No, but I bet you did not expect the extra element," said Kronius.

Standing back up, Setadev shrugged off the impact, as though, he had barely been pushed. "Impressive," he said as he turned toward Kronius and Tyrinion, who stood up near Kronius, "but you cannot defeat me, for I am nothing."

Kronius stared at Setadev. How had that done so little to him?

Charging divine power through his whole body, Setadev emitted a powerful wave of energy across the whole cavern. Everyone was thrown across the cavern and knocked off of their guard. Kevin dropped his sword from the massive force that sent him skidding across the ground.

With everyone disrupted, Setadev jetted over to Kevin, who was on the ground without his sword and groggy. Standing over Kevin, Setadev lit the spark in his fingers again. "I grow tired of your disruptions," he said. "My patience has run thin, so you will be the next to perish."

Frantically, as Kevin regained his consciousness, he started scrambling, looking for his sword. He had no idea where to call it from. Without hesitation, Setadev started to slam the spark down at Kevin.

It was too late. No time to get out of the way. No way to block it this time.

This was the end. I'm sorry, Caitlin, Kevin thought to himself.

Suddenly, the spark stopped. Kevin was horrified at what he saw.

Kronius had jumped in the way of the spark. Setadev had impaled him with it.

"Kronius! No!" Kevin exclaimed.

In response, Kronius had a calm countenance and demeanor, as he smiled in his suffering. "I was hoping that someday I could return the favor to you for everything you did for me. It looks like that day is today." Subtly, he pointed to Kevin's sword on the ground.

Tears started falling from Kevin's eyes. Those who had been shaken up were now able to see what was happening. All around, their eyes were crying.

Then, Kronius disintegrated into the air. Now he was truly gone.

Setadev glared into Kevin's eyes. "And now you are next." He charged his spark again.

Quickly, Kevin looked to his side, where Kronius had pointed. He saw his sword and called it to him. As Setadev prepared to lower the spark to him, Kevin quickly rolled to the side and sprung up to his feet, causing Setadev to miss with his strike. He was now between Setadev and the active dimensional shift.

An arrow shot from Rachel started whizzing toward Setadev's back. He grabbed it in midair and snapped it. Tyrinion then slammed Setadev with a blast of darkness, which Setadev formed his shield of light again to block.

Kevin took his sword and mounted a charge. He was set on impaling Setadev and finishing this once and for all.

In response, Setadev blasted Kevin hard with a wind spell stopping him in his tracks. Kevin tried to push through it, but he would not advance, no matter how hard he tried to keep stepping forward. Seeing an opportunity, Setadev intensified the strength of his wind spell, lifting Kevin up and launching him backward. He was thrown directly toward the dimensional gate.

Surprised, Caitlin took off and flew for Kevin as quickly as she good. She paid no regard to her own safety; she only worried for his.

Moving as fast as she could, she caught up to Kevin and grabbed a hold of him.

Except there was no time to slow down.

Caitlin, Kevin, and the Sword of Purity all passed into the dimensional shift simultaneously. The gate flashed as they disappeared.

They were suddenly gone.

Arthur stared on in awe. "What the…"

"What happened?" asked Rachel. "Did they just go through the gate?"

"What happens now?" asked Necnea, looking to the professor.

The professor lowered his head, tears still in his eyes. "I have not even the slightest bit of an idea," he said.

Turning around to face it, Setadev started laughing. "Well, that turned out to be quite useful, indeed," he said. "An unintended effect, but very nice. Finally, I have rid myself of their annoyance, even if I must give up my desired trophies for it."

The gate flashed again. It was terrifyingly bright.

Then, a blast shot out from the gate and leveled Setadev. He was thrown hard into the cavern wall.

Everyone else looked on in awe. What was about to step out of that gate was something that had never been seen or heard of before.

"You should have known," echoed the perfectly simultaneous voices of Kevin and Caitlin. "You used this gate to combine yourself with the energy of another. You should have realized that leaving it open would allow others to do the same."

For the first time that anyone had seen, Setadev's eyes widened. "You cannot be…"

"What I am is what you fear me to be," echoed the voices again, staying in perfect synchronization, as if spoken by one mind. "You always claim that no one else knows how the game is played. Do you know how it is played, Setadev? You are about to learn, because I am the game!"

I am the game!

The words resonated in Setadev's head as he watched a figure step out of the gate. It had long hair in both red and brown strands, and eyes striped in brown and blue. Dressed in what appeared to be plain white robes also trimmed in white, the figure stood firm. A youthful appearance was clear, but little else could be discerned. A pair of white wings extended from the back, giving an indication.

Rachel stared in stun. "Is… that… Kevin and Caitlin as one?"

"I can hardly believe it," said the professor, surprised. "It is exactly as Larion theorized. The dimensional gate combined them into one form, just as it did with Setadev and the dissipating divine power and energy from Kronius. An angel and the pure one and the divine power of the Sword of Purity as one being…"

"Wow," was the only word Arthur could say, looking on in stun.

Kevin and Caitlin, as one, stood firm against the gate. Raising one hand, they pointed it at Setadev. "You may make your decision now," they said in their simultaneous voice.

"So, what a fascinating discovery we have here," Setadev answered, almost laughing in surprise but more awkwardly than before. "You are the pure one, and the angel, and the power of Vinz Larinion combined all together. How much power do you really have?"

Kevin and Caitlin said nothing.

Setadev's gaze turned into a glare. "Let me find out," he said as he charged them, divine power in hand. He had that deadly spark in his fingers again.

In defense, Kevin and Caitlin only raised a hand. As Setadev impacted with force, a shield became visible, in the same color as the glowing Sword of Purity. Setadev continued to push with as much effort as he could muster, but Kevin and Caitlin stood unmoved.

Using all his might, Setadev pushed his attack. In response, Kevin and Caitlin pushed back, throwing Setadev against the cavern wall. Aside, everyone else stood back, watching in awe as the new combination was effective against the fallen god.

Everyone looked over at Setadev. He was, for the first time, scuffed up. He was not faking this; he was taking significant blows and actually being hurt by Kevin and Caitlin, even in his fully revived form.

Ready to take the offensive, Kevin and Caitlin leapt into the air and energized blades of divine and angelic power in their hands. They lunged at Setadev and engaged hard in close-range combat.

Using his arms to block, Setadev was struggling to defend every shot. Kevin and Caitlin had an immense amount of power and were hitting the fallen god hard. Still, penetrating Setadev's defense was tough.

Then, one strike got through. Kevin and Caitlin got a clean slash across Setadev's chest. He leaped back in midair, stunned to have been struck. With Setadev back on his heels, Kevin and Caitlin went for a stab.

In one motion, Setadev dodged the stab and leveled Kevin and Caitlin with a divine power blast.

They were shot across the ground against the base of the gate.

"Interesting," Setadev said, as he recomposed himself. "It would seem that I have an equal at last."

Scoffing as they pushed off the ground, Kevin and Caitlin said, "We are not equals. You seek to control the realms, and you don't care whose lives you end or ruin to get your way. You're an ethical degenerate."

"And you're any better for seeking to prolong the chaos?" asked Setadev.

Kevin and Caitlin glared into Setadev's eyes. "Chaos is better than what you are trying to achieve," they said. "Let the people decide how they want the world to be."

In response, Setadev laughed. "You just do not see how the game is played, do you? Only the strong can rule. The people are incapable of ruling themselves." He paused for a second. "However, since you clearly believe yourself to be stronger, why do you not try to prove it, and show me that your philosophy is stronger?"

Infuriated, Kevin and Caitlin fired a massive blast of divine power back at Setadev.

Though Setadev threw his arms up to brace himself, he was impacted hard and knocked to the ground. Even for Setadev, that was a hard and unexpected shot.

Fully standing back up, Kevin and Caitlin said, "Your overconfidence shows." They started walking toward Setadev, with the gate behind them.

Setadev stayed on the ground, not moving. Kevin and Caitlin stepped up over him. They formed another blade of divine power and hovered it above Setadev's head. "Game over," they said. "Your reign as the conqueror ends here."

They had no idea what was about to happen.

Without warning, Setadev curled his legs up and kicked Kevin and Caitlin into the air. They were caught by surprise. Then, Setadev blasted them with a wind spell, throwing them directly into the gate.

There was another bright flash. Arthur, Vincent, Rachel, Necnea, and the professor watched on in horror.

Out the back side of the gate, Kevin and Caitlin fell to the ground, separated from each other. The Sword of Purity was in Kevin's hands, but both were out of energy. Caitlin had lost her angel form transformation, as well. Neither one was able to stand.

Laughing, Setadev said, "A feeble effort, but I commend your skills. In the end, the same thing that put you together to let you win tore you apart and led to your defeat."

Slowly, Kevin started to push himself up from the ground, and so did Caitlin. They had lost, and they both knew it.

What was going to happen now? Was this the end? Were they really that weak?

Could no one stop Setadev? Was he going to win?

"Now, then," continued Setadev, "you people have proven that you are resilient. However, I have taken enough lives for the day. I am no murderer, much as you people make me out to be one. As I have fulfilled my objectives, I have no reason to remain here and continue to entertain you." He paused to look at Tyrinion and Necnea. "I am sure that the two of you will alert the gods to be ready for an attack, as you should. For that, I will be waiting for a more realistic opportunity to seize what is rightfully mine."

Tyrinion tried to step forward, but Necnea held him back.

Setadev opened a massive teleportation gate, and began to move it toward him and the dimensional gate. "We will meet again very soon, I am sure. Remember what I have told you," he said. "You cannot defeat me, for I am nothing. And now you see how the game is played."

"Wait, where are you going?" exclaimed Arthur.

Before there was any answer, he was gone.

Chapter 52

Aftermath

"Dammit!" cursed Kevin out loud, now separated from Caitlin. "We were so close!"

Next to him, Caitlin was breathing heavily. "It's over, Kevin," she said. "He's gone."

"But he's not!" exclaimed Kevin, still furious. "He got his power back, killed Kronius and Larion, and escaped!" Suddenly, Kevin burst into tears. He felt like so much of a failure, and knew what had happened would change the world forever.

As he cried, Kevin thought of Kronius. The messenger god had been a special individual. If there was one god who Kevin felt was his friend, despite his flaws and the time he lied to Kevin, it was Kronius. And now he was dead. And now the perpetrator of that was running free, with his full power using the energy that he stole from Larion.

Tears were running down from Kevin's eyes, so impacted by the loss of his friend and his failure to stop Setadev. Beside him, Caitlin wrapped her arms around him, sharing all of the sentiments and tears. Aside from them, Arthur and Rachel each lowered their heads, mournful for the losses they had all suffered. Though he stood firmly, a rare tear could be seen from the professor's eye, as he recalled all of the time he had spent with Kronius in the past year. He had grown connected to the younger god, as well.

Larion was a tragic loss as well. Kevin and Caitlin had not known him as personally as they knew Kronius, but as the king of the gods, his loss would be felt across the entire realms. Tyrinion teared for both his newest friend in Kronius and for the god that stood up for him in Larion. He who had courageously guided the gods in their greatest period of uncertainty was now gone. It felt as though the end was nigh.

Truly, this was the saddest day for the Realm of the Angels since the self-sacrifice of Vinz Larinion. For the mortals present, it represented their biggest loss ever. They had failed to keep Setadev from reviving, and now he was running loose.

Tyrinion came flying over, as Necnea, Arthur, Rachel, and Vincent Stryker ran up to join their friends. "Please, do not be upset," the professor said to Kevin. "You did everything that you could do, both of you. The deaths of our two friends and our failure to stop Setadev is not for lack of effort. We did the things we were able to do, and it turned out not to be enough this time. We must accept it and move on quickly, or else we will always question our actions going forward."

Silently, Necnea nodded. Then, she said, "I praise greatly what the two of you have done. You have shown more courage and valor than anyone, mortal or immortal, that I have seen or heard from."

Though still full of tears, Arthur and Rachel came up to Kevin and Caitlin to offer their encouragement. "You guys kicked some tail," added Arthur. "You certainly gave Setadev a run for his money, that's for sure."

Vincent Stryker extended an arm down to help his son to his feet, while the professor attended to his daughter. "Defeat is inevitable sometimes. It only means that we could not end the war today. As Setadev chose not to end everything today, for whatever reason that may be, the war continues on."

"So it shall," remarked Kevin, as he stood up.

Rachel took a breath as she hung her bow off of her quiver. "Brush yourself off, Kevin," she said. "As long as we all have each other, it's not the end of the world. We've got a long walk back to the Solunar Empire, and it'll be best if we do it together."

Kevin nodded, agreeing. Staying frustrated about it would not do him much good. He had been through so much that it had frayed his nerves, but he understood that anger would not solve any problems right now. He took several deep breaths, trying to get himself calmed down. Normally it was he who was the optimistic one; now, he was needing the optimism of his friends to keep him going. Curious, he then asked, "Where are we, anyway?"

Having stood up herself, Caitlin said, "We're on the Gardolk side of the Peaked Mountains, south of the Southern Pass. This was an old mining camp."

Up and seeing Caitlin, Kevin ran to her and hugged her tightly. "Thank you," he said, catching Caitlin a bit by surprise. "I am glad you are still okay."

Nodding, Caitlin wrapped her arms around Kevin. "I'm glad you're okay, too," she said. Then, she let go of him, a little earlier than Kevin expected.

Smiling and not thinking anything unusual of what she was seeing, Rachel asked, "Shall we get out of this cavern and regroup with the army?"

Suddenly, a voice echoed from the Sword of Purity. *Before you do, I would like to speak with you all.*

For Tyrinion, Caitlin, and Necnea, that voice was familiar.

Surprised, Kevin instinctively took his sword and threw it out of the scabbard, almost afraid of it. It was glowing already. A translucent image started to project from the blade into the air, forming itself as a man with dark skin and silver robes with blue trim.

Instantly, a tear came to Necnea's eye. She recognized her husband, Vinz Larinion.

Tyrinion bowed immediately. "My lord," he began, "your presence honors us. I had no idea you still lived."

"Please rise," said Vinz Larinion back. "I live, and yet I also do not live. I am a part of this sword now, and my conscience holds everything about Vinz Larinion that he saved in here when he sacrificed himself. I am his memories, his personality, everything about him."

"You're still the one I spoke to, right?" asked Caitlin.

Vinz Larinion nodded. "You are correct, my child," he said. "I wanted to have the chance to say some words to each and every single one of you, as I have experienced you through this weapon. However, my time is short, so I must be quick."

It was awe-inspiring. Everyone stood still, waiting to hear what the former king of gods would have to say. Knowing that he had little time, they all listened intently.

"Let me begin," said the former king of gods, "by saying to each and every single one of you that what you has happened today is a defeat, but I commend your efforts greatly. You have done wonders at deferring Setadev, and I would ask that each of you keep your spirits up. I too have now witnessed the death of Ralios Larion, whose nobility and honesty is why I selected him to be the king of gods. Kronius, too, is a tragic loss for us, and I thank him for his efforts."

Vinz Larinion then turned to the professor. "I owe to you my greatest apology for assuming you were a villain, Tyrinion. You were always by my side before, and I was wrong to lose my trust in you. The gods themselves will have to decide who their new king will be, but would you be willing to consider going for it? I know I can trust the Realm of the Angels in your hands."

The professor sighed. "I do not know if I can do that, my lord. There are still scars that run deep, that cannot be healed so easily. Plus," he said, as he looked over to Caitlin, "I am a father now, in case you did not know."

"I do know," nodded Vinz Larinion, "and I also know that your daughter is strong. If you would be willing to at least take part in the rebuilding process, that would satisfy my mind."

Reluctantly, Tyrinion nodded. "I think I can do that part, at least," he said.

With confidence, Vinz Larinion expressed his gratitude. He then turned to Arthur and Rachel. "It must not be easy to have obligations to the empire and to your friends, while helping us try to stop Setadev. Still, I thank you both for your service, and good luck with your new relationship."

Arthur and Rachel looked at each other. Rachel blushed a little bit.

Then, Vinz Larinion proceeded to Necnea. Immediately, she stepped out to hug her husband, only to realize after trying that he was not really there and was only a hologram. After she fell through him, Vinz said, "I am sorry I cannot hug you anymore, Necnea."

Necnea turned around to face him, in tears. "I understand," she said.

"I do want you to know that I miss you as much as you miss me," Vinz Larinion continued. "Someday, I hope that we will be able to talk again, but I want you to know that I want you to take care of yourself even without me. I know what Kronius meant to you as well, and I want you to continue to live your life without misery. I will always live on within you."

Tearfully, Necnea said, "I know. I love you and always will."

Vinz Larinion nodded. "I love you too, Necnea," he said. He gave a second of pause, as he stared at the crying Necnea, his wife.

Then, he proceeded on to Vincent Stryker. "Hello, my chosen hero."

"Hello, my lord," answered Vincent. He then bowed. "I am sorry I failed you twenty years ago."

Again, Vinz Larinion nodded. "Just like this time, you did everything you could do. I want to thank you for everything you have done. Your work is admirable and your son has developed into quite the young man."

"That he has," nodded Vincent with pride.

Then, Vinz Larinion stepped over to Kevin. "Young pure one, you are an inspiration to all of us. You have never believed you are a hero, yet you take more responsibility that most who do. Even in the worst of situations, you have maintained your honor and your sense of right. On your side, I will always be as your sword, guiding you when you need me."

Kevin gave a bow. "Thank you," he said. "I appreciate all of the help you have given me."

With a smile, Vinz Larinion nodded in approval. Then, he stepped over to Caitlin, who started before he could. "Thank you for helping me to find him, and for helping me to see the truth," she said.

"You are welcome, young angel," Vinz Larinion answered. "You too are an individual that I believe we must all aspire to be. Your dedication and devotion never wavered, and you always kept on proceeding forward even when there seemed to be little reason to keep going. What you have endured showcases your resiliency, and I wish we could all follow your example."

"Thank you," said Caitlin, giving a polite curtsey.

"You are welcome," answered the image of Vinz Larinion, as he took a step back. "Sadly, however, my time is up, and I must depart you all now. May you all keep fighting on and showing the world that we will not give in so easily to conquest." He paused for a second and glanced to his wife as he disappeared into the sword. Quickly, he then turned back. "And Caitlin," he said, as the image started to vanish, "perhaps it would be best if you told Kevin how you truly feel inside right now."

As the image disappeared, Kevin looked over at Caitlin and put his hands on her shoulders. Kindly, he asked, "What did he mean by that?"

There was a moment of silence. Then, Caitlin turned her head as she lifted her hands up, placed them on Kevin's, and pulled them off of her body. Kevin was stunned; she had never done anything like that before.

Caitlin took a deep breath. "Kevin, despite the deep feelings we share for each other, the fact is that you hurt me." She paused, as Kevin stared as if surprised. "You showed me who you really are at your core. I don't care whether or not you were under the influence of drugging and a mind shatter; the truth is that I was very hurt by your actions, by what you did. You ran off without me; the reason doesn't matter. And when you kissed Satiana in front of me, you let Setadev shatter my mind." She put her hands over her heard. "That was the most pain I have ever felt in my life, and I felt it for days."

A tear came to Kevin's eye. "Caitlin, I wasn't myself…"

"But you were," said Caitlin. "You weren't being possessed. You were under the control of a substance and had your mind shattered, but you were still you. That version of you that I saw kiss Satiana, was you at your core, at your base level with everything stripped away."

"Caitlin, that's not really fair," Arthur tried to chime in. "It's not fair to judge someone's basic animal instincts when they can't think about their actions."

"It doesn't matter if it's fair or not," Caitlin responded. "It's the truth." She paused, herself starting to tear up. "I suffered for you. I went through the worst traumas I have ever endured to find you, and to find that is how you are at your core, hurt me. And right now, I can't really feel completely like I love you anymore. I was able to transform again because I believed in our love, but I knew how you made me feel and tried to push it aside. It worked for a little while until we made it through this together, but now…" Caitlin was crying too hard to say anything more. Rachel walked up to her and put her arms around her, to comfort her.

After a few seconds of thinking and tearing up, Kevin asked, “Caitlin, does this mean we’re not together anymore?”

There was a long pause.

Caitlin wiped her eyes, as she let Rachel let go of her. “I don’t know,” she said. “I really don’t know.”

Across from her, Kevin lowered his head. He was too sad to say anything.

Then, Caitlin looked to the professor. “Father, can you take me home?”

Saying nothing more, Professor Magnon walked up to his daughter and held her close for a second. Then he opened up a teleportation gate, and started to step through it.

“Is this the end?” Kevin asked, without raising his head.

There was no response. Caitlin and the professor walked through the gate, and disappeared.

In that moment, she was gone.

Left alone, Kevin started to cry harder. This was never what he wanted. Arthur and Rachel, and his father and Necnea came to his side and group hugged him to let him know he was not alone. They too were saddened to see what they had just seen.

He was alone. After so long enduring to see her one more time, how could she walk away?

In the end, Kevin blamed himself, and cried with the thought.

Already, he missed her deeply.

Chapter 53

The Trial of the General

"General Martin Sayo, you stand accused of ignoring orders, destruction of the property of a protected tribe, murder of a great number of the Metoi tribe including Chief Aspectra, unauthorized movement of troops outside of the country, reckless endangerment of soldiers, and treason against the Solunar Empire. How do you plead to all of these charges?"

The setting: the Solunar Empire Court, a room inside the capital building of the Solunar Empire in Seta Archa. The walls were entirely paneled in wood, and all of the furniture inside was constructed of wood, as well. The room was fairly large and held about thirty witnesses, but no jury section. It was constructed in the times of Demonicus's reign, when he served as judge and jury when he wanted to conduct a court case in the few times he did.

One month had passed since the event that would be known in Solunar's history simply as "The Convergence". Now, the war criminal Sayo was being tried for his crimes of rebellion and slaughter. At the high position of the judge was Arthur, the emperor. He had been the one to read the charges to Sayo. Rachel stood next to his high seat at one side, and Rouge and Resa stood at the other. Sayo stood in front of it, in shackles, with two Solunar Empire soldiers as bailiffs. Most of the witnesses present were tribe leaders from the more influential Wastes tribes and representatives from Seta Archa. Two flags were posted in the room corners, bearing the colors of the Solunar Empire: orange and black, in a pattern as though an orange sun was rising from a black horizon.

Sayo's head hung low as he said little. "I plead guilty," he announced.

There was a deep gasp from the witnesses, who seemed surprised by the plea.

Arthur, however, leaned back in his chair. He had been prepared for this. Sayo was, after all, a broken man who had nothing more to fight for. "Very well," he answered. "Then you hereby subject yourself to the law of the Solunar Empire, including its consequences."

"I do," nodded Sayo gravely.

"Then I shall sentence you," continued Arthur, as the ears of those in attendance perked up. "Martin Sayo, what you have done to this country is appalling and criminal. It is true, the Solunar Empire was born of Desolunar only a few short months ago, but it is in every way, shape, and form, still Desolunar. Had you any true loyalty to your country, and not to a man, you would have returned when the orders for recall were dispatched." He paused for a moment, as he pulled out a scroll, which held the official charges against the general. "On the charges of ignoring orders, destruction of tribe property, unauthorized troop movement, and reckless endangerment of your soldiers, I hereby sentence you to be discharged from the military. Your rank will be stripped, and any posting and salary you had are now forfeit."

Sayo let his head down again. Arthur had not addressed the most serious of charges: the murder of the Metoi people, and treason.

"Now," continued Arthur, as witnesses watched on from all around the courtroom, "the next statement I make should apply to all warriors everywhere, military or not, Solunar Empire or any country wherever. War is not a game, Martin Sayo. You do not get to slaughter the innocent. Such acts are highly dishonorable and should never occur. For that alone, you are a war criminal, and execution is a fitting punishment for such an offense." He paused for a second. "Treason, I would consider a lesser crime in this sense, but by committing treason you have made yourself a liability to our nation on a second front, as well. Clearly you have proven yourself capable of betrayal of a trusted position. Furthermore, what would your family have to say, Sayo? What about the families of the men you took out of the country? What about the families you slaughtered?"

Sayo did not look up. He was clearly in distress.

"Still, there is one more fact to consider," continued Arthur. "After all of these crimes had been committed, and you knew we were coming after you, you still came back to help in a campaign against Pseudo, whose list of crimes surpasses that of yours. Because of your efforts, the dangerous Pseudo was driven out of Solunar; and though we failed to capture or compromise him, the power of his Enlighteners from the Shadows have been compromised. Future lives have certainly been protected by this."

A quiet few seconds of silence echoed through the air. Then Arthur was ready to announce his decision.

"It will be considered controversial, perhaps, but I will choose to spare your life today, Martin Sayo. Instead, on the charges of treason and murder, I hereby sentence you to be banished from the Solunar Empire and any of its territory for the remainder of your life."

There was another collective gasp of surprise at this decision.

"Now, there is more to add to this," continued Arthur. "Should you step foot into the empire ever again, you will be immediately captured and imprisoned, with no release for the remainder of your life. If you become active in any military in any other nation, we will track you down and execute you. I have shown you mercy for the good things you have done, but if you press your luck, you will meet the consequences that should be what you experience, instead of what you will. Is that clear?"

Sayo nodded silently. It was clear to him.

"Very well," Arthur answered. "Then it is done. General Sayo, I will now make my closing remarks." He paused for a moment. "The Solunar Empire is grateful to you for your many years of service and for your change of heart in deciding to abandon your support of Pseudo. Your decisions to attack the Metoi village and to take your men on a pursuit of power outside of the empire, however, are most regrettable. It is the decision of this court, and also of your emperor, that everyone is deserving of a second chance. By betraying your people, you have proven yourself unworthy of being here any longer, but by changing your direction and helping to drive Pseudo away, you have earned your second chance." Arthur paused for a moment. "Take your chance in stride, Sayo. This sentence is compassionate with the hopes that you will use it to live a good life and continue to provide good to others. The decisions of whichever country to which you are expelled with not be up to this court. However, this court strongly advises you, no matter where you are sent, to make something that provides for the good of the people of this world. You have always been a leader, General." Arthur glared downward, staring directly into the general's eyes. "Use your talents well." He then looked back up, and grabbed his gavel, slamming it into his podium. "This court is adjourned."

With that, almost everyone in the room stood up and started discussing the verdict. General Sayo looked over to his good friend Vincent Stryker. He stared only in silence, then lowered his head.

No answer was needed. Vincent walked up to the disgraced general, who was still in shackles, and said, "It's okay, Marty. Someday, I hope we will be able to catch back up with John and Milton, and share our old war stories again."

As the bailiffs directed him, Sayo kept his head down and walked past Vincent toward the exit of the courtroom. He would not even acknowledge Vincent's presence.

Seeing this, Kevin stood up and walked up next to his father. "Are you just going to let him walk out like that?"

Vincent nodded. "Yes, son, I am." He paused for a second. "This is not the first time that Martin Sayo has felt disgrace for his actions, I am sure. I can only believe that it has been consuming him, eating him up from the inside for a long time now. For now, it is best that we all let him have some space and some time to gather himself."

After a slight pause, Kevin nodded. He understood. "Do you think that someday you might be friends with him once again?"

Silently, Vincent remained motionless for a second. "Perhaps," he finally said. "Only time will tell for sure. Perhaps, though, it would be best if I went to sit with him outside of his cell until he is ready to be extradited."

"Extradited?" asked Kevin.

Lowering his head, Vincent answered, "Yes, essentially. Even if Arthur has shown Sayo leniency in this court, he will still have to have Sayo taken to the border to force him out. And no matter where Sayo were to be taken, whether it be Aurana, Nuve, Gardolk, or even through Gardolk over to Scurnia, there is not another nation that would not want to arrest him on the spot and try him for war crimes. As Desolunar's most prominent general, Aurana would execute him for treason, Nuve and Scurnia would do the same for crimes as an enemy combatant, and Gardolk would refuse his entry as a potentially dangerous individual and kill him if he were found there. Sayo knows this as well as I do."

With this realization, Kevin lowered his head, too. "Can we do anything for him?" he asked. "For everything he did for us to try and subvert Setadev, he should get a second chance to live, at least."

Vincent let out a sigh. "His best chance would be if we took him to Aurana and you and I leveled with the Auranian courts to spare his life based on what we know. However, keep in mind that not everyone will see it that way. There are many, many people in this world who would love nothing more than to see Sayo dead."

Silently, Kevin nodded. He had that same desire too when this whole ordeal began. He understood the ramifications of what had happened, and knew that Arthur had done the only thing he could to keep from executing Sayo in the empire.

With that, Vincent nodded. "Take care, my son," he said, intent on heading to Sayo's detention cell. "Have some fun with your friends tonight, and I'll meet you back in Rikleifer when we both make it back." He started to step away, and reciprocated one more time, "Only time will tell what will happen."

Kevin understood. Only time would tell on Sayo.

At this second, Arthur had come down from the podium, and Rachel looped her arm around his. She gave him a small kiss on the cheek, as Rouge and Resa came down from the other side. "Speaking of whether or not time will tell," began Arthur, "have you heard anything from Caitlin lately, Kevin?"

With this, Kevin sighed. The answer was clear.

Rouge stepped over to Kevin and put a hand on his shoulder. "Give her a little time to miss you," she told him. "She loves you, Kevin, even if she can't say that out loud right now herself."

Kevin nodded. "I know," he said. "I still can't believe I hurt her so much. I only wish I could remember everything that happened.

Why everything that occurred did, and what I ever saw in Satiana that could have ever drawn me away from Caitlin, or to swear her off."

"You were drugged, Kevin," Rachel answered in confidence. "And you still fought against it and it took a mind shatter on top of that to make you do it. What happened as a result of that was due to heavily impaired judgment because of that." She paused. "Setadev's drugging of you ended up hurting all of us. He nearly split us all apart and broke all of our friendships. And yet despite all of that, you and Caitlin overcame that and became closer than ever, if only briefly."

Looking at his hands, Kevin remembered what had happened only a few days ago. "Quite," he said. "She was so excited to see me when you guys found me in the camp outside of the gate. Then, after Setadev knocked us out of the fight and ran off with his full power, she tells me that she's not sure and she needs time. I guess I'm just not sure what to think, and I haven't heard from her since."

"I'm sure you will see her again soon," said Resa. "Even though all that stuff happened, I still think love like that you two have isn't something you see every day."

Slightly moved, Kevin nodded. "Thanks, Resa," he said.

For a second, Arthur looked away. "There are many things in the world to be concerned of," he began. "The political instability in Nuve is bound to be building even worse with the assassination of Raijin Shane, as well as the death of Arsuf Maxwell. If Arsuf Maxwell's death is ever connected to us, the empire might have hell to pay at the hands of the Cornelia Chimeras. Add into that Setadev's escape, and we're going to have to remain vigilant. There's not a second for us to rest on our laurels."

Suddenly, Rachel looked at Arthur. "You're not seriously going to be like that again, are you?"

Looking back, Arthur rolled his eyes. "Of course not, cynic," he answered.

Rachel's mouth dropped open. "I told you I'm not a cynic!" she exclaimed. Then, she started chuckling, and leaned in to share another kiss with Arthur briefly. Good old Arthur, she thought to herself. He was not any different, after all.

Even Kevin could not resist the urge to snicker at that bit. He responded with a joke of his own. "So when's the wedding, guys?"

Arthur and Rachel suddenly went cold with blank stares. That was clearly not a thought that either of them had had. Behind Kevin, Rouge and Resa laughed in response. "Uhm, Kevin, don't you think it's a little soon to be thinking about that?" asked Rachel.

Then, Arthur dropped his head. "Don't take him seriously," he chuckled. "Let us have some fun this evening. It's only been way too long since we all had some fun together."

In response, Kevin nodded, but looked away. He let out a sigh. "You guys go on ahead," he said. "I just don't think it'll be the same for me."

"Oh, come on, Kevin," interjected Resa. "It's not like you're the only one here who misses Caitlin. We miss her too." She paused for a second. "Without her, my sister wouldn't be alive and well today."

Beside Resa, Rouge looked away for a second. She was a little speechless, but very grateful for Caitlin. Underneath her Vanguard top, there was still a burn scar from where she had been hit by a fireball directly in the chest.

"Do you know where she is?" asked Rachel to Kevin.

Silently, Kevin nodded. "She had her father take her home," he answered. "Back to her home, just south of Haventown, Aurana. I would guess that she's still there."

And as Kevin thought about this, he thought about just how far Caitlin had gone just to find him. He had heard her story by now by way of Rachel, who had made sure to write down Caitlin's account of her actions. He knew now about her trip through the Wastes and her capture by the Aequina. He knew about her travels through Leticon Province and failure at the Fortress of Da Leval. He knew about her continuing to push forward alongside Arthur and Rachel, and what she had witnessed while he was heavily drugged at the Gates to Gardolk. Finally, he was there when she fought Satiana and joined with him to fight Setadev.

She had come so far just to find him. Then, after all of that, she left.

It did not make much sense to Kevin. He had felt bad for hurting her, and he still felt bad for hurting her, but if she was so upset as she should be, then why did she seem so happy to find him before? How did they make the connection for her to transform into her angel form again, when she could only do so by experiencing strong feelings for him?

Maybe it was just her being human. Maybe it was just him being human in not understanding it.

For now, for just one brief moment in time, nothing else really mattered. Not even Setadev, who was sure to return someday from wherever he had disappeared. His friends cared greatly and he was so glad to have all of them, but without Caitlin, there was an emptiness within him. Over the course of the last year or so, she had come to mean so much to him and to his happiness. He had a new reason to live because of her, and now she was gone.

In the end, Setadev had accomplished everything he set out to do. He revived himself and escaped to continue planning his next steps, even if he would be out of the picture for a little while. Though he had managed to kill neither Kevin nor Caitlin, he had succeeded in breaking them apart and exacting at least some level of his revenge. His Enlighteners had lost their "relay point" and quite a few had been defeated at the mountain, but there were still a significant number of them enough that Setadev still had forces working on his behalf worldwide.

And with all of that, such senseless destruction had come with it, too. It was likely now as well that Nuve was permanently destabilized with the deaths of Raijin Shane and Arsuf Maxwell, and would likely head into a civil war fairly soon. If the Solunar Empire were indicted as being involved, including their advance into Leticon, Arthur's new empire could be in serious danger and worldwide war could be possible. Two gods, friends of Kevin and Caitlin, had lost their lives as well.

In the end, it was all so futile. What had all of Caitlin's efforts, as well as those of Arthur, Rachel, the gods, his father, and the Solunar Empire actually accomplished? Kevin's life had been saved, but little good had actually come out of everything that had happened. More harm had come from everything than good, including all of the trauma Caitlin had to face.

He missed Caitlin, so badly. Even with all of the worldwide effects of this incident, all in the name of saving him, nothing meant more to Kevin than missing Caitlin. She broke his heart by leaving, but in a way, he had broken hers first.

Shattered glass rains from the sky. Shattered glass, it rains so dry… they were words from a poem Caitlin had found. They seemed so appropriate in this moment.

Suddenly, Kevin's dark mind was lightened as Rouge and Resa each grabbed him by one of his wrists. "Hey, you can go see her in a couple of weeks and see what she thinks then," smiled Resa. "In the meantime, let's go play some dangerball. I promise it'll make you feel better."

Despite everything that was on his mind, Kevin could not help but crack a small smile at that thought. He was certainly no athlete, but he did love playing dangerball. "Two on three?" he asked.

Rachel smiled, as she kept her arm around Arthur's. "We could do that, or I'm sure we could find some soldiers who'd like to play, and do a full ten-on-ten."

Kevin nodded. "Sounds like fun," he said. "Do you think you guys can meet me outside in a few minutes? I'd like to be alone for a little bit."

Arthur nodded, as the crowd had dispersed from the courtroom. "We can do that," he said. "Just don't forget us, okay?"

Detecting the smart remark, Rachel turned and hit Arthur in his arm.

"Ow!" exclaimed Arthur. "What was that for?"

"For being a smart mouth," answered Rachel.

Arthur shook his head. "Do you just like making fun of me?" he laughed.

"Would you be upset if I said yes?" asked Rachel in return.

Both Kevin's and Arthur's eyes widened. It was rare for Rachel to make such a smart remark. Suddenly, Kevin started chuckling at this, as did Rouge and Reuse, while Arthur put his arm around Rachel and said, "We'll talk about it, okay?"

"Sure," laughed Rachel. She then turned her head toward Kevin. "You want to meet us at the stadium a couple of blocks south of here? Don't be too long." She paused for a second. "I've been trying to talk Arthur into sponsoring a professional dangerball team here, you know."

"I've heard," smiled Kevin. "I'm sure I'd be glad to cheer for them, as long as they're not playing against the Rikleifer Rangers."

Arthur nodded. "Understandable," he said with a smile. "We'll see you out on the field."

Everyone said their goodbyes as Arthur, Rachel, Rouge, and Resa left the courtroom and headed for the stadium. After the door closed, Kevin was by himself. He sat down on the defendant's table and let a moment pass by.

The quietness of the room was soothing. Kevin let out a sigh as he briefly closed his eyes, then opened them as he looked up to the ceiling.

Caitlin was deep on his mind. So much had been lost in this whole affair, and all because he let Setadev lure him out alone to be captured. The following plot of Setadev and rescue efforts from the Solunar Empire led to the deaths of Raijin Shane and Arsuf Maxwell, the souring of diplomacy between Arthur's nation and its neighbors leading to a possible civil war in Nuve and a war between Nuve and the Solunar Empire, the deaths of some soldiers of Arthur's empire and the further strain to their rebuilding efforts in Seta Archa, the destruction of the Metoi and Aequina tribal villages, the sacrifice of Kronius and the death of Ralios Larion, Rouge had nearly lost her life, Caitlin had been beaten within an inch of her life several times, and hers and Kevin's relationship had been torn apart.

In the end, what was gained? In reality, nothing. Setadev escaped and had plans in the works, for sure. It had not been a complete loss, but it might as well had been.

None of that mattered for now, at least. All that was on his mind was Caitlin.

He reached down and pulled out his Sword of Purity, and watched as the venation glowed within the sword. He then relaxed its mind and lit it up in its bright blue power. Then, he glanced at it, held it in front of him, and closed his eyes. "Now I know how you have been able to guide me for the last year, and I thank you for all that you have done, Vinz Larinion. I know you did not mean to lead me into the trap." He then paused for a second. "I trust that you knew what you were doing when you helped Caitlin, then asked her to tell me the truth." Then, he took a breath. "Tell me, if you know, will she forgive me?"

For a minute, Kevin held the sword steady. There was no response.

At this, Kevin let out his breath and sighed.

Then, the sword glowed brighter and flashed as its power dropped and it stopped glowing blue. And for a moment, Kevin thought he heard words in his head:

Only if you go to her when she is ready to see you.

Carefully and quietly, Kevin sheathed his sword as he hopped off the counter and headed out of the room, toward the stadium.

In a couple of weeks, when she would be ready after all of the stress was over, Kevin would go to see Caitlin. And there, he would tell her everything.

For now, though, his friends were waiting for him.

Chapter 54

Second Chances

Two weeks had passed very quickly. Alone, Kevin had returned to Rikleifer via a gryphon transport from Seta Archa. The Solunar Empire would be well now, and things were looking as though as long as they could stave off war with Nuve, Cornelia, and Gardolk, as well as survive the hunger winter, all would come out well for the empire in the end. That would be a tall order for the new empire to fill, but not completely impossible.

There had been some happy times during these two weeks that had passed, including Rachel's nineteenth birthday. Needless to say, she had to make sure Arthur kissed her at least once on her birthday, even if he were still a little reluctant.

Still, Kevin could not shake the feeling about what Setadev had done. The whole mess in western Gardolk had pretty much been worthless. He came out of it, but only after making a stupid decision to go back there alone without his sword. General Sayo had been rescued, but in turn he was banished and likely to be extradited and executed anyway. Satiana had been defeated when Kevin and Caitlin killed her, but the truth was that had they found a way to break her life energy away from Setadev, she may not have been so dark after all. Kevin had never been a fan of killing the innocent, and always believed in second chances. Necnea and Tyrinion had been lucky to escape with their lives, and others such as Raijin Shane and Arsuf Maxwell had not been lucky at all. The gods had been devastated by the loss of Ralios Larion and Kronius, and the Realm of the Angels would never be the same. Kevin had the most sentiment for Kronius since it was the messenger god who discovered him and started him on his journey almost a year ago by now, but also cared for Larion for being a believer in him. And now both were gone.

Truly, Setadev was powerful. He had proven exactly what the

gods had feared for thousands of years: that he was stronger than every god combined. Kevin had tried to do the math in his head repeatedly in the past two weeks to figure out how exactly he and Caitlin were able to hold their own, and just how powerful Setadev was. Within his hands, Kevin held the power of the Sword of Purity, which turned out to be all of the power and life force of Vinz Larinion concentrated into the blade. Theoretically, Vinz Larinion was the second strongest god only to Setadev himself. His energy and life force, combined with whatever strength Kevin himself held and the massive angelic powers of Caitlin were just enough to prove equal to Setadev until they were entirely split apart by being kicked through the dimensional gate. That was a lot of power.

Still, all of that was on the back of his mind. He missed Caitlin, and he missed her badly. He had her on his mind every day. Never did he really intend to hurt her.

And that was why he was here today.

He walked the three days south of Rikleifer, across the Calphos River, through Haventown, all the way to Caitlin's home. It was still cold outside, but spring was coming very soon. For a moment, he stared at her door, thinking hard about his next move.

It seemed like only yesterday that he and Caitlin had met for the first time even further south from here, at a battlefield. From there, they had come here and had their first occurrence of working together as a team here. Of course, at the time Caitlin had lacked any emotion. Her home was small and simple, but well kept even in her absence because little was left to disorganize it. To Kevin, though, it was a special place.

Cautiously, Kevin walked up to her door. It had been a little over two weeks since he had seen her in western Gardolk. He was hoping that she would be ready to see him now. He really wanted to see her.

He raised his hand to knock on the door. Before he did, however, he looked over at his sword and thought deeply for a moment. With a sense of confidence, he drew it, held it up, and in his mind asked it where to go. Then, he let loose his hands.

The sword tugged his arms and swung him to the right, around the house at an angle.

She couldn't be there of all places, Kevin thought to himself. Still, a slight smile came to his face as he sheathed his sword and headed east, deeper into the surrounding forest. As the winter was coming to an end and the spring began, the snow had melted and the tree branches were exposed on the fewer deciduous trees in the forest. The larger amount of conifers were still shining a dark emerald green, as they always had.

Kevin knew exactly where he was heading. Out a little ways from here, there was a fallen log where Kevin had followed her before, and there he gave her a show of confidence that reassured her heart. Could she be there? That was the only thing out this direction aside from more forest.

Onward he walked quietly, anxious for what would become. He hoped beyond all hope that Caitlin would be willing to see him.

Suddenly, he stopped. He saw the fallen log, exactly where it was. Caitlin was sitting on it, facing out toward the east, away from him. She was dressed in her white dress with the red trim, just as he remembered her, but she had her hair done in a style he had never seen: she had a pair of white and red ribbons tied in bows in her hair and used to create a long pair of pigtails between the side and back of her head. It was very pretty to Kevin.

There was a moment's pause. Then, Caitlin said, without turning her head, "Kevin, I want to thank you for coming to see me."

Silently, Kevin walked up to the log and took a seat next to Caitlin. He looked up into her eyes for just a second before lowering his gaze. Unknown to Kevin, Caitlin had considered tying her hair like this for a while, but had never done so knowing that Kevin liked her hair when it was long. She had always been afraid of what he might say if she tied it. However, much to her surprise, he said, "You look very nice. The ribbons are pretty and I like what you've done with them."

Caitlin nodded, but did not show excitement. "Thank you," she said. "I wanted to try something new."

Kevin nodded, a slight smile on his face. The smile faded, however, as he looked back down. "I guess we can't make small talk forever, can we?"

After a second's pause, Caitlin signed. "No, I suppose not," she said.

Another moment passed. Then, Kevin let his heart speak. "Caitlin, I love you," he said. "I know I hurt you, even if I didn't have control of myself. That's still no excuse, though, and I know that is true…"

"I know," interrupted Caitlin, as she looked away for a second. "I don't want you to have to apologize for it. I know it's not your fault, but…"

"Please don't do this, Caitlin," Kevin answered. "Put the drugging and the mind shatter aside for a few minutes, and let me be responsible for my actions." He paused for a second. "Ultimately, the things I did were my responsibility. I never meant to hurt you, and I never intended to betray your trust, but I know I did." Again, he paused.

Before he could continue, Caitlin started speaking without lifting her head. "Kevin, I know you didn't mean it, and it's not fair of me to judge you like that," she said. "When I told you that you hurt me, I did mean that, because you did. Still, I know that that was never your intention." She then paused for a second. "Just answer me one question," she said. "Did you like her?"

Kevin shook his head. "Of course not," he said. "I felt sorry for her when I stabbed her through the chest and disintegrated her, but never did I consciously desire her. Every time when I was sobered out from their drugging, all I could think about was how I could get free and find my way back to you."

Caitlin looked up at Kevin, who kept his head down. "And while you were under the control of the aphrodisiacs?"

There was a moment of silence.

Letting out a sigh, Kevin continued, "I really don't know. The answer seems apparent given what you saw, but my memory of everything that occurred during those times is very hazy. General Sayo told me that it was an effect of the 'blue soup' aphrodisiac that Setadev used to drug me. I think the actions speak louder than the words, in this case."

For a moment, Caitlin looked down again, depressed. Then, she took a breath. "I talked with my father when he brought me home. He told me that I've been a little hard on you, but he understood why."

"I would be hard on me too," sighed Kevin. "I don't like what I did. I can't believe it happened, why it did, how it did…" He paused almost indefinitely, unable to finish his sentence.

"Vinz Larinion knew," Caitlin answered. "Before I came back for you, he talked to me through the Sword of Purity that you left behind. He recognized that the drugging, showing me everything that Setadev did, all of it was a trap to break apart our relationship legitimately and Satiana was a part of that."

Kevin raised an eyebrow. "Are you suggesting that he thought I'd be a carnal pig if I lost my inhibitions?"

"I'd say to an extent that he was right, Kevin," Caitlin answered.

Looking down, a tear fell from Kevin's eye.

"But it's not all your fault," Caitlin then continued, looking at Kevin and trying to reassure him. "We all have needs wired to our instincts, and clearly that comes out when you strip everything away and provide substances to enhance that need. And Setadev exploited it as a clever way to get you to cooperate with him for the Sword of Purity, which he desired to revive himself."

"That didn't happen, though," commented Kevin.

"Exactly," Caitlin nodded. "My father thinks he wasn't counting on gods arriving to fight with us, but they did, and he used them instead." She paused for a second. "Setadev is not afraid of any of the gods. He is afraid, though, of two people: you and me."

Kevin took a breath. "The Sword of Purity and your angelic powers," he said.

"Basically," nodded Caitlin. "Maybe it's that fascination that is why he wants me under glass somewhere in his 'utopia', as he calls it. We proved him right on his fears, though. Even if we couldn't beat him, we were able to contend with him where no one else has ever been able."

Awkwardly, a slight smile came to Kevin's face. "Yeah, that was something else, wasn't it?"

"It was," Caitlin smiled back. "I would have never thought two people could ever have come so close together before." She paused. "It's hard to know for sure because we had a purpose when it happened, but it kind of seems like there may be no more special feeling than when that happens."

Nodding, Kevin said, "I think so too, for that matter, though I have no idea how it happened. All I know for sure is that it was something special, Caitlin, whatever it was."

Caitlin also nodded. Then, there was a long pause.

A breeze of wind blew over the emerging spring landscape. A couple of twigs snapped in the distance. Silence filled the air, as if beckoning the question that was on Kevin's mind, and the one that Caitlin knew she would have to answer.

"Caitlin," Kevin began, "do you still love me?"

There was another second of silence. Then, Caitlin reached under her dress's top piece and pulled out the Key of Hearts that was hanging from her neck. She considered it in her hand for a second. She thought of all of the feelings it had brought her, all of the comfort and all of the love. In all of her struggles over the last few months, and every tribulation she faced on her journey to save Kevin, it was this small piece of jewelry that had kept her going on, that had given her the reminders that what she was doing had a purpose and that no matter the pain and suffering she had to go through, she had to keep pressing on. And in the end, she had accomplished what she had set out to do. She saved him. She rescued the one she loved the most. And this key came from him before, when he had done the same for her.

"I do," she said, as she slid off the log. "I do love you, Kevin." She paused for a second. "But maybe I'm not ready to just go back to how things used to be."

Silently, Kevin nodded. "I understand," he said. He started to tear up, as he turned away.

Caitlin stood up and came over to Kevin's face. She knelt down next to him. "I didn't mean it like that," she said. "Look, let me share something with you."

Quietly, a teary-eyed Kevin looked up.

At this point, Caitlin was also starting to have tears build up in her eyes. Admitting this was the way things were to be was painful to her, too, and having to tell Kevin why, knowing she would hurt him, was making it worse.

"I don't blame you for what happened," she said. "You did go off on your own, but I know you were just trying to do what was right. And what Setadev did exposed what any person would be in that situation. But I guess…" she paused, another tear falling from her eye, "I guess I had you built up in my mind so great that I never would have thought you capable of that. But then the doubts set in because I had you so highly built up that I was afraid of losing you, that I worried about our relationship when it wasn't moving forward fast. And then this happened, and I realized I was wrong to build you up so much." She paused, as another tear fell. "I'm not mad at you, Kevin, and I forgive you for what happened, but I can't forget what I saw and what I experienced."

Kevin listened silently, with his sad eyes open. He gave Caitlin a slight nod of acknowledgment, struggling to find any words to say.

Still tearing herself, Caitlin then said, "I won't say this is forever. Maybe I'm not ready for us to be a couple right now, but I'm still happy to have you here with me. That hasn't changed, no matter what I know."

A tear was still in Kevin's eye. "So what does that mean for us?"

There was a momentary pause. "I still want us to be friends, Kevin. For now, that's the best I can do, and hope that maybe someday we'll have second chances for each other. I hope you can be okay with that." She extended her hand.

Silently, Kevin thought about it for a brief moment. No matter how much he was hurting in this moment, the one thing that would hurt him more would be not to have Caitlin in his life.

Kevin reached out and shook her hand. "You will always be my friend," he said, trying to smile through the tears. "Thank you for saving my life."

"Thank you for being my friend," Caitlin said, as a slight smile came to her face. "My life is better because you are in it."

Epilogue

Night of the the half moon of the second month of spring, also known as identifying date 2048249, at my house south of Haventown, Aurana.

It's felt like forever since I put in a diary entry here, but so much has happened in the last couple of months. I'm not going to write it all down, but I do know that it has changed me so much and has really impacted my life. All I do know is that if anyone ever raises a hand to someone I love ever again, I'll be strong enough to deal with them and any trick they pull.

It still upsets me that Setadev achieved all of his goals and escaped. He must be up to something, or else he would have destroyed us all. He took the lives of two gods and our friends; that alone is a sign of his power. I think he could have destroyed my father or anyone else who has the kind of strength necessary to challenge him. Kevin and I had the ability to contend with him, but sure enough, he was able to defeat us before he left. He keeps saying that we don't know how the game is played, and I do have to wonder now just what kind of ulterior motives he actually has and how many different schemes he has placed back. For now, though, he's left everyone alone, but it will only be a matter of time until he'll try again. He must have left us and the gods alive for a reason, even if simply because he wants us to watch him achieve his ultimate goal.

For that reason, Kevin and I have been training regularly. He's really taking to mastering his swordplay and becoming a master of the art. I know as well that he's visited Rachel quite a bit to practice archery, and wants me to teach him a little bit about magic, too. I've also been working on my magic skills, as well as my angelic power. I'm really curious about this "merging" technique that we used before, and I've asked my father to do some research on it for me to find whatever we can in the old texts about it. Even if it's all just lore, for some reason it's proven pretty true so far. Maybe there's more to it than that, and maybe there are secrets in there to help me grow even stronger.

After the battle at the abandoned mine, General Sayo was put on trial and banished from the Solunar Empire forever. He was taken to Aurana, who was more than happy to accept him and immediately arrest him for high treason and war crimes. Naturally, he pled guilty. Kevin has tried to leverage some support with the Auranian courts to spare his life on account of the recent good he has done, but only time and the decision of the courts will determine what his fate will be. Only recently has he started talking with Kevin's father, Vincent Stryker, who has tried to help the general communicate his remorse and assist in his appeals.

The world's politics look to be pretty much all the worse for wear, too. King Lester of Nuve attended a diplomatic conference in Seta Archa this week, suggesting that he is willing to listen to Arthur on the recent intrusions into Leticon. As to whether or not he'll understand and allow it without retaliation, we'll have to see. Arsuf Zachary, however, has not been so kind, and has declared open rebellion in Cornelia. He has been attempting, we hear, to start a legal referendum on independence of the province instead of declaring war, but may be ready to start one at any moment. As far as we're aware as well, Gardolk knows nothing of the intrusion there, likely because we kept to the mountainsides when we were there and never came close to civilized areas. That has been a relief so far.

My father's been really pitching in up in the Realm of the Angels, too. Unfortunately, the gods are still decimated by the loss of Ralios Larion and Kronius to the point where the whole realm has been thrown into upheaval. My father's reluctance to be there has not diminished, and sadly neither has his stigma with being an outcast, but the others promised how to figure out how to make it easier for him. He says we will have to see how that goes, but he has a legitimate desire to help make sure the gods will be successful in the new era where Setadev is more than a passing threat for conquest but now a real danger for annihilation. It's made me really sad, too; Kronius was definitely a friend, and his loss hurts all of us. We can only take solace in the fact that he's been reunited with his wife as a result of his passing. And Ralios Larion too... one has to wonder who will lead the gods now.

According to Arthur and Rachel, the empire's been running

smoothly, at least. He met with all of the representatives of the Wastes tribes, and issued an apology to the Aequina but silenced them from any more human sacrifices and hostile activities. I'm planning a return trip at some point, too, in order to apologize for destroying their village. The Metoi's village has been rebuilt with help of the empire, which has been good. They also let Marilynn, Lady of the Metoi, assume leadership of the tribe by herself. It's a remarkable development since Metoi culture usually doesn't let women rule, and Marilynn will the be the first female ruler in their history. The troops are all home again in Seta Archa, too, and with the incoming spring, Arthur has pushed his people toward agriculture and trading for food instead of weapons, helping to alleviate the hunger that has been running rampant there since the fall of Demonicus. Supposedly he's making good on his desire to build a city that will be a trading post near the Southern Pass, too. It will be a while until it's no longer an issue, but he's working very hard on making sure all of his people are well taken care of.

He and Rachel have been hitting it off pretty well too, I hear. They have been exploring their feelings for each other for a little while now, and I guess Rachel's really convinced now that somehow she fell in love with Arthur and thinks he should be her everything. Arthur, well, I guess he told Kevin he's not entirely sure yet but is certainly willing to try and see how it will work for a while, and go from there. Rouge and Resa found it kind of awkward, I hear, but they like the idea. As for me, I really like it, too. Arthur's my half-brother and Rachel is my best friend, so if they get married someday, it'll mean that Rachel and I will get to be sisters.

Speaking of which, on the topic of Kevin and I... it took me a long time to think through everything that's happened and what should happen going forward. I know he didn't mean to do anything and that Setadev had him drugged up, but it still hurt me very much to know that inside he would still go for any pretty girl who gave him a second look when his inhibitions were removed. Consciously, though, I know that he still does love me. He does ask questions about it but still believes in us. Having been emotionless for years, I guess I had a tough time relating to that. I've been so convinced that Kevin and I are inseparable and that normal people don't ask themselves those questions and have those tendencies that I let it keep me away and sad. It's certainly not something you see in your ordinary adventure tale or romance novel at the library, just because it is more ordinary than is recognized. However, it is a real thing, and it makes sense when you think about it. Love is a powerful emotion, and a very special thing, but you can't let it blind you. People are people and still are thoughtful, mindful, contemplative, but also impulsive and desiring at their core. Thinking that Kevin would be any different was probably something that led me to my doubts to begin with, those that I promised him I would never have again. Fortunately, Kevin has promised me that he'll start sharing more of his inner thoughts with me so that way I can understand it. It makes me feel better, in retrospect, to know that we'll get to spend more time as friends and we will get to know each other's ins and outs better as a result. That does make me happier to know.

At least tonight ought to help with that; he and I are planning to spend a night on the town in Rikleifer and have a lot of fun. We took a step back and now I'm spending more time at my house south of Haventown, but I still get to see him a lot. I used to think we would get to be really close in a short amount of time and even start doing some of Rouge and Resa's "favorite activities", as they call them, but now I'm actually glad things have slowed down. It means he and I have more time to really get to know each other inside and out, I hope. I know he's sad that we took a step back, but I still feel hurt by everything. I know he's a good person, and I want to be friends with him. I already lost him once. Even if I'm still hurting, I don't want to lose him for good. He means too much to me to give up on us.

With Setadev's return imminent, though, we have to keep remaining vigilant. He put everything into a mess, and we didn't "win" just because we saved Kevin. We lost this war. Keeping Setadev from killing Kevin was only a minor consolation on the grand scheme because now Setadev once again has the power to do as he pleases. Whatever he has up his sleeve, I'm sure he'll be trying to conquer us all and end our lives.

And when that happens, we'll be ready.

Caitlin Amelia Magnon

Bonus: The Dangerball Game

As seen in Chapter 2: Living Life

As she rested her head on Kevin's shoulder, Caitlin asked, "So, I know we played dangerball before with our friends, but can you explain to me how the game works?"

"Sure," said Kevin. He pointed to the Rikleifer Rangers, who were lined up at one side of the field, ready to begin the game. "There's two teams, of course, and one kicks off to the other. The other team retrieves the ball and tries to move it down the field, whether by running with it, throwing it around from player to player, kicking it to one another, and so on. As you can see, the field is pretty narrow, and running it without getting hit or losing the ball is tough, so teams will often plan out some pretty elaborate strategies to move the ball around, usually involving every type of movement and organized formation imaginable. Passes, kicks, sneak handoffs… you name it. Some will even take risks with long throws and hard kicks."

Caitlin nodded, as she listened intently. She was not bored; she was learning. Even with more freedom of emotions, she was still her same self. She never saw her access to emotions as making her lose pieces of herself such as her devotion to studies or her ability to operate logically; she instead saw it as an addition to herself.

Kevin kept explaining, "Since the field is so narrow as well, the game is also very quick. There's always some kind of action around the ball moving very fast. It really takes speed, power, technical skill, and knowledge to be a good dangerball athlete. You score points by taking the ball to the end point. As you can see, the field has two semi-circular ends, and there's a yellow section starting at the semicircle edge, and an even slimmer red section at the very ends. Kids and people playing for fun will usually play with just a rectangular "yellow zone", and a "red zone", as they call it, since they don't have actual fields. Getting into the yellow zone and spiking the ball against the ground there scores two points, while getting into the red scores five."

Simple scoring rules, Caitlin thought to herself.

"It's the job of the other team, the defense, to try and take the ball back. Usually though you can do anything with your players, most teams put one defender just ahead of the narrow red zone to keep people out of it. If you can get the ball to stop advancing without getting a takeaway, like if someone gets tackled but keeps a hold of a ball, a referee will throw the ball in the air and let them try to tip the ball to their own team. Recovering the ball anywhere in the scoring area and taking it out of bounds past their red zone is called a 'trap', which scores one point. If it's intercepted or taken away ahead of the scoring zones, the recovering team has to take it the other way instead. That means good defense where it counts is very important. The game ends when one team gets 35 points, but the last play must be either a five point offensive score, or by a one point defensive trap if the score is greater than 35 on both sides."

"Gotcha," commented Caitlin. She watched someone on the field hit another player hard to dislodge a ball. "I don't remember us hitting each other so hard, though."

"There's a couple of variations depending on who you play with: how violent you can be with attempting to create turnovers, how many players each side plays with, and so on. Most professionals play full contact, but when we're just playing for fun, we usually call it a jump ball if you get touched with two hands."

The loud sound of a whistle signaled the start of the game. As the game began, Kevin and Caitlin watched as the Rikleifer Rangers played intensely. Very quickly, the Rangers were putting up points like crazy, jumping to an early lead. Leading 7 to 2 very early on, Kevin pointed out the strategy they were using to Caitlin, as Kevin was a very big fan of dangerball and knew about it in depth.

"They're using an arrow formation," he pointed out. "It's a very offensive-minded field strategy that utilizes two defenders at the

Rikleifer base circle, five men strung across the middle, and three at the other circle."

At this, Caitlin frowned. "I don't really see it," she remarked. "I just see a bunch of guys running around here and there."

"It's a little more complex than that," laughed Kevin. "They're all running around, of course, but see how they are on the field? They spread it all across very quickly and advance it by passing. By using a thin middle section, they have to rely on passes to move the ball, so they have an extra defender in the back. Leaving the middle open like that, though, lets them have a stronger front to attack the circle with. Three men makes it easier to attack the scoring zone."

Again, Caitlin frowned. "So why not just rush everyone toward the offensive circle, and drop them back after they score?"

"Because then if you turn over the ball, you've basically given them five points," said Kevin. "You might do that if you're really running behind, but otherwise, it's not smart at all. Some teams do play aggressively like that and only keep one back, but it's a good way to wear your players out fast, especially in a long game."

This time, a slightly different look came to Caitlin's face. "I think I get it," she said. "It makes a little more sense."

Kevin chuckled to himself a little bit at that. As long as Caitlin was seeing something in real life and expanding her horizons, he was proud.

Suddenly, there was a fairly dramatic event in the game. In the midfield, an Aurana City player caught the ball from a pass and started running with it. A Rikleifer player then grabbed him and held him hard, trying to tackle him to the ground and strip the round-shaped ball free. The Aurana City player was very big and burly, likely normally a defender who was free in the midfield, while the Rikleifer player was more slim and quicker. With force, the Aurana City player threw the Rikleifer player off of him hard and to the ground. The ball slipped free at the same time, which another Rikleifer midfielder picked up, but from the force of the impact the Rikleifer player was left immobile on the ground.

A gasp echoed through the stadium. A timeout was called, as officials from the team stepped out to assist the fallen player. Within a few minutes, he was walking off the field on his own power, and Rikleifer made a substitution.

Caitlin looked over to Kevin. "Ouch?" she asked, a little surprised by the violence of dangerball.

"A little," Kevin answered, nodding. "I bet that hurt. Normally, though, big guys like that are slow and they're prone to dropping and fumbling the ball. It's round, so it's not made to be easy to carry, even though you can." He paused for a second. "But that's how you stop a ball carrier. You have to hold him, tackle him, even try to take the ball out of his hands. It's only very rarely that people get hurt like that, even despite the size differences in people, just because there are so many things to keep the game balance neutral."

Nodding, Caitlin answered, "I see. Kind of makes tactics important. I hope that guy will be okay, though."

"He walked off on his own power," acknowledged Kevin, "so he should be fine. I wouldn't worry about him too much; he'll be okay."

Within a couple more minutes, the game continued. There was still a lot of dangerball to play.

Rikleifer was the first team to reach 18 points, starting halfscore, a short intermission period to give the teams a break. As halfscore was just beginning, however, a light snow started to fall down from the sky. Caitlin stared into it in wonder, with an amazed and excited smile across her face. Kevin noticed this and, not wanting to interrupt it, only managed to look at her and smile. He was hoping that maybe, just maybe, her mind was really getting to see the world after all and enjoy its wonders.

When the game began again, Rikleifer took total control and prevented Aurana City from scoring again. Within an hour, they had won the game, 35 to 11. A wave of celebrations rippled all throughout the stadium with the Rangers' victory, as once again the city had a reason to be excited.

www.ingramcontent.com/pod-product-compliance
Lightning Source LLC
LaVergne TN
LVHW050908080826
845145LV00001B/10

* 9 7 8 0 9 8 9 7 9 6 6 2 0 *